Where the Herring Run

A Fictional Novel Based On The Life
Of Albert Crosby
CAPE COD

Dorothy D. Leone

Dorothy D. Leone

iUniverse, Inc.

New York Lincoln Shanghai

Where the Herring Run

A Fictional Novel Based On The Life Of Albert Crosby

iUniverse books may be ordered through booksellers or by contacting:

iUniverse
2021 Pine Lake Road, Suite 100
Lincoln, NE 68512
www.iuniverse.com
1-800-Authors (1-800-288-4677)

ISBN: 978-0-595-38372-6 (pbk)
ISBN: 978-0-595-83530-0 (cloth)
ISBN: 978-0-595-82745-9 (ebk)

Printed in the United States of America

Dedication

This book is dedicated to my husband Dan for his continued and indispensable support during the many years involved in the creation of this novel. Dan's unwavering faith in my achievement, and the pride he expressed throughout my endeavor will never be forgotten. He was delighted when I finished the last paragraph and grateful that it happened before his death from lung cancer, on July 22, 2002. He was dearly loved and will be sorely missed. Also, to the Town of Brewster in honor of its Bicentennial Year Celebration. 1803–2003

Acknowledgments

Gifted English teachers and mentors have honed my writing skills over the years. Among them: Catherine Chase Clark of Woodstock Academy, B. Franceschini of Greenfield Community College, Michael Lee and Kip Langello of the Nauset Evening Adult Education Classes and Kathy Mendoza who stimulated my mind and whose guidance and leadership encouraged me to achieve my goals. As a member of her writing group, I became more proficient in the art of writing. Over the past several years, with much practice on my part and an inordinate amount of patience on hers, this novel was finally completed. I also wish to recognize my dear family and friends whose help and encouragement were crucial to achieving my objective and always there when needed: Greg O'Brien of the Stony Brook Press and my fellow associates at the Brewster Town Hall. Without the dedicated efforts of Ginny and Brian Locke, chairpersons of the Friends of Crosby Mansion and the volunteers who have restored the mansion to its original grandeur, this novel could never have been written. Also, my thanks to Elizabeth Hardy whose artistic talents grace the cover of this book and Richard May, 1948 Class Secretary of Woodstock Academy, whose book became my inspiration. I must also include my daughters, Deborah, who suggested the title, Deirdra, Donna and Deanna, their husbands, and my son Daniel and his wife Debby for their indispensable help and support. I'm especially indebted to my sister Gerry for being my listening post and graciously doing the household chores for me while I busied myself with writing. And last, but not least, a very special thanks to my neighbor Kevin Byrne whose computer skills were at my beck and call. I'm beholden to all of you for your time and efforts on my behalf and gratefully extend my love and appreciation.

Author's Note

This novel is based on the life of Albert Crosby who was one of Cape Cod's most colorful and renowned dignitaries. Although it relates the historical facts pertaining to his public life, his personal life is simply imagined and not meant to be interpreted as the truth. Many of the events described in my descriptive style are based on fact and taken from his true biography. Except for his immediate family members, close relatives and historically correct personages, the characters in the book are fictional and do not resemble any persons living or dead. While attempting to stay within the framework of the details that shaped his life, to best suit the relating, I have taken creative license with the personal aspects of it. If I have offended his descendants, it was not intentional and I extend my sincere apologies. However, I seriously doubt that after all these generations, accounts of his intimate private life have managed to survive substantiation throughout the 100 years since his death.

In the case of Albert Crosby, there were many family mysteries and secrets that were concealed or unknown and thus became a source of curiosity. The incidents that shaped "Where The Herring Run" were inspired by these innuendos, rumors and hearsays. I have drawn upon these to formulate my novel. For literary purposes and booklover appeal, I trust the reader will forgive these liberties. In the name of historical fiction, I have endeavored to fabricate the truth.

Also, I plan to donate a percentage received from the sale of this book to the "Friends Of Crosby Mansion." These funds will help toward the restoration and preservation of Tawasentha—Brewster's architectural *Grande Dame*, the historically valued, Crosby Mansion.

Prologue

▼

In early March of 1992, the Friends of the Crosby Mansion Committee, a volunteer group, held a meeting at the Crosby mansion. Its purpose was to plan an open house as part of the "Brewster In Bloom" weekend, at the end of April. The mansion was in its initial stages of restoration. They believed that public tours would help to fund further renovations.

After an extended tour of the mansion to acquaint us with this enormous project, we assembled in the grand foyer. As I sat and tried to listen attentively to the instructions of the chairwoman of the committee, I was surrounded by friends and associates, all with a common cause. At times during the long discourse, I found myself distracted as I scanned each nook and cranny of this once exquisite structure. I began to visualize the resurrection of this stately monument. As the discourse about its illustrious past progressed, I envisioned the former mansion emerging in its original splendor.

The chairwoman then began to lecture on the different aspects of Albert Crosby's life. As she spoke, I imagined ghostly specters from the past materializing into real people and begin to fill the mansion's elaborate halls. The sights and sounds of that era came to life for me. The director's voice droned on as she recited a short biographical outline of Albert Crosby's life. She stressed how much he enjoyed the old homestead, especially when his second wife Matilda entertained. I pictured Albert, in his declining years, recalling his eventful lifetime while sitting in a rocker next to the fireplace of his beloved retreat. The curtain opens, giving the scene around me substance, splendor and soul. It sets the stage for my novel, "Where the Herring Run."

CHAPTER 1

Late-August, 1832

Airborne on a cool, late summer breeze, an intense, reverberating sound drifted in undulating tones toward the bay. Petite Mira (short for Elmira and pronounced Mea'ra) Kerrigan reached and tugged furiously at a rope attached to the crown of an authentic ship's bell. This enormous artifact hung from a solidly anchored bracket on the front fence post. The resonant tone of the clapper's incessant hammering against the large bronze bell, echoed through Brewster, for miles in every direction.

"Oh, damn! It's time to go back, Anne," I shouted, turning to find my eleven-year-old sister bending over in the distance, pail in hand, ready to pluck just one more treasure relinquished by the sea. Although only nine at the time, I was prone to using socially unacceptable language.

"Yes, Albert, I hear the bell! You needn't have cursed about it!" Anne yelled back in an abrupt and reproachful manner. "Miss Mira said she'd ring the bell at four, so we'd have plenty of time to clean up for supper." Because Mira Kerrigan never married, we were required to address her as "Miss Mira" out of respect.

"As if you're telling me something I don't already know," I snarled sarcastically.

"Anyway, the tide's begun to turn now, so we'd better pick up our things from the beach and leave," she said assertively.

It was a picture perfect August day—one that had brought together a rare convergence of two long-awaited events—a sunny afternoon and low tide. The peaceful grandeur of the Brewster flats had beckoned. I grew up watching the relentless ebb and flow of the ocean tides from the upstairs windows of my humble home. I learned at an early age that it took six hours for the tide to go out and another six hours for it to return. I imagined that the sea became weary, intermittingly relinquishing its otherwise relentless hold on the shore to impatient landlubbers—always of course, promising to return. It's as if this ceaseless cabaret of sorts continued to prevail upon this ancient promontory as a needed relief. This happened twice daily, approximately an hour later each day, year in and year out. My many jaunts in the bay at low tide proved to be a fascinating world of discovery. The bay—especially in Brewster—virtually emptied. This picturesque scene was caused by a tide that retreated for more than a mile from the shoreline. Those long stretches of amber, soggy sand exposed at low tide were called the "Brewster Flats."

I always felt that my beloved Brewster, which hugged the inner elbow of the Cape, was one of the loveliest towns on Cape Cod—a 400 square-mile land mass that protruded into the Atlantic Ocean. The map of Cape Cod is similar to an arm and a pugilistic fist seemingly flexed to protect the State of Massachusetts. All through my life, I often found myself closing my fist and bending my arm at a right angle upward and parallel to my shoulders. This makeshift, fleshy atlas helped to pinpoint the exact location of my origins. My native town of Brewster was situated in the curvature between the forearm and what looks like a hand with its fingers bent inward.

The bay waters hug the inner elbow, while the ocean waters slam against the outer arm, from the shoulder to around the bent hand where it meets with the sea in the bay.

When comparing the Oceanside to the Bayside, the latter won when my parents decided to build their homestead. The entire town of Brewster is situated on the bay. The sheltered waters of Cape Cod Bay are decidedly warmer and calmer than those of the outer peninsula of the Cape where the icy, turbulent waters of the open ocean crash in mountainous waves against the shore. The breathtaking splendor of the bay in Brewster is a brilliant jewel—the focal point in nature's regal crown.

My hometown of Brewster, with almost 1300 inhabitants, was incorporated twenty years before my birth in 1803. Before that time, it was a part of the Town of Harwich. Brewster was named after William Brewster, a Mayflower pilgrim. The production of salt was the major industry. The center of town was called the "Factory Village" and was situated around a gristmill on Stony Brook Road—the main thoroughfare through Brewster. It was once known as Stagecoach Road. Most lanes leading to the seashore on the north side of Brewster eventually ended at the Olde King's Highway—a central road that traversed through most of the towns on Cape Cod. Our neighboring towns, which pale in comparison to Brewster are—Orleans to the east—Harwich to the south—Dennis to the west and—Chatham to our southeast.

Anne and I enjoyed meandering along the long stretches of sodden sand exposed by the receding tide. Even at our young age we had a keen sense of appreciation for the wonders of nature as we looked through the lens of child-like awe. These excursions along the flats had become a competitive sport for us. While exploring the flats we aggressively vied for the most extraordinary shells and exquisite polished stones.

We had reached the beach around noon accompanied by our affectionate and faithful rusty colored mongrel, Teddy. He had been a constant companion since I was seven. Fully prepared for our quest, Anne and I arrived carrying pails, nets and a small picnic basket.

"Oh, look, Albert!" Anne shouted with glee as she examined the contents of the picnic basket. "Miss Mira filled it with fruit, corn bread and beach plum jelly! See,…she even gave us a flask of water and a large linen napkin."

"Yes, and I bet you didn't notice Miss Mira also slipped a few freshly baked cookies into our pockets," I replied smugly, knowing that Anne had missed *that* surprise. "She knows how hungry we can get in the afternoon."

While squatting in a favorite hollow between the tall sea grass and beach heather, we ate our lunch and shared some with Teddy. After neatly placing everything back into the basket, we raced down the sand dunes to the shore. Gentle, placid Teddy tagged right along. With my sleeves folded to my elbows and knickers rolled up to my thighs, I waded barefoot through the tawny, dank sand left by the receding waters of the bay. A trail of tiny footprints on the soft, exposed sea floor would remain behind me until it was washed away by the incoming tide. Anne had tied her long dress into a knot at her waist. As we approached the wet, sandy flats, I turned around and started walking backwards. I had developed a habit of looking up at the rolling dunes overlooking the bay.

"Anne, someday when I'm very wealthy, I'd like to build a beautiful castle right there above that high, sandy hill. Wouldn't that be grand! That's my dream!" I said, as I excitedly pointed to the sloping embankment above the shoreline. As I had done many times before, I shared my innermost secrets and aspirations with Anne.

"Dream on, you silly fool!" she scoffed, grimacing. "You, wealthy!…That's a laugh!"

The fitful honking sound of the Canadian geese flying south in a "V" formation occasionally interrupted the stillness of this amazing stretch of sand. The shimmering summer sky was vibrantly reflected in the shallow tidal pools, while the steady, shrieking cry of the seagulls drifting and gliding in the thermals proclaimed their supremacy of the skies. With loud, shrill screeches they circled their prey. Then plummeting with a driving force, they dove for the soft-shelled clams grasping them in their beaks. After soaring to great heights they deliberately dropped them on the stones below to crack them open. The gulls swooped down, drove other scavengers away, and then enjoyed their solitary feast while strutting along the jetties or perched on roof eaves and weirs (large nets stretched over tall posts that were anchored into the sand at low tide). At high tide, large schools of fish became trapped in the nets that extended from the shore into the bay for a half-mile. Fish and shellfish were our primary sources of food.

Another sound indigenous to the flats was the rustling of sails on the moored sailboats. Fanned by an occasional sea breeze the intermittent ping and clang of the metal clamps against the mast was similar to the tinkling tones of a melodic wind chime.

The sandpipers, terns and piping plovers ran haphazardly along the receding shoreline plucking tiny minnows and pecking at the hermit crabs that were scuttling for cover. The distant weirs also served as landmarks. As we rambled along the flats, their presence discouraged straying too far off course.

Anne and I were well aware of all the familiar sights and sounds that surrounded us. Yet in spite of this, we became too engrossed with our task at hand. We had wandered far from shore while searching for unique shells and crustaceans for our prized collections.

Teddy, impatient with our dawdling, returned to the warm, sandy beach for an afternoon nap. The resonant, tolling bell signaled the conclusion of our outing. We decided to gather our treasures and leave. Although conscious of the fact that the incoming tide, once it reached dead low, could steadily creep back unnoticed and trap us in deep cleavages between the sand bars, we nonchalantly went along our merry way.

Anne hopped and skipped along the flats, over a sand bar, and then through ankle-deep water before finally catching up to me. Further ahead by several yards and heading toward the shoreline, I had been wading in water up to my knees. With an awareness and intelligence way beyond her years, Anne stopped abruptly, looked straight ahead, and then turned in my direction.

"Oh, Albert, look at all that water ahead of us!…Some of it must be very deep!" she cried out, terrified. "We've been out here too long! We didn't notice that the tide has already turned!…It's been coming in behind us without our being aware of it. The water must have surrounded us while we were busy searching for shells!"

Although her expressive, blue eyes vividly mirrored her intense fear, for my sake she tried to suppress her panicked feelings. Nevertheless, I sensed her anguish as she urged me to move faster.

"Hurry!…Give me your pail!" she shouted while anxiously reaching out for my bucket and tying it to her apron sash. "Hurry! Hurry! We must leave this very minute! Quickly, give me your hand and don't let go!"

"But-t-t?…Our clothes will get all wet and Miss Mira will be very angry about that." I questioned naïvely, completely unaware of the impending danger.

"Never you mind!" Anne scolded, reaching for my hand. "I just hope the shallows aren't over our heads. We shouldn't have ignored the changing tide," she grumbled, pointing toward the shore and the water up ahead. "I hope it isn't too late…It can get very deep out there." Straining to stay composed, Anne promptly took hold of my hand and grasped it tightly.

"Run! Run, Albert! We can do it,…if we hurry!" she commanded loudly, knowing she had to be forceful and convincing because I could be downright headstrong, especially when it came to following her directives.

"I better do as she says," I reasoned wisely. I had never ventured into water over my head before and was apprehensive about that. Anne and I began to run faster and faster. At first we waded through ankle-deep water—soon, it was up to our knees. We advanced quickly, but the water was waist-deep at this point. Although two years older, Anne was small for her age and just a head taller than I was. When the water reached her shoulders, it was up to my neck. Not able to walk any further, we were faced with a crisis.

"Albert, it looks like it's getting deeper and deeper as we head toward shore. We mustn't waste another minute!" she called out, her trembling voice betraying her anguish.

"But, I can swim!" I hollered back still feeling confident and unruffled. I must have been very young when I learned how. It seemed like I had always known how to swim. Swimming was a means of survival for children reared on Cape Cod, especially those who lived close to the bay.

"I know that!" Anne responded loudly and impatiently while removing the pails from her apron sash and setting them down on the seabed. "We'll have to start swimming and right away!"

"What are you doing, Anne?" I asked, horrified. I was panic-stricken at the thought of losing my precious collection—the valued fruits of my labor.

"The pails are too heavy," she replied matter-of-factly. "I can't swim with them hanging from my waist…They'll be safe here. We can come back tomorrow at low tide to pick them up." Anne knew, however, that the current at high tide would most likely carry our pails and possessions back out to sea. Despite being fretful over my treasures, I reluctantly accepted her decision. Her sense of self-preservation drove her attention to the immediate dilemma at hand.

"I won't be able to hold your hand, Albert, once we start swimming. We'll head for that jetty ahead. The one that's closest to shore," she said, pointing toward a distant mound of stones surrounded by marsh grass. "I'll let you know as soon as I think we can stand. Maybe we won't have to swim too far." Anne covered her mouth with her hand and with a pained expression, whimpered, "Oh, how I wish I'd paid more attention to the incoming tide! I should have been more responsible…It's all my fault. This can't be happening to us!"

"Albert, swim close to me! I'll watch you!…If I see you're beginning to tire, I'll reach over to grab your trouser straps and try to help you along!" she yelled, determined to make the best of a bad situation.

Although encouraged to persist, I was wary of navigating through the vast watery distance ahead. Prodded by masculine pride and youthful innocence, I suddenly felt an urge to prove my prowess. The waves splashed against my face as I started to swim away from Anne.

"All right, here I go!" I shouted. "Race you to the beach!"

"No, Albert!" Anne screamed, frantically waving her arms. "I told you to stay right here next to me!…Oh, you little brat! I'll strangle you when I catch up to you!" she bristled. It was obvious that she was angered and frustrated with my impudence. Frenzied by my disobedience, Anne began to swim furiously through the choppy, spanking waves.

The water in the bay was usually quite calm; however, on this late August afternoon, a brisk east wind whipped up a lather of surging whitecaps. A moderately turbulent surf was licking at the shore.

"Albert, are you all right?" Anne hollered when she finally caught up to me.

"Yes," I indicated with a nod of my head and turning in the direction of her voice. A short while later, she noticed that although I was making a valiant effort, I was struggling to keep my head above water. Exhausted, my flagging little arms wearied from the long swim. I had gradually lost what little strength and rhythm I needed to keep myself afloat.

"Albert, are you sure you're all right?" Anne managed to ask again, shouting and gasping for breath. "You look so tired."

This time, I didn't turn to answer. I was concentrating on putting one limp arm in front of the other. I kept trying to prod my lifeless legs that would not respond to my will.

"Remember, Albert," Anne hollered, instructing and guiding me along, "if we get tired from swimming we can float on our backs for a while! Paddle forward with your hands! The waves will carry us toward shore."

"All right, Anne," I replied. "I'm so glad you thought about that!" I was revitalized by her inspired idea and thankful for her quick thinking. "But,…I'm so tired and we've such a long way to go!" I sputtered feebly.

As I gathered one last ounce of inner strength, I turned myself over on my back, laid flat on the surface of the water, and then submerged my head until it was parallel to my ears. I propelled myself through the swells using a seesaw motion with my feet and spanking my hands against the water. Anne was doing the same, rapidly kicking and paddling fast enough to find herself next to me. She promised to stay close by—just in case I needed her.

"I'm here now! I'm right beside you!" she shouted reassuringly. After floating on our backs for five minutes or so, Anne asked, "Can you swim now? We must hurry, the tide's rushing in right behind us!"

"I'll try! I think I can!" I replied in a feeble voice that lacked my former enthusiasm and confidence.

Together, Anne and I flipped ourselves over again and began to swim toward shore—buoyed by the push of the incoming tide. Progressing faster now toward the beach, we alternated between the breaststroke, dog paddling and floating on our backs. All the while, Anne kept a close watch on me. She realized I was again beginning to flounder. Fatigued, my flaccid arms thrashed uncontrollably above the water. I was determined to keep moving. Yet, as I fought to stay afloat, my vigor was slowly waning. I was at the mercy of the rising sea and the whitecaps that relentlessly splashed over my head.

"Please, God! Help me! Don't let me drown!…I want to live!" I prayed, too frightened to cry. My head began bobbing in and out of the water—sometimes under water for several seconds.

Due to the difference in our ages, Anne's tolerance and physical endurance were greater than mine—this gave her a decided edge in a crisis. Intuitively she sensed the impending danger and took the initiative. Anne promptly mobilized every ounce of her energy, perseverance and wit to save us both. She reached over and seized my britches by the shoulder straps. While energetically kicking her way toward shore, Anne held me above the water with one hand and paddled with the other.

"Oh, dear God, please help us!" Anne prayed, fearing the worse. Although terrified, she evoked the god of her spiritual heritage. She truly believed the lord of her deep Quaker faith would listen to her plea. Anne relied on his help and intervention. "I'm so tired and frightened. I don't know how much longer I can hold Albert and myself above water. I'm afraid we won't make it back to shore. Please, Lord!…Help us!…We must touch bottom soon!"

Anne later informed me of her thoughts and prayers during this ordeal and how they had thoroughly overwhelmed her. She claimed, that at the time, vivid images filled her mind. It superseded even the danger at hand. Anne pictured our grief-stricken parents mourning our loss with numbing disbelief—the accidental drowning of their beloved children—a tragic and inconceivable blow. While trying to dispel these depressing thoughts, Anne said she became acutely aware of something barely touching her toes. She instantly realized it was the hard shell of a horseshoe crab—an ancient creature that roamed the sandy bottom of the bay.

"Oh, thank you, Lord!" Anne exclaimed, looking upward and showing her gratitude for a prayer promptly answered. She turned to tell me the good news. Unfortunately, I had already swallowed a considerable amount of salt water. I made a futile attempt to clear my throat while choking and coughing profusely.

"Albert,…we'll be all right now! We'll be on the sandbar in no time!" she called out nodding her head and elated by our good fortune. "Soon, you'll be able to feel it and walk on your own! I'll hang on to you until then!"

Even though we were still in water up to our shoulders, Anne towed me in by my shoulder straps until we arrived at a point where both of us could touch bottom. As soon as I could stand on my own, she closed her fist and managed to pound several forceful blows against my back. I coughed convulsively, expelling the salty brine from my lungs.

"There now!…Doesn't that feel better?" Anne asked, anxious to hear me speak. She eagerly awaited an answer that would acknowledge the fact that I was all right.

"Yes," I nodded as I reached for her with a trembling hand once the incessant choking and spitting finally ceased. "I guess we were very lucky…Weren't we Anne?" I blurted as soon as I was able to speak, albeit panting, gasping and wheezing between breaths. Shaken and emotionally upset by the whole experience, I turned around to face her. "We made it back just in time…Just a little while longer out there and…"

"I know, Albert," she interrupted. "I hate to think of what could have happened to us if Miss Mira hadn't rung that bell when she did."

Teddy had made it back well before us. Sensing we were in danger, he was pacing back and forth, in and out of the shallow water, ready to bolt homeward to alert Miss Mira. He caught sight of us scrambling toward shore and swam out to greet us. At first we were in deep water up to our necks and shoulders, then waist, knee and ankle deep until we were finally on the sandy beach. The shore-birds darted aimlessly out of our way, skittering along the surf as we made our way through the water's edge. Like a draft beer foaming over a mug, the tidal water spewed its white, effervescent froth on the dry seashore. In a shivering frenzy I began squeezing the water from my rompers and shirt.

"What shall we tell, Miss Mira?" I asked while Anne untangled her ankle-length dress, squeezed the water out of it, and then twisted it into a large, tight roll. Shaking uncontrollably, she firmly massaged her arms with her hands. The preoccupied expression on her face revealed a plausible answer was racing through her mind.

"Don't worry, Albert," Anne replied confidently and without hesitation, "I'll give Miss Mira a believable excuse. I'll make up a good story that will sound quite convincing…I'm sure she'll think I'm being truthful."

"I certainly hope so. She's sure to notice our wet clothing…What will you tell her?" I asked, questioning her brashness and worried that our tale might sound vague and contrived. It was essential that I knew precisely what she was going to say.

"Just you never mind!" she reprimanded, tugging at my sleeve and obviously frustrated by my skepticism. "You just be quiet when she asks! Don't say a word! Let me do all the talking…You hear!"

"All right,…but it better sound like the truth, Anne," I threatened assertively.

"Oh, yes,…it will," she replied. "I haven't decided what I'm going to tell her as yet." I understood Anne well enough to know that she had already concocted the story in her mind and that she had it down pat. She was in complete control of the situation and knew exactly what she would say.

Teddy raced alongside us with his tail wagging excitedly until we reached the beach and jutting sand dunes. He gave his furry body several violent shakes.

"Teddy, stop that!" I scolded, ducking from the cold, startling spray and covering my face with my forearm.

Although a brilliant sun radiated from its foothold in the late August sky, it lacked the penetrating rays of a higher mid-summer orb that soothed and warmed skins chilled by the cool bay waters. Alas, it was too late in the season to expect that kind of comforting, therapeutic relief. Clammy, wet clothing froze our tiny bodies.

"We won't be able to dry off," Anne said, trembling irrepressibly. We hugged ourselves in a desperate attempt to keep warm. "It's been quite a while since we've heard the bell. We should be on our way this very minute."

"You're right, Anne. Oh,...I'm so cold!" I complained, racked by convulsive tremors. The frigid water had soaked my clothing and shocked my small body. "I just can't seem to stop shivering!"

"Neither can I," Anne replied, shuddering. Her plump, small-boned frame was shaking violently. "Look!" she added, pointing straight ahead. "There's a large driftwood log on the beach. We'll sit on it while we dry ourselves."

As we reached the expansive shoreline we found that the sand—long exposed to the sun was warm underfoot—similar to the comforting, heated foot-bricks under our blankets.

"That warm sand certainly feels good doesn't it, Albert?" Anne asked. I nodded my head several times in agreement. We approached the pitted, sun-bleached timber and plunked our drenched bodies on it. I imagined it to be a former mast from a shipwrecked vessel, most likely the victim of a tempest.

"Go over there and fetch the picnic basket. We'll use the napkin to dry ourselves off as best we can," Anne directed, pointing to her right.

Teddy again tagged behind me as I picked up the basket and returned it to Anne. After using the red linen cloth to dry our hair, arms and legs, I yanked the saucer shaped straw hat that I had left behind—over my head. I hoped it would shield my wet hair from Miss Mira's eagle eyes. I stood and handed the fringed square to Anne. Teddy had already darted toward home.

"Here's the napkin, Anne," I said, turning to follow Teddy..."I'm finished with it."

Anne reached for the square piece of fabric and wrapped it around her big, single braid. The cloth absorbed the water as she squeezed and pressed it against her chestnut hair.

Teddy waited patiently up ahead—his tail wagging like a rapid metronome. He bolted toward the homeward path, hesitated, and then returned. Teddy did this repeatedly while Anne and I tried to make ourselves presentable. I hurriedly crammed the napkin into the basket and closed it. It was time to head for home.

"Albert, please pick up the basket?" Anne asked politely. "Now give me your hand...I'm ready." She rose and reached for my outstretched arm.

Anne adjusted her apron and pushed her braid to the back of her head. We mounted a sandy slope covered with bayberry and lavender thistle. It was edged with wild sweet peas and tall sea grasses. Anne and I ran haphazardly along a sinuous, well-worn path that led from the dunes to our Crosby homestead. We were trying to catch up with Teddy, who was already way ahead of us.

"Teddy's probably already home," I thought as we neared the cottage, traumatized by our frightful experience, wet, cold and still trembling.

Our nanny was standing in the front doorway waiting for us to return home. More than an hour had passed since she had summoned us.

Years later when I revealed the truth about our sojourn on the flats and our near drowning in the incoming tide, Miss Mira admitted that she had been nervously awaiting our return and had been intermittently surveying the vast expanse of green and sloping acreage that led to the water's edge. One could enjoy a magnificent panoramic view of the bay from that vantage point. Miss Mira said that she had tried several times to concentrate on her kitchen chores, but found herself frequently stepping outside the door to scan the horizon.

"Where are the wee ones?" she kept asking herself. (Miss Mira affectionately called us the "wee ones.") "I hope me Anne and me Albert haven't gotten hurt or worst yet caught in the late afternoon tide." (Her brogue replaced "me" for my— and "ye" for you.) Miss Mira said she promptly regained her composure and before these thoughts could panic her, she decided, "That's it! I'll wait just a few more minutes, then I'll head straight for the beach!" Just then, her anxiety quickly turned to relief. "Oh! Thanks be to God!…Here comes me Teddy!"

Ultimately, our little heads popped up over the horizon. Miss Mira caught sight of us in the distance hustling along the rambling rose-covered bluff toward home. After concluding that we were fine, she said she heaved a deep sigh and bolted in our direction.

"Come along quickly now!" Miss Mira shouted, running toward us and vigorously waving her arms. "Ye late for supper!" She was keenly perceptive and immediately detected our drenched clothing and quivering bodies.

"Ah, I see ye two have gotten a dunkin' in the bay today! Aye now,…haven't ye?" she scolded in her rhythmic Irish brogue. Miss Mira placed her hands on my shoulders and stopped me dead in my tracks. She bent down and faced me directly. Instinctively, I turned my head and looked away.

"Well, now, me Albert,…tell Miss Mira how did that happen?" she asked, calmly trying to restrain her anger—her vibrant blue eyes sparkling as she spoke. She carefully inspected us from head to toe and continued to question us hoping to get an honest answer. Intuitively, she knew she'd never learn the whole truth. Frustrated because I refused to answer her, Miss Mira grasped my chin firmly with her hand and wrenched my head back to face her.

"Ye weren't caught on the flats by the incoming tide,…now were ye?" she quizzed again, clearly annoyed, exasperated and muttering to herself, in that order. "Ye both been warned about that many times." Suddenly, Miss Mira remembered how worried she had been about us and began to experience a deep sense of remorse. Irritation turned to compassion as she released her grip on my chin. "Ye wee ones were certainly out there for a long time," she said in a more tempered voice. "Ye worried me so!...Ye did! Thank the Good Lord...ye back here in one piece! Ye guardian angels were certainly watching over ye today! I say amen to that,...I do!" she exclaimed, thankful for our safe return.

Miss Mira glanced at our hands and noticed that the picnic basket was the only thing we carried home. "I see that ye have ye picnic basket, but where are ye pails and sea shells?" she asked, deciding to interrogate us further.

I quickly turned toward Anne and waited for her answer. Although she had been in serious thought, Anne hid it quite well behind her freckled face and flippant expression. It spoke volumes about her childlike body that was indeed the temple of an old soul. She braced herself, gulped, and then began to unravel her detailed fabrication. Anne hoped it would be sincere enough to satisfy Miss Mira's curiosity. Certain that her contrived deception was foolproof, Anne started by giving a vague, yet valid summary of what had occurred on the flats. The results being of course, the condition we were in—thoroughly chilled and soaked to the skin. She remained completely composed while relating her fictitious tale, showing no telltale signs of being deceitful.

"Well,...Miss Mira," she alleged accusingly, gesturing and shaking her index finger toward Teddy. "While we were in the deepest part of a tidal pool that naughty dog disobeyed us. Although we told Teddy to stay put and wait for us on shore, he swam through the water to be with us. We decided to walk back with him. All of a sudden, Teddy jumped up to lick my face. His paws pushed against my shoulders and I found myself falling backwards. He was so heavy, Miss Mira, I just couldn't hold my balance and fell into the water. I collided with Albert on the way down and he fell in, too. We both got a drenching...through and through."

"Poor Teddy,...he's so caring and loyal," I pondered sadly. "He's been wrongly accused for what happened to us. If only he could speak and defend himself."

"That doesn't account for ye getting ye hair wet!" Miss Mira said, observing our soggy and droopy hound dog appearance. "And where are ye pails?" she asked again.

Without hesitating Anne resumed her deceitful yarn. "Albert and I decided that as long as we were wet already, we might as well enjoy a little swim," she replied unruffled. "We didn't realize that once we were out of the water,...we'd be so cold. Albert and I left our pails back at the beach," she went on without taking a breath. "We're drying our shells on a flat piece of driftwood. We'll return to pick them up tomorrow after lunch."

Anne's brilliant tale completely charmed me. I was astonished by her resource-ful rhetoric. As far as I was concerned it was inspired. When Miss Mira's atten-tion was elsewhere, I nodded, smiled and winked to show my approval. She responded with a "what-else-could-I-say" gesture. Unaccustomed to deceit, my conscientious sister informed me that she began to suffer pangs of gnawing guilt. Anne was convinced she would be eternally banished to the fires of hell.

"We'll clean up quickly at the outdoor pump, Miss Mira," Anne suggested with a sheepish look, "then we'll come right in to change for supper."

"No,…indeed ye not!" Miss Mira bellowed irately. "I think ye filling me with a whole lot of blarney."

She was not as easily deceived and gullible as we hoped. Miss Mira reached for our hands and held us in tow as we started for home. Teddy tagged along behind. I managed a loud sneeze and when my nose began to gush, I wiped it with my sleeve. We walked back together in utter silence, hand-in-hand toward home over a grassy, sloping rise covered with daisies and tufts of goldenrod.

"Ye come in the kitchen this very minute! Take off ye wet things and be dry in there!" Miss Mira ordered, leaning over to speak directly to us while referring to the small, white cottage ahead. We walked through the metal gate that creaked as it swung open onto the homestead property. Weathered fence posts and vines of wisteria and Boston ivy, which held up the rusted wire fencing, enclosed the acre-age within the perimeters of the cottage. "I'll hand ye wee ones a warm towel and soap to clean ye. Come now,…hurry before ye catch ye death and ye mother's eye. Ye certainly are a sight!"

When we reached the kitchen door, Miss Mira opened it and gently pushed us ahead of her. Teddy sat outside waiting for us to return. Although he was consid-ered a beloved member of our family, I could never understand why he wasn't allowed to enter the house. I guessed it had something to do with his getting a lit-tle too close to a skunk or dead animal, at times. The smell would linger in the cottage for weeks. Teddy usually spent his summer days outdoors—sprawled in a bed of tiger lilies next to the back entrance of the small house.

Large oak beams crisscrossed the ceiling and wide oak boards covered the floor of our unpretentious kitchen. Oak was plentiful on the Cape. Almost all the building materials and furnishings in our modest home were made of oak.

We waited at the black, cast iron sink that had an ornate water pump set deep within it. The pump had a long, curled handle that fascinated my younger sib-lings.

"Can we push the handle up and down to see the water come out?" they often asked. The water pouring out of the spigot seemed magical to them.

My little sisters, Emeline and Kate excitedly skipped into the kitchen to greet us. Ignoring them, I began to wash.

"Anne!" they shouted at the top of their lungs while eagerly reaching to embrace her.

"We missed you! You were gone for such a long time!" Emeline whined. "We've been waiting all afternoon for you to play with us." She was upset and pouting because of Anne's long absence. Anne lovingly bent down and embraced them. "Oh, Anne,…you're all *wet!*" Emeline cried out, obviously repelled by Anne's soaked clothing.

"Sh-sh-sh-!" interrupted Miss Mira, placing her finger over her tightly closed lips.

"Me Little William's napping," she said, speaking softly to quiet the noisy group. "The wee one is plum tuckered…up half the night fussing, he was. I think he's a bit under the weather, again. Ye please be a bit more quiet now. We'll wake him soon,…he mustn't sleep through supper."

"Yes, I know sweetie," Anne replied in a hush voice, turning to answer Emeline. "I'll tell you all about it later." She grinned and inadvertently blurted, "It'll be another one of my famous tales." Suddenly, Anne realized what she said, placed her hand over her mouth, and then quickly looked around for Miss Mira who already had left for the sitting room. "Oh, thank goodness,…Miss Mira didn't hear me say that!" Anne whispered, relieved to find Miss Mira was no longer within earshot.

After leaving the necessary items for us to freshen up, Miss Mira carefully hung a new set of dry clothing on a pegged shelf for our appearance at the supper table. Miss Mira reached for a long wick from a wall bracket and began to flit about from room to room lighting the lanterns. Like a buoyant fairy, she created a magical flame with the delicate touch of her wand. Trying all at once to prepare and serve a hot evening meal for the dinner table, she darted to and fro from hearth to counter and table—whirling about like a spinning top.

Miss Mira had been with the Crosby family for over a decade now. She wore many hats and served the family in various capacities as—housemaid, cook, nanny, servant and nurse. She was also an extremely capable aide to my mother, Catherine. Miss Mira had emigrated from Ireland in the early 1800s. At the time, she was a learned young woman pursuing adventure and a more challenging future.

Our nanny blushed very easily. Because of her fair complexion, her face became beet red at times. She combed her graying, red hair in a long braid that was neatly twisted upward and circled her head several times. Over the years,

Miss Mira had developed a nervous twitch—squinting and wrinkling up her nose at the same time. Her vivid, gray-blue eyes sparkled when she spoke and the evenly spaced squint lines on her cheekbones and across the top of her nose only served to make her smile even more endearing. The sound of her thick Gaelic accent and pleasant chatter was a cadenza of melodic notes to the ears of those around her.

Now in her fifties—her trim figure belied her age. She usually wore a long, black apron over a bouffant, gray dress that swept the floor as she walked. The apron's sash—tied around her waist into a large flowing bow—fell to her dress hem. This otherwise austere garment had a tiny, white eyelet trim edging on the neckline that sufficed as enough finery for her liking.

Miss Mira's cordiality and friendliness were as infectious as laughter. She was cheerful at breakfast, good-natured at lunch and still quite affable at dinner. Calm and even-tempered, she managed every small catastrophe with efficient, resourceful aplomb. Miss Mira made poultices with condiments and herbs and often sent us to bathe in the salt water to soak our sores or rashes. She firmly believed in its healing powers.

I remember slowly shuffling into the kitchen, holding my left cheek while she was preparing a pan of beans for supper. Miss Mira lifted her head to greet me and instantly noticed my pained expression.

"What's wrong with ye, me laddie?" she asked, beckoning me to come to her. "Quick now,…me Albert! Come here to Mira."

"Oh, Miss Mira," I moaned as I hurried toward her. "I have a terrible tooth-ache! The whole side of my face hurts. I thought maybe, I'd put a piece of ice…" Before I could finish my sentence, she opened my mouth to take a look.

"Ah! I see what's wrong…Ye have a bad tooth!" she said categorically. While still holding my chin, she looked straight into my eyes, gestured with her hand, and then held up her index finger. "Aye, me bonnie laddie, I know just how to fix ye problem! A bit of clove oil should do it," she added in her familiar Irish brogue. Alas, the small container of clove oil she took down from the kitchen shelf was empty.

"Not to worry," she said assuredly, turning from the shelf, facing me, and then resolutely waving her arms in the opposite direction. Miss Mira's clever, innovative mind had already conceived of a remedy. She promptly raced around the kitchen, reached for a small bowl, some whole cloves and a wooden mallet. Miss Mira began pounding the cloves, pulverizing them into a fine powder, dipped her index finger into this mixture, and then gestured for me to come close.

"Let me see…if this'll help ye. Open ye mouth again, me laddie," she ordered. Miss Mira forcibly applied the minced cloves to my aching tooth. "There now,…that should feel better very soon, me Albert," she said convincingly, putting her arms around me in a comforting embrace.

Miss Mira seldom appeared irritated or provoked. I surmised she effectively concealed these feelings behind a mask that constantly flashed a bemused smile. She had become an integral part of the family. Not only was she a treasured employee of the Crosby family, but also because of her winning ways she was also an indispensable, and trusted friend. The Crosby children loved her. When Miss Mira chastised or scolded she was fair and evenhanded and always gave us an ardent hug after it was done and over with. We often ran to her for a comforting embrace that was always forthcoming.

"Oh, begorra!" Miss Mira would call out, beckoning us to her open arms. "Come here me bonnie wee ones so I can hold ye close by me." With compassionate and boundless wisdom, she would say, "Aye,…I see ye needs a big hug again, today!" Our nanny would often interrupt her busy chores to listen attentively to our chatter. She would repeatedly surprise us with a treat that she had affectionately put into our pockets. Mindful of our incessant hunger pangs, she thoughtfully left some hasty pudding or molasses and fresh bread on the table. These simple gestures were typical of her acts of extraordinary love for us.

When our parents were away, Miss Mira would set us on her lap and mesmerize our very beings with fairy tales and enchanting fantasies about elves and leprechauns. This was a special treat that she wisely dispensed only at bedtime. A mélange of broken English combined with her Gaelic brogue assailed the text as Miss Mira tried to read our favorite storybooks. It was quite a feat, but she persevered despite her thick Irish accent and limited English diction. She listened to our prayers and affectionately tucked us into bed with a quick, tender kiss on the forehead.

Anne and I heaped our wet clothing in the sink and wrapped ourselves in a towel. With the freshly ironed ensembles draped over our arms, we ascended the staircase to dress in our respective rooms.

Anne later returned to the kitchen—a confident, cheerful and impeccably groomed adolescent. She deliberately inhaled the aroma of the sweet bayberry candles that filled the room. The fragrance was especially delectable to Anne's sense of smell because she had meticulously crafted them herself. The tapers were set in holders and placed on opposite ends of the table. Their tiny flames cast large, darting shadows that exploded into radiant bursts of flickering and dancing languets against the whitewashed walls. This enchanting sight provided an endearing charm and warmth to our cozy cottage.

"Oh, me Anne, how lovely ye look in ye gingham dress!" Miss Mira exclaimed, delighted with the transformation and greeting her with a solicitous compliment. Anne casually slid along the bench to her place at the supper table.

"Thank you, Miss Mira. Oh, the scent of these candles is *so* delightful! Anne said excitedly, taking another deep breath.

"Aye, me lassie, ye certainly can be proud of yeself. Ye worked very hard making them from the bayberry wax. Ye such a smart, industrious child!" Miss Mira said, praising Anne's talents and leaning over to give her a complimentary hug. "And aye, ye didn't practice ye piano lessons today, she added…Ye better find the time after supper," Miss Mira reminded with an open smile and her usual easy-going manner.

"I was just thinking about that," she replied. "Yes,…I will, Miss Mira, unless Father needs to occupy the sitting room. I wouldn't want to disturb him." In my opinion, Anne was an exceptionally talented pianist—a focused and budding virtuoso.

Just then, the family noticed me standing in the doorway. I grinned, certain that my appearance would also please Miss Mira. While extending her right hand in my direction, she smiled and nodded her head in approval.

"Well now,…aren't ye the dapper one? Oh, me how ye've grown! Ye such a handsome laddie," Miss Mira commented favorably. "Ye certainly look a bit better than ye did a short while ago."

Quite self-satisfied with myself for the way I had prevailed over the events of that day, I took a deep breath and stood straight and tall. I was preparing for a future time when intellect, audacity and vigor would be crucial for defeating my quintessentially male competitors.

Undaunted, Miss Mira sent me off in the direction of the supper table—propelling me along with a genial love tap on my backside.

CHAPTER 2

▼

Late-May, 1835

"Sweet rolls!" I exclaimed overjoyed by the smell wafting upwards from the kitchen, still half asleep and sitting straight up in bed. The spicy aroma of cinnamon abruptly awakened me. Like a beckoning finger, it drifted through my bedroom door that had been left ajar. I opened my eyes to the transparent rays of early sunlight that enveloped me with a warm glow. Shafts of radiating light beamed through the bedroom curtains announcing the dawn of a beautiful, new day. They permeated the room, invigorating and prodding me to leap from my bed—a wake-up call for me. A blast of crisp, fresh air shot through the wide-open window of my bedroom and parted the curtains to reveal a cooing morning dove. The bird strutted along the windowsill, pecking at whatever insect it could find. The pleasant song of birds, native to the Cape and perched high in the canopy of nearby trees, filled the open air outside and resonated in my bedroom. They twittered and sang their distinctive songs while the chirping robins adeptly proclaimed the break of day. I pushed the coverlets aside and quickly bolted from my bed.

Miss Mira usually allowed me to sleep a little later on Saturdays. My spirit rejoiced as I stretched and yawned. I felt euphoric on this glorious day—extraordinarily alive and content with the world. She had baked my favorite breakfast treat. While removing my nightshirt, I salivated at the thought of those fresh, warm swirls of cinnamon dough covered with sweet churned butter. Miss Mira usually added a generous portion of tender raisins that truly tantalized my taste buds. I couldn't wait to sink my teeth into those delicious delicacies.

"Albert!" Miss Mira called out from below the staircase. "Are ye up, me laddie? Ye hurry down now,...while these rolls are still warm."

"Yes, Miss Mira. I'll be there in a few minutes…Just need to wash a bit," I replied, standing at the top of the oak stairway. I poured a little water from the large ceramic pitcher into a washbowl and splashed it on my face and hands. I hurriedly dried them with a hand towel and virtually jumped down the stairway into the kitchen. My sisters were already seated around the table—busy nibbling and chatting amongst themselves in subdued voices. They barely noticed me as I slid into my place.

"Where's Little William?"(We called our baby brother, "Little William.")I asked disappointedly, glancing toward his empty highchair. I missed his candescent presence at the breakfast table. He was especially bright and cheerful in the mornings. I looked forward to his laughter and warm hug.

"The wee lad was a bit croupy and had a high fever during the night," Miss Mira replied, clearly concerned as she placed the butter on the table. "Ye mother was up all night trying to ease Little William's breathing. She placed warm flannels on his chest and applied cold cloths to his forehead to bring down his fever. The wee one's finally fallen asleep. Ye mother's still resting while me serve ye breakfast."

"Little William hasn't been his usual chipper self these past few weeks," I thought while reaching for a sweet roll.

For several years now, he had endured reoccurring bouts of croup and fever during the long winter months. It racked his tiny body, taking a distressing toll on him *and* my parents. Little William would usually rally during the spring and summer, but that had not happened this year. Lately, he became quite frail and ashen. After hearing this latest update on his condition, my initial exuberance quickly faded into anguish.

I sat and ate quietly until I suddenly remembered something of utmost importance. I needed to ask permission to walk the several miles to the Factory Village and the Stony Brook with my friend Jonathan. With temperatures that sometimes climbed to summer levels after a chilly and hesitant early spring, the call to the outdoors was irresistible. Due to the glorious weather, it felt like a gift just to be outside and active.

"Miss Mira, do you think Marmmy (we called Mother, "Marmmy") would give me permission to go down to the Stony Brook River?" I asked, gulping down my second helping of sweet roll. "The alewives are already beginning to spawn in Mill Pond. Jonathan will be stopping by around ten this morning. We're planning on returning with a few pails full of fish. His mother would like to serve them for the supper meal this evening. Would you like us to come home with some for you, too, Miss Mira?…If that's all right with you,…I'll fill *my* pails for *our* supper?" I teased, hoping she would approve.

"Well, me Albert,…I guess it'd be all right…It's Saturday," she said, smiling and placing her hands in her pockets under her apron. "With no school today, I suppose ye laddies need to keep yeselves busy." Mindful of the fact that an outing in the fresh air would be beneficial, she went on to say, "It's time ye young ones enjoy some warm sunshine after our harsh, cold winter. Although ye may walk there with empty pails,…it'll be very difficult to return with full ones. I'll ask Japeth to pick ye up with the buckboard this afternoon around four o'clock. Should ye leave before ye parents arise, I'll inform them of ye whereabouts."

"Oh, thank you, Miss Mira," I said appreciatively, getting up from the table and running to her with open arms and a smile that stretched from ear to ear.

"Ye know, Albert,…the herring are very bony," she said, releasing her grip after hugging me tightly. "Ye need to help me clean and prepare them for the evening meal. I'll sear those tiny fillets over the open fire in the hearth."

"Yes,…I'll be happy to do that for you, Miss Mira," I replied after finishing my breakfast and wiping my chin with my napkin. "Jonathan and I may have time to clean them before we return home from the Herring Run. Japeth gave me a very sharp knife just for that purpose. I heard the alewives are very plentiful this year. In fact, there're so many in the run…they're being sold to fishermen in other towns."

"Be watchful me laddies of the many carriages and buckboards traveling along the way," Miss Mira warned, facing me and holding her right hand on my shoulder. "Ye knows I worry about me Albert, when ye out of me sight. Teddy will keep a watchful eye on ye. I filled a knapsack with fruit and such for a picnic lunch. Now mind ye, ye and Jonathan be very careful of those sharp knives,…and no wading over ye heads in the ponds…Ye hear!"

"I promise," I said, reaching for another sweet roll before bolting out the door. "I need to fetch my fishing gear from the barn. I'll be back in good time to greet Jonathan."

Jonathan Eldredge, my chubby best friend who was slightly taller than I, knocked at my door promptly at ten. He was fair-haired and had a rosy, freckled complexion. My young companion was definitely in his awkward stage. His ears were too large for his head and his front teeth—too big for his mouth. Every time I looked at him, I couldn't help thinking he bore a striking resemblance to a beaver. Of course—I probably looked the same to him. We shared everything together—our likes and dislikes, fantasies, and aspirations. Although his family was not as well off as ours, he was never envious of me. We confided in one another and seldom disagreed. He was a true friend. Jonathan never became angry with me or left me to join another. In the summer, we would lie in the grass and stare at the clouds, trying to identify their shapes. We went swimming, fishing, hunting, sailing, and horseback riding or just hiking on the woodland trails. There were many other activities we shared together. Winter found us spreading our arms outward and back and forth, making angle wings as we lay in the snow. Jonathan and I spent many hours sledding, skating or ice fishing on the nearby kettle ponds.

Teddy, who was full of repressed energy, was wildly wagging his tail and eager to get started on our excursion. His favorite sport was running briskly ahead—then returning to join us when we lagged behind. We gathered our knapsacks, pails and fishnets and began the long trek toward the Factory Village and the Herring Run at the Stony Brook Mill site. We would arrive shortly before noon.

The hub of all the existing activities in our picturesque, little town was centered around the Grist Mill. It was the bustling center of Brewster. Its many industrial buildings and water-powered mills hugged the Stony Brook and Satucket Roads. They were comfortably nestled around the junction of the Stony Brook and Lower Mill Pond. The stagecoach made regular stops at the Anguish Mcleod Tavern and Inn where weary travelers could find food and lodging. Several cotton and woolen mills, tanneries, a cobbler's shop, shoe factory and a gristmill were among the numerous thriving businesses in this area.

There were sixty salt works along the Brewster bay shores whose product was shipped worldwide. Salt was also used for softening leather at the tanneries. Brewster was one of Barnstable County's largest manufacturing centers and quite proud of its industrial superiority on Cape Cod.

Nearly a hundred sea captains made Brewster their home. Many generations ago, the sea brought their ancestors to this quaint and quiet town. Brewster's inhabitants were hard working, innovative, friendly and communal. The town also boasted several large fresh water lakes and ponds all teaming with perch and trout. Such was Brewster, Massachusetts on Cape Cod in the year 1835.

After a long, tiring trek, we neared our destination. As he had done many times before, Teddy ran back to join us from around a curve in the road. This time, however, he was barking furiously. Noticeably agitated—his loud bark was a clear sign of danger. Teddy stopped abruptly in front of us, stood up on his hind legs, and then quickly pushed us with his large paws—individually, one at the time, onto the berm of the road. A stagecoach loomed just ahead. It was headed toward the Olde King's Highway. The passengers were guests who had just departed from the inn. We could feel the rush of air as a team of extremely large Morgan horses raced past us. They nearly trampled Jonathan and me to death as we tried to flee from their path. The sound of the horses' hoofs as they galloped by was deafening. Teddy ran to the top of the slope.

"Whew!...That was a close call," I said, thankful that we were able to get out of its way in the nick of time.

"Thank God for Teddy! We owe him our lives!" Jonathan cried out gratefully after catapulting our bodies onto an ivy-covered knoll alongside the roadway. Still unnerved by our near demise, we rose and dusted ourselves off once the stagecoach was out of sight. While standing on wobbly legs, my face paled and my heart pounded like the beat on a brass drum. From a high outcropping above us, Teddy ran down the slope to join us. With his tail lashing back and forth, he stood on his hind legs and licked our faces.

"Good dog,...Teddy!...Good dog!" I said, realizing he was responsible for our survival and appreciative of his spontaneous heroics. Jonathan and I petted, hugged and held him close. I would never forget the unconditional love he evinced for us that day.

"Well,...I guess the only bad thing to come out of this will probably be a good case of poison ivy," Jonathan quipped nervously, attempting to be both composed and amusing as he slapped the sand from his britches. Still shaken and physically rattled by the experience, we chuckled and began to laugh hysterically. The three of us continued merrily on our way.

"Why do the herring return year after year to this very same place?" Jonathan asked curiously, changing his pail from one hand to the other. "I can't figure out why they swim upstream out of the bay, cross the marshes, and then climb up those stone ladders against the current of the Stony Brook,...just to spawn in the Mill Pond. Do you know why, Albert? You've been here many more times than I've been. I'm sure Japeth must have explained all that to you...Hasn't he?"

"Well,...yes," I replied, adjusting the strap of my knapsack on my shoulder. "I asked Japeth that same question several years ago when I helped him fetch some herring for Miss Mira. If I remember well, he told me that these fish aren't actually herring...These bony fish are called "alewives." Japeth went on to say that these spunky, gray fish have been returning here to reproduce long before man ever lived on the Cape or possibly on this continent. Since the dawn of time, they've returned to their birthplace to deposit their eggs. Snakes, frogs and turtles eat their eggs and many of the hatchlings are lost. But the sturdy survivors,...those who do make it to the bay despite many obstacles, continue to forge ahead. The young fish follow their parents out to sea, remain in the bay until they mature, and then return at least twice as adults to swim upstream to the ponds and spawn. The alewives do this every year, Jonathan."

On that late-May afternoon, the rushing waters were teaming with thousands of the tiny, slate-colored fish climbing the stone ladders and going against the rushing waters of the stream below.

"But how do they know when to start their journey upstream?" Jonathan asked while standing on the embankment next to the Stony Brook.

"Oh,…Teddy must be thirsty," I interrupted. Teddy rushed toward a large boulder, pawed at the fish to get them out of the way, and then started lapping up the water.

"I think it has something to do with the temperature of the water from Paine's Creek when it dumps into the bay. It's a two-mile journey from the sea to the ponds," I went on, somewhat unsure about my answer to his question. I removed my knapsack and placed it on a rocky ledge that was jutting out from a mound above the stream.

"Look, Jonathan!" I exclaimed, pointing to the water…"See how the fish gather in the pools below the ladders to pace themselves before they climb the next one!"

"Swimming against the current must make them very tired," Jonathan said, noticing how they huddled together below each stone step.

"They rest before each jump," I replied, preparing to use my fishnet.

"Yes,…yes! I see!" he exclaimed, his curiosity piqued. "Thank you, Albert, for telling me about that…It's amazing how so many of them arrive here in such large numbers. Looks like the gulls also find them to be a tasty treat. There must be hundreds of them overhead. Oh, look! They're swooping down to snatch the ones too tired to go on and swallowing them…whole!"

"Once they've completed this very exhausting swim upstream,…they'll finally enter the pond to spawn," I said loudly, trying to speak over the persistent din of the screeching gulls and rushing waters. "I must say I truly admire the drive and courage of these small, gutsy fish. While struggling to reach their goal, they patiently persist in conquering each barrier, one at a time. I'll always remember these spunky alewives if hardships should ever challenge *me*…in my life."

Jonathan and I squatted to eat our lunch along the shore of this peaceful retreat with its scenic rushing brook—shaded by large oaks and locust trees. We couldn't have asked for better weather. A great blue heron alighted on the pond then glided along the surface searching for food. It bobbed, swiftly snatched a writhing herring in its beak, and then was again in flight. We inhaled the pleasant fragrances of our surroundings—the sweet smell of huckleberry vines and the wafting perfume of lilac bushes in full bloom. These soft lavender bouquets were mirrored in the lucent spring waters below the Stony Mill. White water lilies floating on their verdant pads framed and dotted this vernal pool.

We sat on a lush ground cover of leafy green myrtle as we listened to the refreshing sound of the cascading waterfall. Jonathan and I watched as the fresh, clear water was ladled into the wooden blades of the rotating wheel of the mill. It spilled over from one to the next until it again returned to the pool below. The pond also reflected the weeping willows and wooden bridges. A collection of herring gathered in pools at the bottom of the ladders before making their next assault against the current. The alewives filled the small Stony Brook stream as they struggled up one stone ladder to the next before finally reaching their upland-breeding pond.

With our fishnets dangling from long poles, we quickly scooped up our share of alewives. Just for the fun of it, we jumped into the knee-high water and plucked the fish with our bare hands. We reveled in our catch. The water was still quite cold, but the bright sun rapidly dried our clothing. Soon, Japeth arrived with the buckboard. After sitting and cleaning the fish—it was time for us to return home. Our pails were spilling over with fresh herring for supper.

While I washed and changed from my damp clothing, Miss Mira reached for the utensils and handed them to the girls.

"Will ye help me set the table for supper, lassies?" she asked, hoping to occupy Emeline and little Kate.

"Oh, yes, Miss Mira," Emeline replied, delighted to be of assistance and zealously retrieving them from Miss Mira's hand.

Emeline a sweet, affectionate eight year-old began to place the forks and knives carefully on the table, humming as she went about her assigned task. She had father's olive complexion and similar dark brown hair. It was usually pulled back and tied with a colored bow that hung down to her waist. A small white cap tied under her chin covered her petite round head. Emeline had a tiny, turned-up nose. Her large, expressive brown eyes were fringed with unusually full, black and long curling lashes. It wasn't uncommon for people to stare at her.

"You have such big, brown "cow eyes," they would comment. This remark often made her feel uncomfortable. She could never quite figure out if it was meant to be a compliment or an affront. Despite Emeline's delicate beauty and tender innocence, she was also exceedingly shy and very sensitive. She was a weepy child, prone to wanting her own way. At the least provocation Emeline could make those large "cow eyes" tear—a minor irritation. A mild scolding, a slight hurt or a small disappointment would trigger whining that could last for hours. At times, this became downright annoying to everyone in the Crosby household. We made every effort to calm and appease her so she would end her pouting and eventually gain her composure. Emeline's crying spells exasperated me. I tried everything in my power to make her stop.

"Emeline! For goodness sake…stop your damn crying!" I would say, tugging at her sleeve to get her attention. I often succeeded because she would instantly snap out of it.

"Marmmy says you'll go straight to hell for cursing like that, Albert," she warned menacingly, pointing her index finger directly at me. More often than not, I tried to appease this little tyke with noble gestures by offering her whatever I had to share.

"Here,…I'll give you some of mine," I would say, or "Come,…I'll give you a ride in the pony cart." This type of behavior went a long way toward changing her foul moods.

Prim and proper Emeline was a picture of adorable perfection as she took her place on the highly polished oak bench. She had a small white shawl draped over a linen pinafore that covered a pink, gingham dress. Tan, high-buttoned shoes gave her a darling moppet appearance. Protruding from her pantalets were petite versions of Anne's footwear. Emeline sat directly opposite from Kate.

And oh, my little sister, Kate! She was a veritable enigma who was affectionately named after Mother. Kate was a wholesome waif-like child of six years—a precious pixie—a plump cherub with father's curly hair and mother's fair coloring. She had tiny rosebud lips that protruded in a pucker from a round, chubby-cheeked face. Her shiny pug nose was the size of a tiny thimble. Kate's strawberry blonde ringlets and long cascading curls fell just below her shoulders. The lovely purple bow that fastened her hair matched her stunning violet eyes. Along with a pale lavender dress with elegant pin tucks and tiny pearl buttons down the front, she also wore a miniature version of her sister's fashionable Quaker apron, cap and shawl—complete with the pantalets and tiny, tan, high-button-down shoes.

Kate was as cute and agile as a bright-eyed, bushy tailed bunny. She was also a tomboy full of boundless energy. Kate was a perpetual chatterbox and a miniature whirlwind seeming to be everywhere at once. She was a mischievous rascal—forever climbing, running, chasing, poking, and taunting. Worst of all, she constantly foraged into the other children's things. Miss Mira didn't expect her to stay clean for very long, but at least, through the evening meal. Even so, she usually managed to spill milk or drop food all over herself. Little Kate was an unmanageable child, tiring and a handful. Miss Mira was often exhausted by her rambunctious devilry.

"Oh, begorra…me little Kate! I just can't keep up with ye!" Miss Mira would cry out, thoroughly exasperated by her antics and physically fatigued. "Ye'll be the death of me yet, me wee lassie!"

It had been about fifteen years since my father, Nathan Crosby, Junior moved to Brewster from Chatham. The cozy, eight-room cottage where he lived with his family was situated on a hilly, rolling knoll overlooking the bay. Along with the house, Father added a large barn, stable and caretaker's cottage. The view was indescribably breathtaking. It encompassed forty acres including private rights to the beach.

Father, who was in his early forties, was slim and well proportioned with broad shoulders. He was a muscular man of average height—about five feet, eleven inches to be exact. A native Cape Codder, this dignified, eloquent gentleman was well versed in the arts and social amenities, reflecting many generations of good breeding. He was also active in the social, religious and political circles of his new town. Father stood straight as a picket in his black, hand-tailored suit. He had thick, dark-brown, curly hair and a neatly trimmed beard and mustache. Dense, heavy eyebrows framed his expressive, piercing black eyes that projected his every feeling and thought.

Father had entered into the fishing business and owned several vessels. Due to the financial successes of these enterprises, his family became well known to Cape Cod society. Through his endeavors, Father grew modestly wealthy in his own right. He had a reputation for being a driven, ambitious individual and a strict disciplinarian. Even so, Father was a caring man who capably provided for his children. He was also a perceptive, adoring husband who steadfastly treated my mother with the utmost esteem and respect.

Catherine Crosby, my mother, was in her late thirties. She was a genteel young matron who hailed from a lovely village on the south shore of Cape Cod called Chatham. Mother was an engaging, youthful woman committed to motherhood and devoted to her husband. She was slight and frail in stature with strawberry blond hair and hazel eyes. Her pale, smooth complexion was a fitting tribute to her proud Yankee heritage. She wore her lovely tresses in an upturned chignon that gracefully circled the back of her head. A dainty flower, satin ribbon or bit of lace, color-coordinated with her stylish floor-length dress, often found a resting place in the nape of her neck.

Mother usually wore a soft feminine frock. This evening, as we gathered for supper, it was one trimmed with dainty Chantilly tulle. The material was a pale daffodil shade of chiffon voile. The dress was unforgettable. A large, white satin ribbon circled her diminutive waist. The long flowing bow positioned on her left side held a nosegay of lace and violets similar to the one she wore in her hair. When she left to socialize, matching gloves and parasols complimented all her ensembles.

My mother lived solely for her children and husband, catering to their every need. She nurtured their bodies with patient care and attention—their souls with endless devotion and love. She was a sensitive and tender ministering angel who brought security, joy and comfort to her children. Mother won my father's undying love, respect and support. The parity in their relationship was obvious to family and friends. She was content in her role as wife and mother—devoting many hours to the upbringing of her offspring—educating them about their genealogy and heritage and acquainting them with proper manners, etiquette and religious dogma.

Catherine (Nickerson) Crosby was a descendant of a notable Pilgrim family, whose history dated back to the early 1600's. My parents possessed similar backgrounds. They were both native Cape Codders with comparable education and religious beliefs. Living in blissful harmony, they complimented each other like matching bookends. Their parental love for us mirrored the affection they had for each other. They had six children—Nathan III, Anne, Albert, Emeline, Kate and William—now eighteen, fourteen, twelve, eight, six and four—respectively.

The chimes of the stately grandfather clock in the sitting room heralded the sixth hour of the afternoon. Father asked everyone to bow his or her heads in prayer. When Miss Mira finished her chores, she joined us at the table. She had previously arranged the water goblets and cups at each place setting and had stacked the plates in front of Father, who had just returned from a business meeting. He was seated at one end of the dinner table in an armchair. Mother, who had attended a lecture earlier in the afternoon, sat in a straight chair at the other end. Miss Mira placed a wooden bowl on the table filled with baked potatoes and a crystal one that was filled with green beans, fresh-picked from the garden. A pewter platter was brimming over with the batter crisp herring that I had helped to prepare. How proud I was to have provided this rare treat for my family. A deep cast-iron pot was filled with a hot, apple crisp dessert. A round wheat bread, freshly baked in the side oven of the hearth graced the center of a cutting board that Miss Mira placed directly in front of Mother. Mother sliced and served the bread. Miss Mira took her place at the edge of the bench and sat next to Anne. She joined the others in prayer as she clasped her hands together and reverently bowed her head. Father began with "Grace."

"We thank Thee, Lord, for this food which we are about to receive from Thy bounty," Father recited reverently. "We also thank Thee for watching over us, for our good health and fortune,…Amen."

Everyone seated around the table repeated…"Amen."

"Yes, he certainly was watching over Jonathan and me today," I thought as I envisioned the stagecoach suddenly materializing ahead of us and the way we had eluded it. "Thank you, Lord…Oh, thank you for our Teddy!" I prayed in silence.

"Please watch over our son Nathan at military school," Father petitioned. "And Dear Lord,…we ask Thee to look down upon our William. Fill him with Thy healing graces and make him well again. He's been so frail and feverish of late. We love him so very much. Please, Lord,…listen to our prayers!…Amen."

Again we repeated,…"Amen."

According to custom, the head-of-the-household picked up the plates, filled them, and then passed them around. Everyone placed their napkins on their laps and began to chat and enjoy their food.

"Catherine, my dear, how was your day? Was William doing somewhat better today?" Father asked wistfully.

"I haven't had a chance to check on him as yet, Nathan," Mother replied remorsefully, appearing a bit downcast. "I was late returning from an afternoon lecture. I didn't want to be rude by getting up and leaving, so I stayed until it was over. Miss Mira said he's still asleep. I hope he just has his days and nights mixed up. I'm really beginning to worry about him. He's sleeping far too much during the day and becoming quite feverish and flushed in the late afternoon. William hasn't been his usual happy and contented self lately. His eyes are lifeless and he just wants to be held," she said despondently. "Although my commitment to attend the lecture was long standing, I hesitated leaving him…I should've stayed at home." Teary eyed and outwardly concerned, Mother attempted to justify her absence. "However, it was such a lovely day,…I decided it might be best to turn my attention elsewhere. Miss Mira assured me she'd stay by his toddler bed and send for me if need be. Japeth was kind enough to wait for me with the carriage until it was over. It did help to lift my spirits."

"Was the lecture interesting?" Father asked approvingly, attempting to render a more casual atmosphere to the conversation and allow Mother to feel more at ease.

"Oh, Yes!" Mother replied enthusiastically, eager to converse about something more pleasant. "The ocean voyage of a grand ship that sailed to England and France was narrated and chronicled in great detail. Oh, how I wish we could travel there someday,…it would be such an exciting experience!"

While I munched away on a slice of fresh wheat bread, I thought this might be an opportune time to promise my parents an extended and memorable tour of Europe—when and *if*—I became a wealthy entrepreneur. On the other hand, I had a mouthful of food and didn't wish to interrupt their conversation with my aspirations. I feared being reprimanded or ridiculed.

"We may, my dear Catherine,…we may," Father said nodding his head, hopeful that he would eventually make that dream come true for her. "Well now, Albert and Anne,…what did *you* do today?" he asked, turning his attention to his older children.

"Jonathan and I walked to the Factory Village and the Herring Run," I said, answering first and pleased that I had been asked. "As we approached the Mill, Teddy pushed us from the path of a speeding stagecoach. We're so thankful that he tagged along with us. We both returned with several pails filled with alewives. Japeth picked us up with the buckboard. I also cleaned and boned them into fillets for Miss Mira. That's what we're having for supper tonight."

"Well, thank you, Albert," he replied, acknowledging our contribution to the evening meal, despite the hazard we had encountered. I flashed a satisfied smile. "That dog is certainly a guardian angel in disguise. I hope our dear Teddy will remain with us for many years to come…And you, Anne?" he asked, glancing to where she was seated.

"I helped Miss Mira make rose hip and beach plum jelly. She's also been teaching me how to crochet. I'm learning how to make some lovely bureau scarves for Marmmy," she replied with a sense of accomplishment and pride. "I didn't practice my piano lessons today because I didn't want to waken Little William."

Mother rose from her chair and left the kitchen for a few minutes. She returned and approached Father, tugging at his sleeve to get his attention. He turned toward her and immediately sensed her distress. Tears filled her eyes as she took him aside.

"Nathan, I slipped away to check on William. Despite Miss Mira's effective poultices, he seems more lethargic." Not wanting to unduly alarm the children, she spoke softly—just above a whisper. "I held him for a few minutes. His body was limp and very hot to the touch," she said on the verge of weeping. Her chin quivered as she tried to remain stalwart and composed. "I'm afraid he's not doing well!…If William doesn't improve by morning, I might have to send for Doctor Insley. Japeth will have to leave for Chatham to fetch him." Father pulled Mother close to him and gently put his strong, comforting arm around her waist.

"Now don't you worry, my love,…he'll be fine. It's probably just a slight chest cold," he said persuasively, holding her tightly in an attempt to calm her fears. "I'm sure he'll be up and about soon…If it looks as though he'll need the doctor, I'll accompany Japeth to Chatham and personally see to it that Doctor Insley visits William, if need be."

"Miss Mira and I will spend the night close to his bed caring for him. We'll take turns holding and rocking him," Mother said, becoming a bit more hopeful and cheered by Father's words. Although Father was immersed in his business affairs, I sensed that Mother felt he was now beginning to show some concern—yet she was inwardly dismayed by his nonchalant attitude toward what she perceived was a serious situation.

Miss Mira rose from the bench to get a pot of steeped tea and placed it on the table. She planned to serve it with the apple crisp. Miss Mira scooped this mouth-watering dessert out of the cast-iron pan onto some small plates, spooned a generous dollop of heavy whipped cream on it, and then proceeded to place it on the table in front of us.

"Would ye like a cup of tay, sir?" Miss Mira asked…"And ye, me lady?"

"No, thank you," Father replied, rising from his chair and starting to leave the room. "I'll not have dessert or tea this evening. I must work on some pressing business matters in the sitting room."

"Yes, Mira, that sounds delightful," Mother responded with a forced smile, abjectly glancing at each child and making eye contact with us. "I *will* have a cup of hot tea if you'll join me,…but please…no dessert."

"Children," she instructed in a calm, hushed tone of voice, "please carry your plates to the sink when you're finished and while you wait for me to join you in the parlor, please select your bedtime story…in silence. Your father's preoccupied right now. Be very, very quiet," she repeated, placing her index finger over closed lips. "I'll be there shortly. I must check on William one more time before I linger over tea," Mother said, turning to Miss Mira and setting her cup down on the table.

"I did try to wake the wee one earlier, me lady. He's still fast asleep and flushed with fever,…he is," Miss Mira replied with a frustrated sigh, shaking her head in dismay.

"Although he has no appetite, I'll have to try feeding him a little broth soon. He must eat something before he weakens even more," Mother said anxiously.

"Aye, me lady. Ye stay with the wee laddie as long as need be," Miss Mira said in her maternal way. "If ye shouldn't return by the time me finishes cleaning up here, I'll see to the children and prepare them for bed. Ye need not worry about that! Ye'll need all the rest ye can get right now, as ye'll probably be up all night."

"Thank you, Miss Mira," Mother replied appreciatively, reaching for her hand. "You're so kind and thoughtful. We're so fortunate to have you with us. I really don't know what we'd do without you. The Lord has sent the Crosby family a dear, sweet angel. We thank him for you every day." Miss Mira smiled as Mother left the room. She swiftly tidied up the kitchen, removed and hung up her apron, and then moved quickly toward the sitting room.

The tea in Mother's cup cooled as it sat on the table. Mother found she couldn't possibly return to the kitchen as planned. Little William needed her immediate and undivided attention. His condition was rapidly deteriorating. She tried to feed him, but it was to no avail—he was much too weak. Mother decided to remain by his bedside. At the moment, my baby brother was her primary concern. In the meantime, Miss Mira had taken it upon herself to gather the children at the far end of the sitting room.

"I'll sit here, and ye sit close to me on the floor while I read to ye," Miss Mira instructed. "Mind ye now, ye better all listen quietly or else…it's up to bed ye go," she cautioned. Just as Miss Mira closed the book, she noticed Kate's futile attempt to keep her eyes open. Suddenly, her head dropped forward. "I think it's time ye march yeselves upstairs and change into ye loosies (what Miss Mira called our nightclothes). I'll listen to ye prayers,…quick as a wink," Miss Mira added, pointing to the stairway and giving each one of us her usual love pat on our behinds as we ascended the bottom step.

"But where's Marmmy? Isn't she going to tuck us in and kiss us goodnight?" Emeline asked, whining in her usual vexatious pitch.

"Hush now, Emeline. Our Little William's very sick. Marmmy needs to care for him," Anne explained.

"Ye must pray for the wee one. God willing,…He'll listen to ye prayers. Little William must get well!" Miss Mira said resolutely, tucking us into bed for the night. She quietly closed the door, moved swiftly down the staircase, and then headed straight for the nursery to join Mother. Troubled by Little William's illness, I seized a pillow and coverlet and managed to creep silently down the stairs behind her. I positioned myself on an oak bench at the opposite end of the hallway—out of sight—yet within view and earshot of the nursery.

"Is there anything I can do to help ye, me lady?" asked Miss Mira, placing a ladder-back chair next to Mother's rocker.

"Oh, Mira, I'm so distraught," Mother said plaintively, a melancholy expression distorting her lovely face. "Please, just sit by me and keep me company during this trying time."

"Of course, me lady," Miss Mira replied. "First, let me fetch a nice cup of hot tay for the two of us." When she returned, Miss Mira pushed the nursery door opened with her elbow. She tiptoed toward an end table, positioned it between the two of them, and then placed a woven basket-tray on it. Two dainty teacups, two saucers, a teapot, napkins, spoons and a small plate of sugar cookies graced a delicately laced doily. Mother was rocking William who was cradled in her arms. She was singing a soft lullaby when Miss Mira returned to the nursery.

"This basket-tray's so useful. It's not only sturdy,…but also quite lovely. Anne is so talented!" Mother noted, reaching for her teacup with her free hand as she extolled Anne's virtues. "While you were busy in the kitchen," she added, "William stirred and whimpered faintly. I felt I should hold and caress him for a while."

For one reason or another, Mother had never questioned Miss Mira about her past or her personal life before arriving at the Crosby homestead. Either the opportunity had never presented itself, or if it did—she wasn't bold enough to pry. Evidently, Mother felt this would be the proper time. After all these years, Mother's curiosity must have been getting the better of her. Trying not to dwell on the seriousness of Little William's illness, she asked Miss Mira about herself. I supposed she felt she needed a diversion. It would help to dismiss all those distressing and negative thoughts that weighed so heavily on her mind right now. She took another sip from her teacup and decided to initiate the inquiry.

"Tell me, Mira,…how is it that you never married?" Mother asked inquisitively. "I know it really isn't any of my business, but it's been something I've always wanted to ask you about. You're such a beautiful woman…so caring and so gifted. You must have had some sort of meaningful relationship with a young man in your past. I can't imagine that you haven't. If not,…it's beyond me! Did you ever have a lover, Mira? You've never spoken to me about that,…or could it be the opposite sex didn't interest you? I know you left Ireland in your early twenties to come to this country. Why did you make that decision? Please understand, my dear Mira, you're under no obligation to answer my prying questions unless you wish to do so." While Mother still held Little William in the rocker with her right arm, she placed her teacup on the basket-tray with her left hand, and then reached over to affectionately touch Miss Mira's thigh.

"Oh, me lady Catherine,…I never told ye because I thought that hearing about me past would be of no interest to ye," Miss Mira quickly replied, hoping Mother wouldn't feel embarrassed by her inquiries. "Now that ye have asked me, I think that if ye'd like to listen,…this is as good a time as any to tell ye about me younger days. Ye're not only me lady Catherine, but also me dear, close friend."

"Please go on. Yes,…I *really* would like to know. And Mira,…I also value your friendship," Mother said, trying to make her feel more at ease as Miss Mira was about to reveal the earlier, more private aspects of her life.

"Me dah owned a Pub in County Cork," Miss Mira disclosed, taking a deep breath and setting down her cup of tea. "Me family was very well off, comparing to most,…but I wanted to try me wings,…like a young bird ready to leave the nest. Me long-suffering, day-to-day life in Ireland was sadly unfulfilling. Me unhappiness became intolerable. Oh, how I yearned to travel to America! I think I was about twenty-two when I pleaded with me dah to loan me the funds to sail across the ocean. I promised to repay him as soon as me could find work. Me dah reluctantly allowed me to leave me native land. I can't help remembering the tears shed by me whole family as I boarded the large clipper ship bound for the new country. Delighted to be finally on me own, me heart raced with expectation. It was a long and arduous trip,…across rough and open seas. There were many people on that ship who became quite ill,…some never made it," Miss Mira continued sadly, shaking her head. "We finally arrived in New York on a late October afternoon. I was so amazed by me new surroundings!

"I found a small flat and managed to find work as a nanny for a wealthy family. Me dah had given me enough money to start me new life in this beautiful and magnificent country. I began to repay me dah right off and soon…I was free of debt. Later, I decided to travel to Cape Cod. Me future would be there because it was more like me homeland. I traveled to Boston by stagecoach and from there I boarded a small sailing ship to Brewster. Somehow I knew…I certainly would find work here. Me destination would be a family who lived by the sea. Since that time,…the Cape has been me home. I found happiness and peace here. Although I hope to return to Ireland someday, I never wanted to travel anywhere else in the world."

"Please continue," Mother said, hanging onto each word and taking another sip of tea.

"As to a lover in me life…" Miss Mira went on, hesitating for a few seconds then adding, "aye, of course…there was one,…many years ago. I was introduced to a fine bonnie lad who was just a few years older than meself. His name was

Patrick…So handsome he was. He and his dah delivered fresh fish and shellfish to the kitchen where I worked in New York. On a warm summer day, the cook introduced me to this buckeen. We were putting together a basket lunch for a family picnic. Patrick was there purposely to meet me. Little did I know…she had already told him about me. Fine Irish stock,…he was. Quite charming this Patrick with his neatly combed black hair, his deep blue eyes and a smile that just swept me right off me feet. Oh, I can still remember that day and how me heart jumped in me chest. I guess ye could call it "love-at-first-sight." After that first meeting, he called on me several times. So much in love, we were. When he asked for me hand in marriage I couldn't wait to say,…aye."

"What happened?…Why didn't you marry him?" Mother asked, gently returning Little William to his bed.

"Me Pat was called to serve in the French-Indian War of 1812. He left abruptly promising to marry me as soon as he returned. Me Pat said he would never leave me again. We embraced as the tears flowed down me cheeks. How me heart ached! Me love for him made me feel so complete. When he left…I felt so alone. Patrick had become not only me lover, but also…me dearest friend. The loneliness and yearning for his caress grew more intense with each passing day. It made the waiting for me Pat almost unbearable. I sent letters to him on the front lines pledging me love for him and I eagerly awaited his safe return. His chances of receiving me letters were very slim. Regardless, I wrote to him every day.

"One day in late January, I saw the fish cart from the upstairs window. Fearing the worst, I flew down the stairs after being summoned to the kitchen. I knew it would *not* be good news,…his dah rarely delivered fish during the cold winter months."

"Oh, no!" Mother interrupted, detecting a catch in Miss Mira's voice and shocked at what she expected to hear. "I'm so sorry,…please go on," she said, apologizing and dismayed by her poor manners. Miss Mira lowered her head and placed one hand over her mouth as if to stop herself from crying.

"His dah, a tall, ruddy faced man held me close and calmly tried to comfort me," she went on tearfully, "He knew how upset I would be to hear such tragic news and how devastating it would be for me. 'Aye, me sweet Mira, I bring some sad news for ye,' he said with much sorrow. 'Ye Patrick has died on the battlefield at the hands of the enemy. He was a bloody hero,…he was.' I was gripped in a silent agony. I could feel meself screaming with grief, but somehow,…I couldn't make a sound…me words froze on me tongue. The sorrow and emptiness I felt, dear lady, lasted many years.

"Eventually, time finally healed the melancholy. It slowly faded away,…but I always felt no one else could *ever* replace, me sweet Pat, in me heart. I could never love another. True to his memory, I became content to live the remainder of me days as a spinster. Ye mustn't feel sorry for me, me lady. Me life with you and your beautiful family has been a happy and fulfilling one for me…They're like me own kin," Miss Mira said reassuringly, reaching out to touch Mother on the shoulder.

"Thank you for saying that, Miss Mira," Mother replied appreciatively. "You've already made me feel better about your loss. I'm truly pleased to know we've helped to fill the void in your life." Looking toward the nursery window, Mother glimpsed the sunrise in the distance and the dawn of new day.

"I think…I'd better wake Nathan," she decided reluctantly. "William has barely moved in his bed these last few hours. Nathan must leave quickly to fetch the doctor." Miss Mira immediately left the house to summon Japeth.

Mother, who had been up all night caring for Little William, walked fatigued into the master bedroom and sat on the edge of the sturdy, oak rope bed. Alerted by her words, I followed and watched as she bent down to kiss Father who was still asleep. Although I knew she felt an uneasiness within, Mother composed herself and strained to project an outwardly and placid demeanor.

"Nathan dear, I'm sorry that I must wake you at this ungodly hour," she whispered quietly, gently tapping his shoulder to wake him. "You must hurry and dress quickly." Drained and chagrined, Mother added, "I'm sure William has taken a turn for the worse. Please hurry!" Father sensed the urgency in her voice, sprang from his bed and dressed. "Japeth already has the horses harnessed to the carriage and is ready to leave without delay." Disheveled, he passed his fingers through his hair and darted out the front door to the front fence post and the waiting carriage. Japeth lashed the whip, the horses galloped up the sandy road to the King's Highway, and then raced toward Chatham.

Later in the morning, Father and Doctor Insley returned to the Crosby homestead. Mother and Miss Mira greeted him at the front entrance and smiled while valiantly trying to hold back their tears. Doctor Insley, a rather affable, stout and bespectacled fellow with an unruly head of snow-white hair and a similar thick mustache and beard, tipped his hat, brushed past them, and then headed straight for the parlor. I stood in the front hallway anxiously awaiting his prognosis.

"The baby hasn't moved at all!" Mother cried out hysterically. "He's been still for quite a few hours now! Oh, Doctor Insley, we're so worried about him!"

"I fear the worse, Doctor," Miss Mira interrupted despondently, leading the group toward the nursery and standing in the doorway while they filed past her.

Once inside the room, the doctor hurriedly walked past them. He bent over the toddler-bed to examine Little William, straightened himself, shook his head, and then reached for Mother's hand. His diagnosis was a shocking, cruel blow.

"I'm afraid your son is gravely ill…he has bronchial pneumonia," he said rather pessimistically. "He's already in a comatose state. I'm sorry to say…he hasn't long to live. It's fairly hopeless, at this time. There are tangible signs that the high fevers may have caused severe brain damage. It's best…it ends this way. Chances are,…if he did survive,…he'd most likely be extremely retarded."

"Oh, no!" Mother screamed, covering her mouth. Panic stricken and hoping for a miracle. She began to tug frantically at the doctor's suit lapels, begging and pleading for Little William's life. "Please don't let my son die! Isn't there something you can do?…I can't bear to think we could possibly lose him."

Determined to be realistic and truthful about his prognosis, Doctor Insley spoke directly to my stunned parents.

"Catherine, Nathan,…I'm so sorry!" he said compassionately. "You must prepare yourselves and the children for the inevitable. I will stay with you until the end, which will be very soon,…if that's any solace to you."

"Yes,…please do. It would be such a comfort if you could remain here with us," Father replied, relieved by the doctor's offer. Everyone agreed that Doctor Insley's reassuring presence was eminently needed. It would be a steadfast means of support through this heart-wrenching ordeal.

"Would you kindly explain to the children the seriousness of the situation?" Father asked, appreciative of Doctor Insley's soothing manner. "I would certainly be grateful for anything you could say to ease the pain and trauma they'll undoubtedly experience over this. Albert and Anne are very fond of William. Anne was so attentive to him and Albert wanted so very much to be his big brother. He looked forward to the day he'd be able to take William fishing and sailing…Oh, how dreadful for them! They so loved their baby brother."

"I'll be happy to do that for you," Doctor Insley replied in complete sympathy with Father's grief. "Anything to ease your burden…Where are they now?"

"They're in the kitchen with Miss Mira," Father replied. "She's keeping them occupied while we consulted with you."

Doctor Insley quietly left the nursery and promptly headed toward the kitchen, leaving my parents in a tearful embrace. He reached for Emeline and Kate and gently sat them on his lap. This kindly man held Anne and me in his arms as we stood next to him. Speaking in a straightforward yet sympathetic tone, this genial man informed us about our little brother's imminent demise.

We received the sorrowful news bravely—however, Anne must have read my mind when she asked to return to the nursery.

"Can we please see, Little William, one more time?" Anne begged politely.

"Yes, come. I'll take you to him," Doctor Insley replied. We returned to the nursery grasping each of the doctor's outstretched hands. Emeline and Kate remained behind with Miss Mira. Releasing his grip, he allowed us to step forward. We gazed intently at the pale child in the small bed and touched him gently. Bewildered by the harsh reality of Little William's impending death, the incredulity of his disastrous fate was reflected on our faces.

"Little William doesn't look like himself, I cried, running into my mother's open arms. "He was such a happy little fellow, always smiling, but now, he looks so still. Oh, Marmmy,…why does God want to take him from us? We all love him, so." Just then, Doctor Insley glanced downward into William's bed and shook his head. With a grim expression, he turned to face the family.

"The baby's now one of God's precious cherubs," he said with a sigh and in a cheerless, but soothing tone of voice.

Poorly prepared to cope with the finality of it all, the grief I felt at that moment became overwhelming. Heartbroken, a deep and profound sadness gave way to indignation. I couldn't deal with this surreal event. The naivety of an adolescent mind demanded to know the how and why? "How can this happen to him? Why does my adorable, innocent little brother whom I love so dearly…have to die?" I asked myself as I questioned this enigmatic experience. Overcome by the cruelty of it all, I became lethargically resigned. Feelings of listlessness and inertia sapped my concentration and left me emotionally drained. Much too proud and manly to let anyone notice me crying, I darted from the nursery and dashed up the stairs to my room. I closed the door behind me, threw myself on the bed, and then wept—uncontrollably.

Hysterical ranting, screaming and sobbing suddenly shattered the momentary silence in the nursery. As all hope vanished—the mournful wailing reverberated throughout the Crosby cottage. Similar to a nightmare from which one never wakes, the somber realization of William's death began to penetrate my family's minds and hearts. While trying to deal with his passing and yield to the wishes of a higher power—we were inconsolable. My parents, Catherine and Nathan Crosby, my siblings and my grandmamma, who had just arrived from Chatham, were grief stricken. Our caretakers, Japeth and Miss Mira also lamented his loss.

Despite this distressing depth of despair, our troubled spirits eventually found solace and peace. Although my baby brother's life was sadly shortened by fate, I knew our Little William would always be lovingly remembered—his brief life on this earth—a cherished memory.

C H A P T E R 3

▼

Mid-April, 1838

"Well, Albert, have you made any decisions about what you plan to do with your life now that you're halfway through secondary school?" Japeth asked, looking straight ahead and tugging at the reins. Teddy had joined us in the wagon and stayed right by our sides. He alternated his attention between Japeth and me by poking his head between us and over the rear tailgate to scan the countryside.

"I really haven't given it much thought as yet...however, I've definitely decided to leave Brewster for a while," I replied candidly while contemplating his question. "Father expects me to follow in his footsteps and eventually take over the ship-building business. I feel I'm not well suited for that type of work. I'd like to pursue a more challenging profession," I maintained, wistfully entertaining some vague yearnings of my own. I prefer to do something new and exciting. My dream is to travel to the far corners of the world. It's not that I dislike living in Brewster...I truly love it here. It'll always be my home. Can you understand what I'm trying to say, Japeth?" Before he could respond, I rambled on, "Many of my friends, including Jonathan, have caught glimpses of new and broader horizons from the decks of the packets. (Small sailboats that carried both passengers and cargo to and from Boston.) A desire for adventure and a love of the ocean has prompted their decision to sail on one of those grand seafaring vessels like the *Hottinger*. I may want to join them. I've been giving it some serious thought lately. Anyway, I still have a few years to think about that."

As we approached Crosby Lane, he glanced over his shoulder to face me. After reflecting on my words for a few moments, Japeth spoke at the top of his voice so he could be heard above the earsplitting sound of the wagon wheels and galloping horses.

"Yes, I know how you feel," he replied in a loud yet nostalgic tone. "I'm also a native of the Cape. I've spent most of my life right here in Brewster. Though I love it as much as you do, I must admit I've often had that gnawing feeling deep in my innards to seek my fortune elsewhere…A kind of longing to carve out a niche for myself in the world,…or do something worthwhile…something like returning from a distant land as a war hero or maybe becoming renown as a famous wrestling or boxing dignitary,…I guess," he said, shrugging his shoulders. "But it just wasn't meant to be. I married young, and then by golly…before I knew it, I had a family to provide for. Now don't misunderstand me, Albert, I'm very content with my lot in life and have come to accept it just as it is."

"You're a downright, fine and honorable man, Japeth," I said, duly praising him hoping to make him feel better about himself. I thought this was a fitting time to boost this kindly and unassuming man's sagging ego. "My Father could never have managed without you! At every opportunity he tells everyone about your devotion to us and how dependable you are. Father speaks very highly of you…I want you to know that! You're indispensable to him in every way. Father's so appreciative of all the hard work you do around here, Japeth. We rely on your constant and kindly care. It makes us feel secure just to know that you're close by. You're always ready and content to solve our every problem or emergency. You've committed yourself to our well-being and dedicated your life to our family, farm animals and crops. It goes without saying that we appreciate and cherish your amiable ways. You've always been an exemplary individual, Japeth. I hope that someday, I'll be able to repay you for all you've done for us in a way that truly expresses my gratitude."

"Why, that's real nice of you to say that," he replied with his easy-going smile turning his attention away from me and giving the left rein an abrupt jerk as he turned onto Crosby lane—a bumpy, washed out road. "I do hope you'll be successful. In any case, Albert, just don't be…*ordinary!* I know it's in your make up to be someone special. And you needn't concern yourself about me. The joy your family gives me is gratitude enough."

The Cape was experiencing an exceptionally wet spring. The frequent April showers, so beneficial to nature's resurgence often gave way to heavy rains that made the earthen roadways treacherous. Although the sun's rays were warm, the harsh, chilly breezes off the cold waters of the bay delayed the anticipated celebration of spring already enjoyed inland. The weather—by all accounts—was typical of April on Cape Cod. Despite a nip in the air, a dense morning fog gave way to sunlight that heralded the arrival of spring.

Signs of new life were everywhere. The bogs were filled with a riot of rushes, cattails, fiddlehead fern and luminous white bloodroot whose milky blossoms shone like prisms in the midday sun. The high-pitched calls of peepers drifted toward us from the marsh meadows. Although the landscape was still stark and somber, golden sprays of budding forsythia were awakening from a long winter's sleep. They delicately graced the roadside along with other welcomed splashes of subtle colors. Crocuses and resuscitated emperor tulips, stately pale jonquils and narcissus were all thrusting their bright blooms through the desolate ground around them. Their dramatic presence adorned the walkways and frontage of many homesteads along the Olde King's Highway. As we rode by, I sighted some ring-necked ducks skimming the surface of a roadside pond. A transient breeze carried the rusty, metallic call of the red-winged blackbirds over the bogs. Salamanders and wood frogs frequently crossed the roadway ahead of us as they migrated to the vernal pools. The hardy herring had already begun their journey from the bay, entering the freshwater brooks to spawn in the kettle ponds. The smell of firewood permeated the air as plumes of slate smoke rose high above the cottage chimneys. The buckboard followed every twist and turn down this washboard lane at a fairly rapid gallop.

Japeth Jenkins was a shy private person, a quiet man with strong hands and a soft heart. He was a heavy-set, stocky gent with bulging muscles that were now covered by a gray shirt and a sleeveless flannel jacket. His dark coveralls, cinched at the waist by a wide leather belt, belied his corpulent girth. Wisps of thick, blond eyebrows peered from beneath a black, wide-brimmed hat. Most of the time, Japeth was usually hatless and smoking a corncob pipe. His wide, bushy mustache and dense beard effectively supported his pipe as it dangled from his thin, narrow lips. He was perpetually bronze from being in the fields or on the sea. Born and raised on Cape Cod, Japeth was the son of a commercial fisherman. In the blink of an eye, he could magically transform himself with masterful expertise from—carpenter, farmer and fisherman to an elegantly garbed escort or carriage coachman. Today he was both buckboard driver and deliveryman returning from the Brewster Mill with supplies for Miss Mira.

Japeth, the Crosby handyman, performed a multitude of tasks. This talented man worked energetically in many capacities undertaking just about everything around our farm and homestead. Besides tending to all the farm animals, milking the cows and grooming the horses, Japeth found time to build well-designed, sturdy coops for the poultry to keep out predators. He often made all the necessary repairs to the barn, stable, and the humble Crosby cottage. When free to do what he enjoyed most, he went shell fishing for steamers and quahogs in the bay.

Many of Miss Mira's chowders and croquettes originated from his jaunts out on the flats. With the skill of a first-rate tailor, Japeth mended both sails and weirs and also diligently tended to the sailboats, making sure that they were seaworthy.

In 1823, the year I was born, Father sold his tannery business in Chatham and settled on forty acres in Brewster, concentrating on his ship building business, salt works and farming. Due to Father's frequent absences while tending to business matters, the chores involved with building and maintaining the homestead seemed insurmountable. His dilemma was solved when he befriended the industrious young man working at the icehouse. Father hired Japeth when he was in his early twenties. With Japeth's wealth of experience, he subsequently built the Crosby cottage, barn and carriage house. Japeth was now in his thirties. Father eventually provided Japeth's young family with a small saltbox home in close proximity to the barn. He was genuinely grateful for such a generous gesture from his employer.

Japeth and Victoria Jenkins had three children—Rebecca, Aaron, and Bethany. Rebecca was the oldest child and just six weeks younger than I was. Japeth loved my siblings and me as though we were his own. When I was a young child, he took me under his wing, and as my mentor he taught me the ability to sail, fish, farm, ride and much more. Almost every skill I have ever mastered, I learned from Japeth. His expertise was extraordinary. We spent many hours together cultivating a unique camaraderie. I admired Japeth for his edifying ways, loyalty and competence. I was indebted to him for being such an honorable and steadfast custodian of my father's family and homestead. As I matured, he gave me his undivided attention, patient instructions and manly advice. Japeth had become my close friend and confidant.

After a short pause, Japeth resumed the conversation. "Words can never express my gratitude to..." He tried to verbalize his indebtedness to Father's generosity, but he never got the opportunity to finish his sentence.

Suddenly, the left front wheel of the buckboard sank into a deep rut. With an abrupt jerk, the horses bolted and the wagon began to swerve out of control. Although Japeth tightened the reins, I slid off of the smooth driver's seat and was thrown off the wagon. Teddy, sensing the danger, had already leapfrogged out of the buckboard. Eventually, Japeth brought the horses and wagon under control. Teddy's incessant barking alerted him to my obvious emergency. Distraught, Japeth anxiously raced back to find me clutching my right ankle with both hands and rocking back and forth.

"Oh, Japeth. I landed on this foot. I'm sure I heard it crack." I moaned. "I think it might be broken. My side hurts, too. Oh,…I'm in such pain! Japeth, please help me!"

"It looks like it's pretty badly injured," he announced with a grimace and a sigh after giving the ankle a quick once-over. "It's quite bruised and already beginning to swell. Don't move!…Hang on while I go for help. I'll be right back with Jonathan so he can help me lift you." Teddy was impatient to run off with him. Japeth turned toward Teddy. "Teddy, stay!…Stay with Albert!" he commanded, firmly. Teddy reluctantly squatted his bulky, furry body next to mine and started licking my face.

I watched as Japeth ran through the dense thicket leading to the Eldredge cottage. The Eldredge's unpretentious home was significantly set back from the Olde King's Highway. Japeth followed a well-worn path that meandered through bramble bushes and locust trees. He approached a clearing where juniper and hemlock dotted the landscape. A copper-colored path covered by a thick layer of wet, ochre pine needles was slippery underfoot. The trail skirted a flooded cranberry bog and finally ended at grassy area behind a weathered, wood-shingled saltbox. Japeth knocked loudly on a rear door that lead to the kitchen.

"Oh, Lord! Let Jonathan be there so he can help me," he prayed, panting and breathless. Jonathan, who was now a tall and muscular young man, opened the door. He stood there eating an apple as he looked down on Japeth.

"Japeth!" Jonathan exclaimed, momentarily stunned by the sight of the winded gentleman standing in the doorway. Japeth was greatly relieved to find that Jonathan was at home.

"Quick! Come with me!…Albert's been hurt! I left him with Teddy," he rambled on excitedly. "He was thrown from the buckboard about halfway down Crosby Lane. I'm afraid he may have some broken ribs and a sprained ankle. I didn't want to lift him alone for fear I'd add to his injuries. I need some help getting him home."

Without further questioning, Jonathan quickly turned to fetch his jacket hanging near the door. While dressing, he managed to close the door behind him. As they raced toward Crosby Lane, Japeth continued to babble his account of the accident to a puzzled, but curious, Jonathan.

"We were returning from the Gristmill and within spitting distance from home, when one of the right front wheels sank into a *damn* rut!" he related, gasping as he spoke. "We almost overturned. Fortunately, I was able to right the wagon and calm the horses. I figured it would be easier to help him walk home from there, rather than try to hoist him back up into the buckboard. Besides, the horses were too agitated to go any further."

Jonathan had been my classmate through grade school. He was older than I was by just a few months. In a few years we would graduate from secondary school together. He was not the brightest or wittiest pupil in class—nonetheless, he more than made up for it with his prowess and brute strength. My amiable friend and constant companion turned to Japeth.

"I'm so glad you came to fetch me," Jonathan said. "I only hope it isn't any more serious than you suspect."

"It's probably only a bad sprain," Japeth declared. "Even at that,…it might be quite a while before he can walk on it again."

"Yes, I suppose so," Jonathan replied, despondently nodding his head.

Teddy heard Japeth and Jonathan approaching me from afar and began to bark. He desperately wanted to greet them halfway. While still barking, he ran back and forth. He knew he shouldn't leave my side, but was sorely tempted to do so. Japeth and Jonathan soon came upon a whimpering figure, holding onto his right foot and crouched over in the throes of sporadic pain. I was a pathetic sight. As they approached me, I shielded my eyes from the sun with my forearm as I glanced upwards.

"Miss Mira will have to create another one of her miraculous poultices to ease this pain," I moaned, clutching my ankle. "It's already quite swollen. However, my side seems to feel a little better now. I must have twisted it trying to break my fall. What a fine mess this is," I whined, shaking my head. "Anne's wedding is just a few weeks away. She's counting on me to usher her guests. Please help me up," I begged, reaching for their hands and trying to ease myself up. "I think I can stand on my left foot. Yes,…I can…Let's go!" I said, bravely biting my lower lip. Japeth and Jonathan each grasped an arm and we slowly began our short journey home. On our way there, they provided me with a detailed account about what had happened after Japeth left me. Teddy ran ahead barking and waging his tail excitedly, returning frequently to check on our progress—and then finally tagging along behind us. Favoring my injured ankle, I hopped along the roadway between the two of them, gingerly taking one step at the time with my one good leg.

*   *   *   *

Late-April, 1838

The formal wedding invitations were personally hand-delivered by Japeth to the most prominent families in Brewster, Chatham, Harwich, Dennis, Orleans and Eastham. The elegantly hand printed inscriptions in Gothic calligraphy read as follows:

Mr. & Mrs. Nathan Crosby, Jr.
And
Mr. & Mrs. Simeon Snow
Request The Honor Of Your Presence
At The Marriage Ceremony
Of Their Beloved Children
Anne Nickerson Crosby
And
Robert Whittemore Snow
On Sunday The Twenty-Sixth Day Of April
Eighteen Hundred and Thirty Eight
Two O'clock In The Afternoon
At The First Parish Church of Brewster
The Olde King's Highway
Brewster, Massachusetts

Reception Immediately Following The Ceremony
At Doanes Hall

Bells chimed in the belfry as the guests gathered on the front lawn of the church. While praising the superb weather that prevailed that day, they milled around for a preview peek of the bride. Many of them had come from great distances. Some traveled overland or by sea from Boston and the Islands. The packet and the Olde the King's Highway were now Brewster's indispensable connection to all parts of the world.

What a difference just a few weeks had made! Stimulated by nature's warmer sun and frequent showers, the newly revived grasses on the sloping lawn felt like a lush, green carpet underfoot. Spirits soared as everyone was enjoying this fine, sunny spring day. The guests held onto their jackets or capes. Though the warmth from the sun was becoming more intense with each passing day, the air was still crisp and cool in the evenings. Welcoming hyacinths poked their colorful, delicate heads from under the lavender shrubbery and rows of bright, saucy daffodils. Spring's first signs of hope and promise were heralding the joy and cheer of this *very* special day.

The bridal carriage with Japeth at the reins came to a steady halt at the foot of some large granite steps leading to a white clapboard church with a lofty, prominent steeple. It was aeried high on a hilly knoll adjacent to the Olde King's Highway.

Japeth, dressed in his finest formal suit and top hat, descended from the driver's seat to secure the reins and open the door for the young, radiant bride.

Anne stepped out of the carriage wearing an elegant, ivory satin bridal dress especially designed for this occasion. She was a vision of sheer beauty. Her ensemble was lavishly embellished with delicate Irish lace and exquisitely detailed with yards of seed pearls and pleated tulle.

"My!…What a beautiful bride! How lovely she looks!" one guest whispered to another."

"Anne, I'll hold your bouquet so you'll find it easier to ascend the steps and enter the church without getting your dress soiled," Emeline said, following her older sister out of the carriage. Emeline, who was Anne's maid-of-honor, was now a winsome young woman.

"Thank you, Emeline," Anne replied, grateful for her help as she ascended the wide stone steps that led to the church's vestibule.

After Jonathan and I led them to their pews, the guests patiently sat inside the church awaiting the wedding party. Dressed in our formal attire, we looked stylishly dapper and more mature than our fifteen years.

"How's that ankle of yours?" Jonathan asked as we approached the vestibule where we joined the wedding party. "I couldn't help but notice that you're obviously favoring it."

"It's much better now," I replied, positioning myself in place. "Thank God it was only a sprain. I agonized about performing these ushering duties for her today, but everything seems to have turned out all right. My ankle,…however, is still a bit uncomfortable and painful at times. I'll try not to stand on it too much. That seems to aggravate it."

"You'd better be prepared to lose the Regatta next July," Jonathan warned, hoping to change the subject so I wouldn't dwell on my discomfort. "I've already made some adjustments to my sailboat to increase its speed and maneuverability," he added in a hushed voice. "It'll outrun your dingy any day!" Needless to say, Jonathan was an indefatigable competitor.

"Remember,…it's the expertise of the sailor that wins the race…not the boat," I said, speaking just above a whisper, smiling and shaking my right index finger in his face.

Later on, while chatting with family members, Father revealed his inner most thoughts at the time of Anne's marriage. He disclosed that he was torn by a plethora of ambivalent feelings as he escorted Anne down the aisle to hand her over to her new husband. Father added that although he was bursting with pride because his lovely, young daughter had become a talented and accomplished young woman, his sense of pride turned to sorrow now that Anne would be leaving his home for another. While trying not to be saddened by her loss, he reasoned that at this truly wondrous moment in Anne's life, the all-consuming bliss reflected on her face replaced his distress with profound joy. He realized he had not lost a daughter—he had gained a son.

The wedding march was played at a booming volume on an ornate and newly purchased organ. Large vases that flanked the ministry were tastefully arranged with Easter lilies and a colorful variety of spring flowers, explicitly designed to match Anne's bridal bouquet. Still fresh from the Easter Sunday service the week before, the white floral trumpets dramatically proclaimed Anne's virginity as she approached the pulpit. Their fragrant aroma permeated the far-flung corners of this imposing house of God.

When cordially greeted by the minister, a smiling Anne Crosby and Robert Snow exuded confidence and a profound faith in their future together. Robert Snow was a well-built fellow of average height with blue eyes and a fair complexion. His princely chiseled features were framed by curly, amber colored hair and long, neatly shaped sideburns.

My older brother, Nathan Crosby, the Third, was Robert's Best Man. Nathan had taken leave from his elite military cavalry unit and returned to Brewster to attend our sister's wedding. He was stationed in the Berkshires of western Massachusetts and had to travel three days by overland coach to reach Cape Cod. Nathan was extremely refined and articulate. His polished speech testified to a superior private education. He was the product of a disciplined regimen and staunch Yankee upbringing. As evidenced by his military education and background, Nathan stood erect and straight-faced with eyes focused directly ahead.

Looking suave and debonair in his impressive uniform, my brother, who was slightly taller than average, was a well-proportioned young man with a captivating smile.

"Is that Nathan's eldest son?" I overheard one young lady murmur to another. "We certainly haven't seen very much of *that* one,…these past few years."

"Yes," the other replied, nodding her head and whispering. "He's been away at military school. He's Nathan,…*the Third*. Quite a handsome and dashing fellow, isn't he? I venture they're pretty proud of that "Crosby," too!"

"Why, he's absolutely divine!" the young woman said, giggling behind her gloved hand.

After the wedding ceremony, everyone was invited to attend the reception in Doanes Hall. The music could be heard all the way to the Captain John Freeman House nearby. The hall was directly across the street from the church. It was a small building, but sufficient for our purposes. The men usually stayed outdoors so they could smoke their pipes or cigars and drink to their hearts content without the seething glances from the women who had accompanied them.

"Look at all this food!" Jonathan exclaimed, picking up his plate and filling it to the brim. I was standing directly behind him in a long line of famished guests.

"By the way, before I forget," I said, looking over the lavish buffet table, "Japeth wanted me to ask if you'd help us with setting out the weirs. We'd like to do this on the last weekend of May. Japeth should have them all mended by then."

"Certainly," Jonathan replied despite a mouthful of food. "I'll plan on it. I'm glad you remembered to ask me." He turned toward the buffet table and continued to fill his plate.

Minister Ebenezer Farnsworth stood directly behind me. He was a gangly giant of a man with a thin, prematurely wrinkled face and spectacles that seemed to be an integral part of his nose. The minister tapped me several times on the shoulder trying to get my attention. Startled at first, then curious, I turned around to face him.

"You've grown up to be quite a gentleman, Master Crosby," Minister Farnsworth remarked in a rather ambiguous tone, looking over his eyeglasses. "If I must say so myself, I never expected you'd amount to much. You were such a handful as a child. The way you taunted those poor little girls at service was inexcusable. Well,…I guess Nathan must have had to discipline you firmly…and often…It must have been worthwhile. I must say you've turned out to be a reasonably fine young man."

"Well, thank you," I replied, frowning sheepishly and trying to mask my humiliation when he turned to help himself at the luncheon.

As I approached the end of the buffet table, my eyes momentarily focused on Rebecca. I spied her sedately seated at the back of the hall. I sensed she was patiently waiting for me to notice her in a typical, feminine and flirtatious way. Although Rebecca continued to chitchat with her friends, she tilted her head coyly in my direction and smiled sweetly. I found myself drawn, plate in hand, toward her as if in a hypnotic trance. I chose a seat next to her after her friends got up, one by one, to serve themselves. No longer an adolescent girl, but not yet a woman, this young friend whom I had known all my life had suddenly blossomed into a enchanting seductress.

"Hello, Rebecca. It's so nice to see you here!…How are you?" I asked, aspiring to start a polite dialogue. "My, that's such a lovely green dress! It truly accentuates your eyes," I said, freely dispensing compliments to keep the conversation from fading into nothingness. "Say-y-y, I haven't seen very much of you lately. What have you been doing with yourself?"

"Why, Albert you see me at school almost every day…I've certainly noticed *you*!" she replied, rolling her eyes and trying to suppress her irritation with my rather mundane approach.

"Oh, I'm so sorry!…I didn't mean it that way," I said contritely, wishing I had given more thought to my tactless overture. "I meant…I haven't seen you after school hours," I promptly added. "We had such a great time last summer when you were free from your chores."

"Well,…I really do miss the walks along the flats and all the fun we had jumping the waves at high tide…Especially, sailing with you and Jonathan," she replied, beaming and expelling a deep, nostalgic sigh. After a slight pause, she went on to explain. "By the time I return home from school and finish helping Mama, it's already evening, then I must study and do my homework before bedtime"

After finishing with my plate, I stood and placed it on my chair. "Miss Jenkins, would you do me the honor of joining me on the dance floor for the next dance?" I asked politely. "The musicians have just announced that they're about to play a popular gavotte. My ankle's still a bit swollen and tender,…but maybe it'll be all right. I'd like to give it a try," I said, looking down at my foot and extending my right hand to hers to help her rise from her seat.

"Oh, yes, Albert!" Rebecca exclaimed, nodding her head and smiling while standing close to me. "Why,…I'll be the envy of all my friends!" she whispered. Still favoring my injured ankle, we moved together to the center of the dance floor. I had held her hand in mine many times before, but now the touch of her delicate fingers caused an inexplicable sensation—a spark that ignited an inferno within me.

"I'm not as familiar with the gavotte as you are," Rebecca said, apologizing for her ineptitude with an impish grin as we took our place among the guests on the dance floor. "It's not very often I get invited to a such a grand, social affair as this one. Please bear with me, Albert."

"I'm sure you'll do just fine. Just follow my lead," I replied reassuringly, confident that my dexterity and familiarity with this dance would put her at ease.

A precisely aligned queue of male escorts executed a genteel bow while facing their partners. Their female counterparts wearing lovely, full-skirted gowns responded with a curtsy in complete unison. To the delight of the bride and groom, the musicians played the lively *Francek Overture, Inzugsmarsh.*

As I pulled Rebecca close and stared into her expressive, green eyes, I suddenly felt quite flushed. Her tawny curls, crowned by a wreath of dainty babies' breath framed a face as lovely and lively as spring itself. The next time I held her, our eyes met again. Her pupils were dilated with excitement as she responded with an ebullient smile. "Why am I feeling this way? What's happening to me?" I wondered. This was my first encounter with those unfamiliar feelings. Rebecca, who was also aware of her flushed feelings, was suddenly overcome by a sense of breathlessness, one she had never experienced before. I became conscious of the fact that she was also bewildered and confused by what was happening to her. Again, she smiled demurely. I sensed she had also succumbed to this strange spell. For the first time in my young life, an uncontrollable desire to be much closer to her overwhelmed me. It was all I could do to control myself. I yearned to touch, hold and embrace her. An unfamiliar hunger took hold of my body. I desperately needed Rebecca. Somehow, I had to find a way to be alone with her.

"Rebecca, my ankle's aching. It's not responding very well to all this activity," I moaned, feigning apparent distress with an agonized expression. "It's becoming more painful by the minute. I should take my weight off of it," I added as I bent down and held onto my ankle, which had actually begun to ache a bit. "Don't you think it's getting a little stuffy in here? Would you mind if we left the reception hall?" I asked, concocting several excuses to leave and knowing I was being manipulative. "Maybe we can find a comfortable place to sit outdoors and rest."

"I *could* use a bit of fresh air," she replied, taking my hand as we quietly made a quick exit out the side doorway. When I turned to face her, it was obvious that this winsome schoolgirl with whom I had spent so many hours in the past had now become an extremely attractive young lady. Yes, we had always been childhood friends, but now, she awakened some deep and dormant passionate feelings within me. I had never before experienced such overwhelming emotions.

"Rebecca, it's such a beautiful evening, how would you like to go down to the landing?" I asked, hoping she would be of the same mind. "We can sit on that old wooden ships' mast down there and watch the sunset from the beach."

"Why, that's a wonderful idea, Albert. I'd really like to do that!" Rebecca exclaimed, eager to be on our way. Like the nacreous sheen of a string of pearls, her sparkling teeth gleamed every time she smiled and spoke. I sensed she also savored visions of being alone with me. Rebecca was completely unaware of my ulterior motive for requesting a little jaunt to the bay. I simply wanted the opportunity to make love to her.

"I'm sure we won't be missed,…at least for a while," I said, being somewhat persuasive as we walked hand-in-hand toward the rear of the church. "I'll take the buckboard. The reins are tied to the hitching post back there. I must return it promptly as Aaron will be using it this evening to take your family home. Rebecca, please mount the driver's seat and hold on to the reins while I unhitch the horses. We'll be there in no time." Afraid she might have a change of heart, I hastily limped forward in short, quick steps toward the buckboard and unleashed the horses. I climbed onto the wooden seat next to Rebecca and with a lash of the whip we were on our way.

While I harnessed the horses to the split rail fence that separated the shoreline from the road, we were greeted with an awe-inspiring, panoramic canvas intricately sketched by a cosmic artist. The sunset, ablaze with fluent colors formed a complex mural that filled the heavens with merging shades of pink, purple and orange. This mesmerizing effect was mirrored twofold on the calm bay waters. The setting sun was low in the western sky—although not yet beyond the horizon. A Cape Cod sunset is an exhilarating and mystical experience. Familiar with this particular area, I knew that just around the bend was a small inlet cove hidden from view by tall sea grass.

"Would you like to walk along the shore?" I asked, eager for an affirmative answer.

"Oh,…yes!" Rebecca replied enthusiastically. "You must have been reading my mind. I hoped you'd ask me to do, just that. If you don't mind,…I'd like to go barefoot. I love the feel of the sand on my feet," she added, bending to unlace her footwear.

"Fine, so will I," I said, promptly removing my black leather boots and placing them next to her dainty, high button shoes.

Before she could resist, I reached for Rebecca's hand, put my arms around her waist, and then held her close enough to kiss her warm lips. She positioned her head on my shoulders as we walked arm-in-arm leaving our footprints in the soft sand. The sun on the horizon began to immerse itself into the distant sea. The pink evening sky that overshadowed the bay cast a rosy hue onto the sand. Rebecca and I soon found the secluded alcove and squatted comfortably within its confines. We embraced while intermittently conversing and giggling about the funny, unpredictable happenings of the day.

"This will always be our very own, secret hideaway, Albert," Rebecca said while standing to shake the sand from her dress and repositioning her shawl. "It's getting late. We'd best return before we're missed. My parents will be looking for me."

"Yes, so will mine," I replied, slightly frustrated, but resigned to the fact that the intimacy I had in mind was not to be. I was limited to kissing and fondling. My visceral emotions were left unsatisfied. I would have to be content with that—at least for now. While holding her close, we ambled back to the buckboard. "It's been such a wonderful day,…I hate to see it come to an end," I said, feeling unfulfilled and masking my disappointment.

She smiled and with a few quick nods, I knew she agreed with me. We embraced and kissed one more time before returning to the reception hall.

∗   ∗   ∗   ∗

Mid-May, 1838

"Have you asked Jonathan about helping us with the weirs?" Japeth asked as I entered the barn to find my fishing rod.

"Yes, Japeth," I replied. "I mentioned it to him at Anne's wedding. He just wanted to know *when*. I told him it would most likely be on the last weekend in May. He'll be there to give us a hand. In fact,…he's coming here this afternoon. I'll be sure to remind him about it.

"Is the rowboat down on the beach, Japeth?" I asked. "Jonathan and I will be fishing on the bay. We heard that schools of cod and bass were plentiful out there today. We'll be leaving at high tide with our tackle and rods. I hope we come back with a boatful. Get ready for a tasty codfish supper!" I yelled, walking backwards toward home.

"Thank you, Albert. Good luck!" he shouted, waving good-bye. "I'll certainly be looking forward to that grilled cod. It's been quite a while since we've had such a treat."

I found myself looking toward the Jenkins home hoping to catch a glimpse of Rebecca. "Maybe she'd like to come fishing with Jonathan and me," I thought. Just then, I noticed her mother returning home with a basket filled with lavender and bayberry. Rebecca stood in the doorway waving wildly in my direction and hoping I would see her.

"Rebecca probably needs to help her mother with making soap or candles. I'd better not ask. Besides, it's too dangerous out there for a girl," I concluded, quickly dismissing the idea and waving back. As I leaned my rod against the outside of the kitchen door, Miss Mira greeted me with a smile.

"Ye take this with you, me laddie, and ye catch me a lot of those cod. Me'll coat the extra fish with salt…that'll help to keep them from spoiling." She handed me a basket filled with enough food for the two of us.

"Thank you, Miss Mira," I said, giving her a quick kiss on her right cheek. She rubbed her cheek impatiently as if to erase it—and then shooed us on our way. Jonathan appeared at the door rod in hand and wearing a jacket and hat.

"Hello, Albert! Ready to go down to the bay?" he asked impatiently. Jonathan politely tipped his hat as he greeted Miss Mira. While waiting for me, he began fidgeting with his fishing pole and shuffling his feet along the walkway.

"Yes, I'll be there in a second…I need to fetch my coat," I replied, shouting back from the kitchen table and yanking my jacket off the coat rack. Jonathan handed me the rod as we rushed out the door together.

"Ye wait a minute, Albert! Ye better take ye hat. It can get very cold out there over the water. Ye be gone now and mind ye not to go too far out,…ye hear!" she cautioned in her motherly fashion, handing me my hat, and then returning into the kitchen.

This time, our aging dog Teddy, who was sleeping more often these days, chose to stay behind with Japeth. He was napping—sprawled in some hay in the barn.

"By the way," Jonathan said, surreptitiously trying to mask what could be an embarrassing question. "What happened to you and Rebecca at the reception? I looked for you everywhere, but you were nowhere to be found."

"Oh,…my ankle was really bothering me after having been on it all day, so we left the reception hall early," I replied nonchalantly. "We took the wagon down to the landing and sat on a log for a while to rest and watch the sunset. After that, we returned the buckboard to the hall as everyone was preparing to leave. We joined our families and left for home. I didn't get to see you, either, before I left."

"Oh, yeah,…sure!" Jonathan replied incredulously. "Go on, tell me another tale and maybe…I'll believe that one," he said with a devious smile.

I turned my attention to his fishing rod and began to examine it. Jonathan realized that I was *not* about to divulge the personal aspects of my relationship with Rebecca. Deciding to drop the subject, he began to display his assortment of fishing hooks and describe an adjustment he had made to his fishing rod.

"It's a great day for fishing!" Jonathan blurted, looking up at the sky as we followed the trail to the bay. "Although there's a few wispy clouds out there,…the seas are calm. Can't wait to catch that cod!"

✻   ✻   ✻   ✻

Mid-July, 1838

"The Brewster July Regatta" took place on an exceptionally hot summer day. Despite a morning fog, the sun finally broke through the haze. Crowds filled the bay beaches to participate in this enjoyable Brewster event. At high tide, a sailboat race would take place about a half mile off shore. Many of the surrounding towns took part in this annual rivalry. The participants, about thirty in all and of varying levels of ability, arrived early from the adjacent towns of Harwich, Chatham, Dennis, Orleans and Eastham.

Jonathan and I had moored our sailboats earlier in the day on the landing at Ellis Road. The regatta was designed to showcase the sailing skills of all the young men in the area. Those from fourteen to seventeen competed with one another for a coveted trophy. Most of the observers were relatives and friends of the youthful sailors.

We gathered at the shore around eleven in the morning. The Crosby, Eldredge, Nickerson and Snow families came to bond together as a large extended family. They prepared a clambake on the beach that was an annual event in conjunction with the race.

My grandfather, Nathan Crosby, Senior, and Grandmamma were not able to attend this year. Much to our family's regret, Grandfather had passed away quietly on the 29th of June. He was an ardent supporter of this sporting event and would have wanted it to take place even in his absence. The clambake and the regatta were not the same without him. He would be sorely missed.

Japeth and his family were also there. I purposely searched for Rebecca on the crowded beach. When we caught sight of each other, we eagerly raced to meet and embrace. Our absence was unnoticed by our parents, who were busy socializing. Rebecca's winsome smile made my heart skip a beat.

"God speed, Albert…I'll be cheering you on," she murmured softly. "Be careful out there."

The men had arrived at dawn to start the stone pit so that the clambake would be ready for the festivities at noon. No one seemed to take heed of the ocean spray and the occasional wind gusts that hurled stinging bits of sand against their exposed skin. They dug a hole deep on the beach, lined it with stones from the shoreline, started a hot fire inside the hole with logs, and then covered the burning firewood with more rocks. After the stones were heated for two to three hours, they removed the burning embers from the hole and placed fresh, wet seaweed on top of the hot stones. Working quickly they layered the shellfish and vegetables on top of the seaweed, covered everything with a clean wet cloth, and then placed more seaweed on top of the cloth. The entire hole was filled with victuals and covered with a wet canvas, sealing the steam created by the hot stones. It was left unattended for several hours until the succulent repast was ready to be served.

"Jonathan, do you think we have a chance to win the race?" I asked as we gave our sailboats a final once over before the two o'clock starting time. We carefully examined every inch of the masts, sails, jibs and keels to insure our safety and speed.

"I'm sure we have as good a chance as anyone else," Jonathan replied. "With Japeth's help, we've really gotten our sailboats in tip-top condition…They're truly fast and maneuverable. Yes, I think we could even reach that last buoy in record time. I'm confident about that!" Jonathan declared, pointing to the bay and looking skywards. "Of course that depends on whether the skies stay clear and sunny. We've got more than enough wind right now to sail through this moderate surf."

If one concentrated hard enough while intently looking at the wispy, feather-like clouds that filled the sky that day, one could envision the various shapes and sizes of heavenly angels hovering high above us. I felt that was a *good* sign.

"Yes, I guess you're right, Jonathan," I replied, but not feeling quite as positive as Jonathan. When I took a fleeting glance around me, I experienced a momentary lapse of self-confidence. "Many of those sailboats look mighty swift and sleek, and their skippers seem so rugged…Some are giants compared to me.

What's wrong with me, Jonathan?" I asked. "I'm so small and puny for my age. Why,…Rebecca's as tall as I am. Japeth told me I hadn't hit my growth spurt yet. I certainly hope he's right. I'm tired of having to look up at most of my friends and classmates."

"Oh, for heaven's sake, Albert, stop feeling sorry for yourself! You're probably just one of those so-called late bloomers," Jonathan asserted, annoyed by my whining, yet trying to restore my equanimity. Anyhow, remember what you said at Anne's wedding. 'It's the expertise of the sailor that wins the race…not the boat!' Just keep that in mind! If you really took time to examine those sailboats as I have, you'd be convinced that ours are as seaworthy as theirs,…maybe even more so. Anyway, Albert, it's almost time to sail out to the starting buoy. You'd better fetch your deck hand. He's probably with my brother, Enoch. They need to join us soon."

I gave a loud whistle in Aaron's direction. He and Enoch raced toward us and helped push the sailboats into the sea. We soon reached the starting buoy. We sat and waited until the appointed time. A gunshot would signal the start of the race.

At two o'clock sharp, the sound of gunfire reached our ears, and the race was officially started. While carefully handling the ties and rudder and making sure we caught every bit of wind in our sails, Aaron and I managed to remain clear of the other boats. We could hear a steady uproar of cheers—loud, resonant shouts echoing from the shoreline. Everyone was rooting for his or her favorite sailboat. Above our sails and flying high on the masts were flags with distinguishing emblems or crests. Mine bore—a starfish and Jonathan's—a dolphin. The *Starfish* and the *Dolphin* were side by side until we reached the fourth buoy. Our attention was geared to what was ahead. To insure that we remain within the marked channels, Aaron and I were facing the helm while maneuvering the rudder.

"Aaron just told me that all the others are way behind us!" I yelled over to Jonathan.

"Yes, so I'm told! Whatever we're doing to win this race must be right! We'd just better keep it up!" Jonathan shouted back. "I'll pull up ahead of you when we round that fifth buoy. It should be smooth sailing from there to the finish line!" he hollered self-assuredly while pointing in that direction.

"I wouldn't be too sure about that if I were you! Aaron and I are an unbeatable twosome!" I maintained, pointing to Aaron and bellowing. "Better keep your eyes on the helm rounding that fifth buoy! I noticed there's a shift in the wind as we're approaching that one!"

After it negotiated the fifth buoy, the *Starfish* was two boat-lengths ahead of the *Dolphin*. Suddenly, at this crucial halfway mark, the *Dolphin* began to list. Its sails were almost parallel to the water. It seemed Jonathan could not right his boat. The wind had shifted and the gusts caught in his sails. The *Dolphin* tilted and rolled over—the mast and sails partially immersed in the sea.

"Aaron!…Take the helm!" I commanded loudly, suddenly aware of Jonathan's dire situation. "Hold tightly to the ties and rudder! Turn the sailboat around slowly and come alongside the *Dolphin*! Be very careful and take as much time as you need! Use every sailing skill your father taught you! Remember, you'll be a skipper next year!" Aaron looked at me, dumbfounded. "Dammit, Aaron!…You heard me!…Now do as I say! You know how!" I ordered with unfaltering resolve. "I'm going to swim over to the *Dolphin* and help Jonathan right his boat." After we closed the gap between the two boats, it was now just a short distance away,

"Jonathan, loosen the ties!…Lower the sails!" I shouted as I swam within yards of the *Dolphin*. I was fearful, but guardedly optimistic that together we could right his listing sailboat. I arrived just in time. The boat would soon be swamped and impossible to salvage. Jonathan dropped the sails from the mast into the boat. He and Enoch jumped into the water and joined me alongside the *Dolphin's* hull. We began to push on its keel until it finally righted itself. Jonathan and Enoch boosted themselves up and tumbled into the sailboat. I joined them and quickly started bailing out most of the water that had rushed in. Jonathan and I took up the oars and began to paddle the *Dolphin* toward the *Starfish*. We towed the swamped sailboat behind the *Starfish*. Poor Enoch, he was a pathetic sight as he sat on the centerboard frightened, shivering and in a state of shock.

"I'm so sorry, Albert," Jonathan said apologetically, lowering his head and afraid to face me so I wouldn't see his tears. "I should have listened to you. My stupidity cost you the race."

"Actually, it was your cocksure attitude that did it, my friend." I teased. "They'll be other races, but there'll never be another Jonathan and Enoch. Your safety was my main concern," I said candidly in a firm and somber tone of voice. "Forget about it. We're all safe and sound and so is the *Dolphin*…That's all that matters to me. I'm sure you feel that way, too."

"You're one of a kind, Albert," Jonathan said sincerely, shaking his head. "Thank you for what you did for me and Enoch, out there. You sacrificed a victory for us. I'll never forget that." I boarded the *Starfish* and quickly took over as skipper. I noticed Aaron was almost as distraught as Enoch. While nearing the shore, Aaron was more than eager to relinquish the helm. As we sailed toward the coastline, we could hear loud cheers from the crowd.

"I guess one of the sailboats reached the finish line. I wonder who won," I said, continuing to navigate the *Starfish*.

"I bet it's the *Sandpiper* and that big bully from Eastham, Thomas Bangs," Jonathan speculated. "Oh well,…at this point it doesn't really matter. It was a good try. We did our best. Just a stroke of bad luck, I guess," he reasoned, trying to justify his apparent lack of judgment. The shouts and cheering became louder and clearer as we glided through the surf toward shore.

"Yay! Albert! Yay! Jonathan!" They called out vociferously. Puzzled, Jonathan and I looked inquisitively at each other.

"Jonathan, why are they making such a fuss over us?" I asked, hopping out of our boats onto the shoreline.

"I don't know," he replied as perplexed as I was. "We lost,…in fact, we didn't even finish the race. This is really strange!"

Suddenly, a short gentleman with a large hooked nose, who was as wide as he was tall, stepped out from among the spectators. He wore an outrageous, red outer coat with tails. This block of a man waddled toward us amid the pageantry with a trophy in his hands and bowed almost to his knees. When he handed me the silver cup his gold watch chain almost touched the water's edge.

"It's my pleasure young man to present you with this award," he said in a deep raspy voice. Because of your heroic and unselfish deed today, it was the consensus of the judges and your fellow competitors that we award this cup to you, Albert Crosby. Your sailing skills are exceptional. You certainly would have won the race had you chosen to continue. However, you magnanimously chose to save the life and sailboat of another contestant. You selflessly forfeited the race on behalf of your fellow skipper. For this noble act,…it's my honor to present you with the Brewster Regatta trophy cup." I was so astonished by this reception that his words eluded me.

"Well…I…I, thank you. But…t…t," I stuttered, momentarily stunned by this curious inconsistency. "I don't understand." Before I could say another word, everyone crowded around me, spontaneously offering congratulations and an outpouring of appreciation. My family and friends fondly embraced me. They were especially proud of my intrepidness and delighted that the Regatta Committee had recognized it.

"I'm very proud of you, son. You're a true Crosby! You have honored the family name by your heroic actions!" Father exclaimed, smugly turning to everyone around us to gloat about my proficiency.

The women curtseyed and the gentlemen shook my hand. Rebecca burst through the crowd and brushed my cheek with a kiss. Even Teddy greeted me with his tail wagging excitedly as if he hadn't seen me in ages. Still bewildered by this strange turn of events, I clasped my newly acquired award securely under my arm and surrounded myself for the remainder of the afternoon with my close friends—Rebecca, Jonathan, Aaron, Enoch and Teddy.

CHAPTER 4

▼

"Albert, have ye placed me pies in the buckboard?" Miss Mira asked excitedly. "Me apple pies should win first prize at the fair again this year. Me blue ribbons hang in me room upstairs…I'll add this year's with all the rest," she said proudly, standing in the doorway and wiping her hands with her apron.

"Yes,…I have," I replied. "I'll try to be very careful with them."

A warm sun had melted the early morning frost. The afternoon sky was clear, and although the air was crisp and cool—it was still quite comfortable for late October. The fall harvest had yielded much to be thankful for. Miss Mira had diligently preserved and stored every conceivable vegetable—pumpkins, squash, tomatoes and green beans for the coming winter and spring. The Crosby family would be well nourished, and once the firewood was gathered, we'd be amply prepared for the next two seasons.

"Please keep Teddy in the house, Miss Mira, until I leave," I remembered to say as I headed out the door. "If he should jump into the back of the wagon, he's sure to ruin the pies. Also,…I have all the items the girls want to display in the crafts competition. Emeline's knitted and crocheted work always wins a ribbon, and Kate's pottery is a financial bonanza. I'll be ready to leave in a few minutes. Japeth will be at the reins and Rebecca will also accompany us there. She needs to display and sell her candles at the fair. Japeth will return home with the buck-board. Would you please tell my parents I'm planning on staying until after dark. I'll be joining my friends at the Higgins Barn. Japeth will pick us up around nine."

"The Brewster Harvest Festival" always took place on the last weekend in October.

Like the July regatta, it was an occasion for everyone to come together in a spirit of competitive camaraderie. Friends, relatives and neighbors exhibited their prized farm animals, vegetables, baked goods and crafts for the approval and appreciation of fellow townspeople and visitors. They proudly displayed their wares, livestock, cooking and sewing skills, et cetera with a profound sense of accomplishment. To the delight of all who attended, it was also a festival of good food, games of dexterity and lively music. Races and contests demonstrating strength and prowess in numerous diverse sports were also planned for the upcoming weekend.

"Hello, Albert!" Rebecca shouted from the height of the buckboard seat.

"Here,…sit next to me on the left," Japeth ordered before I could acknowledge Rebecca's greeting.

"It's so nice to see you again, Rebecca," I said with a broad smile, climbing onto the seat and leaning over to talk to her with my hand at the side of my mouth. I wanted to tell her so much more than that; however, I didn't want to alert her father to our more than casual relationship. Except for an occasional comment about how fortunate we were to have such fine weather for the fair, we sat in silence while on our way to the festival. Weather wise, the Cape was having two of its finest weeks so far this fall. We hoped it would continue through the weekend. Although a bit chilly, a jacket was all that was needed to be comfortable.

"Are you entering any of the contests, Albert?" Japeth asked, hoping to end the silence with some meaningful conversation.

"No,…I'm not planning to do that. I'll just sit on the sidelines this year as an observer, Japeth. This'll be a fun weekend for me," I replied. "However, Jonathan has entered the two-man log sawing contest with his brother, Enoch. I've definitely decided to go into the merchant marines as soon as I graduate in June. This outing will be a sort of a farewell gathering with my friends. I want to look back on it with fond memories. We're all so busy with chores and schooling,…it's not very often we can all get together…just for the fun of it. Can you see my point, Japeth?"

"I can't say I blame you, Albert," Japeth replied, turning to look at me and nodding his head in approval.

Rebecca didn't say a word. In fact, she cheerlessly hung her head when I turned to look at her. Surprised by my unexpected announcement, she looked disappointed, saddened and hopelessly resigned.

The anticipated Indian summer had definitely arrived. The fresh sea breezes were much warmer than usual. The early morning mist rolling in from the bay gave way to an azure sky and a radiant sun. Although an occasional biting breeze taunted the hardy sunflowers and Queen Anne's lace, it was a spectacular autumn day—a Cape Cod wonder. As we rode along admiring the brilliant foliage, we gaped at the awesome vista of color around us—so typical of autumn in New England. The swamp maple and oak tree leaves touched by an early frost had changed from their deep, summer green to an autumn palette of breathtaking hues. The ruby reds, vibrant oranges and burnished golds were vividly reflected in the small kettle ponds. We were charmed by the earthen colors of the wetlands, the sepia peat bogs and chocolate cattails. They offered a wealth of natural beauty to the countryside. A half-dozen mallard ducks—all in a row—bobbed atop a crimson cranberry bog that was ready for harvest. Sienna pine needles and cones profusely covered the woodland paths that rimmed the inland ponds. From the wagon we enjoyed a panorama of open meadowlands—rich with dried marsh grass in various shades of yellow ocher that swayed in the distance like soft velvet. It was a view that could be appreciated from either side of the Olde King's Highway. Fields of brass-colored hay were sporadically dotted with evergreen cypress trees. Dramatic scarlet patches of wild cranberries—undiscovered treasures nestled within the salt marshes added a dazzling accent to an otherwise monochromatic landscape.

When we arrived at the barn, it was late Friday afternoon and just before dusk—the day before the judging on Saturday and Sunday. It was a hubbub of commotion. Horses, buckboards and all sorts of horse-driven carriages filled the meadow next to the barn. Swarms of people were vying for space on the craft and food tables.

"Father, let's try to get as close as we can to the side entrance," Rebecca suggested, noting an overabundance of items that needed to be unloaded and carried in.

"I think I can find a space right over there," Japeth said, pointing to a level area between the barn and the mill. "I'll hitch the horses to that split-rail fence and stay here with the wagon. Quickly now,…jump down and get a move on!" he ordered. "Be ready to remove the tailgate so you can start unloading your goods right away!"

As soon as Japeth came to a full halt, we did as we were told and started to carry our wares into the barn. Despite the unruly crowd that was pushing and shoving in all directions, we found our way to a corner table. I carefully deposited the goods that Miss Mira and my sisters had so meticulously created. While I returned to the buckboard to remove our nanny's exceptional pies, Rebecca began to display her wares to their best advantage. I carried the pies to the baked goods table amidst the "oohs" and "aahs" of the ladies in charge. Soon, the buckboard was emptied of its prized goods. Japeth sat smoking his corncob pipe while patiently waiting for us to finish our tasks.

"I'll be coming back for you two around nine," he said, looking at his pocket watch. "Wait for me right here. Keep track of the time and be ready to leave when I arrive. I don't intend to go looking for you."

"Yes,…we'll be here," I replied for the two of us. We simultaneously nodded our heads to indicate that we understood.

"Good luck selling your candles, Rebecca," Japeth called back, cracking the whip and turning the horses toward the highway.

"Goodbye, Father. We'll see you at nine," she shouted, waving farewell.

We walked back together toward the barn. Once he was out of sight and before reaching the barn, I took her hand in mine. When she looked up at me with her demure, captivating smile, I melted and found myself suddenly aroused by her comely presence. We had often slipped away these last few years to our secret alcove on the beach. In my own youthful way, I knew I had fallen in love with her. She was my first and only love. At the time, I was convinced there would be no other. Rebecca had taken me into the deepest realms of what true love was all about. I held her in my arms and we kissed passionately. The vibrations between us had become too energized to be ignored.

"Let's leave for a short while," I suggested, overcome with desire and knowing the need was mutual. "I want to be alone with you, Rebecca. It's not very often that you're allowed to be unchaperoned. We'll escape to our favorite hideaway…Would you like to do that?"

"I was having the same thought, Albert," she confided, looking directly into my eyes.

"But do you think we can make it back before dark?" she questioned. "I do need to sell some of my candles. I'd better return home with a little money…If I show up empty handed, Father will become suspicious."

"We'll leave this very minute." I said, eager to be on our way. "I promise we'll be back with plenty of time to spare."

"Fine," she replied, embracing me one more time before we started our trek to the beach. The Higgins Barn, which was on the south side of the Olde King's Highway, was about a half-mile from the shoreline.

The sandy trail was lined with alternating bushes of sweet everlasting and pokeweed hanging heavy with clusters of dark purple fruit. An occasional dried stalk of chicory sprouted from lucent patches of goldenrod, and deep orange bittersweet vines wound themselves surreptitiously around tree trunks and brambles. In the distance, the sea lavender's muted tufts seemed to float over the dunes like a low miasma of purple wool. As we strolled along the pristine shoreline, the grassy knolls and salt marshes offered a fleeting brilliance of color during this twilight of seasons. After a thirty-minute walk, we reached our own private inlet. Bouquets of delicate beach heather flanked by bayberry bushes were lavishly covered with waxy, silvery berries. The wild rose vines adorned with vivid red hips were profusely scattered amid the verdant dune grasses above us. A tropical storm far out in the Atlantic was creating whitecaps and heavy surf.

"Oh, Albert," she sighed. "I do love you so, and have for such a very long time. I can't imagine not being able to be with you. I was heartsick to hear you were leaving Brewster and that you'll be away for such a long while. If I must,…I'll wait forever for you to return to me."

"I love you *too*, Rebecca. When I return from the merchant marines, I'll ask your father for your hand in marriage," I said, holding her close and settling into our secluded, sandy cove. She leaned her head on my shoulders.

"You have such broad shoulders and strong muscles," she commented affectionately. Flattered by her adulation, I accepted it with a silent smile. "My heart and body are throbbing with my need for you. I ache to be completely yours, Albert," she declared unashamedly as she began to take off her jumper and blouse. Realizing it might be years before we'd be together again, I also had an overwhelming urge to engage in a sexual tryst with Rebecca. I determined the time to consummate our mutual love and desire was long overdue. It would become a cherished memory for us both.

Up to this point, we had only resorted to fondling to satisfy our sexual needs. I wanted her—in fact much more than I'd ever wanted or needed anyone or anything else before in my young life. I began to caress her exposed breasts. Frenzied by a raging physical need, our kisses became more and more ardent. Prodded by innate mating instincts, the passionate embraces became explosive and unrestrained. Enraptured by the eroticism of the moment, the sexual hunger that relentlessly gnawed at our beings demanded to be satisfied. Feverishly, we impetuously ignored every caution—moral or otherwise—and let nature take its course.

We walked back to the barn in ample time, allowing Rebecca to sell some of her aromatic candles. I sought out my friends and met Jonathan standing by the large barn doors. They were opened to expose its contents and décor. The Higgins Barn was adorned with corn stalks, bales of hay, pumpkins, baskets of mums and assorted gourds.

Somehow, I hadn't noticed these fall decorations during previous years' festivities. Lanterns were everywhere. It was indeed a fit setting for the Brewster Harvest Festival.

"Jonathan, Father has asked me to enlist your help again this year," I said, upon greeting him. "Before I forget to mention it,…it's time to collect the cordwood before the cold and snow makes it an impossible task. We need to fill the woodbins before winter. It'll be here in no time. As you already know, the freshly cut timbers need to dry for a few months. Father and Japeth plan to start on the fourth Thursday of next month. Father must tend to business affairs at the beginning of the week. It may take a few days,…maybe through the weekend. That'll give us ample time to chop and stack the firewood. Will you be able to lend a hand again? I asked. "I told Father that most likely you were already planning on helping us with this chore."

"Yes, of course…I'll be there," he replied assuredly while munching on a piece of chocolate fudge. It's something I look forward to each year. Not only do I enjoy the outing with your family, I can certainly use the generous wages paid me by your father. I'll arrive early on that Thursday with all my tools."

"Great!" I exclaimed with my hands in my pockets and looking down at my feet. I was nervously shuffling them on the platform in front of the barn doors, afraid that Jonathan had been aware of my absence and the reason why. "Father will be pleased. We definitely need your help. I wish I were as strong and muscular as you, Jonathan. I truly admire that!"

"Well, maybe I have a bigger frame than you, but you're taller. You've certainly caught up with your classmates and me,…height-wise that is. I remember a few years ago when you were such a runt. You were worried sick about being a dwarf for the rest of our lives. Now,…look at you!" he said with a haughty laugh, shoving me gently on the shoulder to prove his point.

"Thank God, for that!" I replied. "I guess Japeth was right, but I surely doubted him at the time"

"By the way, Albert,…where have you been?" Jonathan asked suspiciously, peeking around behind me as if trying to discover my secret. "I was told earlier that you were already here, so I've been waiting for you to present yourself. I noticed Rebecca also arrived at the same time you did. You're not fooling me one bit! I know what you two are up to! I see the way you look at each other," he went on to say. Intuitively, Jonathan knew that getting an honest answer from me would be hopeless. Nevertheless, I tried to offer a plausible excuse.

"Oh, I just dropped by earlier to deliver Miss Mira's pies and my sister's crafts," I replied offhandedly, assuming the insouciance that was typical of a practiced fibber. "Rebecca's here to sell some of her candles to the venders. She wanted to give them first choice before the crowds arrived in the morning."

"Japeth will be picking us up soon. I'm certainly looking forward to the lively music and entertainment the Bassett brothers will provide tomorrow evening. I promise I'll spend more time with you then. We should have a great time!" I shouted back as I nonchalantly turned around to leave. With a spring in my step, I ambled toward the rear barn door where Japeth would be waiting.

✳   ✳   ✳   ✳

Late-November, 1840

"Hello!" Jonathan shouted as he leaned into the opened door. "I'm ready to go!"

"So are we!" I yelled back, acknowledging his presence and rushing to greet him.

"We left the door ajar so we could listen for you. Father will be here in a minute! Japeth will meet us outside at the front fence post," I said, reaching for my heavy wool coat and pulling my knitted hat down over my ears.

"Enoch has a bad cough. Mother wouldn't allow him to come with us on such a raw day," Jonathan said, running alongside me toward the buckboard. Japeth was stroking the horses and patiently waiting for us. Japeth and his son, Aaron, who was seated next to him, greeted us with a warm smile.

"Hello, Aaron! I didn't know you'd be coming with us," I said, looking up at him. "Good!…The more hands, the better."

"Good morning, lads." Japeth said in a jovial tone of voice. "I hope you're both feeling fit today…You have a big task ahead."

"I'm sure…I'm up to it," I replied, convinced that I was more than ready for the undertaking. "However,…I don't know about Jonathan," I added facetiously and chuckling about it.

"I'll run rings around you, my friend," Jonathan boasted as he gave me a well-deserved shove. "Remember,…Enoch and I won the two-man tree-sawing contest at the harvest fair! And for your information my friend, I've brought every conceivable tool I thought we might need," he added, carefully depositing a large rope, a wide leather belt and some grapple hooks in the rear of the wagon.

"Thank you, Jonathan." Japeth said, nodding gratefully. "I've placed several saws, axes, hatchets and a ladder in the buckboard. I've also added several long planks for unloading the logs and extending the sides of the wagon, if need be. I think we have most of what we need. If not,…we'll just have to make do."

Jonathan and I leaped into the back of the buckboard. Aaron climbed over the seat to join us. All the necessary logging equipment needed for our undertaking surrounded us. Japeth was already seated and had taken hold of the reins. As Father approached the wagon, Japeth welcomed him with the tip of his hat. Father nodded, greeted all of us, stepped up to the driver's seat, and then sat next to Japeth. Japeth promptly cracked the whip. The horses bolted forward and galloped up Crosby Lane toward the Olde King's Highway. We were headed for an expansive wooded area that was directly across from Crosby Lane. It encompassed 1400 acres and bordered the Olde King's Highway for several miles. The buckboard reached a well-worn, winding trail that meandered through this vast woodland. We endured a rather jarring ride en route to the wood lot. This primitive roadway fringed the perimeter of a large, kettle pond. Our quest ended at a thick cluster of tall oak trees.

"Well, I guess this is as good a place as any," Japeth determined after carefully surveying the area. "I doubt we'll find a better clump of trees." Japeth yanked at the reins to bring the horses to a halt and set the brake lever.

"Yes, I believe we can gather much of the cordwood we'll need right here," Father agreed, looking upwards and inspecting the thicket of burnable wood. We leaped from the buckboard and began to unload our tools, each taking as much as they could carry to the site.

It was a heavily overcast November day that was decidedly dismal. The moody, slate autumn sky and the raw biting cold signaled snow. Gray smoke was curling up from the chimneys and the smell of firewood filled the air. Winter's icy breath was close at hand. The crimson reds, potent oranges and the rutilant gold foliage—glorious at the time of the harvest festival had now withered into shades of burnt sienna and fallen to the ground. A soft finely woven mat of titian pine needles snapped under foot. The gusting wind whipped at the tops of the scrub pines and swept the dry, swirling oak leaves into sepia mounds ensnared by green bramble thickets. As they swayed back and forth, the barren oaks in this primitive wilderness formed dark willowy silhouettes against a mackerel sky. Tufts of wild cranberry, scattered along the woodland peeped out from under the dry, copper-tone leaves. It gave this bleak and somber scene a welcomed bit of color. I shivered and drew my arms tightly around my body. The icy salt air assaulted my face, branding me with scarlet cheeks and a ruby nose.

"We'd better get started, the weather doesn't look too promising," Japeth cautioned, looking skyward. "Help me carry the large two-man saw, Nathan. I'll get on the other end…We'll start with that smaller oak tree over there," he ordered, gesturing in the direction of an adjacent clump of trees. "Albert,…you and

Jonathan take these hatchets, climb that tree and chop off those larger top branches. We'll take care of the rest. Once the tree's on the ground, we'll saw it into cordwood." Turning to address his son, Japeth continued to issue his directives. "And you,…Aaron, load it onto the buckboard. I may have to make several trips back and forth to the homestead. With any luck, we can manage to fill the woodbins today. Tomorrow may be too late…It surely feels like snow."

Jonathan and I did as we were told, moving quickly and efficiently with a two-fold purpose—to ward off the bitter cold and finish before sundown. Using large grapple hooks to help us scale the trees, we secured ourselves at the proper place for sawing the branches by using a large leather strap to circle the trunk and fasten it around our waist. Father and Japeth waited until the severed limbs fell from the tree, then they swiftly cut the tree down with the two-man saw. We quickly repelled ourselves downward to the ground, helped to cut the fallen tree into cordwood, and then carried the logs to the buckboard. Japeth, who was joined by Aaron, returned to his small crew after several trips back to the Crosby homestead. It was now late afternoon.

"The bins are almost full," Japeth announced cheerfully, pleased with our progress. "I believe one or two more trees should be enough. We won't need to return tomorrow. That large tree over there should do it," he indicated, pointing ahead and directing our attention toward a massive oak.

"I'll be glad to scale that tree to the top and remove those overhanging branches," Jonathan volunteered, gesturing upwards toward a number of large tree limbs. Anxious to get out of the bone-chilling cold, we agreed and nodded our heads in accord.

"Can't wait to get back to a warm, cozy fire and hot apple cider," I said as I adjusted my toque over my ears, convinced we were all entertaining the same thoughts.

Jonathan sprinted toward the tree and began to scale the trunk, using the grapple hooks to get him to the top. He strapped himself securely to a large branch and started to saw away at a sizable limb.

"Here comes the first one!…Stand out of the way!" Jonathan warned. The bough cracked loudly, broke and fell to the ground.

"We'll start sawing it into firewood as soon as each branch is felled. Then we'll haul it onto the buckboard so we can promptly finish up here," Japeth ordered, taking charge of last minute chores. "One more wagon-full…That's all we need."

"Suits me," I said, delighted with that estimation and tapping my feet against the ground to keep my toes from freezing. I blew a warm breath on my gloved fingertips.

"Yes,...I agree. I'm beginning to feel quite fatigued," Father complained while taking deep breaths that hinted at signs of exhaustion. "I ache all over...Its' been a long time since I've worked this hard. I'm looking forward to my easy chair. Yes,...let's finish up here as soon as possible."

Throughout the day, I patiently awaited the opportunity to ask Japeth about Rebecca. She was noticeably absent from school this past week and I missed seeing her. I wondered if Rebecca was ill or just busy preparing the harvest for the winter. Without exposing my feelings or our romantic alliance, I needed to question him about her. Alas, it seemed as though I was not going to have the chance to do so. It was impossible to be alone with him. There was no time for idle chatter. I'd have to try to catch him later on in the day—maybe on our way home. I decided, that for now, I would concentrate on the task at hand.

While Father and Japeth were sawing a freshly fallen limb, Aaron and I industriously carried each log to the buckboard. Suddenly, we heard a piercing shriek emanating from high above us—then an eerie silence. We looked upward and observed a limp figure strapped to a branch that was severed but not yet detached from the trunk. Just then, the limb snapped loudly and fell to the ground with Jonathan attached to it. The noise and ensuing thud filled the wilderness around us with an ominous echo. Jolted by this sickening sight and sound we stood there paralyzed in various stages of shock. Father ran and knelt next to Jonathan's flaccid, broken body.

"Oh, my God!" Father cried out. "He must have accidentally sawed through the limb he was strapped to!...Quickly! Help me remove the belt! He's still breathing! Hurry, Albert!...Get some water from the pond!"

Although I saw his lips move, I didn't hear him. I stood there dumbfounded and motionless while still trying to fathom what had happened. As I looked down on Jonathan's still form, I could see him lying there—but in disbelief, I doubted the severity of the accident. I simply waited for him to open his eyes and extend his arms so I could help him rise from the ground. "Albert! Hurry!...I must try to revive him!" Father shouted, looking up at me and trying to get my attention.

"Aaron, help me clear the cordwood from the buckboard!" Japeth called out, running toward the wagon. "I'll remove the top plank and place Jonathan on it. We must carry him to the wagon without further injuring him. We'll have to take him to Chatham. Doctor Insley should be at home," Japeth announced after calmly assessing the situation.

I returned breathless, spilling half the water in the bucket. Father removed his shirt, immersed it in the bucket, and then wrung it out. He gently applied the cold compress to Jonathan's forehead. Jonathan opened his eyes, but lapsed in and out of consciousness.

"Please, God,…let him be all right. Please don't let him die," I prayed silently, remembering Little William's death, and how I once asked Him this same favor, only to be rebuffed. "This time you *must* listen, Lord. You've taken my young brother. Now,…I mustn't lose my best friend." While engrossed in these anguished thoughts and close to tears, Father stood and tugged at my sleeve for my attention.

"Japeth and I will take Jonathan to Chatham," Father said. "Here's my coat. Spread it over the plank before we place Jonathan on it. It'll help to cushion him against the bumps in the road. We'll drop Aaron off at the highway so he can alert Jonathan's family as to what's happened here."

"I understand, Father," I replied, hastily performing my assigned task.

"Here take mine," Japeth said, removing his coat and handing it over to my father. "I'm wearing a heavy woolen shirt…I'll be fine with that. You'll need something warmer for that long trip to Chatham. Nathan, please help me lift Jonathan into the buckboard. And please,…don't be thinking the worse," Japeth counseled, lifting one end of the plank that was supporting Jonathan and hoisting it into the buckboard. "He's a very strong young man. I'm sure he'll fully recover in no time."

"I certainly hope you're right, Japeth," Father replied apprehensively.

After Jonathan was gently placed in the rear of the buckboard, I climbed in and squatted close to my lifelong companion. I held the wet shirt on his forehead and stared down at his ashen face. I had seen that awful gray pallor once before. Father quickly joined me while Japeth held the reins. Japeth cracked the whip and we promptly left the dense woodland.

Upon reaching the main road, Aaron jumped out and sprinted toward the Eldredge homestead. Father took his place in the buckboard and crouched alongside Jonathan's motionless and corpse-like body, closely watching him for any change—whether for better or for worse. The buckboard made a left turn onto the highway. Somehow the horses seemed to sense the emergency and galloped at breakneck speed toward Chatham.

"I hope we can arrive before dark," Japeth said, trying to break the uneasy silence between us. "If the horses maintain this gait,…we may just make it."

"Oh, Japeth!" Father cried out, reaching for his handkerchief and weeping uncontrollably. "If that boy doesn't survive, I'll never forgive myself," he sobbed, visibly overcome by this calamity. My stalwart father had only cried a few times in my young life and that was on the occasions of Little William and Grandfather's death. "I feel responsible for this horrible accident. How will I ever be able to face his grieving parents? I should never have allowed him to climb that tree. I should have done that myself." Japeth turned around and extended an outstretched arm. He grasped Father on the shoulder and tried to comfort him.

"Now…you listen to me, Nathan," he said firmly, turning his attention from the reins for a second. By verbalizing his thoughts, Japeth hoped to ease Father's guilt-ridden conscience. He turned to face Father who was directly behind him in the buckboard. "Please, don't be so hard on yourself for what happened to that young man. Jonathan was more than eager to join us today. Why,…he's almost family! He looked forward to earning that extra money for himself. Young people are sometimes oblivious to danger. Their rash actions often lead to dire circumstances. I suspect Jonathan was being a bit too daring and reckless. He endangered himself by unintentionally ignoring his own safety. He should've made sure the limb he was strapped to wasn't attached to the one he was sawing off…Sadly, it never occurred to him…So, please stop torturing yourself," he went on, trying to sustain Father's spirit. "You need to stay calm and clear-headed. We must be prepared for the worse."

"I know you're right about this calamity, Japeth, but I just can't seem to control the morbid thoughts going through my mind right now. This is such a terrible blow!" Father lamented. "I'm feeling so fearful and helpless! These emotions are overwhelming me! Oh, Lord, this seems like a never-ending journey…Will we ever get there, Japeth?"

Finally, the buckboard reached a rather ostentatious Georgian Colonial home. Large white columns stood as stately sentinels along each side of the entrance.

"Wo—o—o—ah!" Japeth called out, struggling with the reins to slow the racing team. The horses came to an abrupt halt directly in front of Doctor Benjamin Insley's magnanimous home. Father jumped from the back of the buckboard and dashed to the front door. The flickering gaslights that illuminated the front room windows could be seen from the outside.

"Thank God, he's home!" Father exclaimed.

"Hurry, ring the bell on the door!" Japeth shouted impatiently. A solemn looking, middle-aged butler opened the front door.

"Is Doctor Insley in? Jonathan Eldredge has fallen from a tree and is seriously hurt!" Father disclosed frantically, his panic-stricken voice trembling and echoing with alarm throughout the house.

"Why,…yes he is. I'll announce your arrival. He'll be here promptly," the butler replied rather adroitly. Just then, Doctor Insley could be heard from inside as he rushed toward the front entrance.

"Quickly now!" he ordered with a histrionic wave of his arms and beckoning the makeshift stretcher toward him. "Carry him in, but be very careful…He may have internal injuries and broken bones."

Father and Japeth had already dropped the back tailgate and began to lift the heavy board on which laid an inert, Jonathan. The planks certainly came in handy in this emergency.

"Winslow, we need you here to help us!" Doctor Insley shouted, summoning his understudy and medical assistant, Winslow Cobb. He was a short, slim and prematurely balding man who had a thin, gray mustache and a well-trimmed Vandyke goatee.

Together we cautiously lifted Jonathan's rag-doll like body onto a padded table set in the center of the doctor's examining room. I stood silently in the corner of the room, still hoping I would soon awake from this dreadful nightmare.

"Please tell me everything you can remember about this accident," Doctor Insley said, directing his question to both Father and Japeth. He was noticeably apprehensive as he meticulously scrutinized Jonathan from head to toe. "Let's see!…His most serious injuries must be tended to first," he judged after his examination.

Taking turns, Father and Japeth thoroughly recounted every detail. They explained that Aaron and I were loading the buckboard at the time and did *not* see what happened. Actually, I had observed the accident, but was much too stunned by it all to be a credible witness.

"Jonathan must have sustained a concussion," Doctor Insley determined. "Although he's a strong young man, his condition is dubious at best right now. He's definitely in shock and in and out of consciousness at the moment…His breathing is also labored. I don't believe I can do very much for him here. He'll need to be taken to a Boston hospital. There's a packet leaving in the morning,…he should be on it," he went on, nodding his head. "Winslow will accompany him to the hospital. He'll keep me advised as to the doctors' prognosis and his progress. Until then, I'll stay here with him. I'll be sure to keep you informed. You're welcome to stay overnight,…if you like. I know you're quite concerned and it's already getting quite late."

"Yes,…I think we should," Father replied. "I appreciate your offer. I really don't want to leave him in this condition. We'll take turns watching over him, alternating the vigil every few hours so one of us can be with him while the others rest."

"We'll return home in the morning after seeing him off," Japeth said. "Catherine will most likely be told about what's happened and assume we wouldn't be coming back until then anyway,"

"Benjamin," Father said, "little did I expect such a terrible tragedy would occur when we undertook the logging for cordwood. Somehow I feel responsible for what's happened to Jonathan. After all, he was working for me at the time. I just want you to know that I wish to assume full, financial responsibility for everything, including your fees for services, transportation to Boston and all the hospital expenses," Father went on, disheartened and wanting to do the right thing. He then turned toward Japeth. "Japeth, when we return, please tell the Eldredge family I plan to do the same for them. No,…on second thought,…I'll tell them myself," he added, hopeful that this generous gesture would help in some small way to ease their pain and financial burdens.

The packet, which was fashioned from oak timbers, was anchored alongside a Chatham dock. The journey to Boston across the bay usually took about six hours providing the tides and the weather cooperated. A wide drawbridge leading from the landing to the wharf allowed carriages and wagons to disembark passengers and unload cargo. Several inches of freshly fallen snow covered the shipping dock and ramp. A kaleidoscope of tracks made by hoofs and wheels were outlined on the wharf—visible evidence that this was a place of extraordinary activity—a Mecca of sorts. Doctor Insley's horse-drawn carriage, designed to carry a disabled person such as Jonathan, came to a halt at the packet landing. We followed behind in the buckboard, ready to return to Brewster as soon as the *Chatham* left port. Accompanied by Winslow and the packet's stewards, Jonathan's gurney was carefully carried inside, wheeled over to the ramp that led below deck, and then disappeared from view.

After turning around, the buckboard left the dock in Chatham, and then headed toward the Olde King's Highway. Father, Japeth and I began our journey back to Brewster shifting our conversation and tortured thoughts from Jonathan's near fatal accident to the likely prospects—he could possibly recover from it.

✻   ✻   ✻   ✻

Mid-December, 1840

Alerted by an arriving carriage, I looked up from my chores just as Miss Mira glanced out the kitchen window into a clear, bitterly cold day.

"Doctor Insley's carriage just pulled up to the front fence post!" Miss Mira shouted, summoning Mother. "He must have some news about me, Jonathan!" Mother had been in an upstairs window when the carriage arrived at the Crosby cottage and heard Miss Mira announce his arrival from the kitchen below. Mother and Miss Mira greeted the doctor at the front door.

Several weeks had passed since Jonathan's accident and his admission to the hospital. Everyone anxiously awaited word of his progress. The Eldredge family had traveled to Boston and remained there by his bedside.

Father and Japeth would soon return with a buckboard filled with winter supplies for our livestock. I was in the barn making room for more hay and feed. Anxious to hear news of Jonathan, I set aside my chores and immediately ran over the snow-covered ground toward the house. I stood inside the kitchen doorway leading to the parlor, waiting for Doctor's Insley's report.

"Good afternoon, Doctor Insley," Mother said as she graciously extended her hand to greet him.

"Good day, Catherine. This will be just a brief visit," he replied, removing his hat and asking, "Is Nathan at home?"

"No,…I'm sorry, he's not here at the moment," Mother answered regretfully. "He left with Japeth to fetch some winter supplies. He should be returning shortly. Nathan will be saddened to know he missed you…How is Jonathan doing?" she asked anxiously, wary of disquieting news.

"Well, there's both good news and bad…to report," he replied ambiguously, finding a chair and sitting down with his cane between his knees. "The good news is that Jonathan is finally conscious and able to communicate intelligently," he chose to say first, hoping it would serve to diminish the impact of his account. "Because of his age and previous good health, he's recuperating at an amazing rate." I observed Mother searching for clues in his facial expressions and words.

"Thank God," I thought, heaving a deep sigh and delighted to hear that my close friend was well on the road to recovery. Elated by this good news, I was ready to burst into the sitting room when I abruptly stopped—dead in my tracks. I was stunned and totally unprepared for the doctor's next sentence.

"Sadly, however, there *is* bad news," he disclosed looking distraught and staring at the floor. "Jonathan shattered his spinal column and is paralyzed from the waist down. In all likelihood,…he'll be a paraplegic for the remainder of his life."

"Oh, no!" Mother wailed upon hearing this shocking and tragic prognosis. She instinctively covered her mouth with her hands as her tears flowed unabashedly. Mother reached into her pocket for a handkerchief and wiped her eyes.

Lulled into believing Jonathan would eventually fully recover from his injuries, my initial excitement was short-lived. I was traumatized by this verdict. "How can this be?" I questioned silently. "Jonathan…a cripple?…He'll never be able to walk again? My robust, vibrant friend will be in a wheelchair for the rest of his life? Oh,…how awful!" This reality was much too difficult for me to absorb *or* believe. Noticeably shaken, I walked across the room to Mother's side, my hat in my hand and my chin almost touching my chest. She assumed I had heard Doctor Insley's report. With empathy for the heartache I was going through, Mother put her arms around me and uttered some encouraging and comforting words.

"Albert, the Good Lord allowed Jonathan to remain with us…He spared him even further trauma. Jonathan could have existed in a comatose or vegetative state or unable to function normally. But, by the grace of God, his mental capacities have remained unimpaired," she said, injecting an optimistic note to the news. "We must be thankful for that…I'm sure he'll eventually adjust to his condition."

"Oh, me heart goes out to that dear lad!…Oh, me poor Jonathan!" Miss Mira blubbered unabashedly, picking up the corner of her apron to dry her eyes.

"I promised Nathan I'd inform him of Jonathan's progress as soon as Winslow returned from Boston. I'm sorry I had to bring you this heart-wrenching news," Doctor Insley said, rising from his chair. "Jonathan should be returning home in a few days accompanied by his family. I thought Nathan would like to be advised about this. He may want to employ a nurse who could tend to him for a while during his recovery period."

"Yes,…I'm sure he will," Mother replied, nodding and supporting his suggestion. "Nathan, will be home soon. I'll inform him of your visit and relay your message. On behalf of my family and myself, I wish to thank you not only for your indispensable services, but also for your enduring compassion toward us. We've come to rely on you as a trusted family physician, but above all, Doctor Insley, you're a dear and cherished friend."

"Why,…thank you," the doctor muttered, blushing and slightly embarrassed by Mother's overture. "Good day, Catherine. I must return to Chatham as I have some gravely ill patients who need my immediate attention," he added, excusing himself and tipping his hat to both ladies in a farewell gesture. "The next time Nathan comes to Chatham,…please tell him to drop by for a visit."

Doctor Insley returned his hat to his head, raised his cane, and then turned toward the door to leave. "He may want to take Jonathan with him when he's well enough to make the trip…I'd like to keep an eye on that young man," he added as he prepared to leave. Eager to be on his way, he dashed headlong out the door toward his waiting carriage. After reaching for their coats, Mother and Miss Mira hurriedly followed behind him to wave goodbye. By the time I approached the front hitching post, the doctor's carriage could barely be seen in the distance. It was already spewing an obscuring mixture of swirling snow and road dust as it sped up Crosby Lane.

▼

CHAPTER 5

Late - June, 1841

I stood in the kitchen doorway ready to leave while Japeth waited for me with the carriage by the front fence post.

"Albert, take this napkin," Miss Mira said, turning from the sink, her hands still wet as she reached for a small bundle on the kitchen table. "I filled it with some sweet cakes for ye. Ye may get hungry on that packet to Boston." After wiping her hands on a towel, she gave me a last ardent hug before launching me on my way. "Now…ye better hurry!"

"Thank you, Miss Mira. It's so like ye to be so thoughtful. Me certainly going to miss ye," I said regretfully and imitating her charming Gaelic accent. I opened the drawstring of my bag, carefully placed her treats inside, and then tossed it over my shoulder. I bent down to kiss her tear-streaked cheek—and then hurried out the door to the waiting carriage. When I turned around to wave a last good-bye, she was dabbing her eyes with the dishtowel she had brought out with her.

"Hurry, Albert! Come up here!…Sit with me!" Japeth shouted, pointing with one hand to the seat next to him and holding onto the reins with the other. "The coach is filled with family," he said, lowering his voice. "The *Sarah* leaves in less than an hour…We must be on our way."

I tossed my knapsack onto the seat, jumped up, and then sat alongside him. He immediately cracked the whip and the horses galloped up Crosby Lane. I twisted myself around and turned toward the small white cottage—my lovely homestead with its rolling green bluffs and panoramic view of the bay. Miss Mira was energetically waving from the doorway. I wanted just one last look at what had been my home for so many years. I made a concentrated effort to brand this nostalgic scene in my mind. I hoped to recall the serenity of this tableau whenever it was necessary—knowing it would always beckon me back regardless of where I traveled. Little did I know how often this comforting image would lift my spirits in the years to come. I even imagined Teddy running alongside our carriage up the dusty road to the Olde King's Highway. It had been several months since he passed away. I yearned for Teddy—that loyal, faithful companion who lived a long life with us, shared our food and slept by our fires.

"What took you so long?" Japeth asked, giving my left thigh a cuff with his elbow. Startled by his question, my thoughts were abruptly interrupted when I realized he was speaking to me.

"I spent some time saying my last goodbyes to the farm animals," I replied, quickly turning around to look at him. "I called on Jonathan earlier this morning. Oh,…Japeth, he looks so pale and weak. Do you think he'll ever regain his ruddy tone and vigor? My heart ached to see him so forlorn and in such despair. It saddened me so when he said he wished we could have left together as planned…How I hated to leave him. The visit was quite distressing for us both."

"I'm sure Jonathan will eventually be his old self, but he may never walk again. I think that one of these days…he'll accept his fate and become a truly useful individual. I'll be sure to visit him as frequently as possible while you're away," Japeth replied, trying to ease my anxiety over leaving Jonathan. As we neared the Olde King's Highway and rounded the corner, he turned to face me and added. "Also, keep in mind that your father's very attentive to both Jonathan and his family's needs. You can be certain they won't be forgotten."

"I know that, Japeth," I replied. "Nevertheless,…he'll often be in my thoughts."

"Well, at least you have a fine day ahead for a sail across the bay to Boston," he said.

"Yes,…it is," I agreed, pleased that he had changed the subject of our conversation.

It was a perfect, early summer day—warm and dry. A jay blue sky, dabbed with a few cottony clouds, allowed the warm rays of a brilliant sun to pierce the light haze of morning and nourish the entire eastern coastline. The flora and fauna rejoiced and thrived. Patches of perky black-eyed susans and clusters of tall sunflowers attracting the goldfinch audaciously faced the sunlight. The rush of air from our speeding carriage caused beds of wild daylilies to bow their jacinth heads as we drove past them. Fields of green marsh grasses and barren Atlantic cedars were visible all the way from the roadway to the bay. The wild rosa rugosa (also known as the salt sea, spray rose)—a perennial Cape Cod beauty—profusely covered the boundary walls along the highway. Their cheerful fuchsia hue was a pleasant contrast against the drab, gray stone. The daisy flee bane, wild mustard and yarrow had embarked on their season and flourished alongside the stone-walls. Dense raspberry bushes entwined with honeysuckle vines, which filled the air with an unforgettable aroma, shared common ground with these wildflowers. A doe and her fawn were feeding on a lush green cranberry bog a few yards from the roadway. They ran into a thicket as a bushy tailed red fox crossed the highway ahead of us. A lone seagull played on the wind and the clucking of wild turkeys could be heard from the brackish salt-water marshes. We rode past the wind-mills—the ever-present sentries of the countryside whose beckoning arms warmly embraced each winnowing breeze. I filled every sense with the unique smells, sights and sounds of Brewster.

"Japeth, I've been meaning to ask you about Rebecca," I said, turning to face him. I decided that this was as good a time as any to mention it. "I haven't seen her since you and your family were invited to our home to share the Christmas festivities with us. We had such a wonderful time together. My classmates said that she'd left the Cape to be with a sick aunt…Is that true?" I asked.

"Yes, Albert," he replied diffidently, looking straight ahead and again cracking the whip. "I'd been meaning to tell you about that. Somehow with spring plant-ing and all, I completely forgot. Rebecca's Aunt Hattie, Veronica's sister, became quite ill with influenza this past winter. She's a widow with several young chil-dren. The missus wanted to help her, but she's carrying our fourth child and isn't well herself. Rebecca chose to take her place. Rebecca offered to nurse her aunt back to health and care for the children. She left at the end of February with one of Hattie's kind neighbors who had arrived by coach to fetch her. Rebecca wasn't able to bid anyone farewell because they returned immediately to Plymouth the next day. She hoped her stay would be a short one. Hattie has fully recovered and is able to care for herself and her children. Rebecca's expected to return home very soon."

"Please give Rebecca my regards and mention that I asked about her," I said, "She's a dear friend…I'll miss her so much!"

"Certainly, Albert," he replied. I know that your relationship with Rebecca is very special. She'll be disappointed to learn that you had to leave before she returned to Brewster."

"Oh,…yes!" I thought, mulling over his assessment of the bond between us. "Our relationship's *more* than just special." Little did her father know just *how* special it was. I knew that while I was away, visions of my sweet Rebecca would fill my thoughts. I cherished the memory of her warm kiss and often fancied her tender body against mine.

The carriage turned right at Packet Landing Road and headed toward the wharf, which was about a mile down a well-worn causeway. We finally reached our destination—the busy Packet Landing wharf. The echoing, clip-clop sound of horse's hoofs traversing the wide gangplank reverberated throughout, as every type of transportation milled about the concourse. Like yellow jackets swarming around a hive, stagecoaches, carriages, surreys, wagons and buckboards circled the docking area. The drivers deposited their passengers, cargo or both on the landing—and then quickly returned via the gangplank back to Packet Landing Road and the Olde King's Highway.

Japeth yanked at the reins to slow the horses as we approached the wharf. The coach finally came to a full stop. He jumped down and quickly opened the carriage doors. I dropped my knapsack to the ground and descended to greet my family. Anne and her husband, Robert Snow, who was carrying their new infant son, were already there anticipating our arrival. She ran toward the carriage to embrace me.

"Do take care of yourself, Albert. I'll miss you, dear brother," Anne said wistfully, clutching her lace handkerchief and drying her eyes.

"I'll miss you, too!" I replied, fondly kissing her cheek and shaking Robert's hand in a farewell gesture. Emeline, Kate, Grandmamma and Mother also took turns in that order to hug and bid me goodbye. "I love you dearly, my son. Do try to stay in touch with us."

Mother pleaded as she started to weep. "When you reach a port, regardless of the distance,…mail us a short letter. Please let us know how you are and your whereabouts."

"Oh, Mother,…please don't cry. You'll have me doing the same," I pleaded, holding her tenderly in my arms. "I'm ready and as well-informed as I'll ever be. I must do this to expand my horizons, to develop and grow as a person. Try to understand, Mother, it's time for me to stand on my own two feet without the support of family and friends. Sailing ships and ocean lore fascinate me. The yonder world beckons and I'm eager to partake of its promise of both discovery and adventure. I remember a proverb by an unknown author that says,…'To detach is not to leave the other…It is to go to ourselves'."

"I know, but I'll worry about you," she replied despondently. "The seas can be relentless and foreigners unfriendly…their lands strange and alien to you. I pray that God will watch over you, Albert, and protect you from harm. May He keep you safe and well until you return to us."

"I'll be fine, Mother," I said reassuringly. "I'll certainly try to keep you abreast of my progress and destinations whenever I get the opportunity." Mother nodded, kissed my cheek, embraced me firmly, and then left my side with Grand-mamma who was trying to comfort her with some reassuring words.

Extending his arm, Father reached to shake my hand, squeezed it, and then pulled me close to affectionately embrace me. He was never an emotional person; however, it was all he could do to restrain his tears. Father removed a tiny velvet sack from his vest pocket and placed it in my hand.

"Albert, this is a little something to ease your way as you journey through that vast world out there," he said. "Use it carefully and wisely, my son. There'll be times when you may need it."

"Thank you, Father," I replied gratefully…I promise I'll be prudent with it. I know you felt you must, but you needn't have been so generous. I've been saving for this occasion and will earn a good wage. Nevertheless, I accept it gra-ciously…I know this gift comes from the heart and that it will ease your mind."

"You're an intelligent, discerning young man and a true gentleman in all respects, Albert," Father said proudly. "Your Yankee heritage and upbringing have produced a splendid specimen of American manhood. We're extremely proud of you and your achievements. You have our blessing. Venture to the far reaches of this world,…conquer it,…make it better, and leave your mark, son."

"I'll do my best, Father," I said assuredly, taken aback by his unusual compli-mentary remarks and placing the small drawstring bag in a pocket inside my jacket. "I hope all will go well and I'll return home hale and hearty at the end of my four-year tour of duty. In the meantime, Father, please look in on Jonathan and…do take care of yourself. Promise me you'll take time to enjoy life and won't let business matters occupy such a large portion of your days."

"Yes, Albert,…I'll try," he replied tearfully, extending his hand to mine for one last handshake. After several rapid, farewell pats on my shoulder, he turned to leave and walked slowly toward the waiting carriage. Japeth stood close by. He decided to remain behind until we were alone together. With both arms, he reached out and hugged me tightly.

"Albert, the Crosby homestead won't be the same without you. I'll truly miss you around there," he said wistfully. "Remember everything I've taught you. You've mastered many skills over the years. There may be times when you'll find them useful,…especially the survival ones. I hope you'll never have to make use of them. If so, maybe then you'll appreciate my instructions and my impatience with your sometimes-flippant attitude. I send you on your way now, feeling somewhat responsible for your mental and physical development. I'm confident that I've help prepare you for any emergency. Strive to be at all times and above all else,…a truly honest man. Success achieved without honor is shallow and ruinous. Abide by your faith in God, for He may be your only connection to sanity. Well,…I guess I've kept you long enough. Be on your way now, and know that you'll be constantly in our thoughts and prayers."

"Oh, Japeth, you've always been a patient mentor," I said. "Your friendship and tutoring have meant so much to me." We walked together toward the packet cabin entrance where a steward waited patiently for everyone to come aboard. "I love my family dearly, but you, Japeth, have a special place in my heart. I'll always try to abide by your sage advice. If I can be half the man you are, I'll consider myself fortunate indeed. Goodbye, dear friend. Again, please be sure to give my regards to Rebecca and your family, and if possible…do try to visit Jonathan. He needs someone like you to bolster his spirits. When I return home, I'll look forward to joining you over a brew and telling you all about my voyages at sea." At the direction of the steward, I turned to enter the cabin.

"Take care, Albert!" he shouted back, waving his hand and turning toward the waiting Crosby carriage.

The anchor was lifted, and the *Sarah* sailed smoothly away from the shore. I joined the other passengers as we viewed the slowly fading coastline from the packet's railing. The voyage across the bay to Boston was uneventful. The seas were unusually calm. The light reflecting off the water in the bay was the most beautiful found anywhere. On such a clear day it was so vibrant—it seemed to dance. The passengers strolled along the deck savoring the fair weather and warm sun. Several clipper-ship captains and merchant seamen on their way to meet their ships in Boston or New York were on board. After building their homes, their farms and mills, the restless men of Cape Cod turned their skills toward mastering the art of building ships and sailing them.

The *Sarah* left Brewster during a mid-morning high tide. The packet docked in the late afternoon. As I scanned the harbor, I felt a rush of excitement and anticipation. Several, massive merchant ships were anchored just off shore. The soaring masts of those vessels—towering shafts of steel suspended with ornate, elaborate rigging were similar to the loose, intricate patterns of delicate crochet dangling from giant hooks. The sun, a radiant disk in the heavens was still glowing despite the early evening hour. I relished the long summer days of June that lingered onto twilight until they finally surrendered to dusk and deepening darkness. The hubbub of people along the pier, cargoes hoisted through hatches, goods carted in and out of warehouses, the horses, carriages and buckboards—all added to the fascination of Boston—its bustling spirit and energetic charm. A deckhand stood at the bottom of the gangplank helping the passengers disembark.

"Could you please direct me to the *Calypso*?" I asked, approaching him from behind.

"It's docked about a half-mile away from here, in that direction," he replied, pointing to the right—and then straight-ahead. "You can walk straight through this warehouse. The road leading to the docking slips is just beyond it. In fact, I'm sure the captain of that full-rigged ship left the *Sarah* just minutes before you came ashore. His name is Captain Joseph Sears of East Dennis. That's his carriage over there waiting for him."

"Really? Hum-m-m! Well, thank you, I'll find my way." I said walking backward and waving farewell. I flung my knapsack over my shoulder—and then headed in the direction of the warehouse. The *Sarah* had arrived in good time. "I still have another day to report for duty. I'll spend a few hours browsing around the shops for a while," I decided, turning and strolling through an enormous storage building filled with soaring stacks of cargo crates. A large, open entrance faced the main thoroughfare and boardwalk.

I stopped at a small café for a hot toddy (a hot drink consisting of an alcoholic liquor, water, sugar, and spices) and a muffin. I had already eaten Miss Mira's cakes while on the packet. I sat at a small table facing the door. A muscular, young fellow with a cap set low on his forehead, stepped up to the food counter and removed a few coins from his vest pocket.

"I'd like a cup of coffee and a sweet roll, please," he said, placing his order with the attendant standing behind the counter. "Also, can you tell me where the *Calypso*'s docked? I've just enlisted in the merchant marines and will be a crew member on that ship."

When I heard the name *Calypso*, I immediately rose from my chair and just as the man behind the counter began to pour his coffee into a large mug, I literately stumbled over to meet him. They both looked stunned by my sudden intrusion.

"Excuse me. Did you say the *Calypso*?" I inquired, joining him at the counter. "I couldn't help overhearing your destination. My name's Albert Crosby," I said, reaching out to shake his hand and noticing that he was about my same height. "I'm also a new recruit and headed that way. I expect I'll be your shipmate. Please join me at my table."

"Why,…thank you. Yes, I will," he replied, pleasantly surprised, extending his right hand to mine and holding onto his hat with the other. "My name's David Atkins. I'm from Nantucket and more than ready to finally get off that *rock*," he said glibly, pulling out a chair and sitting opposite me at the table. "I weighed the love of my native island against a longing to see the world and the latter won. I decided to leave it and seek my fortune elsewhere. I can't wait to join the crew of the *Calypso*. I've yearned to be a merchant marine since my early teens. Where do you hail from, Albert?"

"I'm also from Cape Cod. Brewster's my home town." I disclosed, pleased to know he was a fellow land's end native. "Many of my friends are obsessed with sailing ships and ocean lore. They began their careers coiling halyards on the packets and finished on the quarterdeck of a clipper. Some have already set out for Spain and Liverpool on those new triple-rigged merchant vessels," I went on, managing to gulp down the toddy and biting into my muffin.

"After giving it serious thought, I decided to become a merchant marine just a few years ago. I firmly believe…it'll be my key to a successful future. It's safe to say that no part of the Atlantic Coast has prospered more than Cape Cod right now. Business is being transacted in the far corners of the world. The trading of goods, which has become so profitable these days, is a venture I want to be part of. I plan to work hard and learn well. I hope to be a wealthy ship owner or merchant someday. Oh,…I'm so sorry! I didn't mean to bore you with my aspirations," I said apologetically, realizing I was beginning to monopolize the conversation. David sipped his coffee and took a large bite from his sweet roll.

"Oh, no,…you're not," he replied, shaking his head and swallowing a mouth full of food before he went on. "You sound like someone I really would like to know better. We have a lot in common. I also hope to profit from this experience. My parents passed away within the last few years. I'm on my own now," David disclosed, taking another sip from his mug. A lock of curly, blond hair bounced on his forehead as he spoke. He shrugged his shoulders and heaved a deep sigh. "I have no siblings and only a few relatives. I must make my own way in this world and seek my fortune somewhere,…somehow. I figured the mercantile marine service would be as good a place as any to start." David finished his snack and rose from his chair. "Well,…I'm ready to leave," he announced, swinging his knapsack over his shoulder and opening the door.

"Would you mind if I joined you?" I asked, following behind him. When David turned around, I smiled and added, "We *are* headed in the same direction."

"No,…of course not," he replied, holding the door opened for me. "I was hoping you'd want to accompany me to the *Calypso*."

"I was informed that a Captain Joseph Sears from Dennis would command the *Calypso*. Are you familiar with his name?" I asked. "Do you know anything about him?"

"Yes,…I do. I make it my business to find out about such things," he replied candidly, coming to an abrupt halt—and then turning to speak to me. "Cape

Dorothy D. Leone   87

captains, like Captain Sears have developed their own individualism. They're shrewd and resourceful. Their level of skill and vigor has won for their country the respect of the world. Captain Sears is a master mariner…well known for his expert seamanship. He's one of the best navigators of his time and a respected merchant marine captain who's a cautious yet fearless commander. I learned that he's also an impartial and genial man as long as his crew obeys his orders and dutifully complete their tasks. I'm surprised you don't know him. He lives but a few miles from Brewster."

"There are so many merchant sea captains who live in Brewster and surrounding towns, it's almost impossible to know them all," I said, offering an excuse for my unfamiliarity with Captain Sears. "About three-quarters of all the Brewster men are employed as sea captains or in various businesses relating to the sea such as whaling, salt works, fish weirs, coastal trading and foreign trade. After a short shore leave with their families, the captains are frequently assigned a new command,…spending lengthy tours at sea. It's difficult to keep track of who's captain of what."

"Yes,…I suppose that's true," David said with a few, quick, understanding nods "Now that we've met, maybe we can become bunkmates," he suggested, putting his arm around my shoulder as we continued on our way.

Before I could answer him, I stood in awe at what appeared to be a colossal, quadruple-rigged clipper ship. It was the imposing sight of the *Calypso* that loomed straight ahead. Its mast soared to unimaginable heights. It was a moment of sheer exhilaration. I gulped and took a deep breath.

"Just look at that ship, David!" I exclaimed excitedly…"What a beauty! She's so elegant and sleek! What an unbelievable stroke of luck! How fortunate we are to be members of her crew!"

"Yes, Albert. The *Calypso's* one of the most expensive and lavish freighting vessels on the seas today," he replied knowledgeably. "Its owner is quite proud of this glorious clipper and anxious about the investment this ship represents. Only someone like Captain Sears is selected to be at its helm. His dexterity, grit and experience are vital for a successful and profitable voyage…He's one of the best."

"I must say, David, you've *really* done your homework," I said, duly impressed by his informative answer. "I can see you've apparently researched both the captain *and* his ship and that you've also kept abreast of his progress. I admire your genuine enthusiasm for maritime history. I should be as well-informed as you…however, I've just recently become interested in the merchant marine."

"Thank you, I'll take that as a compliment, my friend," David said appreciatively, executing a mock curtsy and tipping his hat.

"Oh, by the way,…the bottom one!" I mentioned, pointing downward with a smirk on my face.

"What?…What are you talking about?" David asked with a quizzical look.

"Bunkmates, you said…Right?" I reiterated while cocking my head in his direction.

"Yes,…but the bottom one?" he questioned, puzzled by my reference and knitting his eyebrows together.

"Oh, no,…wait a minute! On second thought, you're a bit stockier than I am," I said reconsidering my decision and poking him in the arm. "If you sleep in the top hammock, you'll be right on top of me!…I'd better sleep in the top one!"

We both had a good laugh as we walked together toward our common destination. Somehow I sensed our converging paths had taken us to what was the beginning of a long and steadfast friendship. I had met a soul mate—and it was David.

✳   ✳   ✳   ✳

Mid-August, 1841

As we glided through the emerald waters and neared our first destination, I delighted in the familiar sounds of a maritime setting—it was an orchestration of sorts. Pinging tones, like those of a melodious harp were sounded by strong westerlies singing through the taut rigging. The rhythmic drumbeat of the surging waves against the hull and the percussion made by the swish of the sea as it splashed across the open deck were music to my ears.

"Look!…Look! David!" I shouted, climbing the ship's rail for a better view, gesturing with my arms, and then pointing toward a dark blur on the horizon. As we approached it, the distant outline of an island became a clearer, brighter and more colorful reality. The *Calypso* sailed toward this lush landscape and eased into a lagoon a few miles off shore. The white, sandy beach that stretched for miles in each direction reminded me of the far-away northern coastline of home, but the semblance ended there. A thick grove of royal palms bent and swayed at the mercy of warm, gentle breezes that welcomed us to a verdant, ancient world beyond time—a tropical paradise much like the Garden of Eden.

"I've never seen palm trees before! This is my first time!…Is it for you, Albert?" David asked, agog at the sight and quickly coming alongside to join me on the rail.

"Why yes,…it is!" I replied excitedly. "Since I first read about these exotic islands, I've been eager to feast my eyes on such a place…I can't believe I'm actually here! Some of my friends whose fathers are Brewster sea captains have returned with paintings of such settings. They hang in some of their homes along with other nautical scenes of fisherman, whales and boats. I was always fascinated by the breathtaking beauty of these tropical islands and hoped that someday, I'd be fortunate enough to see one for myself. This must be the island of Haiti. When Captain Sears ordered the first mate to drop anchor here, he mentioned that name. I suppose we'll be advised about it fairly soon."

"Attention! Captain on deck!' shouted First Mate, Elisha Bryant after blowing a whistle. Bryant (we were all addressed by our last names) was a disgustingly obese and ill tempered, scrofulous, middle-aged curmudgeon. He cursed and harangued at the least provocation. David and I made a point of staying out of his way.

We quickly scrambled into place as the captain approached us from below deck. Captain Sears, a deeply tanned and rather fine-looking man in his early forties, promptly swaggered through several rows of saluting seamen accompanied by First Officer, Archibald Howes. Long, tawny sideburns protruded from under the captain's cap and—although he had a rather large mustache—his chin was clean-shaven. His perfect posture reflected confidence and pride in his profession. Captain Sears was a fastidious man who exuded dignity and superiority without being superficial. He was an amiable and discerning father figure to the young seamen—most still in their teens. A patient man, he instructed and encouraged with a grin and an affable nod. "Good job! Well Done!" Captain Sears would say, praising our efforts, smiling and giving us a pat on the back. We admired his ethics and virtues and tried to emulate them. The ultimate responsibility for the *Calypso*, its crew and cargo rested on him. Still standing at attention and looking straight ahead, I noticed several makeshift canoes quickly heading in our direction. Dozens of natives were shouting and waving wildly from the shoreline as others paddled furiously toward us.

"We've dropped anchor at an island in the West Indies. This is the island of Haiti," Captain Sears bellowed, standing erect before the helm with his arms tucked behind his back. In an informative yet authoritative tone, he informed the ship's compliment of the challenges before us. In doing so, he spoke candidly and with composure. The crew stood rigid while listening attentively to his oratory. We were resplendent cavalier midshipmen standing two abreast in our distinctive costumes—red-checked shirts, blue, bell-bottomed denim trousers and shiny, black tarpaulin hats. "We'll stay moored here for just a few days. The *Calypso* is on a very tight schedule. We must return to sea and sail to every island of the Greater Antilles, unload all our cargo, and then fill our hold with valuable imports. Their goods are in great demand in Massachusetts and the Northeast. The Boston merchants and ship owners want to turn a quick and sizable profit on their investments…therefore, there'll be *no* shore leave. Seamen, above all, remember when dealing with the semi-barbarous behavior of these natives, you are at all times the quintessential ambassadors of your country. Be wary of that! You're dismissed!…Move!…Get the lead out!" Captain Sears shouted, pointing to the large longboats dangling from ropes anchored to the deck as they were lowered into the water.

Deck hands were opening the hatchway and yanking on the hold-pulley. Various cargos were derricked up through the hatches. A pallet filled with pine from Maine was slowly raised from below. It would be traded for valuable tropical woods. The *Calypso* remained anchored far off the coast. After rowing to the shore, we waded waist-high in the surf from the longboats to the beach carrying lumber, cotton bales, New England rum, Yankee notions, flour and other goods on our heads and backs. The crew eagerly anticipated trading cargo in exchange for hogs, chickens, fresh fruits, and vegetables. Lately, we were reduced to eating a diet of maritime staples, which were limited to water, hard tack, molasses and salt horse (beef or pork pickled in brine, a staple during long voyages). These meager provisions were beginning to take a toll on our young bodies. My mouth watered at the thought of peeling and eating a large, juicy orange. It had been weeks since I had enjoyed that fragrant smell and succulent taste.

The hot thermal rays of the tropical sun that beamed down from a cloudless sky were unlike anything I had ever experienced before. "It's a perfect day for wading through these lucid, aquamarine waters that are as soothing as a warm bath," I concluded. The fine, white coral sand underfoot felt like talcum powder. I bent down to feel it with my left hand while struggling to balance the load on my head with my right. A small chunk of coral stayed in my hand as the sand slowly sifted through my fingers. I tucked it into my shirt pocket and proceeded toward shore. It would become a cherished souvenir for years to come.

"Wow!…Did you see *that*?" David shouted, gesturing toward the beach and an overhanging palm tree. I immediately raised my head to glance in that direction. A lovely, dark-skinned native girl unaware of civilized modesty was innocently exposing her young, shapely breasts as she bent over to lift some of our wares from the shore. Cinched at her waist was a short swish of silk covering a sensually sculptured figure that rivaled that of Venus De Milo. David and I were unwittingly aroused by a sexual lust we couldn't easily restrain. Our thoughts were filled with an insatiable craving for the closeness of a woman. Captain Sears' habitual directive to his crew immediately came to mind. Quoting him, word for word, we both repeated together, 'Absolutely *no* frolicking with the native women. Many of them harbor serious diseases that can be fatal to unwary white males.' Captain Sears had set clear limits and insisted we adhere to this rule of conduct. Out of respect for his command and because it was in our best interest, we decided to honor his orders without question.

"No shore leave!" I repeated angrily. "No wonder! He knew that after months at sea, we'd be hankering for the company of a woman. The skipper's a pretty shrewd chap, I'd say! Oh well,…I guess he knows best. Anyway,…Bryant is keeping a close check on the likes of us. We'd better hustle."

"Well, no harm in looking is there?" David asked. "What a sight for sore eyes! I don't know about you, but I'm going to get my eyeballs full! She's gorgeous!…Oh, just to hold and touch her soft, female body next to mine," he fantasized. "God!…I ache all over!"

"Will you be quiet, David! You're not helping the situation any. Besides, she's already turned to leave through that thicket of fern and bougainvillea over there," I remarked, tilting and turning my head for one last glance. "So much for your wishful thinking."

We persevered until dusk, carrying cargo back and forth from the longboats to the beach. Eventually, we returned with the other crewmen to the *Calypso* and fell wearily into our hammocks. I placed the small piece of coral under my pillow and was soon fast asleep. Every limb and muscle ached and throbbed with excruciating pain. Although I slept soundly, the soreness in my shoulders kept me from being comfortable.

Inevitably, I awakened around midnight and sat for a short while on a chest made of teakwood. As I looked through a porthole that was next to my bunk, I stared at a remarkable tranquil setting and marveled at the lustrous stars that sparkled like diamonds against a black velvet sky. They seemed close enough to touch. Our quarters were brightened by an enormous full moon that was quite extraordinary. It's gleaming, diffused light hung over the water like a celestial lantern, illuminating an enchanting scene of white beach and royal palms. The trusty sentinels bent in the gentle breezes—their shadowy swaying shapes towered above a glistening silver shoreline.

Dawn found us preparing to repeat the trudge back and forth from the longboats, to the beach. This time we were loading the longboats with goods from the island. Cargos of sugar, tropical woods, cochineal, goatskins and more were being placed in the ship's hold for our eventual return to Boston. Although we looked for her every day, much to our dismay, the lovely Haitian girl never again appeared on the shoreline. We decided she must have been an apparition—a mystical maiden, a vision or mirage much like the legendary mermaid. The *Calypso* soon left Haiti for the islands of Cuba and Puerto Rico.

*   *   *   *

Late-September, 1842

After sailing past a massive, Spanish colonial fortress overlooking the coastline, the *Calypso* dropped anchor several miles outside the large shipping port of San Juan, Puerto Rico. Before we arrived here, the crew had been warned about occasional pirate attacks in these waters. They preyed upon unsuspecting foreign vessels and were a well-known menace. Arms were issued to each crewmember and the few cannons we had on board were fully functional. If need be, we were ready to defend our ship against the hostile frigates. Again, we were instructed as to our whereabouts and duties.

The captain informed us that he would be leaving the *Calypso* to negotiate business matters with Puerto Rican merchants, and that he would be formulating trade agreements with government officials. He said he planned to remain on the mainland for several days. Captain Sears was soon lowered into the longboat with First Officer Howes, two other naval officers and three crewmen.

The first officer was in his late thirties. He was an officious, waffling man who persistently hung onto the captain's shirttails. Archibald Howes was an insensitive, outwardly stolid fellow who was narcissistically full of himself. I must say, however, that he was a handsome, clean-shaven man. Seldom seen without his officers' cap, this ambitious second-in-command had a fair complexion and wavy brown hair that curled at his neckline. Howes' striking sideburns that ended at his chin line outlined his austere and chiseled facial features. As they left, Captain Sears gave command of the *Calypso* to First Mate Bryant.

"David, I guess we'd better follow orders and begin polishing the brass and painting the rails while we're waiting for the captain to return," I suggested, eager to get a good report for getting the necessary tasks done. "Bryant said he wants all these chores completed before the captain comes back aboard ship."

"All right,…you paint and I'll start on the brass," he replied, walking toward the bunker holding the rags, brushes, paint, and polish. As we worked enthusiastically on these projects, we hoped it would help to pass the time. On the third day, while we busied ourselves performing our tasks, I happened to look out through the starboard rails into the distance.

"David, look at all those frigates low and dark on the horizon heading this way!" I yelled, startled and trying to get his attention. David crossed over to join me on the starboard side of the vessel. We stood watching as they closed the distance between us. Bryant quickly pushed us behind some large pulleys. While keeping an eye on the advancing brigands, David and I huddled close to the hatchway leading below deck.

"That's a fleet of pirate ships swooping down on us! They know we're vulnerable because our captain's not on board. They plan to devour us like voracious piranhas…until there's nothing left!" Bryant shouted ominously from the helm. "Quick,…find cover and be ready to use your muskets!" He pointed to several marines and assigned them to the few cannons we had on deck. "Those bandits will find out we're not easy prey! Now, take your positions!…I'll flag you when I think it's time to fire."

Almost a dozen privateer sloops were soon within firing distance. As soon as Bryant flagged us, we poured out shot after shot from our weapons. Although we peppered their decks with cannons and musket balls, only a few made direct hits.

"I'm really scared, David,…my legs feel weak, and I'm shaking all over!" I confided nervously, terrified that we could possibly be sacked. My heart was beating so fast I was afraid it would burst through my chest. "What if we can't ward off this hostile horde of scavengers?" Just as David turned to face me, I suddenly remembered Japeth's instructions and aimed my firearm with renewed confidence and skill.

"Don't think that way!" David yelled, firing another shot. "I'm just as frightened as you are, but we must make a stand! That's what we've been trained to do! Frankly,…I never thought it would come to this. Even though we're noncombatants, I suppose we should have anticipated something like this happening along the way. The *Calypso's* hold is filled with precious cargo. Except for a few minor ports-of-call, we're ready to return home to Boston…They know that! Those privateers are willing to risk their lives to capture this valuable booty."

Captain Sears heard the echoing salvos. Along with his crewmen, he rushed to the shore, pushed the longboat into the water, and then rowed swiftly toward the *Calypso*. Despite the advice of his business acquaintances who told him his attempt to outrun the pirate vessels was suicide, our loyal navigator shoved off with unwavering demarche and equanimity. Captain Sears was determined to save his crew and cargo from these ruthless buccaneers.

At the time, I was baffled by his preemptory behavior and wondered how he could possibly accomplish this feat. Somehow he managed to get through the swells and the swarm of pirate ships. He finally reached the side of the *Calypso* and was hoisted aboard. Unbeknownst to us, Captain Sears' strategy involved a contingency plan using Puerto Rican reinforcements. Their small military boats gave him cover and kept the pirate ships at bay while he worked his vessel to a place of safety under the guns of the El Morro fortress.

This tactical asset was a massive 18th century bastion—a colossal, Spanish colonial castle strategically placed high atop a seaside cliff. This wind-blasted bastion was carved into the sloping lava rock surrounding it and took full advantage of its natural setting. It was built in a semi-circle, giving the caissons unobstructed views on three sides. While entering the port of San Juan that was directly behind it, we were awed by its scope and size.

Fully backed by the El Morro artillery, we avoided casualties and bloodshed. The pirate flotilla was badly shattered by heavy shelling. The *Calypso* emerged triumphant from that dreadful battle. The white flag of surrender was hoisted and flown above a pirate's single-mast corsair. For their role in this act of barbarism, the perpetrators were jailed. The Puerto Rican authorities eventually executed the commander of the pirate fleet. With the assistance of our aggressive new allies, our goods were expeditiously exchanged. Within a few weeks we sailed homeward with a cargo hold filled with exotic goods.

While disastrous for the pirates and their leader, this episode had a beneficial effect. Although a victory had been achieved with the help of the Puerto Ricans, the inhabitants of Puerto Rico and El Morro now regarded American vessels and their courageous masters and yeomen as formidable foes due tribute and utmost respect. The American maritime marines had emerged triumphant over adversity and had proved their bravery and solidarity.

Except for this daunting encounter, bouts of blustery weather, days of drizzle, sudden gales, shifting winds and lengthy periods of dense fog or lolling about in the doldrums—my first two years in the merchant marines were pleasurable, educational and adequately fulfilled my desire for adventure. Despite the rigors of constant hard labor, I became an able seaman—an expert in the old-time art of rigging.

Serving on a Yankee vessel as a maritime cadet was an honored profession. I learned what teamwork was all about. Men of high character and education commanded the Massachusetts maritime. We were the best-paid, best-fed and most competent sailors in the world. David and I served proudly with lusty, seafaring young men as crewmates. Regardless of their cantankerous Yankee mettle, they performed hard and discouraging work at great personal risk. They were the incarnation of all the steadfastness, shrewdness, resourcefulness and vigor attributed to American sailors. My compatriots won for their flag and fledging nation—worldwide respect. It became the rebirth of our country's pride and identity.

Although I sometimes found myself longing for my loved ones, the Crosby homestead and the Brewster flats, I was proud to be a part of what would someday be called the golden age of the American merchant marine. I knew, however, that regardless of distance and locality, like the fresh-water herring of the Stony Brook, I would always find my way back home to Brewster. We are all part of an invisible but powerful circle of belonging. The long stretches of golden beaches and the intransigent tides relentlessly tugged at my very being like an unseen, sinuous thread connecting one to his place of origin. Throughout my life—no matter how hard I tried—it could *never* be severed.

CHAPTER 6

▼

Early-April, 1843

Just after our ship dropped anchor, I received an unsettling telegraph. While my brother Nathan was performing some maneuvers with his cavalry unit, he was thrown from his horse and suffered a fatal head injury. I was devastated by this dire news. I always held a somewhat blasé belief that the pulse of life, like the tides, was a constant ebb and flow of sadness and joy. Nevertheless, at a time like this, it became increasingly difficult to contain my emotions and be rational about this analogy.

"Oh, no! Why did this have to happen again to my dear family?" I moaned while David stood close by. Curious as to its contents, he began to read the telegraph over my shoulder.

"David, would you consider going along with me to Brewster?" I asked, taking a deep breath, sighing as I continued to speak, and then turning toward him with tears in my eyes. "I must attend my brother Nathan's funeral. When my parents heard that my ship would soon reach port, they decided to postpone the funeral so I could attend. I haven't seen my family since I joined the merchant marine,…that's almost two years ago. Although this will be a sad reunion, I look forward to visiting with them. I hope my presence will help ease some of their heartache and be a source of support and comfort during their time of need. I remember the depth of their grief at the time of my youngest brother's death. Little William was just a small child at the time. I can't possibly imagine the impact of *this* unfortunate blow. They'll be devastated. Nathan was only twenty-six and had already reached the rank of major. Death has cheated a vital, honorable young man of a long and satisfying lifetime," I said sorrowfully, shaking my head. "All the hopes and dreams they had for their, dearly beloved, eldest child will now remain unfulfilled. Nathan was their pride and joy…I'm their only son now. The dispatch also noted that passage has been booked for me on the next stage-coach to Yarmouth. A carriage will be sent to meet me there. I'm sure there'll also be room for you, David. The captain's already been advised as to our plans. We must leave within the next hour."

"Yes,…of course, I'll attend the funeral with you!" David replied with com-passion as he draped his arm over my sagging shoulders. "Although it's an unfor-tunate occasion, I could use some time away from this ship. It'll be great being a landlubber again, even if it's only for a short while. We won't be sailing for a least another three weeks or so. Most of the cargo won't arrive for loading until next week, at best."

"Thank you, David," I said, folding the telegraph and placing it in my jacket pocket. "You're a true friend. I cherish the special companionship we share…especially now, when I need it so desperately."

"Albert, I feel honored to have been asked," he said, hopeful that his presence would sustain me through this crisis. "I'm pleased that you want to include me in your plans. It'll be nice to finally meet your family, in spite of the dire circum-stances of our visit…I feel I know them quite well already. I'll get my things together and meet you on the pier in thirty minutes."

With that, David took off as if shot from a cannon. I washed, changed into civilian clothing, and then reached for my knapsack. I hurriedly filled it and headed dockside. David and I hailed an approaching carriage and soon boarded the waiting stagecoach to Yarmouth. A distant sun was hidden in a leaden, over-cast sky that threatened rain. We found our seats across from an elderly couple who were engrossed in lively conversation.

We left Boston just after sunrise and would arrive late that evening—it was a daylong trip. The roads had been widened and graded in my absence, resulting in a faster and smoother ride. Daybreak began with a drizzle that turned to light rain. Heavy downpours soon alternated with soft showers. Shortly after noon, the weather abruptly took a turn for the worst. The incessant, wind-whipped rain became a cascade running like a waterfall down the isinglass panes of the stage-coach doors. As we traveled eastward it was impossible to view the countryside, so David and I drew the shades. We folded our arms, laid our heads back, and then closed our eyes and slept. It promised to be a dismal trip from Boston to Brew-ster, as dreary as I felt inside.

"What was *that*?" I exclaimed, awakened by a startling thud, a loud crackling noise and the braying of the horses. All on board were stunned, jolted and uncer-emoniously tossed to the floor, in that order. David and I helped the shaken elderly lady and gentleman back to their seats. Just then, the driver opened the door. He was holding an opened umbrella and wearing a tarpaulin cloak that was soaked through and dripping wet from the cold driving rain.

"You young lads will have to help me push the carriage through this wash-out in the road!" he yelled over the din. "I'll be up ahead calming the horses and coaxing them on while you navigate around the hole. With your help, we should be on solid ground in no time." He turned to the others in the stagecoach and politely asked, "Will you please step outside for a few minutes?"

The coachman helped them out, one at a time, and handed his umbrella to the elderly gentleman. We jumped out quickly, ran to the back of the stagecoach, and then began pushing with every ounce of strength we could muster. Fortunately, the rain had abated. With our help the coach finally inched itself out of the large, water-filled pothole and we were soon on our way toward Cape Cod. At the end of our journey the driver unequivocally expressed his appreciation.

"Thank you for your help," he said, shaking our hands vigorously. "I was fortunate indeed to have the two of you as passengers. You're both strong, young gentlemen. I don't know what I would've done if you hadn't been on board. I owe you a debt of gratitude and offer you both my best wishes for a bright and prosperous future."

"So happy we could be of service to you, sir," I replied. "Sadly, we're here to attend my older brother's funeral. Thank you for getting us safely to our destination. Goodbye!" Holding onto our hats and bent over to avoid the buffeting wind gusts, David and I ran from the stagecoach stop toward a waiting carriage that had been graciously offered by close relatives.

Despite the inclement weather, the skies showed promise of a better day ahead. The moon and stars were occasionally visible through the dispersing clouds. The fickle spring weather on Cape Cod could change at any moment. We could be bathing in summer-like warmth one day or chilled by frost and snow-flakes the next. I hoped it would be somewhat decent for Nathan's funeral tomorrow. Despite the fact that we had arrived quite late, the family was there to greet us with tears and open arms.

"I don't know what to say!…I'm at a loss for words," I said sympathetically while holding my parents close. "I simply can't express how distressed I am over Nathan's loss…it's unbelievable and heart wrenching. He was a beloved brother whom I'd hoped to emulate. I regret that you have to endure this nightmare again and relive all the sorrow you experienced when you lost Little William. I know I can never take their place in your heart, but as your one remaining son, I promise to help fill that void by always being there for you in your time of need."

"Thank you, Albert," Father said gratefully, his lips quivering as he tried to choke back the tears. "You're also very dear to us. Mother and I are quite concerned about you. You're decidedly pale and you seem to have lost some weight since we've last seen you. The only promise we want from you is that you'll take good care of yourself.

"Goodnight," he added as he affectionately wrapped his arm around my shoulder then turned to leave the room with Mother by his side. "We'll see you both in the morning. The funeral service will take place at the First Parish Church at ten. Breakfast will be served at eight. Japeth will meet us with the carriage at the front fence post sometime after nine."

"We promise to be prompt, Father," I said emphatically. "Miss Mira, would you please knock on my door at seven?" I asked, turning to face her. "David, will share my bedroom."

"Aye,…surely," she replied in her delightful Irish brogue. Somehow without realizing how much—I had sorely missed it. "We've already made provisions for the lad," Miss Mira added with a warm smile and nodding toward David. "An extra bed's already in ye room. Have a good night's sleep me young lads. So happy to have ye home again, me Albert!" She gave me an affectionate hug, a quick kiss on the cheek, and then hurriedly left the kitchen.

Anne and Kate were quite taken by David—my affable shipmate and close friend. He was instantly welcomed and made to feel right at home. As usual Miss Mira lovingly fussed over us. While we chatted, she placed all sorts of prepared pastries, cups of hot tea and toddy on the kitchen table for everyone to enjoy. In the midst of a sad reunion we sat and talked until the wee hours of the morning.

A loud tapping on the bedroom door signaled the time to rise, wash and dress for breakfast. Like a sweet-smelling fragrance, the familiar aroma of freshly baked cranberry nut bread permeated the air throughout the cottage. Despite the circumstances, I couldn't help but appreciate the luxury of being home again.

Since our dress uniforms commanded much attention and respect, David and I chose to wear them to the funeral services. We wore a navy blue pea jacket or watch-coat—as the crew called it—added a black satin ribbon to our hats and a black silk kerchief tied in a neat sailor's knot around our necks. White ducks and black pumps completed our snappy attire.

The sun was shining through a moody sky. It was a gusty spring morning. The chill wind engendered a feeling decidedly more like early March than April. It was a very memorable and impressive funeral. High-ranking officers, resplendent in full dress uniform, served as honor guards. Full military honors were accorded one of their own. After the service they carried Nathan's casket from the church and down the granite stone steps. A horse-drawn hearse waited to transport its noble passenger to his final resting place.

David and I followed directly behind the casket. My grieving parents and family were behind us. Miss Mira, Japeth and his family followed them. I noticed a baby clinging to Japeth. Occasionally, he held the toddler in his arms to quiet him during the service. "That must be Japeth's new son," I concluded. "That little one was expected when I left for the merchant marines. He's an adorable child!" I later learned his name was Nathaniel. I also observed that Rebecca was not with them. "That's strange! Rebecca isn't with her family. Hum-m-m...I wonder why?" I noted disappointedly and questioning her absence.

The church was filled to capacity—standing room only. Jonathan was also there with his family. They waited until everyone left the church to wheel and carry him out to a waiting carriage. I acknowledged his presence and promised to visit him before returning to sea. Jonathan and his family returned home immediately after the services. David and I followed the hearse in the Crosby carriage. Burial was in the Brewster Cemetery on Lower Road.

"You're all invited to attend a luncheon at the Crosby Homestead after the services," Pastor Ezrah Farnsworth announced following the burial service. Many Brewster families and some from surrounding towns were at the funeral. I remembered many of them from the yearly Brewster regattas and Anne's wedding several years ago.

"I see your family's quite well known in these parts, Albert," David commented on our way home. "I've never seen such a large funeral. It was an extremely well attended service."

"Yes," I answered inattentively, deep in thought and inwardly shaken by the events of the last few hours. "Father and Mother are native to these shores," I went on to say, grateful for the genial distraction. "My grandparents were also born on the Lower Cape. Grandfather was a principal participant in the separation of Brewster from Harwich and was present when it was officially incorporated as a town in 1803. Father owned a tannery, a salt works and a large farm. Now he's in the shipbuilding business and owns several fishing vessels. He's also very active in local politics and town affairs. It's quite obvious,...especially at times like this, that they've made many friends."

People filed in and out of the cottage with donations of food and a show of sympathy. After a short stay, they were soon on their way. Again, I looked for Rebecca. Although she hadn't attended the church services, I hoped she would at least make an appearance at the homestead. Maybe she stayed away purposely, cooking and baking for the Crosby funeral buffet. I was puzzled. "Where is she?" I wondered…"And why hasn't she approached me before now?"

"Albert, when are you going to point out that girl you left behind?… Rebecca?…Wasn't that her name?" David asked, tugging at my shirtsleeve.

"Yes,…shush!…Lower your voice," I cautioned, placing my hand over my mouth. "Yes, that *is* her name, but no one knows about us. As far as everyone's concerned, we're just good friends," I said with a quick wink. "I'll have to ask Japeth about her."

"Who knows, maybe she's married and living off Cape by now," David quipped, trying to get a rise out of me. I didn't take the bait, but was completely taken aback and annoyed by his jabbing remark.

"Yes, that could very well be," I thought. On the other hand, it just didn't make sense. Something was obviously wrong. I had received mail from home while docked at some of the *Calypso's* scheduled port-of-calls. I often shared those letters with David because he never expected or received any correspondence at mail call. My family kept me abreast of what was happening in Brewster. However, all the while I was at sea, I never received a post from Rebecca or news that concerned her. While this was quite unusual, I reasoned her letters were probably late in arriving at my points of destination and that somehow the connection was never made. Suddenly, my thoughts were abruptly interrupted by a rather familiar female voice.

"My, you sailor-boys certainly look dashing in your uniforms! Albert,…introduce me to your friend here." I turned to see Hannah Freeman speaking to me, pulling at my jacket sleeve and pointing in David's direction. Hannah was an overbearing young lady, forever on the prowl for an unsuspecting male. At least that was my opinion of her. She was quite pretty, but that's where her good points ended. Hannah was a ruthless shrew who, like Satan, possessed you body and soul once you were in her clutches.

"Why,…hello, Hannah!" I said politely, pulling David away from her. "This is my friend and crewmate, David Atkins." Sensing I needed to act quickly, I fabricated a legitimate excuse with a semblance of truth to it. "Sorry we can't stay around to chat," I went on. "We must leave immediately to run an urgent errand for my parents."

"What on earth's wrong with you, Albert?" David hissed in muffled tones behind her back, questioning my charade. He was obviously not about to leave this lovely stranger and his clenched teeth and stiffened lips clearly expressed his feelings.

"I'll tell you later," I said assertively, repeating the same mannerism and adding an angered groan. "We're out of here…right now! Come on!"

Once out of her sight, I explained the reason for our quick exit. David was thankful to have been saved from a fate worse than death. My little white lie had saved the day. "I certainly outdid myself," I thought. "My trumped-up story would do Anne proud!"

Japeth was nowhere in sight. Probably busy taking care of the horses and carriages; however, I was sure I would be able to catch up with him before I left. There was so much I wanted to accomplish on my short, seven-day bereavement leave. We needed to return to Boston by weeks' end.

"I'll not invade his privacy today," I decided. "He needs time to be alone…to grieve in the only way he knows how and that's caring for his farm animals and silently performing his daily chores." Later that afternoon, David and I took a stroll to the bay. It was nearly high tide as we walked along the shoreline.

"You know, Albert," he said pensively. "Even though we've traveled to some of the most beautiful places on earth, I feel we're truly blessed to call Cape Cod our home. The Cape's *so* exceptional. As far as I'm concerned its flora and fauna are one of a kind. This bountiful headland protruding out into the Atlantic can't be compared to any other peninsula around the world. The islands of Nantucket and Martha's Vineyard also have a unique charm all their own."

"You're right, David," I replied, nodding my head. "I had that same thought every time we went ashore on one of those exotic islands of the West Indies. As lovely as they were, I missed the ever-changing landscape, so attractively altered by our diverse seasons. I've also come to appreciate the receding tide in the Brewster bay that empties for miles exposing an assortment of shellfish. I yearned to see the wild roses, listen for the bobwhite and inhale the delicate scent of the sweet honeysuckle vines. I longed to fish for cod and blues, dig for quahogs, mussels, clams, and scallops, and above all—watch the herring run up the Stony Brook.

"David, see the dunes in the distance overlooking the bay?" I asked, pointing in the direction of the homestead. "One of my life's goals is to build a palatial home right there on that knoll someday."

"Well,…I must say you have some lofty plans, my friend. I hope for your sake you're not disappointed," David replied with a questioning expression while looking toward the rolling bluff. "I also hope to find fortune and success in *my* future. I wish you well, Albert. While we both strive toward our individual goals and reach for the stars, may we never forget the friendship we've shared."

"You can be sure I'll always be there for you, David," I said, putting my arm around his shoulders. "You've become one of my closest friends."

"Let's take your runabout buggy to Eastham tomorrow," David suggested. "I'd like to watch the surf on the ocean side. It'll remind me of Nantucket. Maybe we can take off our shoes and run down the dunes."

"That sounds like a great idea!" I replied enthusiastically, skipping a flat stone across the top of the water and watching it bounce three times. "In any case, before we go there I'd like to stop and visit, Jonathan. We've been friends since childhood. I've told you all about him. Miss Mira will be serving supper soon. I think we should be on our way back." We retrieved our shoes, walked toward the homestead, and then leisurely ambled along the familiar sandy path up from the beach below.

The seagulls, settling down for a feast of minnows and clams, were also ferociously foraging for turtle eggs and fiddler crabs, lured from their burrows by the temperate water. Now, in the early spring, only dusty miller, heather, rose hips and delicate shafts of swaying beach grass touched our legs as we strolled by. The cool evening sun, already beginning to set on the horizon cast a palette of warm pastels. A halo of sepia skies and clouds caught the fading light of sunset over the bay. The heavens were tinted with deep purple, violet, and coral hues that melted into a brilliant, iridescent pink. A rare and awesome sight indeed!—One, I never tired of.

"I remember you telling me about Jonathan, Albert," David said, stopping for a short while to put his shoes on as I did the same. "He's the chap who was paralyzed while logging with your family,...right?"

I nodded and replied,..."Yes."

"That's fine with me," he said enthusiastically. "He sounds like someone I'd truly like to meet."

"I also want to take you to our village center," I went on. "As I've said before, many sea captains have built their homes and settled here in Brewster. The Brewster Mill sits on the site of the Stony Brook Pond where the herring run each year. Though we may see a few earlybirds attempting it, it's a bit too soon for them to be going upstream from the sea to spawn. But, we'll have lunch there and enjoy the site. We'll do that the day before we leave."

"Sounds *great!* I'd like that, Albert. It'll give me a chance to enjoy the beauty of your lovely town before we're back on the high seas again and bound for who knows where," David replied, sighing and shrugging his shoulders. I silently acknowledged his comment with a nod of my head. We reached the cottage and found our place at the table for the evening meal.

"I need to find time to speak to Japeth," I concluded while lying awake in my bed. "I must ask him about Rebecca. Where is she? Why isn't she as anxious to see me as I am to see her?" I wondered. I longed to hold Rebecca in my arms again and savor her sweet kiss. I hadn't received any letters from her, but owing to my uncertain and complex itinerary, I dismissed that. Still, I sensed something was amiss. I planned to rise early and approach him while he fed the farm animals. "Yes,...that's exactly what I'll do," I decided as I turned over in my bed and fell asleep.

I rose at the sound of a crowing rooster and quickly dressed. No one was in the kitchen as yet, not even Miss Mira. I ran toward the barn and overheard Japeth affectionately chatting and stroking each cow as he sat to milk it. I reached for a stool and sat next to him. He didn't seem a bit surprised to see me.

"Well,...hello, Albert. Good morning." he said, looking up and greeting me with a welcoming smile and the familiar nod of his head. "You're up bright and early today. It's so good to have you home again. Needless to say, I wish it could've been under happier circumstances. How have you been, lad?" Japeth asked, releasing his grip on the teat, putting one arm around my shoulder, and then pulling me close with the other. "I've sorely missed you around here. You've always been like my own son. Tell me about your adventures and life at sea," he said, returning to his chores.

"I've been fine," I replied nervously, anxious to get to the reason for my visit. "I'll be happy to tell you about my two years at sea, Japeth,...but first I need some answers to a few questions. I have a feeling you know exactly what I'm going to ask you." Japeth twisted his head, eyed me directly, and then turned around on his stool to resume his task.

"Yes, Albert, I think I know. It's about Rebecca, isn't it?" he asked, anticipating my question. I sensed he was uncomfortable with my inquiry, and I wondered why.

"Where's Rebecca, Japeth? Why isn't she here?" I inquired, unnerved and distraught while waiting for his answer. "Since I arrived, I haven't seen her at all! Rebecca meant a lot more to me than I let on...I think you guessed *that*. I looked forward to her greeting me with a warm smile and open arms. Although she promised to write, I never received a single letter from her. I decided that maybe I was just missing her correspondence at my ports-of call. After sending her several unanswered letters, I supposed that she had her reasons for ignoring them, so I stopped writing. Tell me, Japeth,...is Rebecca married?...Is she living off Cape? I must know."

"No, to both questions, Albert," he replied, finding it difficult to speak, his lips quivering uncontrollably. I could sense his reluctance to continue. "I'm sorry, but I wish it was so." He looked up again, this time with tears streaming down his cheeks.

"What can be so wrong? Japeth's always been sound of both body and spirit. What has shaken him so?" I wondered. I had an intuitive feeling that what I was about to hear would *not* be good news.

"My angelic Rebecca is in heaven, Albert. She's gone to her eternal rest," he said deeply distressed, his tears flowing down his cheeks as he spoke.

"Oh,…no, Japeth! Oh, please don't tell me she's dead!" I cried out, trying to interpret his words and burying my head in his shoulder. "She can't be gone! I can't bear to hear it!" He tried to soften the blow by solicitously tapping me gently on my back while relating the circumstances of her death.

"Soon after you left for the merchant marines, she passed away in Plymouth. Rebecca was ready to return to the Cape when she also became a victim of the influenza epidemic that swept through the area. She contacted that horrible disease and within weeks succumbed to it. The Missus and I are still in shock over her death. There isn't a day that goes by when we don't grieve the loss of our beautiful, Rebecca. I don't think we'll ever get over it. We miss her so very much, Albert. Sometimes the emptiness is so overwhelming." Again he turned to finish his work. "I knew you'd ask about her…so I deliberately tried to avoid talking to you about it. She wanted you to know she loved you dearly, and that she'd be with all of us in spirit. I'm sorry, Albert, you'll have to excuse me. I just can't talk about it any longer. It's too distressing to relive the pain of her passing. I can sympathize with Nathan and Catherine. I also know how it feels to live through a beloved child's untimely death. Parents should never outlive their children,…that's a heartache they take to their graves."

"Oh, Japeth!…I'm so sorry!" I moaned, sobbing and reaching out to comfort him.

"I hope that time will heal the ache in your heart Albert," he said, forgetting his anguish and concentrating on mine. "I know you'll grieve for her as much as you would a member of your own family…probably more so. Although I was reluctant to bring up the subject, I fully intended to tell you about her death whenever you returned home,…no matter how difficult it would be for me. Now, because of the loss of your brother Nathan, it seemed so cruel. How could I possibly compound your suffering?"

"I can't tell you how sorry I am to learn of her death. I loved her, Japeth," I confessed, standing and placing the stool aside. Stunned, sickened and shaken, I abruptly turned to walk out of the barn. I didn't intend to fall apart in his presence. Sensing my despair, Japeth rose from his milking stool and wiped his hands. With one arm around my shoulder, he left with me.

"I knew how you'd react to Rebecca's passing, Albert," he explained compassionately. "That's why I made everyone promise not to tell you while you were at sea. I wanted to inform you of it myself,…in person. You have your whole life ahead of you. Hold dear the good times you had together and remember her the way she'd want you to…as a loving and beautiful, young lady."

"I will," I replied, standing outside the barn door and reaching out to shake his hand before leaving. "Please forgive me, Japeth,…but I had to ask. It was something that truly bothered me. I want you to know how much I appreciate the courage it took to tell me about the death of your daughter. Thank you. I'll always cherish her memory, Japeth. Rebecca was my first true love. She may be gone from my life, but she'll always live in my heart."

Devastated by this unexpected disclosure, I left the barn and ran toward the cottage. I had been dealt a volley of terrible blows. I was crushed and inconsolable. Not only had I lost a much-admired brother, but also the love of my young life. I needed to be alone. David shared my room—that wouldn't do. Feeling intensely wounded and vulnerable, I decided I would go elsewhere. I turned and headed toward the bay. It was low tide. I sought the solace of the seashore and the serenity of the flats. I removed my shoes and wandered along the sand bars and tidal pools.

"Yes, David was right," I thought, reflecting on his remarks about Cape Cod. Despite a slight chill in the air, the morning sun was bright and warm. I took a solitary walk along the isolation of the shoreline toward the curving landscape before me. The bizarre poignancy of the ill-fated deaths of my loved ones was more than I could endure. As I inhaled the salt air and meandered along the flats and through the marshes, I was besieged by an ineffable sense of sorrow that welled from deep within me. While the death of my brother was unimaginable, it was the loss of Rebecca that totally stunned and overwhelmed me. I spread my arms to the heavens in an all-consuming despair that couldn't be ignored, sank to my knees, and then wailed in pain and inexpressible grief. The sound of my fitful sobbing—carried by the wind—bounced off the dunes and ricocheted over the flats. It was effectively muffled by the loud screams of the terns along the beach and the shriek of the gulls overhead. The landscape and nature knew me—the returning echo confirmed that I belonged here.

I wished these dreadful days of sadness and hurt would quietly vanish until this reality was but a memory and my broken heart would finally be healed. The relentless ebb and flow of the tides was a constant reminder that, like the passage of time, it never faltered for a second and simply defied our futile efforts to slow or speed it. As I found my way back to the homestead, the tranquil, extraordinary beauty of the bay became a source of healing peace. I resigned myself to the inevitable and began to accept the will of a higher power with renewed faith and hope for a happier future.

After telling David about Rebecca's fate, I asked him to accompany me to the Eldredge homestead the day before we were scheduled to leave Brewster. My visit with Jonathan would complete my obligations.

"Missus Eldredge, I'm here to visit Jonathan. This is my friend and crewmate, David Atkins," I said while standing on the back steps of the Eldredge home after she opened the door. Jonathan's mother was an amicable graying woman of imposing stature. He had definitely inherited her strength and disposition. "It's a pleasure to meet you, Mister Atkins," Missus Eldredge said, smiling and reaching to shake his hand.

"Please call me David, Missus Eldredge," he replied with a cursory nod of the head. "The pleasure's all mine, indeed."

"We were given a short leave to attend my brother's funeral…however, I wanted to see Jonathan before we left Brewster. I told him that I'd stop by. We must return to our ship in the morning. Will it be all right to see him today?" I asked.

"Certainly Albert, he's been expecting you. Do come right in," she replied, closing the door behind us. "It's so nice to see you. It was such a shock to hear about your brother Nathan's death. My sympathies go out to you and your family."

"Thank you, Missus Eldredge. My parents are still numbed by his death. I doubt they'll ever get over it," I said poignantly, my voice beginning to crack as I agonized over the thought of his and Rebecca's loss.

"Jonathan's in his room. Just follow me and go right in!" she said, leading us down the hallway. His wheelchair was already on the threshold in anticipation of our arrival.

"Hello, Albert," Jonathan said. "I've been waiting for you to visit me. I'm so happy you could find the time to come."

"Jonathan, this is my close friend and shipmate, David Atkins. He was kind enough to accompany me to this tragic homecoming," I said, following behind him as he re-entered his room. I reached for a chair for David and myself. "We would only have been allowed a few days leave when we docked in Boston, but because of Nathan's funeral we were given a little extra bereavement time."

Out of the blue, I decided to ask Jonathan to join us. Although I hadn't discussed it with David, I was sure he would approve.

"Say, Jonathan, we were planning to visit the ocean beaches at Nauset and Wellfleet," I added. "I wanted to show David our part of Cape Cod. I intended on touring the harbor in Orleans and have a picnic lunch at the mill and the herring run. Would you like to join us? I decided to use the open runabout because it's such a pleasant day. If you'd like to come with us, David and I will help you get seated in the buggy. We'll place your wheelchair in the rear,…just in case you might need it. We'll carry you if need be. We'd really enjoy having you join us on this outing. It'll give us the opportunity to get caught up on the last two years. I've missed you, Jonathan…Do say you'll come!"

"Why, yes, Albert! I'd be delighted!…I'd really like that!" he replied excitedly. "It'll be wonderful to be with you both. It's so nice to meet you, David. Any friend of Albert's is a friend of mine. It's been a long time since I've been out on such an excursion. Thank you for wanting to include me in your plans. I'll have Mother put together a lunch for us."

"Oh, no need, Jonathan. I've already made arrangements for a basket lunch at the McCloud House. It'll be ready for us before we get to the Mill Pond," I said, turning toward his mother, announcing our departure, and then pushing his wheelchair toward the door. David and I helped him into the buggy and seated him between us. I took the reins and we began what would be a memorable jaunt. We talked, laughed and had a wonderful time together. Jonathan and David got along famously. Their camaraderie helped me to momentarily forget not only my distress over Jonathan's tragic disability, but also, the agony I had endured during the past week over Nathan and Rebecca's untimely deaths.

*   *   *   *

Mid-April, 1843

We arrived on the pier just in time to start loading freight into the hold of the *Calypso*. This clipper with four masts and mainsails would be leaving before the month's end with its cargo of cotton, glass, lumbers, rice, domestics, gin, brandy, clothes and furniture. After carrying the crates into the hold we secreted ourselves on the pier behind several large bales of cotton to talk privately.

"I overheard two yeomen discussing a rumor that's been circulating among the deckhands. Looks as though we'll be sailing with a new skipper at the helm," David whispered cautiously, scanning the area around us. "Captain Sears has been assigned to the *Wild Hunter*, a newly commissioned ship. Our new commander's name is Captain Cyrus Gorham. Scuttlebutt has it that "CG," as he referred to by his underlings, is a hard taskmaster with a foul mouth. I heard he's a mean, power-hungry son-of a-bitch!"

"Really?" I questioned, surprised by this disturbing hearsay and trying to keep my voice down. "I wonder how much truth there is to *that*! Goddammit, David!…That can't be so!"

"Oh, yes, Albert, I'm sure it is," he replied, disclosing his source. "Several foremast hands working close by were talking about him in terms that really perked up my ears."

"That's hard to believe!" I said incredulously. "A Yankee shipmaster like Captain Sears, who is launching a stewardship,…especially one in the merchant marine, must treat his subordinates with courtesy and respect. He should be a model for his crewman. The captain's demeanor should always be exemplary. As you've already told me before, New England ship owners take pride in their commanders and, on the other hand,…Cape captains are loyal to them, regardless of great personal risk," I went on. "Most of them have a rare mixture of good judgment and experience. Their levelheaded nature insures the safety of the vessels entrusted to them. They're expert navigators of superior character and education,…professionals of the highest caliber!" I pontificated, realizing I was speaking a bit too loud and looking around to see if I had been overheard.

"I *know* all that, Albert,…but I guess it's his last chance to redeem himself," David replied. "He's on notice from headquarters. Unless "CG" improves his conduct at sea, this'll be his last command. Let's hope he'll be on his best behavior and we'll be spared his arrogance."

"I guess Captain Sears will be hard to replace," I said dejectedly. "He was pleasant and always treated us kindly and with dignity. His standards of seamanship were high, yet he was a just and genial man,…caring and fair toward all of us. Captain Sears catered to all our needs and made us feel special,…like each one of us was an indispensable member of his crew."

"We'll soon find out, Albert," David said, pointing toward the ship. "A shiny new coach just pulled up to the gangplank."

The driver descended and opened the door. Without looking around, a stern, slender man in a standard captain's uniform was helped down the steps. His graying head of hair with matching mustache and professionally trimmed beard was exposed when he removed his cap. First Officer Howes and First Mate Bryant, who were disgustingly falling all over themselves trying to make a good first impression, promptly saluted him. While handling his valises, they followed him up the gangplank and into the ships' quarters.

"Yep,…looks like you were right, David!" I said apprehensively. "He's definitely going to be our new captain."

The high-pitched sound of the whistle called the *Calypso* crew to attention. We assembled on deck in our freshly washed and neatly pressed uniforms. Thirty-six seamen, dozens of foremast hands, nine officers, First Officer Howes and First Mate Bryant made up the ship's complement. My shipmates and I stood erect while saluting an aloof and callous Captain Gorham. We cringed as this pompous man—a gargoyle with no heart—walked past us. I found myself terrified of this steely man with a gaunt face and beady eyes. He inspected the ship's crew from our hats down to our shoes. "CG" wielded his chart stick like a menacing baton. In a formidable manner, he fitfully tapped it in his hand while walking past each one of us. The dour new commander ascended the steps to the stern section and stood expressionless before the helm. From that vantage point he bellowed his expectations and infallible rules while we attentively listened to his uncompromising directives. The harsh, resonant sound of his booming voice reverberated all the way from the rigging to the hold of the *Calypso*. He made it known in no uncertain terms that if anyone deliberately got out of line or evinced a slipshod attitude toward an assigned task—it would *not* be tolerated. We would be brought up to the mast and flogging would be our recompense. The crew sensed his strict orders were to be obeyed without question.

"There will be no *sogering* allowed on this Yankee vessel!" he barked loudly. The coarseness in his voice and the wrathful way he rapped his chart stick against the rail was a deliberate attempt to frighten the daylights out of us. "Constant hard work will be the rule! It will make men out of you young scalawags! Merchant marine seamen are expected to man the sails, reef and steer. Each one of you will take turns reeving the studdingsail gear out of the top, furl a royal or flying jib and send down or cross a royal yard. Decks will be barbarized (swabbing a deck with sand and cleanser) daily and all necessary painting, polishing and repairs performed in a timely fashion! Use tobacco sparingly,…if at all, and observe regular hours of sleep!"

With this, we were dismissed. No introduction—not even a word of welcome. Just an imperious, brusque series of commands issued without the slightest hint of cordiality. David and I joined the crew that was hoisting the anchor.

"I wonder if that man knows how to smile, David," I muttered in a hushed voice. "Somehow, I just can't help feeling uneasy about him. We haven't even left port yet, and I already have misgivings about this tour of duty. Oh, well, let's get on with it. Time will tell, I guess…By the way, do you know our destination?"

"I just asked Seaman Perkins that same question," he replied. "The *Calypso* will be sailing to South America. We'll be filling the hatch with Colombian and Brazilian coffee for our return trip to Boston."

"South America!…How exciting!" I exclaimed, returning to our chores and preparing to leave the harbor. "I've often hoped I'd be fortunate enough to visit that continent. I've always envied the seamen who've been there."

To describe the next two years as ominous would be to minimize our tortured existence on the *Calypso*. The ruthless despotism of Captain Gorham was ineffable. The midshipmen were victims of constant vulgar language and verbal abuse. The first mate, petty officer, helmsman, steersmen, boatswain and steward were the butt of his complaints and criticisms and often subjected to tyrannical tantrums. These subordinates and crew masters were publicly reprimanded in the presence of the ship's compliment. Rampant scurvy, dysentery, brutal weather, unfriendly seas and hapless encounters with whales and shoals turned an anticipated adventure into a living nightmare. It could have been instead—a unique learning experience into a world of discovery and diverse cultures for this band of lusty, young merchant marines.

By the time we reached Brazil it was early winter. In bitter cold, we loaded bulky one-hundred-pound burlap bags of coffee beans into the longboats and placed them into the hold of the *Calypso*. The crew was never allowed to leave the ship without Howes or Bryant scrutinizing our every move. Our only connection to land was working from dawn to dusk on the mile-long shipping pier. Captain Gorham's arrogant advice resounded in my mind. "Observe regular hours of sleep."…Now I knew why.

After a brief embargo by Columbian authorities over our lack of proper docking papers, we were finally allowed to sail into the harbor at Puerto Cabello. The hold was filled to capacity with additional tons of coffee beans. At the end of the South American winter season the *Calypso* sailed north for our homeport. Due to the captain's intransigence and poor navigational plans, we arrived in the southern waters of the stormy Atlantic just in time for the hurricane season. Torrential sheets of rain and whipping winds battered the ship. The deck was flooded and pounded by a constant barrage of monstrous waves, flagellated by 120 mile-per-hour winds. The clipper floundered agonizingly in the raging seas of a typhoon that hit fast and furiously. It was next to impossible to navigate a shattered ship through this tempest. I feared we would capsize at any moment and go down with the craft. I firmly believe the weighty cargo of coffee beans kept the

Calypso from capsizing. The vessel sustained substantial damage, however, as soon as the storm was over it was expeditiously repaired.

Not only had Captain Gorham endangered the safety of the ship and crew, he had also failed to provide enough staples to last the length of the voyage. We were reduced to one meal a day that consisted of water, molasses and hard-tack. Fresh water was almost nonexistent and so was carefully rationed. It was common knowledge that "CG" had an ample cache of food reserved for himself, Bryant and Howes. With absolute disdain for propriety, this demagogue disregarded the needs of the men under his command. Weakened by gnawing hunger and the minimal treatment of scurvy, sick seamen rife with fever and chills lay helpless in their bunks. Many passed away and were unceremoniously buried at sea. Due to the apparent hopelessness of the situation, the crew became increasingly disgruntled and vowed to bring Captain Gorham to task for his atrocities. David and I were asked to be included in their grievance. Although reticent at first because of chilling precedents, we were all well aware of an 1835 federal statute that gave seamen the right to file a grievance. If the evidence proved that a captain or officer was guilty of cruel or unusual punishment, the seamen involved would be awarded three month's advance pay. The guilty parties would be decommissioned and dishonorably discharged. We agreed to join the suit against Captain Gorham if conditions didn't improve.

Much to our delight and rousing cheers from a desperate crew, the *Calypso* sailed close to an island in the Bahamas. The ship dropped anchor about three miles off the coast. A small contingent of sailors lowered rowboats laden with water barrels and paddled toward shore. They returned several hours later. Kegs filled to capacity with fresh water and every provision imaginable were crammed into the dinghies. It was the first sight of nourishing edibles we had had in months. The quarterdeck hands quickly dispersed hogs, chickens, fresh fruit and vegetables. The crew devoured the food like hungry wolves voraciously ingesting their prey.

Through the chain-of-command, word had reached the captain that his incensed recruits had reached the point of mutiny. "CG" knew he was responsible for the misery endured by the mariners on the *Calypso*. Although Captain Gorham planned on retiring after this voyage, he feared losing his lucrative pension if found guilty of maltreatment. Also, a conviction would publicly dishonor his prominent Bostonian family. Due to his aberrant conduct and the nefarious exploitation of his subordinates on the high seas, he would ultimately be ostracized and disgraced. For these reasons the captain prudently chose to atone for his indiscretions prior to our arrival in Massachusetts. His sporadic appearances on deck were followed by long absences. Except for an occasional emergence accompanied by Howes and Bryant, he secluded himself in his quarters or the officer's mess for the remainder of the voyage.

David and I vowed we would not reenlist. This miserable voyage would complete our obligation. After surviving the strife and rigors of this terrible tour-of-duty over the last two years, we became disenchanted with life at sea. Seafaring was hard and discouraging work and although it was a lesson well learned, we would seek a safe haven and our fortunes stateside. Also, it was becoming increasingly obvious that the days of the sailing ship were numbered. Nevertheless, ship builders, merchants and shipmasters alike stubbornly persisted to ignore the signs. Like long-lasting daylight reluctant to submit to night, they refused to acknowledge their era was over. They nonchalantly continued to sail as obliviously and boldly as ever—into the sunset.

CHAPTER 7

▼

Early-May, 1845

A cacophony of euphonic sounds sifted through my lethargic brain as I fitfully tossed and turned in a restless sleep. The persistent tantara of a distant foghorn and the clangorous peal of a harbor buoy—its bell tolling isochronally as it was tossed about in the swells—served to create an unambiguous wakeup call. A steady splashing within earshot eventually caught my attention. It was the edifying sound of the surf licking at the bollards. I immediately sat up, jumped down from by bunk, and then glanced through the porthole after wiping the mist with my hand. An early morning fog obscured my view of the pier, but I recognized my surroundings.

"We're here!...We're finally here! Oh, Boston,...how I've missed you!" I exclaimed thrilled at the sight of my beloved homeport. Despite my outburst, David was still sleeping soundly. We had apparently docked while most of the crew was asleep. "David! David wake up!" I shouted, shaking him vigorously. "Hurry! Get up and get dressed! We've arrived! We're here in Boston! The ship's already in Boston Harbor!"

"Oh, that's great!" he replied drowsily, yawning and stretching. "Let's get off this damn hulk right now! We've been cooped up on the *Calypso* long enough! I'll dress and join you in a few minutes."

David and I decided to rent a room together close to the waterfront. We planned to remain there until our discharge papers were issued along with our severance pay. While I would sorely miss the companionship we shared, our destinies would take us on completely different paths.

"I'd like to travel west to California," David confided. "I hear gold is being found out there. If I'm fortunate enough to find a rich vein, I'll stake a claim and build a mine shaft with my mustering-out pay."

"Well,…I'd like to use my wages to finance a tea and liquor business in Chicago," I disclosed with conviction. "Of course I'll need some additional backing to get me started, but I don't think that'll be a problem."

"Say, why don't we travel west together," David suggested, hoping I'd readily agree. "I can at least accompany you as far as Chicago."

"That's a fantastic idea, David," I said while hurriedly tying my shoes. I know I'll hate it when the time comes for us to go our separate ways. I guess I'll have to accept that if we're to make our dreams come true."

From the porthole, I strained to discern the antediluvian warehouses queued along this familiar shipping port. I realized that despite the dense fog our cargo was already being carried down the gangplank, loaded onto the longshoremen's carts, and then carefully stacked in front of a large canopy in preparation for storage. After hurriedly washing and getting dressed, I couldn't wait to leave what had been for me a horrendous voyage at sea.

"Never again!" I resolved, dashing out onto the ship's deck toward the catwalk. "Although, on second thought, I might like to take a world cruise as a wealthy, first-class passenger someday. Then, and only then, would I seriously consider it."

Soon, David was by my side. He bent to fasten his knapsack then followed me down the gangplank to the pier. I raced toward the docking area still struggling with my reefer.

David and I lingered along the wharf checking the various commodities. It seemed that we had indeed accomplished our objectives. The merchandise listed on the requisition orders were now on our ship's manifest. It hadn't been an easy task. Bad backs and calloused knees would probably plague us for the rest of our lives. Even though I had decided that life at sea wasn't for me, I was filled with a deep sense of pride. Due to our valiant efforts, the *Calypso*'s crew delivered some extremely rare and valuable goods to the merchants of Boston. It was indeed a worthy mission. We chose to reacquaint our wobbly sea legs to walking on solid ground.

The center of the city loomed straight ahead. The haze, like a misty curtain hanging over the harbor, had finally lifted. It revealed an early May sun whose welcomed warmth burned through an almost cloudless sky. Nevertheless, I occasionally found myself clutching my hat when an offshore breeze blew over my head.

The month, solidly entrenched into spring, brought forth the lively yellow forsythia—radiant flares that lined the streets and pathways. Nature, awakened from a long winter's sleep, produced a pageantry of color. Vivid tulips and perky daffodils, sprouting majestically between the crocus and the hyacinth, graced the front entrance of each dwelling and business. Leaves were again fluttering on the trees. The dogwood and magnolias, which were in full bloom, tenderly held within their flowering branches various species of songbird. A cantata of incessant chirping filled the air with sounds of lively renewal. I was acutely enraptured by the assurances of these glorious spring days—symbolic of wonderful things to come. I reflected on my purpose in life and looked forward with renewed hope to the fresh and exciting possibilities of my future.

"David, I'm so grateful to be home again from such a trying voyage and in the midst of such beauty…It's so spectacular!" I said, observing the glory of the season and singling out a particular, breath-taking floral bouquet of coral crab-apple blossoms.

"Yes, I agree," David replied with a few quick nods. "We've traveled to distant lands that could easily be compared to paradise, but like I've said many times before,…there's no place like home."

Overcome with an indescribable joy, I spontaneously kneeled and kissed the ground. This wondrous city was the long-awaited portal to my beloved home on Cape Cod. In a short while, I'd be visiting with family and friends whom I had dearly missed these past two years.

David and I walked for a little over a mile along the busy waterfront causeway looking for lodging. As luck would have it, we approached a small three-story brick building. A haphazardly printed sign, hastily painted on a piece of driftwood was displayed in the window of a small tack shop. It read: "Room For Rent—Please Inquire Within." The proprietor and his buxom, top-heavy wife were friendly and accommodating. We followed her up a winding staircase until we reached the top floor. Breathless, she opened the door to a clean, modestly decorated room and stated the rental fee.

"This'll do just fine,…don't you think, Albert?" David asked, giving the room a peripheral glance from the doorway.

"Yes," I replied, nodding my head in approval as I looked in behind him. "It'll certainly serve our purposes."

"I collect my rent in advance. You may pay me by the week," the woman said, gasping as she spoke. "If possible, please try to give me a little advance notice before you leave. One person left in the middle of the night after just a few days. The last person renting this room was asked to vacate it at the end of his week's stay. He was drunken and boisterous at all hours of the night…It was quite disruptive to our other patrons. I expect, you'll both behave yourselves and be considerate of the other roomers here. Your quarters will be cleaned and the bedsheets changed on Saturdays."

"We'll certainly respect your wishes, madam, and we'll be sure to let you know when we plan to leave," I said courteously. "My name is Albert Crosby and this is my crewmate, David Atkins."

"Pleased to meet you," she said with a brisk curtsey, smiling and handing us the keys. As soon as she turned to descend the stairway, I closed the door behind her.

"By the way, Albert," David disclosed while unpacking his knapsack and placing its contents in the oak chest-of-drawers. "I've been told that the Myricks,…my neighbors from Nantucket, also have gold fever. They're preparing to rendezvous with a group in Chicago. The Myricks plan to leave from there sometime next year. We'll all travel together to northern California. I've been invited to spend some time with them before we head west. Most likely I'll be staying on here with the Myricks after you leave for Brewster. They've asked me to help them prepare for the journey. I'm hoping to find work here in Boston. In the meantime, I'll be gathering supplies, tools and equipment, et cetera for our long trip west. I'll be sure to advise you as to my whereabouts so we can stay in touch."

"Well,…David! I must say it sounds like you've really pulled it all together. Your plans seem almost foolproof," I said, impressed with his tenacity. I hung my clothes on the hooks that were near the door. "I wish you success and prosperity, dear friend. May you find the mother lode and be wealthy beyond your *wildest* dreams."

"Say," I said loudly as I turned toward him to get his attention, "If you're willing to pay half the price of my prairie schooner, I'll turn it over to you. I won't need it once I've unloaded my shipment of liquors and teas in Chicago. Now…how's that for a brilliant idea? A bargain,…I'd say!"

"I'll have to think about that one, Albert," he replied with a snicker. "It all depends on whether our plans for the future coincide. You know as well as I that things can go awry. You're such a hustler, Albert!" David scoffed, his voice changing from a scolding tone to a more jovial one as he walked over to me and slapped me on the shoulder. "I'd bet my last dollar that if anyone was going to be rich,…it'd be *you!*

Gales of laughter erupted in our room until David and I realized that the sound of our voices might be heard in the hallway.

*   *   *   *

Mid-May, 1845

The week was coming to a close. Although he would be back, David left to visit the Myricks who were staying with relatives in Chelsea, a small town north of Boston. I lifted the bedroom shades allowing the marvelous morning light to bathe the room with radiance and warmth. We Cape Codders are hardy souls who pride themselves on their ability to withstand long, raw winters and harsh, hostile springs. Nevertheless, today was an exception to the rule. This sunny day was a longed-for change. I had remained in my room during the past week reading to pass the time and formulating my business venture. Braving the outdoors had meant enduring some bone-chilling rainy days, but this was an exceptionally warm, May morning. I welcomed this balmy weather with zest as I opened the window and filled my lungs with the aromatic, salty sea air. The sun's resplendent rays delivered a soothing, beneficial balm that penetrated my whole being like permeating grace.

"The outdoors is beckoning. I must leave this room and venture out." I decided while fetching my coat and hat from the hooks next to the door. "These four walls are closing in on me. It's a good day to complete my errands before I return home. I'll take a walk along the boardwalk, shop and get some exercise at the same time." I donned my jacket and, with cap in hand scurried down the staircase to the street below.

While strolling, at a leisurely pace, through the mercantile district, I found myself gawking at the storefront windows where the owners had artfully displayed their wares. I recognized many of the vendible—some were quite similar to the goods we carried across the open seas in the bowels of our ship. I contemplated returning home with a small trinket or two for Mother and the girls. I also planned to purchase some exotic tobacco for Father's pipe. I decided to enter an elegant bijouterie. I abruptly stepped back and felt an obstruction behind me. I turned to find I had inadvertently bumped into a wheelchair.

"Oh, I'm so sorry!...Please forgive me," I said apologetically, embarrassed by my clumsiness. I automatically babbled this pat phrase without looking at the gentleman seated there. When I turned to face him, I stared in disbelief. "Jonathan!" I cried out, recognizing him at once. "I can't believe my eyes!" I said, stunned and chuckling nervously. "Imagine bumping into you like this,...literally speaking." When I shouted his name, a confused expression flashed across his pallid face—now rimmed by a short blond goatee. "It's such a pleasure seeing you again, dear friend. What are you doing here in Boston?"

"Albert!…Can that possibly be you?" he asked, placing his hand on his forehead to shield the sun from his face. It was evident that as he scanned me from head to toe, he hoped I was actually the person whom he thought I might be. "I dare say I hardly recognized you. Yes, of course…it *is* you, Albert!" Jonathan smiled as he welcomed me with outstretched arms. Elated by this unexpected and emotional reunion, we firmly embraced each other. "It's been such a long time, Albert. I've truly missed you! By the looks of it, I'd say you've been at sea for quite a while."

"Why,…yes, I have," I replied, trying to justify my sloppy attire. "My ship, the *Calypso* is moored here in the harbor for a few weeks. My tour of duty's over and I *don't* intend to reenlist. I'm no longer in the merchant marine service. I've been honorably discharged. I've decided *not* to return to sea," I said decisively. "Those days are over for me. Right now, I'm just waiting around for my discharge papers and mustering-out pay. I plan to find my niche right here…on good old solid ground!"

Just as I finished that remark, I glanced upwards to find an attractive, young woman standing behind Jonathan's wheelchair. Her dainty hands were firmly grasping the handle. Realizing this was an opportune time to formally introduce her to me, Jonathan swiftly raised his left arm and—without turning around—sent his hand backwards toward her.

"This is my devoted and indispensable companion, Margaret Henderson," he said, aiming his index finger at the poised and gracious young lady towering over him.

She responded with a dazzling smile. "Why, she's as beautiful and radiant as this fresh spring day," I thought, quickly removing my cap from my head.

"Margaret, this is one of my oldest and dearest friends, Albert Crosby," Jonathan said with heartfelt sincerity. "You've often heard me speak of him."

I immediately became conscious of my unkempt appearance after catching a glimpse of my reflection in the shop window. "You dumb ass, Albert! You've really botched up *this* introduction," I thought, reprimanding myself and ashamed of my decidedly crude and unflattering image. I must say—I looked like a caveman. I felt her first impression of me would be one of coarseness and repulsion. I think it was the most embarrassing moment of my life. I had become accustomed to my rough exterior these last two years. It had seemed unimportant to me—until now.

"How do you do?" she said politely, extending a tiny, lace-gloved hand. "It's so nice to finally meet you, Albert. I feel I know you quite well having heard so much about you from Jonathan. He always mentions you in glowing terms. The Crosby family has also been very supportive in your absence. We'll never forget their many kindnesses."

Her melodic voice kept reverberating in my head. I had never heard the sound of my name uttered so demurely and so distinctly. Like heavenly stars flickering in the night sky, her sparkling eyes twinkled with each word. As I stepped backward to absorb this captivating vision, I found myself utterly intrigued by this paragon of womanhood.

"We're in Boston for Jonathan's appointment at the medical center. The doctors need to monitor his improvement, every six months," she said, answering my initial question and slowly shaking her head back and forth as she spoke, signaling her frustration with his progress. Her strawberry blond curls peeped from beneath a wide-brimmed chapeau. They bounced delicately around a lovely face with perfectly chiseled features. "Jonathan and I chose to do a little browsing in the small specialty shops along the way to the pier. But I decided to return to our carriage because the physical exams and tests have tired him so. We'll be boarding the next packet ship to Brewster,...shortly," she added. I stared spellbound as she spoke. Mesmerized by her beauty, I heard her speak, but was unaware of her words. Her ruby lips—softly curved like an archer's bow parted to expose teeth that were as white as sun-bleached seashells. Margaret's slight overbite and small, upturned nose only served to enhance her beauty and attractiveness.

"Margaret, there's no need for us to hurry back," Jonathan said. "The *Sarah* won't be leaving for at least another hour or so. Our carriage can wait for us a little while longer. I so wanted to purchase a special gift for you in appreciation for all you do for me. Let's go into the shop for that lovely string of cultured seed pearls you so greatly admired in the window. Please, won't you reconsider?" Jonathan pleaded, turning his head to the side and wishing Margaret would change her mind.

"I think not! You look rather fatigued." Margaret said as she sighed with mock disapproval over his persistence. "You must be exhausted. I believe you've had quite enough for one day," she went on resolutely, undaunted by his plea and forcing the issue by quickly propelling the wheelchair forward over a curb.

"I guess you know best, Margaret," Jonathan said, heaving an inherent groan and obviously crushed by her response—nevertheless, reluctantly abiding by her decision. He glanced upwards searching my face for some kind of reaction. I think he expected I'd agree with him and attempt to argue his case with Margaret. It was a little disconcerting.

"I've never known him to be so passive and condescending," I thought. "What's become of that vital old friend I once knew so well? Jonathan was always the master of his own fate. While I was away, his infirmity must have slowly destroyed that dauntless spirit of his," I concluded. I was heartsick seeing him like this. I remembered him as the most audacious among us, always ready to accept any challenge. I sensed she was being a bit overbearing—however, I applauded her stance. At the moment, Jonathan was her main concern—she cared little about the pearls.

"May I ask a favor of you?" she asked shyly, the apples of her cheeks flushed as she turned to speak to me.

"Why,…yes. Miss Henderson, what can I do for you?" I inquired, curious as to what she might ask of me.

"I'm having some difficulty maneuvering the wheelchair around the curbs. I'd truly appreciate some help along the way," she said with an arresting smile. Her lucid prose spilled like sweet nectar from her rose-petal colored lips. "Our carriage should be waiting for us just around the next block. Jonathan's been ill with a cough, but he seems to be a bit better now. Even so, I don't wish to expose him to this chill, coastal wind any longer than necessary. We'll be sailing home within the next few hours. I hope he'll have the opportunity to rest on board the *Sarah*."

"Certainly. Yes,…of course, I'll help you with the wheelchair. I was planning on walking a short distance with you anyway," I replied, delighted by her request. "In the meantime,…it'll be my pleasure to be of assistance to you both."

The air was filled with Margaret's perfume. Like an invisible aura it surrounded her comely body with the delicate scent of lilac blossoms. Her high-necked, lace chiffon dress defined a figure that was curvaceous and exquisitely shaped. Meticulously clad, she wore a stylish ensemble in a flattering shade of violet. Her shawl, parasol, cummerbund and wide-brimmed hat were delicately embroidered with matching nosegays of spring flowers. Margaret's panache was in perfect harmony with nature and the spring beauty around us. I had to give Jonathan credit—he certainly had extraordinary taste in women. I felt the need to reminisce with him for a while. Quite frankly, I couldn't ignore an ulterior motive—to acquaint myself more intimately with his captivating escort. I was quite enamored with her.

"That settles it," I thought. I was determined to take advantage of the situation. "Somehow I must find a way to join them. There's no denying how I feel about her. I'll also sail on the *Sarah* to Brewster. I'll say it'll allow me to help

Margaret with Jonathan's wheelchair. I'm not quite ready to leave, but if I hurry I can take care of my business within the next hour."

"Miss Henderson,…would you mind if I joined you and Jonathan on the *Sarah*?" I asked hesitantly, hoping she would agree. "I haven't as yet made arrangements for my return to Brewster. Up to now, I really hadn't felt a need to rush. We'll all sail home together. It'll be an opportune time for me to enjoy Jonathan's company and assist you with him…if need be," I said, altruistically trying to justify my spontaneous decision to accompany them.

"Why, Albert,…how thoughtful of you. That would be delightful. We'll look forward to your company and please *do* call me, Margaret," she said, smiling coyly, blushing and instantly shifting her glance from me to Jonathan.

"Fine, I'll meet you later on the packet," I replied, pleased that she had amenably accepted my suggestion. "Don't wait for me. I must return to my room for my belongings. I also need to retrieve my discharge papers and severance pay from the *Calypso*. As I've previously mentioned, my tour of duty is ended. I won't be returning to sea on the *Calypso* or on any other ship for that matter."

I helped them board the waiting carriage and once it was on its way, I hailed another. I returned to the apartment building and asked the coachman to wait for me while I made a mad dash up to my room. Except for a hairbrush and pair of scissors, I tossed all my possessions into a large duffel bag. Then I stood before the mirror, expeditiously snipping away at my ragged beard and mustache and attempting to brush and tame the wire-like hair.

After I became more presentable, I sat at the small desk, scribbled a hasty note to David, and then left my share of the rent on it. I explained my sudden departure and also wrote that I'd attempt to reach him again in the near future. The coachman, who had already been notified of my need to hurry, cracked the whip. The carriage arrived shortly thereafter at the *Calypso*'s slip in the harbor. I flew into the purser's office and collected my honorable discharge papers and earnings. It was an ample amount—more than enough to help launch a future endeavor of my choosing.

"Goodbye, and the best of luck to you and your new crew!" I shouted, trying to avoid an ignominious departure from what had been my home for the last four years. As I passed the captain's stateroom, I noticed that Bryant and Howes were still there tidying it up. They may have seen me; however, I cared little whether they did or not. I dashed past them, ran down the gangplank, and then into the waiting carriage.

With not a moment to spare, I arrived at the opposite end of the harbor where the *Sarah* was docked. The stewards had already begun to haul the gangway onto the small sailing ship. With impatient gestures they summoned me to board at once. Carrying my weighty knapsack over my shoulder, I ran panting toward the packet. I caught a glimpse of Margaret's resplendent form standing alongside the handrails with her disabled charge in tow. They were frantically waving in my direction. An inner warmth, due to my apparent gesture of goodwill, was not enough to dispel the volley of disconcerting thoughts I had regarding their relationship.

"How compassionate of her to be so dedicated to Jonathan's well being. She must truly care for him," I rationalized as I neared the vessel. "How fortunate he is to have such a kindly, refined young woman doting on him,…one who satisfies his every need and showers him with such devotion. I wonder how they met? I'll be sure to find *that* out before we disembark in Brewster."

Margaret and Jonathan had been scanning the docking area, anxiously awaiting my arrival. Without losing sight of them, I hurried to board the *Sarah*. Even as I ran toward them I was focused on her superbly sculptured body and tiny waist. Totally enraptured by her beauty, I could *not* keep my eyes off of her. Margaret's irresistible charisma permeated my every thought. She was a blameless chaste angel, but like *Medea* she had effectively seduced me. I felt a twinge of shame and disgust. "How could I lust after my best friend's companion?" I asked myself as I greeted them with an energetic and amicable wave. I promptly berated myself for allowing my carnal emotions and raging sex drive to run amuck. Lewd and base sensual feelings plagued my conscience.

"Albert, for heavens sake, get a hold of yourself! You pervert!" I thought, soundly scolding myself. I had not only lost my head, but also my heart as well! The same erotic magnetism that had attracted me to Rebecca was again taking hold of my senses. That seemed like eons ago. I had been introduced to many beautiful women in my young life, yet somehow Margaret was different. "Why is she making such an impression on me?" I wondered. The reason seemed to elude me. "Am I falling in love with her? Is this love-at-first-sight?" I had to answer a resounding, *yes,* to both questions. "Dammit, Albert! You're such an idiot!…You know better than that!" Now that I had confronted the truth, I was determined to exercise my self-control. "Under no circumstances must my feelings for her be apparent through inappropriate words or gestures. For Jonathan's sake, I must resist her bedevilment and remember to be a gentleman at all times." As I approached Margaret and Jonathan, I reminded myself of my resolve. I smiled and cordially tipped my hat in a deliberate and casual manner

After a mediocre, yet satisfying luncheon on the packet, I found myself wandering toward the upper deck to breathe in the fresh sea air and enjoy the sunset.

I politely nodded as I walked past others who were there to do the same. I stood on the starboard side at a clearing along the rail. I had an unobstructed view of a blazing pink, purple and orange sky. The sun in its final burst of glory had nearly completed its quotidian decent toward the horizon.

I turned around when I recognized Margaret's greeting from behind me. "Hello, Albert!" she said. Startled by the unexpected, soft and tender use of my name, I felt my heart race wildly as she placed her warm gloved hand over mine. "It's certainly a perfect evening, isn't it?" she asked with an engaging smile, clearly trying to start a conversation. I was elated to see her. Margaret's lovely face left me momentarily breathless. It was radiantly framed by a lustrous aureole of silky, golden curls that were casually tossed about by the ocean breezes. I flashed a spontaneous smile and removed my hat. She gently released her hand to control her flyaway hair while she held onto her wide-brimmed hat with the other. "I thought you might be here," she went on to say. "You seemed to be someone who'd enjoy a glorious sunset over the bay. Cape Cod sunsets continue to fascinate me...They're so spectacular!"

"Well,...good evening Miss Henderson." I said, with a respectful nod of my head and inwardly pleased to see that she was alone. "Yes,...it's my favorite time of day. The seas have been fairly calm. We should be arriving on schedule." Curious, I asked, "By the way,...where's Jonathan?"

"You needn't be so formal, Albert. As I said before, please call me, Margaret. Our common interest in Jonathan will certainly ensure our seeing each other quite frequently from now on," she said. Margaret's facial expressions suddenly changed dramatically as she spoke with a downcast tone of voice. "It pains me to see Jonathan this way,...so sad and frail. I feel so helpless at times. I only wish I could do more for him. How wonderful it would be if his body could be restored through some kind of miracle. But alas, that'll never happen," she sighed, forlornly shaking her head. "Even though the doctors were quite cheerful today, they weren't very optimistic about Jonathan's progress. I'm certain he sensed their disappointment."

"I can sympathize with you, Margaret. I know exactly how you feel," I said, keenly aware of her sensitivities and compassion for Jonathan. "My friendship with Jonathan goes all the way back to our childhood. We were always together. In fact, as you probably already know I was with him at the time of that horrible accident. I relive it often. I fear he suffered another crushing blow when I left to join the merchant marines without him. We had always planned to be together. To be perfectly honest with you, it was dreadful having to leave him behind. Most likely he never mentioned that to you. A day never went by while I was at sea that Jonathan wasn't in my thoughts. I'm not one to pray much, yet I often found myself praying for him. I suppose the outcome could have been much worse. He was unconscious for days. At the time, we feared the trauma and head injuries might leave him comatose or even mentally deranged. Although paralyzed from the waist down, he eventually rallied with all his faculties intact. Thank God for that!" I heaved a deep sigh and looked up toward the heavens. "Although everyone's been supportive, Jonathan's extremely impatient with his disability. It disturbs him because he's so alert and has such a keen mind."

"Yes, you're right," Margaret replied wistfully, agreeing with my opinion. She removed some little bits of bread from her purse and threw them into the water. "Ever since we met, he's pretended to accept his fate. Outwardly, Jonathan's a veritable pillar of strength and courage. Yet deep inside, he's a defeated, tormented young man full of resentment and despair."

While she spoke, the raucous screeching of gulls overhead became more insistent as she tossed each morsel into the bay. They dove down to pluck the tiny handouts from the sea and attacked each other in order to claim their prize. Then, like arrows released from a bow, they shot upwards with their reward securely grasped in their beaks.

"He abhors his dependency on others," she went on to say. "His pride and self-esteem are as shattered as his body. It's so disconcerting to know this about him. It makes me feel so powerless! I know I can't heal his infirmity, but at least I can try to quiet his angry and restless spirit." Margaret's chin quivered as she tried to control her distress. She was close to tears. Curiosity was getting the better of me. Eager to change her train of thought, I decided to ask her about her connection to Jonathan. I threw out one question after another. I felt I had nothing to lose, at this point.

"Margaret, how did you happen to meet, Jonathan? When did you become his nurse and companion?" I asked, dropping all sense of propriety to get a direct reply to my prying questions and hoping not to offend or embarrass her in the offing. When she looked up and smiled without answering me, I went on. "Do you live on the Cape?…Are you also from Brewster?"

"No, Albert. I'm not from Cape Cod or the Islands. Actually,…I hail from Nova Scotia," she replied with a nervous shuffle and looking down at her feet. I sensed she was flattered that I inquired about her background. "My family moved to West Roxbury about ten years ago. My older sister, Abigail, married a native-born Cape Codder, Angus Hopkins from Brewster. His father is Cyrus Hopkins. Are you familiar with that family?"

"Oh, yes,…I do know them!" I replied "The Hopkins own several cranberry bogs in Brewster and elsewhere. Angus is several years older than I am. For that reason,…I really don't know him, personally."

"Abigail married and settled there with him about five years ago," Margaret said, holding onto her dress as a sudden gust of wind threatened to lift the hoop that rimmed her undergarment. "She and Angus have three children now. Jonathan and the Eldredge family are close friends of theirs. I've had the pleasure of spending the last two summers on the Cape helping her with the children and enjoying the seashore. I met Jonathan through them and was immediately drawn to him. I felt an irresistible urge to bring him a little "joie de vivre"…so to speak. I encouraged him to renew his old friendships and tried to rescue him from social isolation. I thought he should travel more and wanted to foster his love of the sea,…but that hasn't happened, as yet. I realized he was subconsciously withdrawing from the outside world." As she spoke, Margaret casually wiped the sea spray from her face with her lace handkerchief and returned it to her dress pocket. "What started out as an act of kindness became an obsession with me. I vowed to rescue him from his depression and inactivity. I wanted to offer Jonathan some hope for the future by helping him reach some measure of fulfillment and self-reliance. Also, he needed someone to accompany him to Boston for his initial semi-annual checkups. I was more than happy to oblige."

"That's extremely gracious of you, Margaret." I said with a nod, smiling and hanging onto the rail while the wind continued to blow across the deck. "He's fortunate indeed to be the object of such devotion and care. I can see that you've dedicated yourself to his every physical and mental need."

"Oh, no! I'm the fortunate one," she replied, momentarily taken aback by my praise. "I believe my presence has made a decided difference in his attitude toward life. It's been so rewarding to see Jonathan eagerly anticipating each new day."

"Well, I must admit you've done an excellent job of restoring his self-esteem," I said. At this point, I hesitated, but felt compelled to ask just one more question. "Margaret,…it's the month of May! How is it that you're still here at this time of year? Did you happen to arrive earlier this year?"

"I remained through the winter, Albert," she replied, walking along the rail toward the lower-deck entrance. "Jonathan asked me to stay. He said he desperately needed me to be here for him. I just couldn't bear to leave him or Brewster. Abigail was also very pleased and appreciative that I stayed on. Angus is usually out at sea when he isn't tending to the bogs. While he's out there fishing for cod and haddock for weeks on end, Abigail's left without adult companionship. It's a lonely life for her. Her small children are a handful. That's very frustrating and depressing for someone who's left alone for such long periods of time. As a result of being homebound, she's become quite reclusive, fearful and tense. Abigail has had several nervous breakdowns in the past."

"You continue to amaze me," I said, shaking my head in awe and admiration. "What a self-sacrificing and kind person you are, Margaret. Tell me, where have you been all my life?" I asked facetiously. I had undeniably fallen in love with this winsome young lady standing before me. I hadn't felt this way about anyone since Rebecca. Everything about her was absolute perfection. No one could be more desirable, praiseworthy or deserving of being loved. Margaret's beauty radiated from within. She was inwardly as attractive and delightful as she was outwardly. "This woman's not about to slip through *my* fingers," I vowed.

"Albert, please excuse me. I hate to leave you so abruptly, but I must check on Jonathan," she said turning to descend the ramp to the lower deck. "He's probably awake by now and looking for me. When I'm with him, he commands my undivided attention. I must return now, to tend to him…I'm sure you understand." While still on deck, I reached for her hand and held it tightly.

"Margaret," I said, speaking softly, yet candidly. She looked up expectantly as our eyes met. I chose my words carefully. "I know this may sound insipid and ill-timed,…but I also need your company. I want to be with you more than you could possibly imagine. If Jonathan's still resting,…please return to me."

I felt a bit unnerved as my heart pounded within my chest. I had unequivocally initiated a romantic relationship. "Now,…I've done it! How will Margaret respond? Will she be offended and angry?" I wondered. "She may not be. It appears I haven't repulsed her at all. No,…not in the least! In truth, she actually seems to enjoy my company." Without uttering a word, I sensed her body language reticently revealed a fondness for me—her straightforward glance disclosed something in her eyes, she couldn't deny. I believe Margaret was equally cognizant of the magnetism between us.

"Yes,…I will," she replied, smiling sweetly, blushing and executing a polite curtsy as she left my side. With short quick steps, Margaret hurried to check on Jonathan. Saddened, I watched as she disappeared below deck. I longed for her return and trusted that she would be back. But alas, I waited in vain. After a while, I took it upon myself to visit them below deck. "Jonathan, must have awakened," I concluded. And yes, he had indeed. As I approached him, he was munching on a small sweet roll.

"Hello, Albert! I guess I dozed off for a while," he said, greeting me with a wide grin and extending his hand to mine. "Thank you for keeping Margaret occupied while I rested...I truly cherish her," he added, looking up at her with an adoring expression.

"Well,...it won't be long now!" Jonathan went on. "We should be arriving at the Breakwater Packet Landing within the hour. Father will be meeting us there with the Hopkins's carriage. You're more than welcome to join us. We'll drop you off at Crosby Lane,...if you like. I'm sure there'll be an extra lantern we can loan you so you can safely find your way home."

"Thank you, Jonathan," I said gratefully. "I appreciate your kind invitation and readily accept it. I wasn't able to make arrangements to be picked up because I left in such haste. It's been so pleasurable joining you and Miss Henderson on the *Sarah*, dear friend. It was an opportune time to be with you and get acquainted with Margaret."

"Oh, no,...the pleasure was ours!" he exclaimed, glancing up from his wheel-chair toward Margaret and me. "I'm so thankful for the circumstances that led to our chance encounter, Albert...I've missed you so. It's meant so much to me to have your company on our voyage home. I'm certain Margaret feels that way, too." She smiled and our eyes met as she nodded in agreement.

The packet glided quietly into its slip at the landing. Although dusk had already settled in as we ascended the ramp to the upper deck—daylight still lingered. I took charge of Jonathan and maneuvered the wheelchair up the ramp and along the gangplank leading to the wharf. An osprey was making its nest above a wooden bollard on the dock and was oblivious to all the commotion below it. Overhead, the familiar screech of the gulls greeted our arrival.

People and carriages were everywhere. I scanned the countryside looking for landmarks unique to my beloved town of Brewster. How welcoming it was to see the sand dunes, the salt works along the shore with their small windmills pumping water into the large vats, the weirs and the white church steeples in the distance. I absorbed the view with elation and gratitude. I heaved a deep sigh as I relished being home.

Despite a distinct nip in the air, May brought forth a feeling of renewal and rebirth. The warmer days of summer would soon be on our doorstep. As we disembarked from the *Sarah*, I found myself thinking of the alewives who were now clogging the herring run of the Stony Brook and climbing upstream to reach the Mill Pond.

The Hopkins' carriage was already there waiting for us. After Mister Eldredge embraced his son, I helped to lift Jonathan into the carriage, and then seated him next to Margaret. I sat down on the seat opposite them. Every now and then, when our eyes met, she smiled and lowered her head. While heading along the coastal road toward East Brewster, Margaret leaned over to speak to me.

"Albert, would you like to join us for supper next Wednesday evening? I'd like you to meet Abigail, Angus and the children. Jonathan will also be there. I'll expect you around six…Do say you'll come," she pleaded.

"How nice of you to ask me," I replied, pleased that I would soon get to see her again. "Yes, thank you,…I accept your gracious invitation. I'll be there promptly at six," I said while descending the carriage steps. Mister Eldredge removed a lantern hanging from a side hook on the carriage and handed it to me as I headed toward home. Before the carriage continued on its way, I abruptly stopped, turned around, waved and shouted, "See you on Wednesday!"

The darkening night sky revealed a mere suggestion of clouds slowly drifting across a waxing moon that poured its diffused light through the evening fog. The sound of the peepers resonated from the salt marshes. Their convivial chorus filled my ears with hauntingly familiar songs. I fairly walked on air all the way to the Crosby homestead. As I neared our cozy bayside cottage where simplicity and necessity were one—long inviting shafts of milky rays glowing from the indoor lamps lay strewn across the ground and—led me home.

Although I had sent a telegraph stating that I would be returning home within a week or so, my unexpected arrival thoroughly surprised my family. With profound expressions of excitement and joy, Mother, Father, Emeline and Kate came racing to my side from every corner of the house. Miss Mira ran in from the kitchen with outstretched arms amid all the shouts, hugs, kisses and tears. "Oh, me Albert, how good it is to see ye home safe and sound," she said in her genial brogue.

"Oh, how I've longed to hear it again," I thought, rejoicing in my homecoming. "Yes!…I'm home at last!"

"Ye certainly are a sight for sore eyes, me lad! Aye, ye look quite fit!" Miss Mira added while looking me over, patting me on the shoulder, and then putting both arms around my waist in an affectionate embrace.

"He looks a little pale and thin to me," Mother injected, sniffling and demurely wiping the tears from her eyes. "He needs some good, nourishing family meals to fatten that bony frame."

Miss Mira set the table with sweet cakes and hot toddy. After hours of chatting with the family and charming them with fascinating stories about my encounters at sea, I eventually bid everyone goodnight. As I picked up my sack and ascended the staircase to my bedroom, I turned around and loudly exclaimed, "Oh,…it's so *great* to be home!"

▼

CHAPTER 8

Late-May, 1845

The day dawned sunny, yet partly cloudy, and still somewhat nippy, even for May. Dark clouds that shadowed the sun eventually moved off. Nonetheless, the unobstructed sunbeams were no match for the cool temperatures surging off the bay.

During the next week, I managed to spend some time with Japeth, even though he seemed preoccupied with his spring chores. I noticed that Nathaniel, his warmly clad son was usually by his side. He was a delightful little boy, but his antics kept Japeth constantly on the run. "Japeth's a bit too old to manage such an energetic child," I concluded as I watched them both from the sidelines.

That evening, the Crosby family gathered before a crackling fire in the sitting room. I held their interest while I recounted some well-chosen aspects of my adventurous years as a seaman. Ultimately, I disclosed my decision *not* to reenlist in the mercantile marine service and the reasons why. As my parents sat in their favorite chairs, they listened attentively. Father leisurely smoked his pipe and Mother embroidered a table runner during the entire discourse. My siblings Emeline and Kate, now refined young ladies, were seated at a corner table playing a quiet game of chess.

"What are your intentions for the future, Albert? Have you made any decisions that you'd like to share with us?" Father asked as Mother raised her head from her busywork. She eyed me directly while anticipating my answer.

"Yes, as a matter of fact, I have," I replied, attempting to satisfy both questions at once. I summarized my goals and aspirations, outlining exactly what I had in mind. "I'd like to establish a wholesale house in Chicago," I said, elaborating on my plans. "I intend to market liquors and teas from all over the world. I'm sure, if given half a chance, I'll be successful. How do you feel about that?...I'd truly like your opinion," I asked, searching their expressionless faces for the slightest hint of approval. I wished to exact a candid response, so I addressed them directly. "Mother, Father, what do you think of my plans?...I'd certainly like your consent before I become seriously involved in this venture. I've been giving this some serious thought for a long time. I feel it's time for me to fend for myself." Although I observed my parents occasionally glancing at one another during my auspicious presentation, they never interrupted me. The moments seemed like years as I nervously awaited their answer. "Damn! Have they judged my idea as downright absurd and foolhardy?" I wondered. "They're probably quite exasperated with me at this point." The quiet in the room was unnerving. Finally, Father broke the silence. I was pleasantly surprised to find that he was enthusiastic and fully supportive of my project.

"It's a well-conceived plan, my son," Father said, rising from his rocker, pipe in hand, and walking over to me. "Your ideas are sound and financially feasible. You're absolutely right...The West *does* need a wholesale liquor and tea business equal to that of Boston's. I'm behind you 100 percent!" Inwardly, I breathed a sigh of relief and grinned from ear to ear.

"If we can be of any help, please let us know," Mother said with a smile, concurring with his assessment. She was noticeably proud of my mature decision to be on my own and financially independent.

"Well...I...I, yes, Father," I replied, hesitantly. "My venture will require some additional funds. What I've saved from my years at sea and my severance pay will not be enough." Undaunted and bolstered by his approval, I continued on with my proposal. "It's a ample amount, but not nearly enough to purchase my initial inventory. I calculated I'd need approximately $10,000 to sufficiently stock my new business. Does that sound unreasonable?"

"No, it doesn't, Albert. I'm sure you'll need at least that much to start such an ambitious undertaking. However, I know you're aware of my financial obligations," he said, trying not to undermine my aspirations, yet trying to be realistic. "I can only afford to give you a third of that sum. For that matter, I'm certain, your uncles Roland and Isaac will be more than eager to provide you with the balance. We'll contact them soon." He doused his pipe with one hand and gestured spontaneously with the other. "I know!...We'll invite them and their families for dinner on Sunday. That should be an opportune time to approach them about financing your new enterprise. They're all shrewd businessmen and always predisposed to investing for profit. You have a reputation for being an honest and industrious achiever, Albert. With those qualifications in mind, they'll be auto-matically assured of a decent return on their money."

"Thank you, for your vote of confidence, Father, and your help in this mat-ter," I said. "I hope to have all the funds I'll need within the next few months. My next step will be to return to Boston, purchase the inventory, and then secure a large prairie schooner to transport it over-land to Chicago."

"Sounds like a workable plan to me, son. The sooner the better," he said, agreeing with my need to get started on what appeared to be a promising future. He shook my hand, put his arm around my shoulder, and then together we walked out of the sitting room. Mother had quietly left for the kitchen, and it had been some time since my sisters had retired to their rooms. We were alone. Quite unexpectedly, I felt a need to share something personal with him.

"Father, I've met the loveliest young woman on my return home," I revealed "She's been Jonathan's nurse and companion for nearly two years now. Her name is Margaret Henderson. I've become quite fond of her."

"Oh, yes, I've had the opportunity to be in her company, several times," he replied. "Your mother and I were introduced to Margaret when we visited Jonathan over the holidays. She's an attractive, gracious young lady,...but rumors have it there's a love relationship between those two," he said regretfully, slowly shaking his head. "If I were you, I'd be a little wary of courting her behind his back."

"Oh, no, Father, I wouldn't do that!" I exclaimed, startled by his warning. "I thought you knew me better. Other than being his nursemaid and close friend, Margaret made no mention of any sort of commitment to him. I realize she's very attentive to his needs, but I gather that's as far as it goes."

"Maybe so," he said with a hint of skepticism in his voice. "Now that you're a young man and feeling your oats so to speak, I have no idea just how far you'd go to win her over. In any case, you'd better take my advice and be very careful about making advances toward that young woman. I noticed the way Jonathan ogled her every time she moved around the room. He literally followed Margaret everywhere with his eyes."

"I know that, Father...You're right!" I acknowledged halfheartedly, hanging my head and placing my hands in my pockets. "Margaret and I chatted at length and ultimately discussed Jonathan while we were alone on the upper deck of the *Sarah*. He was asleep, at the time, below deck. If something existed between them, I'm sure Margaret would've made that clear when I made a more-than-friendly overture toward her. She also seemed to be enamored with me. It's quite possible I may have misinterpreted her intentions. In any case,

Margaret has invited me to dine at her sister's home on Wednesday evening. She wants to introduce me to her family. Jonathan will also be there. It'll be an opportune time for me to uncover the exact extent of their relationship."

"Well, Albert,…I suppose if you're mature enough to start your own business,…you're certainly old enough to find the woman of your choice," Father said, patting me lovingly on the shoulders and trying not to sound patronizing. "The best of luck to you on both counts, my son." We parted and went on our separate ways.

That Wednesday evening was clear and crisp, yet warmer than the previous few days. I arrived at the Hopkins' home just barely after sunset and before the landscape settled into the dark stillness of night. A three-quarter moon—partially hidden by an escort of shadowy angular clouds, patiently waited to make its spectacular ascent into the heavens. While I stood outside the Hopkins' front door adjusting my cravat, the hooting of owls in the oak trees heralded an uncommon contentment with the world. After an initial false start, I was confidant that I was now well groomed and looking my best. I gently lifted and tapped the elaborate doorknocker. Margaret had anticipated my arrival and immediately opened the door.

"Do come in, Albert,…we've been expecting you," Margaret said, welcoming me with a cordial smile and pointing to the sitting room. As I followed her through the foyer, it was almost impossible to keep my eyes off of her. I almost tripped on the hallway rug as I stared at this mesmerizing vision. She was dressed in a lovely, jay-blue chiffon gown that flowed along her body like a sensuous sheath. It was cinched at her tiny waist by a wide, azure ribbon that cascaded to her ankles. A nosegay of blue bachelor buttons was tucked into a fashionable chignon. Margaret positively took my breath away.

"You look absolutely ravishing this evening, Miss Henderson," I whispered in her ear with raised eyebrows and an admiring glance as I beamed at the sight of her. I addressed her using her family name on purpose to emphasize my delight.

"Thank you, Mister Crosby. How sweet of you to notice," she replied with a comely smile, using the same formality and tone of voice. "Jonathan's eagerly looking forward to your visit."

"And how about you?" I asked, taking advantage of the moment while removing my hat and jacket.

"Why, Albert,…of course I am! That goes without saying," she replied, quickly turning around to hang my hat and jacket on the hallway clothes tree. "Frankly,…I'm delighted to see you again." Margaret later confessed that she had purposefully turned away, because her face had become quite flushed.

How I craved her sweet lips. My arms ached to hold her. I was so tempted to take her hand and pull her close to me. Oh, how desperately I needed her! My body throbbed with an indescribable longing. "Dammit, Albert! You simply can't go on feeling this way about a woman who could possibly love someone else," I agonized. "I *must* know how she feels about Jonathan. Until then, I need to find a way to restrain those wayward emotions of mine. I mustn't inadvertently reveal my love for her unless encouraged to do so. That would alienate them both. It would destroy any semblance of love Margaret might have for me...I'd also lose Jonathan's friendship forever. Somehow I can't let that happen." I followed Margaret into the sitting room. Jonathan was delighted to see me. As I walked toward him, he gestured that I come forward.

"Jonathan, dear friend, how are you this evening?" I asked sincerely, yet inwardly resenting the fact that he might be my rival for Margaret's favors.

"I'm doing as well as expected under the circumstances," he replied with a grimace and looking down at his chair. Jonathan reached for Margaret's hand and stared directly up at her with an endearing glance..."If it weren't for Margaret, I'd be nothing but a vegetating hunk of flesh just sitting here waiting to die. She's brought such joy and peace into my life," he said gratefully.

"Dammit!" I thought. "This isn't going to be easy. It's obvious he truly loves her. Father's right, Jonathan idolizes Margaret. How can I tactfully disclose my feelings for her without causing him pain?" Many disturbing thoughts and questions raced through my mind. "I know she's fond of him,...but *in love* with him? No,...I don't think so. Her eyes betray her heart. She looks at me in an entirely different way than she does, Jonathan." I reasoned. "Margaret doesn't embrace or kiss him like she would a lover. I've never seen any visible romantic expressions between them. Still, I could be totally wrong about their relationship." A gentle tap on my shoulder abruptly interrupted my thoughts. I quickly turned around and immediately became aware that there were others on the left side of the room.

"This is my sister, Abigail, and her husband, Angus Hopkins," Margaret said graciously, extending her hand toward them in an introductory manner, then turning around to address Abigail and Angus, "and this is Albert Crosby,...he's Jonathan's close friend," she went on. "Albert, has just returned from a tour of duty in the merchant marines." I shook Angus' hand and Abigail executed a perfunctory curtsy when they stood to greet me. "Pleased to meet you, Mister and Missus Hopkins." I said politely, nodding my head toward them both.

Abigail was thin and gaunt. She was timid and lacked Margaret's sparkling spirit. Dark circles under her ashen-blue eyes, which had long since lost their youthful vivacity, spoke of exhaustion and despair. Her long, auburn hair was twisted and rolled into a large bun on the back of her head. Abigail appeared harried and drained by motherhood—having had three children in quick succession. The young ones had already been fed and put to bed before I arrived.

Angus carried his large, heavy frame in a patrician, pompous manner. He had a full head of dark brown, curly hair that was tied to the back of his head, a mustache and a short beard. Despite a limited education, he was an excellent conversationalist—well versed in many subjects. Angus chewed tobacco. Hence—every so often—he disgustingly spat out the juice into a brass spittoon.

We had a delightful supper that was a credit to Margaret's culinary skills. I made a point of complimenting her for her efforts. Without warning, Angus began to berate Abigail about her ineptitude in the kitchen. The fact that she was the butt of his verbal abuse unnerved me. When Angus momentarily left the room, Margaret proceeded to hug her sister and whispered that she should ignore his taunts. After a considerable exchange of pleasantries over coffee and dessert, the discourse turned to questions about my seafaring adventures. I willingly obliged, eager to avoid a subject that might become controversial or personal.

"Please excuse me. I must leave now," Jonathan interrupted, observing the hour on the stately clock in the hallway. "My father will be arriving in a short while to take me home. I bid you all a fond farewell. It was a delightful evening. You certainly outdid yourself, Margaret. It's been a long time since I've had such a wonderful meal. Would you please fetch my belongings and wheel me to the door?" When Margaret left the room to do as he had asked, Jonathan turned around and went on to say, "Abigail and Angus, I sincerely thank you for your hospitality and,…Albert, it was so fascinating to hear of your travels," he said, addressing me directly. "It truly piqued my interest. I felt as if I was there with you on those exotic islands and foreign lands. Thank you for sharing your exploits with us." Margaret returned with Jonathan's clothing and helped him with his coat. He reached for his hat and held it in his lap.

"I'll see you before I leave, Jonathan," I said, hoping to prolong his soaring spirits. He was familiar with my plans for the future. I had previously disclosed them on the packet while maneuvering his wheelchair up the ramp and toward the gangplank and the wharf where Margaret was waiting for him.

"I'll look forward to that, Albert," he replied. "Do come soon."

"We'll also say goodnight." Angus said, brusquely taking hold of Abigail's arm. "Abigail will most likely be up at dawn with the children. Albert, do plan on visiting us again in the future." He shook my hand as Abigail nodded and curtsied, then he followed her to the hallway where they ascended the staircase to their bedroom.

I accompanied Margaret and Jonathan to the front entrance. Mister Eldredge and the family buckboard were already there. I helped to lift Jonathan onto the front seat and placed his wheelchair in the rear of the wagon. After we waved farewell and re-entered the house, Margaret closed the door behind us.

"Before…you *leave*? I heard you mention that to Jonathan. What exactly did you mean by *that*? Will you be leaving Brewster again? You said you weren't going to reenlist. So where are you going?" Margaret asked in a hushed voice, assailing me with a barrage of questions and clearly disturbed by my words. We returned to the empty sitting room. I placed another log on the fire, reached for an andiron, and then vigorously stoked the burning embers.

"No, Margaret. I certainly did *not* reenlist. I couldn't wait to leave the merchant marine service," I replied emphatically while facing the rekindled flames. "I intend to leave for Boston next month. I plan to establish a liquor and tea business in Chicago. My earnings and the additional funds generously loaned me by family members will allow me to purchase the stock needed to launch my enterprise. I intend to transport the goods myself overland from Boston to Chicago." Having said this, I turned to face her. "I've been eager to get this project started, that is"…I hesitated then added with a crestfallen look,…"until now."

"Why, Albert?" she questioned, bewildered by this disclosure. "Although it's quite an ambitious project, it sounds feasible to me. I'm sure you'll be quite successful. Are you feeling unsure of yourself, or are you having second thoughts about it?"

"No. It's been my intent all along," I replied, turning to face her and sensing a sinking feeling as I gazed directly into her eyes. Without being forceful, I reached for her delicate hand and pulled her closer to me. "Margaret, I think you know full well the reason for my indecision." She looked puzzled. "I just can't leave you," I went on. "Actually, I simply can't pretend anymore. I'm deeply in love with you. It happened the moment I first laid eyes on you. Oh, Margaret, I must know! Do you feel the same way about me? Do you love me as much as I love you? If you say your love is *solely* for Jonathan, I'll understand. That's your choice to make. On the other hand,…if that's so, I won't seek your company any longer. That would be much too painful for me. In fact,…I'd leave Brewster immediately. If my insolence has offended you, Margaret, please accept my apologies." Uneasy about my proclamation of love for her, I anxiously awaited her answer. She moved closer, placed both arms around my waist, and then laid her head on my chest.

"Oh, Albert, my dearest,...I *do* love you." she said. "More than you'll ever know. I love you with my whole being. And yes,...it was the same for me. My heart skipped a beat the first time I saw you. I didn't want to admit it to myself, or to you, because of Jonathan. I've been deliberately trying to hide my feelings for you. Without much success,...I might add." Margaret raised her head, faced me with adoring eyes, and then spoke in a clear, deliberate manner. "He's never said so, but I know Jonathan loves me. Although I'm extremely fond of him, I simply can't return the same kind of romantic feelings he has for me. I love him as I would a cherished family member, but that's the extent of it. Somehow without wanting to address this fact, I think he knows that."

"Margaret, my darling, you'll never know how relieved I am to hear that," I said, thankful to be assured of her avowed love for me. I reached for her chin and gently pressed her lips to mine. Our passionate kiss released an intense, pent-up force from deep within our essence—an explosive and unrestrained outpouring of the love we had for each other.

"Jonathan must eventually be informed about us," she acknowledged with a pained expression. "I'm afraid this will be an another devastating blow for him. I hope time will heal his heartache." She heaved a deep sigh and managed to smile while I held her close and repeatedly kissed her lips, neck, cheeks and forehead.

"I'll be visiting him shortly, Margaret, and when I do,...I'll be sure to tell him, as tactfully as possible, what's happened between us. I promise to be discreet and exceptionally considerate of his feelings for you," I said, trying to ease her conscience. "After all,...he's a dear friend. I wouldn't want to add to his pain. In the meantime, my precious love,...may I call on you? That's if your family will give me their permission."

"Albert, of course you may," she replied demurely. "I would've been saddened if you hadn't asked. My family will definitely accept you. I'm sure they'll be delighted to meet you. I love you my dearest, Albert, and I know they will too!" Again, we kissed ardently.

"It's getting quite late," I said, looking at the timepiece on the mantel and feeling aroused. I concluded I should leave before getting out of line. "I'll see you again tomorrow,...if that's all right with you."

"I'll look forward to it," she replied, embracing me. "Sleep well, Albert. Take my love with you and hold it close to your heart until I see you again tomorrow." With her head on my shoulders we walked slowly, arm-in-arm toward the front entrance.

"I will," I said, placing another tender kiss on her lips. "Goodnight, my sweet Margaret. My heart is fairly bursting with joy and love for you." I kissed her one last time then left her side literally walking on air. "I believe I'll sing all the way home," I shouted from the wagon. I lit the lantern, unhitched the horses and floated onto the wooden driver's seat. Margaret watched from the doorway. She threw me a kiss with one hand and waved goodbye with the other. I cracked the whip and blithely left for home.

*   *   *   *

Early - June, 1845

Every day spent with Margaret was a glorious adventure into the realms of a blissful dream world. Our love blossomed and deepened with each day. I was decidedly her captive—in a welcomed bondage. Margaret and I spent countless hours together fishing, shell fishing or just sitting on the large boulders along the seashore. We also walked barefoot, hand-in-hand for miles along the flats and salt marshes. Sailing across the bay was sheer ecstasy with Margaret who insisted on shielding her face from the sun with a colorful parasol that matched her dainty frock. She was wary of tanning—afraid it would damage her skin and accelerate wrinkles. We enjoyed several excursions on horseback, riding along the shoreline of the bay and through neighboring wooded trails, bordered by dainty lady slippers and mayflowers. On exceptionally delightful days, Margaret and I traveled in an open carriage to Wellfleet and Provincetown to take pleasure in the sand dunes and panoramic views.

As the warm summer days approached, we waded in the pounding surf of the open ocean at Nauset Beach. If the weather was not conducive to outside activities we visited relatives in Chatham. We also enjoyed a friendly game of lawn croquet with family and friends. The green, grassy areas were usually surrounded at this time of year by colorful azaleas and rhododendrons in full bloom. Early evenings found us canoeing on the kettle ponds of Brewster and Harwich or finding the time to watch the sunsets over the bay. After dark, we were often lulled into a romantic mood by walking on the shoreline at high tide. We held each other close while we strolled under a full moon whose light brightened our surroundings and glimmered across the water.

We picnicked around the Mill Pond and Herring Run observing the deer feeding on the gently sloping hillsides. The alewives were on their annual drive to spawn. From shore to shore, the silvery herring, like an undulating gray ribbon—constantly moved upstream to the pond—jamming the tiny creek. Only the most purposeful and hardiest would reach their destination. I must admit I always admired the grit of that small, scaly clupeid.

When we found time to be together, we loved, laughed and played in unspoken joy at every opportunity. Our glorious, ardent relationship was one we wished would never end. It goes without saying—Margaret was spending more time with me than she was with Jonathan. Thoughts of a tryst with her flooded my mind day and night. How I ached to make her completely mine. She was an ethical, refined young lady and out of respect for her, I never exceeded my boundaries. I was at all times a gentleman in Margaret's presence.

Although I rationalized that I had been much too occupied to drop in on Jonathan—guilt was the true reason for my procrastination. Father had rightfully cautioned me against courting Margaret behind his back. Yet, it was exactly what I had been doing! "How can I face Jonathan and confess that Margaret and I are in love? I've deliberately taken her away from him. Will he understand that it was unavoidable? That it's simply something…that just happened between us. Will this admission end our friendship?" These thoughts and questions tormented me day and night. "I can't handle this deception any longer!…I must visit him tomorrow," I acknowledged. "I need to end this torment, and the sooner the better!"

The next morning was quite bleak—drizzly weather prevailed. Low, overcast clouds hid the sunlight. A steady, misty overnight rain had soaked the landscape. Occasional blustery winds caused the treetops to sway like oscillating jibs. It was so dark and dismal that I needed a lantern to maneuver the staircase to the kitchen. "Oh yes,…I almost forgot the Eldredge's oil lamp,…I must remember to return it. I've been too busy to do so before now. I'll take it along with me when I leave," I decided, stumbling around trying to find it. I lit the candles on the table and after locating the lantern, I placed it alongside the flickering candles. I helped myself to some porridge that was still simmering on the cast iron stove. It was mid-morning and except for the family cat curled up and sleeping on the rocker, I found myself virtually alone as everyone was off following his or her own agendas.

"Well,…I've no excuse. The weather's dreadful. I'm sure there'll be no outside activities for me, today. It's a perfect time to visit Jonathan," I reasoned, finishing my breakfast and placing my dish in the sink after rinsing it under the spigot.

Before I could change my mind, I hastily donned my jacket, plopped on my hat, and then bolted out the door with the lantern. Once outside, I decided to return for an umbrella. As I sauntered toward the Eldredge homestead through the scrub pine and cedar meadow, I kept rehearsing some well-chosen words and repeating them over and over in my mind. Again, as I had done many times before, I walked this familiar well-worn path where primrose starflowers sporadically burst forth from the forest floor. The long silence was occasionally shattered by a broken twig underfoot, the howling of the wind and the patter of rain as it echoed through the pines and oaks along the way.

I was inundated with anguished thoughts about my confrontation. "What will I say? If I don't make myself clear, his fragile ego could be gravely wounded…I must be forthright, yet tactful. My explanation mustn't sound arbitrary or defensive as that would alienate him altogether," I reasoned as I neared the saltbox cottage. The frequent wind gusts threatened to tear the umbrella and lantern from my grasp. I held the umbrella tightly with one hand and firmly clutched the lantern with the other.

I knocked on the door and waited. Missus Eldredge opened it, dried her hands on her apron, and then greeted me with a welcoming smile.

"Good morning, Missus Eldredge," I said, removing my hat and placing the wet umbrella inside the doorway. "I'm here to see Jonathan."

"Hello, Albert! Come right in. It's mighty nasty out there today," she said cordially, then pointing to the kitchen. "Jonathan's in there. I'm sure he'll be delighted to see you."

"This lantern belongs to Mister Eldredge," I said sheepishly. "He loaned it to me the night we arrived on the packet."

"Thank you, Albert. Just set it here," Missus Eldredge said, pointing to the entry table. "I'll be sure to let him know that you've returned it." While following behind her, I nervously fidgeted with my hat. "Jonathan's been expecting your visit for days now," she went on, turning the corner toward the kitchen. "Wait here while I let him know that you've arrived. I hope you can cheer him up a bit, Albert. He's been quite sharp and sullen lately…I just can't seem to figure out why."

"I've been meaning to stop by much sooner," I said, trying to apologize for my absence. "I should've been here long before now…I'll try to boost his spirits, Missus Eldredge," I added, feeling rather skeptical about doing that once I revealed the purpose of my visit.

"Dammit! What I'm going to tell him certainly won't help," I thought. "Maybe I shouldn't have come today." It was awkward and unsettling. I began to feel flushed and started to perspire. My first thought was to quickly run in the opposite direction. "Too late, Albert,…you can't turn back now! Pull yourself together!" I told myself. "It's now or never! I mustn't postpone this unpleasant task. I need to confront this right now! He'll be so upset to learn that Margaret doesn't love him in the same way he loves her,…and also the painful truth about *our* relationship," I agonized, shaking my head and following behind Jonathan's mother.

"Jonathan, Albert's here!" she announced. When I walked into the kitchen, Jonathan was facing the window. At the sound of her voice, he turned his wheelchair around to face me. "While you're here with him, I'll run to a neighbor's house," she said as she headed out the door. "I'll be back shortly." Missus Eldredge grabbed her umbrella, donned her coat, and then left.

"Hello, Jonathan! I'm sorry I haven't come sooner. I should have dropped by before now,…my visit's long overdue, dear friend. How are you, today?" I asked. However, before waiting for his reply I went on to say, "Your mother said you haven't been yourself lately. In a sense,…I feel responsible for that. I know how much Margaret's frequent visits mean to you. I must apologize for keeping her so preoccupied since I've been home."

"Though I anticipated your visit days ago,…it's nice to see you again, Albert," he said with a poignant expression and extending his hand to mine. "Mother's right. I guess I haven't been very sociable these past few weeks. I've truly missed Margaret's company. She does, however, drop in once in a while to check on me, but she's usually rushing off somewhere." Jonathan's chin began to quiver and tears welled in his eyes. "I know I should be appreciative, but it's as if she's just making an effort to see me out of a sense of duty. If you must know, Albert, I feel like an ingrate…and I'm downright uncomfortable about that," he went on, looking away from me to hide his tears.

I pulled up a chair, sat facing him, and then took both his hands in mine. "Jonathan, please look at me," I said, trying to be candid and composed. I knew I would have to tread *very* carefully, right now. "The main purpose of this visit is to explain what has innocently transpired between Margaret and me. Actually, it's been the reason for my delayed visit. I know you love her deeply, that's why I fear what I have to say will be quite painful for you."…I hesitated then single-mindedly persisted to blurt out the truth, albeit reluctantly. "Margaret and I fell in love with each other when we first met, Jonathan." He looked at me intently and wide-eyed, the expression on his face—pale and grim. I noticed he began to fidget and tremble, fearing my next sentence.

"Jonathan," I went on, "because we care so much for you, neither one of us would disclose our mutual love. Although it was intensely personal, our feelings eventually manifested themselves. Ultimately, we had to be completely honest about that. Please try to understand that we never intended to hurt you. That's the last thing we wanted to do. Nevertheless, I did reach a point when it was necessary to know exactly how she felt about you. Then, and only then was the truth of the matter revealed. Margaret said she loved you,…but like a dear brother. She added that she had made no pretense about her feelings for you. She was fond of you and that satisfied her desire to be needed and loved…until I unexpectedly entered her life. Now, Margaret says she realizes the difference between what it's like to love…and to be *in* love."

"Are you finished? Must I listen to what you have to tell me? Your insipid excuses are drivel and of little value…frankly, it's demeaning and embarrassing!" he shouted, removing his hands from mine, lashing out and airing his pent up anger. "Don't you think I know what's been going on behind my back? You betrayed me! You violated my trust and dishonored our friendship!" He was incensed and shaken by my words as he questioned my sincerity. I believe he would have thrashed me with both fists had he not been confined to a wheelchair. Frustrated by his inability to fight back, Jonathan quickly turned his wheelchair around and again faced the window.

"I've already been told about your relationship with Margaret. Although it's discreetly hushed up when I'm around, your indiscretions are the subject of the latest gossip in town! For God's sake, Albert!…Don't you know that? I planned to attend a concert in Barnstable and wanted Margaret to accompany me there, so I stopped by the Hopkins' homestead last week. Abigail tactfully tried to tell me that Margaret was not home at the time, and that she'd been with you almost every day since you dined there. That confirmed my suspicions about you and Margaret. You can't imagine what it's been like hearing about the two of you together at every opportunity. You stole her affection from me, you scoundrel!…And you call yourself my friend! Why,…you hypocrite! You're no friend of mine! I'll curse you 'til I die, Albert!" he shouted furiously, becoming malevolent and hostile.

I endured his ire and the humiliating loss of integrity as he vehemently hurled those scathing words in my direction—they were torturous for me. I was aware that his despondency was acerbated by his infirmity. For this reason, I felt deserving of his enmity and submissively tolerated his volatile insults. Nevertheless, I had *had* enough of his diatribe!

"Goddammit, Jonathan! You've got it all wrong…It wasn't that way at all!" I shouted back defensively. "Somehow I sensed you were aware of our need to be together, and I'm also sure you guessed the reason why. I'm sorry you can't accept that! I should've come sooner and been the first one to tell you," I went on to say in a more subdued tone of voice. "That's my only mistake,…and I apologize for that. You shouldn't have had to guess about what was going on between us.

"You mustn't torture yourself over this any longer, Jonathan. The truth is, we're both very much in love. In fact, we've decided to marry in the near future. I have you to thank for that. I would never have met Margaret had it not been for you. I never thought I'd ever find true love again after losing Rebecca. I've never made any unsolicited advances toward her and I assure you, Jonathan, we haven't been intimate. I hold her in the highest respect! Please believe me! We know you feel we've wronged you, yet ours is a genuine and lasting love. Margaret and I never intended to hurt you." I stood and turned toward the door. "Jonathan, I'll leave you now before I upset you further."

"No,...wait Albert! Please,...please stay!" he pleaded, turning his wheelchair around. Puzzled by his about-face, I cautiously approached him. "I must admit I was totally out of line! I knew better than to accuse you of deliberately taking Margaret away from me." He unexpectedly lowered his voice and spoke in a more repentant tone. "Please forgive my outburst. I don't know why I reacted the way I did. I don't know what to say...I'm truly ashamed. You're my best friend and always will be. I can't hold you accountable for what's happened between you and Margaret. It isn't your fault or anyone else's for that matter. I know you always had my best interests at heart. I've deliberately evaded the obvious. The truth is, Albert,...I was jealous of you and also vengeful because of my unrequited love for Margaret. I guess I just needed to vent all that pent up anger. I'm sorry you had to bear the brunt of it.

"I've been so annoyed with myself lately, blaming all the wrongs in my life on my handicap. I'm bitter and impatient with everyone and everything. Somehow that inner peace that everyone claimed would eventually fill my essence has eluded me. I'm afraid I've become too dependent on Margaret. I relied on her to provide me with the happiness and self-confidence that I just can't seem to find on my own. Without her, I don't feel complete or fulfilled. I'm consumed by a loss of self-esteem and indescribable sorrow. As far as I'm concerned, Margaret might just as well have died...I just can't go on without her. The thought terrifies me, Albert...She's my whole world,...the love of my life.

"Like you, I loved Margaret from the moment I set eyes on her. I was ready to ask for her hand in marriage before you came along. Sadly, I wasn't able to muster up enough courage to pose the question. I'm keenly aware of her filial feelings for me, Albert, but I hoped with time she'd eventually learn to love me...the same way she does you.

"Even though I love Margaret more than life itself,…love is all I can give her. She deserves more than that! Much more! There's no way I can be both husband and lover to her. I can't father children, let alone support them in my condition," he acknowledged, looking down at his useless torso and legs. "You're able to give her all those things and more, everything that's needed for a happy marriage…I can't! It was selfish of me to think only of my needs.

"I suppose, after all these years, I just didn't want to lose her," he said with a sigh as his voice began to crack. He bit his lips, but his previously restrained tears began to flow freely down his cheeks. "I cherish each and every moment with Margaret. She was free to choose,…and she chose you. I must learn to accept that. I know that after she leaves me, I'll feel an overwhelming emptiness for a while. It's her devotion and companionship that I'll miss the most! Even though it may be difficult at first, I hope I'll learn to live with that and manage without her…I might even become accustomed to it. Now, you're not to be concerned about that, Albert,…you hear?" he said resolutely, pointing his index finger at me.

"My parents are extremely doting and attentive. They're so thankful that I survived that terrible accident. I must admit I don't always share their sentiment." Again, he stared down at his useless, lower limbs. He heaved a deep sigh and added, "I often wish I had died instead of being left like this."

"Please don't say that, Jonathan." I replied compassionately, bending down to gently rub his arm. "We love you, dearly. Your loss would have been devastating to all of us. Please remember that when you're feeling depressed about your paralysis."

"Albert, with all due respect, I want you to know that I understand your dilemma and appreciate your honesty," he admitted. "I can't blame you for falling in love with Margaret. I did so myself. It's perfectly clear that you're the one she wants…I can't criticize her, or you, for that matter. In the end, I must accept her choice. Margaret's true happiness is the only thing that concerns me now. Please tell her that for me. Actually, if she had to fall in love with someone,…I'm pleased that it's with *you*, Albert! You have my blessing, dear friend. Do promise me you'll always treat her kindly, be sensitive to her needs and cherish her as you would a priceless gem. You lucky fellow!" Jonathan said with a forced smile. He pounded his left fist on my arm and extended his right hand in a final handshake. As soon as I noticed his eyes were tearing again, he quickly turned his wheelchair around.

"Goodbye, Albert," he murmured with his back toward me. He held on to the wheels of his chair and proceeded to rapidly propel it forward. "Before you leave for Chicago, do try to visit me again and take Margaret with you," he went on as he pushed himself out of the kitchen and into the hallway toward his bedroom. "That is, whenever it's convenient for you to do so."

"Yes, we'll do that, Jonathan!" I replied, turning and walking in the opposite direction toward the back entrance. I knew—I would never keep that promise. That would have been like rubbing salt into a wound.

It was almost noon. Exhausted by this confrontation, I mindlessly lifted my umbrella, hat and jacket from the coat rack. While pondering Jonathan's initial antagonism and eventual conciliatory overtures, I quickly put them on and left. Although we had finally resolved our differences in an amicable way, my psyche was tormented and laden with a potpourri of mixed feelings. I felt nauseous. My stomach, like a boiling caldron, was rife with the seasonings of relief, doubt and guilt. They churned turbulently amidst the main ingredients—apprehension, admission and complacency.

The wind and drizzle had abated, but it was still a murky, cheerless day. As I left the Eldredge home, I took a deep breath welcoming the fresh salt air. Totally absorbed in my own thoughts, I placed the umbrella securely under my arm and leisurely walked along the deserted path. The rain gave way to an avian symphony of sorts. The robins, catbirds, cardinals and orioles raised their cheery tunes from nests high in the trees above and in the brushy corners of nearby shrubs. This source of uplifting serenity gradually embraced me with a deep intrinsic sense of well-being. I felt like an enormous weight had been lifted from my shoulders. On that short journey home—nature had subtly revived my troubled body and soul.

▼

With a $10,000 voucher in my pocket, Father and I sailed to Boston. I ultimately received the needed financial backing for my business venture from my uncles. Their confidence in my abilities reflected the many positive aspects of my personality—honesty, tenacity and perceptiveness.

Father insisted on escorting me on my quest. He took the time from his busy schedule to help me formulate a carefully thought-out inventory and list of supplies. How I hated to leave the Cape, particularly Brewster, at this time of the year. Summer was my favorite season. The temperature of the bay waters warmed with each day, and conditions for the many outdoor activities I enjoyed would be excellent for at least another two months. As the packet docked at Rowes Wharf in Boston Harbor, the excitement of beginning my new enterprise prevailed over my angst.

"Well, son, we'll take this carriage directly to the breweries and later to the wholesalers for the wines and teas. Hurry, Albert, before someone else hails him!" he shouted. Father energetically waved his cane trying to get the attention of the driver who instantly spotted us as we neared him. While Father gave him directions, the coachman opened the carriage doors for us and we were soon headed for the commercial district of the North End. Father was familiar with this part of the city as he had been here many times before. I had visited Boston with him during the summer of my tenth year.

At that time, an exposition on the shores of the Charles River had drawn people to New England from all over the world. Father provided the admission fee and money to buy souvenirs, food and drink. He made me promise to be at a specific location after looking at his pocket watch and noting the time he would return for me. I spent the whole day on my own enjoying the various exhibits while he went about his business affairs. I managed to find my way into a majority of the tents where intriguing works of art, unique sculptures and strange artifacts from many foreign countries were displayed. It was the first time I was allowed to be on my own among so many people. It was an incredible experience—one I have never forgotten.

Father was personally acquainted with all the merchants whom he regularly patronized. Earlier in the week, so as to familiarize myself with them, we visited their establishments. He earned quite a reputation for being an honorable, yet astute businessman. His experience was the primary reason he wanted to accompany me. I valued his assistance. Father wanted to be certain I would receive the same courtesy and respect he was accustomed to over the years. Secondly, he was also concerned about the quality of my purchases. His goal was to secure the finest grades for the least amount of money. Father proudly introduced me as his son, Albert, then continued to bargain for almost every product I needed in a most professional way.

The proprietor of a wholesale company we frequented was a rather squatty gentleman who wore a pair of metal-rimmed spectacles. They were set low on his nose and partially hidden under gray, bushy eyebrows. The owner, who had a few sparse strands of hair over his balding head, also had a matching handlebar mustache and a thick beard that reminded me of a well-worn broom. "Well, I must say you've grown up to be quite a fine young man, Albert. Why, I remember when you were no higher than that stool over there," he said in a gravelly voice while pointing to it, crooking his neck upward to focus on my face and exposing a mouthful of gold teeth. "So you're going into the mercantile business,...are you? Well,...I wish you much success, young man! If you've been lucky enough to inherit even a tad of your Father's gumption and savoir-faire,...you can't fail! For that reason, I'll try to accommodate you as best I can. Your requests will receive top priority. Nathan's one of my most valued clients."

"Thank you, sir. I truly appreciate that," I replied, shaking his hand. "If all goes well,...I also hope to be a frequent customer of yours."

It took the better part of two weeks to fill my orders and make arrangements for its storage. The goods would be warehoused until I would eventually take possession of them in the future. We stayed at a nearby inn. Each day after breakfast we expeditiously set out to acquire all the items listed on my inventory. Similar to walking on a hot stove, the cobblestone streets radiated the heat of a blaring sun. I looked for refuge from the oppressive, debilitating humidity of the city. How I yearned for the cool breezes and the refreshing waters of the bay.

"Father, I'm so grateful for all your help," I said appreciatively, wishing him farewell as he boarded a returning packet to Brewster. "I'll be leaving for West Roxbury in the morning. I intend to ask Margaret's parents for her hand in marriage. I'm hoping to include her in my plans to move to Chicago after we wed. If I'm accepted as a suitable husband for their daughter,...and I have little doubt about that, you'll most likely attend a wedding in the spring. In the meantime, I'll return to Brewster...if time allows. I'll be sure to keep you informed. Goodbye, Father. Do take care of yourself. Give my love and regards to Mother and the girls. I'll miss everyone at the homestead. Have a safe trip home." I shook his hand and gave him a quick hug.

"We'll miss you, too," Father said wistfully, returning my show of affection by lovingly grasping me by the shoulder. "Well,...you're on your own from now on. Good luck to you, son. I'm sure you'll do well. And, oh, by the way,...my best wishes to you and Margaret! Goodbye, Albert!" he shouted, waving back after being helped on board by a steward. It was obvious that he was eager to leave the ear-splitting din and mayhem of the city. He looked forward to the tranquility of Cape Cod and being with his family.

∗   ∗   ∗   ∗

Late-July, 1846

The next morning, I checked out of the downtown-lodging house and hailed a coach for West Roxbury. Margaret had been expecting me for several weeks now. After reluctantly saying farewell to Jonathan, she returned home. Although Abigail understood Margaret's position, she was disappointed to see her leave so abruptly. Once our romantic alliance was out in the open, Margaret felt ill at ease being in Jonathan's presence. She decided to leave Brewster, not only for her sake, but especially for Jonathan's. Our friendship with him, precarious though it had been these last few months, had not been irrevocably impaired. He seemed to have survived the impact to his self-esteem. Margaret also intended to announce our engagement to her parents and prepare them for my scheduled visit to their home.

"What will Margaret's parents think of me? Will I live up to the lofty standards they've set for the suitor of their beloved daughter? Will they accept me as their future son-in-law?" I asked myself. "At this stage in my life, I really don't have much to offer her. Will they have as much faith in me and my future...as I have in myself? I'll try to be explicit about how I intend to support Margaret and impress upon them my determination to succeed. I must remember to discuss my business venture with an air of confidence. I hope my sincerity will be convincing." All these speculative thoughts and questions filled my mind as the carriage rode along the cobblestone roadways of Commonwealth Avenue and Newbury Street toward my destination.

While mindlessly gazing from the carriage window, I couldn't help noticing my surroundings with a mixture of curiosity and awe. The horses trotted past long blocks of two-and three-story brick and brownstone buildings. Although these picturesque row houses were similar in architecture and style, each had its own particular characteristic and unique visual richness. The patrician facades were ornately constructed in baroque variations of Georgian, Spanish, Romanesque or European design. Some were constructed with red brick, others with gray, white or various other shades of brownstone. The diversity seemed endless. The large bay windows were elaborately shuttered. Several granite steps led to opulent, distinctive front entrances that reflected the care and pride of their aristocratic occupants. Climbing rose bushes in full bloom were copiously twined around the demarcating iron fencing—their colors carefully selected to compliment the home behind it.

West Roxbury, a suburban, residential area to the south of Boston was home to some of the most prosperous and socially elite Bostonians. Enormous family homes loomed pretentiously behind extensive green, rolling lawns. These bordered the main streets on both sides—one estate more imposing than the next.

"Please stop here!" I shouted as I caught a glimpse of the correct address. We approached an enormous, white clapboard, Greek revival mansion replete with cornerstones, a brick front wall and a hipped roof. I checked the address again. Yes, this was Margaret's grandiose residence. I quickly descended and paid the coachman. He handed me the large carpetbag that I had taken for my trip. I turned toward the walkway to the front entrance. An exuberant Margaret was already out the door flashing a heartwarming smile. She was excitedly waving her arms as she bolted in my direction.

"Albert! Albert! You're actually here! I can't believe my eyes!" she exclaimed animatedly, rushing toward me with open arms and tears of pure joy. "I've been anticipating your arrival for days now. Oh, how I've missed you." She caressingly embraced and kissed me—unhampered by onlookers—be they family, staff or neighbors.

"I've also missed you my dear, sweet, Margaret…More than you'll ever know. I've been counting the days until I'd be with you, again," I replied, delighted by the sight of her and the closeness of her body next to mine. We kissed passionately until we discovered we were being observed, then we walked arm-in-arm toward her magnificent home. "I didn't realize you lived in such elegant surroundings. It's incredible!" I declared, pointing to the prodigious structure ahead. "Honestly,...I'm a little embarrassed. Why, our unpretentious Crosby cottage can't compare to this. You never let on about the size and grandeur of your home, and well,..." I hesitated, uneasy about this unfamiliar environment and feeling a bit like a fish out of water,..."I thank you for *that*, Margaret."

"Oh, Albert. Don't be so foolish." she said, giggling and pressing her index finger to my lips. "I'd exchange all of this for what you have...a wonderful family, a cozy home filled with loving parents and the priceless beauty of Brewster and the bay. As you well know, Abigail's my only sibling. She's married with a family of her own and lives so far away from me...I'm extremely lonely here. That's why I so enjoyed my vacations on the Cape. Most of the time, Father's away tending to his banking business in Boston and...Mother's usually busy presiding over her social and philanthropic functions," she went on dismayed by her lot in life. "For that matter, no one's home at the moment; however, Mother should be arriving any minute now. She'll be disappointed to learn that she wasn't here to greet you," Margaret said, opening a large screened door.

We stood under a delicate, crystal chandelier in the middle of a grand entryway. The foyer was dominated on the right and left by the curved, welcoming banisters of two spiral staircases that soared to a second level. "I've told my parents all about you. They heartily approve of my decision to marry the handsome gentleman from Brewster," she went on, grinning and pinching my cheek. "Come, Albert,...let me show you to your room so you can freshen up. I'll let the maidservants know you've arrived. Another place setting will be needed for you this evening." We ascended the right staircase that led to a long hallway.

Throughout Margaret's home, inlaid of ornately carved, walnut-finished paneling, held a diverse assortment of art-works. About half way down the corridor we stopped and stood before the partially opened door of a richly furnished bedroom.

"I'm so happy. I feel I'm about ready to burst. Having you near, after seemingly endless weeks of longing, is so incredibly glorious," she declared, standing in the doorway with her head on my shoulder. "I'm never letting you out of my sight again, my darling...I love you so!" We kissed feverishly until I released my grip from around her tiny waist.

I had an overwhelming urge to immediately carry her to the bed and make love to her before anyone came home. I know she experienced those same erotic vibrations because she blushed, put her head down, and then albeit loath to do so, she deliberately let go of my hand. As had happened many times before, the need to consummate and satisfy our sexual yearnings for each other inevitably surfaced again. Nothing needed to be said. I knew she wanted me as much as I wanted her. Margaret quickly closed the door and sensuously began to unfasten the tiny pearl buttons that secured the bodice of her dress. She removed her outer garment and enticingly allowed it to fall to the floor—revealing her laced up corset, brassiere, full breasts and petticoat. Needless to say, I instantly reacted to her enticement. Although completely startled by her sudden lack of decorum, I delighted in her initiative and impromptu attempt to seduce me. Grasping my hand again and running toward the bed, she quickly untied her dirndl and had just disposed of her pantalets, when we heard a resonant and inquiring voice call out from below.

"Hello! Margaret,…I'm home! Are you upstairs?"

"Oh, Lord! It's Mother!" Margaret exclaimed, gesturing wildly and whispering with a "caught-with-my-hand-in-the-cookie-jar" look. She quietly unlatched the door and spoke through the opening while reaching for her dress. Moving quickly, she placed it over her head, pulled it over her half-naked torso, and then nervously fastened the buttons. Margaret hurriedly opened a draw and tossed her undergarments into it.

"We'll be right down, Mother!" Margaret shouted back "I've just given Albert the grand tour of the house! Right now I'm helping him unpack his clothing!"

"I'll wait for you in the front parlor!" Madam Henderson yelled back, her voice fading as she retreated to the sitting room. "I had some tea and pastries brought in. Do come down before it cools."

"Whew! That was a little too close for comfort," I whispered after exhaling a deep breath and wiping my brow. "I certainly would've started off on the wrong foot with your family had your mother decided to quietly come upstairs and find us in a compromising position. We'll have to choose a more opportune time to make love, my sweet." We kissed, made a quick exit, and then hastily walked down the hallway—silently snickering as we headed for the staircase.

William and Mary Henderson, Margaret's socially prominent parents accepted me with open arms and readily announced our engagement to family and friends.

"The Crosby's are fine Yankee stock," Mister Henderson disclosed when asked about my social status and background. "Native Cape Codders from way back. Why, Albert's mother is a…Nickerson. You can't find better lineage than that," he acknowledged proudly. I felt like I was being likened to a thoroughbred stallion.

William Henderson was an exceptionally handsome man, who stood a whole head over me. His impeccably trimmed, graying side burns and beard gave him a distinguished cavalier demeanor. He spoke the King's English with mastery and perfect diction. Fully articulate, his slim mustache rose and fell with each crisply enunciated word. Mister Henderson was a sedate gentleman, who although—considered a functioning alcoholic—held his liquor quite well and never slurred his words or appeared to be tipsy. He wore a different suit and starched shirt every day. Attached to his matching vest was a gold chain from which dangled a bejeweled pocket watch. While conversing, he intermittently removed it from his vest pocket to check the time. I suppose it was a habit he developed because of his many appointments with banking clientele. I concluded that Margaret had inherited her father's noble personality and mannerisms. She certainly could *not* be compared to her mother.

Mary (Radcliff) Henderson was a hefty matron of average height. Her sedately styled, brindled colored hair was parted in the middle and tied tightly behind her head in a large bun that was secured by a long, elaborate stylus pick. She was an intelligent and well-educated woman—yet extremely arrogant and domineering. Margaret's mother demanded the biggest and best of everything and was accustomed to getting her own way.

Madam Henderson blared orders to everyone from morning to night and ruled the household with an iron fist. I shied away when she spoke disrespectfully to subordinates, be they servants, housemaids, butlers, gardeners or handymen. She sometimes fired them on the spot. One handyman who had a large family was dismissed for a minor infraction. Any breakage or oversight would be an excuse to garnish their wages. Madam lashed out at her hirelings with ethnic slurs that depredated their race, nationality or religion. If it took place in my presence—I was embarrassed for her. Many were acquainted with her bigotry toward others not of her ethnic background. She had difficulty retaining competent help because of her jarring and sarcastic, verbal insults. The staff was quick to express relief when she was absent from the household.

Margaret's mother, I often recalled after meeting her, would have been the perfect target for one of the Reverend Ebenezer Farnsworth's hell and damnation sermons. The minister shouted his admonition from the pulpit in ear-piercing peals while looking straight into the expressionless, golem faces of his congregation. He would menacingly shake his head and point directly at them and scream, "You, sitting out there in those pews! You know who you are! You're nothing but self-righteous, arrogant hypocrites! Your wretchedness pours out of you like vomit." The parishioners would listen transfixed. "Jesus, commanded you to love thy neighbor as thyself. His "Good Samaritan" parable about the battered traveler clearly defines this precept. You'd better mend your ways toward your fellow man or the devil will certainly claim your soul!...You'll burn in hell for all eternity!" His sanctimonious preaching never really fazed anyone because they inevitably assumed it was directed at someone else.

I personally stayed out of Madam's way, avoiding her sharp tongue like the plague. She was especially obnoxious at supper, either berating the service, the food or the housecleaning.

"Why didn't you come when I rang the bell? Bring this roast back to the kitchen!...It's overcooked! The silverware's tarnished and the crystal goblets are cloudy!" she would holler, throwing the silver on the meat platter, spattering the juices and frightening the poor servant girl to death. I purposefully sat at the opposite end of the table next to Margaret and her father, contributing little to the conversation. When informed about something or someone, she had a habit of mumbling "uh-huh" in a most annoying way. In comparison to the pleasant repast in the Crosby kitchen where love and warmth ruled, the tense, critical atmosphere of the Henderson household—particularly at mealtimes—cast an icy spell that inevitably led to a loss of appetite.

Although manipulative and controlling, Mary Henderson idolized her youngest daughter. She frequently called Margaret, "Princess." In Madam's estimation she was absolute perfection. She pampered Margaret and often eyed her with approving smiles and glances. I began to surmise that Abigail hadn't lived up to Madam's standards and had endured some demeaning behavior and remarks from her mother. Abigail's feelings of insecurity and lack of confidence were most likely the reasons behind her timorous behavior. I wondered why Margaret had not assimilated some of her mother's arrogance over the years—however, as I previously noted she emulated her father.

Madam Henderson kept William at a distance. In fact, they had separate bedrooms at opposite ends of the house. My bedroom was also in that wing. He was informed after the birth of their second daughter that he was no longer allowed in her quarters. While I lived there, they had some heated shouting matches. Mister Henderson would usually throw up his hands, resign himself to her endless badgering, and then immediately leave the house. I wondered why they stayed together. "A marriage of convenience," I concluded, suspecting the wealth enjoyed by the Hendersons was originally inherited from the Radcliff side of the family—thus the reason for her haughty aura and blatant disregard of her husband and common folk. I thanked God she deemed me socially equal and worthy of marrying her precious daughter, Margaret.

Nevertheless, I had serious misgivings about a conversation I overheard one evening, several months after my arrival. After conducting business in Boston pertaining to my venture, my carriage usually dropped me off at the side entrance. On one late afternoon, however, because of a fierce nor'easter, I decided to use the front entrance—taking advantage of the overhanging canopy roof. I heard people speaking in the sitting room while removing my hat and coat. I hung them on the coat rack as the sound of the howling wind reverberated inside the foyer. When I approached the source of the voices, I recognized them to be that of Margaret and her mother. I assumed my arrival had not been noticed.

"They're probably having afternoon tea," I concluded. "I won't disturb them. I'll go up to my room and change." As I ascended the first step I heard my name mentioned and abruptly stopped to listen.

"Albert's persistence in becoming a successful entrepreneur in Chicago is irresponsible...It's complete foolishness and nothing short of fantasy. I hope you realize that, Margaret," Madam Henderson said. Her cautious disapproval had been well rehearsed. "Who's to say...he'll be successful? He's a nice enough fellow, I guess. Nevertheless, I think you could have chosen a gentleman with a more stable future, not someone with such impossible goals and ideals. Selling liquors and teas is below him. He should have a more dignified profession,...one similar to your father's. It's absolutely foolhardy on his part to assume you'll join him in that godforsaken city of Chicago. From what I hear, it's positively uncivilized, impoverished and downright ugly! You'll undoubtedly despise everything about that place. Among other things, it's devoid of paved streets...gaslights and running water,...all the amenities you're so accustomed to here in the East. I suggest you instill a sense of accountability in that young man before he drags you along with him down a path of indigence and into the dregs of that awful city. I'll worry so about you, my dear. I don't want you to get harried and despondent like, Abigail. Promise me, Margaret, you'll try to convince him that this brash scheme of his is absolute nonsense...that he should stay right here in West Roxbury with you and your family!"

"Why,...that bitch!" I cursed silently. Enraged by her deprecating words, I was tempted to bolt into the room and strangle her. "She's trying to undermine everything I consider sacred...my marriage and my future." Just then, Margaret challenged her tirade.

"Oh, Mother, I appreciate your concern for my welfare,...however, I love Albert dearly and would follow him to the ends of the earth if need be," she said in an assertive tone of voice. "He's thoroughly outlined every aspect of his upcoming business venture with me. Albert's confident that Chicago offers unlimited commercial opportunities for someone willing to expend money and hard work. I support his efforts, and hope I'll be an asset to him. As for Chicago itself," she went on, "I'll just have to make it my home, regardless of the inconveniences. I want you to know, Mother,…I have *no* intention of trying to discourage him from his plans. In fact, I applaud his stance to be independent and his resolve to seek his fortune away from family and friends. Please don't pursue this subject any further. I'm deeply offended by your suggestion. My mind is made up. Albert's the man I love and the one I will marry for better *or* for worse."

"Hello!…I'm home!" I shouted, seething inside and purposefully making a racket by slamming the front door and pretending I had just made my entrance.

"We're here in the sitting room, Albert!" Margaret called back. "Do join us for a hot cup of tea."

"No, thank you, my dear," I replied. "I think I'll retreat to my room to change and rest. It's been a long, tiring day for me. I'll join you later this evening for supper."

As I quietly ascended the carpeted staircase, I felt maligned. I was angered by Madam Henderson's harmful and devious words—piercing daggers that assassinated my character and aspirations. I despondently shook my head and hoped she hadn't planted the seeds of doubt in my lover's mind. I saw a future more bleak than I could possibly have imagined. I knew now what I was up against. Margaret would eventually have to make a difficult choice. Would she choose to join me or ultimately decide to remain here with her family? Nevertheless, Margaret's defiance reaffirmed her love for me. I was proud of her determination to be by my side, regardless of her mother's derogatory admonitions.

*   *   *   *

Early-December, 1846

"I have a position open for you at the bank," William Henderson announced after supper one evening while we were in the smoking room. "I know you'll eventually leave for Chicago, but in the meantime, I can keep you productively occupied as an officer at the bank. I hope you won't mind my being presumptuous about your future. I firmly believe that once you've experienced banking as an honorable profession and learned its financial benefits, you'll eventually change your mind and make it your life's work. Why, you may even decide to remain in West Roxbury."

"Thank you, sir," I said somewhat taken aback by his offer and wondering if Margaret had had anything to do with it. "I don't know what to say…I'm at a loss for words. It's very thoughtful of you to provide me with work until I'm ready to be on my own. I truly appreciate your efforts on my behalf. When do I start, sir?"

"Why as soon as you'd like," he replied, putting his arm around my shoulder in an attempt to make me feel more at ease. "How about joining me in my carriage on Monday, Albert? That's as good a day as any to begin your new position. However, we'll need to purchase some additional apparel for you. I'll take you to my haberdashery and have my tailor fit you with a new wardrobe."

"That's mighty generous of you, Mister Henderson. I can't thank you enough," I repeated gratefully. "I'm sure Margaret will be delighted to have me stay in West Roxbury until we marry…instead of my having to commute back and forth from Brewster."

"My sentiments indeed," agreed Mister Henderson, rising from his chair, dousing his pipe, and then setting it on an ashtray. He left the room with his glass of rum while I stood there still trying to assess the discussion that had just taken place. I was now unwittingly employed in banking. "This arrangement could be useful to me," I thought. "I must try to gain from this experience and learn all I can. There may be a time when I'll be able to apply this knowledge to my advantage." As luck would have it—the effort was worthwhile. My apprenticeship in William Henderson's financial institution did serve me quite well in the future.

My first day at the Federal Bank of Boston was an eye-opening experience. I was cordially introduced as William Henderson's future son-in-law. My desk was in close proximity to his office door. Several times a day, a buxom, young woman, only a few years older than his daughters, entered his office with an official-looking writing tablet. She closed the door behind her and stayed for long periods of time. I was told she was his private secretary.

I soon began to suspect the obvious. Miss Caroline Hobbs, I discovered, was the apparent reason for his manifested indifference toward female companionship. Mister Henderson often claimed he would have to work late, compelling him to remain in the city overnight. I often returned to West Roxbury with that message for Madam Henderson. He was leading a double life—engaged in a long standing affair that was discreetly hidden from all—save his banking associates and close friends. If Mary Henderson was intuitively dubious about his excuse or perceived his extramarital dalliances—she never let on. Truthfully, she couldn't have cared less. Rumors had it that years later he died of a fatal stroke while making love to his young mistress. I dare say, I never labeled him "evil" simply because he had my sympathies, and I could relate to his rationale—the need for a loving and compassionate woman.

A formal engagement photo of Margaret graced the society page of the *Boston Herald.* Our wedding date was set for the end of May 1847, and was to take place at a prestigious site in Newport, Rhode Island. Margaret's parents had long decided that our marriage would be performed in the same church where they married before moving to Nova Scotia. Phillip Radcliff, Madam Henderson's wealthy and socially prominent brother insisted that our wedding reception take place at the 48-room Radcliff Mansion. This palatial Italian Renaissance granite structure on 35 acres with a view that overlooked Rhode Island Sound would easily accommodate the hundreds of guests invited. It was to be the social event of the decade. Many sea captains and influential people representing every profession imaginable and traveling from all parts of the Eastern Seaboard, Cape Cod and the Islands were expected to attend.

*   *   *   *

Late-May, 1847

"Margaret, I've misplaced my cuff links!" I complained loudly while nervously groping around the sideboard and fearing that I clumsily dropped them somewhere and irritated at myself for being so careless.

"They're here, Albert!" she hollered. "You left them on the dining room table."

"Oh, yes, I remember now," I replied, approaching her in a more composed tone of voice. "I'm sorry. Please forgive my impatience. You know, my dear,…it's not everyday one gets married. Believe me, I couldn't be happier, but all these fussy clothes and endless preparations have me fretful and edgy." I reached for my black onyx cuff links—a monogrammed gift from Margaret and began to push them through the cuffs of my shirt. My hands were shaking as I fumbled with this supposedly simple chore. I dropped one to the floor. Margaret bent to pick it up.

"I'll help you with that," she volunteered, slipping one cuff link in the shirt cuff and fastening the other. "You must hurry, Albert. The minister will be waiting for you. He plans to give you a few last-minute instructions before the wedding ceremony begins. Be on your way now, my love. Besides, I need time to be corseted and dressed in my petticoats and wedding gown. It'll also take a while longer before the finishing touches to my ensemble are completed to my satisfaction. You know, my dear,…it's not everyday one gets married," she said glibly, giggling and kissing me quickly while pinching my cheek. "And *you* think you've had a difficult time of it! Mother and Abigail will assist me. Go now! The family carriage is waiting," she said, embracing me tightly, not really wanting me to leave. "See you in church my darling, Albert. Your Cousin Uranus will already be there and,…most likely all your family members."

"Oh, Albert! I love you so. I can't wait to be Missus Albert Crosby! I shiver in delight at the very thought of it. I get goose bumps all over. Look!…I've got them right now," she said, lifting her sleeves and showing me her forearm. With one hand already on the doorknob and ready to leave, I kissed her hand, her arm, and then continued all the way up to her cheek and lips. I finally pulled myself away, opened the door and gasped!

There directly under the entrance colonnade was a luxurious, gilded coach suitable for royalty. Margaret's father had hired a regal white carriage to take the wedding party to the church and back again. And there, too—was Japeth. He had been asked to be the chauffeur and he readily accepted. One of the many family carriages that was scheduled to take me to the church was waiting directly behind him. I had found time to chat with him a few hours earlier while he tended to the horses and their finery.

"Japeth, how nice to see you again," I said at the time. I shook his hand and firmly embraced him. "I was delighted when they told me that you had accepted the duty of coachman for our bridal carriage. Did the Missus and family accompany you and Aaron, here? How are you, dear friend? How are your wife and children?" I asked. "I hope everyone's well. I've truly missed you, Japeth."

"I'm doing fine, Albert," Japeth replied, resuming his task of brushing the horse's manes and tails. "Why, I considered it an honor to be asked, especially when Aaron was approached to be an usher. I remember having the privilege of driving Anne's bridal carriage to the church. You were just a young sprout then,…ushering with Jonathan. As we've all said before, your family and I are quite proud of the genteel, upstanding adult you've become."

"Thank you, Japeth. Yes,…I certainly remember Anne's wedding," I said, finding a wooden box to sit on while we chatted. "This time,…I'm the groom. How quickly the years have passed."

"The Missus wasn't able to come because Nathaniel has smallpox," Japeth went on to say. "He's on the mend, but Victoria felt she must remain at home with him. Abigail arrived with the Eldredge family. As you must know by now, her husband, Angus, is on one of his fishing excursions. I also understand that Jonathan wasn't up to the long trip. He's been ailing again. The winter took quite a toll on his fragile health. He sent his wedding present along with his family. I believe it's an oil painting of the Stony Brook. Jonathan said he purposefully selected that particular scenic area because it portrayed a very special place. He said,...'You'd know why'."

"I'm so sorry to hear that Jonathan's not feeling well," I replied, deeply concerned about his health. "I hoped he would've been able to attend my wedding. My dear friend will be sorely missed. His absence will be disappointing to both Margaret and me,...but I understand. I'll certainly treasure the painting. In any case, I'm happy that Nathaniel is recovering from his smallpox. You must cherish that adorable child. Why, he must be almost five now! I'll see you on our return trip from the wedding ceremony, Japeth," I added, taking my leave and waving farewell. "Take good care of my bride. I leave her in your capable hands. I'll be on my way to the church in a few hours, but I wanted to chat with you before I left. Farewell, dear friend."

Now, I waved my hand in Japeth's direction as he sat waiting to drive Margaret and her attendants to the wedding. With my hand still on the doorknob, I looked back at Margaret. From the opened doorway a puff of air made its way between us and sent her white, ankle-length, silk chemise floating up her shapely body like gossamer wings. Margaret was an angelic vision. Each strand of hair was carefully coiffed and studded with seed pearls. Her pale ivory skin shimmered like fine alabaster and her sparkling eyes, like emerald-blue pools, mirrored an unspoken bliss from deep within.

"My darling, Margaret, I simply can't express...my love for you. I love you with every beat of my heart and with every breath I take. You deserve so much more than this poor excuse of a man. I can't believe my good fortune," I said, reaching out for her, pressing her warm, velvet lips against mine, and then kissing her neck and shoulders. "You're indeed a cherished prize. I feel honored beyond words to call you my wife and future mother of my children. Goodbye, my beloved, Margaret."

"Oh, Albert. Don't say goodbye. That sounds so final," she admonished while embracing me once more. "Just say, farewell,...until we're together again...and that should be very soon."

"Yes, I agree. Farewell, my love,...until we're together again *is* better," I replied with another quick kiss before heading toward the roadway where the family carriage awaited my arrival.

"I love you," she reiterated, following me outside the doorway of the majestic Radcliff mansion onto a portico that was flanked by stately columns.

As I checked my pocket watch for the time, I hurried toward the waiting carriage. It was one-fifteen. The wedding would take place at two. Once inside the carriage, I briskly brushed the shoulders of my black formal attire with my hands removing any unsightly lint, hair or dandruff. The cravat was choking me, so I pulled on it to loosen it a bit. The journey to the church would take about a half-hour.

The weather had been seasonably perfect during the past week. Our wedding day was a glorious one with temperatures in the high sixties. The mating songs of birds filled the air and nature's biota searched for love to satisfy their desire to multiply. I joined with them in their overture, singing the saga of the never-ending cycle of life. How coincidental that along with creation, I too, would also procreate with my loved one in the same manner.

As Father had done for Mother, I vowed to treat our relationship with the same tender devotion and utmost respect. Margaret was well aware of that. Except for that one time when I first arrived in West Roxbury, we never allowed our lovemaking to exceed certain boundaries. She feared the disgrace of being with child before marriage. Since that time, we decided to reserve the ecstasy of consummate oneness for our wedding night; nevertheless, it was extremely difficult at times.

Thoughts of the herring beginning their run came to mind. Despite all odds, the feisty alewives were a constant source of wonder and inspiration as they climbed the ladders and swam upstream against the current to spawn in the Mill Pond. It reminded me of my own quest to continue my line, beget children and care for my family. Like the herring of the Stony Brook, I resolved to stay focused—determined to leave my mark in this world and achieve a successful, full life.

The lavish wedding ceremony and reception far exceeded my utmost expectations. Every detail was carefully carried out—nothing forgotten or omitted. It was flawless. There were no social blunders or erstwhile problems to mar the day. Even the weather, which was exceptional, cooperated nicely. Thank goodness for that! Madam Henderson would have been livid if plans had *not* gone her way. It would have ruined an otherwise idyllic wedding.

Margaret was a radiant bride as she approached the minister on the arm of her lordly father. She wore an elegantly embellished, ivory satin gown that greatly enhanced her beauty. It was trimmed with scalloped Belgium lace, seed pearls and crystalline beads. A delicate veil attached to a majestic crown of baby's breath and orange blossoms cascaded toward an ornate train several yards long. William Henderson kissed her, placed her hand in mine, and then left her side. When I touched her soft, dainty hand my heart skipped a beat and leaped with profound ecstasy. Abigail was Margaret's maid of honor and David was my best man. Aaron and Uranus, who was Uncle Isaac Crosby's youngest son, were ushers along with bridesmaids, Emeline and Kate.

The opulent furnishings of the pretentious Radcliff Mansion mesmerized my parents, relatives and friends. They marveled at the multiple crystal chandeliers, marble floors and superbly crafted gold decorations and mahogany wainscoting. The reception was held both indoors and out. An immense canopy was erected amidst the formal gardens and arboretum—breathtaking at this time of year. The table centerpieces of tall, crystal vases were filled with lush rose bouquets and adorned with flowing tulle bows. The extent of the extravaganza was astounding. It ranged from expensive fine china and silver candelabras to the sumptuous dinner of pheasant prepared by a half dozen chefs and a complement of servants. The orchestral music for dancing on the rear veranda emanated from the gazebo. Expensive wedding gifts filled a whole room from floor to ceiling.

It was a most cherished and memorable day for me. Spellbound, I moved in this surreal world in an almost dreamlike state. I seemed to be watching myself in some sort of euphoric trance as I moved slowly through time and space on a celestial plateau where only love, beauty and happiness reigned.

Margaret and I progressed from table to table, from one room to the next. All of our loved ones were present—distant relatives and close friends. Margaret introduced me to those on her side of the family and I reciprocated with mine. We did take part in a few waltzes and gavottes, but generally speaking we mingled with the guests.

"Oh, me, Albert, and me, Margaret," Miss Mira said in her comely brogue, beaming and extending a hand to each of us. "How grateful I am, to be here for ye special day. I think this is the most elegant and grandest affair I ever attended. Thank ye, for inviting me to such a bonnie wedding. Why, I feel like royalty! Please return to Brewster to visit,…if it be possible. In the meantime, I wish ye both the very best of happiness"

"My dear, Miss Mira, we wouldn't think of not having ye here today. Ye like family to us," I said in jest, smiling and turning toward Margaret who nodded in agreement. "We specifically requested your presence. Margaret and I couldn't possibly imagine our wedding, without you. We're so happy that you were able to join my family members. We hope to vacation in Brewster this fall. Do partake of the festivities and enjoy yourself. We'll see you again soon to say goodbye before you leave for Brewster." Margaret shook her head. I corrected myself and added, "No,…we mean farewell, for now."

Mother and Father were in awe of the grandiose surroundings of the Radcliff Mansion. I also sensed they felt a bit intimidated by the Henderson and Radcliff families. I told them I'd be working at Mister Henderson's bank until I was prepared to leave for Chicago.

"Be sure to inform us if you should choose to remain here," Father requested. "In any case, we won't think any less of you. It's your decision to make. Remember, son, it may be a difficult move for Margaret. You'll have to take that into consideration, Albert."

"I know that, Father," I replied, wondering why he would even suggest that—knowing how much it meant to me to be self-sufficient and on my own. Evidently, he had overheard discussions among the guests about my future plans. Father was a very perceptive man and must have concluded that the overtones concerning my venture were not favorable. "I still intend to go ahead with my plans. My move to Chicago may be delayed for a time, but I hope to leave in the not-too-distant future. Margaret will accompany me there. Meanwhile,…I'll be gainfully employed."

Everyone felt I had married well, however that had never been my intention. How could I have known? Margaret seldom spoke of her parents, their background or wealth. When I first laid eyes on this winsome, young lady and fell hopelessly in love, I hadn't a clue as to her financial status. I could have cared less about that. With time, I discovered how refined and educated she was. It only added to her attractiveness. She could have been—a charwoman for that matter. Regardless, Margaret was the only person with whom I wanted to spend the rest of my life.

"Darling, please fetch the valises from our bedroom," Margaret shouted from the staircase. "The coachman's here to take us to the train station."

"I'll be right down," I answered, inspecting the many trunks and bags of various sizes. I won't be able to take them all in one trip," I called out. "Please ask your father to assist me."

I finished dressing and stood before a long mirror. I had to admit the reflection was that of a suave, debonair gentleman wearing an expensive, smartly tailored, Italian wool-blend suit and dress shirt. I was presented with a stylish new wardrobe—a trousseau from my benevolent bride.

"Father will be here in a few minutes. He'll help you carry them to the carriage," she said, approaching the upstairs landing and almost bumping into me as I walked out of our lavish bedroom with a large bag in each hand. "Oh,…Albert, you look positively dashing! I felt my heart skip a beat when I laid eyes on you." She kissed me ardently and sighed, "Oh, my,…I wish we didn't have to leave right now." I smiled, knowing the upcoming honeymoon would be one filled with romance and passionate lovemaking. I was eager for that long-awaited intimacy we would soon enjoy during our first stop—a Providence inn that was in close proximity to the railroad depot.

Our extended honeymoon, a most generous gift from the Hendersons to their daughter and new son-in-law, would last almost a month and cover many cities and states. It was early evening when we entered the waiting carriage. Margaret removed a wool shawl from her bag and placed it on her shoulders. As the sepia hues—cast by a waning sun were slowly being preempted by the inky darkness of night—the cool mist of dusk enveloped us like a dank, transparent veil.

Margaret and I traveled to the southeast by train. We toured Pennsylvania and Virginia. We also visited the capitol city of Washington D.C. and returned home via Niagara Falls and New York City. It was a whirlwind of days on the road. Daytime found us sightseeing and traveling to scenic, historic or intriguing places that piqued our curiosity. We dined in fashionable, elite cafés and tearooms— where violins often serenaded us. Margaret and I spent our evenings attending ballets, operas, stage plays, concerts and orchestral symphonies. We stayed in lovely inns or guesthouses—all elaborately furnished with canopy beds, antique armoires and Persian rugs. I was never happier. While embracing our time together, I experienced—complete gratification. Alas, those blissful four weeks rapidly came to a close. The time spent on our unforgettable honeymoon flew by at an almost unbelievable rate. It was the end of June when we arrived in West Roxbury.

"Margaret, I purposefully haven't spoken to you about my future plans," I said. "I didn't wish to discuss it during our travels together." Somehow I sensed she might be dismayed if I brought it up. I felt it wasn't the appropriate time to broach the subject. We were having such an incredibly fantastic honeymoon—I was afraid to put a damper on it. "I wanted to spare you that unsettling reality. Nevertheless, it's something I need to speak to you about," I continued diffidently while helping her from the carriage. "If possible, I'd like to leave for Chicago next month. My goods are in storage right now; however, I plan on removing them in a few weeks and loading them into the prairie schooner that I purchased before we married."

"Oh, Albert, dearest,…must it be that soon?" Margaret questioned in an uncharacteristically coy manner as she walked up the stone slab steps to the side entrance. "Father will probably expect you to stay on at the bank for at least another few months. Besides, I won't be ready to leave until then. There are so many loose ends I need to take care of. "Thank you notes must be sent as well as sorting and packing the wedding gifts for the trip," she went on in loving, but boring detail.

"Margaret, my love, please don't make it any more difficult for me than it already is," I begged, upset and wide-eyed as I opened the door for her. "Your justifications for remaining here any longer than that...border on the ridiculous! You know my objective is to establish my own company. My new mercantile business means moving to Chicago where there's a need for such an enterprise right now. I'm determined to support my wife and family without the help of family members in a manner of my own choosing! It's bad enough that I owe Father and my uncles the start-up funds. As it is, I'll have to dedicate myself to long hours of hard work so I can repay them as soon as my business becomes profitable. Your father already knows this. He isn't expecting me to return to the bank. I suggest the thank you notes be sent out promptly. As for the wedding gifts, we'll take only the necessary ones with us and send for the rest later, once we get settled," I explained, taking a firm yet compassionate stand against her hesitation.

"Well,...all right, Albert," she said with a huff, resentfully acquiescing to my unyielding objectives. "I guess if I don't dally, I can speedily tend to those details. Oh, Albert, Chicago seems so far away," she whined. "I truly want to be with you my darling, but frankly...I'm reluctant to leave my friends and loved ones. I'll miss them so. I won't know anyone in Chicago. Are you sure you won't change your mind and stay here in West Roxbury? The liquors and teas you have in storage can be sold or returned. Father could see to that!"

"No, Margaret. My mind's already made up about this. I'm leaving for Chicago with or without you,...and that's final! My plans are *not* subject to change! I won't quarrel with you over this!" I replied firmly, firing on all cylinders, angry and upset by her indecision to join me. "If you don't wish to accompany me there on the prairie schooner, I can understand that. In any case, I'd expect you to arrive shortly thereafter," I went on, sensing her adverse attitude. "If she loves me as much as she professes, how can she consider not following me anywhere in the world,...despite the inconvenience?...She said, she would. I truly believe Margaret loves me,...but with conditions?" I wondered. "What's precipitating her indecision? Is she changing her mind? Why is she having second thoughts about this?" These troubling questions distressed me.

Margaret had taken me by surprise. That disquieting conversation did not sit well with me. A feeling of uneasiness gnawed at my insides. Her candid admission and subtle intimation seemingly dashed my hopes for the future. I feared my aspirations might be a weak cause that needed further scrutiny. I had a foreboding reaction to her words and sensed a problem ahead. It was a jarring reminder of the conversation I had overheard months ago. "After reconsidering her mother's desultory assertion, has Margaret decided to do an about-face?" I wondered. It was apparent, that if it was in her power to do so, she hoped to delay the trip or completely dispense of it. Unfortunately, I saw a totally different side of her—one I had never encountered before.

"I've pretty much gone along with your wishes up to now, Margaret. Nonetheless, I've no recourse but to proceed with what's important to me," I said resolutely. I realize…there are always imponderables; however, as you well know, my arrangements have been finalized…It's not as if this was a hasty decision on my part. You've always known my intentions and regardless of your misgivings, I'm sure you're well aware of that fact that I must be financially independent. I'm eager to get started on my journey west. It's only a matter of time before we depart. I hope you'll understand my position and genuinely demonstrate your love for me. I'm eager for you to join me willingly not only as my wife, but also as my helpmate and companion." I flashed a affected grin while I held her saddened face between my hands, kissed her, and went on to say, "Come now, my sweet Margaret,…don't be saddened. Give me one of your *happy* smiles. It pains me to see you so distressed."

"It seems my parents are not here," she noted, wishing to change the subject and end our disconcerting exchange. Margaret looked around to the left of the front entrance then into the living room behind the right staircase.

"Well, we did arrive a little earlier than expected. I'm sure they'll be here anytime now," I replied, jogging out to the carriage to retrieve our bags. When I rejoined Margaret, she greeted me with tears. She was holding a letter in her hand from Abigail.

Obviously upset by its contents, Margaret said dejectedly, "Please sit down, Albert. Regrettably,…it's rather shocking news. Abigail writes:"

Dear Margaret and Albert:

It is with deep regret that I must inform you of Jonathan's death. When we arrived in Brewster from Newport, we were told that Jonathan had committed suicide the very night of your wedding.

"Oh, no!" I cried out, pounding my fist on the sideboard. I felt an arrow of unimaginable grief pierce my heart and—at that moment in time—something inside of me died. "I can't bear to hear any more! I can't believe he'd do that! How horrible! Why,…Jonathan?…Oh, God,…why?"

Margaret tried to sooth my distress with a tender hug. She kissed my forehead and continued to read Abigail's poignant letter relating to the tragic details.

At the very hour you were preparing to leave for your honeymoon, he apparently found a Colt revolver and shot himself through the chest. The Eldredges had left him in the care of a dear friend when they departed Brewster to attend your wedding. The woman had left the house for a short while that evening. When he wasn't in the kitchen to greet her, she knocked on his bedroom door—it was bolted from inside. She frantically shouted his name and ordered him to open it when she noticed a trail of blood seeping out on the floor from within his room. When no response was forthcoming, the friend ran to a neighboring homestead for help. The door was forced open with a hatchet. They found him slumped over his wheelchair—the gun had fallen from his hand. He left a note saying it was better this way. He would no longer be a burden to his loved ones and finally be at peace.

Jonathan begged for forgiveness and asked that he be remembered in our prayers. He bid everyone farewell and left a legacy of love to his family, friends and benefactors that included you both. I know his ill-timed death will be shocking and agonizing for you, but please don't allow this letter to be unduly distressing. Nothing could have been done to prevent it. I guess it was inevitable. Jonathan was a disconsolate man who suffered in a most agonizing way and finally wanted to end the torture. Wracked by debilitating bouts of depression and a mind that was muddled and confused, he rationalized he could no longer live with the hopelessness of his infirmity.

The funeral was well attended by all of us here in Brewster. The Eldredge family was overcome with grief. It was also extremely grievous for your family, Albert. I promised them I'd notify you of his passing. I deeply regret having to write you such a disheartening letter and having to divulge this devastating news upon your arrival home. The children and I are well, but miss you dearly. Until future correspondence, I send you both,

Love and Regards,
Abigail

The disclosure of Jonathan's death by suicide cast an insidious shroud of despondency over our lives. Margaret and I had lost someone very dear to us both. We reasoned that in his frame of mind it was an unforeseen tragedy just waiting to happen. Although his suicide was never openly discussed, Margaret and I felt we were partially responsible. Due to the circumstances of his death, life would never be the same for me. I was so grieved and guilt ridden by Jonathan's untimely demise—it was impossible to dismiss it from my mind. The painting of the Stony Brook Mill remained with me to the end of my days. It was a constant reminder of our treasured friendship.

CHAPTER 10

▼

Mid-June, 1848

"Well,…that's the last of it," David said as he secured the crates with heavy rope so their contents would stay firmly in place inside the prairie schooner. "It's amazing how useful those sailor's knots we mastered in the mercantile marines have become. Can't tell you how many times I found myself utilizing them. That's one skill I've never forgotten."

Although sparsely scattered in the clear, late evening sky, the first scintillating stars visually announced their presence. The days were longest at this time of year when dusk leisurely lingered into the late evening hours—a decided advantage as we prepared to start on our trek west.

"Everything looks remarkably secure. You've done a great job, David," I said, applauding his efforts. "Thanks to your expertise, I don't expect we'll have any breakage should we encounter some of those jarring roadways along the way. The stock is exceptionally well-stacked and fastened."

When it seemed obvious my plans would be unavoidably delayed, I had ultimately decided to purchase the covered wagon instead of leasing it. It had languished in the Henderson's carriage house for almost a year.

"Albert, I can't believe we're finally preparing to leave," David said, excited and energized by our imminent departure. "Say, it's your turn to do a little work around here!" he remarked jokingly. "You fill the water barrels while I harness the team."

"All right," I replied, eager to help. I fetched the pails and walked toward the water pump that was located in the middle of a flower garden and over the backyard well. After making several trips back and forth, the wooden kegs were eventually filled with fresh water. "David, I'm extremely grateful for your help, but above all,…it's your patience with my procrastination that I truly appreciate. I wouldn't have faulted you if you had left without me long ago," I said, placing the covers on the barrels and clamping them in place.

"You should've known I'd wait for you, Albert,…regardless of the delay," David replied, reaching for his carpetbag. "Besides, it gave me more time to work and save for my journey to the West Coast. I was certain you wouldn't change your mind. I know you. You're a man of your word. That's one thing I've always admired about you."

"You *do* know me," I said with a smirk and giving him a sweeping slap on the shoulder. "It's nice of you to say that. And yes,…I guess you're right! I may toy with an idea for a while and thoroughly debate it in my mind, but when I arrive at a decision,…it's definitely the direction I take. It's high time we left, David,…our departure is long overdue. I'm sad to say, Margaret's difficult pregnancy prolonged my stay. I was hoping to leave West Roxbury months ago. In a few months, or as soon as she's able to do so, Margaret has promised to board the train for Chicago. If not, I plan to return over the holidays. I'll sorely miss her and our new baby daughter."

"Do you have the road map with you?" David asked during a last-minute check of the strapping outside the schooner.

"Yes, I do," I replied as we walked over to the two sturdy Morgan horses we had acquired to pull our covered wagon. "I've chartered a path west through the open wilderness just outside the cities and towns. I'm sure we'll be fine as long we follow the stagecoach trails across the country from one town to the next. "With any luck," I added, bending down to feed the horses some hay, "they've carved out a fairly decent route by this time. We'll most likely find lodging houses along the way where we can bathe, dine and spend the night. If need be, we can sprawl across the boxes in the claustrophobic quarters of our wagon or sleep outdoors under the stars. We should have an ample supply of water.

"Furthermore, David," I went on. "I've tucked a sack of hardtack, some beans and dried beef under the seat in case of emergency, otherwise that food will be extra rations for us. We shouldn't need them unless we come upon long distances from one village to the next. We'll purchase provisions of fresh fruit, bread and meat at the town general store along with some hay for the horses. That should last us a few days,…then I guess we'll have to resort to eating what we have. I figure we can cook over a campfire in the evening and dry our belongings should we encounter some foul weather along the way. I think it's a good idea to make camp by some water so we can refresh the horses and ourselves. We may want to wash our clothing in a stream or under a waterfall if the opportunity should arise. I expect we'll welcome that after a long, hot and grueling day on the road."

"Sounds just dandy to me, Albert! Can't wait to be on our way!" David said, eagerly anticipating our sojourn across a third of the United States. "I think we should start out at dawn tomorrow. The way I figure it, we should average a good forty miles a day barring prolonged inclement weather and providing the road conditions are favorable. Chicago's approximately nine hundred miles from Boston. As you already know, it'll probably take us a minimum of at least three weeks to get there. We'll plan on a month," he went on, walking briskly alongside me as we headed back in the direction of the Henderson home.

After being detained for a much longer period than I could have possibly imagined—departure time had finally arrived. I had mixed emotions about that. David had patiently stayed in Boston working and living with the Myrick family. When it appeared that I would soon be able to depart for Chicago, I sent him a telegraph requesting that he travel to West Roxbury where we would prepare to leave together. The merchandise had been delivered there from the warehouse and was stored in the carriage barn. David offered to assist me with loading those goods into the wagon. His help was indispensable. I mentioned aiming for the fifteenth of the month. He said he would arrive around the tenth. It would be wonderful to see my crewmate again. Although David was best man at my wedding, and I had visited him on occasion while working in Boston, it had been months since we had been together.

Shortly after returning from our honeymoon, Margaret announced that I was to become a father in March of this year. It goes without saying, I was delighted by the prospect. My world seemed complete. I felt like everything I had ever wished for was coming true. Unfortunately, Margaret was plagued by nausea and morning sickness throughout her pregnancy. She had a very trying time of it and had lost much of her stamina and weight. The doctor ordered her to postpone traveling indefinitely—at least until a few months after the infant was delivered. Madam Henderson stood by Margaret's bed while she was in labor. Our first child was an adorable baby girl. We named her Irene. Born several weeks premature, she weighed a mere five pounds.

Prior to Irene's birth, I observed Madam counting the months of pregnancy on her fingers. She didn't notice that Margaret also caught her in the act.

"How could you possibly think I was already with child on our wedding day. The baby wasn't due for another three weeks,…it's already been ten months since our wedding day!" Margaret exclaimed, reaching for my hand and angrily chastising her mother. She was visibly upset and deeply offended. Noting the embarrassed expression on her mother's face, I said nothing as Madam left the room.

A few days later, while I was in the kitchen and Margaret was nursing the baby, her mother backed me into a corner. She insisted in her usual intimidating manner that Margaret remain in West Roxbury.

"Margaret will not be able to accompany you to Chicago, Albert. I'm sure you know that," she announced as though it wouldn't make any difference to me. "Margaret can't possibly endure the rigors of such a long trip. She's much too fragile right now. She must remain here a while longer with her father and me so we can care for her and baby, Irene. Margaret needs time to recuperate from this ordeal. If you value her well being you'll certainly concur with our decision. You needn't worry about them, they'll be in good hands, Albert," she went on while filling a pitcher of ice tea and setting it on a tray along with several glasses for the doctor, his nurse and Margaret. "Go and do what you must. You needn't be encumbered by the added burden of having to care for them along the way. Their presence could be detrimental and hinder your progress as you travel west. Margaret and your new baby daughter will be just fine."

While it was against all my principles and what I thought best for me, my wife and daughter, I guessed she was right and halfheartedly conceded to her logic. I had to accept the fact that Margaret and Irene would be well provided for in my absence. Nevertheless, the freedom to seek my fortune came at a high price. I hated leaving them behind. It was *not* at all what I intended. I was profoundly disappointed by this unexpected turn of events. It weighed heavily on my heart. Needless to say, after this lengthy setback I was eager to get underway. I longed to declare my independence from my in-laws' financial help and overbearing ways. It was high time that I asserted myself as the breadwinner. I had a family to support. Their future was in my hands now. It was up to me to make the crucial decisions and shoulder the responsibilities that would eventually benefit all of us.

"I'm sorry to say, I must again accept your generosity Madam Henderson," I said, trying to hide my indignation at her audacity. She had me against a wall, and she knew it. I resented what she posed as obligatory for my loved ones and me. "I really need to leave…and quite soon at that! I've already made arrangements with my friend, David. He'll be arriving in a few days to help me load the wagon. We'll be traveling to Chicago, together. I've also contacted a business associate who'll have my merchandise delivered here within the week. I'll certainly miss my wife and child. I was eager for us to begin a new life in Chicago as a family, but I guess it's not to be,…at least not for a while anyway. Sadly, I must bow to the inevitable and attempt to establish a residence there without her. I hope she'll be able to join me in the not-too-distant future," I said with a lump in my throat and reaching for a handkerchief as unmanageable tears welled in my eyes.

My quest for independence would be costly. The days of wedded bliss and the loving relationship I so enjoyed with the woman I married would now be filled with longing and loneliness. Unless Margaret decided to join me in Chicago, Irene would be eight months old by the time I returned. During my absence, I vowed to wile away the time, tirelessly ensconcing myself in work and business matters. Meanwhile, I would never lose sight of my goal—to become a successful entrepreneur worthy of my beloved wife.

The next morning, I rose at dawn and silently slipped out of bed so as not to wake Margaret. After I dressed, I walked down the hallway and tapped on David's door when I reached his bedroom.

"I'm already up and dressed," he whispered through the slightly opened door. "I'll be down in a jiffy…Just need to wash."

"All right, David," I replied in a hushed voice. "I'll be downstairs putting together some breakfast for us." I made a pot of coffee, cut a few slices of sweet bread, and then sat at the kitchen table waiting for David to join me. While anxious to be on my way, my heart was heavy. I had informed Margaret I would wake her before our departure. David soon appeared in the doorway.

"Have you said your goodbyes to Margaret as yet?" he asked, pouring himself a cup of coffee and approaching the table.

"No,…not yet," I replied, pulling a chair over to the table for him. "I promised I'd wake her before leaving. I won't bid Margaret farewell until we're actually ready to leave. Wait for me at the side entrance while I do so…I shouldn't be too long."

"Looks a little gloomy out there this morning," David said, opening the door, scanning the skies, and then extending his hand out. "It's going to be another hot, humid day. Say, there's lightning streaking across the sky! Can you hear the rumble of thunder off in the distance? It's already starting to rain. Oh, well,…even if it becomes torrential, it shouldn't be a problem for us. At least the cobblestone roads here won't wash away. The storm should be over by the time we reach the outskirts of the city. Let's hope it'll be cooler."

David and I gathered our belongings and ran toward the carriage house. We hurriedly harnessed the horses to the prairie schooner amid the intermittent thunderbolts.

"I'll meet you at the side entrance in a few minutes," I shouted, throwing my sack behind the wooden seat, quickly exiting the carriage house, and then placing a poncho over my head. Taking two steps at a time, I burst into our bedroom to find Margaret sitting on the edge of our bed with Irene at her breast. Momentarily startled, she raised her head as I approached her.

"I'm preparing to leave soon, my dearest," I said, reaching to embrace her and my baby daughter.

"Do take care of yourself, Albert," she said, her cheeks wet with tears. "I only wish I was strong enough to go with you. I guess it just wasn't meant to be," she added, sighing despondently while reaching out to me with her free hand. "I pray to God that he watch over you and keep you out of harm's way, my darling. I can't imagine what my life would be like if anything dreadful ever happened to you. I wouldn't want to live without you...I don't think I could survive it. Remember, Albert, you mustn't endanger yourself needlessly. I'll miss you so, my dearest. I intend to write you as often as possible. You have us to think about now. We love and need you so desperately," Margaret went on to say, looking down at the infant in her arms and placing the sleeping baby on the bed. I bent to kiss her and we embraced knowing there was a distinct possibility we might never see each other again.

"I've made arrangements to return home for the holidays," I said, trying to reassure her that I'd be back and wasn't abandoning her or our child. "Therefore, I won't say goodbye, my love, I'll just say farewell...until we're together again. If all goes well, I'll expect to see you then. I must leave now...David's waiting for me." We kissed again then reluctantly released the grasp we had on each other. I kissed our new baby girl on the forehead, walked toward the doorway, and then threw Margaret another kiss.

Afraid I might give in to my longing to remain with her, I raced headlong down the staircase. I bit my lip trying to suppress my emotions, nevertheless, the anguish I was grappling with eventually overwhelmed me. Unrestrained tears flowed freely as I dashed out the side entrance to the waiting wagon. I ascended the wooden seat and sat next to David. As I neared him, he noticed my downhearted expression and deliberately looked straight ahead. He took hold of the reins, cracked the whip and we were on our way as we sat in silence contemplating our own thoughts. The horses hesitated a bit until they became accustomed to the load they were pulling behind them. Though energized by the prospect of beginning a new venture, I left with a heavy heart. The idea of leaving my loved ones behind put a damper on my exodus. I glanced back at the Henderson home, and although I had just left, I already yearned for my wife and baby.

"Oh, well, through hell or high water, I'll be back for the holidays. Sadly...that's months away," I agonized silently. "I hope she'll come to Chicago before then or else join me on the return trip from here." Engrossed in my thoughts, I suddenly realized David was speaking to me. I turned my attention to what he was saying.

"By the way, Albert, I had an idea. Are you familiar with that old saying, 'It's better to be safe, than sorry.' Well,...I've conjured up a scheme to discourage thieves who might be lurking on the outskirts of the cities and towns that we'll be passing through. I brought along a pinafore, a blond wig and sunbonnet. The bonnet's bright yellow with a wide visor. One of us will pretend to be a woman. I also brought along a small stocking doll wrapped in a blanket. We must be extremely cautious because of our valuable cargo. I believe it's a good idea to journey in disguise once we're out of the populated areas. The husband will wear a wide brimmed farmer's hat, a fake mustache and beard. Bandits are less likely to sack a small, insignificant family rather than two men with questionable cargo under their tarp. I've also brought along a few furnishings...a small dresser, two kitchen chairs and a stool. I'll tie them to the outside of the wagon so it'll look like we're on the move. They'll figure the young man and his family are starting out with their few possessions to settle on some acreage somewhere west of the Mississippi."

"Why, that's an ingenious ruse, David," I said, listening attentively and slightly taken aback by his well-conceived subterfuge. "It's so innovative!...Yes, quite clever, indeed!"

"I thought you'd like it," he replied with a self-satisfied grin.

"And who gets to wear the bonnet and pinafore?" I asked with bated breath, visualizing it, chuckling loudly and expecting to be the ultimate choice.

"We both do," David said, taking his eyes off the roadway and facing me. "When I'm at the reins you'll wear them and hold the so-called "baby." When you take over,...it'll be my turn. Close up, neither one of us could easily be mistaken for a woman, but from far away, who could know the difference? It's important to remain clean-shaven, though. If those outlaws should detect a beard under that sunbonnet when looking through their binoculars, we'll be in for a whole lot of trouble.

"I've also brought along a Colt pistol for each one of us," David went on to say, reaching down under the seat with one arm while holding onto the reins with the other. He raised a small leather carrying case and opened it. "Take this and place it in your clothing somewhere," he said. "You never know when we might need to use them. Actually, we can't even trust some of those innkeepers. I've heard some disquieting tales from folks returning to Boston from some of these places. We'll keep the guns close by and under our pillows when we sleep outdoors or in the lodging houses."

"Dammit, David!" I exclaimed, distressed by his rationale and placing my gun securely inside a lower vest pocket. "I had decided to let my facial hair grow until we reached Chicago. I felt it unnecessary to shave while we traveled. It's such a time consuming task. But, yes,…I guess you're right! I'm sure your imaginative idea justifies the effort. It'll work! In fact…it's brilliant! I've become so preoccupied with the business at hand, I hadn't thought of any safeguards in case of danger. Again, you're one step ahead of me, David. You're so practical and invariably prepared. Your foresight amazes me. I suppose…it's because you've had to fend for yourself for so long. It's not in my makeup to think the way you do,…but I'm learning," I added nodding my head. "I won't relish having to use this pistol, but thankfully,…our skirmishes on the *Calypso* taught me how to defend myself *and* my property."

"I've got mine right here on the seat between us. Anyone attempting to high-jack our wagon won't have a chance against us," David said arrogantly.

He had thought of everything. I felt much more secure. Our welfare was of primary importance to David. Yes, he certainly was an astute and special friend.

"Well, looks like we'll be together again, even if it's only for a month," David said, turning his attention to a busy intersection and tugging at the reins to take a right onto the main roadway. The storm had passed as quickly as it had arrived. "I trust the constant togetherness won't ruin our friendship. If we stay friends after this journey, we'll always be friends. I'm sure that during our cross-country journey…it'll be sorely tested at times," he added with an ambiguous look, a smile and a snicker.

"Oh, I'm not worried about that!" I replied confidently. "We've always seen eye-to-eye on almost everything. In fact, I wish you'd change your mind about going to California. Why don't you stay and work with me in Chicago? We could be business partners. I'd give you a generous percentage of the profits. Do think about it, David…I'll surely hate to see you leave when the time comes."

"Can you beat that!" he exclaimed, chuckling and slapping my thigh. "I was hoping to convince *you* to follow *me* all the way to California! You could haul your cargo west and start your business there. So think about *that*, my friend! I can't tell you how eager I am to start panning for gold in those Northern California hills. I'll most likely stake a claim around Placerville or Auburn as soon as I find a good vein. I just know I'll strike it rich there…No doubt about it."

"I'm afraid destiny has us fated to travel in different directions, David," I responded pensively. "I could no more go to California with you than you could work at a business indoors for me. Our interests are so different. I have a family to think about now, and you're still a free spirit…free to follow your dreams and aspirations no matter how far-fetched they may seem. I hope I'll do well in my chosen field. If not,…I can always follow in my father's footsteps. My father-in-law has also offered me an executive position in one of his financial institutions. Even so, I'm determined to be independently successful in my own right."

"You've got a lot of grit, Albert," David said with conviction. "It'll take a lot of spunk to accomplish what you intend in an unfamiliar city. The road you've chosen may be a fairly bumpy one, but somehow I know you'll make it. In fact,…I'm sure of it. You've got what it takes and more. I wish I were more like you, Albert. Sometimes I feel so uncertain about my future,…but not you. You're so goal-oriented and relentless in your quest to succeed. You've confidently mapped out your life. You follow winding trails with straightforward vision and courageously forge ahead, unafraid as to what might loom around the next corner. That's an admirable quality…I wish I possessed."

"Well, thank you for saying that, David," I replied, turning my thoughts to an analogy I had often made in the past. Two parallel worlds—that of the dauntless herring who in their quest to procreate swim up-stream against the current—and my tenacity to model my life and struggle for success after them.

On one overcast, dreary day while I was at the reins, David reached behind the seat and pulled out a large leather case in the shape of an instrument. He proceeded to open it, and there within its confines was a highly polished, well-crafted wooden guitar.

"I brought along my guitar. I couldn't leave it behind," David announced, noticing my astonishment. He took it out of his case and began to strum a tune on it. "Playing the guitar is my private passion and helps me to wile away the lonely hours. I retrieved it along with all my other belongings when I returned to Nantucket to sell the family home. I thought I'd take advantage of the time and play it before we started our masquerade. It wouldn't look too convincing for a young mother to be strumming a guitar while trying to feed a baby…Now would it?"

"I never knew you to play *any* instrument, let alone the guitar! You never mentioned it!" I said dumbfounded and shaking my head. I came to the conclusion that although David was outgoing, he was at the same time a very private person. "How come you didn't take it with you when you joined the merchant marines?" I asked.

"With all the chores and regimen involved, I figured there wouldn't be much time for it. Like I said before, strumming the strings of my guitar is something I prefer to do to amuse myself when I'm alone," David replied. "However, I knew *you* wouldn't mind me playing it whenever I have the opportunity. I also like to compose my own music, so it's likely you won't recognize any of the melodies. I hope the sounds will be pleasant and soothing to your ears."

"Play to your heart's content, my friend!" I said, holding onto the reins with my left hand and signaling for him to go ahead with the right. "After all these years, I didn't realize you were so musically inclined...or so talented. You've got one up on me! I'm tone deaf. I remember trying to play the piano at home, but finally gave up after the family insisted they could no longer listen to my discordant notes."

David often strummed his guitar until we reached the isolated forests and meadowlands. This was when we had to don our camouflage and start exchanging places at the reins.

As we traveled west, we found the routes sufficiently wide enough for vehicles to travel in either direction. The towns and cities along the way had adequately provided for a transient population. Their easily accessible thoroughfares were paved with cobblestone, brick or rounded stones. These materials afforded a solid base for their main boulevards. Most of the roadways in the small villages and on the outskirts, however, were made of sand, gravel or hard clay. Nonetheless, they were usually traversable, even after a heavy rain. We dreaded the countless miles of black, earthen farmland roads that became rivers of mud after a downpour. Unfortunately, when we became mired in one of these, a farmer's oxen were often needed to pull us free.

Each evening, David and I stopped at a lodging house, hotel or inn along the way where we washed, dined and rested. It would be this way for the next several hundred miles as the East was fairly well populated. In the not-too-distant future, however, we would be traversing open country and lackluster landscapes where the towns were days apart. Farms dotted the distant terrain and narrow trails. Some bordered shallow, fresh-water streams. I became wistful at the sound of the rushing rapids spilling over rock beds in the shallow creeks. It brought back memories of the Stony Brook.

"David,...do you think you'll ever marry?" I decided to ask one day during our sojourn, eager to generate conversation to help pass the time. Actually, it was something I had often wondered about. "You're not getting any younger...you old bachelor, you!" I snickered, elbowing him in the ribs. "You needn't answer that, if you don't want to. I don't mean to pry…I'm just curious. Perhaps I should mind my own business."

"I must say that *is* a leading question, Albert," David replied with a bewildered expression. "I really don't know. I figure…maybe I'm not the marrying kind. I've had some romantic relationships in the past, but at this stage in my life, I just can't seem to make that kind of commitment. Right now, being tied to some woman's apron strings is inconceivable to me. I think you know where I'm coming from. I do enjoy the freedom to come and go as I please. My plans don't include marriage,…at least not in the foreseeable future. Besides, small children annoy me to distraction. I have no patience with their mischievous ways and incessant whining. When I see them misbehave, I'd like to take them across my knee and give them a sound spanking. I'm afraid I'd be a horrible parent."

"I don't believe that, David, knowing you as I do," I said, questioning his reasoning. "You're just making excuses for yourself, but that's your prerogative. If that's how you rationalize your reluctance to marry, then so be it. I can live with that explanation,…although I can see right through it. Enjoy your bachelorhood, dear friend, if that's what makes you happy."

David and I arrived at a small town just as the sun was setting. A lodging house on the main street had a comfortable room for us. As we had done for days now, we secured the wagon in safe quarters behind the inn, dined, purchased provisions, and then subsequently fell into a sound sleep.

The next day, we were up at dawn and on the road before sunrise. We advanced slowly through a morning mist. It would be days before we reached another town. We were thankful for a short period of fairly warm days and cool evenings. Every now and then, David and I enjoyed a moment of rest and relaxation. After sundown, we slept under the stars, often protected by large overhanging rocks or a thick canopy of trees. We reveled in the appearance of tiny forest animals, green grass, meadows, blue skies and the gentle summer rain that often accompanied us along the way. On the other hand, we were always on the lookout for outlaws.

Whenever possible, we made camp on the sandy shores of a kettle pond, river or lake. On the horizon was the dawn of tomorrow. One day tumbled onto the next until David and I reached the halfway mark of our journey. As I traveled further and further away from my loved ones, there were times when I had misgivings about my quest. I kept reminding myself that I was doing the right thing. Their future—and mine—rested on my doggedness to remain steadfast and focused.

We had a few mishaps including a broken axle, but we managed to escape serious adversities. For example, if it became impossible to circumvent the washouts in the road, we placed some wood planks under the wheels. David and I prepared for that possibility by carrying them on the underside of the wagon.

Adventure seekers and prairie schooners alike were familiar sights to the farmers tilling their gardens or tending to their animals. Small homesteads on vast open acreage dotted the countryside. Farm animals—their silhouettes outlined against the sky as they fed in the open meadows—created a tranquil pastoral scene.

We reached an arid passage that weaved through a mile-wide valley surrounded by rocky, mountainous hills. It was a spectacular sight. The sound of a cascading waterfall echoed in the distance. We wondered at the depths of this ancient canyon. It was David's turn to wear the disguise while I was at the reins. He decided to scan the high points of this chasm with the binoculars. From his perspective, David felt we were being watched. He was right.

"There's a band of riders on thoroughbred horses high up on that gorge, about a half-mile away from here," David said after scanning the ridge, quickly hiding the binoculars and pointing to a cliff in the distance. He was noticeably alarmed. "From this vantage point, they look like a menacing group of renegades."

"Could be vigilantes or a pack of thieves," I said, assuming the worse. I felt around the seat with my free hand for David's pistol and clumsily dropped it on the floorboards. I paled and felt my heart race as I hastily reached for the firearm. I instinctively checked my inside pocket to make sure that mine was still there. The real prospect of a bonafide shoot-out loomed ahead. Not only were we vulnerable, but also outnumbered. "I'd better shed this apprehension, or I won't be much help to David," I concluded. "In spite of my anguish, I need to face my fears. I must remember Japeth's training and the dauntless alewives!"

"Keep the horses calm and hold this same steady pace," David cautioned unfalteringly, finding the doll and placing his gun inside the blanket. "I believe if we quicken the gait they'll suspect we've spotted them, give chase, and then try to overtake us."

Anxious and tense, we slowly pushed on in silence. We finally reached the area directly below the rocky ridge where he had spotted the riders. Much to our surprise, the renegades had vanished and were no longer in the area. Our ruse had worked. We both heaved a sigh of relief. The danger had passed,…at least for the moment.

"If they were bandits, they must have figured we weren't worth the effort, and if they were vigilantes, we weren't the ones they were tracking," David reckoned.

I cracked the whip, and the horses galloped at a quickened pace through the ravine until we exited the valley. We decided we would try to reach the next town before nightfall.

"See! I told you our ruse would work," David remarked with a self-satisfied look.

"Yes, it did! We certainly avoided what could have been a disastrous confrontation. Our little masquerade was quite effective against that mysterious group of riders," I replied, thoroughly in favor of David's ingenious idea. "By the way, David, I meant to tell you days ago, that you make a decidedly convincing woman...quite feminine, in fact. I've got a comely little wife sitting next to me," I joked, deliberately taunting him with some cavalier laughter. "You know, David, sometimes we need a bit of mindless humor to ease tensions such as we've just experienced. You really fooled those thugs into thinking you were a nursing mother. I think you should assume the role for the duration of the trip. Then I can let my beard grow instead of using the fake one."

"Oh, no, you don't!" David protested. "We're still alternating! Must I remind you of our agreement? Remember, you're wearing this disguise as often as I have to."

"Really! I'm a bit vague about that!" I replied, grinning from ear to ear and slapping him on the shoulder. "It was all in jest! I knew that even suggesting it would get a rise out of you. No need to fret, my friend,...I'll take my turn tomorrow."

"Whew! You had me worried there for a minute, Albert," David said, exhaling and expressing relief with a whistle. He placed the wrapped doll on the underside of the wagon seat and positioned the gun between us.

"You know, David," I said, "a small measure of humor and trust between friends is always a good thing...Say! I'm hungry. Would you please hand me an apple from that sack?" I asked, nodding in that direction.

"I need a drink," David declared, removing a flask of whiskey from his knapsack as he reached for an apple. He unplugged it, brought the container to his lips, and then guzzled almost half of it before he returned it to his cache. He drank from his flask more frequently these days and actually became mildly intoxicated. His nearness was quite offensive at times because of his liquored breath. I never acquired a taste for hard whiskey. The last time I imbibed, I was on shore leave with my fellow crewmen. I became so violently ill after returning aboard the heaving ship that I wanted to die. I vowed right then and there that it would never happen to me again. Yes, I drank socially, but in moderation. I liked a fine wine, a jigger of whiskey and a brew or two now and then—especially in hot weather—but that was my limit.

When we reached a town or village along the way, David immediately stopped at the nearest tavern to purchase a fifth of the hard stuff even before we procured our supplies. I first noticed his penchant for alcohol at my wedding reception. He consumed one drink after another—his goblet was always full, be it scotch, wine or brandy. I marveled at his ability to mix all sorts of liquors and not become inebriated or deathly ill. After supper, David was spending longer periods of time in the local saloon.

I usually used this time before retiring to tend to the horses and post a letter to Margaret or my family in Brewster. Father insisted I keep him advised about my welfare and whereabouts. I also kept a daily journal that included my expenditures.

There were many evenings when David, who was all liquored up and in a drunken stupor, staggered through the doorway, walked erratically into our room, and then flopped on the bed to sleep it off. No worse for wear—he'd wake up a bit unsteady, yet alert and ready to roll at first light. As long as I had known him, David had never become belligerent after his drinking bouts—merely sullen and lethargic. "What will become of him once he's on his own? Has he become an alcoholic?" I wondered, decidedly troubled by my friend's drinking problem and uneasy about discussing it with him. David needed some guidance. Somehow I felt a responsibility to help him focus on his goals. I was afraid he might become an incurable drunkard, ending up in a gutter somewhere.

"You'd better keep a level head, David," I counseled, trying not to appear righteous and hoping he'd heed my advice. "Furthermore, a nursing mother shouldn't be drinking," I said in jest. He replaced the plug in the flask and returned it to his duffle bag that was under the seat. "Here, drink some water…whiskey won't quench your thirst," I added, handing him my canteen.

"Yeah, you're right…I agree. I guess I've been over-indulging much too frequently these days," he replied contritely, picking up the canteen and attempting to vindicate himself. "I suppose I became a little unnerved by that close call we had back there. I figured a good swig would calm me, that's all. We sure kept them at bay with our little deception, didn't we?"

I nodded, but remained silent. Feeling good about the consequences of an action did *not* obviate the need to discuss his rationale. I was appalled and not about to condone his flimsy excuse for alcohol abuse. "How can he possibly use liquor as a crutch? Does David rely on whiskey to give him a boost in a crisis? Has he become dependent on intoxicating spirits?" I questioned, inwardly concerned for him. I was bewildered because his behavior made no sense to me. I worried that my dear friend was in denial of a surreptitious addiction. Despite any advice I could give him, I realized that David—and *only* David, needed to face and conquer this monstrous vice. If not, it could be detrimental to his plans and eventually destroy him. David's future rested solely—in *his* hands.

───────────── ▼ ─────────────

CHAPTER 11

The oppressive afternoon heat was enervating because of the unusually high humidity. We sought refuge from the hot sun and stopped to rest the horses alongside a clear stream. A spattering of frothy, cumulus clouds drifted quickly across the sky on this typical mid summer day. After leading the horses to the river to drink, we washed them down. David and I decided to take a refreshing dip in the cool rushing water after watching a river otter swim by. We undressed and waded into the knee-deep water. While splashing the water over our sweaty bodies, we scanned the opposite shore.

"David,...do you see, what I see?" I asked, afraid my eyes were playing tricks on me and surprised to see a young female child sitting on a large rock that was partially submerged in the water.

"Yes, I do...It seems we have an audience," David replied, scrambling out of the water to put on his trousers. He had no sooner left, when she realized she was discovered, jumped down, and then crouched behind the rock to hide. David tossed my pants over to me. I hid my body with them until I was out of her sight. I quickly pulled up my pants and together we waded across the shallow creek bed in her direction. We thought she might run away from us, yet when we neared her she began to cry and shake violently.

"Please, don't hurt me," she whimpered in a wee voice, covering her face and shying away from us. I couldn't help noticing the torn, rumpled sundress and the blue shoulder strap that fell loosely down her petit, right arm.

"Don't be afraid. We won't harm you, little girl," I said reassuringly, greeting her with a cordial smile then kneeling down to face her. I looked into her sad, hazel eyes. "All we want to do is help you if we can. I need to ask you a few questions…Is that all right?" She nodded her head. "What's your name? Why are you in this wilderness all by yourself?…Are you lost?" I wanted to calm her down and hoped my inquiries would not add to her fears. I assumed she was momentarily disoriented and searching for her family. "Maybe we can find your parents for you," I said, handing her a handkerchief to dry her large eyes and tiny nose.

"My name's…Molly Duncan, sir," she said hesitantly, between heavy sobs as she plucked several strands of wind-blown hair from her freckled, elfin face. Her straggly tawny tresses were loosened from a limp braid. "I thought you might be the same bad men who dragged my poppa away. Our wagon is just beyond those trees over there." We learned that she called her father "Poppa" as she pointed in the direction of a dense forest grove. "We stopped here late yesterday afternoon. Poppa wanted to water the horses and set up camp for the night. While I left to fetch water from the river, some men on horseback rode in just as poppa was taking the harnesses off the horses. I was going back with the water when I saw them, so I hid behind a big tree…I was so scared. I dared not scream or cry out lest they'd find me. Poppa never told them about me, so those bad men didn't know that I was close by. They beat my poppa, tied his hands together with rope, and then put him on a horse and rode away with him. When I went back to the place where Poppa left our wagon, they were gone and so were the horses. They tore the wagon apart and took all our belongings."

"Oh, you poor child!" David exclaimed, obviously disturbed by the pathetic fate of this small child. "That's an awful thing to have happened to you!…How dreadful!" I took her hand and we walked together toward the clearing.

"Poppa and me lived with my grandmamma in Fremont, Ohio until she went to heaven. We had a covered wagon…but no horses." Molly went on to say shaking her head. "Then one day a few weeks ago, poppa came home with two horses and quickly hitched them to our wagon. We left right away. Poppa said we were going to Goshen, Indiana where my Aunt Julia lives. I'm all alone now. I don't know how I'll get there on my own…I don't even know where I am," she wailed, bursting into tears all over again and wiping her eyes with the back of her hand.

"There,…there…now, Molly," David said, drawing her toward him, picking her up and carrying her tiny form in his arms. "Dry that cute little nose, and we'll see what we can do."

"Where's your mother, Molly?" I asked, posing yet another question and hopeful that she had also escaped captivity.

"My mommy's in heaven with my grandmamma. Grandmamma left Poppa and me last year," Molly replied impassively. "Poppa, was going to leave me with Aunt Julia and her family. She asked him to drop me off there on his way to California. Oh,…where's my poppa? I want my poppa!…I miss him so much! How will I get to Aunt Julia's now?" Molly cried out as she buried her head in David's chest. Consumed by an overwhelming sense of insecurity, exacerbated by her frightful experience and all the uncertainties facing her, she unleashed another flood of tears and sobbed in pitiful waves of anguish.

"Why,…we're traveling in that same direction. We're on our way to Chicago. Goshen isn't too far out of our way. We'll be more than happy to take you with us, sweetie," I said compassionately, sensing it was high time we introduced ourselves. "My name's Albert,…and this is David. David and I will personally accompany you there. We'll take good care of you until you reach your Aunt Julia's home. Just so we'll know where to take you,…what's your Aunt Julia's last name, Molly?"

"It's Aunt Julia Bigelow," she replied, still sniffling.

"You must be famished by now," I added. "When we return to our wagon, we'll make you something nourishing to eat."

"Yes,…Mister Albert…I'm awful hungry. I'm so lucky you came along when you did," she said gratefully. "I don't know what would have happened to me if you didn't see me sitting on that big rock."

"How old are you, Molly?" David asked, completely enamored by this brave youngster who had undergone such a traumatic ordeal.

"I just turned eight, Mister David," she replied, smiling for the first time and revealing a deep dimple on each cheek. "My birthday was June 17th."

"Well, here's a big birthday hug!" David said, setting her back down on the ground and embracing her with both arms. "Now go fetch your belongings. We need to hurry and leave here right away,…just in case those bad men decide to return."

"Maybe they'll bring my poppa back to me," she said wistfully.

"I don't think so, Molly. If I remember well, they don't even know you were here," David said, jogging her memory.

"Yes,…you're right, Mister David," she replied dejectedly in an uncomplaining manner. "I really don't have very much to take with me. Just this small blanket," she said after retrieving it from the rear of the vandalized wagon and scrambling out with it in her hand.

"I'll carry you back to our wagon on my shoulders. How about that?" David asked, eager to make her smile again. He lifted her up to his shoulders and draped her legs over his chest. It worked! We sensed she felt secure with us and that we held her complete trust.

We harnessed the horses to the prairie schooner, and we were soon on our way with Molly sitting between us. When David put on his disguise, she spotted the wrapped doll. After giving him a puzzled look, Molly immediately reached for the decoy "baby" and without saying a word—she cradled it firmly in her arms.

"Poppa wouldn't let me take my dolly with me. I begged him to let me have her, but he wouldn't listen…I cried a lot over that," she said embarrassed and making an attempt to explain her abrupt behavior. "He wouldn't even let me sit next to him. I had to stay inside the covered wagon…I don't know why?"

David and I quickly glanced at each other. We assumed that Molly's father had only been trying to protect her from harm. If those vigilantes had spied a doll in the wagon they certainly would have looked for a female child. While she traveled with him, he was wise enough to conceal Molly from view and careful to exclude any clothes, toys or pets—telltale signs that would have betrayed her existence.

"I wear this sunbonnet and pinafore and hold the baby doll so that I'll look like a mommy, Molly," David explained, wishing she'd stop staring at him. "That way, robbers might think twice before they attack a small family traveling west. Now that you're up here and sitting with us,…we'll look even more like that. Pretty clever, don't you think?"

"Oh,…yes, Mister David," she replied, her wide grin again exposing her adorable dimples. "I don't know why those bad men came into our campsite," Molly went on, clearly bewildered about the motive for the attack. David and I also wondered why their wagon was targeted and pillaged by those thieves. "Poppa saw some riders following us. He told me we might be in danger. Poppa said they were looking to steal our horses and everything in our wagon. Oh, I sure hope my poppa was able to get away. Maybe he's already in Goshen waiting for me."

Again, David and I eyed each other. There was no doubt in our minds that he had most likely met with foul play at the hands of that heartless posse. We had a feeling she would never see her father alive again.

"By the way, just in case we run into him in our travels,…what does your poppa look like and what was he wearing?" I asked, anticipating a general description.

"My poppa ties his long brown hair with a thin leather cord. He has a brown mustache and thick eyebrows. He's about as tall as you, Mister David. Poppa, always wore a black shirt, black coveralls and a black hat," she replied, glancing upwards and completing her father's visual rendering by placing her right hand near her head.

Molly fell asleep on a blanket rolled up behind the seat while still holding the little doll. When it was time to resume our disguise and replace the "baby," David improvised by wrapping his flask with a piece of burlap.

For the next few hours, we journeyed through cornfields and open meadows ringed by thick stands of pines and oaks. It reminded me of the unique beauty of Cape Cod and Brewster with its great expanses of evergreens, kettle ponds and salt marshes. The images of countless varieties of wildlife, which co-existed with man on that headland, were forever etched in my mind. Though I had been gone less than a month, it seemed like years since I had been home. Now that I was so far away from the Cape, I found myself longing for those familiar surroundings. As we moved through this thicket, David picked up the binoculars from the seat.

"Stop the wagon, Albert," he whispered, steadying his hand to indicate a gradual halt so as not to awaken, Molly. "I've spotted something hanging from a distant tree. It's several hundred yards from the road,…definitely a body. I can't make it out, but I'm sure we both know *who* it is. We don't want Molly to wake up and witness this gruesome sight. I hope she'll remain fast asleep."

"David, I'll stay with the wagon while you go to investigate that hanging," I said, tugging at the reins to ease the horses' gait to an eventual halt. "If it's who we think it is, come back and I'll return with you to help bury him."

David quickly removed his disguises then ran toward the tree. He hurried back, signaling that it was indeed Molly's father. He had paid the ultimate price for his thievery. I quietly stepped down, tied the reins to a tree, and then removed the shovels attached to the side of the wagon. Molly stirred, rolled over and went back to sleep. Within a half hour, we dug a deep trench, lowered the body into it and replaced the excavated soil. We covered the gravesite with a large stone then returned to the wagon. Molly continued to sleep soundly through it all. Anxiety and fear had kept her awake the night before, but now that she felt secure, Molly peacefully slumbered in her benefactors' wagon. While caressing her doll, she was relaxed and comfortably curled up under her one possession—the coarse, frayed, nondescript, gray-wool blanket.

✳   ✳   ✳   ✳

Mid -July, 1848

It was just after five on a cloudy and exceptionally humid afternoon. The blackened skies made it appear that evening was arriving two hours too soon. The hues of dusk would soon fade into night as rapidly moving, ebony clouds gathered menacingly over us. We planned on reaching Goshen the next day. David and I decided on a clearing close to a small kettle pond so we could refresh ourselves. We could hear the inimitable sound of thunder rumbling in the distance.

"I think we'd better make camp before the storm hits," David suggested, pointing ahead to a darkened sky and expecting a sudden summer rain. Thunderheads threatened. "We're in for a downpour,…that's for sure. There's a rock formation up ahead, maybe we can find cover somewhere within its crevices."

"We'll stop underneath the overhang at the base of that rocky bluff until the storm passes," I said, navigating the wagon toward a solid mass of stone protruding from a rather steep incline. "We'll find refuge from the rain under that ledge. Those loud claps of thunder hint at lightning that's getting closer by the minute. That nasty storm is quickly closing in on us. Most likely it'll be over us in no time. We must hurry!" I shouted, unbridling the horses, leading them to the water to drink, and then tying them with the guide ropes to a nearby tree. I reckoned the horses would welcome the cool rain on their overheated coats. We decided to wait until morning to replace the water in our kegs with fresh water from the springs.

The ear-splitting sound of crackling, booming thunder and the vicious lightning bolts, like bony fingers from a menacing hand, plummeted indiscriminately earthward assailing all of nature around us. It exploded in the skies beyond the horizon with instantaneous flashes—similar to detonating artillery.

"It won't be long before it reaches us. We'd better get our provisions and set up camp," said David, stretching to grasp the blankets, knapsacks and water canteens.

"Molly, I've prepared a food basket for us. You can help by fetching it for me," I suggested in an attempt to make her feel useful. It was David's turn at the reins, so I busied myself like a good wife and prepared a supper of bread, cheese, dried beef and fruit. I opened a bottle of port wine from my cargo. I felt it was high time we celebrated the upcoming end to our long trek west. We were preparing to exit Indiana. The city of Chicago was but a week or so away. Molly handed David the food basket while I placed a tarp on the ground and began to collect some twigs to start a campfire.

There was an abrupt and dangerous drop in temperature as a cold front made its presence known. A gale hit us with hailstones the size of large marbles. They were bouncing on the ground all around me. I stood erect and gazed westward to where a parched meadow met the ominously inky sky. As the trees arched, their branches were whipped about by a sudden violent wind. These severe warnings and the deafening clashes of thunder frightened us. The landscape sounded an alarm. It was an unusual and startling phenomenon.

"Look,…look over there!" I shouted, pointing to a churning mass the color of soot. "It's a tornado!" I exclaimed, looking through the binoculars. "It just hit ground not too far from here! Oh, my God!…It's directly over Goshen! If that twister unleashed it's fury in that town,…there'll be nothing left of it!"

"Oh, it probably traveled over open country," David reasoned, dismissing it as a common occurrence in this part of the Midwest. "Most likely, it didn't cause any harm or damage."

"I hope you're right, David," I replied, getting out of the rain and sitting on the canvas ground cover. "Even so, I could've sworn that shafts of wood and stone fragments were suspended within that swirling mass. Oh, well,…maybe it was my imagination. We'll soon find out, won't we? We should be arriving there by tomorrow afternoon,…possibly earlier."

After a period of torrential rain and heavy winds that passed as quickly as they arrived, the sun broke through the clouds and the skies cleared. Except for the sound of rushing water, an unnatural silence surrounded us. We enjoyed a leisurely supper, dried ourselves by the campfire, and then as the sun waned, we soon fell asleep.

The persistent chirping of song sparrows along with the staccato notes of the mockingbirds awakened us at dawn. Amidst the morning haze, an incandescent sun cast its shafts of radiant light through the trees, heralding its diurnal entrance like a spiritual presence. Sunbeams glinted off blades of marsh grass, transforming opaque droplets of morning dew into shimmering prisms. The sunlight sparkling on the water glimmered like bits of panning gold rushing along the current.

"It's much cooler today. Yesterday's oppressive heat and humidity are no longer with us. Can't ask for better than this, David!" I remarked, yawning and stretching as he stirred from a deep sleep. "Here's the hat and dress…It's your turn today to play mama to Molly and her doll. It looks like the road ahead is washed out here and there, but I'm sure we can circumvent those loblollies. We'll just detour around them and guide the horses over the grassy areas that abut the road."

Toward noon, we encountered several buckboards heading toward us. Like refugees escaping a ravaged land, these families were heading eastward with their belongings piled high behind them. The children were clutching their pets and small farm animals.

"If you folks are planning to stop in Goshen, I'm afraid you'll be in for quite a shock. You won't find much," an elderly farmer said as he pulled up aside of our wagon. "It's been completely demolished by a severe tornado that came through about five-thirty last evening," added the ruddy gentleman with skin like dried shoe leather. He was wearing a blood-soaked bandage coiled around his forehead. His wife, who was holding a strip of fresh white cotton, was preparing to change it when he stopped to talk to us. This slight, balding man with a long white beard and wrinkled face had a slumped posture that betrayed an untold weariness—as if he carried the weight of the world on his shoulders. "My name's Benjamin Chase and this is my Missus, Bethiah. Our married children are in those other wagons behind us.

"Our farmland's several miles west of town," he went on. "At the time it hit Goshen we were harvesting some crops. We were very lucky. My family and I watched as the twister traveled east and headed directly toward the town. When we returned to Goshen there wasn't much left of it...or our homestead. Some folks fortunate enough to have belowground food larders were saved from its fury, but others were badly injured or killed by that murderous funnel. They were carried into the church. God must have intervened because it sustained minimal damage. The steeple toppled from the roof and the windows were shattered, but other than that...it's still in fairly good shape. The pastor and some volunteers are caring for those poor wretched folk. I got hurt trying to salvage whatever I could from our uprooted home. A beam fell from the roof and almost did me in. We're headed east. My wife has family in Toledo, Ohio. We'll stay there until we can rebuild in Goshen."

"My name's Albert Crosby and this is my wife, Sally," I said, introducing myself and reaching to shake his hand. David hung his head so low the brim of his sunbonnet practically covered his face. "She's extremely shy, especially with strangers. I'm so sorry to hear of your misfortune. Yes,...we are on our way to Goshen. Do you happen to know the Bigelows?" I asked, searching his face for an affirmative answer.

"Yes, I do...But I have no idea what became of them," he replied shrugging his shoulders. "I see your little family's still intact. Consider yourself fortunate indeed, sir. Tragically, the twister claimed the life of our sixteen-year-old grand-daughter, Melanie. She was having a problem trying to breathe. The humidity aggravated her asthmatic condition, so we decided it was best that she remain at home. We found her limp, youthful body several yards away from the house," he went on to say as the tears flowed down his cheeks and Bethiah wept over their loss.

"My sympathies to you and yours, Mister Chase. My heart goes out to you," I said with compassion. "Will this help?" I asked, jumping from the wagon and removing a keg of water from the rear. "You might need some fresh drinking water for your journey. There's enough here for you and the others behind you."

"Thank you, kindly," Benjamin said appreciatively, wiping the blood from his eyes with his shirtsleeve then grasping the keg with both hands. He nodded his head in the direction of the wagons behind him. "They've lost half their children to the fury of that tornado. Their kin worked in some of the shops on Main Street…they're only rubble now. Alas, it was just before closing time." After he said this, I respectfully tipped my hat in the direction of the other wagons to acknowledge their loss.

"We were a day's journey from Goshen when we saw the twister up ahead," I said, helping him to load the water onto his buckboard. "Its spiraling winds had gathered all sorts of debris. I had a hunch the tornado had indeed wrought some serious damage somewhere. Please let us know if there's anything else we can do for you."

"No, thank you. You've been kind enough already," Benjamin replied, nodding as he ascended his buckboard. He sat next to Bethiah and took hold of the reins. "In any case, I'm sure those folks in Goshen will certainly be grateful for any help you can give them, including clothing or food. There are so many victims to tend to. We'll be on our way now. We're hoping to cover another twenty miles before we make camp. Goodbye and a safe journey to you!" he shouted, waving his hand and cracking the whip over the horses as he pulled away from us.

"Humph!…So I'm Sally now!" David quipped, cuffing me on the shoulder. "Great choice of names, I must say! I'll have to think of one for you, Albert. Say…how about Jezebel?"

"That's fine with me!" I replied with a compliant smile while shrugging my shoulders and turning toward Molly. "Do you think it's an appropriate name for me, Molly?" She chuckled and thought that was pretty funny. I released the brake lever, jerked the bits with the reins, and then we continued on our way.

As David and I neared the eviscerated town of Goshen we were stunned by the severity of the pillaging force that had decimated this small town. Large trees were uprooted and strewn across the roadway like matchsticks. We detoured around them by guiding the horses over the grassy fields parallel to the main thoroughfare that led into town. The buildings were pulverized and their infrastructure ripped apart by the velocity of an uncontrollable energy gone berserk. The path of destruction wreaked so much havoc across such a broad sweep that this outlandish scene of some twenty miles remains a vivid memory.

Even though a deep layer of mud covered the homes, which were on the fringes of this 200 mile-an-hour wind funnel, they were still standing. They escaped with broken windowpanes and roofs that sagged under the weight of timber and stones hurled at them. Wooden beams jutted out from rooftops like stilettos ominously thrown at a target. The landscape was strewn with litter, rubble, and large fragments of building debris—testimony to the demonic tornado that had spiraled out of control and splintered everything in its path. Uprooted trees and bushes clogged the streets and were scattered everywhere. As it gained momentum, the dangerous twister moved through Goshen leaving it in shreds. The carnage was unbelievable! The boardwalk was filled with the walking wounded who were dazed and wandering around looking for their loved ones. Some were battered, bruised and bleeding while others lay unconscious along the roadside amid the shambles of what was once a bustling urban town. The result of the unexpected, ferocious assault on this landscape was similar to that of a vast mural depicting a bleak, ravaged countryside. It was a chaotic, catastrophic scene. The magnitude of desolation was mind-boggling.

"Let's try to find the pastor. It's possible he may know the Bigelow family and their whereabouts," David recommended, looking for a clearing behind the church where I could station the prairie schooner and hitch the horses. "He's probably in the church tending to the wounded and dying. I don't think we'll need our costumes,…at least not for a while. Give me your fake beard and mustache," he added, quickly untying the pinafore, wig and bonnet, rolling them into a ball, and then tucking them securely under the seat.

With Molly by our side, I removed my hat as we entered the makeshift hospital using a back entrance. David and I meandered through this refuge overflowing with stretchers and cots. Men, women and children of all ages, ethnic backgrounds and cultures occupied them. Most lay moaning—their blood oozing through makeshift bandages. Some had already died. The specter of death was all around us. The clergyman was much too occupied with the injured to pay much heed to the dead. Through the long hours following the storm he was a source of inspiration, laboring tirelessly and without complaint. This man who went on without rest, concentrated his efforts—solely on the living.

"Hello!" he said, noticing that we were strangers. After tending to an elderly man, he stood up from a bent position, and then addressed us as we approached him. "What can I do for you?" he asked. "My name is Reverend Uriah Thatcher. I'm the pastor here trying to tend to these poor people and except for that woman over there…I'm all alone," he went on, pointing to someone administrating to patients across the expanse of church pews and improvised stretchers that filled the aisles. "It's my responsibility to offer them comfort, and at the very least, a measure of peace and stability. God saw fit to spare this small church,…offering it as a symbol of hope; a beacon shining through the despair and ruins, beckoning all those in need. Even the doctor and his family were among the casualties. Those able to do so have already evacuated the town. An old chap and his wife helped me for a short while, but they were so grieved over the loss of family members that they decided to leave…caring for the injured and the dead was just too traumatic for them." The reverend's efforts were limited to prayer and bandaging wounds. A white coverall apron protected his ministerial black suit, a symbol of his noble calling. This dedicated pastor was thrust into a role that he was completely unprepared for. His dark, blood-shot eyes and flushed complexion indicated his exhaustion and frustration. A halo of white hair circling a bald head and dark-rimmed glasses gave him an aura of both piety and intelligence. He discreetly inspected us from head to toe.

"Yes, Pastor Thatcher," I replied. We encountered those people around noon today. They were heading east and suggested that we help you if possible. My name's Albert Crosby and this is my friend, David Atkins. We're from the East Coast and on our way to Chicago," I said after introducing ourselves, holding my hat under one armpit, and then reaching out with the other to shake his hand. David advanced and repeated my gesture.

"You'll never know how much I've prayed for some strong men like you since this catastrophe. I desperately need some help lifting the dead from these cots," Pastor Thatcher said in a state of semi-desperation, resuming his rounds and moving from one patient to the next. "I've been striving to aid the ones who need it the most. Those pathetic souls with a variety of lacerations, sitting or sprawled on the floors over there can't be properly cared for until a cot is freed for their use. The pews are being occupied with exhausted people that are either resting or waiting for their loved ones to be cared for. Also,…graves must be dug as soon as possible. The unfortunate ones, including the babies and small children need to be put to rest before they decompose in this heat. Several able men who have volunteered their services are assembling caskets as quickly as possible. These brave souls have endured a cauldron of sweat, blood and tears…many are crafting coffins for their own kin. Your presence here is an answer to my prayers. God must have heard my pleas and led you here. I know that now," he went on to say, as he bent down to speak to Molly. "And what's your name,…little girl?" he asked.

"My name's Molly Duncan, sir. Mister Albert and Mister David (she insisted on using the title "Mister" before our proper names) were taking me here to look for my Aunt Julia," she said confidently, continuing to speak for herself and pointing to us. "I was supposed to stay with her while my poppa went to California, but some bad men took my poppa away. I don't know where my poppa is now," Molly sighed, her chin beginning to quiver as her composure slowly deteriorated. Somehow she managed to hold back the tears, then abruptly left us to cheer a young boy resting on a cot nearby.

"Pastor Thatcher, we're trying to find a family by the name of Bigelow so we can hand her over to them. Do you know who they are and where they live?" I asked in Molly's absence. "David, and I found her abandoned east of here a few days ago. Molly said her father was going to drop her off in Goshen and that she'd live with the Bigelows while he traveled west. We offered to take her here hoping we'd locate them. We're fairly certain that bounty hunters, vigilantes or a sheriff's posse were following Molly's father. Evidently, in sheer desperation, he stole the horses needed for his journey to the West Coast. We found his body hanging from a tree. Molly has no idea what's become of him. She was asleep at the time and we weren't about to tell her the truth about his fate."

"Your secret's safe with me," the reverend said assuredly as he fumbled with a length of clean, white percale and began to change a patient's bandage. "You're both decent fellows. I'm honored to make your acquaintance. Yes, I do know that family. In fact, they happen to be parishioners of this church. Good Christian people they are," he added, nodding. "They were delighted that Molly was coming to live with them. Hiram Bigelow confided that unfortunately Molly's father, Reuben Duncan, was a ne'er-do-well…always just one step ahead of the law. I regret to tell you that the Bigelow's home was directly in the tornado's path," he went on in a voice that suddenly turned sullen. "I imagine it's been completely leveled along with all the other homes in that part of town. I assume they're among the fatalities…I don't see them here. It would be a miracle if they're still alive,…but I doubt it. I know where they live, and if you wish, we can ride out there tomorrow. A doctor from Elkhart is due here later today. In any case, there's no way I could possibly leave. I'm sorely needed here right now."

"Yes, we realize it's impossible for you to forsake these people. We certainly understand your commitment to them," I said, scanning the makeshift hospital filled with the wailing sound of infants, the heart-wrenching moans of the injured and the fitful screams of the dying. This humble man worked to accommodate even the lowliest of his flock. Reverend Thatcher's spirit of unconditional love gave solace to the wounded and dignity to the dead and dying. Feeling challenged to help my fellow man and overwhelmed by a profound sense of empathy, I spontaneously offered our services. "We'll certainly try to help in any way we can. We have fresh water in our wagon and a little food supply. David and I will be happy to share whatever we have with you. I also have some alcohol that can be used for medicinal purposes. It might help to sterilize wounds and ease the suffering."

"Albert, what are you saying?" David mumbled without moving his lips. He pulled me aside while the pastor recited a short prayer over a recently deceased body of a young girl. "You know we can't stay here for any length of time! We've got to be on our way as soon as we find Molly's aunt…Time is of the essence," he whispered adamantly with a disapproving look.

"Sh-sh-sh!" I indicated, placing my index finger over my lips. "We can't do anything about that until tomorrow. While we're here, we may as well help this poor soul. It's the least we can do…Don't you agree? Besides, we allowed ourselves a month or so to get to Chicago. We're still well within that time frame."

"I guess so," he said, yielding to my suggestion, albeit grudgingly.

"Thank you for your offer of water," Pastor Thatcher said, joining us again. "All things considered, it seems our wells have survived unscathed. Our water's still fresh and pure…Thank God for that! The only general store in town was also demolished, but the proprietor survived by taking cover in his cellar where he warehoused most of his inventory. He's been kind enough to donate an ample supply of food for these people. His wife and family are preparing meals for us as we speak. I'll be forever indebted to them for their benevolence and generosity.

"Well,…since you offered your services," he added, "I'd appreciate it if you could put the dead bodies in the caskets provided for them and place them in my buckboard for burial. Your strong Morgan horses could also be used to pull the debris from the injured and uncover the dead. I'd truly be grateful for those services. Maybe you can do this while you wait until tomorrow afternoon to find Molly's relatives."

"We'll be happy to oblige," I replied, looking around the church for Molly and finding her sitting next to a small boy with a splint on his arm. I could tell he enjoyed her company. "Molly, you stay here and help Reverend Thatcher," I said when I approached her. "David and I will join you in a few hours. We'll most likely sleep right here on the pews tonight."

The next afternoon, we saddled up and rode to the Bigelow homestead on the outskirts of Goshen. I've never forgotten the nightmarish scene that greeted us. There wasn't a beam in place or stone unturned. A solitary chicken clucked along the rim of what was once the main floor of a wooden, frame home. It was built over a stone cellar, now exposed like a yawning chasm. We called out several times—no one answered. Except for the sound of the wind rustling through the trees and the swishing of water cascading over the rocks in a nearby creek, a ghostly silence encompassed the entire area. The three of us struggled to raise some cross beams—barriers that had fallen across the staircase leading to the belowground level. We poked through and lifted the debris until we found a solid-oak kitchen table. Two small children had taken refuge under it and were crushed when the beams came hurling down. Nearby, we found the bodies of the mother and father who had been killed by falling roof rafters. Hiram Bigelow lay prone in a corner of the cellar. Only his legs were visible under the debris. The family might have survived for a short time, but without immediate aid they succumbed to their injuries. We removed the mangled bodies that were rapidly decomposing under the summer sun. After Reverend Thatcher recited a few, short prayers over their hastily dug graves, we returned to the church and revealed, as tactfully as possible, this tragic news to Molly.

"Oh, no! Who will take care of me? Where will I go?…I'm too little to be left on my own," she sobbed, placing her head in her hands as she ran into David's open arms. His reply took me completely by surprise.

"Don't worry, sweetie. Albert, and I will take good care of you. You can come along with us," he said reassuringly after seeing Molly's crestfallen expression. He held her close and wiped her eyes with his handkerchief. "In fact,…maybe you can come with me to California. Would you like that?"

"Oh, yes, Mister David!" she screamed in delight. Utterly elated by that prospect, Molly jumped into his arms and kissed him on the cheek.

"Wait just a moment," Pastor Thatcher interrupted, quietly pulling us aside. "I know a family who may want to adopt Molly and love her as their own. Their ten-year-old daughter passed away yesterday from internal injuries. The Scranton's have two sons, Daniel and Jacob.

"Molly," he said, kneeling down to face her. "That young fellow you were speaking to earlier just lost his only sister. I'm sure God sent you here to take her place in his life. Come along with me, Molly. His parents have just arrived to take Jacob home with them. I'll take you over to meet them."

He took her by the hand and led her toward the far end of the church where he was preparing to leave with his family. Jacob scanned the area looking for Molly amidst the sea of people. As she moved toward him, he was thrilled by the sight of her and grinned from ear to ear. Although encumbered by his sling, he ran to meet her. A friendship ceremony of sorts took place between the two. The reverend spoke with Jacob's family for a few minutes. They nodded appreciatively, then immediately took Molly under their wing. We couldn't hear the conversation; however, we knew they had made an unequivocal choice. Molly was instantly accepted into their family circle.

David and I were flabbergasted! We looked at each other in disbelief. We felt their decision to adopt Molly should have at least taken a bit longer than it did. "How can this be?…Yes, God certainly intervenes," I thought. "We were meant to be here at this moment in time. It was His plan, not ours. He has purposely directed us on this particular path. David and I could have left at a different time and taken another route. Yet here we are helping in an unforeseen crisis, finding a home for an orphaned child and making life bearable again for some complete strangers."

After giving Molly a firm embrace, we removed her few belongings from the wagon. We handed her the doll and she grasped it firmly in her arms. A case of 100-proof alcohol for medicinal purposes was carried into the church and given to Pastor Thatcher. After helping him with as much relief as David and I could offer during our short stay, we said our goodbyes and prepared to move on.

"We'll rebuild soon enough," Reverend Thatcher said resolutely, reflecting the faith and strength that rose from the dust of this disaster. "We journey forward gentlemen with renewed hope…trusting in the Lord to give us the strength to do what we must. It's a force that sees beyond all the sadness, pain, suffering and death…a spiritual energy that motivates our efforts toward compassion and generosity. It encourages us to reach past our self-centeredness and evokes the best in people. Love and faith provide a healing grace that pushes the human limits of perseverance and courage to that of joy and resolve to begin anew. Our stalwart town leadership will rise above this and the courageous townspeople *will* rebuild. Maybe those who left will return someday,…and as in the past, the likelihood of travelers passing through will decide to settle here. Goshen's revitalization depends upon it. I wish you'd stay here in Goshen and share the promise of that new tomorrow with us. We certainly could use your help, and I *know* Molly will miss you both."

"Thank you, Reverend. I'm afraid that's not possible," I replied, determined to press onward. "I intend to start my own liquor and tea business in Chicago, and David is planning to rendezvous with some friends and journey to California. Thank you for your food and hospitality," I went on, taking hold of the reins and bending to shake the minister's hand as he stood by the wagon. "I hope we've been of some assistance to you, Pastor Thatcher…God speed!" I cracked the whip and, at a moderate gallop, we left the ravaged town of Goshen behind us. Occupied with our own thoughts, I came to the realization that life—as a whole—was indeed a daring adventure into the unknown. We journeyed in virtual silence until we were several miles outside of town.

"Albert, I'll have you know that I became quite attached to that little girl," David eventually confessed, interrupting the quiet. "My heart ached when it was time to say goodbye to her. Why, I may never get to see Molly again!…That's such a distressing thought."

"Well, I must say you've certainly had a change of heart," I replied, not really surprised by his disclosure. "I could tell by the way you fussed over her that you were quite fond of that little tyke. I noticed how you lovingly covered her while she slept and how you made sure she ate well. I realized right then and there that you'd be a great parent, despite what you said earlier. I watched while you entertained Molly with your guitar as she sat close by, and I was impressed by your patience when you taught her how to fish and explore nature. It amused me to hear you relating your various escapades with such imagination and animation. I must say, dear friend, that some were slightly exaggerated," I said nodding my head, smiling, and winking at the same time. "But she believed every word."

"Even though I planned to take her with me after we discovered her would-be guardians were deceased, I know Molly will be in good hands," David said. "She'll be happier now as a member of a family. The Scranton's seem to be good parents. Molly will fill the void in their lives. It's better this way for all concerned…Don't you agree, Albert?" he asked. With a few quick nods, my non-verbal communication expressed an acceptance of his reasoning; on the other hand, I knew David was making a futile attempt to justify her absence—and his bitter loss.

▼

CHAPTER 12

Late-July, 1848

Our long journey was coming to an end. David and I finally reached the outskirts of Chicago. The prairie schooner sat perched atop a slight slope on an otherwise flat terrain overlooking the city. We stopped to view the panorama spread before us. Chicago's vast skyline was a series of unbroken silhouettes—darkened shapes of various widths and heights. Jagged spires, circular domes and towering rectangular structures combined to create a powerful image of a city on the rise.

"Look, Albert! Just a few more miles!...Chicago at last!" David shouted, pointing ahead while guzzling from his flask. He shoved it into my chest. "Here, have a swig...time to celebrate, my friend. Drink to the end of a harrowing but successful journey!"

"Oh, all right,...I guess it's as good a time as any to join you in a celebration of sorts," I said, taking a sip from the flacon to appease him. I twisted the plug back and handed the flask back to him. "However,...we're not there *yet*! Chicago's still a good day's journey from here.

"I think we should resume our camouflage," I added while taking hold of the reins and leading the horses down the incline. "You never know, David...I heard that vagrants abound in these lowlands. It's also common knowledge that most immigrants flocking to this city are indigent and desperate. We should be as vigilant outside these city limits as we've been right along."

"Ugh,...you're right, Albert!" David replied, reaching for the disguises from under the seat, reluctantly placing the bonnet on his head, and then handing me the mustache and beard. "I'm not looking forward to this charade again, but because it was my idea in the first place,...I'll have to swallow my pride and go along with it."

Amused by his change of heart, I chuckled, smiled, and then shook my head. "Since it's already late afternoon, I'm afraid we won't arrive in Chicago until sometime tomorrow," I remarked, noting the beads of perspiration rolling off the horses' hides. "I know we have several more hours of daylight, but I sense the horses are tiring in this heat and need to rest. If possible, let's try to find some shade and water to cool them off."

We traveled across open grassland toward a deep pool of water that was nestled in a small quarry thick with maple and oak trees. After we cooled the horses and ourselves, I started a small fire, cooked a meager fare of beans and knockwurst, and then settled in for the night. Although we hadn't encountered rain for several days, we hoped that while we camped outdoors, we'd be spared a downpour. Even though a band of gray clouds had followed us most of the day, they were now heading south. A scarlet sunset signaled yet another searing day ahead.

From afar, the multi-storied brick edifices of Chicago's financial district looked like the rows of uneven pylons at the end of a dock. As our wagon wound its way on the dusty streets of the city limits, we found we weren't alone in our quest for a better life. Buckboards stacked high with furniture, horseback riders and dozens of covered wagons were entering or leaving Chicago—clogging the already impassible roadways. This transient population was a phenomenon that David and I had never encountered before.

"Where's everyone going and coming from?" David asked, completely mystified by it all, quickly removing the wig and bonnet, rolling up the pinafore, and then tucking them under the seat. "I've never seen anything like this! You know what, Albert,…Chicago's an absolute madhouse! It's fraught with confusion, noise and hostility. Why it's absolutely outrageous! Everyone's pushing and shoving someone else out of the way just to get by."

The sights, sounds and smells of this city overwhelmed our senses as we rambled toward the business district. It was a disquieting scene. Extensive neighborhoods of shanties and lean-tos, which were hurriedly built by the poor and downtrodden with all sorts of scrap wood and tin metal, hugged the streets for blocks. Grimy, rag-tag children were begging everywhere. Intoxicated patrons were periodically ousted from dilapidated saloons, taverns, hovels and dens of iniquity. The gambling houses overflowing with customers, allowed them to wager their monies on the front steps. The din of police wagons chasing criminals, the baying of horses, the incessant barking of dogs, the herding of livestock along the streets and the beckoning shouts of harlots from open windows were deafening.

To make matters worse, the reeking stench of open sewage flowing in the gutters was nauseating. We debated whether we should cover our ears or hold our noses. I was beginning to doubt my judgment. These strange surroundings were so different from Boston and my native Cape Cod. "Have I made a horrible mistake? I wondered with justifiable concern. "Is Madam Henderson right about the pitfalls of this city? Have I been too rash and cocky about choosing Chicago for my business venture? While it's just a meeting place for David, it'll be my permanent home. I don't know about David, but I feel as though I've been immersed in a hideous, bizarre world. Do I want to live in the midst of all this intimidating squalor?"

A sudden burst of gunshots just a few yards from our wagon interrupted my thoughts. A proprietor was shooting at someone who had stolen an armful of goods from his general store. The horses bolted. I forcefully held the reins to control them. It was all I could do to keep my wagon from turning over. If that had happened—I would have lost much of my inventory.

"This place is a veritable hell-hole! I can't imagine people living in this kind of pandemonium and squalor. These conditions are deplorable!" David exclaimed. "I can't understand why the Myricks would want to rendezvous in this god-forsaken place. Unless I'm mistaken, this city has absolutely no surfaced streets, sidewalks or gaslights to speak of. There's no visible means of transportation. At least Boston has a railroad and omnibuses…Not so in Chicago. If I'd known it would be anything like this, I would have planned to meet up with them in Galesburg, instead. I think I'm going to regret my decision to come here…It's unbelievable! Do you feel that way, Albert? Are my expectations unreasonable?"

"Oh, no, David. I can't conceive of a place like this! It's a freak show—a living nightmare! Chicago's utterly beyond comprehension." I said, trying to hide my disappointment. "I just hope it's only a first impression. It certainly doesn't bode well for a city that welcomes strangers with this sort of reception. However, we haven't reached the center of the financial district as yet. The ambiance seems to be getting a little more encouraging as we approach it."

As the wagon progressed slowly along the rough, sandy roadway, David and I welcomed the sight of the four and five-story brick buildings. We assumed the business district would be a short distance ahead. Several church steeples and hotel cupolas thrust their soaring towers above the flat roof tops of numerous plain but functional brick and stucco edifices that were slightly reminiscent of Greek revival architecture. They lacked, however, the ornate windows and porticos of their counterparts in Boston. Nevertheless, in comparison to what we previously witnessed it was indeed reassuring.

"Even though they were built to accommodate the business patrons, many of the temporary wooden sidewalks, which flank the front of these buildings, are in various stages of disrepair," David noted, carefully surveying every aspect of this more respectable neighborhood. "Say, looks like there's some decent hotels in this area! I'm looking forward to a good night's sleep on a soft mattress. Let's pull up behind that one over there," he went on, pointing ahead. It'll be dusk soon. I'd like to clean up and have a large steak for dinner."

"You're always hungry, David. But right now,…I'd say you're more interested in a fine whiskey than you are in a cold shower. You're not fooling me one bit," I said, with a suspicious grin and hint of skepticism in my voice. "All right,…we'll stop there." I rounded the corner and traveled a short distance toward an ostentatious hotel. "Well, this is more like it. I was beginning to believe the Chicago we encountered on our arrival here was a sampling of the whole city. It's certainly no paradise, but at least this district's much more civilized. These residents are obviously better dressed, calmer and more courteous than the unkempt ragamuffins who live in the immigrant settlements on the outskirts of the city. The plight of those poor unfortunate people really bothers me. I'm sure their strong young men would rather be working than wasting valuable time drinking and being idle. If my venture proves to be profitable, I intend to gainfully employ some of them."

The next morning, we set out to find more permanent lodgings—a rooming house closer to the city center. After registering at the desk, David left to find the Myricks and the flotilla of wagons that would be heading west. My first priority was to locate and lease an appropriate property for my new business. After a few days of searching for just the right location, I had the carriage stop at a corner building that faced Chicago Avenue. It was in close proximity to the Chicago River and was exactly what I was looking for. After locating the property owners, I signed the lease for a year and paid my first month's rent up front.

David, on the other hand, was on the move. "Looks like I'll be around for another week. We're waiting for a few more wagons to show up. As soon as they arrive, we'll be on our way. This is the last wagon train heading west for the winter," he said upon his return from his visit with the Myricks. "In the meantime,…if it's all right with you, I'll help you empty the contents of your wagon."

"Thank you, David. You're a true friend. I'm eager to get started. I appreciate any help you can give me right now. I can't wait to unload that wagon. I've been so concerned about my valuable cargo over this past month," I replied while changing into some work clothes. "The first thing I'm going to do is put my sign up over the door. I ordered it the day we started out on our separate ways. I knew

I'd eventually find a satisfactory location. This one's perfect for my purposes. Wait 'til you see it, David!"

David helped me hang my marker from an ornamental cast-iron arm that was suspended over the front entrance. When I realized that my dream of starting my own business was finally coming true, I was overcome with a deep sense of pride. I stood back to scrutinize the sign. It read:

Albert Crosby & Co.
Wholesale
Liquors and Teas

The prairie schooner was soon emptied of the goods we had carried for 900 miles on, more often than not, primitive roadways. The stock was placed on the shelves, labeled, and then priced. I breathe a sigh of relief.

"The help and comradeship you provided me on the way here was indispensable. I don't think, in fact I know, I couldn't have managed without you. You truly deserve the wagon and the horses,…and actually,…much, much more. Take them, David,…they're yours," I said gratefully while handing him the reins. "I wish you a safe journey to California. May you find riches beyond your wildest dreams."

"Thank you, Albert. I know you just want me to take it off your hands," he replied facetiously and jabbing me in the ribs. "Seriously, it goes without saying, I truly appreciate your generosity, Albert. You'll be fondly remembered, my friend. I'll always cherish the memories we've shared.

"Well, the last family has finally arrived," he went on. "After they've rested a few days, our wagon train will leave Chicago. We should reach California before the first snowfall…I'm afraid we're cutting it a little close. It'll be bad enough just going through the mountain passes without having to contend with a blizzard on the way. I'll be busy loading this wagon before we depart,…so I guess this will have to be goodbye," he said chagrined, yet resigned to follow his heart and extending his hand to mine. "I plan on visiting you someday in that palace you hope to build overlooking the bay. Now don't be surprised if I return to Brewster in a gilded carriage."

"I'll look forward to that day, David," I replied. "In the meantime, do take care of yourself and promise you'll stay in touch." I reached for his hand and embraced him firmly. "California's a large territory. You'll probably wind up in the northern part where much of the mining's taking place. In any case, when you reach your destination telegraph me of your whereabouts. You must go your way David,…and I must go mine. I won't say goodbye, I'll just say fare-well,…until we meet again."

"Yes, Albert, I plan to do just that. I'll also look forward to hearing from you once I get settled," he replied, opening the door and taking his leave.

Somehow the future seemed unimportant and the past just memories. It was the present—this very moment that I would treasure forever—regardless of the direction our lives would take. Aware that I might never see him again, I watched as he walked away from me. I was overwhelmed by a profound sense of loss. With a lump in my throat, I swallowed and tried to hold back the tears. Heartsick, I was loath to close the door behind him.

*   *   *   *

Early-November, 1848

I decided to advertise my new business in the local newspapers: The Chicago *Evening Journal* and the Chicago *Tribune*. While the half-page ads were costly, they were worth the price. I also had fliers printed and distributed announcing my opening sale prices. I paid several small boys to slide them under the front doors of homes and businesses for several blocks within the vicinity of my shop. It was a bold initiative that proved to be quite successful. The results were astounding! Within weeks, I had a thriving business. Lines formed outside the doors. It was all I could do to keep up with the inventory. It fairly flew off the shelves. I found myself in a quagmire of work, burdened and overwhelmed.

This urgent situation caused me to hire several industrious young men, mostly immigrants who were willing to settle in Chicago, cast off their shackles of apathy and earn a living wage. Those who worked diligently were assured of a secure future with a stable, rapidly growing company. If they could understand and speak English—they tended to sales. Despite their minority status, their ability to speak a foreign language was quite beneficial at times. Chicago was in the midst of social change—a melting pot of immigrating hordes. They arrived from all corners of the world, looking for work or using Chicago as a rest stop before heading west. Some planned to settle and farm the wide-open prairies of the western frontier or push on to California. In the meantime, I replenished stocks, set up displays, and then plunged into mountains of related paperwork.

"Your financial statement shows your business is becoming more profitable with each month, Mister Crosby, sir. Your early objectives have been realized. Your debts have been paid, and you're already beginning to show a substantial surplus," declared my timid accounting clerk, who insisted on calling me "Mister Crosby." Due to burgeoning business obligations, I decided I needed some assistance with the ledgers. An exceptionally gifted gentleman, Josiah Hathaway had come highly recommended by a client who was moving his business eastward. He opened the books for me to examine and pointed to some figures on an assortment of pages. "I believe you'll need to expand soon," he went on to say. "The lease is up on the building next door. It'll hold twice the amount of inventory you have here. It can be attached to this one with a covered walkway. I'm sure you won't have a problem with the bankers. Your credit is excellent. You've not only established a profitable business, but a reputable one as well."

"Thank you, Josiah. Yes, it sounds like a well thought out proposal." I replied, amazed at his foresight. "I'll certainly give it a lot of thought."

Josiah was a slight, soft-spoken man in his early thirties. He wore a small thin mustache, and also attractive, narrow sideburns and beard that were neatly shaped. They joined at his chin line and framed his boyish face from below one ear to the other. Josiah was married with two children—a boy, ten, and—a girl, five. Above all, I admired his honesty and his industrious work ethics. I trusted his opinion and usually accepted his astute suggestions. I was not yet aware of it, but over the ensuing years, Josiah would become my closest friend and confidant—replacing the void left by the loss of David's camaraderie. Sharp as a tack when it came to numbers and wise beyond his years, he was as indispensable as my right arm. I could depend on him to lend a hand in every capacity imaginable, whenever or wherever needed. If we were exceptionally busy, he would assist with sales. When inventory arrived, he helped to sort, price, and then place it on the shelves. His size belied his tenacity and strength. I was afraid his willingness to lift heavy crates would result in physical injury; nevertheless, he persistently ignored my pleas to let the stronger, larger younger boys do the work. Owing to frequent and sometimes-lengthy business conferences with creditors, I decided to promote him to "General Manager." I needed someone I could depend on in my absence.

*   *   *   *

Late-November, 1848

"I've made plans to leave for the East Coast soon," I informed Josiah after pouring myself a cup of coffee, walking into his back office and nearing his desk. He put down his pen, looked up at me, and then listened intently. "Actually, it'll be at the end of this week. It's been almost six months since I've been east. I promised Margaret that I'd come home for the holidays. I'll be away for just over a month. I plan on returning to Chicago after the first of the year. I wanted to wait until mid-January because business will be especially brisk over the holidays,...but she'd have none of it. I'll leave it to your discretion to hire the extra holiday help. I'm sure you'll be able to handle everything while I'm gone. Telegraph me if a problem should arise and I'll respond immediately. I wanted my family to join me on the return trip, but I don't want them traveling to Chicago in mid-winter. However,...I hope they'll accompany me back here next summer."

"I hope so for your sake, Mister Crosby. It's a lonesome life without your loved ones to share your days and nights," Josiah replied. "Although you hide it well,...I've often seen the longing in your eyes and sensed the ache in your heart. Please put your mind at ease. I'm sure all will go well while you're away. I'll also inform the extra hired help that they're employment will terminate after the holiday rush."

"Oh, that reminds me, Josiah," I interrupted. "While I'm thinking about it, please see to it that the employees receive a sizable bonus. I think two weeks pay should be appropriate. I placed yours in this envelope. Now don't open it until Christmas!" I added lightheartedly with a chuckle.

"Thank you kindly, Mister Crosby," he said, pushing his chair away from his desk, standing, and then walking over to me. "I'll take care of the bonuses, you needn't worry about a thing. I can manage business here, just fine. Enjoy the time with your family. You've been working fourteen-hour days and, sometimes...seven days a week. You need a reprieve from all of this. I know I'm probably wasting my breath, but please don't give this place a second thought."

"I also hope to visit the Crosby homestead on Cape Cod," I said, slowly walking toward the door, my coffee cup still in hand. I turned and stood there a while longer to finish my discourse. "They've been eagerly awaiting my arrival. Letters and telegraphs back and forth no longer suffice. I plan to spend some time with my family members. My parents have always been very supportive. They have a lot of faith in me. I can't wait to tell them about my good fortune and how successful I've already become."

The excursion back to Boston by stagecoach and steamer took almost four days. I encountered a mixture of snow, sleet, blizzard conditions and fog along the way. After reaching Toledo by carriage, I boarded a steamboat that crossed Lake Erie into New York. I disembarked from the launch in Buffalo, then again traveled by stagecoach to Boston.

While journeying eastward, my window seat afforded me a majestic view of the stark winter landscape. The sun was just coming up. It painted a picture-perfect snow scene in a dazzling shade of pink. The large, snow-covered stones and tree branches were swathed in ice along the banks of the frozen lakes and creeks. They glistened under the blinding glare of a high winter sun.

When I arrived in Boston, I hailed a carriage to West Roxbury. On the return trip in January, I would have to journey all the way to Chicago by stagecoach because a good part of Lake Erie would be frozen over. I noticed several inches of fresh snow had fallen earlier in the day. A morning fog had left the branches of the trees heavy with ice, but sparkling like jeweled bangles.

As nightfall descended, an incandescent moon and glittering stars glowed brightly in a partly cloudy, late evening sky. The air was brisk and blustery—the horse's breath visible behind their visors. I retrieved my gloves from my pocket, and I wrapped the wool scarf that dangled from my shoulders loosely around my neck.

Over the horizon, a veil of filmy clouds covered a waning, relucent moon that painted the snow a soft, yellow hue. We rode past a grove of barren trees. Like specters, their macabre, skeletal branches twisting in the wind, were menacingly extended and ready to grasp unsuspecting travelers with their deformed, withered fingers. The moon glow drew inky, hachured facsimiles of each tree trunk on the snow, giving them the frightening illusion of additional height. The eerie stillness and solitude of this sinister tableau caused me to shiver. On the other hand, the thought of being so close to my loved ones warmed my homesick heart.

The carriage came to a halt at the front entrance of the Henderson home. I stepped down, retrieved my baggage, and then reached up to pay the driver.

"Oh, Albert! You're finally here!" exclaimed Margaret, rushing from the front doorway as she ran into my opened arms. Her parents, who were also there to greet me, followed behind her. "It's been such a long time without you, dearest. I've missed you so. Welcome home, my darling!"

"I've also missed you and our little Irene, more than you'll ever know." I said tenderly while kissing her with such burning desire, I couldn't wait to hold her in my arms and make love to her. We held each other tightly as we entered the front hallway. "I'm sure Irene is asleep at this hour," I added. "Although I can't wait to see her, I guess I'll have to put it off until morning."

"Yes, she's sleeping soundly, Albert. I dare not wake her for fear she'll be up all night," Margaret replied. "She's so adorable. As I've written, my darling, she favors the Crosby side of the family. Just wait 'til you see her! Oh, I'm so excited...I'm about to burst!"

"Good evening," I said, acknowledging the presence of the Hendersons, tipping my hat at Margaret's mother, and then shaking hands with her father. "Even though they're here to welcome me into their cozy family circle, this will *never* be my home. I can't imagine living under the same roof with those *two*." I thought as I placed my coat and hat on the clothing stand in the front hallway.

The Henderson mansion was festively decorated with garlands of holly draped over the doorways. Wreaths of spruce and heather embellished with bows of red ribbons adorned the windows and doors. As in most homes in West Roxbury, an enormous, elegantly decorated, Christmas tree, which could be seen from the street, graced the living room.

After a short stay for the holidays, we left West Roxbury to visit family in Brewster. As we traveled along the Olde King's Highway, we could see large chunks of ice pushing up against each other in the bay. In the distance, a pair of gray harbor seals basked in the sunshine as they shared a small ice floe. Icicles hanging from the eaves of the wooden roofs that covered the working weirs glistened like crystalline stilettos hanging from a mother-of-pearl rooftop. Brewster was indeed in winter's grasp.

The serenity of that small town truly captured the magic of the season. Evergreen holly trees heavy with red berries peeked from under the pristine blanket of white that covered the landscape. The branches of spruce and scrub pines bent under the weight of freshly fallen snow. As far as I was concerned there was no fairer scene anywhere in the world. An evening sleigh ride through the drifts in the meadows and under the snow-laden canopies of pines that dotted the countryside, the moonlight skating on the pristine ice-covered ponds and the festive roast duck and turkey dinners, truly embodied the joys of the season.

My parents delighted in their new grandchild. Being home with all my loved ones was short lived; nonetheless—a blissful and cherished visit.

The return trip to Chicago loomed ahead. While I loathed leaving my family again, I was eager to get back to my fledgling, yet flourishing business. Upon our return to West Roxbury, I approached Margaret about my plans.

"Margaret, it's imperative that I leave for Chicago within a few days. I had planned to stay a while longer, but I'm needed there," I said, cautiously approaching the subject and hoping she'd understand. "I received an urgent telegraph from Josiah concerning a business decision that can't wait. It's not something he's able to resolve on his own. I sent him a telegraph this morning advising him that I'd be leaving the day after tomorrow. I decided I ought to respond to this emergency as soon as possible."

I tried to soften the blow by announcing an unexpected surprise. "Tomorrow you and I will sign a contract to build a magnificent home of your choice here in West Roxbury," I said. "It's on a prestigious site,…one that I've recently purchased. Ground will be broken in the spring. It may not be completed for a while, but at least you'll have your own home when you return here from Chicago." When I purchased the land I was confident that by the time it was built, I would have more than enough money to cover its construction.

"Oh, Albert! How delightful!…I'm so excited! What a pleasant surprise!" she cried out, jumping into my arms, and kissing me. "I can't wait to tell my parents. You certainly must be doing well to afford a home in *this* neighborhood. I'm so proud of you, Albert! Why it's a dream come true for me! I'd like to call it "Wildwood.".…Do you approve?"

"It's a lovely name…for a lovely house…for a lovely lady," I answered, smiling, and tenderly holding her face in my hands. I gave her a quick kiss then reclaimed my clothing from the chest of drawers and placed it on the bed. "I'll be back sometime next summer, Margaret. Be prepared to join me on the steamer back to Chicago. Don't worry about packing a large trunk. We'll purchase additional clothing for you and Irene in Chicago. They have some fine shops that cater to the upper classes. My business is doing so well that by June or July, we'll also build a substantial home in Chicago…One I'm certain you'll be quite proud of. It won't be as grand as the one here, but it should suit our purposes for a while. The address is 159 Clark St. I'll wait until you arrive to select the furnishings. That'll keep you busy while I'm at work," I said with a smirk as I folded my shirts and trousers, and then filled my bags. "I'm so eager to have you in Chicago, my dearest. I loathe being away from my loved ones…It's such a dreary existence for me. If you wish, I also intend to hire a nanny so you can have more free time for yourself. I live each day in anticipation of coming home from long hours at the wholesale shop to your loving arms. I want to relax in an easy chair next to a roaring fireplace with my pipe and slippers, sit my beautiful child in my lap, read her a bedtime story or listen to her pleasant chatter. Is that too much to ask of life, Margaret?"

"No, Albert, of course not. That scenario sounds delightful, my dearest," Margaret replied, reaching for my case of cuff links and handing it to me. "The days will be long and lonely for me as well. My arms will ache to hold you and the tears that fall on my pillow will bear witness to the emptiness in my bed. I'll count each day until your return and try to write you as often as possible,...sealing each letter with a kiss. Until we're together again, *do* stay fit, Albert. I understand how dedicated you are to your business venture, but the long hours of work can be detrimental to your health." She took me by the arm after I closed my baggage and we left our room together. "I noticed you've lost quite a bit of weight since you left last June. Promise me you'll take good care of yourself. Again, I won't say goodbye, my dearest Albert, I'll just say farewell...until we're together once more." While the carriage waited, we embraced one last time. As we reluctantly separated, her lips were wet with salty tears that flowed freely down her cheeks.

✳   ✳   ✳   ✳

Mid-January, 1849

Winter in Chicago seemed harsh and uncompromising in comparison to the winters of Cape Cod. It had been an intense season of bitter cold and gusting winds. Josiah met me at the door of the wholesale house when I arrived from my trip east. The high winds and blustery weather of Chicago buffeted my body, making it difficult to keep my balance as I entered the building.

"Welcome back, Mister Crosby. I hope you had a wonderful vacation on the East Coast. On the other hand, I'm so relieved to have you back here at last." he said, looking a bit unnerved and attempting to justify his alarm. "I was doing quite well until this enormous shipment was delivered over two weeks ago," he added, pointing to the disarray in the shop. "There just wasn't any place to store it...Why it's even stacked to the ceiling in both of our offices and in the middle of the shop aisles...It's become a hazard. We simply can't reach our products without climbing over these crates. I have no idea what to do with it all!"

"I'm sorry you had to endure this inconvenience, Josiah. Everything's going to be all right...Please calm down," I said, trying to smooth his ruffled feathers while observing the clutter that was blocking the way to the back offices and creating a narrow path to my desk. "Although my family visit was glorious beyond words, I assure you it's great to be back. I must apologize for your crisis…It's actually my fault. I neglected to tell you that before I left, I leased the building next to us, and also a large neighboring warehouse from a real estate agent who was handling both structures. The lease agreement was mailed to me in West Roxbury to sign and return. This shipment was supposed to arrive long after my vacation. Evidently, the opportunity to ship it out occurred sooner than expected. I'll have this new stock removed and placed outdoors under a tarpaulin until it can be transported to the building next door. There should be more on the way. I'll have that shipment stored in the warehouse."

"I knew that something had gone awry. You've always been on top of things, Mister Crosby," he said, breathing a sigh of relief and reaching for an envelope he had previously placed on my desk. "This telegraph arrived while you were on your way here. And, oh,…by the way, I sincerely appreciate your Christmas gift. I'm extremely grateful, but shocked by the more than generous amount—again, many thanks to you, Albert, on behalf of myself and the family.

"You're quite welcome, Josiah. Thank *you*," I replied, reaching out for the envelope. "And please, Josiah, before it slips my mind again, let's be on a first name basis from now on. After all you're older than I am," I added with a wink and a wry smile.

Thinking the telegraph might be bad news from the East Coast, I opened it immediately. The contents read:

Dear Albert:

Arrived November—Found the mother lode—Will stake claim shortly—All is well—Best Wishes from Auburn, California—David.

"It's from my crewmate and friend, David. Whew!" I said, relieved to know it wasn't an emergency message from home. "I was expecting to hear from him any-time now. We arrived in Chicago together from Boston. I stayed to launch my business and he left with a wagon train headed for the California gold rush. Gold fever's sweeping the country, Josiah. I asked David to notify me of his where-abouts. I'm happy to learn that he's been successful. Sounds like he's doing just fine. I'm sorry to say that I've been so busy, I honestly hadn't given him much thought, lately."

That was the only message I ever received from David. When we parted, it never occurred to me that I might never see or hear from him again. Over the years, I assumed that perhaps like Jonathan, I had lost another dear and cherished friend. I guessed that he might have been drinking with strangers, bragged about his stake, was followed and eventually murdered by claim-jumpers. There was also the distinct possibility that he might have died in a mine cave-in or simply become a recluse—choosing to live a solitary life in the black hills of California until his death. Although I tried, I was never able to find out what happened to him. He just seemed to have vanished from the face of the earth.

$$* \quad * \quad * \quad *$$

Late-February, 1849

"Albert, there's something I'd like to bring to your attention," Josiah announced apprehensively, popping his head in the doorway of my office. He approached me with a set of accounting books in his hands. "Do you have a few minutes? I may be wrong,…but I think this is *quite* important."

"Why,…yes, I do," I replied, rising from my desk and moving toward the coffee urn on the potbelly stove. "In fact, I was just about to pour myself a cup of coffee. How about one for you, Josiah?"

"No, thank you. I dare say, you'll be quite interested in what I have to show you," he said, nervously juggling the large volumes that had red ribbon bookmarks flagging certain pages. He set the ledgers down on my desk for my review. "Look here!" he pointed out, opening the pages to the neatly posted columns of figures. "Liquor sales have almost quadrupled since you started this enterprise. It's actually 95 percent of your revenue. As for the teas,…they aren't worth the effort or the shelf space. Where they're concerned…your profit margin is slim to none. I keep well-balanced books, pay attention to details and note any information revealed by the figures. I've arrived at a definitive conclusion. Just look at this bottom line, Albert! It clearly indicates that you should be focusing solely on the wholesale liquor business."

"I rather suspected that." I replied, sipping my coffee and not a bit surprised by his astute revelation. "I've been giving that some serious thought these last few weeks. You're absolutely right! We'll not replenish our tea inventory. There's no question in my mind that it's actually been a drain on our space and resources. Our sales of tea have declined overall. From now on, Albert Crosby & Company will deal only in the sale of liquors. *That* has definitely proven to be more profitable. It's rather obvious…Chicagoans are *not* fond of tea."

"There's a need for a distillery right here in Chicago. All the wholesale liquor businesses must order elsewhere to replenish their stock. I don't wish to usurp your authority, Albert," Josiah advised, carefully selecting each word so as not to overstep his bounds, "but I suggest that once all the crates are transferred from the warehouse, you should consider converting it into a distillery."

"Why, you must have been reading my mind, Josiah," I replied, looking out the window toward the capacious brick warehouse that was just a short distance from my wholesale business. "You and I are undeniably reading each other's mind. I actually thought that might be an option when I leased the building. The location near the river is perfect for that purpose. I'll order all the necessary apparatus. My primary objective is a distillery that will manufacture a full range of wines, rum, brandy and cognac. That's what the market demands. My aim is to satisfy Chicago's thirst for first-rate liquors and fine wines. I'll purchase the grapes from family owned vineyards in California. We'll use the stone basement to store the wine casks until it ages into vintage stock. Advise the glassmakers that I'll need several thousand bottles. Also, please see to it, Josiah, that we have some labels printed. The operation of the distillery will begin as soon as everything is in place."

"Fine! I'll tend to that first thing in the morning," Josiah remarked excitedly. "I was afraid you'd think my proposal presumptuous of me or that I'd made a factual error. I'm so relieved to know that we're in total agreement…I can't wait to get started."

"This has *certainly* been a productive conversation," I said, shaking his hand as he prepared to leave my office. "Thank you for your suggestions, Josiah. Ever since my friend David left me for California,…I felt I'd lost a close associate and companion. You tend to fill that void for me. I appreciate your enthusiasm and selfless interest in this endeavor. We seem to share the same goals. I owe much of my success to your diligence and shrewd insight. You're as enthusiastic about this business as I am. Not only do I consider you a valued employee, Josiah, but also…a partner and dear friend."

"I'm fond of you too, Albert," he acknowledged, standing in the doorway. "I admire your compulsion to succeed and above all the fair and even-mannered way you deal with your employees. You never order them around or put them down for any reason. You always treat them kindly and in a diplomatic way…teaching with respect and patience. The chores are delegated fairly. By the example you set, there's a polite, cordial standard of interaction between salesperson and clientele,...how they should be addressed and catered to. For these reasons, and many more, I feel fortunate indeed to be associated with you and this company." With these words still ringing in my ears, he left my office. I smiled, took another sip from my coffee cup, and then walked back to my desk.

✳   ✳   ✳   ✳

Early-June, 1849

After the distillery had been in operation for four months, I could no longer keep up with the increased volume of business. The figures from the sales of distilled alcohol and wines soared far beyond my wildest expectations. Stacks of countless orders remained unfilled. In less than a year's time my new venture had mushroomed beyond my wildest expectations. The pressure to meet deadlines exceeded my ability to stay ahead of the demand. I decided to summon my father and his brother, Uncle Isaac. I needed help with what had now become the largest distillery in the West. Uncle Roland and his nephew Uranus, who had also volunteered their services, would arrive at a later date.

"Well, Albert, this is *quite* an establishment you have here!" Father declared upon his arrival at Albert Crosby & Company, removing his hat and descending from the carriage. A light, misty rain fell gently on his face as he looked over the distillery that was prominently set on the corner of Larrabee Street and Chicago Avenue.

"Yes,...it certainly is. I'm quite impressed!" Uncle Isaac acquiesced, following behind him, holding his opened umbrella and gawking at the immense structure before him. "We're quite proud of you. What you've done here in such a short time is incredible! I knew you were doing quite well,...but this is extraordinary!"

Uncle Isaac was about sixteen years younger than my father, Nathan. While Father was a carbon copy of my grandfather, Uncle Isaac favored my fraternal grandmamma, Anne (Pinkham) Crosby. Uncle Isaac had his mother's outgoing personality, coloring and facial features. He was blue-eyed and fairer than Father. Although he was only in his early forties, his hair was prematurely gray and already beginning to recede. Uncle Isaac was a portly, genial man and one of my favorite people. He was an independent spirit, not as stiff and reserved as Father. I always felt at ease in his company. My uncle was a born salesman. Without any visible effort—he could sell anything to anyone. With inbred Yankee wit, Uncle Isaac could charm the most reluctant buyer into purchasing whatever he was selling. He always made it a point to revisit his customers to assure their satisfaction with his product. "Yes, as "Manager of Sales," I decided, "he'll be quite an asset to my business."

It made perfect sense to employ Father as "Purchasing Manager." Father's high standards and decisiveness highly qualified him for that position. I'd grown into adulthood admiring Father's noble bearing and his unequaled eloquence as a skillful haggler and frugal businessman.

"Welcome to Chicago, Father, Uncle Isaac," I said, embracing them both, shaking their hands and escorting them inside. "I certainly hope Chicago will meet all your expectations. I've made arrangements for you to stay at the same lodging house where I've been living since I arrived.

"A home has been built for Margaret, but right now, it's unoccupied and devoid of furnishings. She'll take care of that when she arrives. Margaret has informed me that we're expecting a second child at the end of August. I'm delighted and plan on leaving for West Roxbury around the middle of that month. All seems to be going well with Margaret and the expected infant. I'm hopeful that I'll arrive in time for the birth. From the enthusiastic sound of her letters, the new baby shouldn't interfere with our intended move to Chicago. You should be well-acquainted with the operation of the distillery by that time," I said, after introducing Josiah to my father and Uncle Isaac. "You needn't worry, Josiah knows almost as much about this operation as I do."

I missed my family so much. I crossed off each day on the calendar until it was time for me to leave. The abiding thought of holding them close again made the painful separation bearable. When I arrived, Margaret, who was heavy with child, ran toward the carriage as it approached Wildwood with little Irene in her arms.

"Oh, Margaret, how I've missed you and the closeness of your body next to mine. My days are busy, but my nights are so lonely." I whispered passionately, embracing and kissing her feverishly. I love you and need you so desperately. I've longed for the intimate oneness that alone satisfies the desire we have for each other. I can't wait for you to join me in Chicago." I reached out for Irene, but my infant daughter shook her head, cried, and then turned toward her mother. I suddenly realized that because of my long absences, I was a stranger to her. Only after earning her love and trust would Irene get to know and love me—her father.

The new baby was born shortly after my arrival. She was a fair-haired girl who favored Margaret. We named her Minnie. I was pleased because Irene would now have a playmate and close companion. At the time, I would have liked to have had a son, but I was happy that all had gone well with the delivery. The baby was the picture of health. I couldn't help noticing that Margaret had already packed several small trunks. My wife and family were finally coming to Chicago with me. I was ecstatic!

*   *   *   *

Mid-September, 1849

"Would you please hold Irene's hand, dearest?" Margaret asked after taking the toddler from Madam Henderson's arms. She stepped into the carriage and waved goodbye to her parents. I followed carrying Irene against my chest. I had stayed in West Roxbury about a month. At first, Irene treated me like an outsider, emitting an ear-piercing yowl whenever I approached her. After a few weeks, she began to giggle and chatter when I sat her in my lap. Her facial features, personality and mannerisms often reminded me of my sister, Kate.

"I hope it won't get too hot in the coach for the little ones," I said while holding a sleepy Irene in my lap with one arm, and extending the other to fan her with my hat. "It'll be a lot cooler once we reach the Lake region. As you know, Chicago's often called the "Windy City," Margaret." She smiled and nodded, but didn't answer. Margaret was busy nursing baby Minnie.

Although Margaret enjoyed her new role as fulltime wife and mother, she was not particularly taken with her new, adopted city. In fact, she often let me know about it in no uncertain terms. She constantly compared the secure, civilized life of the East Coast to that of the hardships and uncultured existence of this so-called "Queen of the Lakes." Chicago depressed her with its endless slum villages, saloons and gambling houses. She would remain indoors for days, refusing to venture out for fear of being set upon by the riff-raff who frequented the earthen streets.

She abhorred the revolting sights and odors of human and animal excrement flowing freely in the ditches along the streets. Garbage, waste and sewage, occasionally overrun with mice and large roaches were everywhere. Somehow, I had been able to ignore Chicago's defects, but Margaret despised this city—every effort to placate her proved fruitless. Several times a year, whenever she had had enough of it, she and the children would journey back to Massachusetts and Wildwood.

My wife missed her family and friends and had also developed a need to be in the midst of high society. Margaret enjoyed the luxuries afforded by a city with all the amenities—paved streets, sidewalks, gaslights, omnibuses, railroads and above all—sewers. I didn't object to her trips as it saddened me to see her so unhappy. I became immune to her long absences because of the ever-increasing demands of my business. Her mother's disturbing comments made years ago reverberated in my mind. I often remembered my mother-in-law's grating words about Chicago's shortcomings. I began to suspect that Margaret had indeed succumbed to her mother's influence. She had inexplicably chosen to heed the ominous warnings that would be so disruptive to our marriage. Anguished, I faced the reality of a future plague by extended absences of my wife and family. "Can this be the beginning of the end?" I asked myself. Margaret was gradually weaning herself away from Chicago and all that it represented and—I'm sorry to say—that also seemed to include me.

▼

CHAPTER 13

Mid-September, 1850

At the time of Uncle Roland and his nephew's pending arrival in Chicago by steamer, Margaret had been with me for about three weeks. She had just returned from vacationing in West Roxbury and Cape Cod. Now that summer was waning, a sun that seemed to deny the onset of autumn cast its warmth earthward from a clear blue sky. I thought it would be nice to get Margaret out of the house so she could enjoy a short respite from her monotonous household routine. I left for the distillery at my usual time in the morning, but returned around eleven after making arrangements to have the children taken care of in our absence.

"Margaret, would you like to join me in the carriage?" I asked. "Uncle Roland and Cousin Uranus are arriving by steamboat and are due to disembark early this evening at the dock. A drive through the city might perk you up a bit. We'll stop for a while so you can shop and browse around the clothing boutiques,…then we'll have supper at a fine restaurant. I've hired someone to care for the children. Josiah's wife, Ruth, was delighted to accommodate us. I'll fetch her about one o'clock. Do you think you'd like to come along with me to greet my relatives? Will that allow you enough time to get yourself together?"

"Oh, yes, Albert, it'll be more than enough time. I'd truly enjoy that. It sounds delightful, dearest. Thank you for being so considerate," she replied, untying her apron, pulling it up over her head, and then touching up her coiffure to make sure each strand remained in place. "It'll be wonderful to be together for a few hours, free of the children. Oh, Albert, you can be such a dear at times. I'll be ready!" she said, placing Minnie in her cradle, giving me a quick kiss on the cheek, and then darting toward the bedroom to change.

"I'll be back at one!" I shouted, leaving the house and running back to the waiting carriage.

Since Father and Uncle Isaac had come to assist me with the distillery, Chicago had made some significant strides in the direction of becoming a city equal to its counterparts in the East. Many entrepreneurial-minded young men such as myself had also foreseen the commercial opportunities afforded by this fledging city. As Chicago came onto its own we prospered beyond our wildest dreams. Our success was part of Chicago's "Golden Age." Gaslights now illumined the darkened streets. Canals, railroads and telegraph lines connecting the East and the West transformed a rundown, sluggish city into a bustling metropolis. I was especially pleased that these new amenities had finally found there way west. When I enticed Uncle Roland and Cousin Uranus to join me at the distillery, I admit I had exaggerated the reasons why they should leave the staid existence of Cape Cod and choose to be challenged by the prospects of Chicago—a newly energized and upcoming land of opportunity.

"I can see the steamship in the distance," I said, turning to Margaret as we waited on the dock. The afternoon jaunt had revitalized her spirits. She was beaming. I remembered how smitten I was with her beauty when I first met her on our packet trip back to Brewster. I sensed this romantic afternoon was exactly what the doctor ordered. "It should be docking soon," I added, putting one arm around her waist and holding her close. "It'll be dark soon. For the first time ever, the gaslights are ready to be lit tonight all over the city. I thought you'd like to witness this dazzling spectacle, my dear. That was another reason for today's outing."

"Oh, I can't wait for that to happen. How exciting! Street lights will make the roadways so much safer at night." Margaret replied, holding on to her hat as the wind gusted off Lake Michigan. "Thank you, Albert, for such a memorable day. I'd almost forgotten what it was like to be out of the house and alone with you. The afternoon has certainly flown by. We must do something like this more often. It surely fans the flames of love, my dearest," she whispered in a tone of voice that was filled with desire. Margaret took my hand, looked around quickly, and then concluding no one would notice, kissed me passionately on the lips. "I'll be a lot more grateful tonight," she said. I understood exactly what she meant. If we hadn't been waiting for the steamer, I would have immediately whisked her away.

As the launch began to unload its passengers, Uncle Roland and Cousin Uranus, each carrying a large valise, walked down the gangplank. Through the dim light of dusk, they scanned the waiting crowd for a familiar face. Like burning embers glowing amid charcoal ashes, the sky reflected the crimson rays of a red sunset through the ashen clouds of impending nightfall.

"There they are!" I exclaimed, pointing toward them and waving wildly as they approached us. My relatives smiled and waved back. Almost two years had passed since I had last visited them on Cape Cod. Uranus had matured into a refined young man while Uncle Roland had added a few more inches to his waistline. The throng waiting for passengers to disembark began to cheer and clap loudly.

"My, this is quite a reception! We didn't notice any dignitaries onboard," said Uranus, totally flabbergasted by the boisterous, cheering crowd as he embraced us. Taking note of Margaret at my side, he reached for her gloved hand and kissed it. "My dear, lady Margaret, you look absolutely marvelous!"

"Thank you, Uranus," she said, blushing at what I deemed was a well-deserved compliment.

"Why all the excitement?" Uncle Roland asked, advancing toward us with a handshake and a welcoming hug.

"This is the first lighting of every street in Chicago. It's been an eagerly awaited event,…a *very* special occasion," I quickly remarked, answering his question before he assumed the uproar was especially staged for his and Uranus' benefit.

"Well, I'm relieved to know that!" Uncle Roland exclaimed, glancing around the wharf with an approving nod as we walked toward our carriage. "You mean to tell me you folks haven't had lampposts on *all* your streets before now. Why, that's astonishing! According to your glowing reports, Albert, I fully expected Chicago would have most of the amenities we enjoy back east."

"I must admit, we did have a few areas lit by gaslight such as the financial district, but now *every* street in Chicago has streetlamps that will illuminate the darkened roadways," I replied, taking hold of Uncle Roland's valise and placing it on the back of the carriage. He seated himself inside, and Uranus sat next to him. After helping Margaret ascend the carriage, I followed and sat opposite them.

"Albert, would you mind if I stayed on with you and Margaret until I find suitable living quarters for myself?" Uranus asked warily after arriving at our home and getting settled for the night. "Uncle Roland will be staying at the boarding house with Father and Uncle Nathan. He's already rented a room on the same floor. I don't have too much in common with that generation. Besides, I'm not accustomed to sharing a bathroom with strangers, which is common practice in a boarding house."

"Of course,…that would be fine," I replied. We've already discussed that possibility and agreed that you should remain with us for a while." Margaret had already left the room to check on the children.

My cousin, Uranus Crosby was nineteen at the time of his arrival in Chicago. This demure, good-looking young man, full of purpose and youthful enthusiasm was clearly intrigued by his new surroundings. He was several inches taller than I. Although his auburn hair was a bit bristly on top, it was styled so that ringlet sideburns coiled above each ear. My cousin's piercing blue eyes astride a well-shaped nose were his best feature. His clear, flawless complexion made his adoring lady friends envious. He had a short, professionally trimmed, auburn beard on his chin, but no mustache.

Uranus traveled in aristocratic circles. Due to his patrician upbringing, his interests were far different from mine. Despite the fact that he was ambitious and worked diligently at the distillery during the day, he valued his independence and filled his evenings with the pursuit of cultured activities. He frequented art galleries and attended lectures, concert performances, theater and ballet. Regrettably, Uranus' love of opera was thwarted here because Chicago lacked a structure large enough to adequately house a sizable stage, acoustics and scenery—something he hoped to correct someday.

"Uncle Roland, I'll take you over to the distillery in the morning," I said as we enjoyed a rum toddy together. Margaret and Uranus had already retired for the night. I knew she would be waiting for me and I was eager to join her. Our bedroom was on the main floor while the guest bedrooms were upstairs. "I know you've had a long journey and must be exhausted; therefore, I'll take my leave so you can retire for the night. It's so wonderful to have you here. Your abilities will greatly further my goals. Father and Uncle Isaac are enthusiastically awaiting your arrival at the boarding house. Uranus will stay here with us for a while. He wasn't too keen on having to share the bathroom facilities. Goodnight, Uncle Roland," I said, giving him another hug.

Roland Crosby was a well-educated, cultured gentleman with extraordinarily fine tastes. Wherever he journeyed, he enjoyed gracious living and was also a patron of the arts. Culture was ingrained into his upbringing from birth. Uranus was Uncle Roland's favorite nephew. His influence was unquestionably the rationale behind Uranus' craving for the finer things of life. Uncle Roland was an entrepreneurial tycoon and a real estate magnet who owned several blocks of buildings in Boston and New York. He was also a land broker and proprietor of valuable property on Cape Cod and the Islands.

My uncle was a hybrid of his parents. His countenance and coloring were much like Grandmamma's, but he was built like Grandfather. He wore a goatee and sported a thin, curled mustache whose ends he habitually twisted while in serious thought. Uncle Isaac's personality was more like his brother Nathan who was sedate, reserved and composed. Uncle Roland, on the other hand, could be quite comical and entertaining at times. Despite our differing lifestyles, he was always cordial. Even though his language was quite polished, Roland Crosby was an unassuming man who never lorded his intellectual and cultural superiority over my family or me. I decided that he would manage the distillery and my real estate holdings. Uncle Roland and Aunt Sally had always made us feel welcomed in their home. As unpretentious as it was, I had absolutely no misgivings about having him as a guest in mine.

*   *   *   *

Late-June, 1851

"We need to schedule a very important company meeting at the end of this week," I announced, standing in the new office wing of the distillery. It was now the most imposing structure east of the Chicago River. "Josiah, please notify my family members so they can all convene here. Tell them it's imperative that they attend. I need to discuss some important changes that are relevant to the future of this company, however…I need their input before I implement them. The family members are scattered here, there and everywhere on business assignments. Please see if you can round them up for me. They'll be leaving for the Cape in a few weeks to vacation with their families."

"Yes, Albert, I will. I don't think that'll be a problem," Josiah replied as he placed some accounting logs on the bookshelf. "I've made it my business to be aware of their whereabouts just in case there's an emergency here or back east. I'll send them all a telegram informing them of this crucial conference. Will Friday at nine in the morning be all right with you?"

"That'll be fine," I said as I left for the wholesale shop.

My father, Uranus and my uncles were all present for what would be a momentous announcement. Josiah was invited to attend so he'd be able to answer some pertinent accounting questions, if need be

"Good morning Father, Uncle Isaac, Uncle Roland and Uranus," I said, addressing the curious group who sat there patiently hanging onto every word. "For months now, you've devoted all your energies to the success of Albert

Crosby & Company. The first thing I want to tell you is that I've decided to make all of you associates in this enterprise,…it'll be a partnership. Secondly, I've decided to expand beyond our business into manufacturing camphene and medicinal alcohol…products that are in great demand by druggists all over the country. Diversifying our commodities assures us of a more profitable future."

"Well, thank you, Albert," Uncle Roland said, standing and walking over to me. "You're not only a financial genius, you're also an appreciative and thoughtful individual. We're proud to be associated with you and with a company that has such a fine reputation for integrity. You've already demonstrated your indebtedness to us by your generosity. Allowing us to be partners in this prosperous venture of yours is frankly,…beyond our expectations! I'm sure I speak for everyone else here when I say that because of such an incentive, we'll definitely do our best to insure the future success of Albert Crosby & Company."

"I know that." I replied, glancing around the table toward each family member. "The support you gave me when this was a fledging business hasn't gone unnoticed. I wanted all of you to know how grateful I am for all the sacrifices you've made on my behalf. When I summoned you, you accepted the challenge graciously and with enthusiasm. I recognize how fortunate I am to have a family with such unique talents and expertise. Largely at my behest, you set aside your personal lives, left your families for long periods of time and lived in boarding houses that lacked many of the amenities you've been accustomed to. I've no doubt that Chicago will soon come into its own. Someday it'll rival and perhaps even surpass every metropolitan area in the East. For this reason, I sincerely hope you'll persevere with its challenges. Remember that like others who own successful businesses here, we have a responsibility to provide the leadership and the financial backing needed to develop Chicago's countless opportunities. Our guiding principles will be furthering its educational and cultural development. Again, I sincerely thank all of you. I wanted to express my appreciation for your contributions to what is now *our* company and make it worth your while. I know you'll be leaving soon for short summer vacations with your families on Cape Cod. I wish you a safe journey, and I look forward to seeing you again upon your return. Now, if you're all agreeable, I'd like to treat all of you to an elegant luncheon at Kingsley's." Kingsley's was one of Chicago's finest restaurants and had become my favorite place to dine and entertain my family and business associates.

*   *   *   *

Early - July, 1851

I left for Boston and West Roxbury with my father for a two months' respite from the stress of my flourishing business. Margaret had already returned to Wildwood at the beginning of May. She would be there until September.

"Father, I hope to vacation with you in Brewster for a few weeks," I said as I summoned a carriage on the packet dock in Boston. The lure of the Cape proved impossible to resist. The salt water beckoned me to my origins, much like the ale-wives who return year after year to the Herring Run and Mill Pond. "Of course, Margaret and the girls will visit with me. I know Mother's eager to see her grand-daughters. I miss the homestead and look forward to seeing her, my sisters, Miss Mira and Japeth."

"We'll be expecting you," Father replied, waving goodbye as he walked toward the gangplank for the voyage back to Brewster.

I arrived at Wildwood in the late afternoon. I had forgotten the breathtaking beauty of mid-summer in Boston and West Roxbury. The rolling green lawns and flowering shrubbery that graced the approach to the large colonial homes were lush and flourishing. I stared appreciatively at the climbing rose bushes that were in full bloom. Their beauty covered the white picket fences and the arched trellis gateways of the roadside cottages. The pristine cobblestone streets and side-walks shaded by large elm and maple trees were a welcoming sight. It was so unlike the littered and dusty, Chicago roadways. I took a deep breath and inhaled the fresh air. I could understand why Margaret preferred to be here instead of Chicago, especially in the summertime.

There had been a spell of several days over ninety-five degrees. Today was one of many, which was extremely hot and humid. I carried my jacket over my arm. My shirt was drenched with sweat as I stepped from the carriage and entered Wildwood—Margaret's coveted retreat.

"Hello!" I called out, walking through the back entrance to the kitchen. My voice echoed throughout the house only to be answered with mute silence. It suddenly occurred to me that this homecoming was in stark contrast to earlier visits when an amorous wife excitedly greeted my carriage. I set my carpetbag down and thinking my family might be outdoors, turned around and walked out the back door toward the expansive grounds and gardens behind Wildwood.

"Welcome home,…Mister Crosby!" Moses Porter shouted as he hobbled toward me. The landscaper at Wildwood was an elderly Negro man with a full head of white, curly hair. "Madam Crosby's not at home right now. She and the children left for the lake because it was so hot today. Madam decided to take refuge from this oppressive heat and humidity by cooling down by the water's edge. The carriage will leave soon to pick them up. Madam Crosby wanted me to tell you that she wished to have you join them there, if you arrived early enough."

"Thank you, Moses," I said. "I'll be back in a short while. Please tell the coachman to wait for me.

"I will, sir," he replied, turning toward the carriage house.

I had hoped to be lovingly greeted by my wife and children after such a long absence. I was rather disappointed by this reception; however, because of the high temperatures, I tried to understand Margaret's rationale. I would have to comply with her wishes if I wanted to see her and the girls. I hurriedly placed my valises inside the door, changed my clothing, and then left for the lake.

At the end of the month, we left for Brewster and stayed with my parents until mid-August. I felt like a tourist as I rediscovered its unforgettable charm. I savored the salty scent of the Brewster flats, the slowly turning arms of the windmills facing the bay, the radiant sunrises and ineffable sunsets. As I walked along the shore, which was a short walk from our humble homestead, thoughts of the grand mansion I had always wanted to build on the bluff overlooking the bay came to mind. Now that wealth was within my grasp, I vowed my dream would someday become a reality.

Margaret and I took a picnic basket and enjoyed meandering along the banks of the Stony Brook and Mill Pond. The herring had long disappeared from this clear stream, but the sound of the rushing waters and the splendor of the water lilies languidly floating on the tranquil pond, only served to reinforce the storied quietude and beauty of Brewster.

One day, during my stay there, I visited with Japeth and his family. I couldn't help but notice their handsome and industrious youngest son, Nathaniel, who was now eleven years of age. He was busy pitching hay and tending to the farm animals. Aaron had married and was the successful owner of a large stable in Chatham. Like the spokes of a spinning wheel one day blurred into the next. Although I savored every moment, it was finally time for me to return to Chicago. Father would follow in a few weeks.

*   *   *   *

Late-September, 1851

"Josiah, we're going to need another building for our new brewery," I declared, stroking my beard and in deep thought as I stood outside the brick structure that housed the distillery. "We must hire at least another fifty employees. Would you please take care of that for me while I engage contractors for the new plant? I'd like to do this as soon as possible. I want it completed and operating by the holiday season. We'll be much too busy by that time to start this project. I want to get it underway immediately. There's an ample supply of employable people out there willing to work at this time of year," I declared, walking toward the wholesale shop. "Winter's just around the corner and they'll need to prepare for it. First, let's put them to work helping the builders,…then we'll ask the more industrious ones to continue on as employees in the brewery."

"That plan has foresight, Albert," Josiah replied, joining me on the stroll back. "It's astonishing how Albert Crosby & Company has grown in just three years! It's by far the largest winery and alcohol distillery in the West. And now that you're adding a brewery,…it'll even be more so. You know,…Albert, there are many reasons for this, but the two most important ones are your reputation as a decisive, honest businessman and the superior quality of your products. The finest ingredients that money can buy are used in the bottling of your wines and liquors. As I've said many times before, I'm proud to be associated with a company that enjoys such superior status and is ranked so highly in its field of endeavor."

"Well, then,…Josiah," I said, smiling as I looked at him directly. "You'll be happy to hear that I've also decided to make you a partner and shareholder. I'll see to it that you receive a fair percentage of shares and a sizeable bonus at Christmas."

"Why, thank you, Albert. I don't know what to say," he said appreciatively. "I must say you've taken me completely by surprise. That's mighty generous of you and though I'm exceedingly grateful, you needn't feel indebted to me. After all, I'm well compensated for the work I do for you."

"No, Josiah,…I don't feel you are. You certainly deserve recognition for your dedication, not in title only, but also in a monetary sense," I replied, trying to assure him of his indispensable value to me. "I'd be lost without your sage advice and commitment to Albert Crosby & Company. You've been with me almost from the start, longer than anyone else around here. When I leave this company, and sometimes it's for a lengthy period,…I know it's in good hands. I also feel at ease with your business decisions in my absence. I implicitly trust your judgment."

During the first week of October, Margaret returned to Chicago with Irene and Minnie. Although it was gratifying to have them back again, I was now faced with the dilemma of devoting more time at home to her and the girls, or tending to the expansion of my corporation.

By late fall the new plant was ready for occupancy. The wholesale house, the distillery and the brewery now covered a whole block. The wholesale shop had also been enlarged to house our new beers, imported wines, assorted whiskies, camphene, oil of turpentine and medicinal alcohol. We were inundated with stacks of requisition orders that seemed almost endless. Sometimes we worked seven days a week just to keep pace. The backlog was staggering. Another thirty employees were hired to meet the deadlines and fill the demand.

"For God's sake, Albert! Is it necessary for you to work so much?" Margaret asked, angered by my habitual late arrival every night of the week. It made for a cool reception when the supper meal stayed on the stove for hours. "I might as well have stayed in West Roxbury for the amount of time we spend together here," she nagged, decidedly irritated as she stomped out of the kitchen after angrily setting down a plate of food on the table in front of me.

"Now, Margaret. You know it can't be helped. I admit I've been an absent husband and father, but this is my busy season," I maintained, chasing her into the sitting room and taking hold of her hand. "There's so much that needs to be done. I'm torn between you and my business. You're not making it any easier for me, Margaret. Please don't think of going back east. I desperately miss all of you when you're away. I know that's no consolation, but at least when you're here…I can look forward to spending each evening with my family and my nights with you in my arms. I enjoy amusing and kissing my little girls before I leave in the morning. Oh, Margaret, I beg you,…please try to understand." I pulled Margaret close to me and we embraced affectionately at first, then passionately.

"I'm sorry for my outburst, Albert," she said contritely, lowering her head and leading me toward the bedroom. "It's just that my days are so dreary here. Now that Uranus has found other living quarters, I have no social life to speak about. The girls are the only ones I speak to all day. I need an outlet, something that will pique my interests. Right now, my whole life revolves around caring for Irene and Minnie and waiting for you to return from the distillery. You don't seem to realize what it's like to be left alone here each day, sometimes until after ten at night.

Your days are busy and full while mine are long and empty. Even though you've hired a housemaid and a nanny for the girls, I'm bored to death with Chicago! I'm tired of occupying myself with an occasional outing with Ruth or trying to find goods in shops with their limited supplies.

"Now that your Aunt Eunice has arrived to join your Uncle Isaac, I'd like to entertain them and the other members of the family, including Uranus. Would it be all right with you if I had them here next Sunday for dinner?...I'd really enjoy that! Do you think they'd be available to come on that day or is it too short a notice?" she asked.

"Why that's very gracious of you, Margaret. It's a wonderful idea." I replied as I began to undress for bed. "I'll see to it that they're all invited to gather at our house next week for Sunday dinner. It shouldn't be a problem because they're all here in Chicago right now. I'm certain...they'll accept your invitation. This'll be an excellent opportunity to visit with one another socially. We do need time to be together and away from the hectic business atmosphere, once in awhile."

"Thank you, Albert. I'm so happy that you're agreeable with my suggestion. I'm eager to begin planning the menu," Margaret said, removing the coverlets. A silk gown flowed down her curvaceous body as she placed her fingers in her hair to remove the combs, allowing it to cascade over her shoulders. "You can let them know that dinner will be served promptly at two.

"I've already mentioned this possibility to Uranus. He often stops by evenings for supper while you're still at the wholesale house. I must say I look forward to his visits. He's a delightful guest. Uranus is such a charming, articulate and genteel man. We have so much in common. He and I have a shared belief in the arts that truly inspires me. His knowledge and love of culture fill him with the same enthusiasm you have for *your* business venture. Your cousin often speaks about his ambition to build an elegant opera house worthy of the cultured upper-class society and the nouveau-riche young professionals and their families. It's become his goal. I hope for his sake that he can realize his dream as you have yours."

"I'm beginning to experience a little jealousy here, my love," I said, removing her shoulder straps and letting her nightgown fall to her waist. I held Margaret in my arms and kissed her ardently on the lips, neck and breasts. "I'm happy to hear that he's such good company. Uranus is an extremely fascinating and attractive individual. He's drawn to the social circles of wealthy entrepreneurs and their wives. He feels a responsibility to uphold their upper-class standing in society. Uranus also believes Chicago is sorely lacking in artistic refinements and that its prominent inhabitants,...those of sophisticated backgrounds, are denied those civilities here. He plans to correct this shortcoming as soon as he's financially able to do so. Uranus exists on a lofty plain of aristocratic elegance. Although he arrived here in search of riches, he was quite disappointed to find that Chicago had an environment that lacked cultural services and was deficient in all that he found uplifting. His needs and interests are much too haughty for me. I know you heartily agree with him, however,…I'm content with Chicago,…just as it is. I realize that it doesn't compare with Boston or New York, but it has its own unique charm, my love!"

"Well, I'm glad *you* think so!" she replied adamantly, certain that I'd recognize we had a difference of opinions where Chicago was concerned. "Anyway, you needn't be jealous of Uranus," Margaret added while gently slipping off her silk gown. I was aroused as I felt her soft warm body close to mine. "Your cousin's manner has always been proper in my presence. My love is exclusively for you, Albert."

With that, I turned down the gaslight next to the bed. We kissed passionately and after feverishly fondling each other with insatiable desire, we enjoyed a rapturous night of lovemaking.

✶   ✶   ✶   ✶

Early-December, 1854

Trains were now beginning to pass through Chicago from the East. With them came a surge of commercial opportunities and astronomical growth. Wealthy easterners with goals of tapping into this new robust economy migrated west in search of guaranteed wealth. They came in droves, everyone with their own expertise—prominent architects, bankers, contractors, merchants and professionals from every field imaginable.

Chicago began to emerge from an ugly, latent and undeveloped city where construction spread unchallenged, into one with flourishing and notable advances in architecture, business and the arts. Due to either my astute foresight or my good fortune, I had always anticipated this sweeping change in the city I had chosen to launch my business career.

"Albert, I believe that I'm with child again," Margaret revealed after a bout of morning sickness. "I've been quite ill with this pregnancy. I think I should return to Wildwood. I feel more comfortable with my doctor back east. I'm also concerned for the girls right now. As you know, Chicago's experiencing a severe cholera epidemic. Your father and Uncle Isaac have already left for Cape Cod. I doubt they'll ever return. I believe it would be best if I left, also."

"I'm happy to know we'll be adding another member to our little family," I said, helping her to the kitchen table and offering her a cup of tea and a small piece of toasted bread. "However, I know you're usually in a delicate state of health while carrying a child…and yes, the girls *are* in danger of contracting cholera. I'd never forgive myself if anything ever happened to you or to them. Therefore, I won't insist that you stay here or even argue the point. This time around, I'm in full agreement with you. I'll miss you when you're gone, my love. However, you may as well make plans to leave within the next few days before the deplorable winter weather prevents you from arriving at your destination. I know I'll be concerned about your safety as you travel east at this time of the year. I believe the railroad would be the most comfortable way for you to journey to New York. From there you can board the stagecoach to Boston. Take the girls' nanny with you. I'm sure she'll be delighted to accompany you. Well,…" I hesitated, "at least you'll be back there for the holidays. Business commitments won't allow me the luxury of leaving with you. I envy you being back east during the Christmas season. It means so much to be with close family and friends at that time. If you should feel up to it, my dearest,…please try to visit my parents on Cape Cod. They'd love to see the children."

"How understanding of you, Albert," she said, reaching for my hand as she sipped her tea. An earlier pallor was now replaced by a rosier complexion. "I was hesitant to bring it up, but yes,…it'll be best that I leave Chicago soon," Margaret went on to say. "This epidemic's so frightening. Please take care of yourself, Albert. I'll also worry about you living here in the midst of this deadly epidemic.

"One hearse after another passes by around the clock in front of the house, slowly winding its way toward church services and burial. The sight of buckboards stacked with mounds of body bags, which are most likely the indigent on their way to be buried in mass graves, is unimaginable and revolting to me. My expectations of life in a civilized world are so contrary to this indignation. Yesterday, from the window facing the street, I watched in horror as mourners in small groups grieved their loved ones while following the wagons and carrying umbrellas in the sleet and rain. The unnatural, constant tolling of the church bells is so morbid and depressing. I've been afraid to venture out the door with the girls for fear we'll contract this awful disease. The streets are deserted…no animals and…no people. Except for an occasional carriage or wagon rushing its human cargo to makeshift hospitals, it's like a ghost town. I feel like a prisoner in my own home! I hope that we'll escape the scourge of this unholy plague and return safely to Wildwood. Although Chicago's not nearly as dreadful as it was when I arrived here, I assume your father and Uncle Isaac have had their fill of the persistent, unsanitary conditions that exist here…where infection's allowed to run rampant."

"Well,…yes, I guess that was the final blow," I replied, digesting her tirade against Chicago while putting on my hat and coat and preparing to leave for the wholesale shop. "Actually, they felt that they'd come to my rescue when I needed them and now their mission here was completed."

Father and Uncle Isaac worked diligently and devoted much time and energy to insure the success of Albert Crosby & Company. Now that my company was well established it was time for them to gracefully bow out. I couldn't have reached this point without their help. After extending my deepest appreciation for everything they had done for me, they left Chicago with my blessing. They were aging—it was time for them to enjoy the comforts of home and family. Father was growing somewhat disenchanted with living in the boarding house and with frontier life in general. He made it clear that he was eager to live with Mother for the remainder of his years in the more gracious surroundings of Brewster. I suspect Uncle Isaac also felt that way. In addition, Aunt Eunice was becoming increasingly impatient with the duration of his stays here, and she insisted he return to the Cape permanently.

"I must leave now, Margaret. I have an important business appointment in a half-hour," I said. "I'll see you this evening for supper. I promise I'll try to be on time." I gave her a quick parting kiss, left for my waiting carriage, and then closed the door behind me.

✳   ✳   ✳   ✳

Early - July, 1855

I planned to arrive in Boston for the Fourth of July celebration, but a fierce nor'easter delayed my arrival. Trees had been uprooted and lay strewn across the roadways from New York to Boston. Along the way, I had to stay overnight in several wayside inns. I hoped Margaret would not have our third child before my arrival at Wildwood. She had been quite incapacitated while carrying this baby. Besides being nauseous every day, everything went wrong. Margaret developed kidney and heart problems. The doctor assured her that they were solely connected with the pregnancy and that she'd be fine after the delivery. I was relieved and thankful to know that the cholera epidemic had not yet found its way east. I firmly believed, I had been spared because I stayed put in my workplace and hardly ever mingled with people. I often remained overnight in the office of the distillery or commuted directly from house to shop.

"You have another girl, Mister Crosby," said the doctor, handing me a tiny wrapped bundle. She was tightly swathed like an Indian papoose. Her small round head, which was barely visible, was covered with thick black hair. The baby had dark, wide-opened eyes and definitely had my coloring. While I had hoped for a son this time, I was pleased to find our new infant in such good health despite Margaret's lengthy ordeal.

"I'd like to name her Fanny after a beloved aunt. Would that be all right with you, Albert?" Margaret asked, reaching for Fanny and gently taking her from my arms to feed her.

"Of course, Margaret. You've chosen a charming name for her," I replied, sitting on the edge of the bed. "I'll leave you now so you can rest after you've taken care of Fanny. Thank you, for another beautiful child, my darling. Here's a small gift for you." I said, removing a small velvet box from my pocket that contained a delicate silver broach. A large amethyst—her birthstone—eclipsed the diamonds that surrounded it. "I'm sure you'll cherish it and wear it well."

"Oh, Albert! It's lovely!" she exclaimed, looking up at me. "It's so sweet of you to be so thoughtful. Thank you for such a loving and touching gift. Oh, my dearest, I do love you so."

"I must leave soon, Margaret," I said, rising from the bed and bending to kiss her on the forehead. "I've just been informed that Uncle Roland will be returning to Cape Cod. He's accepted the presidency of a large bank in Barnstable. That'll require my hiring someone to take his place. I'm considering replacing him with Josiah. He's certainly capable of assuming Uncle Roland's duties. Since Father and Uncle Isaac left the company my business responsibilities have mushroomed out of control. And now, without Uncle Roland,…it'll even be more chaotic.

"I know it'll be a while before you can consider returning to Chicago, but do come back as soon as you're able." I said, kissing her on the cheek and the baby on the forehead. "The house is so empty without you and the children. I want you to be there when I arrive home each evening. I need your love and embrace. I long for your body close to mine at the end of each day, the passionate love making and the ecstasy of oneness that alone satisfies our need for each other."

"If you love me as much as you say you do, you'd sell that damn business of yours in Chicago and stay here with us!" she hollered vehemently, lashing out with pent up hostility and twisting my words of love for her into a rebuff of astonishing proportions. "Albert Crosby & Company has always taken precedence over your family. I can't believe your insistence on remaining in that horrible city. It's replete with countless saloons, brothels and gambling houses. Oh, yes,…I forgot! They're the source of your wealth…Their money buys your liquors. You enrich yourself while they become dependent on the alcohol you furnish them. Doesn't *that* bother your conscience, Albert?"

"Margaret, I can't believe you said that!" I replied shaken by her words, recoiling from her bedside and feeling betrayed by her venomous banter. My insides were in turmoil and although I kept telling myself to stay composed, I was unable to cope with her insensitive and uncompromising outburst. I regret to say, I completely lost my temper. "You know better than that!" I shouted back, irately. "You married me knowing exactly *what* my intentions were. I know you heard what I said back then, but you really weren't listening or supposed you could eventually change my mind. My business is *our* source of income. Now you decry my means of support! Your criticisms fall on deaf ears, Margaret. I have no intention of selling it. As my wife it's obligatory for you to live where my work takes me. It's your love for *me* that I wonder about! The fact that I had Wildwood built to appease you was a *big* mistake on my part.

"And no, my conscience doesn't bother me one bit! For your information, if I weren't the one supplying alcohol to those whom you so callously consider the dregs of society,…someone else would be. I'm proud of my products. My wines and liquors grace the tables of every upstanding and prominent Chicago family. And for your information, my medicinal alcohol is in great demand by druggists all over the world because of its superior quality. Where's your sense of fairness, Margaret!

"Oh, what's the use? You don't give a damn about me! You'll never understand my need to have you with me. Come when you're ready,…whenever that is." With that, I left the bedroom in a huff before I said something I'd be sorry for. I returned to Chicago the next day.

$$* \qquad * \qquad * \qquad *$$

Late-May, 1857

"Take a look at the *Evening Journal*, Albert," said Josiah, spreading out the daily newspaper before me and pointing to its front page. "It says here that the mayor's cracking down on the vice and corruption in this city. A large police force descended on the shanties of the north side, which were a haven for that sort of crass and immoral character, and torched that whole slum area this morning. The law officers ousted a list of scum a mile long that included: vagrants, whores, madams, gamblers, thieves, drunkards, rapist and murderers. Maybe now they'll leave the city. I *abhor* that kind of life-style. Chicago is overrun with dilapidated enclaves where this trash finds refuge. I'm happy to see that someone's taking the bull by the horns and correcting this disgusting situation. We don't need that kind of rabble to boost our revenue. We'll continue to prosper without their business."

"You know, Josiah,…you're absolutely right!" I said, scanning the front page and quickly thumbing through the rest of the newspaper. "Chicago's coming up in the world. There's been a dramatic transformation as of late. Whereas these conditions such as the filthy ghettos, muddy roadways, open sewage, polluted water and lack of transportation were once ignored, they're now in the forefront of change. That's all for the better. One by one, every shortcoming is receiving top priority. The leaders of this community are making a valiant effort to eventually eradicate them and restore civility to this city.

"Thanks to the engineers who've migrated here, the carriage drivers can now cross the rivers confident that the newly constructed bridges are sturdy. Chicago can boast a transportation system equal to that of any large city in the United States. Everyday, hundreds of trains pull in and out of the conveniently placed stations. We have countless hotels, inns and accommodations for travelers and business people and more are being built. Did you know that Chicago trades the most lumber and wheat in this country?"

"Yes,…I was well aware of that," he replied, pulling up a chair, sitting down and assuming this discourse might last a while. "Instead of dwelling on the negative aspects of this city, I suppose I should look at all its achievements. I did notice, however, that despite the lawlessness and crime,…religion has also taken hold. Churches of every denomination are being erected and flourishing everywhere in the city. Wherever people congregate, all sorts of spiritual revival meetings are taking place…It's astonishing!"

"Regardless of a vigilant citizenry, which is managing to curtail the unlawful activities of this perverted and transient lifestyle, I'm sure we'll most likely see the evils you mentioned pop up here and there," I said, turning around and placing the *Journal* on the desk behind us. "The only difference is that they'll move about and conduct their sordid dealings in more elegant and refined dens of iniquity."

"Well,…now that we've discussed the news of the day,…I'll take my leave," Josiah said with a grin, preparing to exit the office.

"By the way, Josiah, Margaret has finally joined me again," I said, leaving the office with him. "She arrived from West Roxbury a week ago with the three girls and a nanny. We had a furious exchange of words before I left West Roxbury.

I'm afraid I was somewhat cool and distant while I stayed at Wildwood over the holidays. I didn't intend to be, but I had my reasons. For years, I've patiently tolerated Margaret's reluctance to live here. Margaret loathes Chicago and refuses to adapt and be assimilated into its mainstream. So,…I'm playing my trump card. I promised if she returned to Chicago, I'd build her a large, elegant mansion on Chicago Avenue. I've decided to sell the house on Clark Street and begin the construction of a stately new home this fall. It should be ready for us by '59. I'm bending over backwards in my attempt to please her so she'll choose to stay with me. This time, I hope I'll win this war of wills with a manor specifically built to suit her."

"I wish you luck," Josiah replied, joining me as we walked down the hallway to the plant. "Maybe your new home will be an incentive for Margaret to stay here permanently. I know the visits and meals at my home help you pass the time while she's away, but it's certainly no panacea for your loneliness,…only the loving presence of your family can do that."

▼

CHAPTER 14

Mid-October, 1858

Americans seemed troubled about the failure of the North and South to resolve their differences. As the divergence between the states appeared ready to escalate into an armed conflict between the Northern and Southern factions, Uranus and I were informed that the government was considering a surtax on liquor if war should become a reality.

"It looks as though a war is definitely in our future, Uranus. A revolution of historic proportions is imminent. I've given this possibility a lot of thought," I said after asking him to come into the wholesale shop before it opened to discuss this likelihood. Although he was in the initial process of opening a prestigious art gallery, I hoped he would add a new dimension to my decision-making. "I think we need to be prepared for this should it become a reality. As you already know, a wartime levy may need to be imposed on all liquors. I propose we augment our inventory as soon as possible before this tax is levied on wholesalers. I've decided to lease the Griffin warehouse. It's the largest one in Chicago. We'll purchase and import enough supplies to fill it to the rafters. If war does break out between the North and South, Albert Crosby & Company will be well prepared with an ample supply of tariff-free stock…This will give us a decided edge. We'll be able to sell our products without the added tax. Consequently, our prices will be lower than our competitors."

"Leave it to you, Albert, to figure out how to circumvent the impact of such a tax on our products," Uranus said, looking at me with an incredulous expression as he set his coffee cup down to pick up pen and paper to take notes. "Such foresight! You're so perceptive…always anticipating and planning ahead for the worst…not afraid to take a bold step forward. Now I know why your company is so successful and in such an enviable financial position. A stroke of genius, I must say. I'd never have given that ploy a thought, but yes,…you're quite right. I'll be right on it!"

"Uranus, I'm placing you in charge of leasing the warehouse. Don't haggle…pay them whatever they ask. The cost will be minimal in comparison with the profit. I'm sure…it'll be worthwhile. I'll set about doing the ordering, and I'll ask Josiah to hire more employees to work in the Griffin warehouse," I said, placing tobacco in my pipe, lighting it, and then turning toward the shop window that faced the distillery.

"Fine. I'll plan on doing that first thing Monday morning," Uranus replied, sipping coffee from his cup, then placing it on the counter. "Say,…by the way, Albert, I attended Senator Stephen Douglas' political assembly last evening. He spoke eloquently from the balcony of the Tremont House as a rapt audience of left-wing revolutionaries listened attentively. His discourse, especially when it pertained to slavery was direct, yet somewhat disappointing. He was decidedly adamant about states rights. His opponent Abraham Lincoln is also due to speak there tonight. I eagerly await his oratory and the rebuttal of Douglas' speech. Would you like to join me? It should be an exciting debate, worthy of our presence. We need to support Lincoln's mandate to preserve the Union. It's a case of being overcome by slavery…or overcoming slavery! You know, Albert, because we're such staunch abolitionists, we should be more active in politics. I believe that without compromising our patriotism we must support the movement that guarantees freedom for all. Slavery is a betrayal of America's ideals!"

"Why,…yes. I guess you're right, Uranus," I said hesitantly. I was deep in thought with other things on my mind. I stood and tapped my pipe in my hand, walked from behind the counter, and then sat on the front corner of it for the remainder of the conversation. "Thank you for asking me, Uranus. It should be quite informative and a good diversion for me. I need to cultivate my mind,…expand my horizons, so to speak. As you well know by now, Uranus, your interest in politics and culture is far superior to mine. Nevertheless, they're both as important to the future of Albert Crosby & Company as my financially centered decisions. I'd like to hear what Mister Lincoln has to say. I admire his dovish reputation and absolutely concur with his platform. I intend to donate a sizable amount to Mister Lincoln's campaign if he'll accept it. I can well afford that right now. According to Josiah, our investments and real estate holdings are doing quite well."

"Yes, I agree with you," Uranus said. "But remember that Lincoln's benign tone is not always reflected in his candid words. I'll see you back at the hotel.

Don't plan on working late tonight. If you intend to join me,…be ready around seven." Uranus waved goodbye and took his leave.

Stephen Douglas' Republican opponent, Abraham Lincoln, gave a speech that evening at the Tremont House that was inspiring. His eloquence was unforgettable. Mister Lincoln's expressive rhetoric presented his stance in a clear and concise manner. While his views were heretical, his convictions were straightforward. His articulate presentation was a wholesale rejection of the contemporary prejudices of self-serving authoritarian societies. He deplored the erosion of high standards of literacy available to all genders, races, nationalities or class. Mister Lincoln energized the opponents of African slave trade. He condemned the belligerent proponents of slavery who suppressed true freedom. With the influx of immigrants and their dispersion throughout the States, he said that our principles of equality necessitated that we eradicate ignorance, bigotry, intolerance and conspiracy. If elected, Lincoln promised to simplify reform and preserve those straightforward freedoms so precious to all Americans. I was particularly moved by his proposed agenda should he become the Senator from Illinois.

I was, however, somewhat distracted by the appearance of the numerous sentries who were there to protect him. This security contingent's extraordinary attire—complete with sabers hanging from wide, colorful sashes at their waistline—fascinated me. After a diligent study of these intriguingly clad gentlemen, who were standing guard at various strategic stations around the Tremont House, I nodded in their direction.

"Uranus, tell me what organization do these men belong to?" I asked, curious to know more about these individuals. "I've never seen *them* before. Are they from the Chicago area?"

"Oh, I'm surprised you haven't encountered this unit before now," Uranus remarked in a hushed voice, leading me away while continuing to speak in a more normal tone as we distanced ourselves from them. "They're certainly conspicuous, aren't they? They're an eclectic group of volunteer militia called the Chicago Zouaves. Actually, their outfits are replicas of the colorful Zouaves and Chasseurs de Vincennes of the French Army. Their uniforms with exaggerated enhancements imitate those of the French Algerian Army. These cadets actually perform as an exemplary drill team. They're also called on to volunteer their services for social and military causes. They dominate patriotic celebrations and attract a lot of attention at functions such as this one.

"The Zouaves movement is growing exponentially all over the country. In fact, their commander Colonel Elmer E. Ellsworth is here this evening. He was speaking to Mister Lincoln in the main parlor when I left to meet you. He happens to be one of three law clerks in Lincoln's Springfield, Illinois office. I was introduced to him when I became interested in the Republican Party. His political exploits are well known. As a member of Lincoln's fervent staff, he's become a rising star...continually seeking loftier heights of status and responsibility. We may as well join them at the reception."

"I'd like to meet this Colonel Ellsworth. Do you think that could be arranged?" I asked, walking alongside Uranus. "Yes, let's join the festivities in the main parlor. I'd also like to be personally introduced to Mister Lincoln. He's a brilliant man! He'll become President some day...Mark my word!"

A well-dressed group of women and men with Republican political leanings gathered around Mister Lincoln. When my tall, suave Cousin Uranus approached the group, the ladies blushed, fluttered their fans in front of their faces, and then moved aside to allow him access to the thin, dark-haired man of equal height.

A short, debonair chap in the dress uniform of an Army second lieutenant was standing next to Abraham Lincoln and took pleasure in the adulation and tributes accorded the speaker. I assumed it was Colonel Ellsworth, the commander of the Zouaves. He was a young, handsome gentleman of twenty-four who was clearly quite was full of himself. This over-zealous colonel had a full head of thick, black, curly hair that tumbled down the forehead of his boyishly clean-shaven face. He was a loyal partisan with expressive black eyes that seemed to read every thought by keenly observing one's facial expressions. I later learned that although he charmed the ladies at social gatherings with his gregarious personality, he was always an ethical gentleman in their presence. A portraiture of this youthful hothead, who had an insurrectionist look, must also include the fact that he possessed a compelling charisma. I imagined he was a special breed of human being—one that radiated a magnetic enthusiasm. As Uranus approached the aspiring Senator, Colonel Ellsworth promptly introduced him to Mister Lincoln.

"Uranus Crosby, it's a pleasure to meet you," Mister Lincoln said, reaching to shake Uranus's outstretched hand. "Lieutenant Ellsworth tells me you're planning on opening a distinctive art gallery replete with paintings by several renown artists and legendary impressionists. I'd be profoundly honored to attend your grand opening. It should be a benchmark celebration for Chicago."

"I assure you Mister Lincoln, you'll certainly be the first one on my list of guests," Uranus said. "I intend on sending you and your family a formal invitation, sir. You'd honor me by accepting. However, it may be a while yet as it's still in the formative stages. You'll most likely be quite busy by that time, Mister Lincoln."

"I'll make it a priority," the would-be Senator replied. "It'll be an uplifting reprieve from the rigors of speeches and handshaking for me and Missus Lincoln. And you, sir?" he asked, reaching for my hand after noticing me standing behind Uranus.

"Mister Lincoln, let me introduce you to my cousin, Albert Crosby," Uranus interjected before I had a chance to answer his question. "He's the proprietor of Albert Crosby & Company...a distillery we believe is the largest in the United States."

"Yes,...I'm quite familiar with the excellent products from your distillery," he replied, sipping his wine from a crystal goblet. "Our guests are often served the distinctive wines and superior liquors from your company...It's a pleasure to make your acquaintance, Mister Crosby."

"No,...Mister Lincoln, the pleasure's mine," I said, reaching for an hors d'oeuvre on a tray held by a passing attendant. "I was swayed by your forthright and powerful speech, sir. I'd like to offer my assistance to further your election to the Senate either monetarily or otherwise,"

"Thank you," he replied cordially. "That won't be necessary, but I'd be delighted to be invited to a small reception introducing me to your family and friends. I'd appreciate their support and vote of confidence."

"I'll certainly do that, sir," I said, feeling a genuine attraction toward this imposing figure of a man with soulful, dark eyes who pondered his every word before it was spoken. "If possible, please advise me of a future stopover here in Chicago. I'll be more than happy to gather a fairly large group of people interested in meeting you, Mister Lincoln."

"Please take note of that, Lieutenant Ellsworth. I'll rely on you to notify Mister Crosby of my upcoming schedule," Mister Lincoln said, turning to address his law clerk. "I'll take my leave now, as I must return to my suite. Missus Lincoln had a nasty headache earlier in the evening and had to retreat to her room. I'd like to check on her progress. I hope she's feeling better. Good evening, gentlemen."

"Colonel Ellsworth,...or is it Lieutenant Ellsworth? I'm a little confused," I asked turning toward this debonair young man in uniform after the would-be Senator left our group.

"Do refer to me as Colonel Ellsworth," he replied while watching Abraham Lincoln ascend the spiraling staircase, then turning his attention to me. "Mister

Lincoln and Army personnel are the only ones who refer to me as Lieutenant Ellsworth. As Commander of the Zouaves, I prefer to be addressed as colonel."

"Colonel Ellsworth, I must say I'm quite taken by the regiment of Zouaves posted throughout the Tremont Hotel," I said unreservedly, attempting to praise him for his efforts as their commander and drillmaster. "I've never seen such a striking contingent of militia. Their white pantaloons, colorful scarves, head-dresses and the crescent shaped rapiers suspended from their wide waist-bands…are truly extraordinary. I've also noticed the commanding way they handle their firearms…it's quite impressive. Could I possibly become a member of this remarkable group of volunteers?"

"Why, of course, Mr. Crosby," he replied receptively. "Do come to my office at the Armory if you should decide to join our company. That's where we march in unison, practice our drills and learn to handle the firearms. We perform in many capacities as an efficient unit of volunteer reservists. Excuse me, Mister Crosby, I'm being summoned by our captain. Good evening, sirs," Colonel Ellsworth said, hastily departing from the entourage that had gathered around him.

Uranus and I were staying at the Tremont Hotel. We had rented a suite of rooms and were now roommates until my lavish manor house on Chicago Avenue was completed. Its erection had been delayed because of an embargo on much of its materials. The building supplies were coming from the Northeast and the South, but because of the looming possibility of war, priority was being given to the transportation of needed provisions. Nevertheless, despite this set-back it would be completed in another year and a half. Just as the ground was broken for the newer, more imposing residence that Margaret and I would occupy with our family, the modest house on Clark Street was put up for sale, sold, and then occupied by the new owners. I stayed on at the Tremont Hotel with Uranus who had already been living here for several years now.

Margaret and the girls returned to Wildwood. And again, I was required to subsist without my family and commute from the Midwest to the East Coast. I looked forward to spending the month of July back east and visiting my parents in Brewster. They were aging and now—in their late sixties. As much as I tried to make Chicago my home, Cape Cod beckoned and tugged at my heart. It was my own little corner of heaven on earth.

Sadly, Miss Mira was no longer with them. After returning from a trip to Ire-land to visit family members, she had quietly passed away in her sleep about ten months ago. I was distraught when I heard the news of her death. Japeth, on the other hand, was still as energetic and indispensable as ever. Nathaniel was now in his early teens and still at home with him, his mother Veronica and sister, Bethany.

*   *   *   *

Early April, 1859

"My loyalties are with the North. I agree wholeheartedly with the abolishment of slavery in the states. However, because of my age and number of dependents, I'm not able to enlist in the regular army. I decided that I can best serve my country by joining the Zouaves," I said as I sat next to the large rolltop desk where Colonel Ellsworth was intermittently looking at me and busily shuffling papers.

"I've so many engagements for our drill team that it's becoming a chore responding to all the requests and trying to keep them from conflicting with one another," he interrupted, shaking a fist-full of paperwork in my direction.

The only décor in his rather cheerless, cluttered office was the mahogany paneling behind his desk. It was covered with gaudy medals and ribbons of various lengths, sizes and colors. Several trophies were haphazardly inserted between rows of faded, tattered books on shelves above his desk.

"I'd like to join your corps, Colonel, if you'll have me. It's something I've bandied about for quite a while now. I want to escape the suffocating environment of my hotel room. I've become restless in my leisure hours. I believe that taking an active role in a worthwhile endeavor such as the Zouaves is exactly what I need right now. I'd be honored if you'd consider me a candidate for your drill team," I said, feeling awkward and embarrassed by my excuses. "I've kept track of the Zouaves and whenever possible, I've attended their appearances and made every effort to watch them perform their routines. Years ago,…while in the merchant marines I had some experience with firearms. If I'm given the opportunity to train with a rifle, I'm sure you'll be pleased with my progress."

"You were in the merchant marines! Well, Mister Crosby, I *never* would have guessed it," he remarked with a snicker as he stacked his letters and placed them on his desk. "You could have fooled me…though I should have suspected that. You're from the East Coast. Most young men from there are usually drawn to the sea. How come you didn't make it a career and become the captain of your own vessel?"

"After four years at sea, I found that life aboard a clipper ship was *not* the way I wanted to spend the rest of my life," I replied, uneasily shifting in my chair, correcting my posture, and then preparing to offer an explanation. "Having had my fill of life at sea, I was determined to seek my fortune on dry land. So far that decision has proven to be the right one for me. I'm proud to say that I've become successful beyond my wildest dreams. In spite of this,…I'm desolate and downhearted. I sorely miss my family in Massachusetts. Even though I pass the time away by submersing myself in my work, I've decided I must fill this void with an activity that gives meaning to my life…It'll also serve to satisfy my sense of patriotic duty. Our country's facing an unprecedented war between the states. I intend to do my part."

"You're in luck, Mister Crosby," he said as he swiveled around in his chair to face me. "My usual complement of eighty men is down by five due to relocation or other obligations. In order to fill our ranks, the corps is in need of a few more recruits. We usually march eight abreast…ten rows deep. I've had to improvise by placing five color guards in front of a seventy-member team presentation. So yes, you're welcome to join us at your earliest opportunity…I'll personally train you, myself. It's a rather rigorous and demanding schedule. We meet twice weekly on Mondays and Thursdays. Here's an application and an instruction sheet. You'll be installed at the first meeting you attend…I'll see you then. Thank you Mister Crosby for stopping by."

"Oh, I thank *you*, sir! It's been my pleasure." I said, reaching for the paperwork with one hand while standing and fumbling with the rim of my hat with the other. "For some reason, I expected to be turned down, but you welcomed me with open arms. I can't tell you how much this means to me! Remember, Colonel Ellsworth,…if you should need some financial help to keep this group of volunteer militia functioning, you can rely on me to provide it. I'll do my utmost to carry out my duties to the best of my abilities. I feel honored that you've accepted me into your rank and file and proud to support an organization with such patriotic and noble goals." Colonel Ellsworth rose from his chair and after a symbolic salute and a handshake, I left his office.

*   *   *   *

Early-November, 1859

A cold, misty rain had just begun to saturate the air and moisten the landscape as I stepped outside to view the window displays that had been rearranged for the upcoming holidays. It was just past two o'clock in the afternoon when a carriage came to an abrupt halt in front of the wholesale shop of Albert Crosby & Company.

"Mr. Crosby,…I've come here purposely to ask you if you'd be so kind as to escort me to Washington," Colonel Ellsworth said hesitantly after descending the carriage steps, turning around to ask the driver to wait for him, and then approaching me with his request. I opened the door to the wholesale shop and we stepped inside out of the fog and drizzle. "I'm scheduled to meet with President Buchanan and I'd like you to accompany me there. You're an eloquent and educated gentleman from the East Coast…well versed in social etiquette, diplomacy and protocol. It's imperative that I have your support, advice and guidance.

"Now that a war between the states is imminent, I'd like to recommend that the federal government secure the armed forces of the state's militia and that of the Zouaves. This bold initiative needs to be addressed. There's a possibility that if the White House acts upon my proposal, I could be considered for the Chief Clerkship of the Department of War. While I'm there, I also intend to schedule a performance by the Chicago Zouaves for the President. We'll execute a company drill on the White House lawn sometime next spring. I'd like to familiarize President Buchanan with the corps so he could possibly consider us as an elite guard,…honorary sentries who could defend the White House and Capitol buildings if need be. I dare not wait much longer as the South's already beginning to arm and train their troops. I'd like to leave this coming Saturday…if possible."

"Yes, Colonel, I believe that can be arranged, "I replied, taken aback by his sudden appearance at my business address and confirming my commitment with a handshake. "You honor me by your personal visit and your request to assist you. Of course I'll be pleased to join you on your mission to Washington and help in any way possible to gain a hearing for your cause. I trust your faith in my abilities is well placed. I'll meet you at the railroad station at nine on Saturday morning. We'll discuss your proposal on the train, and also our itinerary and subsequent plans. Everything should be formulated by the time we reach the District of Columbia."

"Thank you, Mr. Crosby," he said appreciatively, standing erect in the open doorway. "I knew I could count on you. I'll await your arrival at the station. See you promptly at nine. You can't believe how relieved I am to know that you'll accompany me on this assignment. You've lifted a heavy burden from my shoulders. When it seemed imperative that I act quickly on behalf of our organization, I immediately thought of you. I believe that in this instance,…two heads *are* better than one. Your assistance will be of infinite value to me in terms of what I intend to accomplish in the two weeks we'll be there. Thank you again." After a quick salute, he turned around, and then ascended his waiting carriage.

We arrived in the District of Columbia on a bitterly cold morning. It took an inordinate amount of fortitude on our part to brave the icy winds. The brightness of the sun in an almost clear sky cast a brilliant glow on dew transformed into ice. Frost covering the branches of the bare oaks was blinding as it reflected the sunlight. A glorious afternoon sun created more comfortable temperatures as we walked to an inn in close proximity to the Capitol and White House.

"I usually stay here when I visit Washington. It's fastidiously clean and the food's superb. It's a favorite of mine because of its informal ambiance. I'm sure you'll concur with me," Colonel Ellsworth maintained as he pointed his gloved finger toward an ornately trimmed, brick structure.

As we approached the front desk to register, I pulled out a large bill from my vest pocket and placed it in the hands of the receptionist.

"Why, Mr. Crosby,…I didn't expect you to pay for our stay here. After all, I'm the one who requested that you join me. Please,…at any rate, accept my portion of the lodging fee," he begged, reaching for his leather billfold and placing the money on the counter. "Let me reimburse you. Your generosity is sincerely appreciated, nevertheless,…I'm fully prepared to pay for our lodging here."

"Let me reiterate that I feel privileged to have been chosen from the corps as your companion on this urgent quest," I replied, returning his money and handing him the keys to a room across the hall from mine. "I can well afford it, so please allow me this trivial monetary gesture."

President James C. Buchanan was absent from Washington. It would be five more days before our audience with him was to take place. We occupied our time outlining, preparing and modifying the colonel's proposal—until it was flawless. That day we rose early and strolled briskly toward the White House. As I looked intently at my surroundings, I remembered that I hadn't been here since my honeymoon. It seemed like ages ago. At the time, I was so much in love—my eyes were only for Margaret. I barely recalled the monuments and magnificent buildings. We telegraphed President Buchanan of our arrival and expected to be in his presence by eleven.

After introducing himself and me, the colonel went on—elaborating his case with eloquence. He spoke clearly, intelligently and without a lot of bravado. The President listened intently as the colonel explained his purpose. Colonel Ellsworth rarely hesitated and referred to me only when he needed to verify or reaffirm a point of information. I must admit the colonel was quite convincing.

"You've put a lot of thought into your proposal to revamp and federalize the state's militias," President Buchanan said approvingly, handing each of us an expensive Cuban cigar and lighting them for us. "I fully agree with your progressive ideas. I shall see to it that both houses of Congress promptly act on it. Due to the secession movement, the dreaded conflict between the North and South is about to erupt. Thank you, Colonel Ellsworth. I look forward to the arrival of your Chicago Zouaves and the colorful demonstration of their skills. Their reputation as an elite precision drill team has preceded them. I'm aware of the many awards they've earned under your tutelage. I'll keep you informed as to the congressional decision concerning your suggestion. No doubt, Colonel Ellsworth,…Washington will see a lot more of you in the future. Goodbye, for now," he added, smiling and tapping the colonel on the shoulder as he accompanied us out of his office.

✳   ✳   ✳   ✳

Early - June, 1860

As planned, a full contingent of the Chicago Zouaves traveled to Washington for their scheduled presentation on the White House lawn. The precision of our drill was flawless. Dressed in our snappy attire and proudly wearing the many medals won in competition, we paraded before thousands—including the President and members of Congress. It was an honor to display our well-honed skills before such an illustrious audience.

"Colonel Ellsworth,…President Buchanan would like to speak to you, sir. I've been assigned the task of taking you to him," a White House aide said during the reception following our program.

"Would it be proper to allow my sergeant, Mister Crosby, to be present with me?" Colonel Ellsworth asked. "While I don't wish to disregard protocol, he's quite familiar with what's to be discussed…His input is of utmost importance to me."

"I suppose…it would all right," the aide replied with a cordial smile. "I don't believe the President will have a problem with that. If he does,…the gentleman can remain outside the office. Please follow me."

"Do come in,…Colonel Ellsworth and you also,…Mister Crosby. I remember you well," the President said, beckoning us forward and again offering us some Havana cigars. Swirls of smoke from the President's cigar spiraled toward the lofty, ornate ceilings. The aide led us to the front of the President's desk, helped to seat the colonel and me in two plush armchairs, and then left us to stand at the rear of the oval office. "I want you to know that Congress is proposing a bill creating a federal armed force consisting of the northern states' militias. It will be a formidable assemblage of reservists. I hope you're aware that your Zouaves, despite their artillery skills will not be assigned to wartime duty because of their age or other grounds. It's also a fact that their uniforms are unsuitable for military purposes. For these reasons and others that I don't wish to discuss at this time, members of the Zouaves will *not* serve their country on the front lines. I've suggested that the Zouaves are best utilized as an elite guard protecting Capitol Hill. Their disciplined presence in the halls of Congress will be reassuring. By the way, Colonel Ellsworth,…congratulations are in order on your new commission. I heard you've just become a second lieutenant in the army. I'm certain your chances of assuming a War Department post will be forthcoming."

President Buchanan turned toward me and without skipping a beat he said, "And you, Mister Crosby,…I hope these uncertain times haven't had a negative affect on your business. I'm well acquainted with your success as the owner of the largest distillery and brewery in the West. Your stand as a staunch abolitionist and your exceptional generosity to political causes are well known. The country needs support such as yours right now. I want to thank you personally, sir," he said, rising from his desk and shaking both our hands before leaving the room with his aides. I was astonished to be addressed personally by the President.

"Well, I must say that certainly was a one-sided conversation," Colonel Ellsworth said in a rather stunned and angry manner. "He said his piece, then left,…just like that! I never got a chance to debate his simplistic reasons for excluding the Zouaves from active duty. I'm truly incensed by his rebuff. It's an affront to the Zouaves!" I nonchalantly nodded my head in agreement with his observation.

"I suppose he's allowed to do that Colonel, sir," I replied with a grimace, surprised by the outcome of our conversation and shrugging my shoulders. "I guess it's one of the privileges accorded a President. Let's return to the festivities…It'll be time to return to Chicago, soon."

*　　　*　　　*　　　*

Mid - January, 1861

The winter seemed long and uncompromising. Snow flurries, blown horizontally by brisk and blustery winds, had been falling all day. Several inches covered the grassless meadows and the ever-present muddy slush of the city—transforming the customary winter ugliness into a pristine, winter wonderland. Like a rendering of an artist's winter scene, the droplets of freezing rain enveloped and illumed each tree branch and radiant daubs of snow dappled the wild, shrubby weeds below. A few hardy gulls floating on the river plucked at whatever drifted by with the current. "Oh, how I miss my loved ones!" I thought, heaving a deep sigh as I looked out from my office window and absorbing this serene landscape.

"Hurry Albert! Colonel Ellsworth will be here to pick you up shortly," Josiah shouted as he stepped through office door and jolting me back to reality. "I hear that as a select member of the Chicago Zouaves you'll be part of a military escort that will accompany Lincoln and his family on the train to Washington."

"Yes, we'll be in charge of protecting the President-elect when the train slows down as it passes through sparsely populated towns or comes to a full stop in the cities. The Zouaves will guard Mister Lincoln while he mingles with the crowds at the railroad depots," I replied, quickly trying to clear my desk "He's quite a popular figure…a little controversial, but nevertheless,…quite amiable. Mister Lincoln understands the necessity of the human spirit to exercise its free will. He enthusiastically champions the cause of the common people, which is an affront to the advocates of slavery and states rights. His vigorous efforts to extend freedom, dignity and justice to every citizen of this country have infuriated the South.

"Now that he's been elected a war between the states is a certainty. The southern states will never abandon slavery. They're ready to fight to the death for their cause. The newspapers are reporting that Jefferson Davis is preparing to become President of the Confederate States. We have our work cut out for us. The Zouaves must shield the President-elect from potential danger. There's a rumor that a network of rebels stationed along his train's route to Washington may attempt to harm him.

"I'm just finishing up some last-minute details. I've brought my valise so I could be ready to leave as soon as the colonel arrives. Thank you, Josiah, for your reminder. I believe all will go well in my absence. Uranus should be able to handle things while I'm away. I'll return as soon as the new President's sworn in."

Seditious crowds provoked by the unrest in Baltimore endangered Washington. The armed forces of the Confederate States of Virginia had now selected Robert E. Lee as their commander. The train passing through Baltimore carrying President-elect Lincoln to Washington was in jeopardy. An attempt to persuade people to assassinate their own leader was encouraged by rebellious factions. Lincoln was in danger of being harmed or killed by a brigade of southern sympathizers who would try to ferment a spontaneous uprising. As the train rolled through to the Maryland state line, the Lincolns and their entourage sang *The Stars Span-*

gled Banner, reminding the would-be radicals that it was written by their compatriot Francis Scott Key during an attack on Fort McHenry in Baltimore harbor.

The inauguration of President Lincoln was uneventful. The transition of administrations was well organized. Lincoln and his team ensconced themselves without fanfare or disruption in the operation of government. I boarded a train for Boston, visited my family at Wildwood, and then returned to Chicago.

Colonel Ellsworth remained in Washington. His parents sent a telegraph to confirm the rumor that although he was recovering, he had indeed contacted a severe case of measles from one of the Lincoln children.

I offered the colonel my best wishes for a speedy recovery and informed him that I would return to Washington around mid-May and again revisit my family in June. Margaret and our three daughters planned on traveling back to Chicago with me at that time.

✳   ✳   ✳   ✳

Mid -May, 1861

"I'll be leaving again for Washington in a few days," I said, reminding Uranus of my upcoming plans. "When I return in June, Margaret and the girls will be with me. I expect they'll remain here at the manor for a while."

"I just want you to know that I'm going ahead with my art gallery," Uranus said, reaching for the saltshaker and using his napkin to dab his mouth. We had stopped after work for supper at Kingsley's. "I'm sure you're aware of the fact, Albert, that I've always intended to put my money to good use. Investing in an art gallery will fill a cultural void that exists in this city. When I arrived here eleven years ago, I'll never forget how disappointed I was to find that Chicago was so lacking in art, theater, and opera. Now that I've accumulated a sizeable financial reserve,…it's become my first priority. After this goal is realized I hope to build a magnificent opera house. In the meantime, I expect the art gallery will occupy quite a bit of my time while you're away," he went on. "I may have to rely on Josiah a bit more than usual. He assumes an incredible amount of responsibility in your absence as it is."

"I know that. Nonetheless,…I believe he actually thrives on it," I replied, smiling and filling our goblets to the rim with a fine sauterne and raising my glass in a toast to his new endeavor. "Here's to your art gallery, Uranus! May it be a prosperous and superior one! Your quest to bring culture to the citizenry of Chicago is a praiseworthy one indeed."

"I've already purchased several valuable paintings and hope to contract a loan for many more from galleries in New York and Boston," he said. "I'll enlist local artists to supply the remainder. I hope to open the display area for public viewing by the beginning of September."

"Where are you planning to do all this? It sounds like quite an undertaking," I asked as I leisurely sat back in my chair and began to smoke my pipe.

"I've had an architect design a building with exceptional lighting and walls that will enhance the beauty of each painting," he replied, reaching into his vest pocket to pay the waiter for the meal. "The gallery will have enormous rooms and other ornately decorated spaces with marble floors and high ceilings. I intend to build it on Washington Street...close to the financial district where people of refined tastes can observe works of art produced by famous artists. They'll begin to enjoy the same artistic and cultural niceties afforded the elite of the East. It will be a magnificent collection of works...a treasure trove of impressionism and fine art."

When I arrived in Washington on May 22nd, I was greeted by the sight of endless rows of tents near the White House. The Seventh Regiment from New York had come to Washington and erected their tents on Meridian Hill. The area was kept in pristine condition. The troops were well behaved—their uniforms were fastidious. They were also orderly and courteous toward the general public. The next day, I spoke to Colonel Ellsworth in the Hall of Representatives. He was meeting with members of Congress about the unruly behavior of some of the Zouaves. Due to his rejection for a War Department post, Colonel Ellsworth had deliberately recruited a regiment from New York City who turned out to be a bunch of hooligans. Their gaudy Zouaves uniforms and armaments were as outrageous as their behavior, which was in stark contrast to that of the New York Seventh Regiment. After his hearings in Congress, he subsequently met with me to address this problem.

"Hello, Albert! So nice to have you back here with me again. The secession resolution has been adopted by a large number of southern states!" the colonel exclaimed, following a salute and handshake. His cordial greeting as he approached me in the Rotunda belied what would be disturbing news.

"Good day to you, Colonel Ellsworth," I replied, returning the formality.

"The city of Alexandria will be occupied and become part of The Union of Virginia!" he said, quickly descending the staircase to the lower level. It was all I could do to keep up with him. "A Mister James W. Jackson is the proprietor of the Marshall House hotel there. He was immediately commissioned a captain in the southern army. For about a month now, he's been flying a monstrous confederate flag from the tower above the hotel in celebration of the secession and to signify his defiance. He also had the star of Virginia placed in its center. It's an affront to the White House as the flag can be seen through binoculars when one looks down the Potomac River. Missus Lincoln, the First Lady, asked me if something could be done to confiscate that disgraceful flag and remove it from its prominent vantage point. I promised her that the Zouaves and I would do our best to remove it from atop that building."

"From the sound of it,...it seems things are really beginning to accelerate around here," I replied as we walked out the Capitol building toward the encampment on the Potomac. "I hope I've arrived in time to be of some help. How do you propose to remove that Confederate Flag from its place of prominence?" I asked, well aware that his ego was at the center of his quest for fame.

"Well,...I've a plan," this fanatical personality replied. "The southern high command has ordered the Virginia militia out of the city. With extraordinary obedience, they dutifully complied, leaving their homes and families to be occupied by the Union army. Foot soldiers from the North are already on their way to Alexandria and about to capture the city as we speak. I've selected about eight good men including you, Albert, to travel by steamboat down the Potomac to the wharf at Alexandria. A Union navy gunboat will cover our landing. I've been given the honor to lead this assault because of my promise to Missus Lincoln. I vowed that if accorded this assignment,...I would *personally* deliver the flag to her. My offer was graciously accepted."

"Is he being arrogant or just idealistic?" I wondered. "Will there be a glorious reward ahead or a tragic conclusion to this daring act? In any case," I concluded,..."he'll need my support."

"You can count on me to assist you," I said decisively, infuriated by the gall of that Captain Jackson. He was the enemy, after all, and like it or not, it was my duty to assist the colonel on this perilous mission. I was filled with righteous indignation and a spirit fired by an inner exactness. "It sounds like a good cause! I'm all for taking down that blasted flag!...When do we leave?" I asked, suppressing a gnawing fear of danger.

"We plan to meet on the pier around eight in the evening," he replied as he pushed the flap of his tent aside and entered. "This will be a night raid. We can enhance our odds for success if we move through Alexandria under the cover of darkness. Oh, incidentally,...that's your tent," he added, casually pointing to the one next to his. "Goodnight! I'll see you in the morning."

✳   ✳   ✳   ✳

Late -May, 1861

On this particular night a heavy cloud cover was a godsend—it obscured the moon that might have betrayed our arrival. Under a cloak of secrecy, Colonel Ellsworth outlined our strategy.

"We'll head down Fairfax until we reach the Marshall Hotel on King Street," he whispered while crouching in a doorway as the rest of us gathered behind him. "You, Albert, and six men will accompany me to the rooftop. Two of you will stay on the ground floor guarding the front entrance."

When we neared the Marshal House we obeyed his explicit orders. Colonel Ellsworth and I, plus six Zouave sentries silently crept up the staircase to the rooftop of the hotel. The single-minded Colonel Ellsworth reached for the flag and ripped it from its pole above the tower. Without warning, an ear-splitting blast reverberated through the stillness. A shotgun carried by a man still in his night-shirt was emitting smoke from its barrel. We stood frozen in a state of shock at the surrealistic sight of the colonel—fatally injured and covered by a blood soaked flag. He was surrounded by a group of terrified colleagues. Private Brownell finally reacted by shooting the man dead. The private eventually received the Congressional Medal-of-Honor for a task well done. The next morning, on May 25th, a special edition of the Virginia newspaper printed a vivid account of the fatal and unfortunate incident. The sensational news read:

> *Mister Joseph L. Padgett followed the assemblage of a Colonel Elmer E. Ellsworth and his squadron from the wharf on the Potomac all the way to the Marshall House. He said, his subterfuge was to enter the hotel before the guards were posted outside the entrance. He watched the siege as Ellsworth and his men ascended the staircase to the roof, and also the planned removal by said colonel of the Confederate flag from its perch atop the tower. Captain James W. Jackson, who was not yet called to active duty, was awakened by Mister Padgett and told what was taking place. He was heard to say, "No damn Yankees are going to take down my flag!" He retrieved his double-barreled shotgun from an adjoining second-floor room, sprinted upstairs to the rooftop, and then shot at the perpetrators, killing Colonel Ellsworth just as he had the flag in his arms. This act of chivalry cost him his life. In the melee, Private Francis E. Brownell of the Zouaves retaliated with a rifle shot, killing Jackson instantly. A coroner's jury has been convened to review the circumstances of Jackson's death.*

It was a significant blow to the Union. Reaction from the citizenry was prompt and trenchant. President Lincoln endured a period of personal mourning. Idealistic individuals like the colonel touch our lives in ways we do not expect. Such was the dedicated patriotism of Colonel Ellsworth—a quirky and determined man who answered to the beat of a different drummer yet—could get everyone else to march to his tune. His funeral services were held at the Capitol. Crowds gathered to view this political activist's lily-adorned casket where he lay in dress uniform. This dedicated patriot would always be remembered as a fallen hero. Private Brownell stood guard in his bloodstained uniform as a captivated public filed past the flower-bedecked coffin. The funeral cortège included President Lincoln's carriage. It followed directly behind the hearse, in front of a lengthy queue of mourners. On the 24th of May, a courageous Colonel Elmer E. Ellsworth, loyal to his God and his President, gave his life for the love of his country. He became a legendary symbol—memorialized as the first casualty of the Civil War.

▼

Late-March, 1862

The War Between the States had been raging for almost a year. It was a time when the barbaric practices of human slavery and wholesale slaughter were the status quo. I received a telegraph from my family in Brewster advising me that many young men from Cape Cod, in compliance with their patriotic heritage, were enlisting in the military. Japeth's son, who was now almost twenty-one years old, was among them.

Nathaniel immediately came to mind. I remembered the last time I saw him. I had accidentally bumped into him a few summers ago before he left Brewster for training at the Maritime Academy. I was entering the icehouse just as he was preparing to leave it. His exceptional good looks and distinctive demeanor took me by surprise. He smiled as I held the door opened for him.

"Hello, Mister Crosby," he said while carrying two large blocks of ice on ice hooks, one in each hand. "Do you remember me, sir? I'm Nathaniel,…Japeth's son? I'd tip my hat, Mister Crosby,…but as you can see my hands are full. It's been several years since we've last seen each other. It's so nice to meet up with you again, sir. My father manages to keep abreast of your whereabouts and the state of your well-being. He's always been so proud of your achievements. You're at the top of his list of exemplary people whom I should emulate."

"Well, it's a pleasure to see you also, Nathaniel," I said, helping him to lift the ice onto the buckboard and watching him climb up to the driver's seat. "You're a fine young man. Japeth must be quite proud of you. Please give your father my best wishes. Regretfully,…I'm here for just a short while. If I had more time, I would have visited with him. Please tell him that for me. I'd love to stand here and chit-chat with you, but you'd better leave with that ice before it melts."

"Yes, you're right, sir. I'd best be on my way. Goodbye!" he shouted with a smile, acquiescing to my suggestion, nodding his head, and then quickly lashing the whip over the horses. It seemed like yesterday. I hoped he would be spared injury or death, not only for his sake, but also for his family's. Tragedy had already befallen them once before with the untimely death of their beloved daughter, Rebecca. "Rebecca!" I heaved a deep sigh and grinned as I fondly remembered our youthful love affair. "Oh,...Rebecca!" My mind drifted to that tryst with my first love. It seemed so timeless—so long ago, and yet—like yesterday.

"Chicago's economically depressed right now," Uranus said, interrupting my thoughts and jolting me back to the present. Uranus and I were Kingsley's most frequent and illustrious patrons. Our table, which was always reserved and pre-set for us, was close to a large stone fireplace with logs sheathed in warm, inviting flames. It was especially welcoming this evening. Although spring was but a few days away, snow tossed by a howling wind was beginning to blanket the city. I sat facing a large, multi-paned window and watched while falling flecks accumulated on the gaslight supports. "Is there anything more beautiful than the gossamer softness of snowflakes illuminated by gaslights?" I wondered.

After being momentarily distracted, I continued to listen to Uranus as he cut into his prime rib, arranged the knife across the top of his plate, and then sat back to explain all the troubling details. "Many banks and businesses have seen their profits evaporate due to this conflict between the states. One by one,...they're failing. Their stocks and real estate holdings in the South have completely vanished or lost their value leaving them destitute and facing bankruptcy. I think we should consider loaning them some funds to help re-establish their financial stability. This may help to keep them afloat until they can recoup their losses. We've accumulated a sizable fortune through our real estate and financial investments. While most partnerships strive to increase its shareholders profits, that should not be our goal. By providing these floundering businesses with financial backing they can remain productive; that'll keep our economy stable and in the end benefit all of Chicago's citizenry. Successful companies such as ours have an obligation to invest in the social welfare of their communities. I believe this makes good sense because...it's ultimately good for business. Our distillery is supplying most of the medicinal alcohol needed by the military, druggists and doctors in this country. An undeniable stroke of luck, I'd say! Now that alcohol is so highly taxed, most people no longer have enough money to buy it. They have no other recourse but to purchase the more affordable medicinal alcohol."

"Yes, so I've noticed. We can't keep up with the orders. The men are working three, eight hours shifts,…seven days a week. The shelves are in constant need of new stock." I replied after taking a bite of food and tasting the wine in my crystal goblet. "It's selling faster than hotcakes! It continues to mystify me as to how they can drink that repugnant drug. Ugh,…it's so bitter! I know that many of the common folk here are consuming alcohol at an alarming rate. I'm sorry to say that I've unwittingly benefited from their addiction. I realize these circumstances are beyond my control. Alas, medicinal alcohol has become the answer to their need for liquor. It distresses me to find that this is so.

"I've been reading the business reports in the *Tribune*," I went on to say, concurring with his assessment of the depressing economic situation while gesturing to the waiter to bring another bottle of the same wine to our table. "I agree with you, Uranus. I must say it's a dismal state of affairs to say the least. If only negotiations hadn't failed because of the South's adamant stand on states rights and slavery,…a truce could have ended a war that has already cost precious lives and resources. It's a damn shame!

"As one of the few solvent entrepreneurs left in Chicago, I believe it *would* be a wise and profitable corporate decision to give our counterparts some financial assistance during their time of hardship. I'd like Albert Crosby & Company to be a business whose integrity and reliability is rightfully acknowledged in the marketplace. One never knows when that sort of aid might be crucial to *us*. Let me add that I've also decided to donate a significant amount of our medicinal alcohol to the army hospitals. This humanitarian deed will serve us well. The Northern Militia needs a staggering amount of funds. Supplying them with this product for medical purposes will be our contribution to the war effort. I figure we can help in numerous other ways. I'll discuss that with you when the need arises. The publicity received through our public good works should result in a well-established tradition of philanthropy. This will be an excellent advertising tool. For now, let's concentrate on notifying the army of our intentions. We'll hire some extra help to pack and ship the freight by rail to the Southeast where it's needed."

Uranus concurred with a nod as we walked over to the coat rack. After dressing for the inclement weather, I put on my hat and gloves then twirled a wool scarf around my neck and face. Uranus did the same. The waiter opened the door for us and we ventured forth. A chill March wind cut to the bone as we walked in the frigid night air. We pushed forward, bent and blinded by the swirling snowflakes. It was as if nature had given Chicago its final, bitter blast of nasty weather before lowering its baton and ending the long, dreary concerto of winter.

*   *   *   *

Mid-April, 1862

"Margaret, I've just been informed that Samuel will be arriving in Chicago some-time in May," I said, finishing my cup of morning coffee and preparing to leave for the wholesale shop. Samuel Nickerson was a good friend and relative through marriage and also Uncle Isaac's son-in-law. "He plans to arrive around the 20th of April. He's already purchased a large warehouse on the river a few blocks from here. Samuel intends to establish his own brewery and distillery. I guess the brew-ery business has become a family affair. It'll be called the S.M. Nickerson & Company."

"Yes, so I've been told. Uranus rather hinted to that effect. Won't that seri-ously hurt your business?" she asked snidely, handing me my jacket and hat and helping me get dressed. "I should think that'll be fairly competitive. Don't you believe that's rather obnoxious of Samuel? I can't imagine he'd have the gall to undercut his own relative! You should have tried to discourage him, Albert. He's a typical self-seeking opportunist. It's inconceivable…an absolute affront!"

"Oh, Margaret,…to the contrary!" I replied, calmly responding to her caveat remark and trying to make her understand by explaining the truth of the matter. "You just don't understand…It's not that way at all! There are more than enough profitable opportunities to go around. Actually, there are limitless prospects for future businesses here. Chicago can certainly use more than one distillery, espe-cially since mine has been completely adapted to producing medicinal alcohol. The potential for industry and commerce during wartime is staggering. There's a rush in supplying all that the people need. Chicago's become the axle in the wheel of supply and demand. We've sent more militia, materials and funds to the war effort than any other northern city," I said while holding and kissing each one of the girls as I took my leave. "That's where *my* fortune's being made. There still remains a need here for a brewery and a distillery that will produce fine wines and liquors…and that's where Samuel comes in. He saw that opportunity and the ability to enrich himself by filling that void. Samuel's a perceptive business-man, a visionary who knows a good prospect when he sees it. Depending on the length of this war and despite the gouging taxes, he's sure to be as successful as I've been,…probably even more so. For some unknown reason, since the conflict began there seems to be an unquenchable thirst for alcohol. So you see, my dear, your assumptions are mistaken. Don't be apprehensive about this. You needn't feel any resentment toward him for wanting to take advantage of the situation before someone else steps in and deprives him of it. Please put your mind at ease…Does that answer your question?" I asked as I opened the door to leave.

"Yes. You've pretty much convinced me that his new venture will not adversely affect your company *or* your profits," she replied, raising her eyebrows, shrugging her shoulders and obviously not persuaded by my explanation. Nevertheless, she smiled and gave me a quick kiss on the cheek.

The brief, beautiful spring season was upon us. Now that it was here in earnest, the weather was bright and balmy. It was a delightful morning when I left for the waiting carriage. We enjoyed sunny skies and temperatures in the upper sixties for a part of every day.

Margaret was expecting our fourth child in early September and seemed to be in much better health while carrying this baby. She had very little morning sickness and as a result she literally glowed—her energy was boundless. Except for the day we married, I never saw her look so radiant. Even so, she made arrangements to again return to Wildwood. She would be heading east around the middle of June. Margaret insisted on having her own doctor for the birth. "Could she possibly be carrying a boy?" I wondered as I looked out from the isinglass window of the coach. "This pregnancy is so different from the others." I dared not hope for fear I could possibly be disappointed again. I told myself that a healthy child was more important than its sex. If fate dictated that another female be added to our family—then so be it.

"Your Cousin Charles is waiting for you in your office, Albert," Josiah said, in a hushed voice before opening the office door for me. "Sounds like he's gotten himself into some trouble again and needs to have you bail him out."

Uranus had a brother Charles who was four years older than he was. At thirty-six, he had a receding hairline and was already graying at the temples. Pleasant and well mannered, Charles was a debonair man of medium height and stature. His tight, curly hair was worn combed straight down to just below his ears. Well-shaped eyebrows framed piercing, teal colored, eyes that flanked a long, straight nose. He had a trim mustache and a small goatee. Charles always wore dark clothing with velour collars, stiff white shirts and silk bow ties at the neck.

He too, like most of the Crosby men had come to Chicago in '57 along with several partners to start his own venture. It was a soap and candle manufacturing business, but it was failing. His associates were displeased with his declining interest in the partnership. Charles' attention to women had become more intense in proportion to the ennui of fabricating the simplistic goods that were beginning to disinterest him. His constant socializing greatly limited the time he spent tending to business matters. Charles, who was a ladies man, much preferred women to soap and candles. He had made some ruinous business decisions in the past and I was certain he was approaching me again to rectify another one of his typical blunders. He was a blasé man with such impractical goals that I simply attributed them to wishful thinking. I braced myself as I prepared to greet him. I was ready for Charles Crosby this time around.

"Well, good morning, Charles. Have a seat." I said cordially, mindful of the fact that he had made a habit of taking advantage of my generosity. With a forced smile and an exasperated nod of my head, I pointed to the chair in front of my desk. I resolutely straightened my vest, walked over to my desk, sat down, and then looked him straight in the eye. "What a pleasant surprise to see you up and about so early in the day. Don't you usually sleep 'til noon? You must have something *very* important on your mind to be here at this time of day. Would you like a cup of coffee? It might help to keep you awake." I added sarcastically, walking over to the coffee pot and pouring myself a cup. I hoped my caustic remarks might arouse a spark of awareness in this automaton of a person sitting in front of me.

"Oh, Albert, cut it out! Stop patronizing me. I wouldn't be here if I didn't need to ask a favor of you," he babbled glumly, lowering his head and fidgeting with his hat.

"Oh, I know *that*!" I replied, nodding my head and walking back to my desk, justifiably annoyed.

"Yes, thank you. I will have a cup of coffee, if you don't mind. I do have somewhat of a hangover. It may help, Albert," he said, reaching for the cup I was handing him and demeaning himself by groveling with each word. "I need to borrow a few thousand dollars to tide me over the next month. I'm waiting for funds from my accounts receivables. I'll return the loan as soon as that money comes in. Albert,…please help me! I'm desperate and really hurting right now!"

"I'd be happy to help you, Charles, however,…my assets are all tied up at the moment. I've made several sizable loans to some prominent businesses here in Chicago," I replied, feeling exploited as I stood and looked out the window with a cup of coffee in my hand. "I know I'll be repaid by them…with interest. On the other hand, I've yet to see a dime of the several thousands, I've already loaned you in the past. You always promised to repay me, yet…you *never* have. I can't believe you're here to ask for more. You've got your nerve, Charles! If only you had made some small effort to reimburse me, I might have loaned you…not *give* you some of my available cash. It makes no sense to further deplete my finances at this time. That would be a *very* impractical business decision on my part. Frankly, Charles, because you're so lazy,...you're truly not worth the effort. You're the most capricious, unstable person I've ever known!...You'll just have to manage on your own from now on

"Let me reiterate, Charles,...you'd better start putting your nose to the grindstone or you'll suffer the consequences." Incensed by his audacity and seething with resentment, I paused and went on to say, "You'll be out in the cold,...a penniless vagrant. You need to change your lifestyle and be productive otherwise...you'll lose your self-respect. Take pride in being a responsible adult for heaven's sake! One is seldom enriched who adopts deceit as a virtue and slovenliness as a way of life! Dedication and hard work are a *must* if one wants to be successful. Life's no joy ride and the sooner you realize that...the better off you'll be! I feel sorry for the predicament you're in right now, but I don't feel wretched enough to throw good money after bad. If I find that you've changed your ways and tried your best to succeed,...then and *only* then,...will I reconsider my resolve not to bail you out of your debts! Goodbye, Charles, I must leave now. I'm needed at the distillery." I left my desk, picked up some paperwork, and then started to escort him out the door.

"Oh, well, I thought I'd give it one more try. Nothing ventured...nothing gained!" he quipped with a frustrated smirk as he rose from his chair. He lowered his head as he walked toward the door and prepared to leave. "Thanks anyway for hearing me out. I won't bother you further. Well,...goodbye, Albert. The truth of the matter is that I'm leaving here empty handed. Even though I'm a family member, you've made yourself quite clear about where I stand...and that's on the outside looking in. Give my regards to Uranus." Without a backward glance, he waved farewell and was soon out the door. I sighed and shook my head with pity for this pathetic character. I hoped for his sake—he'd straighten himself out.

A few days later, Uranus was in my office to discuss the various ways we could support the war effort. We decided to donate some of our inventory along with coffee and tea to fairs and bazaars. The proceeds would benefit war families and widows. Some of the funds would also provide supplies that were much needed by the Northern Armed Forces.

"Your brother was here earlier in the week," I mentioned casually, aware that Uranus would be embarrassed to learn that Charles was most likely looking for another handout. Frankly,...I'm a little reluctant to bring up his name."

"As usual, I suppose he had another fiscal emergency," Uranus said noticeably uncomfortable by my disclosure. "I've repeatedly refused to loan that loafer another cent. I'm sure that's the reason he decided to turn to you. Charles is such a leech! Any day now, his partners will most likely boot him out on his royal ass! I must admit that since he's been here that brother of mine has been nothing but an albatross around my neck. I apologize for him, Albert, and trust he didn't make a nuisance of himself. I hope you didn't give in to his impudence."

"Oh, no! You needn't apologize for him, Uranus. He didn't coerce me into loaning him any more money. I can handle myself quite well when it comes to dealing with Charles," I said assuredly, rising from my chair and again turning toward the window. "The only thing he got from me was a lecture and a dire warning that he'd better put his life in order or else he'd end up a derelict on the streets. I doubt he'll be back." I turned around to face Uranus, shrugged my shoulders, and then added, "It amazes me how two brothers raised by the same parents can have such divergent personalities and principles."

"I know…Isn't it ironic? It's been a mystery to me, too." Uranus replied, picking up the paperwork from my desk and preparing to leave. "I'll see to it that several crates of the merchandise you mentioned are delivered to every charitable organization in Chicago. It should greatly boost their coffers and help them achieve their intended goals."

✳   ✳   ✳   ✳

Mid-September, 1862

"Congratulations, Mister Crosby! You have a son! Here's a cigar for you," announced Doctor Thaddeus Emerson, stepping outside our bedroom, adjusting his jacket, and then addressing me in the hallway.

"Oh, I'm so delighted!" I exclaimed. His words were music to my ears. "How's Margaret and my new baby boy doing, sir?"

"He's a fine healthy infant…robust and ready to take on the world. Your son made his entrance with a big yawn and energetically stretching his arms upwards. Mother is also doing quite well. Margaret's so pleased to have delivered a boy…she said, she's going to name him after you. She knows how much you've yearned for a son. I'm not surprised in the least that Margaret gave birth to a boy. It's a fact that during periods of war, male births far exceed the female ones. You may go in now and visit with them both. I'll take my leave. Although I don't anticipate any problems,…I'll drop by tomorrow. Madam Henderson and my nurse will remain with Margaret and the baby throughout the night."

"Thank you, Doctor Emerson," I said with a grateful handshake. "Margaret thinks so highly of you that every time she finds herself with child, she returns to

West Roxbury from Chicago so you can supervise the birth. I'm surprised she didn't name our son after you." Doctor Emerson, who was a well-proportioned man in his sixties, grinned through his bushy snow-white mustache. He removed his top hat from the coat rack and placed it over a head of straggly, tousled white hair. The doctor found his way down the staircase and after retrieving his umbrella from the holder, he opened the front door. A brisk wind and light rain greeted the kindly doctor when he stepped outside. He had been with us since early afternoon and it was now late in the evening.

"Margaret, my dear, I hear we have a son! It's taken a while, but we've finally succeeded. I'm ecstatic!" I cried out, elated by this joyous occasion. I felt I was walking on air—my feet seemed to race ahead of my body. I hurried to her bedside with open arms. "Not that I don't love my girls,…I adore them. But, oh, to have finally fathered a son! I'm so happy. It's infinitely wonderful! I dared not hope for such a miraculous outcome. This is *truly* a blessed event for me."

"I knew you'd be pleased, my dearest," she said, holding our new baby close to her bosom and reaching out with her free hand to pull me close. I kissed her forehead, sat on the edge of the bed, and then looked down with awe at my new son. He was scratching a small masculine face with a large hand and long fingers. "Albert's as handsome as his father," she said. "I'm sure he'll be your pride and joy. I've decided to name him Albert, Junior. I was sure you wouldn't mind."

"Of course not, Margaret. Why, I'm delighted!" I exclaimed, overjoyed by the birth of a son and pleased to have him named after me. "As I've done before, my dear, when our three daughters were born,…I've brought you a little gift. It's a token of my appreciation, regardless of the baby's sex." I removed the small, black velvet box from my vest pocket and presented it to her.

"Oh Albert how sweet of you!" she said excitedly as she looked up from nursing the baby. "Please open it for me. I can't wait to see what you have for me this time. Oh, how lovely! Earrings to match that beautiful broach you gave me when I presented you with Fanny. Now I have the whole matching set…the necklace, bracelet, broach and earrings. Thank you, my dearest."

She placed baby Albert beside her and went on to say, "You know,…Albert, I find myself transfixed by his manly frame. Even as an infant he's built so differently from the girls. I'm so used to the soft, round plumpness of our daughters with their tiny, chubby fingers and toes,…I just can't get over his flat bottom, broad shoulders and straight body. His hands and feet are so large, and his legs are like that of a chicken's. I keep telling myself over and over again, 'Margaret, he's perfectly fine. That's what a boy baby's supposed to look like.' After having girls, it's a revelation to see such a marked difference in his anatomy. I guess I'll eventually get use to it. Doctor Emerson warned me to be careful when changing him. I could easily be sprayed." Margaret and I had a good laugh over *that* prospect.

"Vive la différence, my dear!" I said with a grin. I got up from the bed and bent over to kiss her again, this time on the lips.

I didn't want to bring it up, but I could no longer delay telling her that I must leave for Chicago within a few days. Although I had arrived several weeks before baby Albert's birth, he had arrived ten days late. I planned on being away from my company no longer than a month, including travel time. I didn't know how to disclose my intentions. I knew if I told her I was about to leave, she would be livid, but I had no choice. I would have to tell her the next day, at the very latest. I was torn between staying on with Margaret and my family or focusing on business affairs that were in constant need of my attention. I was actually becoming quite restless, tired of sitting around and bored to death by this placid existence. The tiresome social obligations, Madam Henderson's arrogance and Margaret's condescending friends were all becoming quite stressful. It was impossible for me to tolerate it any longer. I decided it was time for me to leave.

After Doctor Emerson made his daily rounds to check on Margaret and baby Albert, I went into her room. They were both rapidly getting stronger and seemed to be doing quite well. I decided I'd better get it over with and face the consequences.

"Margaret dearest, do you remember my telling you when I first arrived, I'd only be able to remain a month…less the commuting time?" I asked after kissing her and pulling up a chair so I could sit by her bedside. I took her hand in mine, collected myself with all the tact I could muster, and then went on to reveal my intentions.

"Well,…that time's up for me. I must take the morning train from Boston to New York. I'll be in New York for a few days as I have some business there…then it's on to Chicago. I'm sorry,…but that's the reality of it. I'd love to stay on a while longer, however, that's impossible right now…It's especially so at this time of year when we're so busy with the upcoming holiday season. I do hope you understand. You should be able to travel west before winter settles in. Bring as many nannies as you need to help you. They'll be well compensated and allowed to return to Boston if they wish to do so. All their expenses will be taken care of. Well,…that's it. I'm sure you appreciate my predicament," I added while anxiously awaiting her answer.

"Yes, I remembered what you said. Nevertheless, I assumed you'd change your mind…now that I've given you a son. If you remained here in West Roxbury, you might enjoy watching him grow through his formative years into manhood," she replied candidly, knowing she was being manipulative. Margaret was acutely aware of how much this meant to me. She deliberately touched on a raw nerve—and she *knew* it. When the subject of my leaving needed to be addressed, Margaret was ready to retaliate with a well-rehearsed answer.

"You're wealthy beyond your wildest dreams. Why don't you rid yourself of that burdensome company and take an early retirement?" she said in a calculating manner, her voice becoming increasingly enraged as she went on. "We could live comfortably here for the rest of our days. Can't you understand how much I despise bringing up my children in that crude, filthy city of Chicago! There's nothing there for the children *or* me! I've told you that over and over again, Albert. I refuse to return there and that's final!" She eventually calmed down, collected her composure, and then added, "Why won't you try to look at it from my point of view for a change? I don't think I'm being unreasonable. It would be one thing if we were impoverished, but we're not. Wildwood meets all our needs. There's no excuse for you abandoning your family and living alone a thousand miles away. If you choose to return to your distillery over remaining here with us,…then I believe you need to change your priorities, my dear Albert. I'm begging you to stay here with the children and me. Remember, they're also your responsibility."

"Are you quite finished, Margaret?" I asked, infuriated by her relentless refusal to live in Chicago and aware of a sharp rise in my voice and blood pressure. Completely stunned by her outburst, my breathing became labored, my heart started pounding and a sinking sensation swept over me. As she spoke, I kept repeating to myself, "I must control my temper and hear her out. I need to be sensitive, yet steadfast in my response to her harangue." Although her words were like daggers that gravely wounded my self-esteem, I nevertheless pressed on—determined to make my point.

"Margaret, my dear, this will be the last time I'll *ever* discuss this with you." I replied assertively in a more subdued tone of voice. As I've said many times before, you need not entertain any false hopes. I refuse to sell my business and retire in West Roxbury. You can attempt to shame me all you want and prevent me from being with my son and family, but I won't be threatened or nagged into submission. My future's in Chicago,…not here.

"It goes without saying, I don't propose to stop working. I'm not ready to retire for many more years to come. I'm too young and still exceedingly motivated to apply myself. At this stage in my life, I wouldn't enjoy being idled. I only feel fulfilled when I'm kept active and toiling at something that's pleasurable for me. I do love you and the children dearly, but I must put my own welfare first. If I did as you asked, I'd be extremely unhappy, sulking and languishing with each day,…eventually dying of shear boredom. Would you still respect me if I became a lifeless, insipid shell of a man of no use to you or myself? I'm sure you'd be disgusted with someone like that.

"So you see, my dear, Margaret, I can't abide by your wishes, not for your sake, but for mine. That's my final answer. Somehow I always knew it would come down to this. It was just a matter of time. As far as I'm concerned this subject is closed forever! I'm tired of trying to appease your incessant hatred of Chicago. I'm sorry it has to end this way.

"I still plan on taking the train in the morning. You may remain here for as long as you like. I want you to know, I don't intend to commute back and forth more than twice a year. I'll try to return for a month immediately after the holidays and again in July.

"I leave with a heavy heart. I'm afraid that because of the lengthy separations, I'll become a stranger to my own children. I love my family, and I'm especially distressed about being absent from their childhood and adolescence. My presence is such an important part of their lives.

"Please try to correspond with me often. Do keep me informed about family matters that pertain to you and the children. Now that our family has grown, I'll see to it that you receive a substantial increase in the support check that I send each month.

"I need not upset you further. I'll be in to see you again later this evening and tomorrow before my departure. Farewell Margaret! See, I remembered to say farewell and not…goodbye. I do love you…more than you'll ever know," I said ardently, bending over to kiss her.

She rejected my show of affection by angrily turning to her side and burying her head in the pillow. Surprised at first by her conduct, I realized on second thought that it was typical of Margaret to react that way. Angered by her self-indulgent behavior, I stomped out of the bedroom. At any rate, it was time to begin packing for my journey back to Chicago.

After a very emotional evening, I returned the next morning to bid Margaret and the children a fond farewell. She seemed a bit more receptive. Although Margaret would not accept my reasoning, she had become resigned to the fact that she would *never* be able to change my mind. I left with the memory of an aloof, icy kiss casually placed on my cheek.

*   *   *   *

Late-February, 1863

Uranus bolted into my office, unshaven and disheveled. I was taken aback by his appearance. This was so unlike Uranus—he was usually so fastidious. His grooming was clearly not his main concern this morning.

"Albert, I've been giving a lot of thought to what I'm about to propose," he said completely out of breath as he quickly pulled up a chair and sat squarely in front of my desk. "Even though I've already made up my mind about this, I value your advice and input and think it's time to share my idea with you. As you know, the brewery and the distillery have flourished,…especially since the manufacture of medicinal alcohol. We're wealthy beyond our wildest dreams. We have more than enough money to sustain the business and ourselves. Therefore, I've decided to invest in a new venture,…one that's been close to my heart for many years. The arts are beginning to flourish here in Chicago as well as in all the other major cities in the East. New York already has several elaborately designed opera palaces that are extremely successful and cater to overflow crowds.

"We need a similar structure right here in Chicago that will rival those,…and I intend to build it! It'll be the largest and grandest theater in the Midwest…an academic and cultural first. I'll call it the Chicago Opera House. The auditorium is designed to hold an audience of several thousand.

"I've already reviewed some initial sketches for it. William W. Boyington, a prominent architect here in Chicago has contracted to take over the project. He's taken it upon himself to personally draft them for me. And yes, I've found a perfect place for it on Washington Street between State and Dearborn, right next to the art gallery. The final details for acquiring this land and the existing structures are being negotiated by the builder as we speak.

"I can't wait to get started on this undertaking. According to the specifications, it'll take over two years to build. I'm confident it'll be a financial bonanza. I'd like you to join me in this effort, Albert. I know this whole matter comes, as a bit of a surprise, however,…I'd truly welcome your opinion and any additional ideas on your part. When it's completed, I'll need a general manager. Would you consider assuming that responsibility?"

"Whoa!…Slow down and take a breath…One thing at a time here!" I said, smiling and shaking my head in disbelief. I rose from my chair, circled my desk, and then approached him. "Well, Uranus, it's no wonder you look so harried. I can see you're fully engrossed in this project of yours. Please calm down! I must say you're certainly living up to the bold Crosby tradition. We're famous for assuming colossal risks. At thirty-two, you're already determined to make your mark in this world. I'm really proud of you, Uranus! It's a splendid concept!...I'm sorry I didn't think of it myself. Just joking of course." I snickered as I slapped him on the shoulder. I walked over to the small stove and offered him a cup of coffee after pouring one for myself. "Opera's really not my specialty," I went on, handing him his cup. "I'm sure you're aware of that. I don't particularly take pleasure in that sort of highbrow entertainment. As for my advice, you obviously don't need it. Even so, I'll be more than happy to furnish you with additional building funds if you should need them. Keep that in mind.

"As for being your general manager...only time will tell. A lot can happen in two years. On the other hand, if the possibility still exists at that time, I'd be honored to be in charge of such a prestigious enterprise. Thank you, Uranus. I appreciate the fact that you considered me for that position. By the same token, you could have asked your uncles or even your father. They're just as capable as I am. In fact, I'm certain you can count on all of us. We'll be supporting you and wishing you the very best. I must say, Uranus, that right now I'm as excited about this challenging endeavor as you are."

"Whew! That's a comforting thought," he replied, expelling a gasp of relief, reaching for his handkerchief, and then wiping his brow. "I was afraid you'd laugh me right out of here. I wasn't sure how you'd receive this ambitious pursuit of mine. It's something I've yearned to do for a long while, actually,...since I arrived here in Chicago thirteen years ago. I've always nurtured a love of opera. I dared not hope that I'd ultimately become wealthy enough to see my dream fulfilled. It's simply because of you, Albert, that I find myself able to reach such a lofty vision. Thank you, dear cousin. I'll always be in your debt, and I'll never forget your faith and enthusiasm in my undertaking."

When he stood, I wrapped my arms around him as a further show of confidence. After we shook hands, he placed his empty cup on my desk, and then practically bolted out of the office.

"For heaven's sake, Uranus, pull yourself together!" I hollered, watching him sprint down the hallway and out the side entrance.

"I will!" he yelled back before disappearing from sight.

*   *   *   *

Mid-May, 1863

"Albert, I've just returned from going over the final drawings for the opera house!" Uranus blurted excitedly before taking the time to remove his coat and top hat. I had invited him to the manor on Chicago Avenue and greeted him at the door. I lived alone in the mansion except for a maid, who was away for a few days. When Uranus initially announced his plans to provide a superior form of musical entertainment to the populace of Chicago, I was captivated and wanted to hear more.

"I've brought the drawings for you to inspect! The architect has just completed these prints for me. The art gallery has been incorporated in the sketches as part of the opera house. I've purchased all the additional property on Washington Street that I'll need for this project. The old buildings will be razed next month so that construction can begin immediately. It should be completed by April of '65. It's absolutely magnificent! Wait 'til you see it, Albert!" he exclaimed, beginning to unroll an enormous set of designs on the dining room table. "The opera house will seat 2500 patrons. Its sound system will surpass that of any other opera house in the world. The grand promenade leading to the seat area will be three stories and the auditorium will have an ornately carved forty-foot high ceiling. Think of it, Albert! The Chicago Opera House will be built on such an immense scale and have an interior so elegantly grand,…it'll be the pride of Chicago,…the crown jewel of our country and possibly the most superb on earth."

"Yes, I must say it's incredible. It's more than incredible,…it's extraordinary! Uranus! I know you've accumulated a sizeable fortune through your real estate and investments; nevertheless, this dream of yours seems a bit too extravagant…even for you! Don't you think you're spending an inordinate amount of money on the amenities and that this project may require further study?" I asked, shaking my head and glancing at page after page of embellishments—Italian marble floors, teakwood walls, Persian rugs, gilded adornments, colossal crystal chandeliers and hundreds of solid brass wall sconces. The blueprints included an enormous gas heating and cooling system unlike any other in the world. It was an enterprise of astounding proportions.

"The price tag for the opera house will be approximately $600,000. I have enough funds and financial backing to build it exactly as it appears here," Uranus said, passing his hand over the front page of the neatly assembled stack of architectural sketches. "I intend to cover all the overhead and operating costs by managing it competently.

"I plan to schedule renowned Italian and German opera touring companies as well as prestigious ballet, symphony and orchestral performances. I also intend to enlist the artistic talents of leading theatrical entertainers and vocalists. A heavy schedule of advanced bookings should guarantee continued interest by the patrons. I'll also see to it that the events are well advertised. These "world class" entertainers should play to a capacity crowd. The projected audience statistics call for such a first-rate structure. With any luck, all the seats in the opera house will be filled for every performance. I'm sure…it'll be a huge success!"

"I certainly give you credit Uranus for embarking upon such a massive undertaking," I said, taking a deep breath. Overwhelmed by his extraordinary and challenging scheme, I shook my head in amazement. "It's taken a lot of time, thought and tenacity to realize your dream. I admire you for that. As you said, this is what you've been hoping to achieve since you arrived here. Your persistence to move forward with your opera house rivals that of mine with the wholesale liquor and tea business. The best of luck to you, Cousin! I'm certain it'll be a most successful venture. May your gift of this exceptional opera house to the city of Chicago initiate an epoch of cultural renaissance and become all that you desire it to be."

"Again, thank you, Albert, for your encouragement and support. I know you won't regret it," said Uranus, rolling up the thick pile of drafts, tying it with a ribbon, and then preparing to leave. "Unless there's a particular need, I probably won't be at the distillery very often from now on. I'll be involved with dealings concerning the opera house. That'll keep me quite occupied for a while. I want to oversee every aspect of its construction. I'm sure you understand."

"Go right ahead with your affairs, Uranus. Everything's under control right now," I said, opening the front door for him. "Now that Margaret's staying at Wildwood and I'm no longer active in the Zouaves, I intend to devote all my attention, extra time and energies to the business at hand. The completion of your opera house is of great concern to me. Do keep me posted on your progress!" I shouted, as I watched him descend the stairs and enter his waiting carriage.

*   *   *   *

Early - July, 1863

The erection of the opera house was progressing on schedule. Uranus was exceedingly energized by the construction of his magnificent, cultural institution—a truly elegant, architectural monument dedicated solely to the glorification of the arts. Upon its completion the Chicago Opera House would unquestionably be worthy of awe and admiration. Uranus was already busy scheduling the most popular Italian, German and French opera troupes. He engaged renowned acting companies and famous entertainers with worldwide acclaim. He also signed contracts with the agents of well-known lecturers who would present themselves to full houses. Uranus intended to offer every seat for a reasonable ticket price so that even those of modest means could afford the enriching experiences offered at the opera house. In spite of his enthusiasm for such an ambitious project, I decided to voice my concern. My question was subtly infused with a copious supply of skepticism.

"Uranus, are you sure you have enough funds to complete this gargantuan structure?" I asked. We were both in shirtsleeves and standing across the street from the partially framed opera house on a stifling and airless Sunday morning.

My thoughts wandered to the cool ocean breezes off the refreshing waters of the bay in Brewster. In my mind's eye, I envisioned the vista of whitecaps all the way to the horizon and the steady lapping of the waves against a shoreline that gently curved eastward, embracing an azure sea.

"I'm a bit apprehensive about all this. Somehow the expenditures seem to be way out of proportion to your earnings and investments," I went on, "I appreciate the fact that you're fulfilling your life's dream, but you'd better keep a close eye on the final price tag. You must be prepared to pay for a variety of escalating and unexpected costs or I'm afraid you'll find yourself in dire straights."

"Frankly, Albert," he replied, looking down and shuffling his feet on the boardwalk. "I must admit that sometimes I worry about that possibility myself. In spite of this, I've enough confidence in this venture to know that it'll be profitable. My sponsors and financiers continue to assure me they'll provide all the necessary funds to cover any future deficits, if that should occur. I expect the projected receipts will more than cover the large mortgage payment and other fixed operating costs. I've figured everything down to the last dollar. I hope all will go according to plan. I'm not anticipating any unforeseen problems, but…one never knows."

"I'm leaving in a few days for West Roxbury," I said, walking back to the carriage. "I'll be gone for about a month. If you can arrange it,…I need you to be at the distillery for a portion of your day and manage it while I'm away. Things are quiet right now. I don't expect a crisis to occur in my absence. I haven't seen the family since January. At that time, my visit was cut short because of severe weather conditions that threatened to curtail travel. I wanted to avoid being stranded somewhere, so I left before I planned to. Oh, how I miss Margaret and my family!" I said, entering the carriage and seating myself inside. "I'm ashamed to say that because of my long absences, the children are very distant. Even though they know I'm their father, I'm looked upon as a stranger. After I walk in the door it takes them several days to warm up to me."

"Do you think Margaret will ever return to Chicago?" he asked after telling the driver to drop us off at Kingsley's. "She was always especially cordial toward me. I'm sure you know that I'm quite fond of her. I just can't seem to understand her reluctance to live in that beautiful home you built for her here, especially now that Chicago's future is so promising."

"Oh, she detests Chicago," I said, wiping the perspiration from my brow with my handkerchief. "I've learned to dismiss her negative and judgmental assessments of this city. I've come to the conclusion that it's really not Chicago she dislikes. Margaret loathes the idea of leaving her family, circle of friends, West Roxbury, Boston and New England,…in that order. She insists on staying at Wildwood. I doubt she'll ever return to Chicago. In fact, she's told me so in no uncertain terms. Sadly, but justifiably, I informed her that I'd only be able to return to the East Coast once every six months. To my dismay that seemed acceptable to her. So…I guess that's the way it'll have to be. I must remain in Chicago, but Margaret prefers to stay in West Roxbury. Regardless of everything I've done to avoid this situation, I always had a feeling it would happen someday.

"Every time she brings up the subject of my retiring there, I remember the conversation she had with her mother around the time of our marriage. I overheard Margaret's mother trying to dissuade her from marrying me. At the time, Madam Henderson thought I was being a selfish fool set on a questionable venture so far away from home. Margaret was confident I'd succeed and that she'd adjust to her new surroundings. She said she'd be happy as long as we were together. Margaret tried to convince herself that this was a true reflection of her feelings. I'm sure she desperately wanted a marriage founded on a stable relationship. Nevertheless, as far as I'm concerned Margaret had subconsciously elevated deception to an art form. She wasn't being honest with herself *or* me! I refuse to speculate about the reasons behind her pretext.

"Maybe, I expected too much from her, but I can't convince myself of that. I've done everything in my power to appease her. I've always felt that because I was her husband and the wage earner in the family her duty was to remain by my side. She doesn't mention it anymore, yet several times in the past she insinuated that if I truly loved her and the children, I would sell my business here and retire in West Roxbury. I've become quite weary of the constant nagging and bickering. I flatly refuse to discuss it any further. As a result of having to commute back and forth from Chicago to the East Coast, the frequencies of my visits are now reduced to twice a year."

"Sounds to me like you've locked horns. You're both too stubborn to give in to one another," Uranus said, descending from the carriage. "I hope you'll eventually resolve this stalemate. Give her my best regards and tell her I miss our little chats."

"I will," I replied, leaving the carriage and following him into Kingsley's.

"Oh, yes, before I forget,…you can put your mind at ease," he said, opening the door for me. "I'll be more than happy to oversee the distillery in your absence. I've been much too worried about the opera house lately. Before I become too weighed down by doubt and apprehension, I need to focus on something else for a while."

We were seated by the headwaiter at our usual table by an opened window.

✳   ✳   ✳   ✳

Mid-June, 1864

"Josiah, do you know where Uranus has been lately?" I asked, bumping into him in the hallway that led to the distillery. "It's been awhile since I dined with him at Kingsley's and he hasn't been around here either. I hope all's going well with him and the opera house. Has he spoken to you about that?"

"Why, yes. As a matter of fact, he has," Josiah said, taking a swallow after biting into a breakfast muffin. We continued to converse as we walked together toward the distillery. "A few weeks ago, Uranus asked me to help him with a list of projected costs and what he determined were subtle increases in overall expenses. He wanted some idea of what the final tally might be. Uranus was ecstatically optimistic one minute and inconsolably morose the next. His self-confidence was lost and found from one moment to the next. I'm sorry to say he was noticeably dejected when we finished analyzing the data. Despite the fact that he's a man of substantial means, it was obvious he would require a great deal more money than he has to complete his undertaking. He's going from one financial institution to the next hoping to get additional funds. Samuel offered to come forward with most of the shortfall, but at a very high rate of interest. Because of the war the banks are barely staying solvent. It was impossible to loan him money at reasonable rates."

"Dammit! I had a feeling this would happen! I warned him about that last year, shortly after the exterior walls were erected," I said, pounding my fist on a wooden keg. "I wish he'd spoken to *me* about this. Most likely he's too proud to admit that he was wrong. Uranus was convinced he'd have sufficient capital to finish that opera house of his. The banks guaranteed him a set amount for his mortgage; however,...he'd have to find his own capital beyond that advance."

"Well,...he might have," Josiah replied. "But his need to provide the finest amenities money can buy for the opera house has done him in. Uranus decided to add the art gallery as well as several studios with lavish lounges for the ladies and gentlemen, and also luxurious dressing rooms for the performers. In addition to that, he's also contracted for several other excessive facilities that have never before been incorporated into a building of its size."

"Yes, he's mentioned that in case of fire, he intended to have an extensive water sprinkling system installed," I said, exiting the distillery to return to my office with Josiah still at my side. "Uranus hasn't even *tried* to be prudent. He has no use for the mediocre. He has a tendency to squander his resources with his extravagant concepts. I suppose he expects to recoup his investment many times over. Maybe,...he's right. Even so, I wouldn't be able to sleep nights if I were in his shoes. I'll try to find him and recommend that he be more realistic. I hope he'll be at Kingsley's this evening. If he agrees to be more frugal, I may also provide him with some additional backing."

"That's very generous of you, Albert, considering your earlier recommendation that he limit his expenditures," Josiah said as we parted. "I'll catch up with you later." He stopped short, turned and added, "Oh, by the way,...I'd almost forgotten to bring it up. There's someone who's been asking about you. I've been meaning to tell you about that. When you have more time, perhaps. You've got enough on your mind right now."

"Josiah, I always have time to converse with you no matter the subject. We don't have to discuss business all the time. Come back here and have a seat," I said, beckoning him back and pulling up a chair for him to sit down. "Stay a minute and tell me about this person. You've piqued my curiosity."

"My son, Theodore, is planning to marry a lovely, young woman named Molly Scranton. She arrived in Chicago from Goshen, Indiana to work as a journalist for the *Tribune*. Theodore also works for the *Tribune* as a reporter. When I told her I had a partnership in the Albert Crosby & Company, she said she remembered a kind gentleman by that name. He had befriended her when she was abandoned alongside a river, fifteen years ago. This Mister Crosby and a friend had taken her under their wing and tried to find her guardians who had become casualties of a devastating tornado. They found her a new home with a family by the name of Scranton. The Scrantons had also lost a young daughter to the twister. These people took her in and adopted her as their own. Not only is she personable, but also a highly educated young lady with impeccable manners and speech."

"Oh, Josiah,…that must be Molly Duncan!" I exclaimed, stunned by this uncanny coincidence. "I can't believe that it's actually, Molly. I'd almost forgotten her name until you brought it up. Of course…I remember her. I often thought about that little girl and wondered how she was doing. I assumed I'd never see her again. How splendid! I can't wait to see her. I only wish David was here so we could all be together again. I haven't thought about him for a long time. It saddens me to remember all the adventures I shared with that dear friend. I hope our paths will cross again someday. So tell me, Josiah, when will the wedding take place?" I asked. "I'd like to be invited. Please tell, Theodore, to visit me with Molly, whenever it's convenient."

"Yes, I will," Josiah replied. "You can be assured that you and Margaret will be invited to attend their wedding. It'll take place in September."

"Well, I don't know about Margaret, but I know I'll be there," I said, a bit distressed about what I was about to say. "I doubt Margaret will ever return to Chicago, Josiah. She's content to stay in New England and no amount of coaxing will ever get her to come back here. Despite the fact that I do get lonesome for my family at times, I feel fulfilled by my work. Although Cape Cod has a special place in my heart, Chicago's become my home. I intend to remain where I feel comfortable…in a place that fits my lifestyle."

"See you in the morning, Albert," said Josiah, getting up from his chair and preparing to leave. "It's getting late. Ruth will have supper waiting for me. Please take care of yourself and try not to stay here too late. You need your rest. You've been putting in some long hours lately."

"Yes, I know. And no,…I won't be here much longer, Josiah. I intend to leave right now." I replied, following behind him and reaching for my hat and coat "I must try to contact Uranus at Kingsley's. Have a good evening, Josiah!"

*   *   *   *

Early - November, 1864

I had a delightful time at Theodore and Molly's wedding, in spite of attending it alone. Theodore had taken her to the wholesale shop a few weeks before the ceremony. Molly was everything Josiah said she was—the epitome of genteel womanhood. We became reacquainted and chatted about David and his probable whereabouts. Molly said she hoped she would also get to see him again. Molly also mentioned that she always felt indebted to us and still treasured the doll as a memento of a new beginning and a better life for her.

There was a knock on the door of my home. The maid opened it and returned to the parlor to announce, "Mastah Crosbay, a Mastah Orayness Crosbay's heah ta say yah, Sah. Shah'l I shaw heem in, Sah?"

"Yes, please do, Annie," I said, putting down the evening newspaper and rising to meet Uranus at the doorway of the parlor. Annie curtsied and left the room. She was a genial Negro who had traveled north, just before the war, from the Deep South via the Underground Railroad to Chicago. Annie was a rather heavy-set woman who spoke in a muffled, southern drawl that I found difficult to understand.

"Well, Uranus,…this is an unexpected pleasure. Do come in and make yourself comfortable. How about a little rum?" I asked. Before he could answer, I had already poured the liquor out of the decanter into two shot glasses and handed him one. Though he was fastidiously neat and impeccably dressed, his skin was ashen and dark circles conspicuously rimmed the puffy area under his bloodshot, lackluster eyes. He was a physical and mental wreck.

"Yes, thank you, Albert. My jagged nerves need a boost right now! Needless to say, I'm rather upset and embarrassed about my financial crisis. It's a pressing situation that *must* be resolved," he said, seating himself opposite me on the settee, his eyes downcast as he fiddled with his glass. "Albert, I've come to you as a last resort. At the moment, I find myself in a serious predicament. I'm going to need another $200,000 to complete the opera house. The bank won't give me another cent. I've exhausted every other source of funding. Please see me through this, Albert. I can't allow construction to cease at this point, not when it's so close to completion. I realize that this crisis is solely my fault. I have only myself to blame because of my extravagant tastes and lofty goals. I've refused to allow people, whom I consider boorish, to impose financial limitations on me…those with closed minds that lack vision and imagination. I took their advice as an insult.

"I haven't wanted to approach you about this shortfall because you've warned me in the past about being too free with my resources," he continued. "I truly believed that every item I approved for the opera house was necessary to uphold the superior standards I'd set for it. You know me, Albert, I can't settle for less than the very best. Mind you, once the expected receipts from the sell-out crowds start to fill our coffers, you'll be the first to be reimbursed,…plus interest. Can I count on you to see me through this emergency?"

"You idiot, Uranus! I rather suspected you were in serious financial trouble. You can't say I didn't warn you! Why were you so oblivious to all those escalating costs?" I asked, rising from my chair and walking over to the fireplace. "Despite your extravagances and your "laissez-faire" attitude toward the expenses, I'm definitely in favor of your undertaking." I stood with my back to him while I added another log to the fire. "Chicago needs that opera house to transform it from an uncivilized cowtown to one worthy of envy and esteem,…especially from those condescending eastern cities. It serves no good purpose to terminate the project at this stage. For that reason, and *only* for that reason,…I'll loan you what you need to complete the project. Be at the wholesale shop around one tomorrow and I'll have the money ready for you. Are you sure that'll be enough?"

"Yes Albert, $200,000 should be more than enough. I've allowed for a bit more than I'll actually need in case of some unforeseen costs. I'll return whatever's left over," he replied, reaching for his coat. He put it on and I walked him to the door. "I can't thank you enough, Albert. You'll never know how much this means to me. I'm so thankful you came to my rescue. I've been so worried about this that I haven't had a good night's sleep in weeks. I'll be there tomorrow promptly at one."

"Your not getting off the hook that easily, Uranus," I said with a grin as we descended the front steps toward his waiting carriage. "Although I made it quite clear that I couldn't possibly return to Wildwood at this time of year, Margaret insists that I return for the sake of the children. She begged me to come back to what she calls "home" and spend the holidays with my family. I've told her that Wildwood is *not* my home! My home is the manor right here on Chicago Avenue. Nevertheless, I've decided to accommodate her. I'll be leaving for West Roxbury in a few weeks. I need you to be in charge while I'm away. I know I can depend on you if need be. That means you'll have to be at the distillery everyday to oversee the company business and make yourself available in case of any unexpected problems. I expect you to telegraph me several times a week with a complete, up-to-date production report. I don't think that's too much to ask considering I've just saved your hide with my bighearted contribution toward your treasured trophy."

"I'll be more than happy to accommodate you, Albert. It's the least I can do to show my appreciation," Uranus said, turning to face me as he stopped in front of the carriage door. "How long do you expect to be away?"

"I really don't know. It might be for a few months," I replied, standing there in my shirtsleeves, shivering from a cold blast of wind and placing my arms around my body to warm myself. "I trust you to take over for me, Uranus. Josiah's familiar enough with the operation to be of invaluable assistance. Before my departure,…I'll run through everything you need to know." Uranus ascended his small caleche and took the reins. "See you tomorrow!" I shouted, standing on the front steps and watching as his horse took off at full trot. The carriage sped along the roadway in the shadow of the street lanterns until it swiftly became obscured and vanished into the inky darkness of night.

▼

"Josiah, I'll need an update of our inventory," I said decisively after walking into his office and standing before his desk. "Now that the war's over, I've decided to convert the plant back to producing beer, wine and alcohol. However, I wish to supply these products at an affordable cost to the general public. It's an opportune time to satisfy the consumer demand for inexpensive liquors and medium-priced wines. It'll be a major undertaking, but I'm sure we can accomplish the renovations without much delay...I've given this transition much thought while on my journey back here."

"I'll be right on it, Albert," Josiah replied enthusiastically while gathering a set of inventory logs. "I'll have a complete list of our stock for you by tomorrow morning. It shouldn't be too difficult to reassemble the machinery that we've used before. It's been carefully stored in the rear of the warehouse. The impact of the transition should be minimal. You know,...Albert, I anticipated your desire to do this when the time was right. Oh, how delightful it'll be to inhale that fragrant aroma of hops and fermented grapes again.

"By the way," he went on, "I expect to be a grandfather before the year's end. Molly and Ted are expecting their first child in October."

"Well, congratulations, Josiah!" I exclaimed, tapping him on the shoulder and shaking his hand.

I had just returned from West Roxbury a few days before. Uranus had sent me a telegraph stating that the opera house was completed and ready for its opening. It was crucial that I come back promptly. He was no longer able to supervise the distillery because of this commitment. Actually, I was delighted to be summoned.

In fact, I expected to be recalled long before this and was preparing to conjure up an excuse to return when his message arrived.

After getting out of bed in the morning, I needed to be motivated and know that my day would be filled with decision-making, meaningful tasks and challenging goals. It was crucial that at the end of the day—though mentally and physically exhausted—I could enjoy a well-deserved sense of pride and accomplishment. My stay in West Roxbury was wearisome—one day being more or less similar to the previous one. With each passing day I was becoming more lethargic and bored. How I yearned to feel useful and productive again. Of course Margaret was distressed by this news, but halfheartedly accepted the fact that it was necessary for me to return to Chicago and tend to my urgent business affairs.

I arrived to find that while Uranus had done his best to keep the factory operating efficiently, many of the secondary tasks were left wanting. Josiah had been completely overwhelmed by an overabundance of work—tending to personnel, filling orders and warehousing supplies. I realized that my presence here was mandatory and long overdue. I was quite content to immerse myself in the long-neglected paperwork.

✳   ✳   ✳   ✳

Mid -April, 1865

A vibrant spring sun, whose warm rays beamed earthward through a cloudless sky, kept its annual promise to awakened the flora from a long winter's sleep and prod them to bud and flower.

"What a glorious day! It awakens my heart as well. April is so beguiling and such a free spirit!" I thought as I approached the distillery that morning. I had wearied of the long winters that overflowed into mid-spring. April's warm sun made me feel like it was in the middle of May, but her chill wind sometimes reminded me of being in the middle of March. The nesting birds chirped and filled the air with their songs—adding another dimension to the sense of rebirth and renewal that surrounded me. With the arrival of spring my thoughts turned to the mill site and the herring run. "The alewives will soon begin their yearly ritual of swimming upstream from the ocean to spawn in the Mill Pond. If I close my eyes I can visualize the rushing water cascading over the stone ladders and the water wheel, the welcoming daffodils and the hauntingly beautiful song of the peepers."

"The timetable for the construction of the opera house has been realized. It'll be ready for its grand opening night performance featuring the famous opera singer, Tetrazzini, on the 17th as we planned," Uranus said excitedly, greeting me at the door. "The final details are now in progress and should be completed today. I'll be leaving in a few hours to check on some last-minute particulars. Do you wish to come along, Albert?" he asked.

"I'm sorry, Uranus. I must decline. I can't spare the time today,…possibly tomorrow. A large shipment of supplies will be arriving soon, and I must find a space large enough to store it on the premises. This needs my immediate and undivided attention," I replied, rushing by him toward my office. After overhearing my conversation with Uranus, Josiah made it a point to join us. He also expressed his concern about finding the necessary space for the new consignment. Josiah concurred that it should be done without delay. When it was obvious that I wouldn't be joining him, Uranus left and returned to his carriage.

"Josiah, please bring the inventory logs to my office," I requested. "I must calculate the amount of "on-site" stock needed here. We'll store the remainder in the warehouse."

"Yes, sir! I'm almost finished updating them. I'll return the books to your desk shortly," he replied, heading up the hallway toward his office.

"Thank you, Josiah. That freight should be arriving from the East Coast in a few hours!" I called out, entering my office and closing the door behind me.

The day progressed quite well. My preliminary estimates of the brewery's immediate needs were accurate. The excess was carted away and stored for future use. I cleared my desk and left for home.

The next morning while I dressed, I heard some loud shouting from outside my bedroom window. Curious, I raised the pane to find out what all the ruckus was about.

"Extra! Extra! Special Edition! Read all about it! President Lincoln's been shot! President Abraham Lincoln…assassinated!" The newsboy was yelling at the top of his lungs. "Oh, no, that's impossible! Oh, what dreadful news!" I thought, dashing out my front entrance and straight for the street below to collect my daily *Tribune*. The large bold print of the headlines confirmed my worst fear. I couldn't believe my eyes as I quickly scanned each printed line describing Lincoln's imminent demise. President Lincoln had been assassinated while attending a performance the previous evening at the Ford Theater in Washington, DC. John Wilkes Booth, the suspected killer, was a Virginian from a prominent theater family. His brother was the famed actor Edwin Booth. "What was the reasoning behind this dastardly deed? How will the country cope with the untimely loss of this great man?" My mind raced with distressing thoughts and countless questions. I returned to my sitting room and avidly read each shocking paragraph with utter dismay. As I made arrangements to leave for the day, I rolled up my newspaper, tucked it under my arm and was about to step into my waiting carriage when I unexpectedly heard someone shouting behind me.

"Wait! Wait, Albert!" I turned around to find Uranus running toward me. "Have you heard the news about the President?" he asked breathlessly.

"Of course I have." I said impatiently, agitated and annoyed by his question. I opened the newspaper and practically shoved the headlines in his face. When I realized how rude I had been, I apologized. "I'm sorry, Uranus, please forgive me," I went on. "I didn't mean to do that. It's just that I'm so upset over this reprehensible deed that I inexcusably lashed out at you. You just happened to be the butt of my anger. No offense."

"Apology accepted. If you think you're distraught, how do you think I feel?" he asked despondently. "The grand opening will have to be delayed for several weeks. The funeral train is scheduled to travel from Washington to Springfield. It'll be a slow, melancholy trip from the East Coast to the Midwest. Everything will have to be on hold until after his burial. Why did this have to happen now?" he whined. "I know it's selfish of me to think in those terms, but I've invested three years of my life and all my assets in this endeavor. To have this calamity take place at such an inopportune time is ruinous for me."

"Yes,…you're right. I hadn't thought about that," I replied, troubled by his words. "I was solely focused on the tremendous loss suffered by our now unified country. Actually, the impact on *your* future never occurred to me. I hope you'll survive this setback, regardless of the fact that you must set a later opening date," I said, trying to sound optimistic about the future. "Through hell or high water, Uranus, the Tetrazinni performance will still take place!"

The itinerary of Lincoln's Funeral train was posted in advance of its arrival through Chicago. Because of the utmost respect I had for this man, I planned to be at the train station as it journeyed to Springfield. The crowds gathered quietly and spoke in hushed tones as the somber funeral train, which was draped in black, rolled slowly over the tracks toward them. Except for the echoing click-clack sound of the steel wheels against the metal tracks—there was a reverent silence. It was a fitting and respectful tribute that honored a humble, honest man whom historians would ultimately label the "Great Emancipator." The locomotive bearing its illustrious cargo never halted as it progressed slowly through each station toward the Capitol in Springfield. Long after it disappeared over the horizon, the gathering of people of all ages, genders and races impervious to the weather, stood under large umbrellas wailing and weeping. After weaving through the crowd, I eventually found my way back to the distillery.

A slate sky and a raw mist added to the abysmal gloom of the day. I figured a good, strong cup of coffee would warm and lift me from the doldrums. I walked over to the wood stove and began to pour the coffee in my favorite mug.

"Albert, you're back! I must say you're a glutton for punishment." Uranus teased, smiling and also reaching for the pot to fill his cup. "Were you able to get a glimpse of the train? Was the long wait worthwhile?" he asked. "I decided that I wasn't about to get trampled on by that mob. I can't imagine standing in that chill, dank weather just to view a passing train. Oh, well, Albert,…I guess you and I weren't cut from the same cloth," he added, slapping me on the shoulder.

"No, Uranus,…we weren't! We're very different!" I replied defensively still distressed over the President's death, slamming my cup down on my desk and almost spilling it. "You have no sense of patriotism…You give allegiance to no one but yourself. You're so self-centered, Uranus. I must say it's disgusting! Your apathy truly frustrates me at times! Just getting a glimpse of the train was important to me. I felt I needed to be there…Can't you appreciate that?" I asked. "I became acquainted with Mister Lincoln when I was a member of the Zouaves. He made quite an impression on me at that time. It was an unforgettable experience. His legacy of freedom for all…will live on forever. You should realize, my dear cousin, that I'm not an insensitive clod like you."

"Oh, I'm so sorry! I didn't realize how much this icon of liberty meant to you, Albert. I didn't know him as well as you. I only met him that one time when he debated Senator Douglas. I wasn't aware of your fondness for the President and his ideals," he said, apologizing in a half-hearted, facetious manner. "I didn't mean to upset you. Believe me, I won't ever mention it again."

"Fine! I'll see you at Kingsley's this evening. Are you still planning to visit the opera house afterwards?" I asked, escorting him down the hallway to the front entrance.

"Yes…I expect to be there for just a short while. I need to insure the security of the opera house and the gallery until the date of the postponed Grand Opening," he replied, beckoning his carriage to advance to where we were standing. "Everything's in place for the opening one week from today."

"I'll accompany you there if you don't mind," I said, standing on the curb next to his coach. "Now that the opera house is completed, I'd like to get an overall view of it before the crowds cram the lobby and the aisles."

"I'd like that!" Uranus shouted back, waving farewell from his carriage. "See you later!"

That evening we entered the opera house from the side entrance. Our voices resonated throughout the massive auditorium as we approached the mezzanine and the lavishly decorated proscenium boxes.

"Even though I had to postpone the opening of the opera house, I intend to open the art gallery on the 20th," Uranus announced, leading the way to the comfortable plush sofas angled to face the stage. I watched as workmen removed the outdated billboards that advertised the opening night performance of the renowned opera singer, Tetrazzini.

"I don't see a problem with that," I said, bending over the brass rail to gaze at the expanse of row after row of gilded French provincial seats cushioned in blue velvet. The parquet floor of the auditorium was tilted so that every member of the audience had a clear view of the stage. "In light of the chilling events of this past week the art gallery might be a pleasant diversion for a grieving public. The paintings suspended on the walls of the gallery should help change their mindset and lift them from their melancholy into a more optimistic frame of mind. The art works will promote the marvels of life, such as man's ability to reproduce on canvas the majestic splendor of the world around them. I'm sure the diversity and inspirational talent of the artists will awe the gallery patrons. Also, your clientele should be totally captivated by the elegance of their surroundings. You know what, Uranus,…that's a *good* thing! Will you need help preparing for the opening of the gallery?" I asked, looking up at the ornately carved ceiling and the colossal crystal chandeliers hovering over the mezzanine. These embellishments far exceeded my expectations. "No thank you, Albert," he replied, standing and making his way to the rear of the balcony. "I've already hired a staff, several security guards and guides. I'm sure that'll suffice. As I've mentioned before several paintings are on loan from galleries all over the world. They'll be behind roped-off areas and will be well guarded. It'll be an exceptional assortment of art works,…a collection of paintings worthy of prominent display and admiration."

"I'll be there to give you a hand just in case. As you already know by now, I'm also culturally deprived and a bit curious about the world of fine arts," I said. "I hope to learn why art is so intriguing to people like you, Uranus. An introduction into this area of expertise could prove quite enlightening and also enriching for me. Who knows, I might find it as fascinating and rewarding as you do."

Little did I know it would be an unprecedented, life-changing experience for me. It began on that first day of the opening as I walked along the marble floors of the grandiose art gallery. It was an encounter that resulted in a life-long hobby. I stared with rapt curiosity at the painstaking work and extraordinary beauty of each original painting. I stood before the canvases that celebrated a diversity of styles and tried to delve into the mind of each artist. I was thoroughly captivated by every nuance and stroke of the brush. It was a scintillating experience—an exhilarating mental challenge I had never anticipated or encountered before. Uranus had developed an appreciation for the arts as a young man. I was never fortunate enough to have been introduced or exposed to such inspired talent. The wonder of it seemed almost miraculous to me.

My passion and exuberance for collecting unique and renowned original paintings became an obsession. One work, which I found to be particularly mesmerizing, became one of my most prized possessions. This valued collectable and heirloom eventually graced the blue velvet paneled walls of the opera house. It was Bierstadt's *Looking Down Yosemite Valley, California.*

"This has been a very costly delay for me," Uranus confided soberly, shaking his head in despair while we rode in his carriage on the way back to his hotel. "It's quite serious, Albert…My finances are swiftly dwindling away. I was planning on the proceeds from the first performance to free me from debt. The builders are pressing for payment of their final invoices. I'm also behind by several mortgage payments to the bank. Because this unexpected calamity forced the postponement of my scheduled event, everyone's been more than patient; however,…I'm afraid that'll soon wane."

"You needn't worry," I said assuredly. "Having to delay the opening performance until next week shouldn't be *too* financially painful for you. I'm sure you'll soon recoup your losses. The debut has been well advertised and should be a rousing success. Just promise your creditors that you'll settle with them the next day. That should keep them at bay for a while."

"Thank you, Albert," he replied as we neared his new carriage, which was a four-wheeled buggy with a body of rattan side-panels and a collapsible top. "I feel better already. I won't worry! Somehow you always seem to point out the positive aspects of an impossible situation. You invariably have an answer to every conceivable problem right at your fingertips. I wish I had your confidence and optimistic outlook."

"Uranus, whatever happened to that ebullient young man who had such vision? Have you lost that Crosby passion and initiative?" I asked, bewildered and shaking my head. Without waiting for his answer, I continued my lecture, determined to give him an uplifting talk. "Despite the circumstances,…I never doubted for a moment that you wouldn't persist. I'm a bit dismayed to find you in such a condition. There are usually pitfalls with any endeavor, regardless of well-executed plans. The future's *always* uncertain, Uranus. It seems that sometimes life hits us hard, knocks us flat, and then leaves us wondering…why? These are the times that call for strength, sacrifice and courage; it's when we need to pull ourselves up by the bootstraps and keep going. I've always tried to press on despite the odds. You give up much too easily, Uranus! Like the herring in the run, life's an uphill struggle,…a lesson in fortitude. I suggest you try to emulate the alewives if you wish to succeed! You must learn to adapt and roll with the punches…be strong-willed and decisive. Remember persistence pays!" I reiterated, tipping my hat in a farewell gesture as he left with his rattan buggy. "Here I am," I thought while returning home to the empty manor on Chicago Avenue, "giving Uranus advice about adjusting to the negative and troublesome aspects of life when I can't even make a positive decision about my own marriage."

The April 28th opening night concert was an unequivocal triumph. Everything progressed as planned. With each passing minute, Uranus and I were more at ease. The solo performance of the acclaimed soprano, Tetrazzini, thrilled the overflow crowd that stood to applaud for a lengthy period. This resulted in many curtain calls. The newspapers gave this virtuoso's superb voice a glowing review and marveled at the acoustics of the opulent opera palace where it was performed. "Tetrazinni Concert Starts Cultural Renaissance," they reported. The columnists applauded everyone responsible for bringing such an enriching event to Chicago. The once churlish city had now been introduced to a superior and sophisticated level of entertainment. Everyone agreed that the Chicago Opera house was indeed the finest theater in the country. We were off to an auspicious start. I was ecstatic. Uranus's opera house was a resounding success.

*   *   *   *

Mid-August, 1866

"Albert, I'm so delighted that you've returned to Chicago. You don't know how much I've needed you here, especially now," said Uranus, reaching out to help me with my luggage as I descended the train steps in shirtsleeves—my jacket folded over my arm. "Why did you decide to come back before September?" he asked as we left the railroad station. "I need to tell you about everything that's been happening back here," he went on without waiting for my reply and placing my valise on the rack over the carriage. "Believe me, Albert,…it's *not* good news."

"Oh, Uranus, it's a long story," I replied, pushing and squeezing my large carpetbag alongside the valise. A merciless searing sun beat down on us and the heat undulated in visible waves on the road ahead. I could feel the perspiration running down my back and soaking my silk shirt. "I'll let you know why I've returned in such a hurry…after I find out why you're so distraught."

He looked overwhelmed by responsibility and worry. "Well,…to begin with, he said hesitantly, "The machinery in the distillery is beginning to need attention. It must be replaced. It broke down several times while you were away. As a result, the workmen are becoming quite disgruntled. Also, the liquor and wine sales have been lagging. And aside from all that, I've only been able to schedule three performances at the opera house this summer…That's financially ruinous for me.

"Anyhow, my biggest problem right now is the pollution of the Chicago River. The distilleries that abut the river are being accused of dumping their wastes into it and an uncompromising committee is bringing them to task," he went on. "They've purposefully singled out Albert Crosby & Company. Our plant has been roundly denounced as a prime example of the irresponsible disposal of chemicals and filth. They say we're the worst offenders. The notoriety is downright embarrassing to say the least! I believe I wrote you about that last month. You suggested that I assemble a network of pipelines that would carry our discharge into the grasslands that border the factory. This was done as you directed. In spite of this,…now that summer's at its peak, the people who live in that vicinity claim the odor and pestilence is spreading disease. The noxious smell is carried into their homes by the wind and the effluence breeds flies that are tormenting them to death. Their assertion that we're poisoning the very air they breathe will have to be dealt with immediately. Their ire increases with each passing day. We must act quickly to appease them. There's a council meeting next week. We'll be required to give an exact account on how we plan to correct this situation. Thank God you're here to face them! Your financial backing and pledges of support have assured you of many influential political friends in Chicago. It's time you approached them with a workable solution or ask them to look the other way."

"Don't worry, Uranus. Relax! Calm down…I'll take care of that," I replied. "The equipment will be repaired or replaced. While I can ill afford to do so right now, I'll placate the laborers with a small increase in pay. A large ad in the newspapers announcing sale prices for the liquor and wines should increase our receipts. The problem with the opera house will have to wait. The effluent can be taken care of expeditiously. We'll place drainpipes several feet below ground. All that refuse will drain into a massive underground receptacle that I'll have excavated. A cast iron lid placed on the container should do the trick. The odor will be trapped there. When that fills up, we'll just dig another one, so on and so on.

Will that ease your mind, Uranus? Does that answer your questions concerning this problem?"

"Yes, Albert. I should've known you'd think of something to appease the masses," he said with a nervous laugh. "Now tell me,…how is it that you've returned to Chicago on such short notice?"

"If you must know, when I arrived at Wildwood last month I was greeted by a surly and distant wife," I said, staring out from the open barouche and not really paying much attention to the view as we rode by. "I received a cool reception and was completely ignored by Margaret and the children. They made me feel as though I was invisible. Everyone went about his or her affairs as if I wasn't even there! When I finally insisted on knowing what was wrong, Margaret repeated a nauseating rumor that originated from her gossipy friends. The devious report came from some anonymous, self-righteous people in Chicago. They claimed that I had entertained some female guests in my proscenium box and that I had subsequently had a liaison with these women. I tried to explain that yes,…I did invite some young ladies to join me; however, it was merely a business arrange-ment,…only a cordial attempt to please the agents who were in town accompa-nied by their female clients. I also told her that because most of these women spoke a foreign language, I was unable to converse with them. Their publicity agents acted as interpreters. Margaret, already convinced of my infidelity, rushed to judgment and refused to listen to my explanation. So help me, Uranus, she aggressively accused me of all sorts of debauchery and infidelity. She lashed out at me with such disrespect,…it made my flesh crawl. I told her that she was woe-fully misinformed and I vehemently disputed the rumors. Sadly, my denials were ignored. During my long absences, I've never been unfaithful to Margaret, yet she adamantly refused to believe or trust me. She wouldn't even give me the ben-efit-of-the-doubt.

"After such a long journey, it made for a very unpleasant reception indeed. Margaret's obstinacy and temper tantrums are beginning to exasperate me, Ura-nus. Communication between us has been reduced to ridiculous accusations of deception and betrayal. Every time I return to Wildwood, I feel more and more estranged. This time she moved all my belongings to a guest room. I was no longer permitted to share the same bedroom! I'm tired of her insensitivity, Ura-nus! Her negativity and nagging are beginning to distance me from her and the children.

"The last straw was her manipulative and thoughtless audacity to book passage for a six-month grand tour of Europe for us both. It was an attempt on her part to dispel the notion that our marriage was in jeopardy. I was so incensed by her condemnation and her brazen effort to extract me from what she considered the moral cesspool of Chicago that I abruptly declared my intention to leave immediately. I also resolved to resume my life in the manner…I desire. Nevertheless, a few days later I relented and gave her the option to return with me. I tried to influence her decision by dressing in my best suit and looking as debonair as possible. My efforts were in vain, Uranus…She'll never return to Chicago! I doubt that will ever happen. Margaret considers my lifestyle offensive and degrading to her eastern ethics. She accused me of overstepping socially acceptable boundaries. Margaret despises my friends. She considers them coarse and unsophisticated,…Bohemian, oddball types with nasty moral values. I won't be treated that way, Uranus! It's a deadlock situation. I've come to realize that she married me with the idea she'd eventually change my mind about living here in Chicago.

"Unless there's a serious emergency, I don't *ever* intend to return to West Roxbury! Even though it was an inconvenience, I often endured that long journey simply to oblige her and visit my children. If I should return to the East Coast,…it'll only be to visit my parents. I should have decided to do this long ago! Margaret's incessant demand that I leave Chicago and remain at Wildwood with her and the children is now definitely out of the question. I've made a decision to stay here for the time being." The driver of the barouche led the horses to the curb. We descended the carriage after it came to a stop and entered the distillery where Josiah, the workers and staff, warmly greeted us.

*   *   *   *

Late-September, 1866

The opera house had been opened for more than a year now. Uranus was still wrapped up in his theories and clouded perceptions, yet he remained optimistic. In spite of this, our expectations for continued capacity crowds and unprecedented prosperity were not realized. Due to resisting southern factions, there was much tumult in the Grant administration and his Reconstruction efforts. The clouds of distress, dread, doubt and a disquieting future was shared by the populace of every northern state and permeated these difficult times. It proved to be disastrous for the Chicago Opera House. We had repeated problems in attracting ample audiences for our four-week grand opera seasons. Also—the quality of theater performances had substantially disintegrated in these post-war years. The spectators were often subjected to substandard entertainment. Many talented male performers—brave and dedicated military men on either side of the conflict became casualties of both the grief and glory of the Civil War. It was a revolutionary event that resulted in unprecedented death and destruction. The hard-won peace was purchased at the cost of tens of thousands of outstanding young American men. During the "War Between the States" death had become commonplace. It was similar to the cholera epidemic ten years before. In those days, the incessant hammering sound of the coffin-maker's metal mallets resonated throughout the city. Likewise, a flourishing trade resulting from the war casualties resulted in a boom in the casket industry that produced coffins that ranged from embossed, expensive rare woods for officers to natural pine-planked ones for the average footsoldier.

The price of freedom for the disenfranchised colored people went beyond symbolism. A lingering, dispirited outlook ravaged the economy of Chicago. As a result of this cataclysm the arts lost their popularity with the general public. We repeatedly endured the embarrassment of disheartening performances attended by dwindling audiences. Uranus faced bankruptcy. He was hopelessly unprepared to deal with the catastrophe that now confronted him. I felt responsible because I had unabashedly encouraged him to plunge wholeheartedly into his dream project. Somehow I had to help him out of the predicament he was in. As the manager of the opera house, I decided a meeting of minds was necessary. It was an opportunity to offer Uranus some advice.

"Uranus, meet me at Kinsley's. We need to discuss the future of the opera house," I said with a sense of urgency. "We're in serious danger of losing it. The way things are going right now,…that's almost a certainty."

It was already late in the evening. Nevertheless, it was imperative that we find a workable solution. The fate of the opera house was at stake. I had considered a few options that might help. Kinsley's Restaurant had relocated on the ground floor of the opera house along with the salesroom of the W.W. Kimball Piano Company. These businesses flanked the sides of the two-story arched entrance of the grand promenade that led to the auditorium. One was on the right, the other on the left.

"Would you like to see the wine list, sir?" asked the waiter, placing a set of menus before us.

"No, thank you," I replied. "Just a flask of beer for each of us, please.

"Uranus, I think we should ask Potter Palmer to take over the Opera House. He's in the process of re-developing downtown Chicago," I said after the waiter left the table. "He might be tempted to incorporate it into his plans if it was offered to him at a reasonable price. Then there's William Ogden. His bank could possibly take over the mortgage. I know the opera house is worth more than the mortgage balance, but then again…it's better than filing for bankruptcy. I can only advise you, Uranus,…it's entirely up to you. These are just a few alternatives…I've had in mind. You might want to take them under consideration."

The waiter returned with our flask of beer, placed two steins before us on the table, and then turned to me and asked, "Will you be ordering, sir? The kitchen will be closing soon. I'll be more than happy to take your order now, sir,…if you wish."

"Are you hungry, Uranus? The beer will suffice for me. How about you?" I asked.

"It'll do for me, also," he replied while bringing the mug up to his mouth. "I'm really not in the mood to eat anything right now. In fact, I don't even know if I can finish this stein. Anyway, thank you for asking."

"We don't plan to be here for very long," I said, looking up at the waiter. "The beer will be enough for now. Thank you." The waiter nodded and left.

"Albert,…I've already approached Potter Palmer," Uranus said, dejectedly shaking and lowering his head as he toyed with the handle of his mug. "He's a shrewd investment broker. Although he admits the opera house is the grandest and most elegant edifice he's ever seen, he claimed it would only serve as an albatross around his neck. Palmer said that even if it were given to him as a gift, he'd refuse to take on that debt-ridden money pit!…As for William Ogden, he said that the opera house would most likely have to be sold for far less than the remaining mortgage. Ogden wasn't about to take on a financial burden of that magnitude. So,…so much for your suggestions," he added with a downhearted expression and heaving a deep sigh.

"What are you going to do?" I asked, disheartened by his answer. I began to despair as I considered the likelihood of Uranus' financial demise.

"Well,…there *is* another option," he replied rather offhandedly, looking up from his stein and facing me directly.

"And what is *that*?" I questioned, taken aback and somewhat wary of his answer.

"Albert,…you know as well as I that Chicagoans have always enjoyed playing the odds," he said, taking a sip of his beer.

"Oh, oh!…What's he up to this time?" I wondered. "He's such an opportunist!" I immediately recognized his approach because Uranus had used this equally convincing tone of voice and mannerism on me in the past.

"The sporting and business folk like to take chances on almost anything," Uranus went on to say. "I propose to offer them the chance of a lifetime. For an investment of a mere five dollars per ticket, they could possibly own a palatial opera house. In addition to the building itself, I would also raffle more than 300 additional prizes. The catalog will include many of the paintings adorning the walls of the gallery and opera house. I'll also include all the sculptures. I'm sure the proceeds would more than exceed the initial costs. I would still realize a sizable profit…even *after* you've been reimbursed along with all my other creditors. What's your opinion about offering the opera house as first prize in a lottery?" he asked. "Well, Albert,…what do you think about that?"…Do you think it's a good idea?"

"A lottery,…hum-m-m. I can see you've already given it much thought. It sounds as if you have this lottery scheme all figured out. Yes, you're right! Chicago *is* a gambling city," I replied candidly with several quick nods of my head. I sat back in my chair and folded my arms. I must say, that while I was a dubious about it at first, I began to consider it in a more favorable light after contemplating the absence of alternatives. "It could be the solution to our problem, but it sounds a bit devious to me," I added. "If I'm to be implicated in this so-called "lottery" it must have the blessings of the proper authorities and be legally executed. When are you planning on getting started?"

"I was hoping you'd see it my way, Albert. The tickets have already been drafted and ready to be printed. I'll see the printer in the morning and tell him to go ahead," he replied with a renewed sense of enthusiasm as he retrieved his napkin from his lap and placed it on the table. "The raffle tickets should be ready in a few days. I intend to issue a statement to the newspapers announcing this lottery as an once-in-a-lifetime opportunity and advertise the opera house as the first prize. I'll explain that the exorbitant cost of building the Chicago Opera House into one of the finest theaters in the world emptied my cash accounts and that this lottery will help return me to solvency. I think the community will accept that. After all, bear in mind, Albert,…I *am* telling the truth. Everything should be in place by weeks' end." With that, we rose and left the restaurant.

While writing about the "lottery" in my journal, I was still trying to sort out my misgivings regarding Uranus' seemingly ridiculous scheme. Somehow I was decidedly uncertain and questioned the ethics. "Does the end, justify the means?" I asked myself. "Well, why not give the betting public the opportunity to win the largest prize ever? Or will this lottery idea further exacerbate our difficulties?" Sensing a possible problem ahead, I decided I should give this questionable sweepstakes careful scrutiny before getting involved. Anxious thoughts filled my mind as I tossed and turned all night. I heard each hour and half-hour chime on the grandfather clock. After a futile attempt to fall asleep, I rose from my bed, lit a cigar, and then sat in my large easy chair. When a gentle breeze blew the curtains aside, I gazed out the opened window as the approaching sunrise engulfed the fading darkness. Regardless of trying to focus on other issues, I found myself lapsing into periods of intense apprehension and skepticism. Every time I thought about the lottery gambit,…I shivered and instinctively shook my head.

✳   ✳   ✳   ✳

Late-January, 1867

Tickets for what was now labeled a "National Lottery" sold as fast as they were printed. Saloon and restaurant owners controlled a vast amount of the tickets sold. They ordered them by the thousands, and then sold them to large organizations. These groups pooled their money to allow them a better chance at the top prize. Sporting and business syndicates under such names as Bohemian Club, Bottom Dollar and Dead Broke ordered tickets in lots of a thousand.

The *Tribune* reported that an estimated 200,000 tickets had been sold. This represented a windfall of more than a $1,000,000. While the public cheered, the newspapers questioned the sweeping scope of this corrupt gambling scheme. Strong vocal opposition against the proposal became the outcry of a moral minority—a group of righteous and elitist bullies. Uranus claimed the ownership of 25,000 unsold tickets. I never asked him how much profit he had amassed—he kept that a secret—even from me.

It was too cold for rain and yet too warm for snow. A sloppy, sloshing muck covered the ground. Despite the wet, slushy snowfall the opera house was filled to capacity with syndicate managers and individual ticket holders. A committee of businessmen, lawyers and constables supervised the proceedings. Although the crowd was fairly contained, it whistled and hollered impatiently while waiting for the lottery to begin. It was decided that the top prize would be drawn after all the art treasures had been raffled off. The heavy, blue velvet stage drapes were slowly parted then gracefully anchored by large tasseled cords on each side of the stage. All 305 works of art were prominently displayed to their best advantage. The first tickets pulled out would be for the famous bust of Lincoln by L.W. Volk, followed by several George Inness landscapes, and then paintings by Vedder and Chavannes, in that order. Also included were many minor masterpieces by several famous contemporary artists.

"Uranus,…so far the lottery seems to be going quite well," I said, standing backstage observing an audience expressing their delight with boisterous "oohs" and "aahs." Uranus smiled and concurred. A podium was erected for the hired auctioneer. He held a gavel that was used to signal the end of each awarded prize. All the winning tickets were returned to a large round barrel for the final drawing. It was progressing quite smoothly. My earlier fears that something might go wrong were unwarranted. I had absolutely nothing to fear.

"Albert, the drawing for first prize is next," Uranus said, nervously nudging me to get my attention.

"Yes, I hope the opera house will be won by someone we know," I replied, looking out into the standing-room-only crowd that overflowed into the aisles of the auditorium.

"And the winning ticket is number 58,600," the auctioneer called out. After a few minutes of silence while everyone checked their tickets, garbled mutterings began to resonate throughout the hall as the spectators stretched their necks to look around. Some remained seated while others stood to get a better glimpse of the winner. Unfortunately, no one came forward. The committee scanned the master list and advised the auctioneer that the winning number and grand prize belonged to a Colonel Abraham Hagerman Lee, of Prairie du Rocher, Illinois. The auctioneer shouted his name several times through the megaphone. I was secretly relieved. I heard reports that certain newsmen believed that no matter what number would be drawn—it would inevitably belong to Uranus Crosby. I dismissed that vicious rumor as sensationalism.

"I've never heard of Colonel Lee. Have you, Uranus?" I asked curiously.

He shook his head, and said, "No,…but I'll immediately send him a telegraph to notify him of his good fortune."

Reporters scattered in all directions to find the person who was conspicuously absent from the drawing and who had the winning ticket. Regardless of their persistence they failed to locate anyone who knew this gentleman. It was also discovered that the small village of Prairie du Rocher had no telegraph office and was 275 miles south of Chicago.

"I'll telegraph a lawyer friend of mine in St. Louis and instruct him to send a messenger there first thing in the morning," Uranus promised. We picked up our coats and hats from the front office and prepared to leave. "I expect he'll have to navigate around those torturous, snow covered country roads to find him," he said.

"That shouldn't take too long. I'm sure when they contact Colonel Lee, he'll be pleasantly surprised," I replied, elated for this gentleman as we exited the front entrance of the opera house.

Within a week, Uranus was informed that the winner would be arriving in Chicago under a cloak of anonymity. The whereabouts of the ticket holder would be kept secret until he eventually contacted Uranus.

Somehow several reporters pursuing notoriety for their papers attained this information and managed to catch up with Lee in a Chicago hotel. Their feature stories in the *Tribune* and other competitive journals described him as an earthy gentleman—a decorated war veteran and former riverboat captain. Colonel Lee disclosed a dramatic business deal that occupied the front-page headlines. He stated that because his wife was on her deathbed he had no use for the opera house. He sold it back to Uranus for a sum of $200,000. Uranus had netted a substantial profit. With a seemingly clear conscience and a straight face, he disavowed any knowledge of a scheme to defraud. Nonetheless, it was later revealed that Uranus had hired a calculating and deceitful Joshua Myler as his co-conspirator. For a considerable sum he posed as Colonel Lee and that all of Uranus' 25,000 tickets bore the number 58,600. Before the plot was exposed the remaining tickets were immediately tossed into a barrel and reduced to ashes. I was appalled—as were thousands of disgruntled ticket holders. The subsequent public disgrace and criticism swirling around Uranus and me was similar to drowning in the vortex of a putrefied whirlpool that sucked us into an abyss of perdition. I hoped it was just a bad dream, and that I would soon awake from this nightmarish event.

"How could I have been so naïve and so thoroughly deceived by Uranus?" I repeatedly asked myself. "I should have listened to my intuition. Somehow it just didn't seem right. How could I have sanctioned such a flagrant violation of my beliefs in honesty and fair play? When I conspired to become involved, was it the anxiety over losing the opera house or just bad judgment on my part?" I wondered. From the beginning, I trusted that Uranus was not motivated by greed. Now, to find out that he had concocted a pre-arranged and reprehensible scam behind my back was demoralizing. Although suspect by association, I was entirely innocent of any wrongdoing. My managerial duties consisted of merely overseeing the operation of the opera house, its employees and equipment. I was not concerned with the financial aspects of it. Even so, I was undoubtedly implicated as an accomplice in the plot to swindle the unsuspecting ticket holders. Believing I might be made a scapegoat, I feared for my life. I knew I would be publicly humiliated, ostracized or even banished. I am not without my faults, but I certainly would *never* have stooped to that level of deception. Doing something *that* dishonest never even crossed my mind. "Wait until I get my hands on that cousin of mine…I'll kill him!" I vowed, seething with rage that was becoming progressively more volatile by the minute. "I should have known he had a trick or two up that sleazy sleeve of his."

The ill-gotten gains realized by Uranus were soon made public. The headlines of every newspaper in the U.S. read: Lottery Rigged—Raffle of Opera House— "In-the-Bag"! Several front-page columns exposing this conspiracy harangued both Uranus—and *me*. The news spread quickly among the crowd of saloon, restaurant, sports and business managers who handled the ticket sales. As expected it generated a protest rally that began clamoring for justice. Fully prepared to lynch Uranus, they discussed how they could legally hang him from the nearest tree. Somehow I managed to escape their fury. Although the angry mob often referred to us with inflammatory expressions, such as those—"Crosby Boys," they had their doubts about *my* implication in the scheme. They were not entirely convinced that I was an integral part of the conspiracy. On the other hand, because of my close association with Uranus, they expressed reservations about my innocence as well. There remained an unspoken suspicion of me that persisted for many years.

Ralph Waldo Emerson was scheduled to lecture on "Napoleon" at the opera house in a few days. Those arrangements required my attention. I knew that Uranus was in his office when I arrived. Realizing I was incensed, he decided he had better stay out of my way to avoid an acrimonious confrontation. I burst into his office full of unbridled anger. I lounged at him like an enraged bull facing a red cape, closed my left fist and let him have it squarely on the chin. I was undoubtedly guilty of aggravated assault; nevertheless, he had it coming. He flinched and held his hands up to his face, but he didn't strike back. Like a reprimanded, droopy-eyed hound-dog with his tail between his legs, Uranus pathetically readied himself for a sound scolding.

"Damn you, Uranus!…How could you? Don't you realize that you've committed a serious crime? You're a felon for God's sake! What in hell were you thinking about, you swindler! What you've done is not only stupid…it's scandalous, criminal and inexcusable…It's a fiasco of incredible proportions. You're a brash and arrogant scoundrel. I'd like to hang you myself right now!" I yelled heatedly while pushing him back into his chair. He hung his head in shame. Uranus couldn't face me as I vented my outrage. "I can't believe…I was once convinced you had the legendary Crosby grit to be successful through shrewd and honest hard work. I must say you've done an excellent job of dishonoring our good name and dragging it through the mud. Now, because of you,…the Crosby name has been disgraced and vilified. I'm so disappointed in you. You've really let me down in no uncertain terms. I've always adhered to a strict code of ethics, but you scandalously dragged me down with you. I'm mortified! You're nothing but a thief! If I were in your shoes, I'd make plans to leave Chicago immediately, dear cousin. You deserve everything that's coming to you! Right now…I wouldn't bet a nickel on your life. Get out!" I ordered furiously, pointing to the door. "You louse,…you disgust me! From now on, I'm detaching myself from you and your blasted opera house! I don't ever want to speak to you again!"

Uranus looked at me directly and tried to explain his motives. "Albert, I'm truly sorry that I deceived you and resorted to such drastic measures. I deserve your wrath, but I was at my wits end," he said apologetically. His body language betrayed his shame as he remorsefully lamented his wrongdoings. He lowered his head and shuffled toward the door. "I just want you to know that my financial situation was a lot worse than I let on. I was flat broke and sinking further and further into debt…even with all your support. My income from the distillery and returns from tenant rentals at the opera house were not sufficient to cover my expenses. Not only had the builders sucked me dry of my wealth with their inflated wartime prices, but I also mismanaged the contracts. The agents who charged exorbitant fees for their clients collected their money before I was able to properly tally my receipts and outlays. By the time they left town there was little left to sustain the opera house. I was loath to tell you about that. When I con-cocted the lottery, it was an act of sheer desperation. Once I had started down the path to defraud, there was no turning back. I should *never* have listened to that charlatan, Joshua Myler."

"I'm tired of your self-serving rhetoric and justifications!" I exclaimed, exas-perated by his caveat admonition. "You simpleton!…How did you think you'd ever get away with such a despicable scheme? I told you when you first approached me about the opera house that I'd be more than happy to loan you money anytime you needed it. I gave you an additional $200,000 toward its completion. At the time, you were certain that it would be more than enough," I said, returning to my desk and looking out the window.

Ice clusters had formed on the Chicago River, and in the sunlight, a blanket of glistening new snow transformed the countryside into a landscape sprinkled with sparkling diamonds. A red cardinal had come to rest on a low hanging branch. The contrast of his vivid, crimson hue against the snow-covered limb was strik-ing. The tranquility of this pristine scene induced a sense of serenity and peace deep within me. I let the wonder of it fill my heart with forgiveness and compas-sion. I relented and thought, "I mustn't let my ire and hatred of what he's done prevent me from forgiving him."

I discovered I *could* and *must* forgive him. Despite his sometimes-trying ways, I loved Uranus like a brother. We had always been close. He was not only my cousin, but also a dear friend. Our lifelong companionship need not end this way. I understood that he needed my support—right now more than ever. I would also need to show him a lot less resentment and rage and much more personal forgiveness, mutual understanding and trust. I contemplated my hostility and found it to be irrelevant and a waste of time. The healing energy released was beneficial for us both. I felt composed and relaxed. My previously frazzled nerves calmed considerably as I watched a pair of mallards alight atop the open water and glide through the marsh grass along the shore.

Mentally debating the issues, I rationalized that his passion for acquiring the opera house for himself was symptomatic of a man desperate to prove he wasn't a failure. I interpreted his actions as a man drowning in a sea of debt and grasping for anything that would save his fiscal life. I decided to turn the other cheek. Ashamed of my sudden display of bad temper and abrasive manner, I turned to face Uranus. Not wanting to appear as a hardhearted disciplinarian, my continued questioning was more solicitous. I lowered my voice and asked, "Tell me, Uranus, why didn't you ask for additional funds before resorting to such an illegal plot? Now I know why you so blatantly disregarded my concerns about the lottery. I don't mean to be judgmental, but how can you justify your fraud? I knew your finances were strained, yet I never imagined you were *that* destitute."

"I lived for that opera house…It was my pride and joy. Can't you understand that, Albert?" he replied with a quivering chin and on the verge of tears. "I never wanted anyone or anything to usurp my trophy. I worried that if you or anyone else provided me with additional financial backing, I'd have to forfeit my prized possession and eventually, lose it. Now I regret to say, I can see the flaws in that reasoning. Because of what I've done,…I'll most likely have to give it up, anyhow. If so,…this is a fitting punishment for me. I'll immediately draw up the paperwork and transfer the property over to you, Albert. The deed will be in your name only. After the transaction is completed and the ownership of the opera house is legally binding, I'll leave for New York and the Cape. I plan to remain there until things calm down around here."

Without as much as a goodbye, Uranus gathered a few papers from his desk, rushed by me, and then bolted out the door. I was stunned. When I came to my senses I realized that although it was the furthest thing from my mind, I had just inherited a grandiose and imposing white elephant—and in essence—stolen property!

*   *   *   *

Late-June, 1867

The upcoming year was a pivotal one for me. Not only had I become the sole owner of the opera house, I also became a board member of the Chicago City Railroad in March. That following May, after purchasing a significant amount of income-producing real estate, I had become president of the Chicago Board of Trade. At the beginning of this month, I also assumed the presidency of the Downes and Bemis Brewing Company. Although I still owned the major shares in the brewery, they purchased the business name and changed it at the time of the transaction. It goes without saying my days weren't long enough. I had little time to brood over my rift with Margaret. I longed for my children, but I resigned myself to the fact that they really didn't know me anyway—and consequently—didn't miss me.

As the new owner of the opera house, the first item of business was to change its name from the Chicago Opera House to the Crosby Opera House. Although there had been much dissatisfaction with the outcome of the lottery, fraud was never proven. No one was ever brought to task and it was eventually forgotten. I decided to breathe new life into the dormant leviathan by starting anew and disassociating the opera house and myself from its scandalous past. With a few alterations in administration, I would attempt to manage The Crosby Opera House profitably without Uranus' cultural tunnel vision and his limited, unrealistic guiding principles. Without favoring the affluent social elite over the working middle class or the poor, I intended to make the opera house accessible to all Chicagoans. That would go a long way toward insuring a steady flow of revenue.

Secondly, I would not allow agents to intimidate me. If their clients couldn't wait for payment until a month *after* their performances, then they needn't bother to perform at the opera house at all.

Lastly, along with the ballet, opera, band and symphony concerts, et cetera, I scheduled programs such as light opera, musicals, trendy burlesque ensembles, cabaret musicals, circus acts, minstrels, orchestral ensembles and renowned artists. These included anyone from popular singers and magicians to violinists. To my surprise, sopranos and tenors from all over the world began to compete for dates. Since it had the finest acoustics of any comparable opera palace in the United States, a diversity of artists considered it a rare privilege to play in the

Crosby Opera House. Through political associates, I was also able to schedule the '68 Republican Convention.

"Say, Albert, how do you propose to repay those of us who helped launch Uranus's extravagant opera house?" Samuel asked as he lit his cigar. He had sold his brewery and had now been in the financial business for a few years. Samuel dropped by after his banking hours and was relaxing in a leather wingchair inside my office at the opera house. "I know the responsibility's no longer yours, nevertheless, I've come here...not so much for myself,...but to represent various funding sources and business friends who at my behest invested heavily in this building. They trusted me implicitly because I've always been honest in my dealings with them. I *never* took advantage of their generosity. Now that Uranus has skipped town, I'm in the very embarrassing position of having to make excuses for your deceitful cousin. I assured them that I'd approach you about it, Albert. Some of these powerful men are also some of your closest colleagues. I trust you'll find a way to repay these people. It would show good faith and go a long way toward restoring their confidence in the Crosby name. Do you think it's possible to do something for them, Albert?"

"Well, I'm glad you inquired about that, Samuel. As a matter of fact, I've already begun to set aside some money to pay each one of those creditors," I said with conviction while getting up from behind my desk, reaching for a pitcher, and then pouring some ice tea into a glass. "It's such a hot day, Samuel, would you like some ice tea?" I asked, sitting down opposite him.

"No, thank you, Albert, I can't stay long," he replied, dousing his cigar in the ashtray and walking toward the door. "The Missus expects me home soon."

"Please tell the creditors for me that by this time next year, they'll be reimbursed in full,...plus interest," I said, joining him as he moved toward the doorway. "Although I understand the debt's not mine, I feel compelled to restore the Crosby family honor. I'm genuinely troubled over the whole sordid affair and trust they don't connect me with it."

"No, Albert, they don't. I've assured them...you had nothing to do with it," he replied, before descending the staircase to the side entrance. "They know you never really wanted to own the opera house in the first place and that you've only taken it over to keep it functioning and solvent."

"Yes,...and I intend to do just that!" I said decisively, opening the door for him. "My methods may be a little unorthodox, but I assure you, Samuel, as certain as my name is Albert Crosby, this palace will have continuing performances with sell-out crowds every day of the week."

"Well, that's more like it," he replied, getting into his caleche and taking the reins. (Samuel always preferred to drive his own carriage.) "I've always admired your drive and integrity. The best of luck to you, Albert."

"Before you take your leave, Samuel, tell me,…are you returning to Cape Cod soon?" I asked. "If you spend any time there this summer,…will you please visit the homestead? While I wish I could do so myself, I won't be able to return to the East Coast this year. It's imperative that I stay in Chicago. Give my parents my love and tell them that they're in my thoughts and that I wish them well. They're getting on in years. Regretfully, it seems as though my visits to Brewster have become more and more infrequent," I said with an intrinsic sense of remorse.

"Yes, Albert,…in fact I plan to leave for the Cape next week," he replied before cracking his whip. "I'll be sure to give them your regards. Take care of yourself. I'll see you at the end of August." With that, he lashed his whip over his horse and it lurched forward into a gallop. Before re-entering the opera house, I heaved an envious sigh as I watched the caleche career its way up Washington Street. When it eventually made a right hand turn up ahead—it disappeared from sight.

CHAPTER 17

▼

Early -March, 1868

My Dear Margaret:

Enclosed is this month's family allowance check. As you can see by the amount on this bank draft, I've included a substantial increase. I believe it will help to alleviate some of your financial worries. I understand that you have had increased household expenses with the children's education and other responsibilities. It's my intent that you continue to live comfortably and will not have to forfeit any of the amenities that you've become accustomed to.

Because the ownership of the opera house now takes up so much of my time, and because I am still president of both the railroad and the brewing companies, I've decided to sell the distillery business to Josiah and his son, Theodore. Josiah's been with me almost twenty years now and is well prepared to take over the reins.

Except for a bout of influenza in January, I've been in good health. I keep you and the children in my thoughts and pray that you're all well. Even though my days are full and I'm continually occupied, I dearly miss all of you. I'm hopeful that in the near future my family will return to Chicago. The sound of my laughing children is needed to fill the silent, echoing halls of our lifeless manor. Above all, Margaret, I long for you, my loving and devoted wife. I beg you one last time to give it your heartfelt consideration. If not for our sake alone, then please consider the children. Although I know that I'm extremely engaged outside the home, they need a father in their lives. Please give the children my love. I miss them so very much. Give your parents my regards, and please write soon to let me

know if the amount I've sent will be sufficient. I look forward to receiving
your letters. I love you and send you my best wishes,
Albert

As I braved the elements on the way to the post office to mail the letter, I found myself asking some probing questions that I couldn't answer with any degree of certainty. "Will she answer my short letter or ignore it? Will Margaret be as contentious as ever or be appreciative and reconsider her decision to remain at Wildwood?" I wondered. During the next few weeks, I closely examined every letter and telegraph that came across my desk. But alas, I'm sad to say, I never received any correspondence from her.

At the end of March, my carriage dropped me off at the distillery where I was to make final arrangements for its sale to Josiah and his son. While the business was turned over to Josiah, I still retained ownership of the land and the building. Over the years I succeeded in purchasing all the adjacent mercantile buildings alongside the Chicago River. My holdings now encompassed a whole block.

"I've decided the company should retain the Crosby name,...if that's agreeable with you, Albert," Josiah declared, fumbling with the keys, unlocking the door, and then opening it for me. "It has an excellent reputation nationwide. It'd be foolhardy of me to change it. I'm sure you concur with that."

"Yes, I do. It's a wise decision on your part, Josiah. I'll be sure to legalize that point by indicating my approval on the bill of sale," I replied, lifting my carpetbag onto the desk. "I want you to know,...I'll be more than happy to assist you in any way possible. I'm sure you'll run into a problem now and then; however, if you should,...please don't be afraid to approach me. Regardless of how busy I am, I'll always have time for you. Had it not been for you, Josiah,...I'd never be where I am now. You've been a loyal and devoted employee and have earned the right to sit in the president's chair. Come!...Try it out! I want to leave here remembering just how you looked in it. I can't think of anyone more deserving."

"Thank you, Albert. I'll try not to bother you *too* much," he said jokingly with a wide grin and eyes that mirrored his appreciation as he sat down at the large mahogany desk. "You've always been so supportive of me. When I was hired as your accountant twenty years ago, I never dreamt that I'd eventually become the owner and president of this thriving business. That could never have happened without your faith and trust in me. I thank you for making this possible. Albert Crosby & Company is a successful and lucrative enterprise solely because of your integrity and dedication. I feel honored and fortunate indeed that you considered selling the business to me before anyone else. I hope your confidence in me will be justified."

"I have no doubts about that," I replied, clearing out the desk draws and placing the contents in my bag.

"I hope that Ruth and I will continue to have the honor of your presence at our Thursday evening suppers," Josiah said as he accompanied me to the door with his hands in his pockets. "We truly enjoy your visits. Actually,…it's the highlight of Ruth's week. She occupies her time planning her menu, shopping and arranging a pleasing table setting. Theodore and Molly are planning to join us next Thursday. They'll be bringing, their new son, Jonadah, with them…Please say you'll come, Albert."

"Why, I wouldn't miss it…I'll be there," I replied, bracing myself against the wind, stepping into the carriage, and then waving back. "Farewell, Josiah!…See you on Thursday!"

As I rode toward the opera house alone with my thoughts, the March winds buffeted the carriage and large, wet snowflakes intermingled with the rain and vanished when they reached the surface. I was pleased to find the streets were free of ice and snow. Inclement weather often resulted in a sparse attendance at an opera house performance. I anticipated a full house this evening for the now-popular English version of the Italian opera, *Il Trovatore*.

✳ ✳ ✳ ✳

Early April, 1868

Margaret never answered my letter. I assumed the tension between us had been acerbated by absence and distance. I never heard a word either from her—her family—or her circle of friends. Months seemed to blend into forever. At first, I sought and longed for dialogue with Margaret. Gradually, however, I became distraught, angered and eventually—indifferent and detached. Samuel learned through family members that Margaret, in a perennial snit, was adamant about remaining in West Roxbury. She refused to move to Chicago and was determined never to set foot on its soil again. Her rejection of my entreating letter was the last straw. I decided to go on with my life. At forty-five and graying at the temples, my desire for female companionship had now shifted from waiting for Margaret—to charming another—someone more sensitive to my needs. My love for her faded with each passing day.

I began to seek the friendship of a sophisticated yet worldly woman—one who would enjoy my company and be honored to accompany me to the opera house. While not celibate by desire or nature, it had been my lot in life for many years now. Unfulfilled sexual needs and longings dominated my dreams and were now beginning to spill over into my waking hours. I found myself retreating into erotic fantasies every time a beautiful woman was in my presence. I had the pleasure of having several lovely female celebrities as guests in my proscenium box; however, my association with them was more often than not—plutonic and cordial. I had never sought the services of the so-called "ladies-of-the-night." I was wary of their hygiene and bodies that harbored lice and disease. When tempted, I often recalled the cautionary advice of my fellow shipmates in the merchant marines.

"All the riches I've amassed, and the success I've worked so hard to achieve should make me happy," I thought." Yet in spite of all this, I'm a despondent and lonely shell of a man without a woman to love and a family to cherish," My mind wandered while I checked the lighting in the auditorium and waited for Samuel to join me. "Maybe with time and a little luck, I'll find that one singular woman I'm searching for…one who'll share my life and wealth with me. I won't despair. I'm sure the right one's out there just waiting to be noticed."

While I stood in the mezzanine of the opera house, Samuel approached me from behind. At the sound of his voice, I turned to face him. "Albert, I must say you've done a splendid job of resurrecting this monstrosity," he said, putting his arm around my neck. "My associates have informed me that their faith in the Crosby name has been restored. This about face is evident in their change of attitude toward the "Crosby Boys." We've concluded that despite Uranus' crime, it's been incumbent upon us to forgive him for his grand delusions and shortsightedness. They've gone out of their way to praise your dogged determination to clear up his debts. I've repeatedly told them that unlike Uranus, you're a resolute and trustworthy man. I think they doubted that at first,…but they've come to appreciate the truth of that statement. Your tenacious approach has single-handedly transformed an opera house beset with unsatisfactory attendance and dwindling receipts to one with overflowing audiences and tidy profits. Let me also add that I've always admired your leadership qualities. Your talent for achieving success solely through hard work and honest dealings is highly regarded, Albert. What you've done here is short of a miracle."

"Well thank you, Samuel," I replied. "I think the requirements for the convention hall seating can be effectively adapted to the satisfaction of the National Executive Committee. They're delighted with the opera house possibilities and plan on sending a sizeable workforce here. Only a few adjustments will have to be made to transform it into a national convention center. Needless to say, the committee will make the final decisions about the renovations. I plan to make a few more trips to Washington. Several problems must be addressed before the convention in May. Would you consider joining me the next time I have to meet with the Executive Committee?"

"I'd be delighted. Thank you for asking me, Albert," Samuel replied. "Just give me a few days notice beforehand. I must say, offering the opera house for the upcoming Republican National Convention was a stroke of genius…It should prove to be quite profitable."

"It will be, Samuel. I'm making arrangements to leave sometime next week," I said as I waved goodbye and returned to my office.

The Republican National Convention began at noon on the 19th of May. A crowd of conventioneers with badges from every state filled the opera house to vote for their favored candidate—General Ulysses S. Grant. The convention was a public relations windfall and a financial boon for Chicago. All the hotels were occupied, vendor's shelves were emptied of goods and the newspapers with their augmented circulation cashed in not only on the increased revenue, but also on the worldwide publicity.

"Great job, Albert!…You've exceeded expectations!" Samuel exclaimed, slapping me on the shoulder as we watched the delegates filing out of the opera house. "I believe you've more than redeemed yourself and the family name. Everyone in the business world is beholden to you and the Crosby Opera House for putting Chicago on the political map. It's now considered a city that's as dynamic and worthy of respect as New York and Boston. Thanks to you and your accomplishments, Chicago can discard its image of being a crude and backward city."

"Well, Samuel, coming from you that's quite a compliment. Even so,…like most generalizations things are *not* that simple. Chicago has a long way to go. There are still large pockets of abject poverty. Whole segments of our citizenry live in hovels and shanties…I worry about that!" I said. "My goal was to keep this facility occupied and making money. Nevertheless, a little publicity from pundits and politicians won't hurt either," I snickered with a wide grin. "I couldn't help but notice how the delegates and the well-known personalities gawked at the elegance of their surroundings. Believe me, Samuel, I could tell they were *very* impressed with this showpiece. Word of our hospitality will not only boost the status of the city, but the opera house as well." Having said that, I excused myself and exited through the two-story arched entrance of the grand promenade. After a tension-filled and tiring day—I left for home.

*   *   *   *

Late-June, 1869

Just when I thought the Crosby name had finally been vindicated, my Cousin Charles made the headlines in the *Times* and the *Tribune*. My shiftless cousin was involved in a near-murder. Charles had occupied the living quarters in the rear section of the opera house. Uranus had also lived there before his sudden exit from Chicago. I happened to be there when Samuel, mad as a wet hen, came barging into my office with several newspapers in his hands.

"What kind of a mess has that bad egg, Charles Crosby, gotten himself into this time? What in damnation is wrong with him?" Samuel asked, angrily waving his arms as he entered through the opened door. Infuriated and shouting at the top of his lungs, he pointed to a photograph of Charles. It graced the front pages of both newspapers, which he vehemently slammed down on my desk. "What foolish alibi could that slow-witted, black sheep have for such scandalous behavior? Why, he's crazy as a hatter! I swear…that no-account has the mentality of a moron! You've been good enough to help him along by giving him a place to live and he dishonors it with this kind of debauchery. Goddammit, Albert!" he shouted. "Although I'm a Nickerson, my relationship as a family member also makes me a target. The press seems particularly relentless and wholly without mercy where the Crosbys are concerned. Despite the fact that our family tries to stay out of the limelight, Charles' antics only serve to increase their hatred and suspicion toward us. It seems we're forever under the reporters' close scrutiny. I'm so depressed and embarrassed by it all. I'd like to distance myself from the whole bunch! I find myself entertaining thoughts of getting the hell out of here! You should probably consider selling the opera house for whatever you can get for it and leave with me! This matter concerning Charles is *despicable*! Do you know anything about this?…What actually happened here, Albert?"

"Without condoning his behavior, I must tell you, Samuel, that Charles was having a an affair with the wife of a prominent financier a person you're not acquainted with,…someone not in your clique. I'm sure it's someone you don't know," I replied, trying to calm him down and offering him a glass of wine. We sat opposite each other as I continued the conversation. "I learned of this situation only after his illicit romance became public knowledge. She claimed to have a loveless marriage and seduced a naïve Charles into sponsoring her acting career. Her acting prowess, I fear, was limited to a dual performance as an abused wife and devoted mistress. Poor, Charles, he was badly duped. This manipulating witch was often seen returning from spending the night with him here at the opera house.

"On the morning of the skirmish, her husband was waiting for her. When the unsuspecting couple exited the apartment, he shoved Charles aside and began to strangle his wife until she collapsed in his arms. She was still alive,…but unconscious. After his vicious assault, the incensed spouse flung her limp body at a horrified Charles. The alleged attacker screamed obscenities at them both while decrying her wickedness and adulterous behavior. Thank God the stagehands heard his raucous ranting and raving. They rushed to her rescue and because of their efforts were able to prevent her from being killed or badly beaten by her momentarily insane husband. Unfortunately, she had already suffered several blows to her nose and mouth.

"By this time a crowd had gathered and the reporters were soon getting all the scandalous details from the spectators. They rushed back to their offices to get the whole account into the morning papers. I'm ashamed to say,…this incident was thoroughly exploited by the journalists.

"That's the whole story, Samuel, except that Charles confirmed the fact that she's filing for divorce on the grounds of cruelty. For no discernable reason that I can see, that dim-witted Charles thinks she's going to marry him when she's free. I'm sure that once she's used him to finance her acting career, she'll leave him to wallow in his own misery. Charles said they plan to leave for New York as soon as her divorce is granted. This whole sordid matter is absurd! As far as I'm concerned Charles and Uranus are lost souls wretchedly locked in a cycle of error and loss. They're victims of poor choices and self-inflicted misery,…and only have themselves to blame."

"For all I care, I hope he follows her to the ends of the earth and falls off!" Samuel bellowed, "Charles has done enough damage around here to last a lifetime!

"I've ignored the disapproval of the reporters who assail the way you've been managing the Crosby Opera House," he added. "If it takes packing this place by scheduling burlesques, touring road shows and other bawdy entertainment they consider indecent,…then so be it, Albert. I disagree with your critics…I'm all for it. I don't see those righteous bastards rushing to pay the bills!" Samuel rose from his chair, turned to leave, and then placed his empty wine glass on an end table near the door.

"By the way,…I'll be joining you in your box next month," he went on. "The Missus and I have tickets for the British Blonde Burlesques. We're eager to attend the premiere because of the rave reviews this operatic spoof and its provocative themes have received in Cincinnati. Will that be all right with you, Albert?"

"Certainly, Samuel. There'll be another person there besides myself, and that'll most likely be the booking agent," I replied, rising from my chair and walking him to the door. "You're more than welcome to enjoy the 'Blondes' from my proscenium box. It's an audacious touring group that originated in England. This English version was assembled to counteract the superb French cancan burlesque. I hear it's quite entertaining. The premiere performance is already sold out."

*   *   *   *

Mid-July, 1869

The heat and enervating humidity was stifling on the evening of the opening performance of the "Blondes." As night fell across the city a scarlet sun setting on the horizon signaled a tomorrow that would be another sizzling mid-summer day. For several days now, Chicago had been in the throes of an oppressive, steamy spell that was expected to continue throughout the week. I thanked my lucky stars that Uranus had had the presence of mind to add a one-of-a-kind cooling system when the opera house was built. Although I considered it an outrageous extravagance at the time, I came to appreciate his foresight. The performance could never have taken place without it. In the long run it had eventually paid for itself.

I heaved a deep sigh as Cape Cod came to mind. How nice it would have been to enjoy the serenity of an early evening swim. I envisioned the calm bay waters reflecting the awesome hermosa glow of a sunset on the bay that filled the heavens with crimson, periwinkle and purple hues. I could feel the subtle sea breezes and the cool surf swirling around my overheated body. It was washing away not only the perspiration and fatigue, but also the fears, uncertainties and frustrations of the day. Unfortunately, I was in Chicago by choice on this hot, sultry evening. From my office window at the opera house I gazed out at the darkened twilight sky in the distance. Suddenly, there was a rap on my door.

"Come in," I said, turning around to greet the person who knocked. It was Samuel.

"Hello, Albert, I just wanted to let you know that the Missus and I have arrived for the premiere tonight. I know we're a little early, but I thought you might want to be our guest at Kingsley's before show time. Would you like to join us?" asked this heavyset man who was completely out of breath after ascending the stairs to my office.

"Thank you for asking, Samuel, however…I must decline," I replied. "I'm afraid some last minute details will require my attention before the curtain rises. I need to be available in case the stagehands run into any problems. Also, the florists will be delivering bouquets of fresh red roses for the ornamental containers scattered around the auditorium. Do have an enjoyable time. I'll join you in my box immediately before the start of the performance."

"Fine, Albert…I'll see you then," he said, turning around with a quick farewell gesture and descending the staircase.

I donned my formal jacket and headed for the dressing rooms behind the stage. The producer and publicity agent were nervously awaiting my arrival. The aromatic scent of fresh roses permeated the entire opera palace as the seats were quickly being occupied.

"Mister Crosby, I dare say your opera house is an absolute gem. It's one of the finest my company has ever had the pleasure to perform in," the burlesque troupe manager said sincerely. He was a rather portly gentleman with a salt and pepper goatee, thick eyebrows and bristly head of hair. His large, prominent nose seemed to cover half his face. I smiled and nodded in appreciation.

"Allow me to introduce you to Harold Thompson. He and his wife Lydia are the directors of the British Blondes," C.D. Hess said courteously. C.D. was the opera house booking agent. Mister Hess was a gaunt, clean-shaven man who was fair-haired and wore dark rimmed spectacles. He and I were often at odds due to his overbearing attitude over scheduling and choice of performing arts.

"Would it be all right for him to watch the production from your proscenium box, Albert?" C.D. asked while closing his briefcase. "His wife, Lydia, will remain backstage with the troupe."

"He's perfectly welcome to join our group. Samuel and his wife also intend to sit in my box," I replied, shaking hands with both men. "Oh, I'm being summoned by one of the stagehands. You'll have to excuse me…I'll see you both later."

The first call for the seven o'clock performance was announced backstage. I finished supervising the adjustment of the curtain pulleys and gaslights over the stage and ascended the staircase to the balcony. I opened the door to my box where four people were already seated and waiting for the show to begin. Samuel and his Missus were in the upper settee while Messieurs Thompson and Hess occupied the lower one. My box held two such sofas on each level. There were times when I entertained a party of eight. I made my way down to where the two men were seated. After politely addressing them both, I sat down. The noise level in the crowded auditorium was deafening. A diverse group of rowdy patrons were loudly conversing with each other several rows away. The people who attended this type of entertainment were less reserved and not as well dressed as those who attended the operas of the Uranus era. Nonetheless, I was pleased with the turn-out. The theater was darkened as the lights began to dim. Only the stage lights remained lit.

"These folks are in for an incredible evening of entertainment," C.D. whispered. "I've seen this same performance in both New York and Cincinnati. The comedians are sidesplitting and the women shapely and gorgeous. The program includes the audience in variety of ways, such as inviting them onstage and asking them to sing along with the catchy music."

As advertised, the young women in the British Blondes' chorus line were exceptionally beautiful and curvaceous. They wore similar blonde wigs, identical corsets and short, sheer, layered outer garments. My jaw dropped as I gawked in awe. I was thoroughly fascinated by these buxom young ladies who were all smiling and dancing in unison. Their high kicks were faultless. They turned and lifted their petticoats to expose their scantily covered backsides to a delighted crowd. The energized patrons clapped and stomped to a rousing rendition of Strauss's *Tritsch Trastch Polka*. The audience was thoroughly enjoying itself—including me.

"Why, it's absolutely marvelous!" I exclaimed while still clapping along with the infectious rhythm as I turned to address C.D. All of a sudden, there was thunderous applause and laughter from the standing-room-only crowd. I quickly turned to face the stage and noticed that one of the young ladies had lost her blonde wig, revealing a head of long, brunette hair fastened into a chignon. The embarrassed young woman quickly replaced it—at a hilarious angle. Pandemonium reigned as the amused throng exploded with whistles and shouts, cheering her on. I removed my opera glasses from the pocket on the settee and focused them on the stage. "Oh, wow! What a beautiful woman…her body's superb and her face is mesmerizing!" I thought, completely charmed by her stage presence. I watched as she eased herself out of the chorus line while the rowdy crowd screamed in delight and clamored for more. The "Blondes" closed ranks as she made a quick exit off stage.

"That's Georgia Garrison!…That young woman is *fired!* I knew we should *never* have hired her in the first place!" Harold Thompson shouted vehemently. He was noticeably incensed as he stood, crumbled his program, and then threw it wildly against the seat.

"Oh, it wasn't *that* disastrous," I said lightheartedly, hoping to defuse his anger so it wouldn't result in her dismissal. "In fact, I think it was rather comical and so did the audience."

"That was *not* supposed to happen! The performers were told they'd be sacked if the production was disrupted for any reason. What just occurred out there," Harold Thompson said in a livid and uncompromising manner as he pointed to the stage, "was a prime example of inexcusable incompetence! People have been fired for a hell of a lot less! Please excuse me, I must find my way backstage. I need to tend to this immediately. Lydia will be quite upset as well," he maintained, getting up from the settee and heading toward the door at the rear of the proscenium box. I also decided to leave because I felt an irrepressible empathy for the poor girl. I sensed her employers might be too embarrassed to fire her in my presence. With this in mind, I bid Samuel and his wife goodbye, ascended the steps of the proscenium box, and then followed behind Mister Thompson.

"Lydia works hard with these girls and after repeated training and rehearsals, she expects them to achieve perfection," he groused, trying to explain his indignation while we descended toward the stage. "She's a hard taskmaster and demands a certain amount of dedication and commitment from her performers."

When we reached the backstage wings, the attractive young lady was nonchalantly hiding behind the theater draperies. With youthful naivety, she watched the remainder of the performance from the wings. Lydia, who was on the opposite side of the stage, also approached her from behind the scenery. I expected to see a distressed young woman traumatized by the whole sorry incident, but her insouciance startled me. She was quite unruffled and smiled sweetly as we neared her. After a few private words together, Harold and Lydia Thompson, who were quite perturbed, beckoned her to move toward the dressing rooms where we were standing. Ultimately, she came forward to face them with her head held high and holding the wig in her hands.

"I'll save you the embarrassing chore of having to fire me…I quit!" she said with the bearing of a mature adult. She addressed each one and made a brief, yet succinct statement to the surprised duo. "In spite of everything that's happened here, I do want to thank you for your patience with my shortcomings. It's not your fault. I just can't seem to adapt my talents to burlesque. I'll pick up my things from the dressing room and be on my way."

"Georgia, you're a very talented and engaging young woman with allure and a lot of potential," Lydia said. Lydia was a straight-laced, middle-aged, motherly type who kindly removed some folding money from her pocket. This energetic woman had a fine figure and few wrinkles. "I've never before encountered such sophisticated presence and dramatic promise. You have a fine soprano voice and you dance like a prima ballerina, but your heart's not in it. With your education and polish, you've got too much class for burlesque," she went on, putting her arm around Georgia's shoulder and offering her some practical advice. "Seek loftier heights, my dear, and nurture your aptitude for music,…it's a major component for fulfillment and growth, Georgia. You should try to find employment in a musical theater company. That would be more to your liking,…something more intellectually challenging for you. Why you ever joined the burlesque is beyond me. Here's a little advance on your pay. Please remember to pick up the balance at the end of this engagement. Good luck to you, Georgia. Actually, we had reconsidered and had decided to let you stay on. Despite your occasional blunders, we're quite fond of you. You have a bright future ahead. If you should need any references, we'll be happy to furnish them. Now go out there with the others holding your wig for the final curtain calls. And,…oh, before you leave us, let me introduce you to this gentleman," she said, pointing to me. "Georgia Garrison, this is Mister Albert Crosby, the owner of this opulent palace."

"How do you do, Miss Garrison," I said, kissing her extended hand while she held onto the wig with the other. She responded with a dimpled smile and a quick, lively curtsey. "I'm honored to make your acquaintance. You certainly gave the audience a good laugh. Your little "faux-pas" was very funny. In fact,…I thought it was part of the act until Mister Thompson, here,…became so agitated, "I added, nodding in his direction"

"Thank you, Mister Crosby. You're very kind to say that," she replied surprised but grateful by my comment. "Your Crosby Opera House is just about the most elegant performance center I've ever seen," she went on. "Oh, that's the curtain call…I must join the others on stage." With that, she turned and rushed from my side to the center of the stage. The audience applauded enthusiastically with boisterous hoots and howls that increased several decibels when Miss Garrison made her appearance. I stayed in the wings waiting for her to return. I was utterly charmed by this delightful young woman whose soulful brown eyes had captured my heart. I wanted to get to know her better. "What will she do after she leaves here? Does she know anyone else in Chicago? How will she manage by herself? Will she be able to find work somewhere?" I asked myself, decidedly concerned for her welfare.

Eventually, she exited the stage with the performers and was about to walk past me when I offered my hand. "Miss Garrison, may I have the pleasure of your company this evening. If you can find it in your heart to indulge an old man,…I'd like to have you join me for a meal at Kingsley's."

"I'd find that quite pleasurable, Mister Crosby," she replied enthusiastically with an engaging, toothsome smile. "Please don't consider yourself an old man. I've known younger men who could learn a lot from you. Their boorishness can't compare to your social graces and genteel manner. Besides, you're quite fit for your age…whatever *that* is! I'll be a few minutes. It shouldn't take too long as we always travel light. Some members of the troupe have become my good friends. I'd like to take some time to say goodbye and wish them well. I'll meet you at the restaurant in about twenty minutes, if that's all right with you," she said, leaving my side.

"That would be fine, Miss Garrison," I replied, pleased that she had accepted my invitation. "I'll take it upon myself to order for you. Is there anything in particular you'd like to have?"

"I'm very easy to please. I don't have a large appetite, but I'm not a fussy eater. So, yes,…please don't wait for me. Do…order our meals, Mister Crosby," she said, gesturing while walking backward toward the dressing rooms.

Kingsley's was bustling with activity. The waiting line queued out the door. Even so, my usual table was waiting for me. I informed the maitre-d' that a guest would be joining me.

"Good evening, Mister Crosby. I understand the burlesque performance was sensational! I've heard nothing but glowing remarks about this frolicsome farce at your theater," the Asian waiter said as he placed the plate, silverware and wine goblet opposite me. "I plan to see the matinee tomorrow. As you can see we're very busy tonight. Will your guest be joining you soon? Would you like to order now or later, Mister Crosby?" he asked, standing next to me with menus in hand.

"I'll order now. My guest will be arriving a little later," I replied, reaching for the menu from his outstretched hand. "Please bring a bottle of Chablis to the table. By the time you return, I'll have selected the entrée." He left to fetch the wine while I scanned the menu. I selected a filet mignon for the two of us. I was sipping the wine and reading the daily newspaper when Miss Garrison approached the table. I instinctively looked at my pocket watch.

"Hello again, Mister Crosby, I hope I haven't kept you waiting too long," she said with a sunny smile, noticing that I had checked the time of her appearance. Miss Garrison had arrived a half-hour past the original twenty minutes she had previously stated. However, I could appreciate her tardiness. She was stunning in a light chiffon dress that flowed gracefully as she walked toward me. The golden fabric reflected the iridescent colors of the candlelight. I couldn't help noticing how the men at the adjacent tables, even those who were accompanied by women, gawked at this striking brunette as she sashayed past them.

"May I serve your dinner now, sir?" the waiter asked.

"Yes, please do," I replied, pouring the Chablis into her crystal goblet. "I'm honored by your presence at my table. A toast to you, Miss Garrison, for a memorable evening! You were a big hit!" She raised her goblet to join me in the toast. "I absolutely concurred with the rest of the audience. Your little gaffe was exceedingly funny. Why, you were the star of the whole performance!…You stole the spotlight!" We clicked our glasses together and enjoyed a good laugh.

"You needn't be so formal, Mister Crosby. You may call me Matilda…That's really my first name. My full name is Matilda Georgia Sourbeck. Georgia Garrison is my stage name. I combined Georgia with Garrison solely for theatrical purposes," she said before taking a bite of her meal.

"Well, in that case you may call me, Albert," I replied. "What do you expect to do Matilda, now that you've left the burlesque? Do you have friends or family here in Chicago?" I asked noticing her delicate perfume as I bent over to speak to her. "Oh, I'm sorry, I don't mean to pry,…it's just that I'm truly concerned about you."

"Actually, Mister Crosby,…are you sure I may call you, Albert?" she asked as I nodded in approval. "I'll be fine," she said. "While I have no friends or family here, I've saved enough money from my salary to hold me until I find work. Aside from singing and dancing, I'm also a pianist and able to accompany myself musically. I expect to find employment in the entertainment field. I hope my talents will assure me a string of engagements at some of the finer restaurants or other reputable places."

"How did you come to join the British Blondes Burlesque in the first place?…Or should I ask?" I inquired, eager to get an answer without trying to sound intrusive. "According to the Thompsons, you weren't particularly suited to that bawdy type of entertainment."

"It's a long story, Albert…Are you sure you want to hear it?" she asked. "I don't know if I should bore you with it, but if you're interested…I'll try to make it brief."

"Certainly. I'm eager to know more about you, Matilda," I replied without hesitation. "It sounds like it might be intriguing…You've definitely piqued my curiosity."

"I come from a fairly affluent family," she disclosed. "I was born and raised in Washington, D.C. My father's a lawyer and a judge. Before they married, Mother, was a gifted musician and a member of a symphony orchestra. I guess I inherited her aptitude. She was aware of my talents and insisted that I have a well-rounded musical education. I was constantly being shuttled from voice lessons to piano recitals. The dance and ballet also occupied much of my time. I spent a few years at the university after graduating from secondary school. While there, I met a male student from New York, whom I eventually married. Within a few months, however…I knew I'd made a horrible mistake. He was a jealous and abusive husband. I endured his threats and battering until the day several sheriffs arrived at my door. He was handcuffed and dragged off to jail for having committed a serious crime. I was told his wife had him arrested for bigamy. She learned that he had married me while still wedded to her. My marriage was nothing but a sham and a mockery. Although I was ashamed, I can't tell you how relieved I was to know that I was finally free and well rid of him.

"In spite of this, he had a strange notion that he could still force himself on me upon his release from jail. He vowed he'd find me if I didn't wait for him. I feared his murderous madness. The British Blondes Burlesque had arrived in New York at the time and was preparing to leave for Cincinnati and Chicago. I was attracted to a posted advertisement for talented young women who were needed to augment their chorus. I decided to vanish into a fog of anonymity. Traumatized by my experience and afraid that he'd return to harass and harm me again, I gave this opportunity serious consideration. Afraid he'd eventually discover my whereabouts, I auditioned, was hired, and then joined the troupe.

"I've since advised my parents as to the reasons why I left, and also why it should be kept a secret. I told them I saw it as a way out of my predicament,…that I was fine and making a life for myself. I've taken all the necessary precautions to hide my identity. That necessitated changing my name to Georgia Garrison. I created a new self by wearing a blond wig in public. It would be the perfect disguise. Although everyone was kind and understanding, being in a burlesque chorus wasn't at all what I had expected it to be. I not only found it personally degrading, but also, an inappropriate use of my talents. That's primarily my reason for leaving the troupe. Please don't feel sorry for me. I'm finally at peace with myself and relieved to know that I've most likely evaded the violent repercussions of my ex-husband's revenge. I hope I never see that horrible man again. So there,…you have it!"

"A blond wig! What a coincidence! Has the blond wig of my past become a link to my future?" I wondered. I suddenly remembered how well that ruse had worked for David and me.

As she spoke, I realized how different Matilda was from Margaret. Their personalities occupied opposite ends of the spectrum. Matilda was an effervescent, poised and self-sufficient young woman who had willingly left the security of her family. Margaret was demure, prim and proper, but extremely insecure. Her happiness derived from clinging to the sanctuary provided by her parents and circle of friends. "How strange," I thought, "that I'm so attracted to this liberated icon of individualism with traits so opposite from Margaret's."

"Well, I must say, Matilda,…that's quite a poignant account," I said, gasping and shaking my head in amazement. "Yes, I certainly hope he hasn't followed you here. At the risk of sounding flippant, he's in for a whole lot of trouble if he should even *try* to contact you. I have several friends in law enforcement. I'll see to it that he's arrested and driven straight out of town with bullets fired at his heels." We laughed again. It had been a long time since I enjoyed the company of a woman, especially one so attractive and personable. This charming female had completely captivated me. She had me in the palms of her hands.

"I've been doing all the talking. Now it's your turn," she said, taking another sip of wine and putting her goblet back on the table. "Maybe it's a little presumptuous of me to ask,…but are you married? Do you have a family? I'd really like to know more about you,…a compassionate man who's so concerned about my welfare. I must admit I like that about you. Even though I'm a bit intimidated by your influence and wealth, I do find you quite fascinating and personable, Albert."

"I rather like you too, Matilda. I feel quite comfortable and very much at ease in your company. Your straightforwardness is so refreshing," I replied sincerely, reaching for her hand. "I guess I owe you an explanation for asking you to join me this evening. I hope you won't be overly disillusioned by my disclosure and all the perverse nostalgia associated with it. Yes, I *am* a married man with a family of four children. I have three daughters and a young son. I've lived here in Chicago without my family for about seven years now. My wife, Margaret, refuses to budge from our home in West Roxbury, Massachusetts. Shortly after our marriage twenty years ago, I left the East Coast to seek my fortune here in Chicago. For the next thirteen years and after the birth of our children she intermittently lived here with me. But regrettably, she inevitably missed her family and her aristocratic, social circle of friends and would regularly return to what she considered *home*. She despised the uncivilized, low-class people who lived here and would eventually pick up and leave me for months at a time. I desperately tried to please Margaret by having an elegant mansion built for her and the family in Massachusetts so she'd have a place to stay during the summers and on other occasions. That was a terrible mistake;…one I've since learned to regret. I thought Margaret might decide to stay after I had a palatial manor built for her, here. She did remain in Chicago for a while, but even the manor didn't help. Several times a year I had to journey east to visit my wife and family, whom I sorely missed.

"Nevertheless, after the birth of our son seven years ago, she informed me that she'd *never* return to Chicago again. I was given an ultimatum. Either I move back to West Roxbury and retire there, or else I'd never see my family unless I continued to commute. Sadly, it became a contentious issue. My life is *here*, Matilda…This is where I make my living. I wasn't ready to retire and become an indolent gentleman of means. I wasn't cut out for that type of lifestyle. I wrote to her in March of last year begging her one last time to return here with the children, but she never responded. I live by myself in our oversized house. The only other person there is an affable housemaid…a Negro woman from the South who comes everyday to tend to the household chores.

"I'm planning on putting the manor up for sale soon. I've decided to move into the Sherman House on Clark and Randolph Streets. So,…as you can see I don't have a marriage,…at least not in the true sense of the word. Sadly, my children are growing up without their father. I'm sure…I've been forgotten. All I have are a few family photos and lingering memories of them. It pains me to have to tell you all of this. While I've never revealed the particulars of my private life to any other woman since our separation, I feel completely at ease telling you that I'm often depressed and guilt ridden over my failed marriage.

"Perhaps my zest for wealth was destructive for my loved ones and me. I wanted to make my mark in the world and though I may have succeeded financially…my personal life has been a complete failure. But realistically, I'm a driven man and have no wish to live any other way. That's the situation. I hope you won't take offense by my tale of woe and my desire to socialize with a young woman such as yourself."

"Oh, no, Albert, I fully understand your dilemma. In fact, you have my heartfelt sympathy. It's impossible for me to understand your wife's reluctance to be with you. Maybe she didn't love you enough to separate herself from her eastern roots. It's her loss, Albert, not yours!" Matilda said, rising from her chair. "I hate to have to leave, but I must find a place to stay tonight. It's already getting quite late…It'll be difficult to find a room at this hour."

"I was fully prepared to offer you a small apartment that's on the premises of the opera house, Matilda. You're welcome to stay there tonight until more suitable quarters can be found for you," I said, helping her with her shawl.

"Well, thank you, Albert. I believe I'll take you up on that offer. I didn't relish the idea of being out on the street right now and looking for a place to sleep," she replied as I summoned the waiter and paid him. The restaurant was almost empty as we walked toward the door.

"You needn't have worried about that," I said assuredly as we ascended the staircase to the apartment. "I certainly would have escorted you wherever you had chosen to go and made sure that when I left you,…you were safe and secure in your room. Needless to say, I'll also make sure that all is well here before I return home." I opened the door and turned on the gaslights. "Matilda, here's the key. You're welcome to stay as long as you like. I'll be back in the morning."

"I appreciate your generosity and promise not to take advantage of it," she said. "Again, Albert, thank you so very much. This certainly must be my lucky day. I look forward to seeing you again. I know!…Come for breakfast! I'll venture out in the morning to buy some scones. The coffee will be ready…Do come!"

"Thank you…I'd like that! I'll see you around nine," I replied, turning to leave. Uranus and Charles had previously occupied the apartment. Uranus was now a curator of an art gallery in New York City, and Charles had permanently returned to Cape Cod after his mistress, who failed in her attempt to become an actress, finally rid herself of him.

My carriage ride home found me mulling over the events of the evening. I felt I'd met the ideal woman I was searching for. She was pleasing and perfect—an attractive, fun loving—yet refined young lady. Matilda seemed to enjoy my company, even though she was much younger and just a bit older than my daughter Irene. "Can Matilda possibly be interested in me as a suitor…a man twenty years older than she…already middle aged and graying at the temples?" I wondered. All the same, I planned on offering her employment at the opera house. I would also approach her in the morning about remaining in the small residential suite.

"Good morning, Matilda. Did you sleep well?" I asked while entering the apartment after she opened the door. She still looked as ravishing as she did the evening before—not a hair was out of place. Matilda was wearing a lovely plaid, silk dress that fell stylishly to the floor from her tiny waist and swished around her feet as she walked. Her eyes sparkled as she spoke.

"And good morning to you, Albert. I hope you're hungry. I'm feeling quite domestic this morning," she replied with a dazzling smile as she pointed to a chair opposite her. "I've just brewed the coffee and the scones are still warm.

Please sit here at the table. I slept quite well, thank you. There isn't a thing missing in this apartment. I must say it's quite comfortable. Thank you again for allowing me to stay here last night."

"I'm sorry to say that my time is quite limited this morning. I've arranged to meet with Mister Hess at ten. The final settlement with the Thompson troupe needs to be negotiated," I said, pulling out the chair for her. "But before I forget, I did want to speak to you about something that occurred to me last night while I lay in bed. I'm in need of a bookkeeper,…someone who can help me with all the tasks associated with the opera house. Actually, the position calls for a clerical worker who could tend to the receipts and banking accounts, et cetera. I thought that maybe, aside from your engagements in the evening, you might like to work for me a few hours during the day. I just can't seem to accomplish all the lesser chores related to managing the opera house. I could certainly use some help. And as I mentioned before, you're welcome to stay here for as long as you'd like. You needn't feel that you must give me an answer right now. Please give it some thought, Matilda. You can inform me of your decision at a later date."

"That's extremely kind of you, Albert," she replied, pouring my coffee then placing a dainty napkin and a plate with some pastry on it in front of me. She sat, sipped her coffee then began cutting into her scone. "I appreciate your generous offer of employment, and I believe I'll give you an affirmative answer about that, immediately. However,…if it's all right with you I prefer to find another place to live. There's definitely nothing wrong with this apartment. In fact, it's absolutely perfect! It just wouldn't be the proper thing to do. That's the reason I'm declining your offer to live here. The newspapers would have a field day. They have a habit of distorting even the most casual friendships into lurid affairs. You certainly don't need that kind of detrimental publicity and neither do I. I wouldn't want that bigamist ex-husband of mine to find me through the gossip columns. I hope you understand, Albert."

"You're absolutely right, Matilda. I hadn't thought of that," I replied, getting up from the table and walking toward the door. "You may commence whenever you like."

"Your offer of work is very considerate, Albert," she said, rising from her chair to join me. "Would it be all right to start as soon as I find appropriate lodgings?"

"That'll be fine, Matilda," I replied. "My reasons for hiring you are self-serving. I'm not only trying to help you, but I'm also looking out for my own interests. Believe me, any help you can give me with all the administrative details will be greatly appreciated. I should have had a secretary long ago. I'm afraid you'll find a backlog of paperwork on the desk. My Cousin Uranus once occupied that office. He was the original builder and owner of this opera house. I've since taken it over, and I've tried to handle it more profitably. I must be on my way. I hope you find lodgings that will suit you. Please don't worry about the key. I have another. You may return it when you report for work. I look forward to seeing you, again. Goodbye, Matilda. No,…I'll just say farewell until we see each other again. Oh, by the way don't forget to pick up your back wages from the Thompsons before you leave," I added as I descended the staircase.

"I'll remember, Albert," Matilda said, standing in the hallway and waving goodbye.

Delighted that she had accepted my offer and realizing that I would soon be seeing more of this beautiful and engaging young lady, I rushed down the stairway with a youthful spring in my step.

✻   ✻   ✻   ✻

Early-May, 1870

"Albert, I noticed a "for sale" sign in front of your home. I assumed that you'd most likely want to sell it one of these days," Josiah said after I stopped by the distillery to visit. I made it a point to stay in touch with Josiah, usually to show my interest and support and also to find out how he was doing with the distillery. If time permitted, I'd greet the old-time employees and chat with them for a few minutes. Some had been hired when I had first started the distillery and were still employed there. They were always pleased to see me.

"The house is much too large for me," I said as I took a seat in what was once my office. "Living there alone these last few years has been very disheartening for me. There are *too* many memories associated with it. If it weren't for Annie, I'd be living a solitary existence. It's impossible to converse with her because of her southern drawl. Socially, that's not much help. There are several prospective buyers who are interested in purchasing it. Scores of affluent people are moving west in search of profits. The size and prestige of my Victorian manor with its desirable location is exactly what they're looking for. I'm moving into the Sherman House next week. I wanted to let you know of my whereabouts in case you needed to be in touch with me,…that's my principal reason for visiting you today."

"I thought that might be why you stopped by," he said after offering me a hot toddy that I politely declined. "It's always a pleasure to have you drop in on us, Albert. There isn't one person on these premises who doesn't look forward to your intermittent visits. We all know how busy you are and truly appreciate the fact that you always seem to find time to call on us. All is going well, Albert, and so far,…thanks to you,…the disposal of our chemical wastes appears to be under control. We shouldn't run into any further problems this coming summer."

"That's great news! You're doing a fine job here, Josiah," I replied. "I'll make a quick trip through the plant to greet everyone, then I'll be on my way. Goodbye for now, I'll return again, soon." With that, I left and walked down the hallway toward Theodore's office. I leaned in and said, "I hear you have a new addition to your family. Congratulations to you and Molly! Please give her my regards."

"I will, Mister Crosby. Thank you," said Theodore, waving a cheery greeting and a similar farewell.

A sun-drenched, balmy spring day greeted me outside the side entrance of the distillery. I decided to walk to the front entrance where I asked the driver of my carriage to wait for me. Refreshed and uplifted, I felt as cheery as the weather—celebrating the pure joy of being alive on such a pleasant day. My relationship with Matilda was accelerating into one of constant companionship. While we were together, I was always a gentleman and respectful of her. Without revealing my fondness for her, I acquiesced to appreciative caresses as a show of gratitude for her efforts, and also to kissing her gloved hand as we parted. Matilda escorted me everywhere. She accompanied me on business trips to New York and Washington, D.C. where we would visit with her family. Matilda usually dined with me at Kingsley's and joined me in my proscenium box.

Unfortunately, I was always under the close scrutiny of the newspapers. A few unforgiving reporters were incensed about my audacity to replace opera and ballet with provocative burlesque and other less sophisticated entertainment. They considered this a corruption of moral values. There were also several commentaries on certain aspects of our relationship. Using apparent truths to misinform the public, frequent gossipy references filled their columns with my supposed clandestine encounters with a young female by the name of Georgia Garrison. We were described as having secret meetings in private dining rooms and in the opera house itself. As a result, our social liaison raised eyebrows. I had warned Matilda about that. Nevertheless, because her real name was never used, she dismissed their hyperbole and innuendos as merely a ruse to sell newspapers.

As the carriage meandered slowly on the now cobblestone streets of Chicago and across the city to the opera house, I couldn't help but compare the Chicago of the present to the one in '48 when I first arrived here. In the last half of the 19th century, Chicago had taken a dramatic turn. It had enjoyed a cultural and aesthetic renaissance. The skyline had changed significantly. Due to the transformation of its business district, Chicago was now a proud, self-respecting city. Several blocks of five-story buildings stood side-by-side in all parts of the city. Multi-colored species of azaleas and rhododendrons in full bloom added a wealth of dazzling color to Chicago's spring landscape. This profusion of plants and flowers amid these commercial properties softened an otherwise monotonous setting. The creamy blossoms of the late-spring shrubs and trees glistened in the sunlight like cultured pearls. The ornately fabricated cast-iron fronts on the sophisticated granite buildings were reminiscent of Parisian architecture. Their European flavor gave the city an appearance of eminence. An array of church spires and the Chicago Avenue Water Tower gave the illusion of being in London. The imposing Crosby Opera House in the midst of these edifices added an air of opulence to its environs. As the carriage came to a halt in front of the opera house and Kingsley's Restaurant where I was to meet Matilda, I was filled with an overwhelming sense of pride and satisfaction.

CHAPTER 18

▼

Late-April, 1871

"Samuel, have you spoken to your banker friends about my proposal?" I asked during a scheduled tour of the opera house. "As you can see, the opera house needs some extensive renovating if I'm to attract a well-heeled audience. The carpeting is badly soiled and worn…It's beyond repair as is the upholstery and wall hangings. We need new floor covering throughout and new cushions for the seats. Also, the interior should be repainted from top to bottom. I've had the main staircase redesigned and plan to change all the gaslight fixtures and wainscoting. I estimate the transformation will cost approximately $100,000. Considering all that needs to be done, will that be adequate?"

"Yes, I believe it'll take at least that much to accomplish your goals," Samuel replied looking down at the dirty rug, shrugging his shoulders and shaking his head. "Its certainly in sorry shape. Yes,…I agree, Albert, it *does* look quite grimy and rundown," he concurred with a deep sigh as he examined his immediate surroundings.

"I've already spent $25,000 of my own money to replace the heating and cooling systems. The sprinklers that Uranus installed in case of fire must also be repaired," I said, pointing to the ceilings. "Frankly, Samuel,…I'm not sure if I should go forward with this project or sell the building. I can't make up my mind. I've been debating this for several months now. I've come to the conclusion that since the opera house has been profitable for the past several years, it would be a good business decision to restore it to its original opulence. In spite of this, it certainly can't be accomplished without additional funding from the banks that hold this mortgage."

"We're having a meeting in a few days to discuss advancing you the funds you've requested," Samuel said, pausing for a moment to light his cigar. "Of course you're expected to attend and present your argument for refurbishing the opera house. I already know they'd like to see it converted into a multiuse, business building. The bankers feel this would fetch a more lucrative return on their investment. Regardless of their stand, Albert, I want you to know that I thoroughly support your decision to give this place a complete overhaul. If we're to urge my partners to vote in favor of your request, it's essential that you come up with some convincing statistics to counteract their mindset. This proposition is bound to be controversial and trigger a lively discussion,...opera house versus business complex. You'd better be ready to answer their questions accurately and skillfully. Honesty will go a long way towards overcoming their objections. It's entirely up to you, Albert. It goes without saying, you'll need all your past and present financial statements and future projected revenue."

"Have no fear, Samuel. I'm as ready as I'll ever be to plead my case," I replied.

The day before the scheduled conference, a late spring snowstorm had deposited a sloppy eight inches of wet snow. I feared it would persist throughout the day resulting in the cancellation of the meeting. However, I was pleased to find that although the skies remained gray—no snow had fallen during the night. The streets had been cleared to allow an adequate passageway and a warm sun quickly melted the remaining snow.

Eight influential businessmen attended the meeting, which took place as scheduled. These dignified gentlemen were meticulously groomed. They wore custom-made tailored suits and sported mustaches and beards that ranged from slate gray to snow white. The future of the opera house had become a contentious matter for this group of financiers. As I stood before these unflappable men of prestige and influence, I positively shook in my boots. Interestingly enough, after much discussion and debate against my proposal, the tide gradually turned in my favor. I eventually swayed them toward favoring a complete remodeling of the opera house. I convinced them that the opera house had a bright and prosperous future; nonetheless, it all hinged on funds for the renovations. I reminded them of the immeasurable educational and cultural contributions, which were once presented at the opera house. Such offerings would again produce a cultured and literate citizenry that society required. I maintained that reviving a higher standard of living could be to our benefit. It could foster a burgeoning economy that would provide ample employment for all Chicagoans. The majority agreed with this line of thinking. After considering my reputation and honest dealings with them in the past, they voted unanimously in favor of the resolution to supply me with the requested financial backing. As was expected, it was not without constraints. They stipulated that the restorations commence without further delay and be completed as soon as possible. I gave them a tentative grand opening date of late September or early October. They were satisfied with that, and they wished me well. I was relieved. I felt I had conquered another ladder in my quest to succeed.

✳   ✳   ✳   ✳

Mid-July, 1871

The renovations begun in May were progressing quite well. The opera house was now closed to the public due to its complete remodeling. This was done so that the auditorium, mezzanine and balconies could be worked on simultaneously without obstructions or delays. Scaffolding and workhorses were everywhere. Ladders blocked the aisles as an army of tradesmen, each with their own expertise, worked feverishly toward the completion date. The blue velvet seating was replaced by red brocade and the wood trim was painted a rich cherry-mahogany hue. This same material would also be inserted within the sizeable, ornate wainscoted panel of the auditorium walls. I planned on displaying prestigious artworks on these sections. They would be flanked and illuminated by crystal and brass gaslight candelabras. The installation of plush crimson carpeting would be the finishing touch. Despite a debilitating heat wave, the cooling system kept the opera house at a comfortable temperature. After being in the cool opera house, I wasn't looking forward to stepping out into the oppressive 95-degree temperature.

"Are you still performing at the Emporium, Matilda?" I asked, standing alongside her in the grand promenade. Matilda had again accompanied me on an excursion to survey the transformation of the opera house. Her long brunette hair was gathered in a fashionable chignon and adorned with delicate rose buds. She looked fresh and lovely in a sheer, pink-pearl chiffon dress that clung provocatively to her young, shapely body. Matilda carried a wide-brimmed straw hat with matching chiffon ties in her hand, along with gloves and a small beaded bag. "Matilda, I've never actually had the pleasure of watching you perform. Would you mind if I joined the audience while you entertained?"

"Not at all, Albert,…I'd be delighted!" she exclaimed, taking my arm as we descended the steps in front of the opera house. "And, yes I'm still there and I certainly wouldn't mind you being in the audience. It's been so terribly hot lately…I've actually had the piano moved out onto the patio," she went on. "There's an occasional, refreshing evening breeze out there. The restaurant tables have also been set outside and enclosed under a screened canopy. Do come, Albert! I certainly hope I live up to your expectations," she said with a sweet smile. "Now that I'm no longer working at the opera house because of its closure, it seems we just don't get to see much of each other these days…I miss that!"

"I also miss seeing you, Matilda. That's why I'd like to visit you at your place of employment some evening," I said, helping her into the waiting carriage. "Thank you for your company today. Your opinions and suggestions mean a great deal to me. I value your excellent taste and exceptional insight. You're such a gifted woman, Matilda,…so worldly and wise beyond your years. I'll drop you off at your hotel," I added. "Josiah and Ruth are expecting me for supper this evening. Before I leave you, I'd like to ask you to join me at the Sherman House this Monday. Weather permitting…we'll dine outside on the terrace. I'll send my carriage to pick you up if you choose to come. Am I correct in assuming that you're free that evening?"

"Yes I am, Albert. The restaurant's closed on Mondays," she replied as she stepped down from the carriage and headed up the walk in front of her hotel. The Emporium where she worked was just around the corner from her apartment. "I'd love to join you! I'll look forward to seeing you…Can I bring anything with me?" she called back.

"No,…Matilda, just yourself," I shouted as I watched her poised, agile figure strut through the hotel lobby.

A week later, I made it a priority to dine at the Emporium. I thoroughly enjoyed the musical diversion that Matilda provided the patrons. She was an vivacious and exceptionally talented entertainer who was very well received.

*   *   *   *

Late-September, 1871

The dry, moisture-less heat of summer had continued into fall. The Midwest was experiencing a drought of unprecedented proportions. So little rain had fallen in Illinois and our neighboring states that a permanent cloud of dark smoke emanating from forest and prairie fires hung forebodingly over Chicago. Distress signals, alarms and fire bells rang out from every corner of the city. Newspapers warned that the weeks of drought, rising temperatures, decreased nighttime humidity and increasing winds made for a critical situation. According to the journalists there was a high risk that the fires would spread. They wrote that Chicago was in grave danger and doomed to experience a catastrophe. I judged the public was being misinformed. I felt that the tabloids were creating a false impression and that their calamitous reports were premature and misleading. They claimed that the makeshift homes of the impoverished immigrants dwelling on the city's outskirts would ignite like paper. Even though conditions were steadily worsening, no one paid much attention to the admonition—relegating it to typical newspaper sensationalism.

"Albert, I think that as long as you're renovating the opera house it might be prudent to remove the wooden shingles on its roof and replace them with sheet metal," Uranus suggested. Uranus had been here for just a few days when I gave him a tour of the nearly completed renovations. We were inspecting the on-going revitalization of the opera house. I promised the mortgagers I would pursue a higher caliber of musicians and performing artists such as the ballet, concerts and symphonies and would also arrange for German, Italian and French opera. I needed to put forward an impressive schedule of events if I were to remain in good stead with the investors. Unfamiliar with these superior productions, I found I was at a loss when it came to selecting the most prestigious among them. This was Uranus' expertise. He had quietly returned to Chicago unnoticed after I had sent for him. Uranus believed the time was right for his reappearance at the opera house and was delighted to accommodate my request. With a swagger supported by his refined skill—he was a man on a mission.

"Do you realize what the cost of exchanging the wood shingles for metal sheeting would be?" I asked, taking a look at the original plans of the roofing. "It's astronomical! Besides, I've just enough money to repair the interior let alone the roof! Trying to extract more capital from that bunch of misers would be like pulling teeth. The roof is in good condition. I'm afraid…it'll have to do. I doubt it actually needs a metal roof, anyway."

"Well, Albert, maybe you're right. It's just that I'm concerned for the opera house in case of fire," Uranus replied, pointing to the lofty ceiling of the auditorium. "The sprinkling system should keep the interior intact,…however, the sprinklers above the ceiling may be damaged if flames engulf the roof."

"I guess we'll have to take our chances and hope for the best," I said, rolling up the plans and securing them with a thin roping. "I'm confident this structure is built to withstand any kind of onslaught wrought by nature."

"I want you to know that I've already taken the initiative and publicized the artists for our grand reopening on October 9th," Uranus announced enthusiastically. "A large, one-page advertisement promoting the ten-day concert tour of the Theodore Thomas Symphony Orchestra will appear in the *Times* and *Tribune* tomorrow. I expect there'll be a run on tickets,…so be prepared! I'll pick them up from the printer this afternoon."

"Fine,…I'll alert Matilda. She'll take care of selling them from the front office," I replied as I replaced a painter's cloth that had fallen off of a row of seats. "I'm arranging a grand reopening celebration on the evening of the 8th. Matilda has taken care of the "By Invitation Only" guest list for me. Everyone I could think of is invited: newspaper reporters, politicians, bankers, business owners and prominent citizens. Of course, Kingsley's will be the caterer. I intend to give the visitors a grand tour of the newly remodeled opera house. I'm sure they'll be awed by all the embellishments."

"You should be proud of what you've accomplished here, Albert," Uranus admitted as he meandered toward the front of the grand promenade. "I'm delighted that the opera house will again become a beacon for cultured interests. I trust it'll stay that way. I know you felt a need to augment the box office receipts, but your choice of bawdy entertainment is precisely the reason this costly and extensive overhaul is now necessary. Your offering of one lowbrow performance after another attracted a vulgar class of people who cared little for the premises. Their muddy, manure-covered shoes, dirty clothing and disgusting habits of smoking, chewing and spitting tobacco certainly hastened the downfall of this once pristine palace. I hope you understand that while you had a full house,…you really didn't profit from that slovenly, indifferent crowd. Without intending to do so,…you alienated the nobility of this city. Maybe you've learned your lesson, Albert…I certainly hope so! From now on, if you have the best interests of the opera house in mind, you'll give me full rein to choose what I believe will attract only the most elite citizenry.

"There will definitely be some obvious changes beginning with the grand reopening performance," I said, thumbing through a stack of signs. "As you can see, I've already given that a lot of thought. These "no smoking" signs will be posted in the lobby. I've converted part of the men's restroom into an antechamber with sofas and standing ashtrays. That'll be the only place where smoking is allowed. Spittoons have also been strategically placed in every aisle. I also intend to have staff members handle the coat closets. Ushers on duty will see to it the patrons' shoes are clean before they're allowed into the auditorium. As these signs point out, anyone seen abusing these regulations will be politely escorted out the door. I don't believe…I'll have a problem."

"Every performance of the Theodore Thomas Symphony Orchestra has sold out!" Uranus exclaimed, much to my delight. "His orchestral concerts were a sensation across the world. This reopening night extravaganza will be enriching and an uplifting influence on an appreciative, intellectual Chicago audience."

*   *   *   *

Early-October, 1871

Gale winds greeted me as I stepped down from my carriage. I clutched my top hat tightly, while trying to avoid the flying debris in the dust devils that swirled around me.

"We've had such a drought! We need a drenching rain to alleviate this tinder-box situation," I concluded as I looked up and ascended the stone steps that led to the opera house. Its Italian facade and mansard roof loomed majestically before me. I glanced at the notices that advertised Monday evening's upcoming special attraction. They were positioned on the right and left-hand entrances to the grand promenade. The smell of smoke permeated the air and a murky haze greeted me as I entered the opera house. I dismissed both as merely annoying.

I had a four o'clock appointment with Melville Stone who was the owner of the Stone Foundry. He had agreed to loan me an extra thousand chairs for the overflow crowd. Although Melville was an amiable yet astute businessman, he had a gruff appearance and was well known for using what we Cape Codders call "salty language." His long, well-manicured handlebar mustache was his pride and joy. He had a rather chubby, round face with a double chin and bulging bug eyes. I likened his spherical shape to that of a walking rain barrel.

George Upton, the music critic for the Chicago *Tribune*, would also be there. He was a tall, lanky fellow with bushy, ginger-colored hair and matching eyebrows, beard and mustache. His assignment was to review the renovations and the orchestral rehearsal.

"I'll take just one final tour of the Crosby Opera House," I decided as I wandered proudly through the grand promenade. I could have entered through the side door, but I wanted to experience the full impact of the extensive remodeling. Specifically designed to draw affluent audiences, it would be the spectacular lobby that would make the first impression. After a short stroll through the art gallery that hadn't required renovation, I ascended the mahogany staircase. The plush scarlet runner was striking. All the carpeting and matching upholstery had been made to order in France.

"Yes, by golly!…It's as wondrously grand and elegant as I imagined. Indeed, it's fit for royalty!" I exclaimed, grinning from ear to ear and exceptionally pleased with the finished product. "I must view the stage and the whole theater from the mezzanine."

The crystals, like sparkling diamonds, encircled the brass chandeliers and cast their shimmering light on the intricately sculptured walls and ceiling. Exhausted from a long day's work, I chose a front-row seat in the balcony to the right of the stage. I sank comfortably in a plush Queen Anne chaise lounge that was decidedly restful. I was overwhelmed by the panoramic view.

"While the renovations closed the opera house over the past two seasons, and the costs soared way beyond the initial $100,000,…it's a successful endeavor worthy of the delay and expense," I rationalized as I sat back and rested my head for a few seconds.

A panoramic outdoors scene that was colorfully painted on a mammoth canvas, slowly ascended to the rafters. Next, scarlet velvet drapes parted to reveal yet another set of brocade draperies that hung in graceful folds. The crimson material matched the upholstered theater seats. They were pulled back to expose the Theodore Thomas Symphony Orchestra behind a final curtain. The musicians were all seated in place and could be seen through its sheer, delicate creases. When this curtain was raised the renowned orchestra, whose reputation had packed the house, was ready to perform. The opening day audience clapped in ecstatic anticipation. An overflow crowd of 2,500 filled every permanent seat, plus several hundred extra chairs. The flawless performance of Beethoven, Mozart and Strauss was inspired. The acoustics magnified the dulcet notes of this music throughout the theater, catching every gradation of sound and tone. The blaring pitch of the brass section was pleasingly diminished. Every nuance was clear and sharp. "Yes!…Perfect!…Superb!" I exclaimed as the audience gave the orchestra a fourth standing ovation. I sensed their enthusiastic applause was not only an appreciative expression of this splendid orchestra, but also a fitting tribute to the most magnificent opera house in North America.

I felt a forceful tap on my right shoulder and instantly opened my eyes. The scenic canvas was still in place. The booming voice of Melville Stone, who was bending over me, echoed through the auditorium and shattered the sudden silence.

"Sleeping on the job, eh! Well, I'm sorry to have to wake you, Albert," he said half-heartily, "however, I know you'd like to get this shit over with as soon as possible."

"Whoa!" I exclaimed drowsily and cringing at his vulgarity. I jumped up and turned toward him while still trying to open and focus my eyes.

"I need to know where you want me to set up all those goddamn folding chairs you requested from my foundry," he went on. "I've been told you want them in place by Monday evening…I'll meet you on the stage."

"Yes! Oh, yes! Thank you, Melville. I'm sorry,…it's been a long day," I replied, shaking my head to awaken myself. "I became so relaxed sitting here, I must've fallen asleep. The orchestra will be rehearsing early Monday afternoon. The chairs must be in place by that time. You should deliver them here no later than Monday morning."

The next day the courthouse bell tolled continually, summoning every available volunteer to help extinguish a fire that had spread from a paper factory to several adjacent blocks of manufacturing buildings. Chicago's strong winds, an integral part of life in this city, became arsonist and predator. This culprit carried within its hot breath the sparks that ignited its targets, enveloped them with all-consuming flames, destroyed them, and then moved on. As predicted many of the temporary dwellings erected for sheltering the indigent were engulfed in flames, as were many suburban residences.

"The hotel is directly in the fire's path. I believe we should move our belongings from the Sherman House to the opera house," Uranus suggested when it was apparent the hotel was in imminent danger. "I've already packed a valise. I'll wait for you to do the same. The carriage is at the entrance of the lobby waiting for us, and so is,…Matilda. I had the driver picked her up at her hotel. I knew you'd be concerned about her safety so I sent our coach to fetch her."

"Yes, I think you're right,…we should leave here immediately. Thank you, for thinking about Matilda and taking the initiative. We'll need to return to the opera house this evening for the reception, anyway. This is as good a time as any," I replied, swiftly gathering my clothing and tossing it into a carpetbag.

"When you left Chicago I was so infuriated with you, I never expected to forgive your deceit,…let alone be beholden to you!" I added. "It took a while for me to realize that you were a desperate man facing insolvency. Regardless of being disappointed with you at the time, I always admired your sophistication and subtle aura," I said while locking the door to my room. "In spite of everything, I *have* forgiven you,…primarily because I'm still quite fond of you, dear cousin."

"I've found it difficult to live with myself since that awful day when I chose to betray you and the citizens of Chicago," Uranus said remorsefully as he grasped his valise and followed me down the hallway with his head and eyes lowered. "I was especially ashamed of my criminal wrongdoings,…it was bound to reflect on you and imply that you were involved. I failed you and as a result of my actions,...your integrity was severely damaged. You've always been an honest man, Albert. I hope to spend the rest of my life making it up to you."

"You needn't apologize further. All I can say is that you should consider yourself fortunate not to have been hanged or indefinitely incarcerated," I said, descending the stairway to the lobby. "As far as I'm concerned,...it's a closed subject."

The carriage wound its way through a dense haze. The atmosphere was one of apprehension. I could tell that Uranus was worried about the opera house. I assured him that the advancing flames would not be a threat to it and that the building would most likely be all right. Matilda thanked us both for thinking about her during this trying time.

We arrived at the opera house to find it basking in its newfound glory. Large banners blowing in the wind advertised the upcoming reopening. They hung down from the third story to just above the grand promenade entrance. Within a few hours, strategically placed gas spotlights would showcase and illuminate the whole façade.

Despite their angst over the precarious conditions outside, the invited guests arrived for the reception. They were awed by the spectacular transformation. The monstrous auditorium, which was once a seedy, burlesque theater in the past, was now a dazzling, majestic opera house—its ambiance even more splendid than it was when it first opened. It was a memorable occasion for me.

"Uranus and I are getting together after the reception. You're welcome to join us at Kingsley's for a few drinks," I said, addressing Samuel and his wife at the reception. Matilda and one of Uranus' women friends will accompany us there. The evening's still young and we're in celebratory mood. Would you like to join us?"

"That sounds like a great idea," he replied. "We'll definitely be there!"

We toasted our triumphant reopening festivity. A renaissance of sorts had been introduced to Chicago. Our party, which was basking in the glory of the new Crosby Opera house, had a pleasurable evening. As we were preparing to leave Kingsley's, some patrons at the next table told us that the fire had spread to the western part of the city. They claimed that while the river area was threatened, it looked as though the business district would be spared. We were relieved to hear that. The alarm bells rang incessantly throughout the evening. It was around nine when we left the restaurant.

"Oh, my!...Look at that fiery western sky!" Matilda exclaimed as she stepped into the street outside the opera house. A curious crowd had gathered to watch the spectacle. In the distance, fountains of glittering sparks, like fireworks, filled the night sky and glowing embers churned in the hot winds hurling their fury toward a defenseless city. Confident the opera house would most certainly be spared and tired after a long day, I decided to retire for the night. I had already placed my belongings in my office and planned to sleep on the sofa. Uranus said he would join me later. The two ladies headed for the apartment in the opera house. Samuel and his wife decided to return home.

It seemed as though I had just dozed off when clamoring voices became audible from outside my emergency quarters at the opera house. A series of loud knocks soon followed.

"What's all that commotion?" I wondered as I rose from the leather sofa, reached for my shirt, quickly put it on, and then still half asleep, staggered toward the door.

"Wake up! Wake up, Albert! The opera house is doomed!" Uranus shouted with alarm.

"No,…that can't be possible! It's not happening! I must still be asleep! Yes,…wake up, Albert!" I told myself, shaking my head back and forth in a frenzied stupor. "Wake up from this hellish nightmare!" Alas, it took only a split second to realize I was conscious and standing in a smoke-filled room.

"Please hurry!…Open the door, Albert! The fire's worsening by the minute! There's black smoke everywhere!" Matilda screamed hysterically while frantically pounding on the door. I promptly unlatched and opened it. Uranus, Matilda and Samuel were standing there in wet ponchos and gesturing wildly.

"All the buildings in this block,…including the opera house are in the path of the fire-storm!" Uranus yelled, gasping and giving me a wet poncho to put over my head. "It's extremely windy out there,…the air is filled with smoke! The sky is a steamy, churning mass of ashen soot. Albert, it's so thick we can barely see through it. It's almost impossible to take a breath! The courthouse is in flames! We must try to save as many of the paintings as we can before the opera house and the art gallery also ignite. Hot embers are already falling on the roof…It won't be long before we lose them!"

"Oh, no! That can't be!" I said in disbelief, hastening to find my shoes and slipping them on untied. I passed my arms through the poncho and placed the hood over my tousled hair as we descended the smoke-filled staircase. "We can't lose the opera house. Not now!…Not after all this!" I wailed.

"I'm afraid we have no say in the matter." Samuel replied as he hurried down the stairs ahead of me. "We returned here after the Missus and I were told that our house was in one of the residential areas leveled by the flames. I left her with some neighborhood friends who were heading eastward. I came back to assess the damage to the bank. The streets are filled with people, Albert! There's confusion and panic everywhere!…Believe me the situation is chaotic!" he said panic stricken and opening the side entrance doorway.

As we entered the street, we covered our faces with scarves. The thick, black smoke stung our eyes and we gasped for breath. This choking mass of soot rose some 20,000 feet above the ground in some places. Burning rooftops belched a pungent smell of charred wood. Coal yards that had ignited earlier also produced a caustic odor. The extremely dry weather, which persisted over a long period of time and the unusually windy conditions, created the most devastating firestorm of the century. Beginning with a warehouse fire on the South Side on September 30th, followed by a planking mill that went up in flames a week later on the west end, the tinder-dry city of Chicago had become one enormous bonfire. The wind-driven fire fanned by 60 mile-an-hour gusts splintered in two directions. The firestorm started east of Dearborn Street and wiped out the northern end of the city as far as the river. Now it was headed toward Adams and Jackson Streets. The opera house at State and Washington Streets was directly in its path. The treacherous shifting winds carrying blazing bits of debris had already ignited the roof of Samuel's First National Bank.

"The fire's totally out of control!…The whole downtown's ablaze! Chicago's in jeopardy!" Matilda cried out with dread bordering on despair. She had to holler to be heard over the din of the fire bells and street noises. "Uranus and I will stay here and try to salvage the most valuable paintings and other treasures from the opera house! I'm afraid the flames will soon engulf the building!"

Before I had a chance to answer her, a large stable at one end of Washington Street burst into flames. The barn doors were opened and dozens of horses were released. They ran wild down the middle of the street. Amid the shrieks and pandemonium, the crowd scattered in every direction fearing for their lives. Suddenly, we heard a deafening explosion. The streets became darkened, deepening the atmosphere of shock and terror. Our only source of light was now an alarming sky emblazoned in vibrant shades of red and orange—highlighted by glowing sparks of swirling ashes in a turbulent wind. At irregular intervals large, torch-like flares menacingly plummeted to the ground around us. We assumed the gas plant had also become a victim of the ravenous flames.

"You'd better go immediately!" I shouted. "The sprinkling system won't be operational as it's activated by gas. Samuel and I will head for the business district near the river. We might be able to salvage some of our properties there. The distillery and the brewery are also in it's path…What time is it?" I asked Matilda.

"It's about one-thirty," she replied as she rushed up the steps to the grand promenade. "Uranus left to fetch a gallery cart so we can place the paintings on it. I'm to meet him here. I'll catch up with you later, Albert!…Good luck!"

"Do take care, Matilda! Remember nothing's worth endangering yourself or Uranus!" I called back while waving farewell. Samuel and I had already started to push our way through the hysterical crowd.

I was stunned by the loss and devastation. As we proceeded on foot toward the business district, which was next to the Chicago River, the streets were clogged with people towing their belongings. It would have been impossible to maneuver a carriage through this swarm of displaced persons and animals. The horses, alarmed by the flames and flying sparks, would have bolted in terror, anyway. All across the city, as far as the horizon and beyond, the raging inferno was relentlessly consuming everything in its path.

Tongues of flame licked at the imposing new buildings that had become the pride of Chicago. Entirely made of wood, but with facades of brick or stone, these structures were fire hazards to begin with. I tried not to dwell on the unthinkable—the demise of my prized opera house. The financial loss would be staggering. I began to focus my thoughts on how my other properties could possibly be salvaged. As we sprinted toward the brewery and distillery, I turned to Samuel.

"Many of the buildings in this block are built with bricks,…theoretically they should be fireproof," I shouted over the roaring flames and the clang of the fire engines. There's a chance we might be able to save them if we soak the rooftops with water."

In the distance, I caught a glimpse of Josiah, running toward us.

"Hurry! Come this way! Move away from the fire lines! I see a clearing in the crowd!" Josiah yelled as he was trying to reach us by weaving in and out of the horde that was blocking the street. "What a nightmare!…It's beyond comprehension! I'm so pleased to see that you and Samuel have arrived safely. I feel so helpless! There doesn't seem to be anything I can do to stop this fiery onslaught. Ruth has joined Theodore and Molly at their home. It's far enough east to be spared."

"My home's also gone, Josiah," Samuel announced dejectedly. "I'm here to see what can be done about the distillery and brewery. Maybe there's something we can do to save them."

"That's why I hurried here, also." replied Josiah. "It's a shocking scene to say the least! All these people are homeless,…hapless casualties of the fire. There's a mass exodus of families toward safer ground. Many people engulfed in flames have already lost their lives as they tried to flee…while others have been maimed or killed by collapsing buildings! It's horrible!" Josiah exclaimed, saddened and terrified. "These refugees have been forced out of their homes. They've had to abandon them to the unrelenting blaze. As you can see,…most are women and children. Their men are vigorously pouring water from storage tanks over the roofs of the remaining buildings. They're attempting to douse the sparks that would eventually ignite these structures. Others are turning water hoses on the outside walls of the insurance and mercantile buildings. I've heard their efforts were futile,…the buildings are a total loss."

As he spoke, I looked around and discovered that firefighters on the few remaining fire engines were incapable of functioning. Exhausted from having to fight the stubborn onslaught and intensifying flames since early Saturday, the volunteer firemen were totally unfit for duty. It was a sorry sight. Without hesitation I took the initiative and stood in the middle of the street.

"All you people out there! Get busy! Pitch in and help! Grab all those abandoned buckets and form a line along the street down to the river," I shouted at the top of my lungs. The crowd was traumatized—everyone was standing around in a catatonic state. They remained at the street intersections passively watching the advancing firestorm. I took command and began to organize a bucket brigade. "Stand just a few feet apart from each other," I ordered loudly, straining to speak over the din. "If we're able to keep the bricks and roof wet,…there's a good chance we can save these buildings! If we do, you're all welcome to move your belongings in them and stay there until you can find better lodgings!" I yelled with unhesitating authority while gesturing in all directions, much like an auctioneer at a public sale. Time was of the essence. Charred, coal-like embers had already begun to ignite the rooftops of the distillery. It would take an effort of enormous proportions to defeat this fiery assault. Fortunately, it hadn't yet reached the brewery.

Before long the flames began to consume the interiors of the distillery. I quickly realized that trying to salvage it would be a losing battle. The heat was so intense that it twisted girders as easily as a hickey bends pipe. A bank suffered this same fate along with all the other commercial businesses in this block. The veracious fire leveled all of them. I turned to a downhearted Samuel who was feeling defeated and resigned. He felt it was an act of God—a punishment for his single-minded pursuit of wealth.

"Snap out of it, Samuel!" I yelled, shaking him out of his doldrums of self-pity. I was determined to fight back and needed him to help me. "Somehow we'll lick this thing! We'll survive this horror! We need to pray the wind will dissipate and not jump to the brewery. If the roof and exterior walls of the brewery can be kept intact, it could be salvageable. We could be back in business within a week. We must hurry!" I reached for an abandoned pail and shouted, "Here, take hold of this bucket and come with me. If we work together, it can be done!"

With that one goal in mind, I began drawing water from the river, filling every pail that was hopelessly discarded by its owner. I passed one along to Samuel who passed it to the next person along the bucket brigade. Josiah, who was already there, took over for me as I ran ahead. I removed a ladder from an abandoned fire engine and leaned it against one of the buildings. When the first full bucket arrived, I grasp it, ascended the ladder until I reached the top, and then hastily emptied the pail. I splashed its contents on the rooftop and down the sides of the building. I repeated this process every time a bucket was hoisted up to me. At first, I lifted them as if they were empty. Somehow I had tapped into a hidden reserve of strength and endurance. My steadfast objective to save the brewery, exploded into raw energy—my vigor seemed limitless. Like the alewives of the herring run, I steadfastly battled the flames with drive and seemingly little effort. I inched the ladder forward, hurling the water against the blackened, steaming bricks of the third story.

Regrettably, my initial surge of energy began to fade before my mission was completed. I was slowly tiring. My arms felt like they were being pulled from their sockets. Two thirds of the way, I switched from my right arm to my left as I reached for the buckets. The pain in my shoulders was excruciating. My wrists, which were strained from the twisting and heaving of each weighty pail, ached and throbbed. Blood from my blistered hands mixed with the water in the buckets and every finger remained bent in a claw-like grip. "Will I *ever* be able to straighten them out again?" I moaned while reaching backwards for another full bucket. "I must maintain this pace or all will be lost." Intermittent, sharp and painful spasms stabbed the overworked muscles of my back. "I must find the stamina to finish…just a bit further," I kept repeating to myself. My legs were cramping as I wearily climbed each rung of the ladder. By this time, Josiah had joined me at the bottom of the ladder and offered to relieve me.

"Josiah," I shouted, looking down at him, "as soon as I finish soaking this rooftop and these bricks, I'll continue at ground level! With help from the fire brigade we should be able to reclaim a good portion of the brick exteriors…Only a few more buckets to go!" Finally, I descended the ladder for the last time. After working feverishly for several hours, exhaustion had finally set in. My lungs were filled with searing ash and soot causing me to cough profusely. The queue leading to the river's edge had thinned considerably. I was distraught over the gaping spaces left unattended by the volunteers who had eventually tired and dropped out of sight. I'm sure they left their stations assuming their attempt to stem the onslaught of the flames was hopeless. "We must double our efforts! Quickly now, close ranks! Let the older children help!" I hollered, prodding into action those who had persevered. "You adults,…this is a critical! Pick up the abandoned pails and splash the water against the second stories! Children drench the lower levels! We mustn't surrender these valuable properties to the flames! Just a little longer now! Please stay put! The firestorm is progressively moving away from this block!"

The fire hazard had greatly diminished—the wind gusts seemed to be abating. Due to our persistence, we triumphed and won a decisive battle against a brutal force of nature. Motivated by a sudden burst of civic pride, the pace quickened and the task was promptly completed. "Because of your perseverance,…we've survived this disaster and have accomplished a nearly impossible feat! This is a testament to your labors! I couldn't have done it without you!" I announced loudly over the ecstatic uproar of an applauding crowd. Hundreds had gathered in the square to lend a hand and witness our battle. As the empty buckets were finally deposited on the cobblestone street, the bystanders hailed our success with raucous cheers.

"Hurrah! Bravo! Hurrah for Albert Crosby!…Long live, Albert Crosby!" shouted the volunteers who had now become unsung heroes and impromptu champions. As Josiah and Samuel approached me, they were still cheering and applauding wildly. Samuel placed his hand on my shoulder.

"I must say, Albert, because of your tenacity and cool head you almost single-handedly saved the Downer and Bemis Brewery from being consumed by a fire that leveled nearly all of Chicago," he said appreciatively. "You should be quite proud of yourself for being so courageous and composed in the face of calamity. I'll never forget that! Your grit and intestinal fortitude continue to amaze me. Go along now, Albert, and get those hands bandaged! You've done enough for one day. I'll stay here to guard the safe until the constable arrives. Let's hope its contents are intact."

"Yes, Samuel, as a matter of fact,…I'm extremely tired, but the effort was unquestionably worthwhile," I replied, visualizing the rebirth of our financial district and the city of Chicago. "Roll up your sleeves, Josiah! Even though the distillery's gone we'll start removing the rubble and rebuild again. We *will* recover! This will become the core of our *new* financial district.

After a hellish night, it was the dawn of a new day. The destructive winds had finally relinquished their hold on Chicago. Like the wildfire, word spread that the brewery was still standing and was no longer in danger. The plant workforce and their families had already brought in blankets, pillows and food from their nearby homes, which were destroyed by the flames. They kindly shared their meager belongings with us. Despite being worried about Matilda and Uranus, we moved into the offices and prepared to rest for a while.

Josiah, who was still outdoors surveying the damage to his distillery when we entered the brewery, came rushing in. "I've just received word that Uranus and Matilda are on their way here! They're pulling a large wooden cart toward the brewery!" he exclaimed, animated and out of breath.

"Sit, Josiah!" I said, pulling up a chair for him. "Why, that's great news! Here, I've poured some hot coffee for you…Relax! You need to compose yourself. You've had enough excitement for one day. We're all safe and sound and that's all that matters right now." I turned to address Samuel.

"Samuel, since the brewery horses have been spared, I'll hitch them up to a wagon and meet Matilda and Uranus before they go any further. I'll help them transport the paintings back here," I said, dashing out the door. After summoning several workmen to join me, we were soon on our way. The brewery wagon managed to make its way through the crowded roadway. People were covered by a charcoal, powdery dust and in a state of shock. While pushing their belongings through the streets in all sorts of handcarts, wagons or baby carriages, they moved forward with expressionless faces and blank stares. Families carried their children and pulled anything that had wheels, behind them.

"There they are! I see them. Stay right here! I'll help them reach the wagon," I yelled, jumping down from the buckboard and running toward Uranus and Matilda. I was so overjoyed by the sight of them.

I began furiously waving my arms until they could see me bobbing up and down on the crowded street. While it was only a distance of several hundred yards, it seemed so much longer as I ran toward them. This calamity had made me realize how much Uranus and Matilda meant to me—especially Matilda. I was so relieved to see them both. We affectionately embraced, took one look at each other, and then began to laugh uncontrollably. It was such a joyous reunion! My heart warmed at Matilda's infectious laughter. We were covered with a combination of soot and ashes. Our faces were dirty beyond recognition and our hair was matted flat. Once he was made aware of it, Uranus was appalled by his appearance.

"Oh, Albert! It's so wonderful to see you!…Is everyone all right?" Matilda asked, wiping her hands on what was once a lovely, turquoise satin gown especially designed for the reopening reception. It was now pinned up high just below her waist. "You're still soaking wet, Albert!" she said with compassion. I had been so pre-occupied with my efforts to save the brewery, I hadn't noticed that my clothing was drenched. "It's a good thing we brought along your carpetbag. Uranus snatched it along with his valise as we left the opera house. Why, you'll catch your death!"

"I've got a brewery wagon waiting for us just down the road," I announced, confident that after pulling a heavy cart across the city, it would be music to their ears. "I'll help you with this, Uranus. Matilda, just walk beside me."

"But your hands are all bandaged. I should pull the cart, not you, Albert. How did you hurt them?" she asked while sympathetically placing her hand over mine.

"They'll heal quickly. They're not bothering me right now," I said assuredly, helping as best I could to carry the cart forward with Uranus. "We're almost there. I think you can catch a glimpse of the buckboard from here." We unloaded the contents of the cart into the wagon, jumped into the rear, and then surrounded by our precious cargo, we were soon on our way.

"We heard the brewery had survived the fury of the fire. That's the reason Matilda and I headed this way," Uranus said, trying to brush away some of the soot from his clothing. "At least our prized collectibles and artworks can be stored there until a safer place can be found. I'm afraid that along with the opera house, Samuel's First National Bank Building is also a total loss…I guess he rather suspected that." Business owners huddled together like members of a large extended family consoling one another after being burned out of their offices and shops. It was shocking to see the tragic results of such a horrendous and destructive power.

"So tell me, Matilda, what happened after I left the two of you?" I asked, handing her and Uranus a warm blanket. I began to feel chilled, so I also wrapped myself in one. I had come prepared. The temperature was now more seasonal and just in case some quilts might be needed, I had decided to toss them into the rear of the wagon.

"As soon as you and Samuel were on your way here, Uranus and I managed to stack most of your paintings on the gallery handcart," she replied, shivering as she huddled under her blanket. "We covered them with some of the brocade drapes we salvaged, and then hung your bags on the handles," Matilda went on, relating in stunning and frightening detail the events prior to their arrival. "Unfortunately, once we were out on the street, ruthless and intimidating people accosted us. It was revolting! I'm ashamed to say that the general public displayed an astonishing indifference and cruelty when compassion and kindness should have prevailed. When they dared to lift the cover on the handcart and tried to steal the paintings from us, Uranus and I shoved them out of the way. We felt like we were adrift in a sea of incivility. From that point on, we kept a close watch over our precious cargo. Uranus paid a hefty price to an elderly man with a horse-driven farm cart so we could transport our treasures out of harm's way. After the transfer we carefully covered them again with the torn drapery material. We were especially careful with your most prized painting, *Looking Down Yosemite Valley, California.* The terrified horse refused to budge, so we unhitched him and began to pull the farm cart ourselves. Uranus enlisted the help of some young boys. After offering each of them a few dollars, we moved on."

"Where did you go from there? How did you decide what direction to take?" I asked, bewildered and shaking my head.

"We were told to head for Wabash Avenue because the fire hadn't reached there as yet. People said that it might completely escape the fury of the raging firestorm," Matilda continued breathlessly. "We entered Wabash Avenue about three-thirty in the morning. There was total mayhem as a blizzard of hot embers surrounded us. People cowered in terror as the explosive sounds of the growling, hungry flames consumed the buildings all around them. A monstrous ball of fire rolled from block to block burning everything in its path,…right down to the foundations. It was unbelievable! The sound of buildings crumbling amid the shrieks and wailing of a panicked crowd was horrifying. Death and destruction were all around us! I really thought it was the end of the world! The clanging gongs of the fire engines, the braying horses, the tolling church bells and the moaning foghorns echoing from the river, all added to the chaos. From where we were standing, an alarming scarlet sky indicated that the flames had consumed Dearborn Street and the opera house. Like hurling comets, a hail of fire ignited the roof then traveled down from the ceilings to the walls. The banners advertising the Theodore Thomas Concert caught fire. Flames shot up three stories high and ignited everything behind them. That's when the hot winds also caused the demise of Samuel's bank. The façade of the opera house collapsed inward around four-thirty this morning. The St. James Hotel went down at that time as well.

"We thought that only the western part of the city was aflame and that the fire was headed in a northern direction. By the time we reached Wabash Avenue we found gridlock, confusion and turmoil everywhere. Abandoned goods and people still in sleepwear sat atop whatever they could salvage. They occupied every bit of space on the roadway. The number of people in exile grew by the minute as residents from the west and southwestern parts of the city abandoned their homes. Elongated tongues of flames licked and devoured the buildings on both sides of the street. The fire, which was carried by hurricane force winds, soon enveloped us. The frightened crowd screeched in horror, left everything behind, and then began to run eastward. It became obvious that everyone would have to leave

Wabash Avenue in a hurry and find safer ground. I decided that I needed to run faster and maneuver more easily, so I removed my petticoats and corset. I dropped them to the ground, twisted my dress up to my waist, and then pinned it there. Besides,…airborne sparks had already burned several holes in it. Uranus and I continued to pull the farm cart toward the Chicago River through a sea of people. By seven in the morning the massive flames had engulfed both sides of Wabash Avenue. That's when Uranus and I arrived here."

The paintings were placed in a storage area of the brewery where they'd be protected until a more appropriate place could be found for them. All of us slept most of that day, which was Monday, only to awake on Tuesday to find a smoldering desert-like landscape.

Where once stood the proud city of Chicago, basking in its transformation from an untamed frontier city to one of splendor and respectability, there was nothing but miles of desolateness. As the sun rose on the horizon—only a few chimneys, several brick fireplaces and partial walls were all that remained. A barren, smoldering landscape—testimony to the scope and scale of this unbelievable disaster, stretched out for miles in every direction. It was devoid of trees, grass or bushes. Nothing was left—only vast, ghostly acres of scorched shells that stood amid a smarting haze of gray smoke. Due to the low visibility from the smoldering ashes in the air, we were unable to discern where the opera house had once stood. Uranus, Samuel, Matilda and I were alone as we looked over this ravaged scene. We gaped at our surroundings through a veil of vapors curling up from the debris on the ground. The landscape was littered with mounds of rubble, charred shingles, wood, brick and granite steps that led nowhere. The echo of a barking dog broke the unnatural silence. A lone soldier on duty from General Sherman's battalion stood guard over the devastation. The troops were summoned to prevent sightseers and looting. The slow, steady peal of mournful bells in distant church towers rang out across the land proclaiming the death of a city.

Numbed by the events of the last few days, I kept repeating, "I can't believe this! It can't be! Why has this happened to me?…How will I ever recover from this disaster?" My heart sank at the thought of the enormous financial loss I had incurred. We lingered stunned and motionless in the midst of the incinerated remains of the opera house. I bemoaned the fact that before its destruction only a handful of people had been fortunate enough to see it in its newly renovated glory. I heaved a deep sigh and tried to hold back the tears. I was wallowing in my own self-pity when I noticed Uranus who was shaken and distraught. He sat on the granite steps covering his face with his hands, his elbows resting on his knees.

I walked over to him and touched his bent figure that was swaying back and forth, and then sat down next to him.

"This was the crowning achievement of my life," Uranus wailed, chagrined and inconsolable as he placed his head on my chest. This calamity has abruptly ended a cultural revival. My vision of furthering an appreciation of the arts in Chicago has vanished. The opera house is nothing but a crumbled pile of rubble and debris. I've sacrificed my honor and devoted half of my life to this cause and now,…it's over. I refuse to remain here any longer. I'm leaving for New York as soon as I can. I've decided to pick up where I left off before you summoned me here,"

"Well, I plan to keep the brewery in operation," I said. "Chicagoans are a thirsty lot. They'll want to drown their sorrows with a brew or two. Sadly,…but fortunately for me, most of the other breweries are gone. You know, Uranus, there's a possibility I just might be able to recoup some of my losses," I added, contemplating the ever-changing joys and heartaches of life as I forcibly led Uranus away from the ruins.

The human toll of the fire was immeasurable. Rebuilding the economic, social and cultural life of Chicago would call for strength, sacrifice and courage. I had sustained a loss of nearly a $1,500,000. It was the largest capital loss incurred by anyone in Chicago—a sobering fact. Nevertheless, instead of crushing my spirit it motivated me to forge ahead and rebuild my financial empire. Great tragedies can change one's priorities and goals dramatically. Even though I was distressed over the destruction of the newly renovated Crosby Opera House and knew that it would be sorely missed, I decided against rebuilding it. Instead, I would definitely focus my energies on the restoration of the brewery.

The Chicago Fire was a turning point in my life. After moving into a furnished room on Calumet Avenue, I began the process of restoring water to the brewery. My first objective was to construct a pipeline that would deliver water from Lake Michigan to the brewery. Within three days, the Downer and Beamer Brewery was operational—the only Chicago brewery to be functioning at the time. Along with a lack of gas, the fire had destroyed most water systems in Chicago. Water wagons lined up for miles at our pipeline where my employees dispensed a never-ending supply of water—free of charge.

In the midst of this convulsive world, the reconstruction process began without delay. The Chicago Fire would be remembered as a moment when the collective will triumphed over misfortune. A cohesive effort of men, money and supplies poured in from every state in the union. Confident in a new beginning—anxiety was replaced by hope. In the face of adversity it prevailed, staring fearlessly into the daunting abyss of the future. Chicagoans foresaw the manifest destiny of their once magnificent city rise from its ashes. They resuscitated its heart—it was resurrected—and soared majestically. After an uphill struggle, a motivated citizenry exemplified an indomitable spirit to achieve its vision of a new and revitalized city of Chicago.

▼

Early - January, 1872

The Downer & Bemis Brewery was up and running again, just three weeks after the fire. As anticipated the sales of beer soared. The brewery was operational around the clock. Many of the employees who were hired were jobless after the great fire and content to work regardless of any inconvenience to them. After having recovered the contents of the safe from his former bank, Samuel continued to operate his banking business in a reclaimed building on the same block as the brewery.

Slowly but surely, I was beginning to recover my financial footing. In due course I decided to rebuild the distillery, but blizzard conditions and one snowstorm after another hampered its reconstruction. I never realized how harsh the winters could be in the Midwest until I had lived here a few years. From the time I decided to migrate to the Plains States, every succeeding winter had become more frigid and with a heavier accumulation of drifting snow than the previous one. Due to the howling winds, the ordeal of waiting for a carriage on the streets of Chicago in January was intolerable. In comparison, the winter seasons on the Lower Cape were positively balmy.

"I'm considering selling the distillery, Samuel, once it's built and operational," I said as our carriage left the brewery. He and his Missus were also staying in the rooming house on Calumet Avenue until their new home was ready for occupancy. "I'm sure to realize a sizable profit from the sale. I plan to use that money to wipe out the mortgage on the opera house. I've already given the bankers half of what's owed them. I hope to erase the balance and still have enough to reimburse Josiah for the amount he invested in his lost business venture. I won't attempt to sell it until it's fully functional."

"I always knew you'd find a way," said Samuel, looking out the window at the falling snow and turning to face me. "Your resilience is astonishing, Albert! Again,…you're one step ahead of me. I'd given that some thought, but decided it wasn't my place to approach you about it. I wondered how you intended to pay the mortgage, let alone the renovation loan on the opera house. You should be able to get top price for the distillery. My fellow financiers will be relieved to know you plan to repay your debt in the near future. They never doubted that you'd eventually do so, but they never guessed it would happen this soon," he went on. They'll be pleased to know their confidence in you hasn't been misplaced. You're an honest man, Albert. Like many other business owners who lost everything in the Chicago Fire, you could have left them with a tremendous deficit."

"Among other things, I've also decided to return to Brewster for a six weeks vacation, Samuel," I said as I handed him a lit cigar while enjoying mine. "First, I'd like to visit aging parents while they're still in good health, and all my other family members.

Secondly, I need to make a decision about my relationship with Margaret. I intend to confront her about our lengthy separation. I'll be leaving in a few weeks and plan to stay until the end of February while the distillery is being rebuilt. Josiah will oversee the construction and also the installation of the new machinery. If possible, I'd like you to be in charge of the brewery in my absence. Matilda will be here to assist you with the paperwork. She's very obliging and capable." I went on. Now that the opera house was gone, Matilda had taken over the bookkeeping chores for me at the brewery.

"I plan to visit West Roxbury on my return trip to Chicago. It's been several years since I've seen or heard from Margaret. I'd like to see my children,…although they probably won't recognize me or even remember who I am. I'm married in name only, Samuel. Perhaps I shouldn't concern you with my personal problems, but I feel it's time you knew exactly what's been transpiring all these years. Margaret's a changed person,…not at all the woman I loved and married so long ago. The last few times I saw Margaret she was cold and unresponsive. Her kisses were icy and her smile, forced. She had forgotten the words "I love you" and cared little about the memories we shared as husband and wife. As far as Margaret was concerned there would be no more lovemaking. This had been going on for many years, even before I left permanently. That was when she took off her wedding ring and threw it at me. 'Leave, Albert! I'm tired of your long absences and your womanizing!' she shrieked like a mad woman. 'Go now! All your belongings are packed in a trunk! Take them with you! Leave and never return here again!' It was a dreadful scene. I haven't seen or heard from her since. I need to know what she intends to do about this non-existent marriage of ours. I just can't go on this way. I'm at the end of my rope. I think you know what I mean,…don't you, Samuel?"

"Frankly, I don't how you've managed to live like a bachelor for all these years," he replied as we approached the rooming house. He doused his cigar, put on his gloves, and then prepared to leave the carriage. "Your relations with prominent women in your proscenium box are common knowledge,…though, I know you were only being cordial to them and their agents. While these occasions have received a lot of adverse publicity, as far as I'm concerned you've always remained true to your marriage. The Missus and I have always held Margaret in the highest esteem, but I understand your dilemma. I hope your visit to Wildwood will be a fruitful one. I agree…It's time for you to finally resolve the situation you're in and find an answer to your future. I'll do my best to take care of things on this end."

*   *   *   *

Late-January, 1872

Illumined by the lantern outside my office window, a mystic flurry of snow fell silently like an astral shower hurling earthward across a darkened sky. I sat at my desk completing some pressing last-minute paperwork before my trip east. It seemed like ages since I visited Brewster and the Crosby homestead. As cottony clumps accumulated along the windowpane my thoughts turned to Wildwood. My body yearned for the closeness of a woman. While my heart longed for Matilda—my spirit harkened back to Margaret and the children. It was becoming impossible for me to exist in this hellish netherworld of unrequited love and desire. I had endured the torment of suppressing these yearnings for the last twenty-four years—a painful past that blurred into nothingness. After extensive soul-searching, I found it necessary to assume control over my fate. The time to bring body, heart and spirit together in absolute harmony was *long* overdue.

Though I wrestled with the idea and dreaded the long arduous trip that loomed ahead in the deep of winter, I also looked forward to seeing my parents and children. How they must have grown since I last saw them! Albert, Junior was an infant—he would be almost ten now—Irene and Minnie—young women of twenty-four and twenty-two, and Fanny—a youthful seventeen. Sadly, my last visit to Wildwood had ended in an unfortunate impasse between their mother and me.

I was overwhelmed by self-doubt and a wrenching guilt. "Wealth hasn't brought me happiness," I concluded, trying to come to grips with the quandary I was in. "I've traded independence and security for the loneliness of a joyless, empty life. I have only myself to blame. It was my choice. I'm partially responsible for the estrangement. I suppose we make what we want of our lives. It was never my intention to live apart from those I loved, but in my quest for riches…I've lost so much. Was I wrong to have stood my ground?" I asked myself. "No,…we're both at fault. Margaret deceived me, whether intentionally or not. In retrospect, I should have seen the warning signs. Every effort to make her happy was futile. The only thing that would have satisfied her was to give up everything I'd ever worked for. The sobering reality is that in either case, my marriage still would have failed." My thoughts were abruptly interrupted by a knock on my office door.

"Hello, Albert! I returned this evening because of some rather mundane matters pertaining to the second shift," said Josiah, poking his head in my doorway. "I saw the light still burning in your office so I decided to drop by for a minute. I wanted to see you before you left and wish you well. It's getting late, Albert. Are you almost ready to leave soon? Your train leaves at seven in the morning."

"I know, Josiah. I haven't even packed my valise as yet," I replied, shaking my head and troubled by my lack of enthusiasm. "I'm dreading this trip to the East Coast."

"Yes, traveling at this time of the year can be trying," he said, sensing the apprehension in my voice. We'll certainly miss you, Albert." Without commenting further, Josiah approached me and firmly grasped my hand as I rose from my chair. "Have a wonderful vacation! It's been a long time coming and well deserved. We all want you to enjoy being with your family. Promise me you won't worry about anything back here."

"Thank you, Josiah, I won't," I replied while affectionately wrapping my arm around his shoulder. I reached across my desk for a small envelope and pressed it into his hand. "I intended to do this in the near future, but because I've had such a profitable three months, I'm able to reimburse you for your initial investment in the distillery business. You lost everything in the fire. This might help you get back on your feet again, dear friend. I truly appreciate the fact that you stopped by my office to wish me well. You actually saved me the hassle of trying to find you. I'll be forever grateful, Josiah, for your support throughout this whole ordeal. It was extraordinary."

"Well, I must say this is certainly unexpected, Albert!" he exclaimed, pleasantly surprised. He looked down at the envelope in his hand. "You always seem to be there for me when I need it most. I don't know what to say! Thank you, Albert! You're a dear friend, indeed. You've had so many setbacks yourself this past year. My losses were minimal in comparison to yours, but I should have known you'd do something like this. You're such a thoughtful person."

"I wish it could have been more, Josiah," I said, returning to my desk and neatly arranging ink, pencils and pens into a top draw. "You and your family have been so kind to me over the years. And please don't hesitate to approach me if you should need any further financial assistance."

"You needn't worry about that, Albert," he replied. "No more commercial businesses for me. I plan to invest in real estate from now on and continue working in the management and accounting fields. Do you need transportation to the train station in the morning?" he asked while still in the doorway. "I'd be more than happy to pick you up in time to board your train."

"No thank you, Josiah," I replied. "I've already made arrangements for a carriage. It should be at my door by six-fifteen. As usual, I'm depending on you to take care of things in my absence. Be sure to inform me if any problems should arise. Samuel's also been advised to keep an eye on things. I'm sure all will go well. Farewell, Josiah! I'll see you at the end of February."

"Goodbye, Albert! Have a safe journey!" he said, waving as he left and closing the door behind him.

I leaned back in my leather chair and lit my pipe. I finally finished the paperwork and cleared off my desk. While leisurely inhaling a fine vintage tobacco, I swiveled around to face the outdoors. It was as if my nose was pressed against the window of my life. Transfixed, I found myself staring reflectively at the steady, hypnotic snowfall racing past the lamplight. I began to question my reluctance to visit the East Coast. "I should be eager to see my family and my children again,…but I'm not. Why is that?" This question and many more raced through my mind. "What's happening to me? When did I change? Have the long absences distanced me from them?" I wondered. "When I last visited Wildwood,…why did I feel more like a stranger than a family member…a visitor completely out of my element? After all this time, I know I'll feel uncomfortable in their presence. It'll be especially so with Margaret.

"Oh, how I resent her spiteful ways and lack of fairness. I can't believe she ever truly loved me. She has purposely kept the children from knowing me,…their *father*! Margaret feels her actions are justified because I refuse to live with her and the children. Well, that will never be. My life is here. I realized long ago that the only connection I have to her and the children is the fact that I'm the sole provider. Over the years, this has proven to be a major bone of contention. I resent her financial dependence on me. Her lack of compassion, self-indulgence and obstinacy has become repugnant to me. It's no wonder my feelings for her have slowly disintegrated from that of ardor and passion to antagonism and alienation. Well, this is it! I'm not getting any younger. I've been living a bachelor's life for much too long now. I'm damn tired of it! I must be released from the shackles of this loveless marriage and free to live my life as I see fit. How gratifying it would be to come home after a long day's work to a loving and attentive woman. Is it wrong to want this kind of relationship?" I asked myself.

Just then, my thoughts turned to Matilda. "We've shared so much these last few years. She's become the sounding board for all my frustrations and made this last year bearable for me. Without her compassion and empathy, I would certainly have gone to pieces under the pressure. I have a feeling that Matilda's deeply in love with me; alas,…it's been a one-sided affair. She's never received even the slightest commitment from me. While she senses the breakdown of my marriage due to the long separations from my wife, she still prefers to remain on the sidelines. Matilda's never brought it up or forced the issue. While she's only slightly older than Irene, she's a mature adult with whom I have so much in common. Her love for me, her encouragement and kind spirit provide energy to all my endeavors. She's given my life new meaning. Matilda has never questioned my reluctance to commit to a lasting relationship. She understands that it's a dilemma that only,…I can resolve. I've been so grateful for her support and ongoing patience during all the uncertainties in my life. Ever since I've known Matilda, her faith in me has never wavered."

Suddenly, it became quite clear. With an insight that was profound and penetrating, I realized that Matilda was the single, most irrefutable reason I was reluctant to leave Chicago. I dreaded being away from her,…let alone for six weeks. The thought of being without her smile, vivacity and tender touch overwhelmed me with sadness. I understood that indecisiveness and procrastination had clouded my perceptions. In essence, I needed her by my side not just for the next six weeks, but also for the rest of my life. Enthralled by thoughts of her charm and beauty, my heart took flight. "Face it Albert," I told myself, "you're hopelessly in love with her. Only Matilda's love can fill the emptiness in your life." I was instantly focused on the truth of the matter. What once seemed like an insurmountable impasse was now unmistakably clear. I knew what I must do!

With a crack of the whip the carriage was on its way from my office at the brewery to my room on Calumet Avenue. The stillness of the late evening was shattered by the clip-clop sound of the horses' hoofs against the cobblestone street. After leaving the coach, my footprints marred the unsullied, ermine mantle of snow that covered the walkway. It peppered my face with wet droplets as I glanced upwards. The brightly lit windows of my room faced the street. My heart skipped a beat at the sight of the shadowy figure standing in the window. It was Matilda!…My sweet lovely, Matilda! She smiled and waived excitedly as I ran toward the hallway of the rooming house. As I fairly flew up the stairway, I wondered, "Why is she here? Is she here to bid me farewell? Yes, of course,…I'm sure of it!" I ached to see her again before I left. I was overjoyed that she had come.

"Let me help you with your hat and coat, Albert," she said when she met me at the door. "I thought it would be nice to be together this evening before your departure in the morning. I knew you'd most likely have to go out again to dine, so to save you this inconvenience,…I've taken the liberty to prepare a simple meal for the two of us. I hope you don't mind, Albert. And oh, by the way," she added, pointing to the dresser, "while I waited for you, I packed your valise."

Momentarily stunned by her spontaneous thoughtfulness, I grinned and finally managed to say, "What a pleasant surprise!" It was so like Matilda to be so thoughtful. "Why, I'm delighted, Matilda! In fact, I planned on seeing you after I finished my packing. I was going to stop by your apartment this evening and ask you to join me at Kingsley's…*This* is a much better idea!" I said, taking her into my arms. I looked around the room—an inviting fire roared in the fireplace. The crimson glow, the warmth of the flames and the fragrance of the burning wood transformed a lackluster boardinghouse room into a cozy retreat. Carefully positioned in front of the hearth was a small table covered with a lace scarf. A place setting for two was complemented by a set of fine crystal goblets. Matching lace napkins embellished the dinner plates and a solid brass candleholder graced the center of the table. As Matilda lowered the gas lamps and lit the candle, the flickering wick cast an enchanting silhouette on the walls. "Why, Matilda,…this is *just* splendid! You've thought of everything!" I exclaimed, looking around with a giddy grin. I was amazed by her resourcefulness. It was so romantic!

"I have supper right here in this basket. I've even included your favorite,…a classic French Chablis," she said, uncorking the bottle and pouring it into the wine glasses.

Matilda reached down, handed me one goblet and held the other. "Cheers to you, Albert and bon voyage!"

"And best wishes to you, my sweet, Matilda!" I replied, looking into her penetrating dark brown eyes as the high-pitched ping of our clinking glasses echoed throughout the room. "Oh, this Chablis is superb!" I exclaimed after taking a sip.

"I mustn't drink too much of it, my dear, or I'll certainly leave with a horrible headache in the morning." She smiled with her heart, giggled and fell into my arms.

"Oh, Albert, I'll miss you so! I've been in love with you from the moment I was introduced to you," she said wistfully, placing her arms around me and leaning her head against my chest. "When I first met you I was fairly swept off my feet by your sincerity and,…sensuality as well. I lost my heart *along* with my wig, and I lose it again every time I see you, my dearest. It was especially so tonight when I saw you outside the window."

I reached for her dainty chin and as our eyes met, I kissed the tears away from her lovely face. Her all-encompassing love for me radiated from deep within her soul. We finally yielded to the reticent, ardent love we had for each other—a love that had been suppressed during all our time together. I kissed her passionately. Our lips melted together as the smoldering sexuality inside us erupted like a dormant volcano.

"Oh, yes!…Yes, I do love you! I love you,…beyond all reason, my dearest Matilda!" I repeated fervently. "I promise, I'll never leave you again. I can't even bear to leave you,…now!" Our lips met again, igniting the spark of burning desire I'd forgotten existed within me. "Oh, Matilda, you make my life worthwhile. How fortunate I am to have you love me, so! I want to spend the rest of my life with you. I need you to be forever by my side." As an idyllic euphoria enveloped us, she silently accepted my total surrender.

Drawn together like steel to magnet, our ardent embraces continued unabated. With an insatiable craving and frenzied gestures, we undressed. She removed the hairpins from her chignon. Her hair, like soft, downy cashmere cascaded past her shoulders and over her voluptuous maiden breasts. Matilda's young, shapely body was fragrant and soft as a rose petal as it pressed against mine. Love became passion as our bodies melted into a single entity. The oneness we shared gloriously satisfied every secret longing and erotic need. Our ardent lovemaking lasted until dawn. It was an amorous, unforgettable experience—one that would always be eagerly anticipated and often repeated in my lifetime. Right then and there, I decided to make my darling Matilda, forever mine.

*   *   *   *

Early-February, 1872

After a lengthy, arduous journey to Massachusetts and Cape Cod, I arrived in Brewster. As the train weaved through the Cape Cod countryside, I lifted my head from reading a periodical and glanced out the window. Small ice flows floated with the current in the bay—remnants of large chunks that had pushed up against the shore. Now—in early-February—the snow had melted due to some unseasonably warm temperatures. It was actually shirtsleeve weather. In spite of this, the lakes and ponds were still frozen over because of a long, severe winter. The blanket of ice was almost three-feet deep in some places. It reminded me of the thick layer of paraffin that Miss Mira poured over the homemade fruit jellies and jams to preserve them. I squinted as I looked out into the bright sun that reflected off the opaque surface. Skaters with varying degrees of expertise glided across the large lake. It was crowded with fishermen who were sitting with poles that dangled over openings in the dense, ice cover. While adults leisurely walked in their midst, children played with long sticks—sliding flat stones across the frozen lake toward a barrier net. Families sitting in horse-drawn carts meandered along the perimeter enjoying the scenery and the sunshine. They rode under a clear blue sky, gaping at the flora and fauna that bordered the lake. Cart tracks crisscrossed the thick frozen surface and formed a quilt of sorts. The sun's ray reflected on the surface in varying monochromatic shades of gray—ranging from iridescent white to shimmering silver. This was quite rare as the sun usually melted the ice fairly rapidly; however, as I mentioned before, it had been a harsh winter with temperatures way below normal.

The Town of Brewster had changed a bit since my last trip. A group of women from Brewster had sponsored and built a library on the Olde King's Highway adjacent to a newly constructed Baptist Church. Also, a new gristmill was being built to replace the one that had stood there from the days of my youth. The main street was widened to accommodate several new mansions. Each one was more imposing than the next. Wealthy sea captains, who were now in their retirement years, owned many of them.

On the carriage ride to the homestead, I was spellbound as I absorbed the ambiance of my native town. As we drove through the bucolic meadows on a sandy road, I gawked at fields of fiddleheads, phragmites, pussy willows, rosehips and barren cranberry bogs.

Fortunately, toward the end of my vacation, the Cape was experiencing some blissfully mild days. Every now and then, I enjoyed moderate temperatures—in the high forties or low fifties. The countryside was free of snow and the roadways were clear. The landscape, however, was still brown and stark. The precipitation was usually in the form of rain or snow flurries. The moist air froze on the bare oaks and transformed the branches into sparkling shafts, which glistened against a backdrop of ever-changing billowy clouds that floated in a sunny, azure sky. Brewster's stark countryside was in the grip of winter awaiting its rebirth.

It had been years since I visited with my parents. Despite her aged skin and white hair, Mother was as lovely and vibrant as I remembered her. Father was now in his late seventies and walked with a cane. Other than that, he was still as agile and alert as ever. While I was there, my sisters came to visit with their children. I was pleased to learn that in my absence Anne had become a grandmother and I—sad to say—a *great* uncle.

"I see Japeth's still working around the homestead, Father. How is he?" I asked at breakfast a few days later. "I'd like to have a long chat with him before I leave."

"Japeth and his family are quite well," he replied, gesturing to Mother to join us. "He and Veronica have almost as many grandchildren as we have. Aaron has a prestigious position with the Boston Railroad. Bethany and Nathaniel are married and live in Truro and Harwich, respectively. Like us, Japeth's getting on in years. Consequently, I've hired another young fellow to help him with the chores. His name's Hudson Ellis. He'll eventually take over when Japeth can no longer keep up with it all. This is such a large homestead. It's become too difficult for Japeth to handle the farm animals, livery and gardens, et cetera. Japeth's mentioned that he'd like to move to Plymouth so Veronica can be with her sister. I'm sure he'd be delighted to have you visit, Albert. Although he was as saddened as we were when he heard about your losses in the Chicago fire, he was pleased to know you had persevered." As he spoke, I noticed that Mother forlornly lowered her head.

"You needn't worry about me. I've already begun to recoup my losses through my brewery, railroad, real estate and banking facilities," I replied, taking mother's hand across the table. "It's one of the reasons I decided to visit you. I wanted to assure you that I'm still financially secure. My distillery's being rebuilt as we speak and I plan on selling it as soon as it is finished. I expect a profitable return on my investment. Samuel's been a godsend. His assistance has been invaluable. Actually,…it's been the key to restoring my financial foothold. Uranus has started a real estate business in New York and I hear he's doing quite well. I plan on stopping by to see him on my return trip to Chicago.

"To be perfectly honest with you," I went on, "it's my personal life that needs attention right now. I'm quite frustrated with my failed marriage. It's been years since I've seen Margaret *or* my children. This is also another reason for my journey to the East Coast. Margaret has consistently refused to leave West Roxbury and live with me in Chicago. She never had the decency to respond to a letter I sent begging her to return and reaffirming my love for her and the children. I also explained that I'd be sending her a sizable increase in the family allowance. I haven't heard from her since, Albert, Junior, was born. I must admit that I'm a parent in name only and have never been involved in my children's daily lives. I'm nearing fifty now. The years of being without my family and the resulting loneliness are beginning to take their toll. When I married, I looked forward to a lasting union like yours,…one filled with love, mutual respect and devotion. So far,…that's eluded me. Just so you'll be aware of it, I intend to divorce Margaret. I need the companionship of a loving woman. My subsistence and livelihood are rooted in Chicago. Margaret never intended to spend her life there with me. I hope you both understand and appreciate the position I'm in."

"We *do* understand, Albert," Mother replied. The subject continued to be intently discussed as Mother placed a platter of freshly baked cranberry sconces on the table. "Frankly, your father and I have been dismayed by Margaret's refusal to remain with you in Chicago and fulfill her obligation as your wife. When your father left to help you, he made it clear that I needn't accompany him because it would only be a temporary situation, whereas,…your move was a *permanent* one. Father and I reasoned that she was much too attached to her roots and preferred being with her family and friends instead of living with you. It stands to reason that when it came right down to it, she never loved you enough to stay by your side, Albert. Her indifference to your wishes all these years has deeply saddened us. You have our heartfelt sympathy.

"Margaret did come for a short visit a few summers after the birth of your son, but that was the last time. When Father and I stopped by Wildwood about six years ago, on our return trip from Europe, we noted a marked difference in her personality. People change,…I guess," she went on with a dejected sigh. "After the European voyage, which you so graciously provided for us, our ship docked in Boston. By the way, this gives us the perfect opportunity to personally thank you for such a generous and considerate gift on our 50th anniversary. It was truly the highlight of our lives.

"Well,…to go on," she added, "We eagerly anticipated a stopover to see our grandchildren. However,…we received a polite yet cool reception. It was thoroughly unexpected! We had to wait at least a half-hour in the parlor for her to greet us. She never even bothered to offer us a cup of tea. When she finally summoned the children, the girls remembered who we were, but young Albert had to be introduced to us. It was a heart-wrenching experience. Your father and I were appalled. We couldn't stand another minute of her rudeness and inhospitable behavior. Fortunately, we had asked the carriage driver to return for us in an hour. We vowed we'd never visit her again. You have no idea how distant and aloof she was toward us." Father glumly nodded in agreement while reaching for his coffee cup.

"What you decide to do about your future is entirely up to you, son…It's your life.

In any case, despite your decision, we'll always love you and respect your judgment," Father declared, reaching over to affectionately place his hands on my shoulders as Mother nodded in agreement. I could tell she was visibly saddened by the instability in my life. "I'm sure you're aware that divorce is quite scandalous and frowned upon these days. Of course, gossipy tongues will be wagging, but don't let that influence your choice. Do what you must. It's a shame that it had to come down to this. You deserve a better lot in life than the one forced upon you by a spiteful woman. We know that you married Margaret with the intention of living with her "until death do you part." Her duty as your wife and the mother of your children was to be with you, regardless of her sentiments. She failed you in that respect," he maintained, rising from his chair and walking around the table toward me.

"I appreciate your trust and support, more than you'll ever know," I said. "Thank you, both for being so caring and perceptive. I guess my biggest disappointment is that I expected my marriage would mirror yours. Sadly, it wasn't meant to be. I'm troubled over what I must do. On the other hand, being able to share it with you has somewhat lightened my burden. I believe I'll take a stroll along the bay," I said, getting up from my chair, putting on my hat and coat, and then walking toward the kitchen door. "I'd like to take advantage of the sunny day and the mild temperatures. It may help to clear my head and calm my nerves."

As the refreshing salt spray carried by the offshore winds greeted me on my way to the bay, I searched within my soul for answers that seemed to elude me. I needed to face what was happening in my life and sort through all the contradictory feelings that had preoccupied me lately and the courage to deal with them. I feared I might be intimidated into settling for less than what I truly wanted out of life. My happiness and peace of mind were predicated upon achieving a clearly defined objective. As I meandered along the seashore, my thoughts soon became secondary to the message that Mother Nature was trying to impart. Through the ages, the sea with its relentless, powerful force hurled a continual series of frothing, breaking waves over the shoreline. The whooshing and splashing of the surf added sound and motion to the otherwise tranquil serenity of the seashore. It whispered some compelling words of wisdom. The longer I walked in solitude along the craggy inner elbow of the bay, the more determined I became to leave my past behind me.

As I walked up the sandy path toward the homestead, the goals I had set for myself as a child came to mind. Again, I imagined the grandiose castle of my dreams set high above the dunes that overlooked the bay. I wanted Matilda to be a part of that. "Matilda!" Oh,…how I miss her!" I thought with an unbelievable longing. I wished she were by my side enjoying the tranquility of the deserted seashore and wind-swept dunes. I sensed an overpowering urgency to tend to my unfinished business. After a long overdue visit with Japeth, I planned to leave for West Roxbury.

"Hello, Japeth," I said, quietly approaching him with an extended hand as he sat milking a cow. "It's Albert,…old friend. How are you?"

"Oh my goodness! It *is* Albert!" he exclaimed, startled by the sight of me standing so close to him. He took his time getting up from his stool, as if coaxing his arthritic bones into allowing him to stand. "I'm fine…and so is my family,…just getting on in years as you can see. Old age is really taking its toll on my body." Japeth looked me over from head to toe. "I heard you had arrived in Brewster," he added. "It's so wonderful to see you again, Albert! You've really made a name for yourself. You're somewhat of a celebrity in these parts. Every so often your name appears in the local newspapers for one reason or other."

"I hope the articles are not *too* unfavorable," I said with a wide grin.

"Of course not," he replied. "I see you haven't lost your sense of humor, Albert. We're all so proud of your achievements. Your generosities during the war and your bravery in the Chicago Fire for example,…have been front-page news. We were all saddened by the loss of your opera house, but pleased to know that you had escaped injury and financial ruin. You certainly fit the description of a prosperous gentleman in your fine clothes and well-trimmed hair and beard. I always knew you had the mettle to make something of yourself."

"Japeth, over all these years, I've never forgotten my mentor and the many hours you spent teaching me how to make my way in this world," I said, reaching into my coat pocket. "You took me under your wing as if I were your own and showed me how to live my life with dignity, honor and purpose. I have a small token of my appreciation for all that,…right here in this folder. Please open it, Japeth."

Japeth carefully opened it and gasped at the bank note inside. "I can't accept this from you! It's much too generous!" he insisted, wide eyed and shaking his head. "Thank you, Albert, from the bottom of my heart!"

"You're welcome, Japeth," I replied. "And yes, you can accept this because it's a promise I made to myself and you,…years ago. I heard you're planning on moving to Plymouth soon. This'll be enough to build or buy you a new home. It should also see you through for many years to come. I give this to you with a grateful heart,…for it's well deserved. This is strictly between us, Japeth. No one else need know about it."

"But, Albert, your father has always been so generous to me and my family," he pointed out. "Through the years, he's done so much for us,…more than what was actually necessary. This is way above and beyond what I'm truly worthy of. I was always fond of you,…and only did what I would have done for my own."

"I know that!" I replied, preparing to leave. "That's precisely why it's been such a pleasure to be able to do this. What my father did for you is what he felt he *must* do. Apart from that, I'd like to reward you on my own for all the priceless, lifelong lessons I learned under your tutelage. It's simply a way of expressing my gratitude for your patience and guidance. Say no more, Japeth. Enjoy! And that's final." I reiterated, walking toward the barn door. "Goodbye, dear friend. No,…I mean farewell…until we meet again, sometime in the future. If not, I wish you the best in your retirement years. May you stay well and live long!"

✳   ✳   ✳   ✳

Late-February, 1872

The rail line had been extended to Brewster in '65. The train trip to Boston that began at six-thirty in the morning—took a whole day. The passengers, cranberries, salt, shellfish and mail that were once transported by packet ship were now cargo on the trains. I found a seat close to the coal stove to keep warm. A few inches of snow had fallen the evening before my trip to Boston, but the tracks were clear and there were no delays.

After bidding my parents farewell, Hudson, who was a fair-haired, tall and muscular young chap, drove me to the train depot with the buckboard. He was energetic and very courteous. Hudson was an amiable fellow who spoke volumes with his face. He had a pleasant demeanor—always smiling and endeavoring to please.

"It's been a pleasure to meet you, Hudson. Take care of my parents," I said, preparing to board the train. "Thank you for rising so early to take me here. Goodbye! Give, Japeth, my best!" I waved farewell, heaved my valise onto the train, and then ascended the steps. My retreat in Brewster had proved to be exactly what I needed. I felt relaxed, renewed and galvanized. My future was clear-cut. I knew precisely where I was headed and what I must do. The Cape Cod countryside with its bay, cranberry bogs, rolling hills and meadows left me longing to return. The Cape—and Brewster in particular were in my blood. Like the alewives, regardless of wherever life would take me, I would return to my origins. And similar to the osprey, I would build my home along the seashore. I wasn't ready to do so as yet, but I knew that my life-long dream would someday become a reality. It was only—a matter of time.

"Boston!" the conductor shouted as the train rolled into an extraordinarily large railroad station. It was early evening when I waved for a carriage. I decided to stay at a nearby hotel during my stay here. I would return there after my visit to Wildwood. Boston had become quite cosmopolitan over the years. Imposing theaters, elegant restaurants and inns bordered Massachusetts Avenue. Unlike Chicago, Boston was pristine—devoid of shanties and slum areas. I began to appreciate Margaret's reluctance to leave Massachusetts. I had to admit it certainly had an appealing charm. I dined in the hotel restaurant and then retired to my room. I would start out for West Roxbury in the morning. A few days before my departure from Brewster, I sent Margaret a telegraph advising her of my arrival date. I couldn't help speculating, "How will she look after all this time? How will I be received? Will she be civil? How will she react when I declare my intention to divorce her?" I tossed and turned for hours before I finally fell asleep.

"I'll be leaving for the day, but will return this evening," I announced as I handed the desk clerk the keys to my room. "I plan to board the train tomorrow for New York. I'll be leaving around nine in the morning," I went on, turning to exit the lobby. I looked at my pocket watch. It was already ten o'clock. I wanted to look my best, so I bathe before breakfast, got a fresh haircut, had my beard trimmed and my shoes polished. I summoned a carriage and was soon on my way to West Roxbury and Wildwood.

The coach traversed the circular roadway in front of the gracious white manor and pulled up to the front portico. I asked the driver to return for me in an hour. A snow covered landscape glistened in the warm sunlight. I dodged the melting icicles hanging low and dripping copiously over the front door. An elderly maid-servant opened the door, took my hat and coat, and then hung them on the coat stand.

"Madam will be here momentarily, sir," she said, leading me into the front parlor.

"My name is Olga. May I fetch you a cup of tea, sir?"

"No, thank you, Olga," I replied, choosing to sit in an armchair near the front entrance. Olga was a buxom Scandinavian woman with white hair that was twisted in a braid around her head. She curtsied and left the room. "How different it was twenty-four years ago," I thought, "when I was so eagerly welcomed by an adoring woman,…one I believed would love me forever," Unfortunately, fate had conspired to crush my aspirations and send us on our separate ways.

"Hello, Albert," Margaret said in a rather aloof, solemn tone of voice as she walked into the room. It was an exceptionally reserved greeting.

"It's so nice to see you again, Margaret," I said, standing to greet her with an extended hand. She ignored it and sat on the sofa. I took a seat in a wingchair opposite her. "How are the children? Will I be able to see them while I'm here?" I asked. Although I was ill at ease, I was indifferent to her presence. It was apparent that I was no longer in love with her. I sensed absolutely—*nothing*. While we conversed the maid brought in a tray with a silver tea set and placed it on a small table in front of us.

"The children are fine; however, they're not at home right now," she replied in a civil, but aloof manner. "Irene and Minnie have accompanied Mother on a trip south. Fanny boards at the academy and Albert's in grade school at the moment. I believe it's just as well that they're not here," she said without explaining why. Margaret poured a cup of tea for me, but I politely declined it. She poured one for herself and took a sip. I couldn't help but notice how much she had aged. Not only had she become quite wrinkled, but she had also gained a considerable amount of weight. I'm sure I would have gradually become accustomed to her outward mien, had we not been apart for such a long while. Margaret would have always been beautiful in my eyes. However, I was completely taken by surprise because my memory of her was in such contrast to this actuality. She was wearing a dowdy, black dress with a small, white collar. Her hair, which was parted in the middle, was pulled back from her face. It was twisted into an austere bun and fastened behind her head. Except for her lighter hair color she bore a striking resemblance to her despicable mother. "Like mother like daughter!" I thought. I was revolted and felt the hair rise on the back of my neck. I found the similarity wonderfully ironic. Had she retained her former beauty, I might have been dissuaded from my purpose. Somehow she noticed that I was taken aback by her appearance.

"Well, Albert, I must say your graying sideburns make you look quite distinguished," she said in a subtle attempt to remind me that I had also aged in the last ten years. "What brings you to Wildwood in February? I believed that if you ever returned to the East Coast,...it would at least be during the summer."

"As you know, Margaret, I lost the distillery and the opera house in the fire," I said, fidgeting and trying to make myself comfortable in the chair by crossing my legs. "Nevertheless, I was able to salvage the brewery and it's operational right now. The distillery, however,...was a complete loss. I plan to sell it after it's rebuilt, but I will retain the brewery. After such a disastrous experience, I found it necessary to get away. I decided it was high time to reflect on my future. I needed to resolve some weighty decisions about my life. What better place than in Brewster with my parents. I've been there for the last month, thus the reason for my visit here."

"And what is that, Albert?" she asked bluntly, aware it must concern her. Margaret became defensive and eventually resentful and manipulative. In previous encounters the tension had been palpable. Now it was so intense you could cut it with a knife.

"Margaret, as you pointed out I'm not getting any younger," I said, trying to stay composed, yet forthright. "Because I've been estranged from my loved ones, the last ten years have been a time of abject loneliness for me. I can't go on existing this way,...isolated in a rooming house and living a life without even a modicum of affection. I'm here to tell you that I intend to divorce you. Whether or not you object to it is of no consequence to me. As in the past, you and the children will be well provided for. I will give you a final cash settlement of your choosing and the deed to Wildwood. I'm sorry to have to do this,...but I must be liberated from this arrangement. I can no longer tolerate this lifestyle. I want to share the remainder of my days with a loving spouse. I've met such a lady...A wonderful woman who throughout my ordeal last fall was caring and supportive. I plan to marry my friend and companion as soon as the divorce is granted. I believe that's all I have to say right now,...Margaret."

"Divorce!" Margaret exclaimed with a huff, infuriated by my disclosure. She became wide-eyed and rigid as she sat straight up on the settee. "I can't believe you'd go that far to rid yourself of me! I dare you! Oh!...I won't hear of it!" she shrieked. "I should have known you'd do something that contemptible! Oh, Albert,...a *divorce*! How rude and thoughtless of you. I can't believe you could be that spiteful. Don't you care that conventional Bostonian social circles frown on such a thing! It's rare and unheard of in these parts. Why, it's decidedly scandalous! I certainly hope you'll reconsider that decision, Albert. It's ludicrous! I can just imagine what my relatives will say about that! It'll be the topic of conversation from here to the Pacific. I must say you certainly have a cavalier disregard for socially accepted customs.

"Why do you need a divorce? Why can't things just stay as they are? Why don't you just decide to live with your paramour? No one will be the wiser. I've already been informed about her through various sources. I believe her name is Matilda Sourbeck,...also known as Georgia Garrison, a former member of a burlesque troupe. Why, she belongs in a brothel! Honestly, Albert, you should be ashamed of yourself for being involved with a young woman of that caliber. How disgusting to learn that she's just a few months older than Irene...You pervert! What are you trying to prove? For heaven's sake, Albert,...act your age!"

"Dammit, Margaret! You're impossible! Listen to yourself." I bellowed as I shot up from my chair. "Your insults aren't worth a reply!" I was so furious that I had an urge to lash out and slap her. It might have happened had I not been sitting so far away. Despite her outburst, I composed myself and lowered my voice so as not to betray my hostility. "I believed I was doing the gentlemanly thing. I thought I should grant you the courtesy of approaching you about my intentions, but I can see,...it doesn't matter. You care little about me. All you're worried about is being the object of gossip and ridicule. I'm not here to argue or grovel, Margaret. First of all, I didn't come here for permission to divorce you...I've already *made* that decision.

"Secondly, I *will* marry Matilda whether you approve of her or not! Her age shouldn't concern you. She's mature beyond her years. Matilda has always respected my marital status and would never have intentionally become involved with a married man. I haven't lived with her as yet,...and don't intend to until we're married. That's not the kind of relationship we want for ourselves. You abandoned me long ago. Due to your self-serving and uncompromising disposition, you've broken every promise made to me at the time of our marriage...I have no marriage!" I sensed my resentment intensifying and ready to explode. "Is a loving and lasting relationship too much to ask for? If living alone is how you intend to exist for the remainder of *your* days,...that's *your* business! It's not my idea of a fulfilling life!"

I was acutely aware that I must remain calm and cool-headed lest the discussion end in a regrettable argument. I stopped short of a crescendo of confrontational words. "The repercussions could be dangerously explosive...I must avoid that," I concluded, as I prepared to leave the room. One reason for my reticence may have been an awareness that my words could come back to haunt me. Again, I tried to regain my equanimity and without raising my voice, I went on to explain, "I always loved my children, but you managed to turn them against me. Because of your bitterness and hatred of me, they were poisoned by years of acrimony and disrespect. You used *them* to punish *me*.

"If you had been a more compassionate partner, one who was clearly sensitive to my needs, I might never have fallen into the arms of another woman. You only have yourself to blame for that, Margaret. You've behaved like a spoiled child! Your obstinacy, egotism and inability to understand my point of view were your downfall. I've lived for years in silent agony. The longing for a tender and loving woman to greet me after a long day's work and to share my bed will soon be over for me. Although we were alienated from each other, it might have been permissible for me to live with Matilda without the benefit of marriage,…but that's *not* who I am. My presence here is solely out of respect for you as the mother of my children. I will not defend Miss Sourbeck's character except to say that she's a lady,…a refined young woman who would never stoop to your level of vindictiveness."

"You have the audacity to criticize *me*, Albert! You should talk!" she admonished vociferously. Margaret pointed an accusing finger at me and began to shed any pretense of decorum. "Come down from the inflated view you have of yourself! I know you better than that! You're not exactly a model of moral integrity, my dear! I've read about your shenanigans involving the opera house lottery, the bawdy burlesques you introduced to a crude public and the raised eyebrows you managed to evoke in cultured circles. Your transgressions with prima donnas and actresses are common knowledge. You're a philandering womanizer…an adulterer having one affair after another and living a life of debauchery! I'm familiar with your drinking and carousing night after night! I've also been told about your affair with that seductive little hussy. As far as I'm concerned that gold-digger has coerced you into marriage because you're financially secure."

"That's it, Margaret!…I've had enough of your accusations! I don't care if you insist upon damning me, but I won't sit here listening to your judgmental criticisms of someone you don't even know. Your outburst against Matilda doesn't warrant or deserve denial! Your insinuations are based on unsubstantiated rumors that are phony and steeped in hypocrisy! You *know* better than that!" I replied, seething inside and furious at myself for being uncertain about my grounds for divorce. I refused to be intimidated by her verbal abuse. I walked over to the coat rack, reached for my coat, plopped my hat on my head, and then headed for the front door.

While sounding conciliatory, without actually being so, I turned toward her and said, "I had hoped for a civil dialogue and an amicable dissolution of our marriage; however, I guess it just wasn't meant to be." I could feel my temper flaring again.

"Your self-indulgent arrogance and asinine behavior are repulsive. Frankly, Margaret, you've been a calculating and controlling bitch throughout our marriage. I can't wait to be free of you! Your pompous grandiosity is insulting, to say the least. You don't hold a candle to Matilda. She's an intelligent and sophisticated woman,…more cultured and ladylike than you'll ever be! I've fallen in love with a wonderful, sensitive and compassionate person. You, on the other hand, are insolent when it's least fitting. In my opinion you haven't done or said anything in years that could be construed as endearing! The way I feel right now,…I don't care if I ever see you again!

"In fact, as of this visit, Margaret, I'm ending all communication with you and the children! Anyway,…thanks to you they never got to know me. I might as well be dead as far as they're concerned! It's time for me to leave. My carriage will be waiting. I'll take care of all the legal aspects from my end. You'll soon hear from my lawyer." Not wanting to acerbate the situation, I merely said, "*Goodbye*, Margaret! And believe me this time,…it's *not* farewell!"

Incensed, yet relieved that this was now all behind me, I opened the door and without looking back, I left abruptly. It was over! My love for Margaret and the monogamy I once cherished would soon become a distant memory. The waiting carriage returned me to my hotel. The next morning I left for New York. After visiting my Cousin Uranus, I spent a few days tending to business matters, and then continued on to Chicago.

▼

CHAPTER 20

$Mid-March,$ 1872

"I have some good news for you, Albert," Samuel announced while seated at his desk. After offering me a chair, he leaned over to give me a handshake with one hand and a cigar with the other. "I have a buyer for your distillery. I quoted a ridiculously high price to a group of wealthy entrepreneurs. I told them if they wished to purchase it, you wouldn't take a dollar less. They never flinched and immediately proceeded to sign a Purchase and Sale agreement. The H.H. Shufeldt & Company will take it over on the first day of May. So,...Albert, I believe congratulations are in order. You're on your way to regaining your fortune. I knew you'd eventually recoup your losses. I must say it certainly hasn't taken long! Your brewery, real estate and land holdings along with the sale of your distillery have put you in the black again. The losses you've sustained would have shattered a less resilient spirit, but you're made of stronger stuff. You've stubbornly surged forward with unbridled energy to recapture your position in the grand scheme of things. I can't say that if I'd been in your place, I would've had the courage to go on. I've said it many times before, and I'll say it again,...Albert, you're one of a kind! I'm proud to be related to you."

"Whew! Well, that's a relief! I needn't concern myself with the distillery any longer. Thank you, Samuel, for your usual business savvy. I guess that's why you're in real estate and banking,...and I'm into beer, wine and liquors," I replied, delighted by his announcement and commentary. I rose from my chair and prepared to leave.

"You can be sure I gave myself a hefty commission," he said, taking a long puff on his cigar, smiling and feeling quite pleased with himself. After enjoying a toast and a good laugh, he rose from his desk, walked over to me, and then patted me on the back. "By the way, the Missus and I would like to have you come for dinner next Sunday afternoon. We moved into our new home about two weeks ago, and we'd like to have you visit so you can see it for yourself."

"Sounds wonderful, Samuel! I'd like that!...However, I'd like Matilda to accompany me, if that's all right with you. I believe your Missus isn't too fond of her due to the malicious and unfounded rumors about us. Do you think she'd mind?" I asked as I stood with my hand on the doorknob preparing to leave.

"Matilda's *always* welcomed in my home, Albert," he replied assuredly. "I'm sure the Missus will be hospitable and cordial toward her,...if only superficially. She knows how I feel about you two. Anyway, she's definitely changed her attitude toward Matilda since the fire. Whether she minds it or not,...isn't my concern,...nor should it be yours. I'll be looking forward to your visit next Sunday."

"On a more serious note, Samuel," I went on while standing in the doorway and facing him directly. "I want you to know that I made it a point to stop in West Roxbury before returning to Chicago."

"Did you get to see, Margaret?" Samuel asked as he doused his cigar in the sand-filled container next to the doorway.

"Yes, I did," I replied, eager to share that experience with him. "I sent her a telegraph informing her of my arrival. She was home at the time; however, the children were away. Sadly, I didn't get to see them. The older girls were traveling, the youngest was attending the academy and my son was still at school. I was there for about an hour. It goes without saying that she was quite upset about the divorce, but I stood my ground and departed after stating my case. It wasn't a very pleasant scene. By the time I left, I was happy to have the dreaded encounter behind me. Things are certainly beginning to change for the better. After the separation and divorce is finalized, I'm going to ask Matilda for her hand in marriage. I missed her so much while I was away. It seemed like decades since I had last seen her. Samuel,...I won't ever leave her again."

"Although I should feel elated that you've found true love with Matilda, who's an extraordinary woman,...I'm truly saddened by it all and sorry that you'll be estranged from your children," he said with a pained expression as he shook his head in dismay. "I can understand the reasons behind your decision,...still it seems so tragic that you and Margaret could never resolve your differences. I'm sure the Missus will be in a state of shock and apt to side with Margaret when I tell her. She was always so close to her. They still correspond whenever possible."

"Ah, hah!...Now I know how Margaret got all the scuttlebutt about me and the goings-on in Chicago." I said with a snicker so he'd know I meant no offense. "Women thrive on gossip. I suppose I've been the subject of their banter for quite a while now. Frankly, I could care less! Aside from the press, they seem to savor sharing the more salacious aspects of my life and all the scandalous gossip about me. I hope that will end with my marriage to Matilda,…but I think not! Oh, well,…I can't let that bother me."

"You're probably right. Women will be women…They stick together like glue," Samuel said, holding the door open as I made my exit. "It should take a few weeks to finalize the sale. I'll let you know when you need to turn over the deed to the distillery. Take care, Albert."

*   *   *   *

Early - June, 1872

Unfazed by the controversy over my legal proceedings, I filed for a separation and divorce from Margaret shortly after the sale of the distillery. I was able to prove that for two years prior to my filing the complaint, she had willfully refused—without reasonable cause—to remain by my side as my spouse. Consequently, I was expeditiously granted a divorce on those grounds. The Cook County Circuit Court judge also decreed that Margaret would no longer have claim to, or be the beneficiary of any proceeds derived from my land and real estate holdings. I gave her enough money at the time of the settlement to permit her a life of luxury until the day of her death.

"Matilda, my love, will you marry me?" I asked as soon as I returned from the courthouse. She was in her tiny apartment awaiting word from me. I was ecstatic as I held her in my arms. "Matilda, I beg you,…please say you will. This aging man is deeply in love and can't imagine living without you. You have shown me a love *of* life and given me a love *for* life. *You*, Matilda, are the love of *my* life. I need you to share my days and nights. I promise to love you *beyond* life itself, my darling, Matilda."

"Oh, Albert! Of course I will!" she replied, feverishly kissing me on the lips, cheeks and forehead—her tears wetting my face. "I'll never leave your side and will also love you forever. I could hardly wait for the day you'd be free of your loveless marriage, my dearest, Albert. I purposely kept my distance until you were able to acknowledge your love for me and ask for my hand in marriage. Even though I knew you were well aware of my feelings for you, I didn't want to interfere with the relationship you had with your wife and loved ones. I'm not a promiscuous woman. My conscience wouldn't allow me the luxury of yielding to my affection for you before that time. If I had, I couldn't have lived with myself. You were a married man with a family and I respected that status. Needless to say, I've been pacing back and forth hoping all was going well for you. These are tears of pure joy! I'm so happy I just can't help crying. Oh, Albert, I do love you so!"

"In fact, everything went quite well, my love. The divorce was promptly awarded without delay on grounds of desertion," I said. I wiped away her tears with my handkerchief and discreetly passed it over my face. As I did so, I thought, "For once in my life, I have someone who truly loves and needs me." Like the alewives that were now clogging the small stream of the Stony Brook, I felt I had just successfully ascended another ladder in my quest for fulfillment.

"I must return to New York next week on business for the railroad," I went on. "I'd like to have you accompany me and,…if it's all right with you, we can also be married there. Uranus will be both best man and witness. I'm sure you must have a friend or relative who can do the same for you."

"Why, that would be perfect," she replied, while pouring some champagne from a bottle into two goblets. "I will telegraph my parents immediately to tell them the good news. They'll be delighted to know that their daughter's marrying such a fine gentleman," she acknowledged with a girlish giggle as we toasted our future. "My family has already been informed about you. They've known for a long time, how much you mean to me, Albert. They wished me well and hoped that I'd find true happiness with you someday. I'm sure my older sister, Sarah, will be more than happy to be my maid-of-honor. Oh, Albert my dearest, I'm in seventh heaven. Please stay, my love. I'll make us something simple to dine on, and well,…we might want to finish this bottle." I smiled and held her tightly as we ardently embraced. After a light yet satisfying meal and a passionate manifestation of our love, we fell asleep in each other's arms.

∗   ∗   ∗   ∗

Mid-June, 1872

With the summer solstice just a week away, New York was wearing its premium, late-spring finery. It was a stellar day. The emerald green lawns and the flowering dogwoods of the parks beckoned a modish public to picnic in the shade of the weeping willows and leafy maple trees that surrounded the small ponds. The beautifully landscaped flower gardens were neatly mulched and weeded. Their array of dazzling rose bushes, voluptuous peonies and salmon-pink poppies were breathtaking. For those who wandered along the meandering paths, the gardens provided a vista that was in sharp contrast to the city itself. It was a quiet respite from the blaring city noises, congested streets and bustling humanity.

"Let's contact a justice of the peace who will marry us on the eighteenth," I suggested, walking arm-in-arm along the streets of the city abutting Central Park.

"That sounds just fine, Albert," Matilda replied, gaping at the displays in the department store windows. "That'll give my family time to get here from Washington. Maybe we can make reservations for them at the same hotel where we're staying.

"Look, Albert, at that haute-couture in this window!…It's the slimmer silhouette!" she exclaimed, pointing to a storefront manikin. "It's called the new "mermaid shape." I can't get over the avant-garde fashions here."

"It looks like it would be a little difficult to walk in, but it's not the least bit overstated…It's actually quite pretty," I noted, stopping to gawk at the many fashionably dressed manikins with matching parasols and hats of diverse styles and shapes. "Why don't we go in, my dear, so you can purchase one for our marriage ceremony and several more for your trousseau. I can just imagine how lovely you'll look in one of those."

"Oh, Albert, darling," she said, heaving a sigh and moving forward past the doorman who opened the door for us. "Most likely they've just come from Paris and are quite expensive."

"I never want you to worry about that while you're married to me," I replied as we neared the ladies apparel section. I lovingly took hold of her chin. "There's nothing I'll relish more, my sweet Matilda, than to grant your every wish and offer it to you on a silver platter. While you're making your selections, I'll spend some time browsing through the haberdashery department. After you've made your purchases, we'll take an open carriage through the park, dine, and then attend a theater of your choice."

"That sounds heavenly, Albert!" she exclaimed as she left my side, waved goodbye with one hand, and then threw me a kiss with the other. I started for a lower level of the store.

Matilda's parents eventually arrived to attend our ceremony. We were married in one of the hotel's elaborate reception rooms. Uranus and Matilda's sister Sarah were our witnesses. Sarah Ann Gray was in her middle thirties and differed from Matilda in every way. She was a strawberry blond with hazel eyes. Sarah had a larger frame and favored the Sourbeck side of the family. Matilda, however, bore a striking resemblance to her mother. Her equally robust husband and their young daughters accompanied Sarah. Uranus had a fairly pleasant and attractive lady friend with him. Also present were several of Matilda's classmates from her university and a small circle of our intimate friends, including several politicians, dignitaries and renowned theatrical artists.

The words of the justice of the peace, "until death do you part," echoed in a familiar way through my mind. I had no doubt that *this* marriage would be a life-long journey for us both. I knew that unlike my first, we would grow old together. I smiled at my beloved as I placed an ornate, diamond, heirloom ring on her finger. It was one that had been in Matilda's family for decades. She was dazzling in the dainty, chic off-white gown—purchased purposely for this occasion. Matilda carried a bouquet of red roses and babies' breath that flattered her radiant, pink complexion. My bride wore her long, silky hair in a loose chignon under a flattering chapeau. Her hypnotic, dark eyes and tiny, straight nose over rose petal lips had captivated me from the moment I first laid eyes on her. Nevertheless, there was no doubt in my mind that it was her dynamic spirit and buoyant personality that attracted me to her. Matilda proved to be a remarkable woman. She was composed and self reliant—fearlessly facing life with a superfluity of optimism and verve.

"You may kiss the bride," the justice of the peace said at the end of the ceremony. He was a rather officious looking, middle-aged gentleman who rarely smiled. His head was sparsely covered with flaxen, curly hair and his spectacles dangled over a long, thin nose on a skeletal face. We turned to embrace each other when a boisterous, enraged voice emanating from the back of the room was heard over the applause of the gathering.

"Oh, Albert!…That's Henry, my ex-husband!" Matilda screamed in horror. She was pale from fright as she placed her hand in front of her mouth. I instinctively reached out to hold her close. Her body shook all over because of his presence and I could sense her fear. In seconds, this treacherous ex-husband was halfway across the room and advancing menacingly toward us with hatred on his face and a loaded gun in his hand. He had an obvious demonic obsession to commit murder. Wild-eyed and crazed beyond reason, he intended to kill us. Although neatly dressed, he was surly and unkempt. His black hair was disheveled and his face partially concealed by a scruffy mustache and beard.

"Take your hands off of her, you bastard!" he shouted in my direction. "She's mine! You can't have her, you son-of-a-bitch! You're a dead man!" His loutish words were shocking and frightening.

It so happened that there were several robust hotel employees in a conference room next-door setting up chairs for a business meeting. These men heard the shouting and shrieks of the women and immediately ran into the room. They came up from behind Henry—at the very moment he fired the shot. They jolted his arm upwards causing the bullet to hit the ceiling. One of these rescuers raced from the hotel to summon a police officer while the other two quickly overpowered and disarmed him. They held him until he was shackled and taken away by several police officers.

"How did he find me? Who could have told him about this? He could have killed us all!" Matilda sobbed, holding me tightly and looking up at me for support. Our brush with death was mirrored in her horror-stricken face as she placed her head on my shoulders. "Oh, Albert, despite the fact that I tried to be discreet, I feared something like this might happen. Please forgive me for this dreadful debacle. I'm so sorry!"

"It's all right, Matilda, my love." I said in a comforting manner while kissing and wiping the tears away from her face and trying to still her shaking body. I spoke softly and calmly over the bedlam that surrounded us. "Thank God no one was harmed…We're all fine. That predator will never be able to try that again. This time his offense is attempted murder. I'll see to it that your ex-husband rots in prison. It wasn't your fault, my dearest. He most likely heard about our wedding ceremony from someone closely connected to your family. Actually,…it could have been anyone.

"Well, we're married now my love, so please don't let this intrusion spoil our special day. Smile…and promise me you won't ever give it another thought."

Everyone breathed a sigh of relief and tearfully embraced us. The euphoria of the occasion—momentarily dampened by a near-tragedy—again prevailed. Before I had the opportunity to invite him to the wedding luncheon, the justice of the peace, who was mortified by the whole episode, congratulated us and promptly left.

"Please join us in the hotel restaurant as our guests," I announced, inviting the several dozen or so people present to accompany us there.

Followed by our guests, we walked through the hotel lobby toward an opulently furnished restaurant. "I love you, Matilda," I whispered as I held my beautiful bride tightly around her waist. Somehow it seemed so right. The simple yet profound ceremony of my second marriage meant more to me than the pretentious, grandiose affair of my first. I knew in my heart that my union with Matilda would not only be one of devoted love, mutual respect and indefinable happiness, but also one that would be harmonious and permanent. If I had to recall just one day at the end of my life, I would choose this day—this moment when Matilda smiled and said, "I do."

*   *   *   *

Early - July, 1873

"Matilda, you must hurry. The carriage will be here to take us to the train station in about fifteen minutes," I said, looking at the mantle clock and checking my pocket watch. "I have our valises ready to be placed in the rack as soon as it arrives. I'll wait for you downstairs."

After our marriage, I moved out of my room in the lodging house and joined Matilda in her small, cozy apartment. We were about to journey east. It would be Matilda's first visit to Cape Cod. I wanted her to see the Cape and Brewster where I had spent my adolescent years and where I hoped to retire, someday. It had always been my home away from home. The Cape was heaven on earth to me. I was also eager to rediscover it through her eyes. The modest Cape Cod cottage on Crosby Lane was ever my destination as I followed my heart eastward. I hoped Matilda would love it as much as I did. I also wanted my parents to get a chance to meet her. I was sure she'd make quite an impression on them.

My heart sang a song of pure joy. I was never happier. To say that my life was now all that I dreamed it would be—is an understatement. Although in my late forties, I felt young at heart and evinced an inner contentment that had eluded me for such a long time. Matilda was everything to me. She made every day a romantic adventure. Her unwavering love, selflessness and devotion continued to astound me. Matilda's heartwarming smile was like a beacon shining from the shoreline into the distant darkness of night. It was a blissful lure that could have beckoned me from the farthest corners of the world.

"I'm ready, Albert!" she called out. "I'll be right down! Have you seen my parasol?" she asked from the upstairs hallway. "It's misting outdoors…I'll need it today…I must protect my chapeau."

"I have it right here with the valises," I yelled back. "Yes, I knew you'd need it, so I purposely left it out along with my umbrella. Be sure to lock the door on your way out, my dearest." Matilda rushed down the stairway. We stood outside and under the canopy of the front entrance when the coach pulled up at the curb. I entered it first so I could help her up the narrow steps into her seat.

"I'm so elated about this trip to Cape Cod. I can't wait to meet your family and visit all your boyhood haunts," she said excitedly as she closed her parasol and adjusted the skirt of her dress. "I hope your parents will approve of me. I'm a bit nervous about that,…considering the difference in our ages."

"They already know all about you, Matilda, my love. When you told your parents about me, I was informing them about you," I said as we rode to the train depot. I was determined to put her at ease and calm her fears. "My parents were pleased that I'd finally found a woman who would be loving and supportive. I believe they're the most forthright and understanding people in the world. I thank them for the person I've become. I've always been grateful for their strict but loving upbringing. Their enduring patience, sage advice and sacrifice have carried me through many crises in my life. I know you'll be warmly received. I have no doubts about that!"

"Whew! That's good to hear! I was a bit apprehensive about being welcomed by them," she replied, exhaling a deep breath.

"Let that be the least of your worries, my dearest," I said, reaching over to hold her hand as we pulled up to the train station.

A mighty locomotive that devoured coal, breathed steam and belched ashes waited on the railroad tracks. Behind its massive iron engine it towed a lengthy caravan of freight and passenger cars.

"All aboard!" the redcap shouted, standing outside the train.

Matilda and I found our seats in the first-class section. We traveled through covered bridges and tunnels that had been carved through hillsides. At times, the train perilously hugged the mountainsides or teetered over trestles that were high above cascading rivers. I had traveled this route many times before, but now, accompanied by my bride, I seemed to be much more aware of my surroundings.

Matilda's enthusiasm, like that of an energetic, inquisitive youngster was infectious. She pointed out the grazing animals and rich farmlands ready to yield their bounty of wheat and corn. Along the way, we tried to guess the names of the small towns we passed through. Their church steeples, which were visible over the distant rooftops and trees, were especially intriguing. Matilda and I were thoroughly captivated by the fleeting view of the countryside. We also dined, read and managed to doze off for a while. Before we knew it, we arrived in New York. From there, we journeyed to Boston, Cape Cod and Brewster.

"It's so nice to have you back in Brewster," Hudson said while politely removing his wide-brimmed hat and opening the family carriage door for us.

"Hudson, this is my wife, Matilda Crosby,…it's her first trip to Cape Cod," I said, shaking his hand. The salt air, the sights of the bay, the windmills and cranberry bogs, along the way, have already endeared her to its charm. I plan on spending much of my time pointing out all the captains' homes, the herring run and other points of interest while we're here."

"Pleased to make your acquaintance, Madam," Hudson acknowledged with a smile and a quick nod of his head. "Your parents are quite excited about your visit, Mister Crosby. Your sisters and their families have also gathered here to greet you and your Missus."

"I telegraphed them a few weeks ago about our intention to vacation here,' I went on. "After we've been with them a while this evening, I'd appreciate it if you would take us to the McCloud House,…the old stagecoach stop. We've arranged for a room during our stay here. My parent's home will be fully occupied with all their company."

"I'd be happy to accommodate you, sir," he replied, lifting the valises onto the back of the carriage. "Just tell me when you'd like to be taken there. I'll be waiting for you with the coach, at that time."

"Thank you, Hudson. I believe nine-thirty would be fine," I said. "Will that be all right with you, Matilda?"

She quickly nodded her head and answered, "yes."

"By the way,…how's Japeth these days?" I asked, curious to know how my old friend was getting along.

"As far as I know, he's doing quite well, Mister Crosby," Hudson replied as he helped Matilda into the carriage. "After you left us last year he had a house built in Plymouth for himself and Veronica. He moved away last May. My family and I are living in the custodial cottage. His son Nathaniel is still living in Harwich."

"Oh, I'm so pleased to hear that," I said, stepping into the carriage after Matilda.

Hudson closed the carriage door, ascended the driver's seat, and then headed toward Crosby Lane and the family homestead. Everyone was there to greet us when we left the carriage. Matilda was welcomed and cordially received. After the initial introductions and embraces, the family accorded us a belated yet intimate—surprise wedding reception.

*   *   *   *

Late-September, 1873

"Matilda, I've just been approached about becoming the president of the Chicago Railway Company," I announced as I walked through the doorway of our apartment. I removed my jacket and kissed her fondly. She held a wick in her hand, pulled up a chair, and then sat at the table. Matilda was preparing to light the brass candelabra in the center of the room. A place setting with a hot, appetizing meal was already on the table. I assumed she had been watching for me and had quickly placed it there the moment I entered through the door. "I've been mulling it over, but I won't give them my answer until I've had a chance to discuss it with you," I said as I reached for a slice of bread and placed it on my plate. "I also intend to keep my position as president of the brewery. I believe I can handle both positions. It's possible that I'll be traveling quite a bit, and I'll be away from you for what could be several weeks at a time. How would you feel about that? Believe me, Matilda, it's not something I'd relish doing…It's entirely up to you, my dear."

"No,…Albert, it's not up to me. It's your decision to make, my dearest," she stressed, gingerly wiping her mouth with her napkin before speaking further. "Yes,…I'll certainly miss you when you leave me, but I know you'll return at your earliest convenience. Your happiness is all that matters to me. If you believe that position will be rewarding, then by all means,…listen to your heart. If there's an occasion when I can join you on your business trips, I'll be more than happy to do so. Otherwise, as you well know, I'll keep myself occupied while eagerly awaiting your return. Either way, my dearest, if it's something you'd like to do, you have my wholehearted consent."

"Well, Matilda, as long as you put it that way," I replied, rising from my chair, extending my arms, and then gratefully embracing her, "I guess, it's settled then! I propose a toast to the new president of the Chicago City Railroad Company!" At the ping of our wine glasses, we giggled like school children. I lifted her from her chair, carried her into the bedroom, and then dropped her on the bed. We fervently embraced and undressed. Overcome by the excitement of the moment, we were filled with such bliss and passion that we inevitably melted into an ecstatic oneness. Matilda, my wife and lover stayed nestled in my arms all through the night.

"I'll have to go to New York around the holidays, Matilda. Would you like to join me?" I asked one evening in early November while adding another log to the fireplace. We had just retired to the parlor for the evening.

Matilda was busy sewing some tiny buttons on the sleeves of a lovely emerald-green, satin dress she had just finished. She was an accomplished seamstress. Her many talents continued to amaze me. I suggested that she not bother to sew her own clothes, as we were wealthy enough to buy them ready-made; nevertheless, Matilda claimed that it was something she thoroughly enjoyed. She maintained that sewing was her hobby, and that she derived great pleasure and pride from the end product of her talent. Designing her own clothes was not only satisfying, but also allowed her to choose her own fabrics and the latest styles.

"That would be grand, Albert!" she replied, startled by my proposal. "I was planning on finishing this dress in time for the several Christmas socials we'll most likely to be attending,...but that's a much better idea! I'm delighted! Will we have time to visit my family in Washington?" she asked. "It's been quite a while since I last saw them." I might also have some exciting news for them by that time."

"Of course we'll spend time with them. I've already purchased the train tickets for our trip to D.C. What do you mean, Matilda? What news?" I asked, puzzled by her statement.

"Well, I haven't wanted to say too much about it until now, but I've missed two of my menses. I believe I may be with child, Albert," she announced, looking up from her work in an apologetic manner.

"Matilda, my dearest! Is that so! Why,...that's incredible!" I exclaimed, completely flabbergasted by her astonishing disclosure. I raced across the room, picked her up from her chair and firmly embraced her. "I didn't realize that even at this late stage in my life, I could still father a child. Why, that's wonderful, Matilda! I'm delighted! I hope those are tears of joy and not...of sadness," I said when I noticed that she was crying.

"If you must know, Albert, I've been quietly despondent lately and quite apprehensive about how you'd receive this news," she replied with tears flowing down her cheeks. "I didn't know how you'd react when you learned that you might become a father again. I wouldn't have faulted you, Albert, if it upset you. You already have grown children. It also occurred to me that you'll be an elderly gentleman by the time our child reaches adulthood."

"That matters little to me! Right now my main concern is you. I love you and will love our child as well," I said, taking my handkerchief from my pocket and dabbing her tears. "How are you feeling, Matilda? You don't seem to be ill or nauseous. At least, I haven't noticed that."

"Actually, I've been feeling fine,...no different than any other time in my life," she replied as she returned to her chair and picked up her busy work. "I've heard some horror stories about morning sickness, but I haven't experienced any discomfort as yet. Maybe I'll be lucky and enjoy a relatively easy pregnancy. Thank God for little favors!" Matilda perked up, smiled, and then went on to say, "Oh, Albert, you'll never know how relieved I am to know that you're excited about my announcement and to hear a genuine concern for me in your voice. I should've realized that you'd be loving and supportive. Every once in a while, I'm reminded about why I love you so dearly. I hope it'll be a boy. I'd love to present you with a son."

"Oh, my darling, Matilda, it doesn't matter if it's a son or daughter as long as we have a healthy child," I said in an attempt to discourage her from setting her expectations on one sex or the other. "Do you think you'll be well enough to take the trip to New York?"

"I don't foresee a problem with that, Albert," she replied. "I've made this dress a few sizes larger just to be sure it will still fit me by late December." We chuckled over that as I held her close and lovingly passed my hand around her waist and over her abdomen. After deciding to turn in for the night, the new mother-to-be and I walked arm-in-arm toward our bedroom.

*   *   *   *

Mid-December, 1873

The snow had been falling all day—adding just the right touch to the holiday decorations hanging outside the shop windows. The snowfall, like a white frosting, clung to the holly and pine wreaths that were embellished with red bows. Spruce and heather garlands adorned the jewelry store entrance and a strap of sleigh bells rang melodiously as I entered to make a purchase.

The shopkeeper smiled as he cordially approached me. He was a gentleman of medium height with prominent blue eyes, a thin raven mustache, beard and hair to match. A small, round loupe hung from a chain around his neck. It dropped down his chest and dangled over a gray bib apron cinched around his waist.

"I'd like to see your assortment of emerald rings, sir," I said as I stomped my feet inside the door to release the snow. He nodded and turned to retrieve a jewelry case at the rear of the store, carried it back with him, placed it on the counter, and then proceeded to opened it.

"This assortment of rings with various sized stones are expertly crafted and set into lovely silver, platinum or gold settings. I'll be happy to answer any questions you might have about any of these. This ring has a one-carat emerald stone placed in an exquisite silver marquis setting," he said, pointing to the ring and removing it from the display box. "I'd say it's the loveliest one of them all. I also have a matching necklace and emerald earrings that complement it,…if you're interested."

"Yes, I agree. It's by far the most dazzling," I replied, delighted that I had found exactly what I was looking for in such a short time. "I'll purchase that one and also the matching necklace and earrings." As I fumbled around inside my coat pocket for a small case with one of Matilda's rings in it, I thought, "Yes, this will be the perfect accessory for her new dress. I'm sure she'll be delighted with this Christmas gift."

"This is the size I need for the ring and here's a bank note for the whole lot," I added. If it's all right with you,…I'd like to wait while you make the necessary adjustment."

"Certainly, sir," he replied, staring at the bank note. "I see by your signature that your name is Albert Crosby. It's been a pleasure dealing with you, Mister Crosby. I must say that you've just made quite a significant purchase." He chose a matching ring size, removed it from a large hoop, and then returned Matilda's to me. "The least I can do is size it for you while you wait. As a goodwill gesture, I'll also have one of my clerks wrap your gift for you. Excuse me while I go to the rear of the store. I'll be back shortly." True to his word, he soon reappeared with my beautifully wrapped gift. "Thank you for your business, Mister Crosby,…and happy holidays to you and yours! I hope you'll return again soon," he said as he handed it to me.

"I don't think I'll want to spend this much money very often!" I joked, waving goodbye. I placed the valuable gift safely in the inside pocket of my coat, walked out the door onto the snow-covered streets, and then flagged down a carriage. Before long, I arrived at the front door of our apartment building. I asked the driver to wait for me.

Since Matilda and I were destined to become parents, a celebration was in order. I planned to surprise Matilda with an outing to a fancy restaurant where we would enjoy a delectable meal and a champagne toast. I also wanted to present her with an early Christmas gift so she could wear her emerald jewelry with her lovely, new dress.

"Matilda," I shouted boisterously through the opened door. There was no answer—only a disquieting silence. That was unusual because she always watched for me every evening. Matilda usually had the door opened and was ready to greet me on the staircase landing with a tender and welcoming embrace. I bolted inside. When I didn't see her close by, I again shouted, "Matilda!"

"In here, Albert. I'm in here," she said in a feeble tone of voice that came from the direction of the parlor. Terrified, I could feel my heart pounding as I rushed in to find her moaning and bent over in a wingchair next to the fireplace.

"Matilda! Oh my God, Matilda!…What's wrong?" I asked, panic-stricken. I knelt down to face her and picked up her chin. She looked at me with unfocused eyes that were barely opened. It was obvious that Matilda was in excruciating pain—it distorted every feature of her ashen face. I thanked God my purchase had not taken long and that I had returned promptly. I was also relieved to know the carriage was still waiting for us.

Instead of an anticipated pleasurable outing it would be an emergency journey to the hospital. I hurriedly placed a coat over her shoulders, picked up her limp body, and then carried her in my arms down the stairway. As I approached the carriage, the driver instantly jumped down to help me with her.

"Please take us to the infirmary immediately! My wife's quite ill and needs immediate care!" I shouted frenetically as I gently placed Matilda on the seat. After fairly leaping into the carriage, I sat down next to her. I wrapped my arm securely around her and held her close. Matilda leaned her head on my shoulders and every so often she moaned and smiled pathetically while gazing up at me with drooping eyelids.

The coachman, sensing the emergency lashed the whip and the horses were off at a gallop. The carriage sped through the city streets until we reached the hospital.

Because she was still bent over in agony, Matilda needed to be carried into the hospital. Once inside, she was immediately placed on a gurney. At that moment, a rather refined, young doctor and an elderly nurse approached her. After I answered a few questions, they placed a blanket over her feverish body and prepared to take her away.

"We'll take care of her from here on. Please wait here, sir," the doctor ordered. "I'll be back later to inform you of her condition." Having said that, they rolled her bed down the hall and were soon out of sight and were soon out of sight.

While I sat in the foyer the minutes passed like hours. Every five minutes, I found myself glancing at the large pendulum clock. I tried to read some of the periodicals spread out on a table before me, but was unable to concentrate and put them back. My concern for Matilda permeated my thoughts. I had never been what you would consider a prayerful person. Although I was not an atheist and firmly believed in God, I was repelled by organized religion. I guess you could call me an "agnostic." However, throughout my life, I often found myself calling upon God's help. Realistically, I was too proud and independent to rely on someone else to solve my problems—especially a questionable, supernatural being with supposedly omnipotent powers. Nevertheless, this was an exception. I needed God's help now more than ever. The outcome of this crisis was completely out of my hands. Matilda's fate rested solely in *God's* hands—not mine. She was wholly at his mercy.

"Now that I've found complete happiness with Matilda, please don't take her away from me…I'm so worried about her!…I beg you to let her live!" I prayed closing my eyes and lowering my head. "Please return her to me and restore her to good health for the rest of her days. You alone have the power to grant this plea, if it be your will."

At that moment, I felt a gentle nudge on my shoulders. I lifted my head and looked up. It was the doctor.

"Mister Crosby, sir, Missus Crosby's had a difficult time of it, but she's going to be all right," he announced reassuringly. However, his expression soon changed from one of comfort to one of empathy. "Her condition was perilous at times. We almost lost her, but she's a strong young woman and rallied. Unfortunately, it's my sad duty to tell you that she'll never be able to bear another child. Your wife was carrying a fertilized egg in her fallopian tube. As it grew, it burst through the vessel and the resulting infection destroyed the tissues of her womb…It had to be removed. I don't know how she was able to withstand the unbelievable pain. We did the best we could to repair the damage. I believe she'll regain her strength shortly. She should be able to leave the hospital in about two weeks, maybe sooner."

Matilda was out of the infirmary in twelve days and although weakened by the trauma, she soon began to feel like her old self. We discussed the fact that we would be childless. I assured her that above all else—her health was my primary concern. I was thankful that she was still with me and—as I pointed out—I already had grown children from my first marriage. When she realized we would be free to socialize and travel together unimpeded, she began to accept the inevitable and the idea gradually gained favor with her. We left for New York as planned and also visited her parents in Washington, D.C.

Nothing was ever mentioned about her hospitalization. Years later, when her mother questioned our childless marriage, Matilda candidly explained why she was barren and requested that her mother keep her confidence. While on the train I presented her with her gift of jewelry. Although only a few weeks had passed since it had been purchased—it seemed like an eternity. Matilda was speechless, overjoyed and appreciative—in that order. Happy and secure in our mutual love and content to be together in good health, we went on with our lives and never mentioned it again.

▼

CHAPTER 21

Late - June, 1874

"Governor William B. Washburn is visiting the Cape. We've been invited to be present at a reception in his honor," Father announced shortly after our arrival at the homestead. "All the local political dignitaries and everyone in our circle of friends here on the Cape have also been asked to attend. I'm sure that you and Matilda will also be welcomed. It'll take place next Saturday evening at the Freeman Cobb Mansion right here in Brewster. Would you and Matilda like to honor him with your presence by attending with your Mother and me?"

"Yes, Father. Thank you, for including us in your plans. We'd be delighted to meet Governor Washburn and your close associates," I replied enthusiastically as I placed our valises inside of the guest room door.

Matilda and I traveled to Brewster to enjoy a month's vacation on the Cape. I had hoped that she would come to appreciate all the wonders of Cape Cod, but I often heard her saying with an exasperated huff, "If Albert can stand it,…I guess I can." I wanted to change her attitude and hoped to foster a love for the seashore, its gentle winds and restorative salt water. While she had to admit it was lovely, it was a bit too boring for her liking. Matilda was always in a celebratory mood and looking to be amused. She sought a livelier lifestyle—either entertaining or—being entertained. We stayed with my parents as other family members were arriving later in the season. Mother and Matilda got along famously. I often heard them laughing together as they sat with their embroidery. They had similar personalities and seemed to enjoy each other's company.

As we walked barefoot along the flats, we enjoyed some exceptionally fine weather. "See that bluff up there, Matilda," I said, pointing to a grassy dune ahead of us, I've always wanted to build a castle on that knoll overlooking the bay and someday,…I will."

"Yes,…I can imagine you'll do just that, Albert," she replied, batting her long, dark eyelashes. She was a ravishing beauty in her sheer, melon dress with matching sash that billowed with each gust. As she spoke, Matilda brushed aside some flattering, wispy, wind-blown locks from her face. The warm breezes off the distant coastal waters managed to scatter her long, brunette tresses. "I hope your future will be as prosperous as your past so you can realize that wonderful dream of yours. Yes,…I'd like to be a part of that vision."

"Oh, you will be, my love!" I replied, squeezing her tightly around the waist. "You're the focal point of the whole idea. You make my fantasy worthwhile. One,…I now visualize as a distinct possibility."

It was time to prepare for the reception. At this time of year, a ground cover of violet sweet peas, magenta vines of wild roses and clumps of heather interspersed with dusty miller brushed our legs as Matilda and I took the familiar path back toward the cottage.

The family coach with Hudson at the reins deposited us at the Freeman Cobb Mansion at about six in the evening. Dozens of carriages from Brewster and surrounding towns were arriving and leaving the estate. As I led Matilda into the front parlor and removed her shawl, I realized how incredibly privileged I was to have this attractive woman as my escort and wife. I was always amazed by her ability to stay thin without the slightest effort on her part. Matilda was radiant in a white chiffon and lace dress—a stunning, chic design she had created for just such an occasion. Miniature orchards in her chignon accentuated her lovely features. She was by far the most attractive woman there. While we meandered through the crowd to the hors d'oeuvre table, I noticed that every man in the main parlor was ogling her. Her charisma was so mesmerizing that the ladies were noticeably unhinged by the attention given this svelte beauty. They also disliked being upstaged by an uninvited "wash-ashore." Envious of her captivating charm and good looks, they found fault and secretly criticized her behind their fluttering fans. Matilda noticed the disapproving glances and raised eyebrows. She also sensed the rather bewildering and tense atmosphere that prevailed when we emerged from the reception line after greeting Governor Washburn and his charming wife.

"Albert, is there something wrong with me?…Do I look all right?" Matilda asked, whispering behind her lace-gloved hand.

"Like I said before, my dear, you look positively stunning," I replied reassuringly. "Pay no attention to those women and their jealous banter. They're undoubtedly resentful of your striking assets and regal bearing. I'd say they're green with envy. Many of them were old classmates of mine. They haven't changed one bit. Their small town ignorance and holier-than-thou attitude has always repulsed me."

As the evening progressed, my parents and I noticed that no one came forward to introduce themselves to Matilda, so I took it upon myself to present *her* to them. The guests were polite yet aloof and reserved. Although I sensed the men would have preferred to engage in conversation because of Matilda's effervescent personality, their female escorts impetuously pulled them away. These people never remained to chat. Instead they immediately turned away and distanced themselves from us. Matilda decided to primp in the ladies powder room where the women had gathered. The men retreated to a drawing room to discuss the politics of the day and smoke their pipes and cigars.

"Can you imagine the audacity of that Albert Crosby to show up here uninvited with his parents, especially with that "hussy" he calls his *wife!*" criticized one of three women seated on a settee with their backs to Matilda. Matilda had entered unnoticed and was standing before a mirror when she overhead snippets of the conversation between them. She quickly hid behind the entrance wall.

"I heard she was a *burlesque* dancer. He was having a salacious affair with her while still married to his first wife. It's scandalous!" remarked the second woman.

"Yes,…and from what's been rumored around here, he divorced his first wife to marry this fortune-hunting burley queen! Why, she's young enough to be his daughter! I've often heard that she's commonly referred to as "an old man's darling." How shameful for his parents. They're such decent, moral people," disclosed the third.

"Hum-m-m,…that's mighty interesting," interjected a fourth woman who was bending over to speak to the other three. "His attempt to include that,…excuse my figure of speech,…"little whore" in our social circles will definitely be a futile one,…no matter how much he tries. The only way she could ever live or own property on Cape Cod would be to marry into it! She's severely damaged his social standing by dragging him down to her level of decadence. Albert Crosby will no doubt be dropped from the Cape's social register."

These local women had callously made it quite clear why Matilda was made to feel so unwanted. Their remarks wounded her deeply. To have them deride her in such a way was demoralizing. She had unwittingly become the butt of scandal and local gossip. Matilda wanted to confront them, but left undetected. Overwrought by a sense of shame and resentment toward the malicious scandalmongers, Matilda summoned me from the smoking parlor and tugged at my jacket sleeve until we were alone and out of sight.

"Can we please leave, Albert?" she begged, her face twisted with grief. Matilda dabbed her tears as they flowed freely down her cheeks. "Please take me home," she sobbed…"I'm not wanted here. I overheard a nest of female vipers defiling my reputation,…*and* yours. The women in the ladies parlor weren't even aware that I was there and listening to everything they said about us." Noticeably chagrined by their denigrating and smarting remarks, a traumatized Matilda went on to repeat everything she heard. "Oh, Albert, I feel so demeaned and unwanted here! It wasn't so much what they said about me, but their vicious character assassination of *you* was reprehensible! As far as I'm concerned their spiteful and crude mannerisms are definitely not in keeping with acceptable upper class behavior,…at least not where I come from. Albert. Please notify your parents that we're about to leave. I don't care if I have to walk all the way home!"

"I can't say I blame you for being upset," I replied compassionately. "Those backstabbing, insolent women will tear someone apart just to further their own self-importance. Their judgmental criticisms are uncalled for! What they've said about you is not only untrue, but also rude and unforgivable. You certainly have a good reason for wanting to leave. In any case, my dear, please don't let yourself be troubled over this. Right now, I happen to be the target of their small talk and insulting remarks. My expulsion from the social register was automatically set in motion as soon as I obtained a divorce and married a theatrical performer. Believe me, symbolically speaking, those fat cows have hoof and mouth disease! Their seething resentment of me created a mistaken image of you! As far as they're concerned, you're a social outcast,…regardless of your educational background. Those ignorant women place little value on intellect and academic achievement. On a sliding scale from zero to ten, the magnitude of their insensitivity falls off the charts! Matilda, my dearest, I could care less about what those vain people think or say about us! They'd best stick to subject matters that should concern them, such as ancient folklore or the ecological consequences of mythological fish stories!" I added facetiously. Matilda grinned and began to snicker over my sarcastic comments. "Those women don't begin to compare to you in any way, my love. I understand your reluctance to stay here and I'll certainly honor that,…however, Hudson's been advised to return for us in less than an hour. Can you endure to remain here until then? It's such a lovely evening. Why don't we take a short walk while we wait for transportation home."

"Yes,…that's a fine idea, Albert. In that case, I'll stay and wait for our carriage to arrive," she replied, resigned to my suggestion. "Oh,…there's a falling star,

Albert!" she exclaimed, revitalized and pointing toward the sky. "Let's make a wish." I was sure our spontaneous wishes were similar—a long and happy marriage together. "It's quite possible that I've overreacted to the whole situation, but I felt quite hurt and discriminated against, by it all," she went on, plucking a rose from a nearby bush.

As we entered the terraced mansion gardens, we were greeted by the scent of fragrant flowers, the sight of flashing fireflies and the sound of chirping crickets that intermingled in the descending darkness. Whereas Matilda was a strong-willed, enlightened woman, she was naïve when it came to understanding that a second wife with a stage background would certainly be rejected by the puritanical culture of New England. The onset of new ethics was long overdue in the so-called "polite" society of Cape Cod. Maybe, I expected too much from traditions that were rooted in old colonial concepts of morality and decorum.

*   *   *   *

Mid-September, 1874

"Samuel, Josiah tells me that several of my real estate investments have made me a rich man. My sizable fortune will allow me to enjoy an early retirement," I announced after removing my top hat and entering his office at the bank to discuss my future plans. "I've decided to resign my positions as president of the railroad and the brewery."

"What do you intend to do with all your free time?" he asked, taken aback by my unexpected disclosure.

"I've always wanted to travel abroad and now that I have the money to do so,…I expect to do just that!" I replied, taking out a packet of brochures from my vest pocket and placing them on his desk. "Matilda and I will be enjoying a long-delayed European honeymoon. We'll be sailing out of New York in about a month. We plan on visiting as many countries as possible. We're likely to be away for approximately ten years. It'll take that long to visit and stay awhile in every country on our itinerary. I'll be back to visit you again before I leave Chicago."

"I wish you well, Albert," Samuel said, glancing at the leaflets then returning them to me. "Though I've never yearned to travel to Europe or Asia, I envy you the opportunity to do so. Anyway,…the Missus would never hear of it. She couldn't bear to venture that far away and leave the children and their families behind. All I can say is that it's well deserved. I trust all will go well for you and Matilda while you're there."

"Samuel, you can be sure that Matilda and I will be traveling first-class all the way," I said, putting on my top hat and preparing to leave. "We intend to stay at the best hotels and dine in the finest restaurants. I'll purchase my own carriage and hire a chauffeur and valet for the duration of our stay abroad. Many of our friends whom we've met through the opera house,…renowned political dignitaries and theatrical performers, have already invited us to stay in their homes."

"Give my best to Matilda, and please keep me posted as to when you'll be leaving, Josiah. I will want to plan a small "going-away" party for you. You'll be gone for such a long time. I know we'll miss you both," he said forlornly as he shook my hand.

After extensive preparations, the day arrived when we boarded our ship. It left from New York City on the 10th of October amid the sounds of a cheering throng and bellowing foghorns. It was quite different from the clipper ship I had sailed on during my days in the merchant marines. This luxurious vessel was propelled by steam engines. The days of the sailing ships were long gone. How technically advanced we'd become in the last thirty-five years!

We arrived in England within two weeks. While there, Matilda and I were guests of Queen Victoria. After spending the good part of a year there, we moved on to Ireland. Our itinerary eventually took us to every country in Europe and parts of Asia. The months and years literally flew by. We were enjoying an extraordinary adventure together. Matilda always dressed the part of a wealthy man's wife. My vivacious spouse and traveling companion brought me recognition and fame. Matilda flaunted her exquisite jewelry and stylish Parisian fashions as casually as a duchess. We were cordially received in every country we visited. Monarchs, dignitaries, famous celebrities and people of great wealth throughout Europe and Asia repeatedly requested our presence at royal functions and affairs of state.

As we toured and traveled through each country, Matilda and I shopped incessantly for items that were not available in the States. We painstakingly selected valuable paintings by the Masters and ornately framed, lesser-known works of art. We purchased superb sculptures and priceless antiques—French carriage clocks, Italian marble statuaries and bronze art treasures. We accumulated numerous ornate and gilded furnishings for a home that we planned to build someday. Most of the objects we acquired were being warehoused with that goal in mind. Uranus saw to it that everything I shipped would be placed in a storage facility in

New York City. Matilda and I decided that when we returned to the States, we would rent an apartment there.

During our ten-year travels, Samuel was kept abreast of our whereabouts. We telegraphed him often, regularly informing him of newsworthy items from across the Atlantic. I received this telegraph on May 10, 1876 while we were in Italy. It read:

> *Dear Albert and Matilda:*
>
> *This is to inform you—Daughter Irene married yesterday—Husband-George Cropsey—Attended wedding-West Roxbury—All well with your parents—Purchased land in Brewster for summer estate—Best Wishes—Samuel.*

Unfortunately, all our telegraphs were not about joyful occurrences. One sent me on November 23, 1882, read:

> *Dear Albert and Matilda:*
>
> *Sending our regrets—Death of your Father-Nathan—Ill-several months—Summer retreat almost complete—Ready by '83—Looking forward to your return—Samuel.*

"My father has passed away," I wailed as I turned toward Matilda who hurried to my side to embrace me. "I hoped he would have hung on to life until we returned. I loved him so, Matilda. He'll be deeply missed by all who knew him. Mother must be especially grieved. I'll send her a telegraph and offer my support and condolences. Though I know Father adequately provided for her in the event of his death, I'll send her some additional funds. I realize now that I should've prepared myself for such an occurrence,…still it comes as a dreadful shock." I tried not to blubber, nevertheless my eyes welled up and the teardrops dribbled down to my chin.

"I'm aware of how much your father meant to you, my dearest," said Matilda, holding me close and trying to sooth me with comforting words. "He was your idol,…your inspiration to succeed through dedication and hard work. Your father wouldn't want you to grieve for him. He'd expect you to remember him fondly for the kind of man he was and the manner in which he lived. Nathan was a gracious Yankee gentleman who cherished his family and lived an exemplary and honorable life."

"Yes, you're right, Matilda," I replied, easing myself from her arms. I reached for my jacket, put it on, and then left for the telegraph office.

In January of '84, shortly before Matilda and I prepared to return home, we received another tragic telegraph from Samuel. It read:

Dear Albert and Matilda:

Regret to inform you—Josiah sustained heart attack—Attended funeral week ago—Summer home completed—Visit us this summer—Have safe trip home—Samuel.

Again, I was shattered by another heart wrenching death. This time, I mourned the passing of Josiah, my dear friend and close associate. I looked forward to seeing him when I returned to Chicago. That was never going to happen now. I decided to send a telegraph of sympathy to Ruth and the family. I couldn't picture being in Chicago again and not having him there. Josiah and Chicago were synonymous in my mind. I mourned his loss for a long time.

Matilda and I sailed from England in February of '84. We arrived in New York on a clear and cold Sunday afternoon. Like a long twilight easing into nightfall, a subtle change had crept over the waterfront. Still—despite the fact that we had been gone ten long years—it seemed as though we had just left. Nonetheless, when we looked around we realized the skyline had changed dramatically. It looked as if we had taken a step from a familiar past into an unknown future. As we approached the harbor, the sight of a massive figure of a woman holding a torch astonished us. It stood on a small island outside the city and was completely surrounded by workmen and scaffolding. We learned that it was a gift from France and that it would be called the "Statue of Liberty." Matilda and I made it a point to attend the dedication ceremony in '86.

"After our trunks are delivered to our Park Avenue apartment, we'll contact your family in Washington and invite them to visit us once we're settled in," I said, turning to Matilda as we traversed the gangplank to the docking area.

"Matilda! Albert!" Our names were clearly heard over the clamor and pandemonium on the wharf. It was Uranus. He was vigorously waving both arms, trying to catch our attention.

"It's Uranus, Matilda! He's over there by his carriage…Do you see him?" I asked, pointing to where he was standing in the midst of the milling crowd.

"Why, yes,…it *is* Uranus!" she exclaimed, delighted to see him after such a long absence. "What a pleasant surprise! How nice of him to be here to welcome us back! Maybe he's come here to celebrate my birthday, today," she said jokingly. Matilda had significantly matured in the years we were away. Like a fine wine that excels with age, she had graciously evolved from a naïve, vulnerable young lady into a poised and sophisticated woman. Dressed in a white ermine coat, hat and muff, she turned heads as she made her way through the horde of people on the dock.

"I sent him a telegraph telling him when we'd be leaving England, the ship we'd be coming back on, and also our arrival date and time," I said. "Evidently, he made arrangements to escort us to our apartment."

After weaving our way through the disembarking passengers and the welcoming crowds, we pressed forward toward an enormous array of trunks. Ours were already sitting on the dock waiting for the porters to take them to Uranus' carriage. As soon as he caught sight of us, Uranus raced in our direction. Following several embraces and handshakes, he led us through the pandemonium where his coach was waiting. Uranus had noticeably aged. Though he was discreet about it, I'm sure he realized that we, too, had also matured over the years. His sideburns matched the gray of his top hat and several new wrinkles were permanently etched on his face.

"Oh, it's so grand to have you both back here on home soil again! It seems like you've been gone for ages. I must admit it's been beneficial for you both. Albert,…Matilda,…you look *great*! Why, Matilda,…you're positively radiant!" he exclaimed as he placed our valises on top of the carriage. I nodded and smiled in agreement with his assessment.

"According to Uranus, the apartment he's leased for us will perfectly fit our lifestyle," I said as we ascended the carriage. "It's situated in mid-town Manhattan, close to the theaters and fashion districts," Uranus grinned and tipped his top hat, silently expressing his delight with my satisfaction. We left the pier, and then headed toward the city to what would be our new home.

*   *   *   *

Mid-April, 1884

While Matilda and I were in the parlor, which was furnished with many items from our trip abroad, the sound of the doorbell momentarily startled us. I was reading the evening papers while Matilda was stitching lace onto one of her dresses. When I opened the door, a messenger handed me a telegraph. Beset by a sense of foreboding, I rapidly signed for it. After the messenger made a quick exit, I closed the door and scanned the envelope. Hoping it was not bad news—I immediately opened it and read its contents as I walked back toward the parlor.

"Who was at the door, Albert?" Matilda called out.

"Matilda, my dear, I've just received a telegraph from Chicago. Evidently, while we were away Mister Downer retired from the brewery. It's been taken over by a John H. McAvoy who's now president of the company," I announced as I approached her.

"Go on, Albert…Why are you being informed about that?" she asked, looking up from a book she was reading.

"They heard I was back in the States and thought I might want to come out of retirement," I replied. "In any case, they wanted to contact me about becoming the vice-president of the Bemis & McAvoy Brewing Company. They're also offering me the position of superintendent of the brewery. It seems they require my expertise to help increase their profit margin. I've heard that it's becoming a very lucrative business under McAvoy's leadership."

"Well, I must say that offer sounds quite challenging!" she commented nonchalantly, searching my face for my reaction. "Is it something you might be interested in?…Would you like to go back to Chicago?"

"It's an exciting prospect. Just the idea of it stimulates me. It sounds like something I'd really like to do," I replied, returning to my chair and hoping that she'd catch the enthusiasm in my voice. "I really hadn't given much thought to returning to work, however,…I've been a bit restless since we've been back. I've enjoyed a long hiatus from being employed as the executive of a promising company,…but I've missed that! You should know me by now, Matilda. It's an invigorating challenge for me…It's part of my make-up. I know we've just moved here and settled into a somewhat leisurely lifestyle, but my heart yearns to be actively engaged and accomplishing something worthwhile."

"Albert, dearest, as I've said repeatedly,…your happiness is my primary concern. If you're content,…then so am I!" she said, putting down her sewing and speaking directly to me. "The expression on your face and your tone of voice reveal an inner excitement you can't possibly hide from me. I can tell that you're positively elated by that telegraph. I could never deny you the fulfillment you seek or your need to feel valued by your colleagues."

"I knew you'd understand," I said, rising from my chair to kiss and embrace her for her compassionate response.

"Don't wait another minute, Albert…Answer them directly. Send Mister McAvoy a telegraph telling him you'll accept his offer, and that you'll arrive next week," she suggested, putting down her book, getting up from her chair, and then walking over to me. "I'll start packing in the morning while you purchase the tickets. That should be soon enough for them."

"We'll keep our apartment here just as it is and return as often as possible," I said, embracing her. "It'll be a nice change for us,…a vacation retreat from the busy, work-a-day life in Chicago. Besides,…we can travel to Boston and Cape Cod more easily from here. I'll ask Uranus to keep an eye on it for us. He'll be surprised to learn that we'll be leaving so soon."

We arrived in Chicago a week later. It wasn't very long before I remembered how chilly Chicago could be in the spring. When we left the train, Matilda and I held onto our hats as we pushed forward against the cold, buffeting winds off Lake Michigan.

"Welcome back!" Samuel shouted, greeting us with an embrace as he took hold of our valises. Surprisingly, his hair, mustache and beard were now snow-white. "It's just grand having you back here in Chicago! Everyone's waiting to see you. Congratulations are in order! I've been notified of your new positions at the brewery, and I've arranged a reception for both you and Matilda,…a small celebration in your honor. It'll take place tomorrow afternoon at the bank."

"Well, thank you, Samuel,…that's quite thoughtful of you. Oh, how I wish Josiah could have joined us. Chicago won't be the same without him," I said forlornly. Samuel nodded sadly, agreeing with my remark. "And how are the Missus and the family? We've returned with some gifts for them."

"Everyone's fine." he replied. "We're looking forward to spending the summers in our new mansion in Brewster. It's the largest and most elegant one in town. I must say it puts those lackluster captains' homes to shame. Speaking of homes, I've taken the liberty to rent a lovely modern apartment for you in one of our newest hotels. It's in one of the nicer sections of the city. I think you'll find it to your liking," he went on, addressing us both. "After we have something to eat,

I'll have the driver take you directly there. By the way, Matilda, I must say you look absolutely fabulous!"

"Thank you for that nice compliment, Samuel," Matilda said graciously, taking my arm as we approached Samuel's carriage. We had always loathed Chicago's blustery winds and were grateful that transportation was waiting for us in front of the train station.

*   *   *   *

Mid-March, 1885

"Matilda, I've received some disturbing news," I announced dejectedly. "Uranus sent me a telegraph informing me that Mother has a life threatening illness and that her health is gradually deteriorating. It hasn't come as a surprise. As you well know, I've been acutely aware of Mother's declining health. I'd like to leave for Brewster as soon as possible. She's been asking for me. Since I wasn't there for her when Father died, I feel I must be with her now. I hope you understand."

"Of course I do, Albert. I'm so sorry to hear that she's not doing well." she replied, holding me close. "We'll leave on the morning train to Boston. I must say it's fortunate that we've been vacationing here in New York. At least we won't have so far to travel."

Matilda and I had planned on spending the month of March in New York. I had worked long hours through the holiday season. It was time for a short respite from the exhausting schedule. I wanted to spend more time with Matilda and also escape the fierce March winds of Chicago that chilled to the bone.

Just before the holidays, Uranus left his real estate business and moved to Brewster. After some fruitless dabbling in the stock market and investments, which had generated negligible profits, he had finally decided to retire. He managed to live comfortably in the family home and become a well-known, respected citizen who supported music and the arts on the Cape.

Hudson met us at the train in Brewster with the family carriage. It was decidedly warmer on the Cape than in New York. While Cape Cod experienced an occasional snowfall, the precipitation at this time of the year was usually rain. The frost-free landscape of the Cape was ready to break out from its somber winter hues to the more verdant tones of spring. Even though I was returning home under rather sad circumstances, I relished being back in Brewster again. It dawned on me that except for my stint in the merchant marine and my long honeymoon abroad, I had always managed—regardless of the distance—to revisit my beloved native town. "I enjoy walking the trails through the salt marshes," I reflected. "The pitch pine forests, the "flats" and the ever present shoreline,…all these pleasurable experiences and much more are forever beckoning me to return…It's my past, present and future,…an integral part of my being…It's in my blood…It's who I am."

"I'm so pleased that you've been able to come, Mister Crosby," Hudson said, opening the door for us when we arrived at the homestead. "Madam Crosby has asked for you many times, these past few weeks. You'll find her in the downstairs bedroom behind the parlor. My wife, Aurelia, is with her and tending to her needs at the moment. Your sisters have all taken turns being by her bedside. Kate is due to arrive tomorrow. Aurelia's been her caretaker in the interim. Madam is growing weaker with each day. Thank God, you've arrived before her passing. She has no idea that you've come to stay with her. It'll be a wonderful surprise!"

"After we visit with Albert's mother, Hudson, Aurelia may leave. I'm sure she'll appreciate being able to return to her family," Matilda said while removing her hat.

"Thank you for everything you and your Missus have done for my mother, Hudson," I said appreciatively, hanging our coats and hats on the familiar hooks next to the door. Matilda walked ahead of me as we moved through the parlor and to the bedroom behind it. I sat and took hold of Mother's limp hand as Matilda stood by my side. The person in the bed was almost unrecognizable. I was shocked! My heart sank. Although she was still a beautiful woman, Mother looked so *old*, thin and pallid. Her once attractive coiffure was now tousled and matted like white virgin fleece.

"Hello, Mother,…it's Albert! Matilda's here with me. We love you…dearly," I said, kissing her on the forehead as she opened her tear-filled eyes.

"Oh, son! You *are* here! I *knew* you'd come!…I've missed you so, Albert!" she moaned in a weak, droning voice that became less and less audible as she spoke. Mother reached out with feeble arms to pull me closer to her. She was welcoming me home with an embrace and love beyond measure. "Nathan's waiting for me, Albert. I can't wait to see him again."

"We'll be here with you, Mother Crosby, for as long as we need to be," Matilda said, taking Mother's hand gently in hers, then reaching to stroke Mother's forehead. "If it's all right with you, we'll relieve Aurelia so she can be with her family." Mother forced a feeble smile and nodded.

Aurelia was a sedate, dark-haired woman of Indian descent whose high cheekbones and square jaw betrayed her heritage. She advanced toward Mother and held her hand. "I'll be close by in case I'm needed here, Missus Crosby," she said reassuringly, wiping Mother's brow with a wet cloth. "I'm leaving you in good hands. Goodbye for now, my dear, sweet lady." Aurelia quickly turned away from her and fearing she might break down and cry in Mother's presence, she hurriedly left the room. Matilda left with her while I remained with Mother.

Every once in a while she asked about the gentleman standing next to me. When she mentioned him a third time, I asked her to describe him for me. In a weakened yet exasperated voice, she said, "I don't *know* who he is!…I've never seen him before!"

"Who *is* this unseen person?" I wondered as I looked around the room. "Is he the "Angel of Death" come to retrieve her spirit and take her to her heavenly home?" I guess I would never know—until it was my turn to leave this world.

"Thank you, Aurelia. I'm sure Mother Crosby appreciates your devoted and tender care," said Matilda, quietly leaving the door ajar behind her. "I hope we'll be able to do as well."

"Although we know she's experiencing a lot of pain, she's a very kind and soft-spoken lady. Missus Crosby's a strong and composed woman who never complains," Aurelia said, putting on her hat and coat. "Please be sure to send for me whenever you think it's necessary. I'll be more than happy to return at any time."

"I promise I will," Matilda replied assuredly as she stood in the kitchen doorway. "It's quite foggy out there and night is settling in. Will you be able to negotiate the path to the tenant cottage in the dark?…I'll ask, Albert, to accompany you home if you wish."

"Oh, I'll be just fine, my dear. I can find my way home with my eyes closed," Aurelia said assuredly while on her way out. Matilda closed the door behind her, put on an apron, and then started to make supper.

"I've made a chicken stew. I hope Mother will eat a little bit of the broth," Matilda said, entering the bedroom with a tray in hand. "I'll try to feed her some of it."

"I doubt you'll be able to do so," I said apprehensively, shaking my head. "Mother hasn't opened her eyes since you left the room with Aurelia. She hasn't been responding to any of my efforts to keep her awake. I believe she may be comatose. We've arrived just in the nick of time. I'm afraid she won't be with us much longer." Consumed by indescribable sorrow, I turned away, bit my lips and wept.

Throughout the night, my sisters and I kept a constant vigil over Mother as she slipped in an out of consciousness. She passed away about six o'clock in the morning. Although she was no longer in pain and looked so peaceful, we all stood sobbing by her bedside. Countless family members and friends from near and far attended her funeral. Matilda and I said our goodbyes, returned to New York, and then subsequently went back to Chicago. The family home and the waterfront acreage on both sides of Crosby Lane were bequeathed to me.

I eagerly looked forward to spending the summer months with Matilda at the Crosby homestead. However—interestingly enough—she believed that all the women who lived on Cape Cod had "web feet." Despite that mind set, I hoped she would someday share my affection for this peaceful escape with its panoramic view of sea and sky.

✳   ✳   ✳   ✳

Late-August, 1886

We had just returned to Chicago from spending most of July and August in Brewster. There was a decided change in attitude toward us. Our savoir-faire fairly dazzled the straight-laced Yankee Easterners. Due to the fact that we had become more sophisticated and self-assured, they seem to have forgotten our "notorious" past. Matilda, too, had long since forgiven their self-righteous attitude. Our travels abroad had allowed us to develop a unique and cosmopolitan outlook on life. Matilda and I became the spark that ignited the otherwise drab existence of our peers. Our close friends included a mélange of royalty, dignitaries and an endless list of well-known politicians and entertainers. The once distant and staid social elite of the Cape considered it a privilege to be included in the company of such intriguing individuals. We had won a moral victory of sorts. Our presence was constantly in demand at every gala occasion. Matilda and I began a social whirl of dizzying proportions.

"As you're well aware, Albert, dearest," Matilda said, approaching me with an expression and tone of voice that revealed a request would soon follow. "When we stay at the homestead next summer, we'll again be inundated with invitations to all sorts of social affairs. I'd like to reciprocate, but the small Crosby cottage is grossly inadequate for my style of entertaining. Remember when we discussed building the castle of your dreams overlooking the bay? Well,…now that we plan to spend our summers in Brewster, I think you should give it some consideration.

"Yes, Matilda,…if you must know, I've been giving that some serious thought lately; however, I don't think I'm quite ready to commit to that right now," I replied. "Although my many and varied investments are really quite profitable at the moment, I've invested a considerable amount of money in an enormous expanse of woodland acreage in Indiana. Samuel and I intend on manufacturing wooden barrels. It's a new venture for me. I've co-signed a promissory note at Samuel's request. He's informed me that one of his largest accounts comes from such a company. His financial foresight is usually so uncanny,…I thought I might as well give it a try. Evidently there's money to be made in barrels."

"You know best, Albert. I'll try not to trouble you about it any further," she said taking my hand across the table. Although Matilda feigned acquiescence, she was clever enough to appeal to my lifelong dream. "It's just that I picture all those lovely furnishings we purchased stored in a dismal warehouse when they could be magnificently displayed in a grand palace such as those we visited in Europe. If, perhaps, you'd think about that in the future,…I'd truly appreciate it."

"I will, my dear,…I will," I said. "By the way, I have some important business to tend to in New York, next week. Would you like to accompany me? It'll give you time to shop while we're there. You may want to purchase a new fall wardrobe or attend the theater."

"Why, yes of course, Albert! My schedule's always flexible where your concerned, my dear. I'd love to return to our charming apartment, attend the fashion previews for the next season and take in the newest theatrical productions," she replied, raising her wine glass to her lips.

In the next six months we made numerous excursions to New York. Some were business trips while others were merely for pleasure. In February of '87 we chose to make New York our permanent and legal residence. My venture into the barrel-making business was faltering. It provided an inadequate return on my money and was a constant drain on my wealth. As a safeguard against possible debt and bankruptcy, I decided to transfer all my assets: properties, investments and bank accounts—to Matilda.

▼

CHAPTER 22

We arrived at our Park Avenue apartment from Chicago at the beginning of the month. Urgent business necessitated my return to New York. However, on the 21st of February, I purposely limited the length of a Board meeting with the New York Railroad administrators. This would allow me sufficient time to prepare for Matilda's fortieth birthday celebration.

"Happy Birthday, my love!" I said as I presented her with a bouquet of red roses. "I've planned a surprise for you this evening. I'll wait for you to change into one of your finest dresses,...one of those intended for a special occasion. You must hurry as the carriage will return for us in an hour."

"Oh, Albert, my hair needs to be done,...but it won't take long. Please wait! The roses are lovely! Thank you, my dearest. It was so thoughtful of you," she replied, taken aback and flustered by my unexpected announcement. Matilda grasped the bouquet, hurriedly added water to a vase, and then placed them in it. "I'll be ready shortly," she promised, quickly exiting the room to change. I read the daily paper while I waited for her.

It was at least an hour before she left her boudoir to join me. Aware of Matilda's stylish coiffures, I knew it would take at least that much time to arrange it to her satisfaction. I had taken this into consideration when I decided to dine at a choice restaurant. I also planned to surprise her with tickets to the opera, *Il barbiere de Siviglia* that was being presented at the New York Grand Opera House. Matilda was still stunning at forty. She was wearing an azure-blue satin dress and the exquisite cultured pearl necklace and earring ensemble I had given her on a previous birthday. I grinned when I saw them again. I remembered that when I presented her with this set, in the company of friends, they remarked that the pearls were as big as marbles. At the time, the sound of laughter filled the restaurant.

"I'm sorry I kept you waiting, Albert," she said, walking into the parlor and giving me the impression that she was truly contrite about the length of her toilette. "I wanted to look my best for this milestone birthday. Reaching forty certainly doesn't make me feel good about myself."

"As always, it was worth the wait and,...as always, my dear, you look positively lovely. Your faultless complexion and shapely figure belie your age. Actually, you look more like twenty-five," I replied as I helped her with her coat.

"Thank you for that compliment, my love. I really needed that today to boost my spirits," she replied as she adjusted her hat. We had dressed warmly with heavy winter coats and scarves to brave the bitter cold outdoors. An evening fog and freezing temperatures covered the landscape with sheer ice. Soon, we were out the door and on our way to her birthday celebration.

"I have a very special gift for you this year, my sweet," I announced upon my return from the restaurant cloakroom. I carried a thick wad of rolled paper, which was wrapped with a large pink ribbon, back to the table. I had purposefully waited until we finished our meal to retrieve it from inside my coat and to reveal its contents. As I placed it in front of her, I said, "In the last few years, I've been aware of the charming and persuasive way you've off-handedly badgered me with those poignant hints concerning the sort of home you hoped to have someday. Well,...happy birthday, Matilda! Here it is! I love you, my dearest, and I always will. I intend to spend my remaining days with you in this,...our dream home." She looked at me with a bewildered expression. After removing the ribbon, Matilda shrieked in delight.

"I don't know what to say! It's just breathtaking! It's the most beautiful house I've ever seen! These blueprints are extraordinary! Why it's much more then just a house,...it's an elegant mansion! I'm so excited! I-I-I'm just speechless!" she exclaimed, stuttering and gasping as she looked at one page after another. "Oh, Albert,...I see that "Mrs. Crosby's House" is written in script on top of every page. How sweet of you to do that! Oh, thank you, Albert," she added gratefully. "My goodness!...When did you find time do all this work?...It's so professional."

"I began this project months ago. I secretly drew up my own plans for a home that incorporated everything we ever wanted. I got my inspiration from the imposing manors along Chicago's Gold Coast," I confessed with a smile. I rolled the designs together then fastened them with the pink ribbon.

"Do you remember mentioning that we needed an art gallery for the many paintings we have stored in the attic of the homestead? Well, my dear,...there's also a plan for that. While it's principally my design, I enlisted the help of an architect to guide me through the finer aspects of it. I'm happy to see that you approve. We'll start construction this spring. Is that soon enough for you, Matilda?"

"Of course, Albert!...Of course it is! Spring can't come soon enough." she replied ecstatically, rising from her chair. "It's so magnificent! Its design and grandeur are more lavish than I could have ever imagined. I noticed that you've also incorporated many of the opulent features we fancied in the lavish European and Asian palaces we visited. When do you think it'll be finished?"

"Sometime in '88, I believe. We'd better hurry or we'll be late for your next birthday surprise," I said with a sly grin as I helped her with her coat.

"Oh, Albert, it certainly can't compare to this last one!" she said with an appreciative embrace as we boarded the carriage toward our next destination. Once inside, she giggled and kissed me tenderly on the lips.

Although we enjoyed the opera, Matilda was clearly distracted by thoughts of her extraordinarily grand, birthday gift. She continued to ask questions about it and elatedly prattled on about the celebrities she intended to invite as guests to our imposing new home. I smiled as I conscientiously listened to her hushed chatter while at the same time trying to be attentive to the opera. It was a birthday—she would *never* forget.

✳   ✳   ✳   ✳

Early -April, 1887

"I've decided to retire from the vice-presidency and also the superintendent's position that I have here at the brewery," I announced at a meeting of the board of directors. "At sixty-four, I've reached a time in my life when I'd like to return home to my roots on Cape Cod and Brewster,...in particular. The salt water and sea spray are as vital to me as the blood that runs through my veins and the air that I breathe. I intend to build a new home along the shores of the bay on some ancestral land that I've inherited. You're all cordially invited to visit Matilda and me when the mansion is completed. I've already prepared for my departure. Everything is in order. My resignation is effective immediately. Goodbye, dear friends and colleagues. No,...I'll just say farewell until we meet again. I thank you for your support and hope you'll wish me well as I begin my retirement years."

My disclosure didn't come as a surprise. Since giving Matilda the plans for our new home, I had often spoken about my intention to retire. I wanted to supervise every step of the construction. To do that—I would need to be free of my responsibilities.

"Matilda, I gave my notice today at the director's meeting. I'll be picking up my things and cleaning out my desk in the morning," I said upon entering our Chicago apartment. I took her in my arms and gave her a convivial kiss. "I'd like to leave for the Cape next week. Once we're established in Brewster, we'll give up our apartment in New York and move the furnishings into our new home along with everything else we have in storage. Most likely, we'll return to New York during the winter. When we do, we'll rent a furnished apartment there. I doubt we'll ever need to revisit Chicago, again."

"That's wonderful news, Albert," she said as she prepared to place our evening meal on the table. "We can stay in the cottage for a few summers until the house is built. Moreover, the spacious attic can also hold all our furnishings, antiques and art treasures until we're ready to incorporate them into the mansion."

"Yes, that's exactly what I planned to do," I replied, pulling up a chair. "Speaking of the homestead," I went on. "I've been contemplating what's to be done with it. The small house has such sentimental value to me,…I've decided to preserve it exactly as it is. In fact, I've already made some significant changes to the architectural design of the mansion. Our new home will be L-shaped and built *around* my father's home. It'll be incorporated as an almost invisible wing to the rear of the mansion. I just didn't have the heart to demolish it. I value my childhood home and cherish the fond memories associated with it. I hope you're in agreement with that, my dearest."

"Whatever makes you happy, Albert," she replied, seating herself at the table. "For that matter, I thought you planned to build your dream home on the grassy knoll directly above the dunes,…the homestead is slightly beyond it. However, it really doesn't make any difference to me, dearest,…if that's what you want."

"Although my dream was to build my castle on the bluff overlooking the bay, I decided to keep the old homestead and its original furnishings. The new house will be close enough to the seashore for my purposes," I said, reaching for my wine glass. "A door that I've included in the design of the mansion will open into the cottage. It will complement the ornate interior of the mansion on the outside,…but on the inside it will reflect the simple décor of the homestead furnishings. The family home will be completely hidden from view," I said, taking a sip from the goblet and returning it to the table. "The only thing that will be visible from Crosby Lane will be the arched veranda that wraps around the front of our lovely, three-story home. I've also added a sixty foot observation tower that should provide a commanding view of the bay and a large portion of the lower cape shoreline."

"That's fine with me, Albert. My only concern was having an elegant manor large enough to entertain our many friends and visiting dignitaries. Whether it's situated directly on the bay or not,…is of little consequence to me," Matilda replied, placing her napkin on the table. "This way, we'll both be happy with the finished product."

＊   ＊   ＊   ＊

Late-March, 1888

Construction of Matilda's new home was started shortly after we arrived from New York in early May of '87. Because it was such a huge undertaking, the Old Colony Railroad laid down a sidetrack from the main line on Depot Road in East Brewster to the construction site on Crosby Lane. The tracks were needed to transport lumber and other materials to the site overlooking the bay. It would also serve to take our future guests directly to our home. The contracting company, John Hinckley & Son of Yarmouth, was in charge of the carpentry. Most of the men enlisted to work on our home were exclusively from Cape Cod.

By the time the actual construction on the mansion was started, it was spring of '88. Matilda and I had spent the winter months in New York. It had been a week since we returned to Brewster. Once the tracks were completed the materials began to arrive for construction and the framing started to take shape.

I eagerly anticipated spring's contribution to a winter-weary world. The first signs were unmistakably beginning to appear on nature's workbench. Without a doubt, the symphony of spring had begun. The sun was shining with a warmer radiance and the trees were starting to bud. For me, the awakening of the natural world from its long winter's sleep was a constant source of inspiration and wonder. The explosive burst of color, the return of the bluebirds and the fresh scent of wildflowers were incredible delights that I could see, hear, feel and enjoy everywhere—everyday. Soon, a triumphant spring would end with the warming of the waters in the bay—the precursor to the yearly migration of the alewives on their excursion from the sea at Paine's Creek to Mill Pond. The calm ribbon of the Stony Brook exponentially turned into a gray surging current, full of activity and life.

"Mister Crosby, I've been appointed supervising foreman for this project. I work for the firm of John Hinckley & Son. It's so nice to see you again, sir," Nathaniel Jenkins said as he reached to shake my hand when I appeared on the site. I hadn't seen him since he was a young man. Although I recognized him immediately, he had noticeably matured. "We should have the exterior completed by the end of this year providing the weather co-operates. I'd like to have it all enclosed by November so that the inside can be completed through the winter and spring. We have a workforce of about forty men. A few additional detailers have been recruited for mantel and lintel ornamentation. Frank Hinckley, who's the junior member of the firm, will oversee the whole task. The Hinckleys have set an especially high standard of workmanship for your mansion. Because their reputation is at stake, the quality of the craftsmen's work is of utmost importance to the company."

"The construction couldn't be in better hands, Nathaniel. I'm delighted to have you onboard," I said, looking at the workmen setting up the staging and scaffolding. "I'm sure your father trained you well. He was a hard taskmaster…How's my dear friend, Japeth? Have you heard from him lately?" I asked. "Why, he must be in his eighties by now."

"Thank you for your confidence in my ability, sir," he replied, glancing over the specifications after opening the roll of plans. "Father's well, but he's walking a little stooped over these days. Actually, he's living with me and my wife, Millicent, in Harwich. When Mother passed away a few years ago, we felt it was best that he spend his remaining days with us. That way we can watch over him in his declining years."

"Please give Japeth my regards," I said, deciding to leave so as not to interfere with his duties. "I think of him often,…especially when I'm here in Brewster. If there's any question about the plans, please check with me. My wife and I will be staying in the homestead until the fall."

"I'll be sure to tell, Father, you asked for him," he said as he smiled, waved, and then started to leave. "So far the plans seem clear and forthright…I'll definitely consult you if there's a problem."

Nathaniel who was in his late thirties was a rather handsome young man with dark-brown, wavy hair. He was a well-built chap with broad shoulders. Although I recognized a striking resemblance to his sister Rebecca, Nathaniel's features and mannerisms were decidedly his own. He didn't look at all like his brother, Aaron, who favored Japeth. I enjoyed being in his company. He was polite and accommodating. It was eminently pleasurable to have him in charge.

"Matilda, I'd like to give our mansion a special name. I've been giving this a lot of thought lately," I said, putting down a book of poetry that I was reading. "I'd like to call it "Tawasentha" from *The Song Of Hiawatha* by Henry Wadsworth Longfellow. It's one of my favorite poems. The first line reads: "In the vale of Tawasentha," which is serene and picturesque. Our home will be such a place. I believe it deserves this fitting name."

"Why, that's a beautiful name, Albert! Tawasentha it is then!" exclaimed Matilda. "It sounds as elegant as the house itself."

"I'll have the name Tawasentha prominently placed on the mantel of the most conspicuous fireplace in the mansion," I said as I left my easy chair to retire for the night.

✳   ✳   ✳   ✳

Early - June, 1889

While we were in Paris for the spring, the John Hinckley & Son Company held an open house. The construction company was so proud of our imposing new house that it sent out "By Invitation Only" notices of its near completion. The engraved invitations were sent to dignitaries, public officials and correspondents from several prestigious publications. They were encouraged to inspect the newly erected Crosby Mansion—undoubtedly one of the grandest homes of its day on Cape Cod. One journalist submitted this report in one of the local newspapers:

"The exceedingly elegant and roomy, Romanesque Crosby manor constructed by the John Hinckley and Son Construction Company, is situated on the site of the family home that has been preserved with the utmost care. The old homestead, whose frail split fence is heavy with roses, has been harmoniously incorporated into the new structure. The Crosby's summer retreat, called 'Tawasentha' is located on the West side of Crosby Lane in East Brewster. Oaks and willows shade the road leading to the Crosby's Landing. Fragrant grasses and sweet fern cover the winding path through pastures and woodland. Crosby Lane leisurely follows to the sand dunes that edge the shore and border the grounds of the mansion. The Crosby home sits serenely by the sea overlooking the bay. The mainly 'Queen Anne' mansion integrates several architectural interpretations, including, among others, 'Colonial Revival' or 'Palladian Revival' The house, with its conglomeration of architectural periods and details, is quite elaborate. It boasts intricate gables, dormers and a collection of chimneys, small towers and classic urn finials on the roof corners as well as Victorian bow windows and a lighthouse. The ornamentation, though imaginative is tastefully done. The use of a dazzling array of materials adorns the inside

and out. The Crosby's, clearly obsessed with grandeur, spared no expense in build-ing the Brewster Mansion. A long, graceful veranda with its columns and Roman arches graces the front of this grand Victorian home. A tower 60 feet high sprouts from the rooftop above the main entrance. The reception hall is said to have been inspired by a room the Crosbys visited in Buckingham Palace. A spiral staircase with delicately crafted balustrades lead to the upper floors of the mansion and a balcony that overlooks the sea. From the viewing tower one can survey the whole inside shoreline of the Cape Cod Peninsula. The bedrooms, situated off a balcony that forms a hallway over the front entrance are large and airy. The estate contains 35 rooms and 14 fireplaces. Designed with English tiles and mantels imported from Europe, each fireplace has its own unique features. The floors on the entire first level of the new Crosby mansion are of polished oak. The library is finished in mahogany panels with exquisite Japanese hangings. The Crosbys duplicated the parlor, called 'The Versailles Room' after a personal tour of the palace in Versailles, France. The billiards room is finished in natural woods and resembles an indus-trial baron's hunting lodge. The elegant dining room in antique oak has a large fireplace and a sizeable ornate music box. This reporter noted that the scalloped arches bordering and topping the wainscoting painstakingly matched those on the outside façade of the building. The rooms are finished with a colonial flair. The furnishings, decorations and hangings are the best obtainable. The mansion boasts an incongruous mixture of massive, gilded furnishings, elaborate foreign finery, exquisite porcelains, solid brass fixtures, art works and life-size marble statutes throughout. The structure has steam heating devices and is illuminated by gas that is manufactured in the basement. Fresh water is supplied to the building by engines and pumps. The Crosby's installed a communication system throughout the mansion for the convenience of the residents, servants and guests alike. A large three-story carriage house in close proximity to a caretaker's home is located where the barn of the old homestead once stood. The mansion also boasts a fireproof art gallery. The thickness of the walls consists of four courses of brick hidden beneath the clapboards. The gallery is 70 feet by 50 feet and two stories high. It is placed directly to the south of the billiards room and connected to the house by a foyer. Its design includes a precision-designed clerestory and glass ceiling to provide even illu-mination for the gallery. Dainty chairs and plush sofas are scattered everywhere in the room so one can sit and admire the impressive taste and wealth of its owners. Within its walls, Mr. Crosby has exhibited a plethora of rare collectibles that include priceless paintings, statuaries and bronzes acquired by the Crosbys during their many years abroad. I found the Crosby mansion an imminently imposing landmark. Brewster can be particularly proud of this most elaborate and expensive showplace. The architectural heritage incorporated within its walls is the most superb in all of Barnstable County. Also, its gallery undeniably contains one of the foremost and valuable collection of art treasures in the Commonwealth of Massa-chusetts—and possibly all of New England.

Matilda and I thought it was an excellent article that aptly described our perfect and beautiful new home. We were especially pleased with the gratifying announcement that our collection of art works was the largest and most imposing in the county. It helped solidify our standing in the Cape Cod community and social circles. Matilda immediately began to make plans for a grand and magnificent "open house" reception.

$$*\qquad*\qquad*\qquad*$$

Mid-September, 1889

I had a chance encounter with Hudson at the carriage house. I inquired about Nathaniel who had been conspicuously absent from the premises.

"Hudson, I haven't seen Nathaniel since I've been back from France. He hasn't been around to direct the final touches, yet there's still quite a bit of work left to be done on the mansion…It's not nearly finished. Has he been transferred to another project?…Has something happened to him in my absence?" I inquired.

"Unfortunately, Nathaniel was critically hurt when a scaffolding gave way from under him." he replied despondently while grooming the horses. "He fell from the second story and suffered some internal injuries. It happened sometime in late May. He's at home in Harwich,…but from what I hear he's not doing very well. Nathaniel's been replaced by another foreman. It doesn't seem the same around here without him."

"Oh, I'm so sorry to hear that!" I said. "I hope he recovers. Japeth will be devastated if anything happens to that young man…It'll kill him for sure. Hudson, please let me know if you hear anything more about him."

"I will, sir," he replied, walking out of the carriage house with me. "Many of the workmen are his good friends and stop by to visit him every once in a while. I'll be sure to ask them how he's doing and keep you informed."

"Thank you, Hudson. Missus Crosby and I will need the carriage this evening," I said. "We've been invited to attend an anniversary celebration at the Captain Elijah Cobb house. We'd like to leave about seven. Please have the carriage ready for us at the front entrance."

"I'll be there and waiting for you at seven," he replied, turning toward the tenant house.

"Matilda, a detailer from Boston is arriving sometime next month to engrave the woodwork and wainscoting. I plan to have the name "Tawasentha" placed in raised letters on this mantel," I announced while standing next to the fireplace in the dining room that was adjacent to the front entrance. The mansion will officially be called by that name from this point on."

"Why, I've been calling it Tawasentha from the day we moved into it, Albert," she insisted with a questioning smirk and an annoyed humph. "I've just about completed the arrangements for the open house. I believe it'll be festive to have it just before the holidays. Tawasentha will be elegantly decorated with an enormous, twelve-foot Christmas tree in the entrance hall. I'd like to stay here as long as possible. It's like living in our own palace. We can leave for New York soon after that. Does that meet with your approval, Albert?"

"I must say that's a *great* idea, Matilda! It'll be pleasurable being here at that time of the year," I replied, holding her close and embracing her. "I'll also hate to leave for the winter. I'll miss the view of the bay from our bedroom windows and our leisurely walks along the shoreline and the flats."

A few hours later, the doorbell rang on the side entrance. Our butler, Luis, who was newly hired, answered the door and announced that it was Hudson. Luis was a soft-spoken gentleman in his late forties. He had emigrated here from Spain as a young man with his family. His slightly graying, black hair and mustache, his intense dark eyes, olive skin and melodic Spanish accent gained much favor with Matilda and me.

"Please show him into the kitchen," I instructed. "Luis, would you be so kind as to make us a hot toddy? There's a fall chill in the air. It'll help to warm him."

"Mister Crosby, as you know I've been keeping you informed about Nathaniel Jenkins," Hudson said, seating himself down at the table. "He had stabilized these last few months, but took a turn for the worse a few days ago. Regretfully,...I must tell you that Nathaniel passed away sometime last evening. One of the carpenters still working on some unfinished detail work stopped by to inform me about it. I know how fond you are of Japeth and his son. During the years we worked together, we also became close friends. The funeral will take place in two days. I'll be more than happy to accompany you,...if you should wish to attend."

"Oh, Hudson, that's such distressing news!" I said, shaking my head in dismay. "It just so happens that Matilda and I have a commitment that day. Even so, I'll plan to attend the funeral with you. She can manage to fulfill that obligation without me." I took the hot toddy from the butler's tray, handed it to Hudson, and then took one for myself. "I'm sure she'll be fine with that. If it's a nice day we'll use the Victoria carriage.

"Fine, sir, I'll pick you up around eight," Hudson replied. "I'm not looking forward to seeing poor old Japeth so grief stricken, not to mention Nathaniel's wife and her three fatherless children. The death of that young man is so tragic," Hudson added in a melancholy tone while sipping his toddy. "Just when we thought he'd recover,...he unexpectedly succumbed to his injuries. No one would have predicted that. It's unbelievable! Life just isn't fair sometimes...It's so heartbreaking! Excuse me for blubbering. I thought the world of Nathaniel. He was such a strong, vibrant person and a gentleman at all times. Goodbye, Mister Crosby...I'll see you on Thursday." With tears welling in his eyes, he finished his hot drink and left.

On Thursday morning, Luis summoned me to the door. Hudson had arrived to pick me up for the funeral.

"I had to take the town coach, sir. It looks as though it's about to rain any minute now. In fact, it's already started to drizzle a bit," Hudson said as he stood in the doorway with an umbrella.

"That's fine, Hudson," I replied as we walked briskly toward the carriage. I clutched my hat as we made our way through the wind blown rain and fog. "It might be best after all. Some folks might need transportation to the cemetery. This way we'll have room to accommodate them if need be. Missus Crosby's not feeling very well today,...she has a mild cold. She's chosen to postpone our appointment and stay at home."

Our somber trip to Harwich took about an hour. We arrived just in time to see the horse driven hearse carrying Nathaniel's casket stop in front of the church. We hurried past it, went inside, and then sat in a rear pew. I was surprised to see the church overflowing with mourners. The minister delivered a glowing sermon. He eulogized Nathaniel as a model of absolute perfection. Nathaniel exemplified the very best of human virtues—someone who was filled with love for his fellow man, a paradigm of charity and propriety. We learned that Nathaniel had been a devout Christian who helped his church in every possible way. He not only held a bible class, but he was also a church deacon who gave generously of his time, energies and money to support his place of worship.

After the funeral service, weather had taken a turn for the worse. I offered the coach as transportation to the cemetery. Two young couples were delighted to join us. I was happy to oblige. Hudson and I introduced ourselves as they ascended the steps to the coach.

"Are you related to the deceased?" one of the young women asked. "Nathaniel and his wife Millicent are dear friends of ours. We're devastated by his death."

"No, I wasn't related to him," I replied. "Nathaniel's elderly father was the caretaker of my family's homestead for most of his life. He was born after I left for the merchant marines. From there I moved to Chicago. It sounds like Japeth raised a mighty fine chap. I haven't as yet had the opportunity to offer him my condolences."

"We heard that Nathaniel was injured while inspecting a mansion being built in Brewster," the young woman's husband said. "You introduced yourself as Albert Crosby from Brewster. We read about that palatial home in the newspapers. The article stated it belonged to a Mister Albert Crosby. We knew Nathaniel was a carpenter foreman for the John Hinckley & Son Company and that he worked on that mansion. Is that your home?"

"Yes,…I'm sorry to say it is," I replied, lowering my head. "I never found out about his fall until my wife and I arrived here in Mid-September. I kept abreast of his progress and was relieved to know he was slowly improving. I was shocked to learn of his death. Nathaniel's father is a dear friend. He taught me every skill I ever needed to get along in this world. And above all, he set exemplary standards that I've tried to live up to my entire life."

"Well, his father must have raised Nathaniel with that same set of values," the other woman injected while removing her handkerchief from her purse and drying her eyes. She was seated directly opposite me. "Although he was unpretentious," she added, "Nathaniel was the cog in the spiritual wheel of our congregation. Our church services and socials won't be the same without him."

"We thank you for offering your fine coach for our trip to the cemetery," the second woman's husband said gratefully. "A carriage will be there to pick us up after the graveside services."

"It looks as though we've arrived at the cemetery," I announced, glancing out the window and noticing that the rain had abated. "I don't believe you'll need your umbrellas," I added…"The skies seem to be clearing. The mourners are gathering over by that large willow next to the stone wall."

We walked over as a group and with lowered heads stood around the casket. At least fifty people were present. After a long silence, broken only by chirping birds and whistling winds, we joined the minister. The cleric reiterated that Nathaniel was now in God's hands and that heavenly peace would be his reward.

The minister returned to his carriage. The grief stricken widow, who was a rather pretty, yet plain young woman advanced toward the casket with her small children and immediate family members. They took turns placing flowers on it. As everyone was turning to leave, I approached a disconsolate Japeth and shook his hand. I embraced him and offered my condolences. Hudson, who was just behind me, took his turn to do the same. I repeated my gesture of sympathy with Aaron and Bethany whom I hadn't seen since my childhood days. Japeth introduced me to Nathaniel's family and told them that I was the owner of the mansion on Crosby Lane.

"Japeth, I'd like to talk to you privately if I may. Can you spare a few minutes before you leave for home? I asked. "I'll walk back to the carriage with you,…if that's all right?"

"Of course…Thank you so much for coming today, Albert," he replied. "You don't know how much this means to me. What would you like to speak to me about, Albert?"

"I'm sorry to say, I only had few opportunities to converse with Nathaniel while he was alive, Japeth," I went on. "However, when I did, I couldn't help but admire his genteel, sensitive nature. I've heard nothing but glowing accolades about him from everyone who knew him. I'm honored to have attended the funeral of such a fine young man. You certainly can be proud of his legacy. It's definitely a tribute to your upbringing.

"I know that it wasn't anyone's fault, Japeth. Nevertheless, just the fact that he was working on my home at the time of the accident is quite disconcerting for Matilda and me," I added, removing a leather folder from my jacket pocket. "I'd like to present you with this bank note for his family. Will you see to it that they receive this? It's a contribution made in his memory and a token of my concern for their welfare. It's the least I can do to lessen their financial burdens and make life easier without him."

"Albert, as usual you're much too generous," Japeth said, tucking the folder in the inside pocket of his coat without opening it. "The construction company he worked for paid him all the while he was incapacitated. They wanted to show their appreciation for the efficient and timely completion of your home. Nathaniel was one of their most dependable workers. In any case, I thank you on behalf of myself and the family."

"You're entirely welcome, Japeth," I said with a tip of my hat. We stopped in front of his carriage. "And how have you been,…dear friend? Despite the circumstances,…it's so nice to see you again."

"I can feel myself failing by the day," he replied. "Living to bury another one of my children can hasten the death of an old man like me. Regardless, I'm in good hands. Millicent is very attentive and caring. Anyhow,…Albert, before I leave here today,…there's something I must tell you."

"And what is that, Japeth?" I asked, bewildered by the dire sound of his ambiguous statement. "You've never kept anything from me, dear friend."

"Even though I've often felt you should have been told before now, I made a solemn promise that somehow,…I've managed to keep," Japeth said with a heavy sigh. "Now it seems rather senseless to continue the deception, especially since you've been so generous to Nathaniel's family. Albert,…I believe you should know,…*you* were Nathaniel's father,…not *me*!"

"Japeth, that can't be so!" I exclaimed loudly, quickly looking around to make sure I wasn't overheard. "N-o-o-o,…that's impossible! How can you say that! I know you wouldn't lie to me. Please,…please, Japeth,…tell me it's not true! Why are you telling me this *now*?" I asked staggered by his revelation. My mind was racing backwards trying to remember all the circumstances that could have possibly led to this traumatic moment.

"Albert, I wish for your sake that it wasn't so,…but so help me God,…it's the honest truth. Nathaniel was *your* son and Rebecca's. I'm sad to say he was conceived when the two of you became intimate with each other. Veronica and I raised him as our own. It's a good thing you left for the merchant marines when you did. I was so furious with you,…I wanted to whip your hide! I would have thrashed you right then and there if I had had the opportunity to do so.

"I was adamant about telling your parents, but Rebecca begged me on her hands and knees not to do that. My anger soon turned to compassion when she made me realize how much she loved you. Rebecca said she loved you more than life itself, and that she was even more to blame for what happened,…than you were.

"While on her deathbed she made us promise never to tell you,…Nathaniel,…or anyone else for that matter, lest it might inadvertently be revealed someday. Rebecca actually died of complications from childbirth. The attendant couldn't stop the hemorrhaging. For her sake, I fabricated the cause of her death.

"In a way," he went on,…"it was a relief not to have to tell your parents. After all, it was the least we could do. We felt so beholden to them for their many kindnesses and generosity toward us. If you revere the love you had for my daughter and your friendship with me,…you'll promise me that what I've just disclosed will stay solely in your heart until your death."

"Oh, Japeth,…I'm so sorry that I've put you through such pain for all these years. I loved Rebecca. I planned to marry her when I returned from the merchant marines. Alas,…it was never meant to be. Rebecca has always held a very special place in my heart. I've never forgotten her, Japeth. I promise to honor your secret and never violate your sacred trust…No one will ever know," I replied as I struggled to make sense of what I had just heard. I took his frail body into my arms and embraced him tightly. I needn't have said another word because that gesture forever sealed the pact between us. "Farewell, dear friend. Best wishes to you and the family. May your broken hearts be healed by the passage of time and the loving support of those dear to you."

I was in deep thought as I walked toward the coach. Sadly, I contemplated my paternal and filial ties to Nathaniel. I tried to face the unspeakable truth that had emerged from my conversation with Japeth. Hudson was already in the driver's seat patiently waiting for me. When I neared the carriage, he jumped down to open the door. .

As I sat there alone staring out the coach window and trying to reconstruct my past, I suddenly became aware of something that had truly bothered me for a long time. Somehow without knowing why, I had always been intuitively ill at ease where Nathaniel was concerned. My life had become similar to a complex puzzle—one that was almost finished, but nearing its completion—an odd, missing piece, which had purposely been left out because it didn't seem to fit anywhere, was discovered and positioned exactly where it belonged. When finally in its place, it became quite obvious—the remainder of the puzzle could never have been finished without it.

*   *   *   *

Late-October, 1889

"Albert, Mister Robbins has arrived here from Boston. You'll have to advise him as to where you want him to apply his skills." Matilda said, leading him into the billiards room and immediately leaving us. I was leisurely reading the newspaper and smoking my pipe.

"Please have a seat, Mister Robbins," I said, indicating that he should sit in a chair opposite me. "Your craft is among the last finishing touches needed here. I'll point out the areas where I'd like to have the carvings done. Some of the lintels, wainscoting and trim around the windows and doors require your detailing expertise. However, I do have one special request. The name my wife and I have given this mansion is Tawasentha. I'd like to have that name carved in raised letters and placed on the fireplace mantel of the dining room. It'll be called the Tawasentha room. My request is that when you place the letters of this name onto the mantel,…you reverse the "N." I know this may sound strange, but I have my reasons. Let this be your last project. Please complete this particular task immediately before you leave."

"Well, I must say that is an odd request, Mister Crosby," he replied skeptically as he got up to leave the room. "Nevertheless, I'll do as you wish, sir. I just hope it won't reflect on my work."

"Don't worry about that. I know exactly what to say," I assured him. We walked out the door toward the mantel in question. "I'll just explain that you had a young apprentice place the lettering onto the mantel and that several hours after you took your leave, I noticed the error. I decided not to have you return for such an insignificant error and,…I'd just leave it that way."

"Sounds credible to me, sir," he replied, shrugging his shoulders. I'll do as you say. After all,…it is *your* home, not mine."

Once I had regained my emotional equilibrium and come to terms with the fact that I was Nathaniel's father, I wanted some sort of reminder of him. I could never comprehend the reason behind Nathaniel's death. He was so young and so vital. Nathaniel's passing served no purpose and seemed so senseless. It dawned on me that the dining room near the front entrance would be the one place most often used during the day. I would have the letters denoting the name Tawasentha whittled and positioned onto the mantel with the letter "N" reversed. From that point on, every time I sat down to eat or walked by it, I would be reminded of Nathaniel. It was a discreet legacy to his memory—one that would live on for decades to come and for as long the mansion existed. No one would be the wiser. It was my own unique way of paying tribute to a son I barely knew.

"Albert, did you notice that the "N" is reversed in the name Tawasentha on the mantel in the dining room?" Matilda asked…"Why, that's an eyesore! I should think you'd have that error corrected," she admonished with righteous indignation, a few hours after the detailer left for Boston.

"Oh, Matilda, I doubt he'll come back from Boston just to fix such a minor mistake," I replied, dismissing it as inconsequential. "It'll make for a fine topic of conversation,…don't you think?"

"No,…not really!" she answered with a huff as she left the room, obviously annoyed by my indifference.

Every time someone brought up the subject of the inverted "N," Matilda would shrug her shoulders and indignantly remark, "For some unknown reason, Albert's not a bit concerned about it. So,…I guess if it doesn't bother him,…it shouldn't bother me, either."

*   *   *   *

Mid-June, 1890

While in New York this past winter, Samuel, who had now retired on Cape Cod, had written me that Japeth, my dear friend and confidant had died at the end of January. His secret died with him and was ever safe with me. Samuel also advised me that our combined venture into the barrel business was failing miserably. Enormous debts were beginning to deplete our once bountiful accounts. The financial effects could be devastating. As co-signer of the note, I was slowly being plunged into bankruptcy.

"Matilda,…just in case I'm taken into bankruptcy court, I think we should see to it that the deed to this house is solely in your name. Otherwise, I may lose the mansion to the creditors," I declared after receiving an alarming telegraph from Samuel. "We'll make the trip into Barnstable in the morning,…if that meets with your approval."

"That sounds like a wise move on your part, Albert." she said approvingly as she checked the clean linens for the guest bedrooms. "I'll be ready to leave about eight. In any case, my dearest, while you haven't wanted me to worry about it, I've been keenly aware of the problems with your supposedly "risk free" undertaking with Samuel. I've noticed that you haven't been sleeping soundly at night. You've been tossing and turning and finally rising at dawn. I wish you'd be more approachable and confide in me, Albert.

"You'll be surprised to learn that since we've been married, I've used portions of the generous allowances you've given me to make some shrewd investments of my own. I've been speculating in real estate, railway and brewery stocks among other quite profitable commodities. I suggest we place those securities on the market while the price is still high and apply it toward your debt. I'll sell my valuable jewelry and stocks that are in the vault at the bank and also give you some cash from my personal account. If you remember well,…all your properties, investments and precious art works are in my name. I believe my assets should be enough to cover your note without having to touch what's actually yours…Are you agreeable with that?"

"Matilda you're an absolute marvel! You're astonishing! It's no wonder I fell in love with you!" I exclaimed, coming up from behind her and placing a kiss on her cheek. As usual, my intuitive Matilda was invariably prepared for my possible financial downfall.

"You don't know how much this means to me, my dearest Matilda. I feel like a weight has just been lifted from my shoulders. Being married to you is the best thing that's ever happened to me. Thank you for coming to my rescue. I'm sure I'll sleep well tonight and wake up in your arms in the morning." We giggled like honeymooners as I poured each of us a goblet of our favorite Chablis. Matilda and I toasted to our success over possible financial ruin and future happiness.

That summer we experienced some fierce thunderstorms. Lightening flashes frightened Matilda to death. She managed to concoct some silly things to protect herself from them. Matilda usually put two chairs together with rubber pads and lay across them with her feet off the floor to insulate her against the lightning bolts. Her absurdities were hilarious. I frequently split my sides laughing at her bizarre idiosyncrasies. She placed barometers in every room of the house and ordered that *no* water be drawn throughout the mansion.

Matilda also worried about the dry hay catching fire in the barn. If she thought a storm was on its way, she enjoined Hudson to get the hay out of the barn, run out, and then throw pails of water all over it. Fortunately, there was never a fire. Nevertheless, before every storm my strong-willed wife could not be dissuaded from her routine. After each tempest had ended Matilda invariably took credit for saving the barn. It would take volumes to describe her sometimes funny—sometimes sad—and sometimes infuriating struggle to defeat Mother Nature.

Matilda was also quite patriotic. A large American flag flew every day without fail from a pole on a high knoll overlooking the bay. To Matilda's dismay lightning bolts frequently struck the flagpole. Eventually, she had the pole taken down for days during the summer—for fear it would attract the lightning.

Thursday was Matilda's "Health Day." We seldom planned to be together on that day of the week. If we had guests, she informed them upon their arrival that she would be preoccupied on that day. Matilda let it be known that she was to be excluded from any plans made on Thursdays. The fifth day of the week was purposely set aside for her personal beauty and health needs. She spent most of the day tending to her grooming from the tip of her toes to the top of her head. The results were usually extraordinary. Matilda always emerged from her Thursday rituals looking fabulous.

Accustomed to this weekly routine I invariably made myself scarce by visiting with friends or family. During the summer months, I enjoyed shell fishing or an excursion on my sailboat in the bay. I took pleasure in being free to do whatever I chose to do on that day.

Matilda's fabulous complexion belied her age. She refrained from being out in the sun for fear of damage to her fair skin. Like Margaret, my wife shied away from tanning because she abhorred a bronzed, wrinkled face and limbs. That was their only similarity. In her estimation, a ruddy appearance was unbecoming and signified that she toiled outdoors on a farm or in the gardens. Refined ladies would never do such as thing. Regardless of the heat, whenever she ventured into the sunlight she wore a large brimmed hat and a garment with long sleeves.

My dear wife also had one fault that seemed to worsen with the years. She was never on time! Matilda was *always* fashionably late no matter how important the occasion. It became a mild aggravation that continually frustrated me. On our twentieth anniversary, I gave her an expensive piece of jewelry. It was a diamond pin that spelled out "Hurry Up." Although appreciative, she found it to be quite amusing—of course—she never wore it. My sweet, precious Matilda eventually had diamond earrings made from it.

▼

CHAPTER 23

Mid-August, 1890

"Albert, I'm planning on hosting an "End-of-The-Season" social gathering the first week of September. Will that meet with your approval, my dear?" Matilda asked somewhat timidly while rocking in a wicker swing on the veranda. "You know how I dearly love to entertain. We've been the guests of so many of our friends,...I thought it'd be nice to reciprocate. I intend to invite every one of them to our gala party. I'd like to have it during the late afternoon and early evening...I might also enlist the services of a small musical ensemble. If it's a pleasant day we can have it out here on the veranda and on the grounds."

"Sounds as though you've already begun making plans for it," I said, sensing her extraordinary enthusiasm. I held my pipe in one hand and a glass of ice tea in the other as I sat in a cushioned wicker armchair with my feet on a matching hassock. "In the future, Matilda,...just so you can plan ahead, why don't you make it an annual event? It'll be an excellent way to repay our social obligations while we're still here at the Cape and before everyone leaves for the winter season."

"That's a wonderful idea, Albert!" she exclaimed with a semblance of exuberance. She got up from the swing and stood before me. "As a matter of fact, I've given that some thought myself, but now that you've also mentioned it,...that's exactly what I'll do! I've thought of some great ideas for our yearly parties. It'll be such fun to plan and think of innovative ways to make our yearly get-togethers different and exciting each year. This year's social event will reflect a plantation-like atmosphere with appropriate southern dishes and popular music originating from the south," she went on to elaborate.

"How many people do you plan to invite, Matilda?" I asked as I doused my pipe, put down my tea, and then prepared to return inside. "Please, don't forget to invite, Uranus, and one of his lady friends."

"I believe there'll be about fifty people not counting the celebrities and the musical ensemble. Uranus will be here and so will Samuel and his wife. I knew you'd be agreeable,…so I've already sent out the invitations," Matilda replied. She followed my lead and entered the house ahead of me as I held the door open. "I stated that it would begin promptly at five in the afternoon. You know how much I dislike people who habitually arrive fashionably late. I also hope they understand that "adults only" are to attend." I nodded my approval and headed toward the door leading to the old homestead—a peaceful oasis where I often sat undisturbed in my favorite rocker until I fell asleep. I chuckled to myself as I thought of the countless occasions when *we* were the last couple to appear at someone's doorstep.

"I assumed you already had a head start on the party when you started to talk to me about it," I said with a grin. Assured of my blessing, she sauntered into the kitchen to begin preparations for her upcoming soiree. She would be devoting every spare minute to this endeavor. Matilda was at her best organizing gala occasions and arranging the entertainment for her guests. She was a gracious hostess who seemed to make everyone feel welcomed and special. Matilda accompanied herself on the piano as she sang the popular melodies of the day. She invariable used music as an icebreaker to liven things up and could easily charm others into following her lead. Matilda would ask her guests to join her in a sing-along, clap to the rhythmic beat or harmonize as she played along on the piano.

She had invited her good friends, Shakespearean actor John Drew and leading actress Minnie Maddern Fiske. They would be arriving next week for a two-week stay. That meant an exhausting round of sightseeing, dinner parties and receptions.

Matilda had boundless energy. Her days began at dawn and ended at all hours of the night. Regardless, I was determined to keep up with her. She kept me alert and active. I was thankful for that. Otherwise, if left to my own devices I would probably have been happy at my age to be dormant in my rocker—a doddering, dim-witted and dawdling old man.

*   *   *   *

Early-September, 1890

"You summer people certainly know how to put on a damn good party!" said one of the guests whose superlatives were rather slurred and garbled. He was a bit tipsy and almost fell off his chair when he reached out to me as I walked past his table. "Why, I haven't had an imported cigar this good in years,…and the liquor,…it's the best I've ever had, anywhere!"

"Well, thank you, Benjamin…Do enjoy!" I replied with a nod of my head and waving to the butler to refill the glasses on the table.

"Matilda, your first "End-of-the-Season" get-together is a *tremendous* success!" I said as we surveyed our guests who were thoroughly enjoying themselves and pleased with the turnout. Some were chatting, singing and laughing loudly while others were taking part in lawn games and touring the art gallery. I'm sure Matilda was delighted with the outcome of her comprehensive planning.

"Thank goodness the weather cooperated," Matilda said, looking up at a cloudless sky as we walked arm-in-arm. "Everything's gone off like clockwork. It's wonderful to have the tables out here on the veranda. Everyone really enjoyed the food, and I must say our houseguests Mister Drew and Miss Fiske made quite an impression.

"The landscaping we completed last year appears to have taken hold," she added, glancing around the premises. The new pines and maple trees are giving us some shade this summer and the grounds are a lush green. Many of the annuals we planted are still blooming,…the flowering wisteria's flourishing and the rose bushes are just lovely! Oh Albert, I'm so happy with our new mansion,…I can barely contain myself! It's everything I ever wanted in a home."

"Remember, my dear, this is my gift to *you*. It's Missus Crosby's House," I reiterated, squeezing her close. "I'm pleased that you love it as much as you do. It does my heart good to see you so ecstatic over it."

*   *   *   *

Late-November, 1890

Although we gave up our Park Avenue apartment as I had previously suggested when Tawasentha was built, Matilda and I continued to enjoy a rich, full life. Every time we returned to New York City we stayed at a different luxury hotel.

We also enjoyed being able to travel whenever and wherever the spirit moved us. If we decided to board a steamer for Europe—then that's what we did. Matilda was the spark. By the time Matilda planted the idea in my mind, she had already acted upon it.

"I'd like to visit Washington, D.C., Albert," Matilda suggested one evening as we returned to our suite from a Broadway opening. "It's been quite a while since I've seen my sister Sarah and my nieces. Sarah's a grandmother now. My niece has two daughters of her own. I hear they're adorable little tykes. Would you mind if I invited them to spend the summer at our cape house? (Matilda sometimes inadvertently referred to Tawasentha as the "cape house.") The sound of children at play will be music to my ears. I'm sure they'll be accompanied by their nanny."

"I won't mind having your niece and her daughters visit us next summer as long as they don't get underfoot. Tawasentha's not exactly adapted to frolicking children," I replied. "I have a few business acquaintances I'd like to contact while we're in D.C. When would you like to leave?" I asked, knowing damn well—she already had the tickets in her purse.

"I thought it might be pleasant to be in Washington for the holidays. I was able to save some money on our train tickets because I purchased them early last month. I received a newsy letter from Sarah saying she hoped we'd consider it," Matilda announced as she dug into the stack of mail on her desk to retrieve Sarah's letter. "Ah, here it is! You might want to read it,…if you should you find the time. Sarah said their nanny is responsible for their care and will keep them quite occupied while we're there. We'll know more about the girls when we visit. I might not be anxious to have them at the Cape if they turn out to be spoiled brats! Somehow,…I seriously doubt that."

"Well, I guess that settles it! Washington it is,…for the holidays!" I replied, resigned to following her wherever she wanted to go.

We traveled to the District of Columbia and stayed with Matilda's sister. Her grandnieces were there with their mother and much to my delight they were polite and extremely well behaved. They were also curious and intelligent—a pleasure to be with. I became quite fond of the girls and after being with them for a few months, I actually looked forward to seeing them again next summer. During the time spent with the little tykes, I often thought of my own children. I realized I had missed most of their childhood and—probably had several grand-children the same ages as Matilda's grandnieces. "It's possible I could even be a great-grandfather," I thought. "I wonder what they look like? What's become of them and where do they live?" I asked myself. "Actually, it's sad to say if I acci-dentally bumped into them on the street,…I wouldn't even know them. Now that I've lost Nathaniel,…a son, I barely knew,…it might be wise to get to know Albert,…a son, I've never known."

Not wanting to repeat a nagging mistake, I acted on my future by recalling my past. I decided to put pen to paper and send Albert a letter. I was uneasy about reaching out to him and what I would write. Even so, I decided I would begin by apologizing for my absence in his life and attempt to explain that I had not inten-tionally abandoned him. I would try to justify my decision to divorce his mother—a separation that prevented me from ever getting to know him. I would also tell him that he had always been in my thoughts. I planned to invite him to Tawasentha next summer.

Uranus was somewhat knowledgeable about Margaret and my family. He was informed about them through various sources. He told me that my son had not yet married. Maybe it was wishful thinking, but somehow I hoped that Albert, Junior might be independent and mature enough to visit me despite the intimi-dating and spiteful disapproval of his mother. "Yes, I'll write to him." I made up my mind to do it without delay. "I won't procrastinate any longer," I resolved, choosing to do so before I lost my nerve and capitulated to a defeatist attitude.

"My investments in stocks and bonds continue to be quite profitable, Albert," Matilda disclosed upon our return to New York. "I've been fairly successful man-aging my own money; however, I must admit my broker's advice has been phe-nomenal. I'm sure I wouldn't have done as well without it. He's done an exceptional job of protecting my assets. Financially,…we're in good stead. We may want to take a vacation from our mundane day-to-day existence and spend our next winter on the French Riviera. I'd also like to spend more time in South-ern Italy or the Greek Islands. Give it some thought, Albert, and let me know how you feel about that."

"My dear, Matilda, it's fair to say that you're an absolute marvel!" I replied, giving her a kiss and a loving hug. "Italy's a fine choice. I look forward to attend-ing the Italian opera and touring that country's fascinating cities and the charming towns that are nestled in the verdant valleys of its majestic mountains. While there, we can augment our collection of sculptures and priceless art works."

*   *   *   *

Late-May, 1891

"I heard about the letter you sent to Albert, Junior," Uranus said discreetly after arriving to greet us and waiting until Matilda was out of the room. We had just returned to Tawasentha for the summer season. "Needless to say, his mother was incensed. You'll be happy to know that in spite of Margaret's hostile mind-set he stood his ground and said he was keenly aware of what had transpired years ago. Albert said he'd accept your invitation to meet him; however, because he didn't wish to further acerbate the situation, he'll stay at my home when he arrives in Brewster. It's been years since I've seen, Albert. I often stopped and visited Wild-wood while on my way back to Brewster. He was just a youngster then. I'm really looking forward to seeing him again. Why, he must be almost thirty now!"

"Oh, that's great news, Uranus!" I exclaimed as we sat in the art gallery. The gallery was always the first place Uranus wanted to see when he visited me. Now that he was almost sixty, a white-haired Uranus was still fascinated by works of art. He inevitably wanted to see the latest acquisitions that I had purchased while on my sojourns from Brewster. "I'm delighted to know he'll be here at the Cape this summer. My son's a complete stranger to me. I hope that after all these years of hearing about my apparent failings,…he'll keep an open mind and evaluate me free of Margaret's influence. I must admit, I'm a bit anxious about that! I'd like to get acquainted with my son and have him get to know me before it's too late. Who knows how much longer I have to live. I don't want to die without at least trying to redeem myself in his eyes. If I can,…I intend to eventually earn his approval."

"I see you've purchased a *Monet.* How did you manage *that*, Albert?" Uranus asked, a bit curious about where I had acquired it.

"The usual way, my dear cousin, I *paid* for it," I said factiously while slapping him on the back. We both had a good laugh and after imbibing a brew or two, he left. Matilda was not at home. She had left to attend her social group's welcoming tea. I had not as yet spoken to her about my intent to contact my son for fear it might prove to be a futile effort on my part. Until now, I was uncertain about this likelihood. I decided to tell her everything that had transpired, at my first opportunity.

"Matilda, would you like to visit the Herring Run and the Stony Brook Mill with me today?" I asked while at breakfast that next morning. "The alewives are swimming up the ladders in the "run" right now."

It was an unseasonably warm day around the first of June. I was elated by the pending arrival of the summer season. Like nature, my spirit was revitalized as I enjoyed life to the fullest.

"The weather's perfect for it," I added. It would be nice to spend some time together before we're preoccupied with an onslaught of guests. Maybe you could ask Lydia to put together a small basket lunch for us." Lydia, our young and energetic kitchen maid, who was slim and fair-haired, had lived in Brewster all her life.

"We can visit the mill, walk along the trails, and then picnic on the green knoll under the willows," I went on. "Don't wear anything too bulky or something you wouldn't want to get wet. It's such fun catching the alewives in a net and scooping them into a pail…I haven't done that in years. We'll both fill a bucket with herring. The cook will know how to prepare this delicacy for us. I'll take the caleche and we can go there on our own…Would you like to do that?"

"Yes, I would, Albert!" she replied as she took a sip of her morning coffee. "That sounds *so* romantic. Why,…I'm all for it! However, *I'll* make the picnic lunch. You know I enjoy doing that, my dear. Don't you remember the little tête-à-tête we had a long time ago in your apartment before you left for the East Coast?" she asked with a sly grin. She got up from her chair and walked toward me. I put my arms around her waist and held her close while we blissfully reminisced. She kissed me tenderly on the lips and I responded with a long, fervent embrace.

"Oh, I certainly do!…I recall every moment of that heavenly night!" I replied in a purposefully hushed voice as I squeezed her close to me. I glanced around the room to make sure none of the servants were nearby. "How could I ever forget? That's when I realized just how much I loved you,…and how much you meant to me."

While we sat on a soft wool blanket covered by the contents of a large picnic basket, we took in the beauty of our surroundings. I inhaled the crisp fresh air, as one would breathe in the fragrance of a vintage wine after it has just been opened. Matilda did likewise.

"This was a delightful idea, Albert! It's so peaceful and quiet here. The sounds of the splashing waterfall spilling over the mill wheel as it turns and the gurgling of the rushing water of the brook,…are so restful," Matilda said, sitting with her back braced against a willow tree. "It's amazing how many alewives are in that narrow, spring-fed stream. How they strive to continue their legendary ritual, swimming against the current and up those stone ladders to their destination! You did call them alewives, didn't you?"

"Yes, Matilda, those small, gray herring are called "alewives." It's a mammoth feat for such a tiny fish; nevertheless, most manage to conquer all the obstacles and find their way upward to spawn in the Mill Pond," I said as I poured each of us a glass of fine port wine. "As you can see,…they're also easy prey for the gulls. In the distance where the sea meets the current, you can hear the echo of their incessant shrieks. In a short while we'll go down to the brook with our nets and fill our buckets with alewives. You'll have to tie up your dress if you want to wade in the stream."

"I know that, silly!" she replied with a giggle and a gentle shove. "Let's just sit here awhile so I can digest my lunch."

"It was a fantastic picnic, Matilda. Almost as appetizing as that first one when we became intimate," I teased. "While we're sitting here, my love, there's something I need to tell you."

"And what's that?" she asked with a shocked expression, knowing I wasn't one to keep anything from her for very long.

"Oh, no! I haven't been unfaithful!" I replied with a hearty laugh…"It's nothing like that!"

"Ugh, that's a relief!" she said with a deep sigh. "I must say,…I felt a bit faint for a moment there."

"Matilda, I took it upon myself to write to my son, Albert, Junior," I said, looking down at the ground and pensively swirling a branch around in a doodling pattern. "I sent him a letter trying to explain my absence from his life. So help me, Matilda, it was one of the most difficult things I've ever had to do…It was such an agonizing decision,…a life altering choice of enormous proportions for me. I asked him to visit me this summer in Brewster. I would have always regretted not contacting him. I believed I had nothing to lose. I'm not getting any younger,…who know how many more years I have. It's been something I've wanted to do for a long time."

"I can understand your motives," she said with empathy, putting her arm around my shoulder as a sign of her loving support…"Did he ever answer you, Albert?"

"Actually he didn't,…but Uranus heard from him," I replied as I stood up and took hold of the pails while Matilda returned the picnic paraphernalia to the basket. "Uranus was always fond of Margaret and kept in touch with her through the years by way of her sister Abigail and Samuel's wife. Albert wrote and told

Uranus that regardless of his mother's objections, he also felt he wanted to meet me. He'll come sometime in July. Albert intends to stay with him while he visits."

"I'm so happy for you," Matilda said as we walked back to the caleche. She placed the basket on the seat between us while I deposited the pails on the floor of the buggy. "I realize now why you hadn't mentioned it before. If nothing had come of it, you would've felt as though you had at least made the effort and let it go at that. It's a personal thing,…no one else need know what transpired between the two of you."

"Thank you for being so understanding, my love," I said, taking her by the hand as we walked barefoot over the warm, rich soil. The canopy of luminous greens allowed a smidgen of dappled sunlight to shine through. As usual, Matilda's insight was profound, focused and penetrating—it thoroughly put me at ease. Hand-in-hand, we again strolled toward the rocky shore of the stream before we left for home. The darkened, rushing brook below us was swollen and teeming with alewives.

✳   ✳   ✳   ✳

Mid-July, 1891

It was a hectic summer season. Matilda's niece Dorothy and her two daughters had already been here a few weeks. Several celebrity guests that included Samuel Clemens had appeared at our door this week and were expected to remain with us for a minimum three-week stay.

"I've planned a formal reception for our guests, Albert. Our Cape and Island friends will want to meet them," said Matilda, catching me on my way out the door. I was headed toward the small buggy that Hudson had readied for me by the front fence post. Uranus informed me that Albert had arrived within the week. He requested that for the initial meeting I should go to his home, which was less than a mile from Tawasentha. Albert, Junior maintained that he'd be more comfortable there with my reticent cousin Uranus by his side.

"I'll leave you in charge of that chore, my love," I said, turning to face Matilda. "I'll take the buggy to visit with Uranus and Albert.

"Albert, are you nervous about meeting your son?" Matilda asked, walking out the door with me. "It'll be the first time you'll have seen him since he was an infant."

"Yes, I am,…a little. I wonder what he'll look like and what sort of person he's become," I replied. "I suppose he's thinking the same about me. I hope I live up to his expectations."

"I'm sure you will. Be your poised engaging self. Your self-confidence and wit should get you through this awkward and long-delayed encounter," Matilda said reassuringly. "Just be comfortable and composed in his presence, my dear," she added with a spontaneous smile as she stood on the veranda to wish me well…Give my regards to your cousin *and* your son. Young Albert will most likely want to join Uranus at my formal welcoming party for Mister Clemens and Miss Kellogg. (Miss Kellogg was one of the most renowned sopranos of our day.) I'll get to meet him at that time. Don't forget to remind Uranus about the reception and be sure to personally invite your son."

"I will!" I replied, waving back as I walked toward the carriage. After a short drive, I pulled up to Uranus's home. It had also been the homestead of my Uncle Roland, who had passed away in '74, and Aunt Sally who died and left it to Uranus in '88. An aging Uranus greeted me with a handshake as I descended from the carriage. Behind him stood a fair-haired young man who was at least a head taller than Uranus. His blue eyes reflected his joy at seeing me for the first time. I noticed he was not as muscular as Nathaniel—nonetheless, well proportioned. He also approached me and shook my hand. My eyes welled with tears as we embraced each other.

"It was so nice of you to be in touch with me," Albert said. The three of us walked a few steps toward some rockers on the front porch. "I'm so pleased to finally make your acquaintance, Father. Ever since I was in my teens I've longed to meet you. Now that I'm a grown man, I want you to know,…I've always felt that what happened between you and Mother was no reflection on the love you had for your children. Because of your extreme generosity, we were always well provided for. I respected you for that Father, and I hoped that someday I'd get to see you. All I needed to know was that you *also* wanted to meet me.

"I'm my own person, sir…I pretty much follow my heart," he went on to say. "Many times in the past and even up to the present, Mother has tried to prevent me from meeting you, and I'm sorry to say that so far she's been successful…however, I'm beyond that now. Thanks to Uranus's hospitality, I intend on being here for a while. I hope we'll see each other often so that I can get to know you better."

"Yes, I'd like that, Albert," I said, listening intently to every word. I detected no hypocrisy in his speech or bitterness in his tone of voice. While he spoke I noticed how much he favored Margaret's father. He had Margaret's coloring and her family's stature; nonetheless, I was pleased to detect a semblance of my own personality and demeanor. Although I sensed something deeply sensitive about him, he was spirited, perceptive and forthright. Though Nathaniel had my coloring and features, unlike Albert, Junior, he had Rebecca's distinctive personality and the Jenkins' distinguishing family characteristics.

"Oh, by the way, Uranus," I added as I turned toward him. "Speaking of seeing each other again, Matilda wanted me to remind you about the reception she's having for Mister Clemens. She requested that I extend the invitation to you also, Albert."

"Mister Clemens?...Mister Samuel Clemens?" My son asked repeatedly, clearly impressed by the mention of his name. "Why I'd be honored to be in his presence! Of course,...I'll be there! Thank your Missus for wanting to include me in her festivities. I look forward to meeting her and seeing that lovely mansion,...I've heard so much about."

I asked Albert about his sisters—Minnie, Fannie and Irene. He said that they were well and that each one had several children. And, yes, Minnie was a grandmother—and as I had supposed, I was already—a great grandfather. He doubted they would ever be in touch with me. Unfortunately, they grew up listening to their mother's host of vitriolic attacks and malevolent rants about their father. They learned to loathe me and would most certainly live their lives following Margaret's lead in that regard. We engaged in lively conversation for a few hours, I said my goodbyes, and then I left for home.

*   *   *   *

Early-August, 1892

Matilda and I were spending another summer at Tawasentha taking pleasure in everything that Brewster and the Cape had to offer—the weather, the seashore, the seafood delicacies and the social whirl. In July, Matilda hosted a formal reception for the Prince of Wales. It was the largest gathering *ever* on Cape Cod. Everyone on the Cape Cod and Islands social register was included along with famous and intellectual elite from all over the world. A lavish buffet was provided for the guests and an eight-piece musical ensemble was hired for an evening of dancing. The finest liquors and cigars were copiously offered to our guests. The Prince was visibly awed and gratified by the hospitality and the gracious welcome he received on our shores—particularly in our home. Matilda again lived up to her reputation as an extraordinary hostess.

While the festivities were in full swing—and when I found I had had enough of Matilda's parties for my simpler Cape Cod tastes, I slipped away toward the unobtrusive door on the ground floor. It led directly to the sitting room and the warmth of my old family homestead. I had escaped this sort of bedlam quite often in the past. It was a place where I often stepped back in time whenever I tired of the revelry and needed to relax. In the simplicity of its surroundings I would find myself reminiscing about my boyhood, contemplating the meaning of my life and counting my blessings. The old farmhouse always retained its charm—it nourished my soul and breathed new life into my being.

In contrast to the opulence of the mansion with its gilded furnishings and atypical riches, my father's unpretentious home was left exactly as it had been when I was growing up. Nothing was disturbed. It was furnished with the plain country accessories of its period. On top of the rope beds were feather mattresses, handspun linens and quilted coverlets. The oak milk cupboards and sideboards containing the original pewter goblets and serving pieces were still in the kitchen. Cobbler's benches were placed alongside the functional cabinets that were filled with old china and cooking utensils. Rush-bottom chairs were scattered throughout. A spinning wheel was set on the left-hand side of the fireplace and a comfortable rocker was placed directly in front of it. A century old carpet graced the floor of the parlor where I relived the simple realities of an earlier, more tranquil period. I tired more easily these days and found it increasingly difficult to keep up with Matilda's pace. When I was discovered missing from the hustle and bustle of socializing and after the last guest had gone, Matilda could always find me serenely rocking by the old-fashioned hearth and staring at the uneven oak floorboards.

As in past summers, Matilda's niece was visiting with her daughters. One day when they bolted through the front door, I overheard Matilda calmly chastising her young grandnieces. At the time, I was rocking on the veranda and quietly laughed at the conversation between them.

"Girls, please be careful when you walk or run through the house," Matilda said in a soft-spoken yet firm manner. "Do *not* step on the Persian rugs and the runners in the hallways. Make sure to walk around them and on the wood floors only. The carpeting is extremely fragile and expensive. I don't wish to replace them because they've become soiled, abused or worn. Do you understand, my sweeties?"

"Yes, we do, Auntie Matilda!" one of them replied while the other stared at Matilda wide-eyed and nodding her head in agreement. "We'd like to go up to the tower to view the bay and the fishing boats through the telescope…Would that be all right, Auntie?"

"You have my permission; however, you must be very careful up there and remember not to step on the carpeting as you ascend to the third story," Matilda warned, shaking a menacing index finger at them.

"Another one of her eccentricities," I thought, smiling and shaking my head after hearing her cautionary instructions to the children. From that moment on, when they regularly climbed the staircase to the third floor and the observation tower, it was laughable to see the girls carefully skirting Matilda's precious hall runners.

Hudson had befriended Matilda's niece and grandnieces from the day they arrived. He spent much of his time bending over backwards to make sure they all enjoyed their days at the Cape. As Japeth had done for me ages ago, Hudson became their personal guide. He introduced them to the thrill of the hunt by demonstrating how to find soft-shelled clams and quahogs for steaming and chowders. After Hudson showed her how, Matilda often took her guests digging for clams. He also taught the girls how to sail and fish. As they walked the flats, Hudson familiarized them with a new world exposed by the receding sea. With his help Matilda's grandnieces flew their homemade kites on the exposed sand. They took long hikes through the marshes following some well-worn trails to explore the beauty and delicate balance of the Cape's wetlands.

He also kept the girls busy by teaching them useful crafts, such as how to make soap, candles, pottery and wampum jewelry. Due to his efforts their days at Tawasentha were full and productive. Matilda became quite attached to Hudson and was ever appreciative of his sincere interest on their behalf. It made for a very relaxing summer for me.

"My theme for this year's "End-Of-The-Season" lawn party will be Parisian," Matilda announced as September approached. We chatted and strolled casually along the bay. The ebbing tide was exposing a bonanza of crustaceans for the gulls whose loud cawing shrieks penetrated the calm of that late August after-noon. "It'll center around a café-like theme with French gourmet food. Every-thing will be French, including the menus, the entertainment and the music. French and *only* French will be spoken. I think everyone should have a glorious time. What are your thoughts about that, Albert?"

"If I must say so,…it sounds a bit outlandish to me, Matilda. It might become something of a fiasco," I warned hesitatingly. While it was my honest opinion, I already knew it wouldn't make much difference, anyway. When Matilda made up her mind about something it was almost impossible to dissuade her from her plan of action. "Most folks in these parts aren't particularly familiar with the French language. It could be construed as a deliberate attempt to confuse or belittle the guests. Your dream party could possibly end up being a nightmare with negative social undertones."

"I know, Albert, but most folks are *not* in our social circle," she replied rather pompously. "Our close friends are intelligent and as equally well-versed in most European languages as we are. We've closely identified with these people and their cosmopolitan life-styles. It'll be fun, Albert, you'll see! It'll also give us a chance to practice our conversational French. It might prove to be a challenging mental exercise and help reacquaint us with the language." It was obvious that she couldn't be persuaded to change her mind. I simply shrugged my shoulders and bent down to pick up a piece of blue seaglass.

My son had returned to Brewster again this summer and was staying with Uranus. We frequently found time to be together. Young Albert was an exceptionally intelligent scholar who was working on his dissertation for a doctorate in physics. He was about to begin a professorship and head a symposium at Harvard University in the fall. I wished him well and acknowledged that I was quite proud of him.

"Father, I'd like to discuss your relationship with Mother, now that I've gotten to know you better, and I'm more comfortable in your presence," Albert declared the day before he left for Boston and Wildwood, "I feel I'm able to express myself more freely, where she's concerned."

It was an extremely gray day. Dark, ominous clouds moved slowly above the shoreline. As we stood high up on the dunes looking down at the monstrous waves and towering surf, the chill from the overcast sky was in sharp contrast to our usual late summer warmth. It was more like October—a preview of fall. We had taken the caleche to the ocean in Eastham; however, we rode with the hood sheltering us from the wind and possible rain. Albert had taken over the reins.

"Despite Mother's lack of civility toward you, I love her dearly. However, I realize how insistent and intimidating she can be at times. Nevertheless, Father, I've always had an open mind and given you the benefit of the doubt. Maybe it's because I'm a male and view her from a different angle than the women in the family. In their eyes she was completely justified for having stood her ground and refusing to join you in Chicago. Regardless, it's always been my contention that a woman should follow her husband and always be by his side. Her refusal to live with you and raise the children in a two-parent family never sat well with me. Although I never mentioned it to her, I always felt that just because she despised Chicago, it was no excuse to force you to live alone. Also, it was very self-centered on her part to make us pawns in the marriage and deny us the love and presence of a father figure. As you must know by now, she's defiled your name and accused you of every sort of debauchery imaginable. That rings even more hollow several decades later. I thank my lucky stars that I was perceptive enough to see through her negative and biased judgments. Even though Cousin Uranus has emphatically denied her fabrications,...I can see for myself that you're an upstanding, moral man of honor and integrity."

"Well, thank you for saying that, Albert," I replied as we stood high on the dunes gazing out at the wonders spread before us. Stretched out for miles below us was a spectacular expanse of pristine, golden beaches and frothing cobalt surf that curled in mammoth waves and crashed along the shoreline.

"I was completely enamored by your mother," I went on. "I was so deeply in love with her that every time we were separated, I missed her so much my body ached to hold her close. I needed her so desperately. Somehow,...I couldn't make her understand that. She just didn't seem to share my sense of loneliness. Margaret made it quite clear that she was perfectly content being away from me. I had an intuitive feeling that she just didn't love me as much as I loved her. I often wondered how a marriage that seemed so right at the time,...go so wrong?"

"I know that," he said, placing his arms around my shoulders in a gesture that indicated he understood my dilemma. "Four children can attest to that! You're quite prolific, Father, I might add," he went on, chuckling and tapping me on my shoulder.

"Your mother came from an affluent background and lived a pampered lifestyle, Albert. On the other hand, I was a struggling entrepreneur striving to make a living for my family." I said. "While living at Wildwood, nannies cared for the children while her days were filled with bathing, fixing her coiffure and primping, putting on a dainty frock and going out into the garden to cut fresh flowers. She frequently had afternoon tea with friends and also went on shopping excursions or luncheons. Her evenings were spent attending concerts, theatricals, ballet or opera among other entertainments.

"Try to understand, Albert, it was much different in Chicago because of my business commitments and her refusal to acquaint herself with new friends and surroundings. She never gave it a chance! And of course,...we didn't have all those amenities. I don't wish to criticize your mother by saying deprecating things about her,...and I'm certainly not trying to polish my halo, either," I insisted while grasping my cap when a sudden gust of wind blew off the water. "In any case, I believe you should know I did everything in my power to make Margaret feel at home in the Midwest. That included having a manor in West

Roxbury and a beautiful Victorian mansion in Chicago. *Nothing* pleased her,…if it meant remaining there with me. I'm sure she married me with the idea that she'd eventually change my mind.

"After you were born I grew weary of her obstinacy and gave up trying. I realize I could have given in to her demands, but at the time my work and my future were in Chicago. The collapse of our marriage was also my fault. Every time I returned to Wildwood, I felt more and more estranged. Finally, your mother moved all my belongings to the guest room because she didn't wish to be intimate with me. She claimed she had had enough children and was afraid she'd be with child again.

"I guess people change. Sometimes we're utterly unable to cope with that. Your mother and I should have sought some sort of compromise to mitigate the damage to you and the girls, but we were both hopelessly ill equipped to do so. My visits became more and more infrequent. Years of loneliness, isolation and separation from my loved ones all served to extinguish my love for her and separate me from my children. Those were the darkest days of my life.

"The ramifications were disastrous to our marriage. The divorce wasn't entirely my fault, as your mother would have you believe, son. I was actually pushed out of my family's lives. If I'd been welcomed back with loving, open arms, I would have continued to commute to the East Coast indefinitely, despite the ordeal. She was the ultimate cause of the breakup of our marriage, although she'd never admit to that.

"Disheartened by it all, I lived a hellish existence as a lonely bachelor. I craved the companionship of an affectionate woman. I despised living in one rooming house after another. Then I met,…Matilda. She restored my manhood. Her infectious smile and tender touch became the sole source of my joy and happiness. My life took on new meaning and purpose."

"If it's any consolation to you, Father, I *do* understand. You're right about the breakdown of your marriage to Mother!" Albert replied as we turned to leave the bluff and return to the caleche. "To this day, she considers herself maligned and completely blameless,…someone to be pitied for having had such a disastrous marriage."

"Actually, my love for Margaret was a lot different than the love I have for, Matilda," I said as we walked through the sea grass along the narrow sandy trail. "With your mother it was love from the first "hello,"…an all-consuming, passionate attraction that was definitely sexual. While physically attracted to Matilda, it started at least on my part as a cherished relationship, one that gradually matured into a deep, abiding love that has grown more intense and meaningful over the years. We found that we were utterly miserable when we were apart from each other. It was heartening to know that she missed me in the same way. After every reunion, I realized that I couldn't visualize living my life without her. That's when I knew I needed to divorce your mother and marry Matilda.

"Matilda later confessed that she fell in love with me from the moment we were introduced. Although she was sympathetic about my solitary existence and marital difficulties,…it was never discussed. Matilda knew I was still a married man with a family on the East Coast. She accepted this reality knowing she might never have a romantic alliance with me. When I finally redefined my priorities, I divorced your mother and asked Matilda for her hand in marriage."

"I find the fact that Matilda respected your status as a married man says much in her favor," Albert said. "She could have taken advantage of your situation, lived with you and eventually seduced you into marriage. With your wealth and good looks,…you're not exactly a bad catch," he added with a wide grin and a gentle slap on my shoulder. "You're very fortunate to have found such a devoted and adoring wife. After all, wives should be lovers, too! Matilda's so pleasant and vivacious. Above all else, one can easily tell that her life revolves around you and that she absolutely worships the ground you walk on. I can understand why she's so precious to you."

"Please stay in touch, son. I've become quite fond of you during your stay here over the summer," I said as I glanced up at the sky and noticed a change in the weather. Dark, ashen clouds in a smoke-gray sky were heading our way. "I suppose we'd better be on our way. It looks like rain."

Shortly after Albert left the Cape, Hudson told us that severe weather was making its way up the coastline. This was the season when a tropical storm could quickly escalate into a nor'easter of hurricane force.

"I'm afraid I'll have to call off my lawn party. Thank goodness my nieces have already left Cape Cod for home," Matilda said downheartedly while going through her list of guests and deciding to write each one a note of cancellation. "The storm will probably get here either just before,…or on the date of the party itself. Either way, everything will be a soggy mess. I wouldn't want to endanger my guests by having them venture out in such dreadful weather. It won't be possible to reschedule the festivities as everyone's expected to return home within the next few weeks." Looking annoyed and muttering to herself, she grumbled, "I guess when things don't flow,…they just aren't meant to be!"

"I think that's a wise decision," I said, trying to reassure her that she was doing the right thing. Nonetheless, I was secretly relieved to be rescued by Mother Nature. The "French Fiasco" would have been a fate worse than death. "I'm sorry it turned out this way. We can pretty much control everything in our lives, my dear, except the weather."

Hudson busied himself by hurriedly bringing in the hay and storing the tools in the barn. He rounded up the farm animals and tied down the newly planted trees. After securing the barn and carriage house, he pulled the small sailboats out of the water and dragged them up onto the grassy bluff. When Hudson finished he left for the tenant house to join his family. I brought in the lawn furniture and anything else that could be blown away. I was a bit concerned about possible damage to the art gallery, clerestory windows and the tower. I would simply have to hope for the best.

"I'm so frightened, Albert. I've never witnessed such violent weather. The force of the torrential rain and gusting winds is terrifying," Matilda said, trying to look out the windows that were made almost opaque by the downpour. The eighty-mile-an-hour gale force winds drove the driving rain at a slant. The windowpanes were plastered with an assortment of wind-blown willow and mimosa leaves, pine needles and ferns.

"I think we'd better go below ground level, Matilda," I suggested, looking out our bedroom window. "We'll be safer there in case the storm accelerates into a hurricane." I could see the wild surging waves in the bay reach an alarming height of at least eight feet. They slammed against the shore and over the bluff sending sheets of spray toward the mansion. "We must alert the chambermaids, servants and butlers and bring them down from their upstairs quarters. It'll be foolhardy for them to remain on the third floor. That will not be a safe place for them. They must join us in the basement."

Soon, we assembled in the cellar with some lanterns and chairs. The chef put together a small lunch and everyone sat there throughout the storm. We played games, read and sang along with a staff member who played a harmonica. Although apprehensive about our safety and the survival of Tawasentha, Matilda and I halfheartedly joined in the revelry to help pass the time and ease our concern.

At about four in the afternoon, the gusting winds diminished and the torrential rain became a drizzle. By the time we emerged from our dismal basement shelter, sunbeams shone behind silver-rimmed, slate clouds signaling the end of what had been a disastrous gale. The storm left us with roof damage, broken glass in and around the mansion and several downed trees. The beachfront suffered a great deal of erosion from the extraordinarily high surf. Several ships and many lives had been lost at sea. Aside from minor flooding in low-lying areas and wash-out damage to the roads from wind-blown high tides, the Cape had fared quite well. In spite of this, as it passed through the elbow of the lower Cape, we had endured the brunt of the tempest along with Chatham, Orleans and Eastham. Some older, more fragile homes were completely demolished by the storm's deadly force. Hudson worked feverishly for days on end to make the necessary repairs to the old homestead and the mansion. As soon as the restoration was completed and Tawasentha was again intact—Matilda and I left for New York.

▼

CHAPTER 24

Late-July, 1893

"Uncle Albert, please come with us down to the bay," pleaded Eugenia, the elder of Matilda's grandnieces who was tugging at my sleeve while I was reading the newspaper on the veranda and not inclined to move. "The tide's dead low this afternoon. Alexandra and I would like to walk the flats and look for some miniature treasures, like pretty shells and sea glass. It's such fun watching the hermit crabs and catching minnows in our nets. Auntie Matilda won't let us go by ourselves...Our nanny has left to do some shopping in Barnstable. Please,...Uncle Albert, do come with us!"

"Oh,...all right," I replied, putting down my paper and getting up from my favorite wicker chair. I remembered when I was their age how much I enjoyed walking the flats. I recalled standing at the edge of the bay in Brewster and being awed by the vastness of the space that stretched out before me. How it awakened my heart! It would be a fine way to escape the heat of the day—the cool, wafting breezes off the bay would be refreshing. "Get your pails and nets and we'll leave momentarily. Let's tell Aunt Matilda and your Mother that we're heading for the seashore."

"We already have everything right here," said Eugenia, showing me all the required paraphernalia for our sojourn over the flats. "I'll run to tell Mommy we're leaving."

With one little girl on each side of me, we found our way down to the shoreline. Now that I was seventy, these sprightly children were visibly impatient with my unhurried gait.

"You girls go ahead. I'll watch you from here. I prefer taking my time when I walk along the flats. Don't worry,...I'll eventually catch up with you," I said.

They excitedly scampered ahead while I lagged behind…"Don't go any further than that rock out there!" I shouted before they were out of earshot.

Seagulls, soaring and shrieking in the sky above, occasionally disrupted the serenity of the flats. As I had done so many times before, I couldn't help but marvel at the quiet beauty of the seaside and the spectacular panorama. The action of the receding tide and wind created an intriguing pattern—a rippling blanket that stretched endlessly across the summer sandscape. Only the distant silhouette of two small children, who were bending over their pails and intensely absorbed in their discoveries, disrupted the distant vector at the horizon between sea and sky.

On impulse, I turned to look toward the sandy bluff and the grassy knoll that led to the mansion. The lone figure of a man stood there shielding his eyes from the sun as he scanned the flats and seascape before him. He started frantically waving in my direction, scrambled down the dunes, and then was soon within shouting distance.

"Can that be someone I know?" I questioned, keeping an eye on the girls as I walked toward this mysterious person who was approaching me. "It can't be Uranus or Albert, Junior? This person's gait's unfamiliar." I was bewildered as to *who* this could be and why he would want to join my grandnieces and me on the flats.

"Albert, old friend and shipmate!…It's me, David…David Atkins!" he bellowed, racing toward me with outstretched arms. "How wonderful it is to see you again after all these years!…I've never forgotten you!"

"Oh, my God! It can't be!…David Atkins!…What are you doing here? I never thought I'd ever see you again!…This is incredible!…I can't believe my eyes! I exclaimed running toward him. I was completely flabbergasted by the sight of this well-dressed gentleman. "Have I died and met my friend again in heaven?" I wondered for a brief moment. Once I realized it certainly *was* David and that he was actually standing before me in the flesh, we unreservedly embraced. The tears flowed freely as we faced each other. "Why, you haven't aged a bit," I added. "I'd have recognized you anywhere!"

"Oh yes, Albert! That's why you looked at me with such a puzzled expression, dear friend!" he chuckled, slapping me on the shoulder. "Now let's be honest! We certainly don't look the way we did when we parted forty-five years ago. Although I must say, Albert,…you look positively robust and fit!"

"Thank you!…And so do you, David!" I replied with a wide grin.

Except for a ring of white tresses, David had lost most of his hair. His equally white mustache curved around his mouth to meet a short Vandyke goatee. While his face and limbs were not heavy, he did have a potbelly.

"I'm accompanying my grandnieces while they scour the flats for treasures and sea life." I added. "I must get their attention as it's time for us to return home. I want to know everything that's happened to you since '48?" I added while walking out toward them with my arm over his shoulders. "I'm overjoyed at the sight of you,…but still dumbfounded by your sudden appearance. I was led to believe you most likely met with foul play and died after reaching California. I'm so happy to know I was wrong. Thank God for that!"

"Well, you weren't too far off base, Albert," David replied, expelling a deep sigh. "It's a long story,…but it looks like we have an equally lengthy walk ahead. So,…I'll try to get to the point and explain why I haven't been able to contact you before now."

"Please do, David…I'm damn curious as to where you've been all these years!" I said. "I received only one telegraph from you after you left me."

"When I arrived in Auburn, California in the late-fall of '48, I worked for a while in a livery stable," David went on as he splashed through a tidal pool. "I wanted to get accustomed to the area and find out exactly where I should go before I set out into unknown territory. After several months, I decided to venture out on my own. I found some gold nuggets in a small mountain range 25 miles out of town and began to dig in that vicinity. It looked quite promising,…so I staked a claim and returned to town to file and record my entitlement."

"That must be when you telegraphed me in Chicago," I said, eager to hear the rest of the story.

"Yes," he replied. "I took the time to do that before leaving town again with my wagon and all the materials and tools I'd need to build a mine shaft,…wooden beams, boards, axes, picks, et cetera. It took me almost a year to finish it, as I had to dig it out myself,…one shovel full at a time. I made several trips back and forth to the town for supplies. By the way,…I've been sober since I left you. I realized I'd need to be if I wanted to make a go of it. I couldn't let liquor get in the way of my goal."

"Was it safe for you to return to town?" I asked. "I should think you would've been a bit apprehensive about doing that for fear of being followed and bushwhacked while returning to your claim. When I didn't hear from you again,…I imagined the worse."

"No, I was exceptionally careful not to lead anyone toward my mining operation," he replied. "In fact, I was doing quite well until one day while I was busily chipping away at the stone deep inside the mine, I heard a rumbling noise and felt a powerful vibration. It was an earthquake! I ran toward the entrance as the beams began to fall. I had been warned about the possibility of tremors in that area, but I dismissed that notion. Now,…I was running for my life. I could see the entrance and the light ahead, but that was the last thing I saw for weeks."

"Were you seriously hurt?…How did you escape?" I asked.

"Members of an Indian tribe called the Wintun discovered my limp body just a few feet from the opening of the mine," he replied. "I had received a severe blow to the head from a beam that landed on my chest. The Indians had been hunting in that region on the day of the earthquake. As they rode by the entrance to the mine they saw me lying just beyond it. They carefully transported me to their village while I was unconscious.

"The Wintun are a group of three friendly tribes that inhabit the Sacramento Valley of north-central California. Although some tribes eventually fought back after white settlers and gold miners plundered their land, these Wintun were peaceful and very responsive to my needs. They carried me into a tepee and made me comfortable. While I lay unconscious on a straw mattress, for days on end, a squaw kept my wounds clean and cooled my brow with a wet cloth. When I finally opened my eyes, I found that although I was eventually able to speak, I had forgotten everything. I couldn't even remember who I was!"

"Oh, David,…that's dreadful! It must have been awful not to remember anything from your past," I said forlornly shaking my head. "But evidently your memory must have returned because you're here. You seem to be fine,…now."

"My recollection slowly came back in bits and pieces as the years progressed," he continued. In the meantime they gave me the Indian name "Yellow Feather" and I married the devoted Indian squaw who took care of me. We have three grown children and nine grandchildren. In due course, I slowly regained my memory and returned to the mine, but I'd lost interest in gold mining for fear of another earthquake. The tribe is extremely adept at cultivating a flourishing forty-acre vineyard. The grapes grown there are ideal for vintage wines. I became their liaison with the white man and the wine producers. Actually, I was their representative and salesperson. It was profitable for the tribe,…but I never became wealthy.

"It's only been about twenty years now that I've remembered you, dear friend. I met a gentleman from a Chicago winery who had come to California to purchase grapes from our vineyards. I asked if he knew you. He said he knew *of you* through the company he worked for. He added that you had been the president of his company until you resigned and moved to the East Coast. It took quite a while for me to find the time and money to return to Cape Cod. Even so, I was determined to visit you before my death. My longed-for wish has finally come true.

"Although I've had a good life and a fairly uneventful one,…another misfortune has befallen me. There's a sense of urgency in my visit because I've recently been diagnosed with a terminal illness. I was told that if there was something I wanted to do before I died, I had better do it soon. I remembered your dream to build a castle on the bay in Brewster, so I immediately headed this way. I could've telegraphed you that I was coming, but because of the uncertainty of my disease, I decided to surprise you, instead."

"Well, David, you certainly did that! I'm still in a state of shock!" I exclaimed as I beckoned the girls to return without delay before the incoming tide arrived to fill the bay. "Though you seem to be fairly healthy right now, I'm sorry to hear that you're ailing. I hope you'll stay well for a while longer.

"Do you remember Molly Duncan,…the little girl we found on our way to Chicago?" I asked.

"Why, yes, I do. The memory of her came back to me at the same time I remembered you, Albert," he replied. "Have you seen her?"

"Yes, David. In fact, she came to Chicago as a young woman and married my accountant's son, Theodore Hathaway," I responded excitedly. "They have several children."

"Did you ever tell her about her father?" he asked.

"No," I replied, "I wondered if I should,…but I decided to leave well enough alone. I didn't want to dishonor her memory of him." David nodded in agreement.

"My wife and I left Chicago and built the mansion we call Tawasentha in '87," I went on. "It was completed, in '88. "When I say *my wife*, I mean my second wife, Matilda. Margaret refused to stay in Chicago. After years of being alone there, I finally divorced her and married Matilda. I've never been happier. Matilda is everything to me. Although we're childless, I did have four children with Margaret,…three daughters and one son. However, the only one who visits me now, is my son, Albert, Junior."

"The lady who answered to Missus Crosby when I came to the door certainly didn't look like, Margaret," David said, wide eyed and shaking his head back and forth. "I thought I had the wrong house at first until I was told that this was your summer home and that you could be found walking along the flats. I must say that's quite a *summer home*, Albert. I see you had it built around the old family cottage. It's not exactly the castle of your dreams set high on the knoll overlooking the bay,…but it's damn close to it! I'm happy for you. I always knew you'd be a wealthy man someday."

"Yes, David, but my drive to succeed was very costly. My personal life suffered a disastrous blow and I had to start all over again after the Chicago Fire," I replied. "I do hope you're planning on staying with us for a while. We have so much to talk about. You must stay…I won't take "no" for an answer."

"Thank you, Albert. I'll stay for a few days if you insist," he said. "I also plan on visiting Nantucket while I'm here. I doubt I'll ever be able to return to the East Coast again."

"By the way, David, do you still play your guitar?" I asked as we leisurely strolled behind the girls who were running home ahead of us. "When I recall our journey west, I have fond memories of you strumming your plaintive melodies on it."

"Yes, but I had to teach myself to play it all over again when I found it among my belongings…It still comforts me," he replied with a smile.

David picked up the jacket and shoes he had left behind on a beached rowboat. After slipping into our shoes, we walked back with an arm over each other's shoulder toward Tawasentha, chatting, laughing, and reminiscing.

*　　　*　　　*　　　*

Mid-August, 1895

"Mister Crosby, I'm sorry to bother you sir, but there's an official-looking gentleman at the door with something he insists must be delivered to you,…personally," Lydia said apologetically. I had been weeding around the day lilies of the old cottage when she approached me from behind. I took pleasure in being outdoors in the summer. For many years now, I had assumed the chore of cleaning, pruning and trimming the shrubbery and flowers around the homestead. It was a project I thoroughly enjoyed.

"That's perfectly all right, Lydia. I'm just about finished here, anyway. I'll follow you back through the house," I said, getting up off my knees and brushing the sand from my pants and hands

"I'm the constable from Barnstable County. Are you Albert Crosby?" he asked while standing in the doorway. He was a courteous and well-dressed gentleman.

"Yes,…I'm Albert Crosby," I replied, curious as to the reason for his appearance at my door.

"Sir, this is a formal summons for a libel suit being filed against you in the Massachusetts Supreme Court. Please sign here to verify that you've personally received it," he said without a change of expression or tone of voice. He handed me a pen and an envelope filled with paperwork to sign. Annoyed by this intrusion, I took everything from him and proceeded to complete it on a sideboard inside the entrance hallway. When I gave it all back to him, he handed me a larger envelope, briefly thanked me with a quick nod of his head, and then raced back to his waiting carriage.

I promptly opened the formal, wax-sealed envelope and began to read its contents. My hands trembled and my heart raced while I looked around for the closest chair. I decided I had better sit down as I was becoming a little shaky and faint. It contained several claims totaling an excess of $500,000 that had been obtained against me by the City of Chicago and the States of Illinois and Indiana.

"Why am I being sued for this excessive amount of money after all this time?" I wondered. "I realize I left several unpaid bills when the Chicago Fire destroyed the opera house, but even so,…I endured the greatest financial loss of anyone in Chicago at the time. I've always assumed everyone else had to absorb his or her own shortfalls as well. As far as I'm concerned,…it's a closed chapter. I never imagined I'd be liable for those debts plus the interest accrued over all these years. I guess I was obviously wrong about *that*!" I could feel myself getting more agitated by the minute as I slammed the envelope and its contents on the sideboard. I needed to find out how this had happened.

"Matilda, please join me in the dining room. I need to speak to you," I bellowed from the foyer of the front entrance. She was in her sewing room, which was just above the upstairs hallway and to the left.

"What's wrong, Albert?" she shouted back, sensing the emergency in my voice and bending over the balcony to look down at me.

"It's private, Matilda. If possible,…please come down right now," I said with a sense of urgency. I walked toward the dining room to await her arrival.

Matilda immediately put down her sewing, hurried down the stairs, and then ran into the dining room where I stood transfixed by the paperwork spread out before me on the table. She supposed that something was very wrong because I seldom called for her from below the staircase. If I needed her, I usually ascended the stairs and quietly summoned her.

"Sit here, my dear," I said dejectedly, pulling up a chair for her. "I've got some troublesome news…I feel you should know about it straight away."

"I can certainly detect your concern, Albert," Matilda said as she carefully scrutinized my face. "I can't help but wonder what has you so upset. You have a pained expression on your face and it's completely drained of color. I'm almost afraid to ask."

"Well,…I've just been handed a summons to appear in the Massachusetts Supreme Court. I must answer claims filed against me by several sub-contractors seeking remuneration in connection with the opera house. Here are the documents," I went on. "Evidently, someone has discovered where I live and has decided to sue me for debts left unpaid after the fire. I'm dumbfounded by it all. I never expected anything like this would ever happen to me. I thought those outstanding bills had long been forgiven because of the heavy losses I incurred. Dammit, Matilda,…I'm angry as hell over this!" I said, pounding my fist on the table. "I'll find out how this happened even if I have to question everyone in our so-called circle of friends."

"I think I may be able to answer that, Albert," Matilda replied calmly as she reached across the table to hold my hand. "One of the women in my garden club lives in Chatham. She informed me that she recently had a former judge as a guest. He was now a senator from Illinois. He and his wife stayed with them this past summer. This friend said that she and her husband had taken them on an extensive tour to view Brewster's many superb captains' homes and the grand residences of its wealthy entrepreneurs. The judge and his wife were avid art collectors, so they included our home and art gallery as a place that would be of special interest to them. She claimed that because the name Crosby is quite prevalent on the Cape, the judge made no connection with you until he saw the showpiece of our gallery,…Bierstadt's *Looking Down Yosemite Valley, California*. He instantly recognized it as a painting that had been prominently displayed in the Crosby Art Gallery in Chicago. A sketch of the Crosby Opera House also caught his attention. She said he instantly realized that you were *the*, Albert Crosby. My friend said she didn't understand why, but after sending a few urgent telegraphs to Chicago,…he left abruptly. This lady was embarrassed and mystified by the whole affair. She wondered if she or her husband had committed a social faux pas. Now, unfortunately, I know what was behind the judge's sudden departure."

"If he was a judge,…he must have been a lawyer at the time of the Chicago Fire," I concluded. "Apparently, he was hired by my creditors to recoup monies spent refurbishing the opera house." I held my face in my hands and tried to cope with this bewildering turn of events. "It states here that I'm liable for an amount over $500,000. That could ruin us, Matilda!"

"Not unless I'm also liable for your debts, which I certainly am *not*! In any case, we need to contact my lawyer," she replied. He'll act not only as our consultant, but also as our legal representative. I'm sure he'll advise us as to what we should do. Please don't upset yourself over this, Albert," she said trying to bolster my sagging spirits. "It's been years since all your assets were wisely turned over to me. Right now, everything we own here in Massachusetts is in my name and has been for a long time,…that includes the land, the mansion and all its furnishings. Only the most well heeled defendants, such as you and I can take on those greedy creditors. Justice will be served, my dear. Come now, put these documents aside until we've appointed my lawyer to look into these claims for us. We'll retrieve these legal papers later and deliver them to him promptly when we reach New York."

"I feel better already. Just having spoken to you about it has eased my anxiety and lifted a heavy burden from my shoulders. Thank you, Matilda," I said, getting up from my chair and giving her an appreciate embrace. "Somehow my dearest, I knew you'd be able to help me. I needed you to pull me out of the despondent frame of mind I was in. I worried about becoming impoverished and possibly losing our home. You've directed those negative thoughts toward a more positive outcome. I can see that I was needlessly beginning to panic. At my age, the loss of financial security becomes a frightening prospect. Your levelheaded approach has given me a renewed sense of confidence. In your usual perceptive way, you've restored my faith in our future. Again,…thank you for that, Matilda!"

*   *   *   *

Mid-May, 1898

"There's a letter here for you. It's from your son," Matilda announced while sifting through a stack of mail retrieved from our box at the New York City Post Office and handing it over to me. As I slit the envelope with the letter opener, I wondered why Albert had written me. The letter read:

Dear Father:

I thought I'd take pen in hand to inform you of my decision to join the Army and take part in the Spanish-American War. I've been given the rank of corporal. Most likely I'll already be on my way south by the time you receive this letter. I'll miss seeing you again in Brewster this summer. I've

*also written to Cousin Uranus. I hope all will go well with you and Matilda
in my absence. Please keep me in your thoughts, as you will be in mine.
I'll try to stay in touch. Until then, I send you my love,*

Albert

"Albert has joined the armed forces and is off to the Spanish-American War,"
I said. I was so unnerved by the news that I became short of breath and could feel
beads of cold sweat on my forehead as I reached for a chair.

"I know how upsetting this news must be for you, but I'm sure he'll be *fine*,"
Matilda said, standing beside my chair. She passed her handkerchief across my
forehead, stroked my shoulders, and then kissed my cheek. "He has the Crosby
mettle and sense of self-preservation. Albert's in his late thirties now, and he
probably needs to venture beyond his East Coast boundaries. His enlistment will
be a broadening experience for him."

"Yes,…I guess you're right." I replied, nodding my head. "Since I first contacted him we've spent a lot of time together and become quite close. He's a wonderful son and I love him dearly," I said in a quivering voice. Tears were welling
in my eyes. "If anything should happen to him, Matilda, I…well,…I just can't
even think about that!"

"It's out of our hands, Albert. All we can do is hope and pray that he'll come
back safe and sound. Come now, let's have our afternoon druthers," she said.
Matilda made a hot spiced-tea toddy for herself and me. "Here, drink this…It'll
make you feel better on this dreary, raw afternoon."

*   *   *   *

Early-December, 1898

Matilda and I had been in New York for two months when I received another letter from my son. I was heartsick to learn that due to an unknown illness, he had
been honorably discharged on November 23rd. All efforts to treat him had been
fruitless. He was told that his condition was incurable and that he would only
have four months to live—at most. This cruel death sentence was an unbelievable
and devastating blow for him—his family and friends. Albert would be staying at
Wildwood and cared for by his mother.

"I'd love to see, Albert, again,…but I guess it's not to be. I won't even be able
to attend his funeral," I said, after revealing the contents of the letter to Matilda.

"Why is this happening again? I've had to endure the deaths of so many of my loved ones,...my brothers, my parents, my dear friends and now possibly my son, Albert." I immediately thought about the loss of my brother Nathan, my friends Rebecca and Jonathan and my son Nathaniel,...all young people who had lost their lives before they had even lived them. "Oh, Matilda, how tragic that at age thirty-six,...the prime of his life,...he should be cut down. Albert, Junior was the picture of health. He should have lived a long life."

"Albert, dearest, I'm so sorry to hear such dreadful news. I know how much your son means to you. But who knows, miracles do happen," she said with empathy and hoping to lift my spirits. "At least you can take pleasure in the memories you have of him. What if you had never contacted him? You would have never forgiven yourself."

"Yes,...I certainly made the right decision when I decided to get in touch with him," I replied, nodding my head and placing the letter in the slot of the desk. "At the time,...it was *my* death I worried about,...not his. I'll write him every once in a while. I only hope he gets my letters. It would be just like Margaret to discard an envelope with a New York postmark on it. I hope she won't sink that low." Sheer exhaustion overwhelmed me. I felt sapped by the traumatic news. I rose from my chair and made preparations to retire for the night.

✱   ✱   ✱   ✱

Early -March, 1899

Matilda and I seldom rented the same apartment or hotel in New York during the winter months. For this reason, as soon as we were settled, I made a point of informing Uranus exactly where we were staying. I felt it was important for him to know our whereabouts in case of an emergency. On March 9th, I received a telegraph from him confirming my worst fears. It read:

Dear Albert and Matilda:

Deeply regret to inform you—Death of your son, Albert on March 8th—Cause of death-unknown—Will attend funeral in West Roxbury—Burial at Forest Hills. Will be in touch with you soon—Uranus.

"Oh, Matilda, I had hoped for a miracle. Oh, how I wanted him to recover and come back to visit us again this summer...I guess it just wasn't meant to be," I said, wiping the tears from my face with my handkerchief. "I'll miss him and our pleasant father and son chats. As Japeth once said, 'Parents should never outlive their children. Life's never the same for them after such an agonizing loss.'"

"You've had more than your share of grief, but the death of your only son whom you dearly cherished must be so distressing for you," Matilda said compassionately. She held me tightly in her arms. "Always remember Albert, Junior, the way he was,...full of energy and vigor. Thankfully, you never had to see him frail and gaunt. That would have been agonizing for you. I doubt you could have coped with that."

"Yes, you're right, Matilda," I replied, pulling away from her and retreating to the parlor. "I need some time to be alone. I'm sure you understand that."

"I do, Albert. I'll be preparing a little something for dinner. Relax and smoke your pipe," she said, turning to leave and stopping to ask, "Can I get you something right now?"

"No, thank you, Matilda. Actually,...I'm not very hungry," I replied wearily. I was heartsick and emotionally drained. "I'm feeling a bit queasy and tired. I may go into the bedroom and lie down for a while."

"That sounds like a good idea, Albert," she said. "I don't feel much like eating myself. While you're resting I'll write a letter of condolence, and I'll also have some flowers sent to Wildwood from us both."

✳   ✳   ✳   ✳

Mid-April, 1899

"Matilda, I've made a decision to file for bankruptcy," I announced while I sat at my desk, putting together a stack of papers and placing them in a folder. "The lawyer has advised me that this would be my best option,...otherwise your assets could also be attached. He'll soon gain a hearing for me in court. Bankruptcy's the only way to get out from under this burden of debt in Illinois and Indiana. Ever since I was discovered in Brewster, a mountain of claims has been piling up against me. I've been mulling it over and decided I must do something about it. As long as the claimants think I have money, they'll keep hounding me. I've just been informed that I'm to appear before the bankruptcy judge at the end of May."

"I think that's a wise course of action, Albert," she said, walking over to the desk and putting her arms around my shoulder. "Those creditors are motivated by greed as far as I'm concerned. They feel they have nothing to lose by taking legal action against you. You can't possibly be liable for all that money!"

"I know, Matilda,…but it's such a disgrace to file for bankruptcy," I said despondently. "I'm a proud man and no one has *ever* had to do that in my family. That's why I've put it off for so long. Rumor has it that I've lost my "Midas Touch." However, in spite of the shameful publicity we've endured recently, I'm surprised to learn that our friends have remained loyal and uncritical."

"Of course they would, Albert," she agreed. "There isn't one of them who hasn't been touched by some sort of financial problem. It's how one handles the reversals that count. You mustn't let it depress you. I'm certain everything will go well for you at the hearing. Yours is a just cause…I insist on being there with you and the lawyer."

"I was hoping you'd want to be there with me," I acknowledged as I rose and moved toward the wingchair by the fireplace. I sat opposite Matilda who had retrieved her needlepoint on the settee. "Matilda, I've been giving some thought to a subterfuge of sorts," I added while smoking my pipe. "I'd like your opinion of it."

"Well, I must say that sounds intriguing, Albert" she said, rapt and wide-eyed. "I remember you telling me about the ruse that you and your friend, David, concocted to avoid bandits on your trek to Chicago. It worked then, and whatever you're hatching in that shrewd mind of yours will most likely work for us now…Please tell me."

"Although it was David's idea, I learned a great deal from that little deception. Since that time, I've made it a point to be prepared. I'm very seldom caught off guard. My plan is that we should appear before the judge as a broken, impoverished elderly couple looking ill and destitute," I replied, after lighting my pipe and inhaling the fine tobacco. "It would help foster some compassion for our financial demise."

"Sounds like a credible strategy to me, Albert," she said. "Please go on."

"No one knows us here in New York except for your lawyer and a few close friends," I went on. "Matilda,…you'll have to excuse my appearance for a while. I intend to let my white hair, mustache and beard grow long and disheveled. We'll go to a used clothing shop and purchase a black, ill fitting, cotton fiber suit and a shabby, out-dated Prince Albert style coat,…one that's changed color over the years from black to an iridescent green. I'll wear that over a distasteful outfit.

My paupers costume should be complete with a cane and a pair of well-worn shoes."

"Why,...that's hilarious!" Matilda chuckled, slapping her knee in hysterics. She could barely stop laughing when she asked,..."And what have you planned for me? I can hardly wait to hear it."

"You, my dear, won't look nearly as poverty stricken as I will. You'll pad yourself to look like a prosperous, hefty matron and arrive at the courthouse wearing crutches and feigning a bad knee. I think that should garner a little sympathy for us poor old folks," I said, smiling wryly. I handed Matilda a goblet of dry white wine. Let's toast to this clever deception. With a little bit of luck this ploy should work in our favor."

"I must say, Albert, that's ingenious! I'm fascinated by your resourcefulness," she exclaimed, joining me in the toast.

"Yes," I reflected. "Like the more perceptive alewives in the herring run, I'll be clever enough to position myself safely along the edges of the current and save my strength until it's needed to climb the ladders." My quest to overcome adversity, despite all obstacles, had always been the dominant characteristic of my life.

$$* \qquad * \qquad * \qquad *$$

Late-May, 1899

On the day of the court hearing, Matilda and I rose early to dress in our carefully selected wardrobe. It was uniquely designed for our appearance before the judge. We left unnoticed through the back entrance of our hotel. Once on the street, we mingled with the crowd, and then took a public coach to the courthouse. The weather was as nasty and ugly as our drab attire. Due to the rainy conditions, a large tattered umbrella had been added to our costumes. Even the patrons ascending into the coach moved out of our way to avoid contact with us. Before closing it, we snickered behind the opened umbrella. Our disguise had passed a crucial test.

"Good day, Mister and Missus Crosby," our lawyer said as he approached us at the entrance of the courthouse. Ezra Paine shook my hand and tipped his hat to Matilda. "I wasn't sure at first if it was actually the two of you. I must say I heartily approve of your masquerade. Quite clever indeed!...It'll certainly make my efforts to plead your case much easier."

Ezra was a likeable fellow with a stentorian voice. He wore his black hair parted in the middle and slicked back. Ezra sported a short pointed beard and a thin mustache that curled up the sides of his cheeks to join his sideburns. He often used a monocle that hung from a gold chain around his neck to read his legal papers. Although he was of medium height, his posture was faultless. He stood straight and tall and spoke with confidence and authority. Ezra represented us wearing a starched white shirt, bow tie and a dignified tailor-made suit.

Matilda had been his client for many years, but this was the first time I also needed his services. Despite the fact that we had a lawyer, the judge asked to speak to us directly.

"I see that you're answering this injunction from Massachusetts by claiming bankruptcy here in New York…How is it that you're filing for bankruptcy, Mister Crosby?…Have you no assets, sir?" he asked."

"No, Your Honor," I replied, bending over my cane and directing his attention to Matilda. "Years ago, my wife and partner, Matilda Crosby, risked her life to save most of my priceless art works during the Chicago Fire. I was so thankful for her selfless deed that I had everything I owned legally transferred to her. I retired in '87 as vice-president of the McAvoy Brewing Company. I receive a small retirement stipend amounting to about $1,000 a month. It's often necessary for my wife to lend me additional spending money."

"Is that correct, Missus Crosby?" the judge asked, addressing Matilda.

"I'll speak for Matilda Crosby," Ezra said as he approached the bench and indicated that I should also be seated next to Matilda. "Let the record show that Missus Crosby has been my client for decades now. She is the sole owner of the Crosby mansion and the forty acres surrounding it. Matilda Sourbeck Crosby has $160,000 in the bank, mortgages amounting to $160,000, also real estate, paintings and furnishings totaling $150,000. Over the years, she has advanced Mister Crosby in excess of $50,000."

"Do you reside in Massachusetts year round or is New York your home state?" the judge asked…"Where do you cast your vote, sir?"

"Yes, New York is where we live seven months out of the year, but my wife and I do not have a permanent address here. We hardly ever stay in the same hotel preferring the freedom to choose lodgings at our own discretion," I replied, grimacing in pain as I took my time to stand, leaning on my cane, and then holding onto my back. "When we return to New York from Cape Cod, we choose to live in different areas of the city and state. The Missus and I spend the summers on Cape Cod because the weather in New York City can become quite unbearable for us old folks. I've never voted in either Massachusetts or New York…I have no interest in politics."

"What if your wife were not available and you needed money?…What would you do in that case, sir?" the judge asked impatiently. There was a hint of exasperation in his voice as he tried to understand the complexity and contradictions of our situation.

"My wife is *always* by my side," I said with a timid and withdrawn expression. "As for myself, except for my tobacco and medical needs,…I seldom require money, your honor."

"Your case will be deliberated…You're free to go. Your lawyer will be advised as to my decision," the judge said as he pounded the gavel on his bench, gathered the paperwork, and then left the courtroom.

In June 1900, just as we were preparing to leave for the Cape, Ezra informed me that I had been declared bankrupt and that the judgments against me had been dismissed. The Massachusetts Supreme Court was notified of the decision handed down by the New York Court. The demands for payment were found to be non-binding. Matilda and I were ecstatic. Our attempt to protect ourselves from the vultures, who would have picked our financial bones clean, had been successful. With this heavy burden of debt lifted from our shoulders we began to prepare for our journey back to Cape Cod and Brewster. Now, we could now look forward to living on the Cape in blissful happiness for many summers to come—until the end of our days. I had finally climbed over the last ladder. Matilda once mentioned that time was like a bottle of rare perfume. We're apt to use a lot in the beginning, but when we reach the bottom—we savor each and every drop. Such was our life during the next seven years.

✳   ✳   ✳   ✳

Late - July, 1906

"Uranus is here to see you, Albert!" Matilda shouted, speaking through the mansion's communications system. I was resting in the upstairs master bedroom that overlooked the bay. I needed to do this quite often these days. I hadn't been feeling well for several months. Depression and inertia associated with my physical illness sapped my energy and had plague me for an incredibly long time. As a result, Matilda had kept the entertaining to a minimum. I was gradually losing the stamina and the will to attend the many social functions that were often required of us while in Brewster. All those extraneous obligations no longer mattered to us. Due to my deteriorating health, Matilda saw to it that these past few summers at Tawasentha would be a tranquil retreat for us both. She assumed the role of a devoted matriarch, diplomatically insisting that everyone be aware of my need for peace and quiet. "Don't come down!…Uranus will visit you upstairs," she added. "He'll be up to see you shortly."

Rested and in fairly good spirits, I hollered back through the contraption, "Do come upstairs, Uranus!…It's been quite a while since we've visited together."

I rose from my bed and put on my slippers. While I managed to get fully dressed everyday, I seldom wore shoes except, perhaps, in the winter. At this stage of my life, any kind of light footwear sufficed for my purposes. I had always hated shoes anyway. From the time I was a child I couldn't wait for the warm weather to arrive so I could discard those cumbersome things that weighed so heavily on my feet.

I walked into the adjoining bathroom and splashed some water on my face. When I glanced into the mirror, I saw the reflection of a balding, white-haired octogenarian. "Where has the time gone? My, the years have certainly flown by! We're here for such a short time," I thought as I closely examined the old, wrinkled face staring back at me. At this point in my life, I was convinced that my earthly days were numbered.

With the looming onset of death, thoughts of an afterlife and the supernatural crept into my mind. I remembered Minister Ebenezer Farnsworth preaching about damnation and our immortal souls. I understood that we were composed of body, spirit and soul. "I know the body is mortal,…but where is this abiding soul of ours,…and what is it?" I questioned. "Does the soul exist within our spirits or is it one and the same?…In what part of our being does our soul exist? What happens to the soul when it leaves our bodies at the time of death? Does it leave with our spirits? Is the spirit our personality,…*who* we are?" Could it be that when we die,…we don't know it? Or like I've often heard said, 'When we're dead,…we're dead!' "I knew we lived on perpetually through our progeny as my ancestors did through me, but until now, I had never given death much thought. It was a profound and unplanned psychological experience. I meditated on these mysteries and how I viewed my own existence in this world. It struck me as a moment of truth—the thought that our lives are but a speck on the eternal continuum—an infinite universe that flows endlessly.

I always compared life to the seasons of the years. I believed that the naivety and exuberance of youth was like the spring, while the drive and enthusiasm of middle age—similar to summer. The acceptance and sense of achievement as we reaped the harvest of our efforts was analogous to fall. And finally, the quiet resignation to life's imminent end became the winter of our lives. It was our destiny from the day of our birth. We were born—we lived—and we died. I guessed it was as simple as that!

"But why is life so fragile and death so final?" I asked myself, choking back the tears. "It's ironic,…a cruel paradox! Oh, how I love life with its feelings, dreams and aspirations,…all part of the human condition! I want to enjoy each and every minute of these precious gifts for as long as I can!"

Then my mind turned to Matilda. It seemed like yesterday when we married. A photograph taken on our wedding day graced the mantel of the fireplace in our bedroom. "She's the reason I'm so loath to leave this world. From the depths of my heart springs a fountain of love for her," I thought as I heaved a deep sigh. While trying to sort out all these feelings, I heard Uranus ascending the staircase. I quickly wiped my face, took hold of my cane, and then met him in the hallway above the balcony.

"How are you, Albert?" he asked, walking toward me. Although he had a full head of snow-white hair, unlike me Uranus still maintained a dignified and erect posture. "It's so good to see you again, dear cousin. I thought I'd pay you a short visit," he said, extending his hand toward mine.

"It's so nice to see you also, Uranus. I truly appreciate your concern for me," I said, showing him into the bedroom and offering him a chair while I chose a rocker. Uranus led a quiet, communal life in Brewster. His dedication to public service was surpassed only by his professionalism. "I hear you've been appointed to the Town Council. Along with your deaconship in the First Parish Unitarian Church of Brewster, you must be kept quite busy."

"Yes, I am, Albert,…but never *too* busy to stop by and see you. You never did say how you were doing…Are you in any pain?" he asked.

"No, I'm not the least bit uncomfortable," I replied. "But I'm quite weak and extremely tired most of the time. I seem to have lost much of my energy. My sensitivities to exertion are quite noticeable these days. Even going up and down the stairs is an effort that leaves me breathless," I lamented with a trace of despair that Uranus easily recognized. "I'm so happy that you've come by, Uranus. I've been meaning to speak to you so you could help me put some of my anxieties to rest. I have some important matters I must discuss with you. It's essential that Matilda is well cared for and that she have a confidant whom she can trust and rely on for support and guidance after I'm gone."

"Don't talk that way, Albert! Why,…you'll probably outlive me!" he said emphatically, turning toward the window so I wouldn't notice his anguished expression. "Of course you can count on me to look after Matilda. I'll always be there for her and make myself available to assist her in any way I can. Needless to say, you know as well as I that Matilda's a strong woman who'll most likely do quite well on her own."

"Tawasentha's an enormous responsibility for a woman living alone. I'm a sickly old man, Uranus. The specter of death is breathing down my neck. Matilda and I have already discussed my passing," I said candidly. "If anything should happen to me, she said she would spend the winters in Washington, D.C. with her family. Our assets are in order and due to her astute financial planning, she should be monetarily secure for as long as she lives."

"Yes, Albert,…I agree," Uranus replied. "The upkeep of this mansion could be a problem, but I'm sure that as in the past,…she'll have family with her during the summer months here. Matilda's grandnieces are married now with young children of their own. I'm certain they'll be happy to visit and keep her company in the summer. She's also learned to rely on Hudson for the maintenance of the estate while she's here and in her absence. Please don't worry about how Matilda will manage without you. She's an exceptional woman! Matilda has attained personal standards that few will ever match. Her love for you is incredibly profound. Even though she'll deeply grieve for you and you'll be sorely missed,…I'm confidant she'll do quite well on her own."

"Thank you, Uranus," I said, gratefully. "Lately all my thoughts have centered upon leaving her behind to fend for herself. I can't seem to dismiss these morbid feelings that weigh so heavily on my heart. I knew you'd help me gain a better perspective. Thank you, Uranus, for your encouragement. You've truly made me feel much more confident about leaving her. You've convinced me that her life, although dramatically altered,…will go on without me."

"I'll leave you now,…so you can get your rest," he said, excusing himself. "I only wanted to stop by for a short while."

"Wait,…wait just a minute for me, Uranus," I said getting up slowly from my rocker and reaching for my cane. "I'd like to accompany you downstairs. You can help me descend the staircase to the front entrance. It's much too hot to stay up here cooped up in my room. I need to fill my lungs with some fresh air…I believe I might enjoy sitting out on the veranda for a while."

I stood on the front porch alongside Matilda to wish Uranus farewell. We watched as he ascended his caleche and cracked the whip. After taking the bend in the road on two wheels, Uranus was soon out of sight. While we sat admiring the mansion's well-manicured grounds, Matilda had two tall glasses of ice tea brought out to us.

The neatly pruned cedar shrubs and shade trees were now full-grown. Voluptuous hydrangeas—vivid-blue mop-heads—surrounded the veranda. Rambling, ruby-red roses clung tenaciously to the rail fencing while lively day lilies, like a colorful rainbow, cast their beauty from one end of the estate to the other. Every so often a cool sea breeze fanned us as we sat sipping our tea.

All of sudden, I was overcome by a twinge of nostalgia. I had an urgent need to connect with the sea. For some reason, I felt drawn to the bay.

"Matilda,…I'd like to take a walk to the seashore. Would you join me? You may need to hold me up at times as we negotiate the sandy path over the dunes. Do you think you could manage that?" I asked after finishing my tea and placing the empty glass on the wicker end table. "When I looked out our bedroom window, I noticed that it's an afternoon high tide. I haven't been down to the beach at all this summer. Besides, it's such a hot day,…it would be nice to cool off a bit! I know I'd enjoy the revitalizing sea spray on my face and soaking my feet in the refreshing surf."

"Why, I'd love to accompany you to the water, Albert," she replied, picking up the tray with our glasses and carrying it into the house. "I'll be right back out, my dear…Sit here until I return."

In no time, we were out the front gate and heading toward the shore. An occasional gray gull soared overhead. We were met by bouquets of salt spray roses on sprawling vines coiled around clusters of lavender and heather. Matilda held a tight grip on me as we gingerly navigated the sloping dunes to the sea. Her resilient presence facilitated my trek over obstacles I might never have tackled on my own. As we moved closer to the water's edge, tufts of ground-hugging, violet, sweet peas and silver dusty miller carved their way up from sandy depths to cover the sloping terrain. I had almost forgotten the splendor of the swaying sea grasses—those soaring, green sheaths whose growth and density protected the nesting terns, and also the shoreline from erosion.

A shimmering sun burned through a few feathery clouds. It was an exceptionally perfect day. A placid sea sent small, metrical waves surging and swishing along the shore. The gentle surf licked at the tawny ribbon of beach, teasing the sandpipers and plovers with its bounty of minnows. As always—I was captivated by it all. I inhaled the heady aroma of the salt air and scanned the vista of sea and sky. It was an unforgettable canvas. Like a sponge, I absorbed the unique beauty around me and heaved a poignant, heavy sigh. As I stood there on the shore, I relished this moment as I embraced the shadows of my past and became peacefully resigned to my fleeting future.

Since the dawn of time, the lapping of the waves and the abiding tides have flowed and ebbed ceaselessly—and so it would be—evermore. I realized that this breathtaking and humbling experience might never again be repeated for me.

The calming and steadying effect of this sandy promontory brought my thoughts into focus. "My mortal lifetime is merely a second on nature's timepiece," I thought as I approached the water. "I'm satisfied with the outcome of my life despite some regrets and failures. My hopes and dreams have been fulfilled, and above all, I'm so grateful that it will end here in Brewster,…my little corner of heaven on earth."

"I'd like to take my slippers off and sit on this rock for a while," I said, reaching for Matilda to help me as I approached it. She gently cradled my arm in hers until I sat down. "I'll dangle my feet in the water for a few minutes…Oh, my, this feels so good!"

"I'll sit with you," Matilda said as she waded barefoot into the water with her still-girlish gait. Although her hair was now an attractive shade of gray, her skin still glowed like lustrous ivory satin. It was a perfect time and place to be reflective and enjoy our intimate relationship. "I don't think we should stay here *too* long. I'm afraid you'll get a chill and tire from this rather cavalier exercise." We laughed quietly as she joined me, placed an arm around my shoulder, and then dangled her feet in the foamy brine. The cool waters of the bay effectively refreshed our overheated bodies.

We sat and chatted about what was happening around us. Cognizance is intimacy with all things—a horseshoe crab moving slowly along the bottom—a sailboat on the horizon and a school of cod swimming by and attracting a noisy flock of herring gulls. All of this against a backdrop of high tide in the neighboring salt marsh where the osprey waded in search of fish—just below the surface. I picked up some flat stones sanded smooth by the tides and skimmed them across the water. Among them was a broken quahog shell shaped like a fan and rendered smooth by the pounding surf and sand. I turned this shiny, purple and white piece of wampum over in my hands for a few seconds then placed it in my shirt pocket. Sadly, it was time to return home. I was reluctant to leave this serene setting. On the other hand, I was beginning to feel fatigued, so I surrendered to the needs of my aging body. I hoped I'd be able to climb the steep, twisting path through the dunes.

When I looked up from the shore, the watchtower above Tawasentha came into view.

"Look, Matilda, there's the tower of our magnificent mansion overlooking the bay! The stately castle of my dreams!" I exclaimed. "No matter how many times I've done so in the past, I never tire of seeing it from this perspective. Tawasentha is my crowning achievement,…the culmination of my life. In spite of nearly insurmountable obstacles, through the dark forests and bright rainbows of my life, Tawasentha's been well worth everything I've sacrificed for it. Like the dauntless herring of the Stony Brook, I faced my fears,…conquered the challenges and succeeded in my quest. It's given me a deep inner satisfaction and wonderful sense of accomplishment, Matilda. I'd like to leave this remarkable edifice behind as my legacy to Brewster and the whole world. I hope it'll be a lasting monument that survives the test of time and remains through future decades as incredibly elegant and serene as it is now. Above all, I've been fortunate enough to share it with you, my dearest Matilda. I want you to know that I love you,…so very much!"

"I know that!" she replied, tilting her head. Matilda flashed a heartwarming smile, took my head in her hands, and then kissed my lips. She helped lift me from the large stone and after putting on her shoes, she helped me with my slippers. Eventually, we trudged upward toward Tawasentha, and as we did so, Hudson caught a glimpse of us and came running. He took hold of one arm to keep me steadied and Matilda held the other.

"I'm very tired…I'll rest in the cottage and come out in time for supper," I mumbled wearily as I headed for the door to the old homestead. Exhausted from the long walk, I shuffled in, sat in my rocker and started to rock. Calm and content, I reached into my shirt pocket and held the glossy piece of shell in my hand. While feeling its even edges and silky-smooth surface, I envisioned it as a whole entity—part of a living organism that was once the coarse outer shell of a crustacean sea creature. I turned it over in my hand and contemplated how the turbulence of the sea had buffed, reshaped and polished it to its final, glossy finish. "My life's a lot like this strong, beautiful shell that's been left for all to enjoy," I thought. "Each one of us is molded by adversity. It strengthens and empowers us to enrich the lives of others and exposes the most commendable aspects of our own unique spirits. I trust I'll be fondly remembered after my passing and that future generations will take pride in my accomplishments and benefit from my endeavors."

The rays of a mid-afternoon sun filtered through the lace curtains. Touched by these thoughts, I envisioned the shadow of a young man dressed in white and standing in the midst of these ephemeral shafts of light. "Oh, yes!…There he was!" At that moment, I smiled and instantaneously recalled my mother's death. I knew he was an angel. I felt a tear roll down my cheek as my surroundings began to blur and fade. I could feel my life—like the precious shell I grasped in my hand—slowly slip through my fingers. As my spirit followed this heavenly escort into the hereafter, I turned to find my lifeless body peacefully rocking by the old-time hearth.

Epilogue

▼

Albert Crosby died at the age of 83 in 1906, in his mansion called "Tawasentha." He is buried in the family plot in the Brewster Cemetery on Lower Road. After his death, Albert's former wife Margaret (Henderson) Crosby asked the Chicago courts to set aside the divorce granted to her husband on grounds that she had only agreed to a separation. Margaret claimed that she had not deserted her husband, and that Albert had been a philandering husband who did not want her there while he amused himself with his lady friends. She also alleged that Matilda's marriage to Albert was illegal because Matilda had obtained a fraudulent divorce in New York from her own husband.

Margaret's petition was denied. Undeterred by that setback, she and her daughters, Irene and Fanny formally requested to have themselves made administrators of Albert's estate. They were subsequently appointed as such by the probate court of Brewster. However, when Matilda disclosed the fact that she and Albert were fulltime residents of New York and only summer residents of Massachusetts, and that Albert owned no property, personal or otherwise in Massachusetts to be dispensed of, the court concluded it had overstepped its authority. Judgment was subsequently vacated, thus Margaret and her daughters were no longer involved in the Crosby estate.

Matilda continued to enjoy her summers at the Crosby Mansion until her death at age 81 in 1928. She spent the remainder of each year with close relatives in Washington, D.C. Matilda left her estate, including the buildings and 150 acres of land to two grandnieces. Matilda's family members continued to use the mansion. However, the taxes and the upkeep of the mansion became a financial burden for the families whose husbands were career military men. The grandnieces and their husbands were stationed around the world and their service wages were not nearly enough to meet the obligations of the mansion. For these reasons, it was eventually vacated and abandoned.

The imported antique furnishings, the priceless art works, the oriental rugs and the many marble and bronze sculptures along with all the contents of the carriage house were eventually auctioned off to clear the property of tax liens owed the Commonwealth of Massachusetts. The auction, which took place just weeks before the Wall Street Crash of 1929 was attended by hundreds of people on the mansion grounds. The paintings were practically given away. The entire collection netted $6,000. Bierstadt's *Yosemite* was sold for a mere $250.

To avoid having it seized for back taxes, The Cape Cod Institute of Music purchased the mansion in late 1930. Martha Atwood became the owner and administrator. A long list of talented and now, famous personalities attended sessions in this once-renowned school of drama and music.

The estate was sold again in 1950 and rejuvenated as an elegant inn and restaurant and called the "Gold Coast Inn and Restaurant." The business proved to be unprofitable for the owner and in 1970 the mansion was sold to a Doctor John Spargo who called it "Seascape." He converted the mansion into an exclusive dieting and finishing school for obese, wealthy young women, which was quite successful. However, the mansion suffered structurally as the result of accommodating these students. The oversized rooms were sectioned off into resident dorms and a large cafeteria building was attached to the side of the mansion facing the bay, thus obstructing the view. After the doctor's death, his associates lost interest in the summer camp and decided to permanently close it.

The State of Massachusetts has owned the mansion and about 90 acres along Cape Cod Bay since 1987. When it purchased the area through eminent domain as an extension to Nickerson State Park, its purpose was to give saltwater access to campers in the park.

From 1987 to 1992 the mansion was stripped of its former dignity and in various stages of disrepair. With the blessings of the Town of Brewster, the Friends of Crosby Mansion, an all-volunteer group undertook the massive restoration project in 1992. During the following years, the renovation of Tawasentha continued to be the object of much time, effort and money, which was enthusiastically donated by specialty workers and volunteers. This endeavor is still an ongoing project and funded by tours, holiday open houses and also social and community affairs.

After lengthy legal negotiations by Chairpersons, Brian and Virginia Locke and Brewster town officials, the Town of Brewster subsequently approved a

25-year lease agreement with the State in 2003. Now, in 2005 the State has agreed to help finance some of the major undertakings. Tours are still given on the 1st and 3rd Sundays of July and August. Once the mansion is completely restored to its former grandeur, it will be opened to the public as a historical site and museum.

978-0-595-38372-6
0-595-38372-6

Breinigsville, PA USA
15 April 2010
236237BV00001B/13/A